MW00397277

LEGITIMACY

BOOK ONE OF THE VANILLA CYCLE

BY

M.H. VAN KEUREN

Also by M.H. Van Keuren

Rhubarb

Copyright © 2013 M.H. Van Keuren

All rights reserved.

ISBN-13: 978-1-4841720-5-6

Cover Design: Damonza.com
Formatting and Print Design: www.awesomebooklayout.com

Editor: Little Media Empire (little_media@yahoo.com)

Written in Montana.

Website: mhvankeuren.blogspot.com

This is a work of fiction. Names, characters, places, and events either are the product of the author's imagination or are used fictitiously. Any resemblance to actual persons, living or dead, businesses, events, or locales is entirely coincidental.

PART ONE: BIRTH

FEBRUARY 2108

The finance director's stylus hung in the air where it had fallen from the corner of his mouth.

"Those are the facts in black and white," the mayor said. "We'll all be dead in three days."

Kyi glanced around the table at the dozen other gaping members of the Angel-37 executive council. The mayor scattered the contents of a small pill bottle onto a grip pad. He scooped up a handful and gulped them down with water.

"How could this happen?" the planning director asked. "Aren't there safeguards? Weren't we assured that we would be safe here?"

"Valdosky and the UN are doing everything they can to determine the cause of this lapse," said the UN Space Authority liaison.

"Lapse? Sixty thousand people, including you, are going to die while Valdosky covers its ass."

The vice mayor signaled for order. Even if an explanation was eventually put forth, Kyi realized, none of them would live to hear it.

"Who else knows?" asked the finance director.

"The UN and Valdosky alerted me a few minutes ago," the mayor replied. "I called us together immediately."

"Are we going to inform the populace?"

"Dangerous," said the chief of security, shaking his head.

"But you must," the UN liaison said.

The vice mayor interrupted. "The question is not if, but how. There are no secrets on this asteroid. If it gets out that we tried to hide this, we'll all be killed."

"It sounds like we're dead anyway," the facilities director said.

"We mustn't panic," said the vice mayor.

"We need to provide people with options," Kyi said.

"Options?" the chief of security asked. "Like what?"

"People should be given time to say goodbye in their own way," Kyi said.

"Can't we get away?" the finance director asked.

"In what, exactly?" the facilities director replied.

"Pressure suits? Cargo containers?"

"Cargo containers could never hold enough air or food," the facilities director replied. "And we wouldn't have time to retrofit more than a few. People will die even quicker in pressure suits."

"If some can be saved, it will be worth the effort," the UN liaison said.

"I'll do what I can." The facilities director ran his fingers through his hair.

"No," the security chief said. "Our first priority must be to protect critical systems. People will want to shift. We need to let them. The more the better."

"This still doesn't address how to tell the people," the vice mayor said. He glanced hesitantly at the mayor, and then looked to Kyi. "Perhaps it should be you."

"Me?"

"They respect your voice."

"I am not my father."

The security chief slapped the table. "We need a plan before we go making announcements. I hate to shock you, but there will be panic. This colony is a barely-post-adolescent time bomb. Organize suicide sing-ins later. We need to lock down mission-critical sections now."

"I don't disagree, but do you honestly expect chaos?" the finance director asked.

"We have to expect the worst."

"A sudden lockdown might start a panic."

"Not doing so will create needless suffering. Those who wish to spend their remaining time in peace can do so only if they feel safe. What's the greater sin?"

The mayor grunted, and the room fell quiet. "Not one of us will live to be judged," he slurred. "I'm sorry. You each do what you must. I will not decide." He rose but drifted clumsily. The UN liaison moved to help him, but the mayor spasmed and slipped out of his arms. Kyi gasped.

"How many of those did he take?" the vice mayor asked. The pills on the grip pad were gone.

"Someone call medical."

"No!" The security chief grabbed the drifting, convulsing body of

the mayor and pushed him into his chair. "He's made his choice. We can't wait…" His attention fell to the table screen in front of the mayor's seat. His face grew concerned, and he looked to the upper corners of the room. Kyi followed his gaze to the cameras that captured the regular executive meetings for broadcast to the station.

"No," the vice mayor gasped. "Has everyone seen?" The chief nodded.

"Why would he do that?" the UN liaison asked. As if in answer, the mayor let out a breath flecked with foam.

"I suggest we all leave now," said the chief, drawing his stun gun and heading to the door, pulling the facilities director with him.

"God help us all," said the finance director.

"I think we're long past that," Kyi said.

CHAPTER 1

We can see the asteroid now. The sun has lit one edge like a jagged moon. I expected a primordial roar, or a growl. Instead, we cower from the radar tone, as if this threat were something electronic.

—from the message from Shwe Kyi Myiang to her father, Professor Lah Maung Lwin, recorded February 23, 2108

OCTOBER 2076

"Where are we going, Mommy?" Teague asked as his mother knelt to tie his shoes.

"It's a surprise. And a secret," she replied.

"A secret?"

"Other foot," she said. Her brown hair was down, not pulled back, and she had put on dangly earrings.

"A secret means I can't tell anybody. Is that like a promise?" Teague asked.

"It's kind of like a promise."

"How are we getting there?"

"By taxi."

"Can't we take a tuk-tuk?

"No."

"Will we—"

"No more questions, Tiger. It's a surprise. Don't you like surprises?"

"I don't know," Teague replied. His mother's mobile rang and she answered it.

"The taxi's here. Let's go."

The cab hadn't yet reached the end of their block when Teague's mother patted the seat. "Settle down, Tiger. We'll be there soon enough," she said. Teague sat but stretched to see out. For a while, he recognized the buildings from their neighborhood, but after several turns they pulled onto a broad, sunny boulevard, and Teague lost his bearings. Whenever the cab drew to a stop, which it did often in the heavy traffic, Teague looked up, but each time his mother smiled and shook her head as if to say, "Not yet."

Soon, enormous glass-and-steel skyscrapers rose up on each side of the street. "Almost there," his mother said, even as the traffic thickened. A few minutes later, they pulled along a wide sidewalk, bustling with pedestrians.

"Is this the surprise?" Teague asked, craning to find the top of a towering building that seemed to be their destination.

"It's inside," his mother said as she paid the driver.

"What is it?"

"This is a shopping mall."

"Do we have lots of money?" Teague asked. "Kids at school say only rich people go to malls." His mother took his hand.

"No, we don't have a lot of money. But we are going to a store with very expensive things, so you need to be careful. Can you do that?"

"Yes, Mommy."

They shuffled through a revolving door, and chilled air erased the memory of the humidity outside. A screenbot zipped forward, welcomed Teague's mother by name, flashed pictures of her posing in a series of colorful dresses, and offered to lead her to a store.

"Look, Mommy, it's you," Teague said.

"It's a sales gimmick," she said and skirted around the bot.

As she led Teague along the concourse, he studied each storefront for some clue to their destination and began to worry that he was going to have to try on new clothes or shoes. A few moments later, the mall's central atrium yawned above them like a golden cavern. Shoppers were riding a set of towering spiral escalators to and from five glittering levels. At the foot of the escalators, water was spouting from four raised pools, leaping in measured jets over a tile mosaic.

Teague looked up at his mother and pointed. She nodded and let go of his hand. He darted ahead, but when he ran under the water, the splashing became bubbling and the water filled with fish. He spun in place, but stepped back when several fish looked his way. The water disappeared, and the fish morphed into birds.

"Mommy, come in here," Teague called, but she only smiled.

One tile conjured a chorus of dolphins. Another sent arcs of buzzing lightning overhead. Teague hopped and stretched to mix the effects—rainbows and laughter, crackling blue fire, popping bubbles—until his mother called.

They took the spiraling escalator up and up and got off at the fourth level. Teague kept close to the glass railing, eager to see the fountain from above, and almost stepped on a baby panda.

"Hi there," the panda said. "I'm Ping-Ping, and I'm a Zubot. Would you like to come inside and meet all my friends?" Teague had heard of Zubots but had never seen one.

"Can we, Mommy?" Teague asked.

"We'd love to," she said to the panda.

The panda waddled toward a bright green arch topped with an animated sign. They followed it through a spray of mist into an ersatz sunlit jungle clearing filled with wild noises and soft, rhythmic music.

"Hello," said a pot-bellied pig.

"*Sawadee ka,*" a penguin added.

A miniature elephant lumbered forward. "Welcome to Zubotix of Bangkok," he drawled.

A squirrel jabbered in its own little language and scampered away.

"Nice to see you," said a baby orangutan hanging from a tree branch by one arm.

A man dressed like a zookeeper waded through the menagerie with a bright-eyed polar bear cub toddling along at his side.

He greeted Teague's mother with a wai. A Labrador puppy circled Teague, yipped twice, and sniffed at his shoes.

"Everyone's happy to see you," the salesman said. Teague looked to his mother for reassurance.

"It's all right, Tiger," she said. "This is why we're here. You can choose any one you want."

"Really?" Teague asked.

"What's your name?" the salesman asked, and Teague told him. "How old are you?"

"I'm five."

"A big boy. Do you have a favorite animal?"

On the far side of the clearing, a long, black-and-white tail bobbed in and out of view. It skirted a herd of little dinosaurs, disappeared behind a tree trunk, and reappeared by a stump, on top of which a lamb and a duck were playing checkers. Teague rose on tiptoe.

"You can go closer," the salesman said. "Everyone's very friendly."

Teague edged around a kitten and a Hello Kitty playing hopscotch, keeping his eye on the banded tail. Then the animal stood up on its back legs as if it wanted to see Teague, too. It was covered with gray fuzz. Its friendly eyes glistened and blinked. It cocked its triangular head, curled its black snout into a smile, and waved one gray, hand-like paw. Teague waved back. The animal dropped back onto all fours. Its tail swayed as it approached, catlike, and then it sat up again, almost as tall as Teague, and chirped happily.

"Ringer, this is Teague," said the salesman.

"Hi, Teague. It's very nice to meet you," Ringer said.

"Can I pet him?" Teague asked the salesman.

"Why don't you ask him?"

"Okay. Can I pet you?"

"I like to be petted," Ringer replied. He grinned as Teague cautiously stroked the soft fur on his head, and then asked, "Do *you* like to be petted?" Before Teague could answer, Ringer stroked his arm and squeezed Teague's biceps gently. "Wow, strong muscles."

"You're funny," Teague said. "Mommy, he's funny, right?"

"Do you like this one? What kind is it?" she asked.

"It's a monkey," Teague said.

"Actually, it's a ring-tailed lemur," the salesman said. "Not an exact replica. Zubots are designed with friendlier features—eyes, hands, teeth, mouths. Nature can be a little too real."

"I like your tail," Teague said.

"Thanks. I like it, too." The lemur cuddled his tail for a moment, and then burst out, "Do you want to play a game?" He scampered across the room to a sawtooth wall of counters dotted with devices and hopped up onto one. "I can connect to lots of games, and I come with a screen like this one, and two of these." The lemur handed Teague a game controller dotted with red, blue, and yellow buttons. "Want to be on my team?" he asked.

Soon, Teague and Ringer were collecting coconuts marked with lowercase letters before tropical birds could carry them off. "Watch out! Incoming!" Ringer called as they played. "Goofy birds. You're no match for Teague and Ringer."

The adults came up behind them, and the salesman spoke again. "All Zubots are shift-ready. Its avatar will behave just like the real thing. E-shift and U-shift compatibility are standard—"

"I don't think we'll be needing that," Teague's mother cut in.

"It's standard, so…it's there." The salesman hesitated for a moment. "Let's see. It's always on Uni-Fi and will interface with any Uni-Fi device. Personality is customizable for traits like gender, helpfulness, and playfulness. The settings are dynamic. It can be a playmate around your child and family and a quiet pet in public. But it's not just a playmate. Zubotix has an extensive list of learning games and activities designed around interaction. Your son's school curriculum is probably already part of our library."

Teague and the lemur moved on to a number-stacking game. When their sum got to one hundred before the birds', Ringer leaped to his feet and held up his hand.

Teague put his hand up, too, and the lemur slapped it with a tiny clap.

"We make a great team," Ringer said.

"Tiger, do you want to meet any of the other animals?" his mother asked. "Look, there's a baby kangaroo, and little dinosaurs. Do you like dinosaurs?"

The lemur smiled and cocked his head.

"I like this one," Teague said.

That evening, Teague watched the blinking light of the charging pad while his mother stuffed a mountain of packaging into the largest Zubotix box. The lemur looked asleep, curled up between Teague's bed and his desk.

"How much longer, Mommy?" Teague asked, climbing into bed.

"Sixteen hours. Not until after school tomorrow."

"Can I sleep on the floor with him?"

"Don't be silly. He's right here." She draped Teague's covers over him.

"Thank you, Mommy."

"You're welcome, Tiger. You should think of this as a gift from Gran and Grandpa."

"Because of the money you got when Gran died?" Teague asked.

"Where did you hear about that?"

"I heard you talking on the phone."

"Yes, when people die, they sometimes leave money or belongings for their families. I decided to use that money to get you something special."

"What about Daddy? Did he leave us any money?" Teague's father had never been more than a picture on his desk and a few videos on his mother's mobile. He'd gotten sick and died while helping people during a flood in Myanmar.

"We get a little each month from the church because of Daddy," his mother replied.

"So is Monkey from him, too?"

"Monkey? Is that his name?"

"Yeah."

"How'd you pick that name?"

"He's just Monkey."

"Then I suppose Monkey is from your father, too."

"If I ask, will Jesus tell them thanks for me?"

"Of course he will."

She prayed with him, kissed him, and turned off his light. The little LED blinked in the dark.

* * *

The light was still blinking when Teague's mother woke him for school. The Zubot's fur was cool except for a warm spot near the tail. Teague picked up a game controller and tapped the buttons. He ran his fingers around the edge of the inert screen, careful not to smudge its pristine surface. His mother called him to breakfast, and Teague dragged himself away to find his uniform.

"Can we come right home after school and play with Monkey?" Teague asked as his mother scraped scrambled eggs onto his plate. "I can't wait to tell Vit about him."

"Teague," his mother said, "remember how I told you that this Zubot needs to stay a secret?" Teague nodded. "I'm very serious about that. I know you might want to tell your friends at school or at church, but I'm asking you not to. Monkey will just be our secret for now."

"Why, Mommy?"

She paused, and then pulled out a chair and sat down. "He was very expensive, and that might make the other children feel jealous. Do you know what 'jealous' means?"

"That they will want Monkey?"

"Yes, but they might also think you're bragging. In the Bible, Peter quotes Proverbs and says that God opposes the proud but gives grace to the humble. Do you understand what that means?"

"God doesn't want me to talk about Monkey?"

"It means God doesn't want you to brag about yourself. Yes, you have a very nice thing, but it might hurt others to know. Does that make sense?"

"Yes," Teague said, unsure if it did.

"Good. It's important that I can trust you. Plus, it's fun to have a secret, isn't it?" She tickled him. "Now eat up or you'll be late."

Teague liked walking the few blocks to school with his mother. She knew many of the shopkeepers, and they always had a friend-ly wai and a smile. She ignored the mechanics at the motorcycle shop, who whistled as they passed. At the open iron gate of the schoolyard, she tugged his backpack over his arms and kissed him on the forehead.

"After school, come straight to the reading room," she said.

"Yes, Mommy."

"I promise I'll try to leave early today, okay?"

"Okay," Teague replied. He leaned close. "I'll keep our secret," he whispered and then ran into the courtyard to find his friends.

That afternoon, Teague quivered as his mother consulted the instruction page on her screen and found a slit in the fur of the lemur's chest.

"One click, two clicks," she said. "It says this takes a few seconds. Don't worry, Tiger."

Teague held his breath and then witnessed creation. The creature's eyes opened sleepily. His tail curled and uncurled. He yawned and rolled onto his hands and feet and stretched. He looked at Teague, looked at Teague's mother, and then gave them an enormous smile.

"Hello," the lemur said. "Are you Teague Werres?" Teague nodded. "That's a great name. Do you like to be called Teague?" Teague nodded again. "That's great. How old are you, Teague?"

"I'm five and a half."

"You're a lot older than me. I'm only five and a half seconds."

Teague grinned. "You're funny."

"Now I have a weird question, Teague." The Zubot leaned close and whispered. "What's *my* name?"

"Monkey," Teague replied.

"Can you spell that for me?" Monkey asked. Teague did, carefully. "Monkey. Monkey. I'm Monkey. I like my name." Monkey danced and sang his name over and over. Teague laughed and clapped along. "Let's do the Monkey dance." Monkey waved Teague to his feet, and they danced as Monkey sang the Monkey song, which became the Teague song, which became the Teague and Monkey song. Monkey's tail brushed Teague as they twirled, and he squealed. The song climbed to a climactic crescendo, and they collapsed on the floor, laughing.

"I like you, Teague," Monkey said. He sat up in front of Teague's mother and cocked his head to one side. "Are you Naomi Werres?"

"I am," she replied.

Monkey held out his right hand. She shook it gently. "I'm very pleased to meet you. Shall I register you as Teague's parent or guardian?"

"Sure, I'm his mother."

"What should I call you?" Monkey asked.

"Call me Mom," she replied.

"Mom, you have not configured parental content and behavior controls. I can walk you through the wizard or connect you to your Zubotix.com account right now."

"Oh, no. Later. You two play."

"Is this your room?" Monkey asked Teague after Naomi had left. "It's a great room. Want to show me around?"

After Teague had shown off his few favorite toys, they explored the rest of the apartment. Monkey asked about the house rules and sniffed at the screen in the living room, his mother's mobile, the hairdryer, the kitchen appliances, the alarm clocks, and even the doorbell.

"Where do you go to school?" Monkey asked.

"All Saints kindergarten."

The screen on Teague's desk brightened. "This one? All Saints Evangelical Mission School?" Monkey asked. A website for the school had loaded. Teague knew the buildings in the photos, but he didn't recognize anyone in the slideshow of smiling Thai children and Western teachers. "Do you like it there?"

"I guess so. The chapel time is weird. It's not like our church at all, but Mommy says it's okay. Can we play some games?"

"I like to play games," Monkey said and passed Teague one of the controllers.

At dinner, Monkey sat in the chair that had always stayed empty at the kitchen table. He rested his chin on a bare placemat, smiling as Teague described their games to his mother. A few minutes into the meal, Monkey perked up. "You're receiving a call," he said. A second later, Naomi's mobile trilled from the entryway.

"I'm impressed," Naomi said and went to answer it.

"How did you know?" Teague whispered.

"I have big antennas." Monkey waggled his ears. Naomi returned, listening to her mobile. She gestured at Teague to eat and took her own plate away.

"Who is it?" Teague whispered.

"Margaret Stevens," Monkey whispered back. Teague made a face.

Naomi leaned against the counter, repeating "Uh-huh" and "I know." She notched the mobile between her ear and shoulder and started the dishes.

"Was that Mrs. Stevens?" Teague asked after she disconnected.

"Finish up quickly. She's coming over here in a few minutes with Mrs. Chaiprasit."

"Will Mrs. Chaiprasit bring candy?"

"Doesn't she usually? But don't go pestering her."

"Can I be excused?"

"Finish your broccoli," Naomi said. Teague offered a piece to Monkey.

"I don't eat food," Monkey said, shaking his snout. "Placing food and liquids in my mouth can harm me and may void my warranty. You should eat your broccoli like Mom says. It's good for you."

Mrs. Stevens, the pastor's wife, was a large woman, and she seemed even larger when standing next to Mrs. Chaiprasit. Teague stayed out of her way, hoping that Mrs. Chaiprasit would still see him waiting in the hall. He wasn't disappointed. Mrs. Chaiprasit gave him a hug and offered him a sucker. She smelled, like always, of the restaurant she owned with her husband.

"Thank you," Teague squeaked. His mother gave him an approving nod, and he scurried back to his room and the blanket tent he'd built for Monkey to hide in.

"Can you hear what they're talking about?" Teague asked as he chewed the sucker down to the stem. Monkey listened and shook his head. "Maybe they're talking about something secret. Let's be sneaky like Shakiro Squirrel and find out."

"I have lots of Shakiro Squirrel games, books, and videos. Do you want to select a game?"

Teague dug into his closet and emerged with a ragged towel. He started to tie it around his neck like a cape but stopped. "No, *you* be Shakiro Squirrel," he said, and tied the towel around Monkey's neck. "I'll be Dr. Yokona." Teague returned from his closet wearing a yellow rain jacket. "We're going to spy on the Snow Monkeys of Doom. They've got a bomb that's going to make it snow on the whole world and another bomb that's going to boil the oceans."

"This sounds fun," Monkey said.

"But be real quiet so they don't hear us," Teague said. "Ready, Shakiro?"

"Super-hyper-duper-mega ready, Dr. Yokona," Monkey replied in Shakiro Squirrel's voice. Teague opened his door a crack, and Mrs. Stevens's voice got louder. He poked his head out. Monkey peeked out below him. Teague put his finger to his lips. He dropped to his hands and knees and crept toward the living room, staying tight to the wall. Monkey's ears were pricked up over a gleeful grin.

A meter from the living room, Teague could see the King of the Snow Monkeys, making his grand speech from the wide throne of the couch. Teague fell to his belly and crept forward. One snow monkey minion was sitting in the glider in the corner. Another sat on a chair brought in from the kitchen. Her eyes met Teague's, and they weren't happy. Teague took flight with a little shriek. Monkey deftly avoided Teague's legs, dragging the towel back to the bedroom. Teague and Monkey scurried under the blanket tent, and Teague pulled a pillow across the opening.

His mother opened the door and hissed, "What's going on?"

"We're just playing."

"You can come out, but please leave Monkey in here."

"Okay, Mommy."

"Monkey, please stay in this room when other people visit. Do you understand that? I don't know if you can."

"I understand," Monkey replied.

"Mommy?"

"What?"

Teague poked his head out of the tent. "Can I call you Mom, like Monkey?"

"That's fine, but please remember what I said."

She shut the door. The muffled voices resumed.

"Do you want to play another game?" Monkey asked.

CHAPTER 2

Everyone is praying. Inside, the chapels and temples are filled. Out here, men and women kneel in the dust. I find that I can only bear witness.

OCTOBER 2079

Teague raced ahead to push open the heavy glass door for his mother, glad to be heading out into the sunlight after Sunday services. Once she was through, he hopped down the YMCA's front steps until he heard a shout from behind him.

Kevin Stevens had let the door close on him and was faking trauma. "Teague-man, you trying to squish me?" He freed himself with a grin. "Don't worry about it," he said, and whopped Teague with his motorcycle helmet as he sauntered past. At the sidewalk, Kevin turned around. "I'm running the kids' activities on Wednesday night," he warned.

"Kevinball?" Teague asked.

"You better believe it. Come ready to play."

"Super-hyper-duper-mega ready," Teague said. Kevin grinned, settled the helmet over his messy red hair, the same color as Pastor Stevens's, and zipped out into traffic.

"Can I take the subway home alone?" Teague asked when he caught up to his mother. "I know where to go."

"I know you do, but no. It's a nice day. We're going to walk."

Teague pouted, but not for long. He was free after a long morning in the sweltering activity rooms.

"What did you learn about in Sunday school today?" Naomi asked.

"Nothing."

"Nothing? Didn't you pay attention?"

"I couldn't," Teague said.

"You couldn't or you didn't?"

"Kahn and Manu were bothering me."

"Surely not the whole time."

"They were," Teague said. "And Manu told the teacher that he saw me smoking."

"Why would he do that?"

"I don't know. He said it to her and the whole class."

"I doubt that Miss Lalana believed that a third-grader was smoking."

"She didn't."

"Well, just remember, until the Stevenses adopted them, Kahn, Manu, and Nan didn't have all the blessings that you have."

"At least Kevin's nice," Teague said.

A few blocks from the YMCA, they crossed an expansive park that had been trampled by the previous evening's night market. At a plaza in the center, Naomi bought iced cups of fresh pineapple from a cart vendor while Teague chased an indifferent sweeper bot.

"I'm going away tomorrow, for a few days, to a town up north," she told Teague as they sat on a shaded bench to eat.

"Is someone sick?" Teague asked.

"No, I'm helping to reorganize their reading room."

"Who am I staying with?" Teague asked.

"Mr. and Mrs. Chaiprasit."

"Good. Mrs. Stevens's food tastes weird."

"That's not nice. I hope you don't tell her that."

Teague shook his head. "Can I bring Monkey this time?"

"No, Tiger," she said. Teague huffed, but his mother had never changed her mind about keeping Monkey secret. Naomi sneaked the last piece of pineapple from Teague's cup with her fork. Teague protested as she chomped it playfully, but he knew she'd let him eat the rest of hers.

* * *

Teague was surprised at first to see Mrs. Chaiprasit waiting at the gate after school the next day. "Hurry, now," she said. "I've got customers."

Not far from the school, Mrs. Chaiprasit veered onto a narrow street that had been closed to vehicles and threaded her way along several bustling blocks where vendors were beginning to unpack their wares under pop-up tents. Teague's backpack pounded on his shoulders as he jogged to keep up with her, darting around the plastic crates and handcarts blocking the walks. A few minutes later, she paused and took Teague's hand before turning onto a wide, clear sidewalk along a busy boulevard. He wished she hadn't, especially as they passed the salesmen smoking cigarettes in the entrances of noisy electronics stores—he was old enough to walk alone near traffic without holding hands.

At the next corner, Mrs. Chaiprasit skirted around the two entrances of a dark parlor where dozens of people lay on bunks half-hidden in the shadows, seemingly asleep. There were places like it all over the city. Teague looked back for a few steps until Mrs. Chaiprasit released his hand and he spotted the gold and red awning of the Chaiprasits' restaurant halfway along the next block.

Teague heard Mr. Chaiprasit's greeting before his eyes had adjusted to the thin light that filtered through the poster-covered windows. Only two of the restaurant's four tables were occupied: one with a pair of professionally dressed women, the other with a set of mechanics in overalls. Steam billowed from the buffet, fogging the sneeze guard and thickening the air. Mr. Chaiprasit was perched on his usual stool at the register counter at the end of the buffet under framed portraits of the king and queen. His nose and thick glasses were, as always, buried in a screen. His black hair was plastered to his head.

Mrs. Chaiprasit put Teague at the table nearest her husband and brought him bowls filled with soup, rice, vegetables, and chunks of breaded chicken. Then she disappeared into the back, calling to the cook.

The faded poster over the table advertised several dishes with strange garnishes. As Teague ate, he tried to decipher the Thai captions and wondered if Monkey would be able to read the flowery script. Mr. Chaiprasit cleared his throat loudly as if he had sensed Teague's secret thoughts.

When he'd finished, Teague peeled the backs of his thighs off the chair's upholstery and carried his dishes around the register counter into the steamy kitchen. A hair-netted cook greeted him with a nod and poured a bag of frozen vegetables into an enormous wok.

"Did you get enough?" Mrs. Chaiprasit asked, looking around the door of a stainless steel refrigerator.

"Yes, thank you. Can I go out back?" Teague asked, and Mrs. Chaiprasit waved him away.

Teague left his bowls teetering on a pile of lunch dishes and ran toward the blue sunlight at the end of the hallway.

The alley behind the restaurant felt like a different world from the street outside its front door. The buildings were not the even row they were along the sidewalk. Their jagged brick and concrete faces sheltered smelly recycler bins and stacks of emptied crates and pallets, while weeds strained through cracks along the foundations. Teague jumped onto the hump between the deep grooves pressed into the asphalt by countless delivery trucks and ran, scattering a muttering clutch of pigeons.

Half a block away, the alley intersected with another. On the far corner of the intersection, tall, white stucco walls stretched out like an angel's wings, twenty meters long on each side. Where the walls met, a narrow gateway arched over a short set of steps. Teague took them at a hop, dragging his fingertips over the smooth porcelain and rough mortar of the arch's walls, and ran inside.

A stone path, overgrown with elephant-ear leaves and outlandish flowers, led from the arch to the portico of a tile-roofed temple near the back of the garden. Even though his mother had often reminded him of the second commandment, curiosity sometimes drew Teague inside. In the tiny room, a golden Buddha no bigger than Monkey sat cross-legged on an altar among candles and the remains of offerings. Today, Teague stopped at the temple's doorless entrance, patted the two stone guard dogs on the head, and ran out onto the garden paths.

Teague imagined himself the ruler of a labyrinth. Rocks, sticks, and fallen leaves became pawns in an epic struggle. Champions gained power, while others fell in disgrace. He spoke for them all in a quiet murmur, mimicking the sounds of their battles, heralding the victors, and exiling the defeated. Shadows had fallen over the garden by the time Mrs. Chaiprasit's voice sang through the archway.

That evening at the Chaiprasits' apartment, Teague organized races among the little cars from the wicker basket of toys that Mrs. Chaiprasit kept for her grandchildren. At bedtime, she spread sheets over the futon in the second bedroom and then sat with Teague as he knelt and prayed, asking blessings for his mother, Mr. and Mrs. Chaiprasit, and his friends at school. Finally, Teague recited the Lord's Prayer, and Mrs. Chaiprasit rewarded him with a smile. She wished him goodnight and turned out the light.

Teague's mother had taught him not to pray for Monkey, because Zubots didn't have souls. But once Mrs. Chaiprasit closed the door, Teague whispered one anyway. A few minutes later, he fell asleep to the drone of the city.

"Teague?" Mrs. Chaiprasit whispered. "Teague?" He felt shaking, and he tried to roll away.

"He's not waking up, Vipada." The lights snapped on. "Teague, you need to wake up. Something's happened."

"Jettrin, let the pastor talk to him," Mrs. Chaiprasit hissed.

Teague groaned and sat up on his elbows, squinting. Mrs. Chaiprasit was sitting next to him, her expression twisted. Mr. Chaiprasit cinched a robe closed over his pajamas. A third figure loomed in the doorway—a sweating Pastor Stevens. He wore glasses that Teague had never seen before.

Mrs. Chaiprasit rose, and Pastor Stevens took her place, sitting awkwardly. The futon frame creaked and tilted.

"I need you to get dressed, Teague. Your mother needs you."

"Mom's not here. She's taking a bus."

"Your mother's been in an accident." Pastor Stevens placed a meaty hand on Teague's shoulder and urged him out of bed. "Where are your clothes?"

Teague wobbled as he stood on the cool rug. He pointed to his bag.

"Get dressed quickly," Pastor Stevens said. "I'll be back in a moment."

Teague's shirt went on backward and then tangled as he tried to fix it. The only socks he could find were yesterday's, and one of his shoes was under the futon.

When Teague stumbled into the hallway, Pastor Stevens was whispering to the Chaiprasits. "Ready?" he asked Teague.

"Bless you, child," Mrs. Chaiprasit murmured, giving Teague a brief hug.

"He's welcome to stay with us as long as is necessary," Mr. Chaiprasit said.

"Thank you, Vipada, Jettrin," Pastor Stevens replied.

The empty city seemed stripped of color, except for the orange ovals of streetlight shattered on the wet pavement. Block after block of security grates had been drawn as if to cage the shops in. Every few minutes, Pastor Stevens shifted in the undersized bucket seat. Teague let himself be frightened by the shifting shadows on the pastor's round, usually pink, face.

Many silent minutes later, they turned onto a brightly lit street, and their pace slowed to a crawl.

"A hospital?" Teague asked, reading the red-and-white signs.

"I thought you were asleep," Pastor Stevens replied.

They bumped into a parking garage and spiraled up a maze of ramps and columns. Pastor Stevens jerked the car into a parking space and turned off the engine. He twisted to face Teague and cleared his throat.

"Your mother's bus had an accident. She's been hurt very badly. They brought her here, but we need to bring her out. Do you understand why?"

"So God can heal her?"

"That's right. She doesn't want to be here. They've given her drugs and performed surgery. They say she needs more, but we know she needs to be with a practitioner instead."

"Can I talk to her?" Teague asked.

Pastor Stevens paused. "Your mother is asleep," he replied.

The squeal of an unseen vehicle echoed through the garage as they crossed a skywalk over the street. Sliding glass doors yawned open at the end of the bridge, and a blast of conditioned air breathed them inside.

Pastor Stevens's sermons had always made hospitals out to be evil, menacing places, but the corridors were as bright as day, clean and ordered—perhaps, with their soothing colors, even beautiful. Why wouldn't God want his mom to be here?

They took an elevator down several floors to an expansive, low-ceilinged lobby, half-filled but strangely quiet. A news program murmured from the ceiling-hung screens. Periodic coughing broke the hush. Pastor Stevens spoke with a woman behind a glassed-in counter.

"We've got to go up to another floor," he told Teague.

The next lobby was smaller and ended in a forbidding set of wooden double doors. A man had stretched out across several chairs to sleep. Pastor Stevens tapped a screen at the counter, and the face of a nurse appeared. After a brief conversation, the doors opened with a whisper.

As they entered the octagonal room beyond the doors, Teague sucked in his breath to see the science of medicine at work. The floor-to-ceiling glass walls protected an electronic world. Behind each facet lived a bed so surrounded by equipment that it was difficult to separate the occupants from the machines. A live image of each patient's face was projected on the glass, surrounded by scrolling readouts. The nurses' station in the center might have been the bridge of a spaceship. Passages led to similar rooms several meters away on two sides. A nurse in blue scrubs pointed, and Pastor Stevens guided Teague around the arc of the nurses station.

On the fourth facet, Teague read the name "Werres" and

searched for familiarity in the projected face. The eyes were bruised and swollen. A brace held the head in place. A tube snaked into the mouth. An awkward white bandage covered the right cheek and nose. Then Teague found the curve of the left cheek. "Can I go in there?" he asked.

"I'm sorry, no," the nurse replied.

"I need to talk to her."

The nurse exchanged a look with Pastor Stevens.

"Can we bring a chair for the boy?" Pastor Stevens asked. "I need to speak to Naomi's doctor as soon as possible." Before he left, he turned to the face on the glass and said, "Pray for her, son. That's what she needs most now. True prayer by those who love her. Can you do that?"

Teague started when someone touched his shoulder.

"Sorry. Were you asleep?" Pastor Stevens asked.

"I was praying," Teague said. "It hasn't worked yet." He had mouthed the Lord's Prayer again and again, ending each one with an imploring "amen" and then allowing himself another look at his mother's face. Once he had found a figure dressed in white from head to toe standing by her bed. His imagination had conjured an angel, but then he had seen the all-too-human features—a nurse attending to his mother's machines.

"Come with me," Pastor Stevens said.

They took an elevator and several wide corridors to a set of frosted glass doors, but before they entered, Pastor Stevens put a hand on Teague's shoulder. "We're going to talk to a very important person, the doctor in charge of this place," he said. "I've explained that your mother doesn't want to be here, but he may ask you some questions. You believe God will help her, don't you? And you'll help me tell him that she wants to come home?"

Teague could only nod.

"Let's say a prayer before we go in." Teague bowed his head as Pastor Stevens asked for God's will to be done, and for strength and courage and faith for them and for Naomi. He ended with a hushed amen.

Soft sunlight filtered through the blinds and reflected off the broad glass desk. The very important person looked so much younger than Pastor Stevens that Teague wondered if there had been some mistake. Another person, a woman wearing green scrubs and a stern expression, was waiting for them as well.

"Thank you for seeing us so promptly this morning, Dr. Srisati," Pastor Stevens said. He greeted the woman with a nod. "Dr. Aromdee."

"We have received the documents concerning Ms. Werres." Dr. Srisati tapped his desktop, and several pages glowed open. He studied them for a moment. "This is her son?" he asked.

"Yes," Pastor Stevens replied.

The administrator took a deep breath and studied Teague with deep, intelligent eyes before turning back to Pastor Stevens. "Mr. Stevens, this hospital received four of the critical casualties from this tragic accident. Thanks to the work of skilled physicians like Dr. Aromdee, we expect each to survive. But recovery from trauma can be a long and difficult process. Ms. Werres has sustained very serious injuries. Taking her off pain mitigation and antibiotic regimens will seriously compromise her condition. I have reviewed Ms. Werres's status with Dr. Aromdee and concur that there are a variety of therapies that may expedite her recovery, even from her brain injury."

"Dr. Aromdee explained the options to me earlier," Pastor Stevens said. "However, my position is firm. As her living will stipulates, she does not consent to any further procedures or care."

"Her left lung was collapsed," Dr. Aromdee interjected. "She suffered severe blood loss. Without the artificial blood supplement and oxygen—"

"I understand all that," Pastor Stevens said.

"If she is moved, there is a significant chance of continued internal bleeding—" The administrator put up a hand to silence Dr. Aromdee, but she kept talking. "—changes in her pulmonary activity, infection. We haven't even been able to assess the extent of her brain injury due to her coma."

"Are there any administrative issues with the living will, payment, or release request?" Pastor Stevens asked the administrator.

"There are no issues, but—"

"Then as Naomi's designated representative, I ask that all medications be suspended immediately, including the Universal Treatment booster. I've made arrangements for her to be moved this afternoon."

Teague swallowed. Had they given his mother the Universal Treatment? He'd learned in church that Vanilla was a drug born of evil, separating souls from their God. Its promise of hyper-extended life—no one even knew how long exactly, but at least several hundred years—was a mockery of God's gift of eternity. It treated a condition that needed no remedy.

"Sir, I want my fullest objection on the record. I disagree with allowing this man to remove Ms. Werres," Dr. Aromdee said. "Mr. Stevens, does this boy understand what is happening to his mother?"

"We've spoken. He understands."

"I would like to hear that from his own mouth," Dr. Aromdee said.

"Doctor, please," the administrator chided.

"Does he understand that his mother will die if she is removed from this facility?"

Pastor Stevens stood, looming over Dr. Aromdee. "That is your opinion," he said, his pink face turning red.

"That is fact," Dr. Aromdee said, glaring up at him. Dr. Srisati put a hand on Dr. Aromdee's arm.

"Dr. Aromdee," Pastor Stevens hissed, "Naomi's faith in God will heal her. Her faith will transcend your medicine. Jesus Christ heals and will see her through." Teague hated the silence that followed and feared not knowing whom to believe.

"Tell her, Teague. Tell her what your mother would want," Pastor Stevens said. Teague looked at the floor. "Son? Do you want your mother to leave this hospital so that God can heal her?" Teague's eyes welled with tears, and he felt his head move up and down. "The boy says yes."

Dr. Aromdee burst out, "That's no answer. Of course he wants his mother to be healed."

"Doctor," the administrator said, "I'm afraid that hospital policy is clear, and I must agree to the request of the patient's representative. She'll be released with informed consent. Please make the necessary preparations."

"I will prepare the informed consent document personally, so that Mr. Stevens will fully understand his responsibility," she said.

"God bless you for making the right decision, doctors," Pastor Stevens said.

That afternoon, Teague awoke in the backseat of the Stevenses' car when its tires crunched to a stop on gravel. He sat up and saw that Mrs. Stevens had brought him to their house, a bungalow on stilts set back in a narrow, overgrown lot behind a high chain-link fence. Mrs. Stevens flipped the passenger seat forward for him before heaving herself out of the driver's seat.

Teague stumbled behind Mrs. Stevens up the long steps to the deck that wrapped around two sides of the house. She let him in through the front door, and then disappeared into the kitchen. "The children will be home from school soon," she called.

Teague shuffled into the living room, a dim space with yellowing walls and a picture window that overlooked the deck and the driveway. The floor was filled with rows of folding chairs facing a spindly lectern at the far wall. Teague had been here often when the church couldn't meet at the YMCA. During services, the house bustled with activity: the scraping of chair legs on the wood floor, dozens of voices, music from the piano. The quiet now, like everything else, was an inversion.

A crucifix on the wall behind the lectern was an ugly, stabbing thing, an object of suffering, not solace. Pastor Stevens had been so angry when the doctor had said his mother would die. Teague wished he could talk with Monkey. He was sure he could bring up a website with some answers.

A mobile rang, and Mrs. Stevens answered with a singsong greeting. Teague strained to listen, but she had stopped speaking. He sensed Mrs. Stevens's approach even before she appeared with a hand over her mouth. She gestured for Teague to come to her.

"No," he said and backed away, keeping chairs between himself and Mrs. Stevens. His bottom lip quivered. His breathing wavered.

"My poor dear," Mrs. Stevens whispered.

Teague jumped when she moved, but she crossed the room and knelt beneath the cross, her back racked with sobs. Teague thought he should join her, but he considered the crucifix and found no reason to pray.

Teague had been removed to Kevin's room and put onto the bed with the curtains drawn. In the hallway, whispers preceded footsteps like a conspiracy. Mr. Stevens had returned at least an hour before, but when the door cracked open, it was the lanky form of Kevin that cast a shadow into the room.

"Hey, man, you awake?"

Teague sat up, sniffed, and wiped his sleeve across his face as Kevin sat down on the bed.

"I'm so sorry. Your mom was great," Kevin said. Teague nodded and fought to keep his lower lip still. "I'm supposed to take you to your place to pack some things. You're going to stay with us for a few days."

Teague hoped this meant his first ride on Kevin's motorcycle, but he found himself once again in the Stevenses' minuscule car. Halfway to the apartment, Kevin asked, "You going to be okay with this?"

"What do you mean?"

"Just—everything's happening so fast. Want to make sure you're okay."

"Now you can meet Monkey," Teague said.

"O-kay," Kevin said, drawing out the vowels. "I'll meet your monkey."

A few minutes later at his building, Teague darted out of the elevator ahead of Kevin. He buzzed open the apartment with his code and ran straight to his bedroom, arriving before Monkey had had time to get off his charging pad.

"It's good to see you, too," Monkey said with a giggle as Teague held him close.

"Mom's..." The words caught in Teague's throat.

"I don't understand, but it's all right. You can tell me later," Monkey said.

"We have to go."

"I like to go new places."

"Teague?" Kevin called and turned on the bedroom lights. "Where would—holy shit, you do have a monkey."

Monkey cocked his head, chirped, and waved.

"Is that a Zubot?" Kevin asked. "Teague-man, you are wicked Kelvin." Kevin crouched, and Teague let Monkey down.

"Hello, I'm Monkey."

"I'm Kevin," he replied and shook Monkey's paw. "How long have you had him?"

"Since kindergarten."

"Is he shift compatible?"

"I don't know."

"I'm E-shift and U-shift ready," Monkey replied. "M-shift, J-shift, and MV-shift upgrades are available through Zubotix.com. Sat-X shift capability will be available in future upgrades." Teague had only heard Monkey talk like this to his mother.

"Wow. Come on, let's get you packed up. Mom wants you back for the prayer and dinner thing. Clothes in here?" he asked, pointing at the dresser.

Teague collected Monkey's accessories in his backpack. Kevin grabbed Teague's school uniforms from the closet in one handful, wrapped them around their hangers, and stuffed them in the duffel bag from the hall closet. He yanked out Teague's raincoat, leaving the hanger swinging. Even after he'd emptied most of Teague's dresser drawers, the bag was only about half full.

"Anything else? Toothbrush? Toys?" Kevin picked up a hinged photo frame from Teague's desk. One side held a close-up of a man wearing sunglasses and a collared blue shirt, the first two buttons open: Teague's father. He was leaning against a peeling, yellow-painted doorway. The room behind him was dark. His mother had taken the picture at a Phuket motel before Teague had been born. The man looked happy enough, but Teague had always wished he could see his eyes. The other photo was of his mother and himself. He was a baby in a backpack, head lolling to one side behind his mother's shoulder. She was dressed for hiking, standing on a dirt road in front of a wooden sign covered with illegible paragraphs of Thai script. Her mouth was open as if she was speaking. She'd told Teague the picture was special because it had been taken the day that she took her Tiger to see the tigers.

"I think you'll want this," Kevin said. Teague nodded and put it in his backpack.

In the car, Monkey purred as Teague stroked him from neck to tail.

"Kevin, what were you and Monkey talking about? M-shift and all that?"

"Shifting. You know," said Kevin. Teague shook his head. "Do you play games online?"

"I play games with Monkey."

"Hmm. How to explain this? Say you're playing a game with Monkey, but Monkey's on Mars."

"God doesn't want us to go to Mars."

Kevin snorted. "We'll talk about that some other time. Let's just say Monkey's on Mars."

"Okay."

"How would you play the game together?"

"I don't know. We'd just play, but separately?"

"Okay, but Mars is, what, eighty or ninety million kilometers away. If you talk into a radio on Earth, it takes several minutes to hear the signal on Mars."

"Are you talking about the speed of light?"

Kevin pointed a congratulatory finger at Teague. "Exactly. It's hard to play a game, or talk, or whatever, when you're that far apart. To make it easy, you shift."

Teague wrinkled his brow. "How do you do that?"

"You put on a shift set. It connects to wires you have to have installed in your brain, and the software puts you to sleep. When you wake up, you're in the Virtual Internet. You're an avatar, and your brain is synced up with Mars time, and so is everyone else there. That's M-shifting. If you E-shift, you're on the Earth real-time grid. Earth, Moon, local stations, and stuff. U-shift is somewhere in between."

"Does it hurt?"

"Not a bit. I'm going to get all set up after I get enough money. Don't tell Mom and Pastor Dad, though. They'd crap a rhino."

"I won't," Teague said. Kevin's secret was safe with him.

* * *

The evening after the funeral, Teague huddled on the hard living room couch that had been made up for him to sleep on. He wanted to hold Monkey, but Mrs. Stevens insisted that the Zubot stay quiet and out of sight, and she was still busy in the kitchen. At least she hadn't taken him away. Better yet, she had forbidden her other children to touch him.

If Teague closed his eyes, he could still see his mother's casket at the front of the chapel at the funeral parlor. He'd had time to burn it into his mind as Pastor Stevens droned on about how death was just a transition, as if she had left the world cleanly and beautifully, as if she weren't locked in that box, mangled and torn. He'd claimed again and again that she now existed with God as if he was trying to convince himself. When Pastor Stevens had prayed, Teague bowed his head and closed his eyes but sang the Shakiro Squirrel theme song in his mind.

Teague had overheard enough in the past few days to piece together the facts. His mother had died in the ambulance as she was being taken to a practice to be healed. She had died while three healers, Pastor Stevens among them, were deep in prayer with hands laid on. Pastor Stevens had watched her die, but Teague didn't dare ask him about it. Had she cried? Had she spoken? Could she even breathe?

Teague pretended to be asleep when Mrs. Stevens turned out the kitchen lights. She hesitated briefly in the living room before heading toward her bedroom. When she had gone, Teague whispered to Monkey, and he crept out of the duffel bag, hopped onto the couch, and curled up in Teague's arms.

"There's a mention of you on the Internet," Monkey whispered. "Do you want to see it?

Teague dug his screen from his backpack. Monkey had loaded a page from the website of the church's headquarters in Boston,

Massachusetts. Sure enough, there was a picture of Teague standing in front of a lectern, the encircled crown and cross of the Christian Science logo prominent over his shoulder. It had been a wide shot of the children's choir at last year's Christmas program, published on the church's newsfeed. The other six children had been cropped away.

Light still seeped from under Kevin's bedroom door, so Teague tapped quietly. Kevin was in his pajamas but welcomed Teague in and closed the door.

"I wondered what this was about," Teague said, handing over his screen.

"Those bastards," Kevin muttered as he read.

"What?" Teague asked.

Kevin lowered his voice. "I know your parents were cool and all, but they're making them out to be martyred saints."

"Why?"

"This is so slimy. Did anyone talk to you about this?" Teague shook his head. "Do you want to stay in Bangkok?"

"Where else would I go?"

"Because it sounds like they're raising money to keep you in foster care here. That probably means with us, knowing Mom and Pastor Dad. You really don't have any other family?"

"I don't think so," Teague replied.

"It looks like they sent this to churches all over, and not only to Tellurites," Kevin said. Teague flinched to hear the slang term for their church. "They're basically using you to raise money. They're probably going to collect lots more than they actually need to take care of you. You shouldn't let them use you like this. You want me to say something?"

"I don't want to make trouble," Teague replied, shaking his head.

"This stupid church," Kevin said. "It's so dying. As soon as I'm old enough, I'm going to take Vanilla, get a shift set, and never look back. I might even go to the Moon."

"You're going to take Vanilla? But—"

"Teague-man, don't believe everything you hear, even in Sunday school. When you get older, you can decide for yourself, but don't believe anything blindly. Does that make sense?" Teague nodded, unsure if it did. "Tellurites aren't going to be around in twenty years anyway. I've heard Mom and Dad talking. They used to get a hundred people at Sunday services. Now they're lucky to get thirty, and that's in a big city."

"Would Vanilla have saved my mom?" Teague asked, taking back his screen.

Kevin shook his head sadly. "I don't think it works like that. Sorry."

CHAPTER 3

Most are shifted and, in a way, already dead.

MARCH–APRIL 2080

"Can I go to the Chaiprasits'?" Teague asked Mrs. Stevens.

"Don't you have homework?" Mrs. Stevens asked over her shoulder.

"No, ma'am. I did it already," Teague said. This was true enough. He'd worked ahead and completed all his math lessons for the year. It had been simple, especially with Monkey as a tutor. "So can I go?"

A timer beeped, and she waved him away from the oven door. A blast of heat and a strange smell wafted across the kitchen. At the table, Kahn and Manu pretended to gag. Mrs. Stevens clucked her tongue and gestured for them to focus on their schoolwork. "Not now," she said to Teague.

"But they said I could come over anytime."

"Dinner's almost ready and, besides, you'll see them tonight; it's Wednesday," Mrs. Stevens replied. Nan toddled into the kitchen banging a toy tambourine.

Teague shuffled back to Kevin's bedroom and shut the door, muting the incessant jangling. He fell onto his foam-topped cot in the corner opposite Kevin's tangled bed and hugged his pillow.

Monkey wriggled out from his charging nest underneath Teague's bed. "Can we go?" he asked. Teague shook his head.

"That's okay. We can have fun here. You just got a birthday message from Zubotix. Want to see it? It's full of great offers. No? Do you want the lights on?"

Kevin's burgundy paint seemed to swallow whatever afternoon light was finding its way in through the little window, leaving the flexi-posters to advertise their ever-changing stream of bands in the shadows.

"Do you want to play a game?" Monkey asked, and after a moment, he hopped onto the bed and stretched out next to Teague with his chin on his paws.

Out the window, Teague could see only tree branches and the neighbor's roof.

When Mrs. Stevens called him to dinner, Teague urged Monkey under the bed and emerged to find plates being set around the still-unfinished homework. Nan was kneeling on her chair, banging a spoon on the table.

"You can sit here," Mrs. Stevens said with an affected lilt, guiding Teague to Pastor Stevens's usual seat at the head of the table.

"What about Pastor—?" Teague asked.

"He's at the Y getting ready for Bible study," she replied.

"Why does Teague get to sit there?" Manu asked.

"It's his birthday today. Remember? Eat quickly. We have to go soon."

"Where's Kevin?" Teague asked.

"Where do you think? He's at work," Kahn said.

Halfway through dinner, Mrs. Stevens produced a wrapped box, and Teague took it hesitantly. Usually Kevin handled the family's obligations to him: the trips to shop for new shoes, haircuts. "I'd hoped to sing 'Happy Birthday' as a family, but we'll do it over cupcakes at church tonight," Mrs. Stevens said.

The present was a backpack, which was nice enough, except that he already had a decent backpack. He thanked Mrs. Stevens and tested some of the zippers. Kahn whispered to Manu, and they laughed. Mrs. Stevens barked at them to eat and to finish their homework.

Kevin's motorcycle was parked in the carport when they returned from Bible study. Teague followed the Stevens family up the stairs, wanting to dawdle, but he had nowhere else to go but Kevin's room. When Teague entered, Kevin swiveled around in his desk chair with Monkey on his lap. "There's the birthday man," he said. "Sorry I couldn't be there tonight. Is that your present from XX and XY?" He waved to the backpack on the end of Teague's bed. Teague shrugged. "Close the door and come see this."

Teague bristled when Kevin slid Teague's own screen over for him to see. The pink and black webpage announced that Mati, whoever that was, was "adrift in a cloud of nothingness," whatever that meant. Kevin tapped a video, and the girl began to spin in place on a stage, her pink bass guitar slung low on a strap embroidered with pink skulls. Her sweeping black hair obscured her face. Kevin glanced at the door and edged up the volume. A brooding, ephemeral punk soundtrack murmured over the desk.

"We've been going out for a couple of weeks," Kevin said. "Isn't she a Helen?" Teague frowned. "Trust me. Someday you'll understand. Her band's name is—" A knock rattled the door. Kevin snapped his fingers, and Monkey made the page disappear.

"Teague's bedtime," Mrs. Stevens called through the door.

Kevin gathered up his own screen and homework. "Happy birthday," he said as he left. "Should I turn the lights out?"

"Whatever," Teague answered.

As Teague tried to go to sleep, the house seemed to churn around him. Kahn and Manu wrestled and flushed the toilet more than necessary. Nan shrieked and cried. Mrs. Stevens shouted and tromped up and down the hall. Pastor Stevens mumbled from the master bedroom. Teague kicked off his itchy covers and pushed Monkey away.

"Go charge," he said, and Monkey dutifully crawled under the bed.

Long after the house had quieted, the bedroom door creaked open, and a wedge of light reconnoitered the room. Kevin undressed in the dark and got into bed. The day seemed over at last.

"You still awake?" Kevin whispered.

Teague hesitated. "Yeah."

"I'm sorry your birthday sucked." After a long silence, Kevin said, "I'll make it up to you. We'll go to the e-mall, hang out, eat junk food, and play Immer-Sims until we collapse. How does that sound?" Kevin had promised to take Teague to the e-mall months ago, to show him where he worked, to take him to the arcade, but he'd never followed through.

Another silence.

"Come on, don't be like this."

Teague didn't know how else he was supposed to be.

* * *

Teague sat up, surprised, when Kevin burst into the bedroom. Kevin dumped his messenger bag on his bed, opened the curtains, and then shouted when he noticed Teague. "Dang. Scared me. What are you doing in here?"

"Nothing."

"Have you been in here all day? It's Saturday afternoon."

"I know."

"Are you sick?" Kevin asked.

"No."

"Were M and K picking on you? Mom's lunch give you the farts?" Teague refused to be amused. "Sorry. Want to play Sector Sigma? I've got a little while before I'm meeting Mati." Teague shook his head. "Come on, Teague-man," Kevin said. "What's up?"

"Nothing's wrong! Just leave me alone!" Teague raked away his tears, stuffed his screen in his old backpack, and called for Monkey to follow.

"Where are you going?" Kevin asked. Teague ran, going out the front door to avoid Mrs. Stevens. Kevin came out onto the deck and called after him.

Teague ran and ran—taking alleys so he wouldn't be seen—to his only refuge. He dumped his backpack at the guard dogs' feet, charged into the temple, and stopped at the top of the altar. He slapped the Buddha once, hard, on the side of its head. The statue only continued to smile. Teague slapped it again and then again and again with both hands until his hands stung and his eyes burned. When he was out of breath and out of tears, he stumbled down the steps and fell to the floor. A few minutes later, he slid his shoes off.

"Monkey?" he asked. "Can you take these outside?"

* * *

Teague opened his eyes in the dark, unsure why he was awake, or if he'd ever been asleep. He was about to turn over when he sensed a presence near his bed.

"Monkey? Wake up," a voice hissed. Teague froze.

"Hi, Kev. What do you want to do?" Monkey replied from under the bed, mimicking Kevin's whisper.

"We need to help Teague."

"I like to help."

"No one's helping him with coping—with his mom dying," Kevin said. "I think that's what's wrong. You have a grief program, right?"

"I understand now," Monkey whispered in his serious voice. "Please wait while I access Zubotix Parent Resources." Teague tried not to breathe. "Welcome to the Zubotix Child Grief Support Program. This program, developed by leading child psychologists, expands the relationship of a Zubot with a grieving child in his or her time of loss. Subtle interaction gently and compassionately guides the child through the grieving process at his or her own pace. Also included are exclusive support materials for guardians, a configuration guide, and access to certified child grief counselors. The program is compatible with all Zubotix models, Beagle Series or later."

"That sounds perfect," Kevin said.

"Would you like to learn more?"

"No. Let's do it. Use my account to pay for it."

"The cost is three hundred and twenty-five UN notes. Shall I convert that to baht for you?"

"No, unos are fine."

"Shall I register you as the guardian?" Monkey asked.

"Yeah. Do that. Thanks, Monkey."

Monkey returned to his nest and Kevin to his bed. Teague rolled over, forgetting that he was pretending to be asleep, and wondered if three hundred and twenty-five unos was a lot of money.

* * *

The next Saturday, Kevin woke Teague early. "Get up and get dressed," he said. "I won't take no for an answer."

A few minutes later, Teague shuffled into the kitchen, and Kevin pressed a breakfast bar into his hand. "What's going on?" Teague asked. Kevin zipped Monkey up to his neck into Teague's old backpack and then made Teague put it on.

"I like to go new places," Monkey said over Teague's shoulder.

Kevin handed Teague a motorcycle helmet. "Don't ask questions," he said. "Just eat up and put that on."

Teague shivered in the cool morning air under the carport as Kevin donned his helmet. "Can you hear me?" Kevin's voice rang clearly through Teague's helmet, and Teague nodded his weighted head. "Good. Get on behind me. Hold onto this bar here or around my waist. Rule one: Don't fall off. Rule two: Enjoy the ride, but not at the expense of rule one." Had Mrs. Stevens approved this? She'd never let Teague ride with Kevin before.

The bike wobbled as Teague got on, and before he felt settled, the whiny electric motor began to vibrate the seat. "Hang on," Kevin called, twisting his wrist. The bike jumped forward, and gravel spun out from under the rear tire. Teague clung to Kevin's waist as they bumped through the gate and accelerated onto the street.

"Whoa, loosen up," Kevin said. "I do need to breathe." Teague relaxed as much as he dared. "You doing okay back there, Monkey?"

"I'm doing fine," Monkey said over the helmet speakers. "Did you know you're exceeding the speed limit?"

Kevin laughed. "Get used to it, my lemur friend."

Cool wind breathed through Teague's clothes, but the sun

warmed him through the intermittent gaps in the city's shadows. Soon, Teague began to enjoy the feel of the ride, to understand the changes in vibration and the angles of the turns.

Kevin slowed, veered across the oncoming lane, and stopped at the curb near another bike parked on the sidewalk. Teague released his grip on Kevin's gut as Kevin took off his helmet and ran his fingers through his hair.

A door between shuttered shops opened with an electric buzz. Teague felt a twinge of resentment when the girl with the flowing black hair emerged, wearing a leather jacket and loose pants covered with pockets. As she swung her hair aside and kissed Kevin, Teague noticed the telltale glint of a shift implant behind her ear.

"Mati, Teague. Teague, Mati."

"*Sawadee ka,*" she said kindly, and Teague felt the twinge melt away. He greeted her in return, all too conscious of his face scrunched in the motorcycle helmet.

"Monkey's back there, too," Kevin said. Monkey chirped.

"Cute," Mati said. She slipped her helmet on, flipped a dark visor over her face, swung a little backpack around her shoulders, and straddled the other motorcycle. Kevin tugged his helmet back on.

"You ready?" Kevin asked.

"The question is, are you?" she replied over the radio. Her bike accelerated silently, bumped off the curb, and zoomed away.

"Oh, yeah," Kevin laughed. Seconds later they were close behind her, moving easily on the quiet streets. They exchanged the lead several times in a friendly, flirting race, and then ventured side by side onto the highway.

The still-rising sun stuttered between the skyscrapers as they traveled north. The high-rises eventually gave way to lesser buildings, which soon smoothed to farms, where the light strobed off rice paddies. Teague's arms and legs began to stiffen. Every few kilometers, they passed an enclave of roadside stores and service stations clustered close to the highway or the turn-off to a town, and Teague studied each for some clue to their destination.

At an announcement from Kevin, they exited onto a two-lane highway heading northeast and rolled through a quiet town. They turned on a road that began to climb into the hills beyond. Twenty winding kilometers later, another turn took them onto a narrow, roughly paved road. A forest rose high and dark around them. A yipping dog chased them when they slowed to pass through a roadside village carved out of the trees. Three elderly men looked up from their game table on the store's porch to watch them pass. Just past a solar station at the far end of the village, they scattered a flock of chickens.

"Where are we going?" Teague begged.

"Hang on. We're almost there," Kevin replied. A few minutes later, the pavement ended and the road climbed higher and deeper into the hills. They passed a platoon of monks, mere boys in orange robes, who cheered to see them. Teague risked a wave through the plumes of dust.

They continued on for a few more kilometers, and then Kevin skidded to a stop in the middle of the road. "We're here," he said.

Teague stumbled onto solid ground, confused. There were no buildings or parking lots, not even a widening in the road. He squeezed out of his helmet, and Kevin pointed to two signs twenty meters farther on.

Feeling began to return to Teague's stiff legs as he approached the signs. The first read "Khao Yai Mountain Tiger Conservancy" in English and Thai. Teague recognized the second. The lines of dense Thai script had nearly been weathered away, but he didn't need to decipher them to know what they meant. He had been here before as a baby in a backpack. His mother had stood right here, and a monk had taken their picture.

"Did you know we were coming here?" Teague asked Monkey.

"Kev asked me to keep it a secret," Monkey replied over his shoulder.

Footsteps crunched on the gravel behind Teague. "We thought this might be a good place for you to think about things for a while," Kevin said. Teague knew that meant his mother but was glad Kevin didn't say so. Kevin unzipped Teague's backpack, and Monkey hopped to the ground.

"Look this way, gentlemen," Mati said. She held up her mobile. Kevin put his arm over Teague's shoulder.

Monkey leaned against Teague's leg and said, "Cheese."

The rest of the morning, they rested in the shade on the decks that overlooked the seemingly fenceless habitats. Occasionally, a yawning roar echoed through the trees like a primal warning, or one of the keepers slipped by on some business. Teague found that he didn't mind when Mati and Kevin held hands.

They ate lunch in the village under an umbrella advertising Singha Beer and returned to the conservancy in the afternoon. While a pair of cubs wrestled playfully, Teague tried to match his breathing to that of their dozing mother, wanting to feel the raw strength and power in himself. His mother had called him Tiger, and she had brought him into these mountains; maybe there was a reason.

* * *

The e-mall might once have been as grand as the one where his mother had taken him to buy Monkey, but any magnificence, along with any potted plants or public art, had long been displaced. The wide, tiled promenades were choked with makeshift booths and stalls. Even the permanent storefronts on the perimeter had been subdivided, as if rented by the square centimeter—a night market come in from the rain.

Teague had never seen so many mobile covers and cases in his life. Millions of them dangled from pegboards, were crammed on shelves, or were dumped in bins. The remaining space was packed with gadgets, widgets, and accessories, the most valuable of which were showcased under shiny glass counters. It was almost impossible to tell one vendor from the next, and each promised the best prices, one-of-a kind customizations, and life-changing hacks. At one large stall, a proprietor promised to make almost anything with his long row of spattered, rattling object printers. Everywhere flexi-signs flashed prices in a dozen languages, and Teague was sure he'd heard people speaking a dozen more.

Kevin and Mati pushed right through the teenage throng in the aisles, and Teague forced himself to keep up, even when he wanted to stop and stare. Nearly everyone had visible shift implants, and many had proudly incorporated them into glowing, articulated tattoos that spilled down their necks and covered their shoulders and arms in seemingly functional filigree. The hentai that played blatantly on so many screens left Teague both curious and terrified. In almost every stall, people were sprawled on padded benches, couches, or even the floor—shifting. Why did Pastor Stevens let Kevin work in such a place?

They spiraled up a set of escalators to a floor with even narrower aisles than the first. Two enormously tall and lean men loped by, their heads almost scraping the ceiling. Their faces were Chinese, but long and stretched. Their spindly legs and torsos were framed with sleek, humming exoskeletons. "Martians," Kevin explained, seeing Teague gape after them.

"They might be from the Moon," Mati remarked.

"No. Definitely from Mars," Kevin said. "Lunatics are even taller."

"Don't be rude," Mati said.

They soon arrived at a four-by-four-meter stall little different from the hundreds of others. "This is where I work," Kevin announced. A chime sounded as he crossed the plane of the entrance. Electronic parts hung in little plastic bags from a pegboard along one wall. On the opposite side, open cardboard boxes of ancient comics weighed down a folding table. The hand-labeled tabs of the dividers—Thai, Japanese, English, and Chinese—had nearly been worn away by untold browsers. Kevin skirted around a glass display counter stacked full of used mobiles and ducked through a black-curtained opening in the back wall. There were no shifters here, only a vacant recliner, its upholstery more duct tape than vinyl. Several faded piñatas, including a Shakiro Squirrel, hung among the light strips from the spidery grid of truss overhead. Teague imagined kids beating Shakiro Squirrel until candy spewed from his body and shuddered.

Kevin returned. "He must have gone to the restroom or something."

"Isn't your boss afraid people will steal stuff?" Teague asked.

"No one steals from Badass Bondi," Kevin replied.

"Why do they call him...?" Teague began, but decided he didn't want an answer.

Outside the Virt-plex on the top floor of the e-mall, Teague deduced the current Immer-Sim titles from the half-functioning marquee as Kevin bought them candy and enormous bottles of energy drinks at the concession stand. What were they going to play? *Seven Seas: Captain Bloodwell's Revenge*? *Li Ping, Superspy IV: Invasion Taipei*? *World Cup '76*? Or maybe *Dragonhold: The Siege*?

"Don't tell Mom I let you drink this stuff, but trust me, you're going to need it," Kevin said, loading Teague up with the bottles. Teague headed for the Virt-plex's entrance, but Kevin called his name. "Where're you going?" he asked, and nodded his head to one side. "This way."

In a dark recess of the nearly abandoned arcade, Kevin presented Teague and Mati to a man with a pencil-thin mustache and hard eyes. He looked them up and down and admitted them to a dim, concrete back corridor. They followed in silence until he stopped at a metal door no different from the dozens they'd already passed. Kevin and the man conducted a quick transaction with their mobiles, and the man unlocked the door.

Inside, a single bare fixture cast a dull pallor over what was probably meant to be a storeroom. In a near corner, Immer-Sim gear—goggles, gloves, plastic guns, and vests, all piled on charging pads—covered a folding table. A thick bundle of wires spewed out of a portable equipment rack and disappeared under a black curtain that had been draped across the room. Teague peeked through the curtain to find the gridded sensor array of a not-quite-Immer-Sim-brand Immer-Sim suite.

"We've got twelve hours," said Kevin, and Teague gaped. The only other time he'd played Immer-Sim, at a friend's birthday party at the science museum, they'd been allowed only fifteen minutes. "Are you ready to *really* play Sector Sigma?" Kevin asked.

It was a grisly death. Teague yanked off his goggles and plopped down on the gridded floor. If his head had been pounding—from the sugar, the noise, the caffeine, the virtual battle, or the weight of the gear—he hadn't noticed until now. His arms and trigger finger ached, but he had to laugh.

"That was some hit," Kevin said, removing his own goggles.

"I think I need to stop for a while," Teague said, pulling out his earbuds. This Sector Sigma made the game they played at home seem like checkers, even when they played on the big screen in the living room when Kevin's parents weren't home.

"I guess we should have brought Monkey," Kevin said. "We could have used Corporal Monk's nuculizer to bring down that Devastator."

They shed their gear and sat on the floor to eat the takeout Mati had brought.

"Do you want to play something different?" Kevin asked.

"What is there?" asked Teague.

"They've got a great Muay Thai boxing game."

"You don't box," Teague said.

"Yes, I do."

"Since when?"

"For a couple of years now," Kevin replied. "At a gym near the school."

"When do you have time? Do you even *have* a job?" Teague asked.

Kevin raised an eyebrow and chuckled. "Of course I do. How do you think I pay the gym dues, or for the mobile I don't officially have? And save for college to appease XX and XY?" He set his lunch aside, went to the control screen, and selected a game. "Okay, pay attention. I'm setting it to Advanced."

"Why not set it to Master?" Mati asked with a wry smile.

"I don't want to make a complete fool of myself," Kevin replied as he stripped off his shirt.

"Show-off," Mati said. Kevin blew her a kiss, donned his goggles, pushed buds back in his ears, and pulled on a pair of sensor gloves.

On the screen, Kevin appeared under harsh spotlights in a crudely roped ring with a muscled Thai boxer and a tattooed referee. A shadowed crowd cheered savagely around them. A bell chimed, and music began: drums and cymbals and a recorder in seemingly random rhythms. Kevin circled his opponent and then struck, but landed in a clinch. The boxer scored points on Kevin's ribcage, but after a flurry, Kevin had the boxer pressed against the ropes. The referee separated them. Kevin landed a good punch, followed by a solid kick to the boxer's side. The boxer stumbled and recovered, but from then on it was Kevin's round.

"Not bad," Mati said when Kevin emerged from behind the curtain glistening with sweat.

"Do you believe me now?"

"Can you take me to your gym?" Teague asked.

"Are you kidding? Mom would banish you to Kahn and Manu's room so fast. But I'll teach you a few things."

That evening, Kevin kept his promise. Monkey played along, mimicking the stances, punches, and kicks.

"First, you've got to get in shape," Kevin said. "Run to school instead of walking. Use the pull-up bar in the carport. Do push-ups every day. As many as you—" He was interrupted by Mrs. Stevens calling for Teague to go to bed.

"Sounds like you had a fun day," Monkey said after Kevin left. "You'll probably sleep well tonight. But I've noticed it usually takes a long time for you to go to sleep. What do you think about?"

"I don't know. Stuff."

"Would you like to talk to someone about those things? I'll always listen, but maybe there's another person, like an adult, you might feel like talking to."

"There's not," Teague said. But a few minutes later, he realized—there was someone.

* * *

The lobby mural had celebrated the work of Thai doctors through the ages—from centuries-old two-dimensional traditional medicine to tomorrow's 4-D telerobotic nanosurgery—more times than Teague cared to count. And dozens, if not hundreds, of people had filtered past, their footfalls muted by the carpet. The vacuum that had been crisscrossing the lobby since they'd arrived finally edged up to their bench and then swerved away, seemingly irritated at their presence.

"Are you sure they called her?" Teague asked.

Kevin laughed. "Settle down. It's a big place."

Dr. Aromdee arrived from an unexpected direction. She wasn't angry or exhausted, like Teague remembered her. Her hair had been fastened in a thick ponytail, but a few stray hairs fell down the sides of her face. She wore purple scrubs and carried a screen and a large silver travel mug. "Hello, Teague," she said as they stood. "And you must be Kevin."

"Yes, ma'am."

"Thank you for bringing him."

"It was his idea," Kevin said.

"Are you hungry?" Dr. Aromdee asked Teague.

"A little," he replied.

"How about we find a snack? My treat."

"Take your time," Kevin said and plopped back onto the bench with his mobile.

As they waited for an elevator, Dr. Aromdee said, "You've found a good friend."

"He's Pastor Stevens's son. They're my foster parents now."

Dr. Aromdee pursed her lips and nodded. "Kevin cares about you."

"I guess so," Teague said.

They rode the elevator down one floor and crossed a busy corridor into a sunlit cafeteria. Dr. Aromdee took the top tray from a pile by the entrance, swiped her badge across the corner, and handed it to Teague. "They have cookies over there. Sandwiches if you're really hungry. Fruit. Drinks in that case. Help yourself." She picked up another tray and headed straight to the coffee machine.

"I was—I am," Dr. Aromdee began after they'd found a table, "very sorry for your loss."

"Thank you," Teague said, having months ago learned the proper response. He picked at the plastic around his cookie, a huge thing, as big as his face.

"Go ahead," she said, tearing into her own. Teague opened

his and broke off a bite. "Good?" she asked. Teague nodded as he chewed. "Are you going to school?"

"Yes."

"I'm glad. I'm certain your mother would have wanted you to get a good education. I understand that she was a healer."

"Not like you," Teague said.

"No," Dr. Aromdee agreed. "But I'm sure she cared for her patients just as much."

Teague let himself look Dr. Aromdee in the eye. "She would've lived, wouldn't she? I mean, if she had stayed here?"

"Yes. In all probability, she would have."

"I was really confused."

Dr. Aromdee sighed. "I did everything I could for her. And so did you. You mustn't blame yourself."

"You were the only one who told the truth that day," Teague said.

"Mr. Stevens did what he believed was right. And it's what your mother believed, too. You understand that, don't you?"

"You can believe a lie, though," Teague said. "I think they believed a lie."

"How old are you now?"

"I'm nine."

"You still have a lot of growing up to do. But, yes, people often believe lies. And perhaps your mother and your pastor did. That's unfortunate, but that doesn't make them bad people."

"I think..." he began, and then restarted. "I understand."

"I've worried about you," she said.

"You have?"

"Of course. To be going through all this at such a young age."

"Everyone keeps saying that there's a purpose."

"That's a big question," Dr. Aromdee said. "Anyone can look back and say that because something bad happened, and then something good happened, that the first event must have had a purpose. But I don't think that's how it works. I think that people in general want to do good. So when a bad thing happens, most people try to return good to the world. If you become a good person, a stronger person, it's not because your mother died. It's because you chose to do so."

"But why did it happen?"

"I can't answer that. Human beings are fragile creatures. We often forget that these days."

"Are you talking about Vanilla? The Universal Treatment, I mean?"

"I suppose I am."

"Do you take it?"

"Of course."

"My mom didn't."

"A brave choice."

"Why brave?" Teague asked.

"Not everyone is strong enough to really live according to how they believe." As Dr. Aromdee spoke, her mobile buzzed. She frowned at the screen and then tucked it back into her pocket. She plucked a pen from her breast pocket and pulled a napkin from the dispenser. "I'm afraid I need to go, but I want you to keep in touch. This is my eddress. Message me anytime you need to talk. I can be your friend, someone who might give you a different perspective on things."

"Thank you," Teague said.

"I'm very glad you came. I'm sorry we didn't have more time. Can you find your way back to the lobby?" Teague nodded. "One last word of advice."

"Yeah?"

"Think something good about her every day. A memory. That she loved you. Anything."

"I will," Teague said.

"Good. Don't lose that." Whether she meant the napkin or his memories, Teague didn't know.

"That wasn't long," Kevin said.

"She got called back to work."

"You didn't tell me she was a Helen. Did you get her eddress?"

"Yeah."

"You got the stuff, Teague-man," Kevin said and elbowed him with a laugh.

"Shut up." Teague elbowed Kevin back.

* * *

As Pastor Stevens said the blessing for the evening meal, Teague caught Kevin staring at him. For Kevin to be at dinner was strange enough, but when he looked away, Teague knew something was wrong. "Family meeting after dinner," Pastor Stevens announced after the prayer.

"About what?" Kahn asked.

"After dinner," Pastor Stevens replied. Kevin didn't look away this time but shook his head slightly.

Teague ate a little and asked to be excused.

"Don't go far," Mrs. Stevens said.

Teague had barely shut the door when Kevin came in the bedroom. "God, I've been wanting to tell you," he said, sitting down on Teague's bed.

"Tell me what?"

Monkey emerged and began to glance back and forth between them as they spoke.

"Mom and Dad are moving. There's some bigger congregation in India that needs a pastor."

"I don't want to go to India."

"*We* don't have to," Kevin said.

"What do you mean?"

"They're figuring out a way for you to stay here with the new pastors."

"I don't get a choice?" Teague asked.

"I think you do, but…do you really want to stay with them?"

"What about you?" Teague asked.

"I'm not going to India."

"You're staying here?"

"I'm going to the United States. I'll finish school there and start college in a few months."

"But you—"

"Hey. Forget about me. You need to worry about yourself right now."

"What do I do?" Teague asked.

"When they ask if you want to stay, just be honest."

"And they'll agree?"

"They only get about one thousand American dollars a month from the church to take care of you."

"How do you know that?"

"I've overheard them talking."

"So what?"

"It's not very much, now, is it?" Kevin said.

"I don't know," Teague said.

"Trust me, it's not, and most of it goes to pay for school. So I'm saying that if you want to stay in Bangkok, you can. I know my dad feels guilty about your mom. He's never said it, but I've noticed how he avoids you."

"But you won't be here," Teague said.

"We'll keep in touch. Maybe someday we'll hang out in the shift grids together."

Teague patted his lap, and Monkey climbed on. Teague hugged him close and rested his forehead on Monkey's head. He didn't want to cry, especially not in front of Kevin.

"I'm sorry. Don't be angry," Kevin said.

"I'm not." Teague had meant this as a lie, but when he considered that he might never see Pastor Stevens again, he realized it was the truth.

CHAPTER 4

It isn't safe in the public areas. I had hoped this hysteria would pass. Why do we fear for our lives when death is so certain, so soon? Or is it pain we fear the most?

JULY 2080

Teague dismounted the bus cautiously. He hadn't been expecting such a hammered-together, monsoon-scoured neighborhood, even on this side of the river. He had pictured something more... safe? But Monkey insisted that this was the stop. The utility poles were tangled with hundreds of haphazardly swagged wires and distressed transformers. The road surface crumbled into the dried earth at its edges. Monkey leaped into Teague's arms at the sight of two stray dogs, but they were more interested in an overflowing recycling bin.

No one would worry for hours—Teague often went to the library or visited the Chaiprasits after school—but he was certain that Pastor and Mrs. Varner would not approve of him being so far from the bricks, curbs, plate glass, and traffic control of their neighborhood, no matter what time he returned.

The bus rolled away, and Monkey pointed across the street to a path between buildings, more surveying error than alley. "Stay close," Teague said, letting Monkey down. He took a deep breath before darting across the street through a gap in the traffic.

Teague was used to stares wherever he went, especially with Monkey at his side, but he hurried past the silent, suspicious attention of a street-side barber and his customer under a ragged umbrella. He forced himself not to break into a run when, from an alcove full of motorcycle carcasses, a mechanic squinted at him and Monkey in turn and then spat into the dirt.

A hundred meters along, Monkey scampered to a rusting screen door set in a plywood wall. There was no sign or address, only three pairs of sneakers moldering by the door as if they'd been there for several rainy seasons. Teague pressed his nose to the screen and shaded his eyes to see into the darkness beyond. He knocked, but the tiny bangs dissipated into emptiness.

"You're sure this is right?" Teague asked, checking the alley.

"The coordinates match," Monkey replied.

The screen door creaked as Teague let Monkey in ahead of him. Once his eyes had adjusted, Teague found himself in a small, windowless office with bare plywood floors and a cluttered desk without a chair. A ceiling fan turned lazily in the stifling heat. A hammock dangled across one corner. But this had to be the right place. The walls were covered with layers of posters announcing boxing tournaments long past. Voices filtered through a doorless opening beyond the desk.

"Hello?" Teague called. He poked his head around the corner and found a cloistered courtyard with a raised, weathered boxing ring at its center, surrounded by rickety bleachers. The voices were coming from a dark passage straight ahead along the cloister. "Stay here," he said to Monkey.

At the other end of the cloister, the courtyard shared a wall with a grungy locker room. Rust streaks dripped from a row of showerheads to the drain in the concrete floor. A peeling divider barely concealed a single toilet, and two wobbly benches sat askew in front of a bank of leaning lockers. A medical kit had been left open on the scarred upholstery of a training table. Teague's feet began to crunch on sand as he crossed to the end of the passage.

Teague stopped as he entered another cloister, this one surrounding a square sandpit. About thirty boys, mostly teens, had turned their backs on duct-taped punching bags and mismatched free-weights under the awnings to focus on the center of the sand. There, among a milling clutch of six more boys, a man was kneeling by another boy lying on his back.

Teague watched for several moments, trying to discern what had happened, until he realized that someone had noticed him—a man, blond and severe. He wasn't large, but strength brimmed from his narrow frame. This must be Josiah, the gym owner, the prize-winning boxer turned coach for underprivileged boys. Except for his scruffy red beard, he looked just as Teague had imagined, with sinewy muscles and the eyes of a fighter. The man made a stern announcement in Thai and waved a bloody towel, not taking his gaze off Teague. The boys began to return to their exercises.

The man skirted around the scene in the sand and marched toward Teague. "What do you want?" he barked.

"Josiah?" Teague managed through a tight throat.

"You want to see Father Josiah?" the blond man asked.

"You're not—?"

"Josiah, someone to see you," the man called.

Back on the sand, the real Josiah helped the boy to his feet and clapped him on the back. As he strolled over, Teague took stock: a hairy barrel chest, a gnarled nose that overwhelmed his face, unkempt gray hair, dirty khaki shorts, and a sweat-stained tank top that looked as if it had been worn for days. Teague had expected brawny arms, but not a potbelly.

"What do you want, boy?" he asked.

"I want to learn Muay Thai?" Teague squeaked, hating that it had come out as a question.

Josiah harrumphed and walked into the locker room, leaving the scent of sweat in his wake. He bent over the locker room sink, cupped his hands under the tap, and splashed water over his head. The blond man began to repack the medical kit.

"It's hot as fuck, Ned," Josiah said. "You'd think after all these years..." He splashed again, leaving his shirt even more transparent.

Josiah barreled out without a look at Teague. Teague waited a moment, confused, and then hurried after him. As he approached the dark office, he heard a scuffle and a shout of surprise. Teague ran in to find Monkey cowering in a corner, shrieking defensively. Josiah had backed against the desk and was brandishing a flyswatter.

"He's mine," Teague shouted.

"Get that fleabag out of here before I stomp it to death!"

"No, he's a Zubot," Teague said.

Monkey jumped into Teague's arms. "Hi. I'm Monkey. I'm a Zubotix Beagle Series Ring-Tailed Lemur."

"Just what I need today," Josiah muttered. He opened a desk drawer, removed a flask, and took a long pull. He screwed the cap back on but didn't put the flask away. "Do your parents know you're here?"

"No."

"Even better. Look, kid, I don't know where you think you are, but this is not a membership gym. I can recommend some places for you if you want. This isn't some place for rich kids to slum it."

"I don't understand."

Josiah laughed coldly. "You probably don't. How old are you?"

"I'm nine, sir." Monkey held up two paws with one of his fingers curled down.

"Cute," Josiah said. "Go home."

"Why?" Teague asked, putting Monkey down.

"This is not a charity. Well, it is a charity, but not for you."

"Why isn't it a charity for me?" Teague asked. "I don't have any money."

"Well, go home and ask Mommy and Daddy to give you some."

"But your website—"

"Bah. The website," Josiah interrupted. "Are you Thai?"

"I was born in Thailand. I've lived here all my life. And my parents are dead."

Josiah stared at Teague for a few moments and then looked at his flask. "So what? Where do you live?" he asked.

"I live with foster parents, but they won't pay for classes."

"Bullies at school? Neighborhood kids busting your ass?"

"Huh?"

"Why do you want to learn to box?"

"I just do. It seems fun." As soon as the word "fun" escaped his lips, Teague knew he'd said the wrong thing.

"Get out."

"That's not what I meant."

Josiah rounded his desk, taking a slide of debris with him. "You heard me. Fuck off." He stomped out of the room.

"Stay here, Monkey," Teague ordered, and ran after Josiah.

"Sir?" Teague shouted, before Josiah got to the locker room. "Khru?"

Josiah spun around. "What did you call me?"

"I called you khru. Teacher."

"Do you understand what it means?"

"Yes," Teague replied, desperately trying to remember if Kevin had told him anything else.

"What's your name?"

"Teague Werres."

Josiah considered Teague with a hard glare, and then said, "Why don't you tell me why you really want to learn to fight?"

Teague swallowed. "Because…because my parents are dead, my only friend moved away, and everyone I know would tell me I can't do it." He sensed that he shouldn't break Josiah's gaze.

"You're not the only one who's had a rough go in life, you know?" Josiah said.

"I know."

"Most of the boys here have lives that make yours look like a fairy-tale picnic. I'm hard on them to keep guns and drugs out of their hands. I won't go easy on you just because you're the lazy spawn of some pasty ex-pats."

"I don't know what that means."

"It means you won't get any special treatment."

"I can't come every day," Teague said.

"Do you understand what I'm telling you?"

Teague nodded.

Josiah threw up his hands. "Whatever."

"Thank you," Teague said.

Josiah snorted derisively and then bellowed, "Ned!"

The blond man appeared from the locker room. "Yes, Father?"

"This is Teague. Let him know what he needs," Josiah said.

"Yes, Father," Ned replied.

"God help you if you're lying about any of this," Josiah yelled as he walked away. "And leave that fucking lemur at home."

"What lemur?" Ned asked.

* * *

Teague changed into the shorts and T-shirt that Ned had suggested he buy, borrow, or steal. Then, barefoot, he stepped gingerly over the sandy concrete to the training area of Josiah's Muay Thai Gym, A Program for Boys. Across the sand pit, Father Josiah was holding pads for a wiry teenager and barking instructions at the boy in Thai. Did Father Josiah ever change his clothes?

"Werres."

Teague spun around to find Ned looming behind him. "Yes, Teacher?" he replied, eager to display the respect all the sites said was so important.

"Run," Ned said. "On the sand. Around the edge. Do not stop until I tell you."

"Yes, Teacher." But he hesitated, trying to formulate a question.

"Go," Ned ordered.

The first step onto the sand nearly drove Teague back to the wet concrete of the locker room, but he clenched his teeth and set off counterclockwise into the shade. He turned his first corner and then stepped onto the truly hot, sunlit sand. Boys began to tap their neighbors and nod in his direction.

Like all the others, the boy with Father Josiah had paused to gape at Teague. But as Teague turned his second corner, Father Josiah rebuked the boy for his inattention. Teague stumbled and flailed to keep his balance. Laughter.

Teague rounded the third corner, squinting, sweat already pouring down his forehead and back. A boy flung out a string of Thai invective Teague didn't understand, and several other boys laughed. Teague turned the final corner and shuffled back onto the shaded sand. Now it came as a welcome relief. Ned had gone, so Teague began another lap. On the third lap, a boy spat on the sand in Teague's path. Teague stumbled as he dodged it but kept moving, fighting for each step in the deepening troughs.

The other boys soon moved on, the novelty spent, their own training to do. Teague's clothes grew heavy and his pace slowed, but any speed was better than surrender. Father Josiah disappeared. Teague kept plodding, marking his progress by the burlap-covered posts, where Father Josiah had stood, the insulting boys, the ball of discarded tape, the shade, anything to keep his mind off the next searing, squeaking footfall. After a while, one boy began to teach several others a kick, punch, and block sequence in the center of the sandpit. It was a welcome diversion. Teague was about to begin another lap when he heard his name.

"That's enough for the day. Go home," Ned called from the locker room entrance.

Teague hobbled onto the solid, cool concrete, grit stabbing into his soles, but his only thought was of the sink. He alternately swallowed handfuls of water and poured them over his head. When he could drink no more, he plopped on a bench, closed his eyes, and sucked at the thick air. He wasn't sure his quivering legs would hold him, let alone carry him to the bus stop.

"My goodness," Mrs. Varner said when Teague came in the kitchen door. "Are you all right?"

"Yes, ma'am. I played soccer at the park with some friends."

Teague edged around the Varner toddlers and their sticky toys on the kitchen floor. Hannah, the oldest, babbled at him. Robert Jr. began to cry as his mother bent to wipe his nose. "Clean yourself up quickly. Dinner's in less than half an hour," Mrs. Varner called.

Teague fought not to grimace as he took painful steps out to dinner in fresh clothes. Mrs. Varner had changed, too, from her daytime sweatpants into a long, homemade dress. The children's faces had been cleaned, probably with Mrs. Varner's own spit. He'd witnessed that too many times.

Pastor Varner parked in the carport, climbed the front stair, entered through the front door—he never used the kitchen door—and came immediately to his spot at the table. He was many years older than his wife, but almost as thin and narrow-shouldered. Mrs. Varner herded Hannah and Robert Jr. into place behind her own chair, and Teague stood behind his. When the children had been hushed, Pastor Varner bowed his head, said a brief prayer, and then sat and began to eat.

Despite his ravenous hunger, Teague forced himself to eat slowly, taking just one forkful for each of Pastor Varner's deliberate bites. Mrs. Varner fed her children from her own plate, placing morsels in front of them and eating next to nothing herself. Robert Jr. began to fuss, and when Pastor Varner glared at her, Mrs. Varner took the boy out of the room. When they returned, the toddler apologized to his father and did not speak again.

* * *

The next day, Teague's feet were tender and his legs painfully sore. But on the second day, the day he'd planned for his next excursion, he awoke to find them healed and ready.

When Teague entered the dank locker room that afternoon, several boys ceased their conversation and gathered to leave. Teague stood aside to let them pass, but one boy pushed him hard against the lockers. Teague's head banged against a metal edge, and he fell. He staggered to his feet, holding his scalp, and heard another commotion. In the passageway, Father Josiah was holding the boy against the wall and growling in Thai.

After Father Josiah released him, the boy waied, mumbled an apology, and then turned to Teague.

"I apologize," the boy said in Thai and waied again.

"It's forgotten," Teague replied, returning the wai. The forgiveness did not warm the boy's scowl.

"Werres, you will run again," Ned said, as if he hadn't noticed the scuffle.

Father Josiah had gone without a word.

* * *

"It sounds like you got yourself a real old-school khru," Kevin said. Teague edged the screen's volume down again. It might be late morning in America, but in Bangkok his foster family had all been asleep for at least an hour.

"I can't afford to go anywhere else," Teague whispered.

"How much are they charging you?"

"Nothing."

"You're kidding. Where is this place?" Teague told him, and Kevin searched for the details. "I'm not finding it. Oh, here it is. Wow. You're going all the way over there?"

"It's the only place I could find."

"That area's like gangland central. Do you know that?"

"So?"

"I'm not going to tell you not to go, but…" Kevin shook his head. "Did you check this place out?"

"A little," Teague replied.

Kevin's face slipped out of view for a moment. "What's your khru's name?"

"Josiah," Teague replied. "People call him 'Father', but I don't know his last name."

"Father Josiah Muay Thai," Kevin murmured as he searched. "Is this him?" A page appeared, including a photo of a young Caucasian boxer throwing a punch; the other fighter was a blurred silhouette.

"He's older."

"He would be. He was born before Vanilla. Josiah Coward. American. Wow. This guy was pretty good, if this is him." Kevin skimmed the text. "Regional championships. Medals at the Pan-Asian Championships. Pro for a few years, first in Thailand and later in an Australian circuit. Looks like he caused a stir performing unusual wai khru dances because he was a Benedictine priest."

"Benedictine?" Teague asked.

"Catholic, not Buddhist." Kevin read more. "Wow. It looks like he killed a guy during a bout in Australia. Or the guy died during the fight. He was pretty much forced to quit after that. Both boxing and the priesthood. I don't know, Teague."

"I like him."

"Be careful," Kevin said.

* * *

Each afternoon Teague went to the gym, Ned issued the command to run, and Teague ran. Kevin had guessed that the days of circling the sand were a test. "They're trying to weed you out, make sure you're serious," he'd said. Teague ignored the other boys and instead focused on Father Josiah, looking for the young boxer from the photo in the old man's face and hoping that he'd get to meet him after he passed the test. Teague crossed the finish line on a Monday but didn't find out until the next Thursday.

That day, he emerged from the locker room steeled and hydrated for another bout of running, barely feeling the grit on the concrete under his feet. But he stopped, shocked to find a skinny Thai boy about his age slogging the circuit, gasping for breath, glassy eyes focused on some distant phantasm. Was that what he had looked like? The boy stripped off his sweat-soaked T-shirt and tossed it like a dead fish, leaving a wet skid on the concrete. Teague jogged onto the scorching sand.

"Werres." Teague turned. "Not today," Ned said. Teague fought to keep from smiling as he stepped out of the pit in time for the other boy to struggle past.

Ned led Teague to a shadowed corner behind a set of bleachers in the first courtyard. He demonstrated a proper stance, and Teague tried it out. Ned adjusted his feet with a nudge. He had Teague bounce on the balls of his feet and return to the stance. After several repetitions of that, Ned demonstrated a basic punch. As Teague punched the air over and over, Ned asked, "Why do you fight? Don't stop. Answer the question."

"I don't know," Teague said.

When Ned let him put the bouncing, the stance, and the punching together, his efforts barely made a sound against Ned's palms. Still, it was satisfying.

"Why do you fight?" Ned asked again.

"I don't know."

"You must know. I fight because the fight is in me. I carry it inside me. Keep going. Who wins the fight?"

"Um…the person who knows how to fight best?"

"Knowledge is not enough. Again. Knowledge is nothing without practice. Practice is nothing without discipline. Again. So who wins the—?"

"Herbert," Josiah's voice carried across the courtyard. "The Tam brothers are kicking the shit out of each other, and I think our new runt is about to stroke out."

"Yes, Father." Ned assigned Teague a daunting set of push-ups, sit-ups, and pull-ups and then hurried away.

On his way out for the day, Teague passed behind Josiah, working bent over the office desk. Teague was almost out the door, sure that he'd gone unnoticed, when Father Josiah grunted. "I've been watching you run," he said with an approving nod. "The real trick will be to survive Ned's Spartan, Klingon, crypto-Lutheran bullshit. Keep it up."

Teague had no idea what any of that meant, but he resolved to do it.

CHAPTER 5

The last three days have been surreal and difficult.

APRIL 2081

The boys on the bleachers cheered as Teague climbed into the ring—but not for him. They were hooting and clapping for Ran, the boy who had drawn the privilege of facing him in the first round of Teague's first gym tournament. Teague had sparred with Ran before—he'd sparred with all the boys his age—and it had always been humiliating. And from the way Ran began to showboat for the boys in the stands, this afternoon would probably be no exception. "You learn more from losing. Absorb from your opponent," Ned told Teague every time he sparred. Teague sometimes wondered if Ned was trying to be funny.

Teague performed his wai khru, ignoring the whistles and hisses from the near bleachers. On the platform near the ring, four elderly musicians smoked pungent cigarettes and chatted as if they were waiting for a funeral. A dozen other men—scouts, supposedly, from clubs and leagues—lounged in the sun on the far bleachers.

"This is no time for fear," Ned said as he checked Teague's headgear. Teague wondered what last-minute advice Father Josiah was giving to Ran. "You have the reach advantage; use that," Ned continued. Teague knew that his extra centimeters meant little against a quick and vicious opponent.

A scrawny, wrinkled referee in a grubby shirt wheezed unintelligible instructions. Teague touched gloves with Ran. The bell rang, and the music began.

Teague bounced on the balls of his feet, skirting away from Ran to the almost-random rhythms. The flute and horn twittered and hopped like a flock of birds. Teague barely blocked Ran's first lightning-fast punch and then missed a kick to the ribs. He fell forward on Ran and tried to bring up a knee, but Ran pushed him away, against the ropes. Teague blocked another punch and tried to throw one of his own. A glove met his head from the left, and the ring became a blur. When the music stopped, Teague staggered back to his corner, unsure of how he had stayed on his feet.

Ned sprayed water in Teague's mouth. "You know him now. He's strong on the right but leaves holes on the left. Hold the clinch harder. Knees are weapons. Use them." He clapped a hand solidly on Teague's thigh. "I want you to start with the monkey-lizard combination. He won't be expecting it."

"I don't know it that good," Teague mumbled.

"Teach it to him," Ned said and shoved Teague's mouth guard back in place.

When the music restarted, Teague found himself on his feet, so he attacked as instructed. His flailing felt nothing like it had in practice. Ran backed away, seeming to lose his balance, but then struck. Teague blocked, too slowly, and went down. The prune-faced referee bent over and mouthed a question with sour breath. Teague heard laughter as he staggered to his feet. Seconds later, in a clinch, Teague kneed Ran repeatedly, ignoring the pummeling against his own ribs. The referee pulled them off the ropes. Before Teague found his bearings, Ran kicked the side of his head. Teague staggered and fell on his rear. The referee bent over him and spoke as if from a great distance. Ran was holding his arms up to the cheering boys. Teague made to stand, but the ring spun. Ned lifted him to his feet, set him on the crate in the corner, and began to remove his headgear and gloves. Teague spat, and his mouth guard dribbled down his chest.

"Can you stand? Then on your feet. There is no shame here," Ned said.

In the center of the ring, the referee grasped Teague's wrist with a painfully strong grip and then raised Ran's arm. Things had actually gone better than Teague had expected. He had expected to die.

Teague shuffled through the deserted locker room to the shadows in the training yard and collapsed on a weight bench as far as possible from the cheers and the music of the next bout. He held his head in his taped hands. Ran's foot had come so fast, so unexpectedly.

"Put your arms above your head. You'll breathe deeper, recover faster."

Teague looked up, surprised to see Josiah coming across the sand. He sat next to Teague but said nothing.

"I lost," Teague said.

"True, but not as badly as you might've."

"What does that mean?"

"It means that Ran thought you'd fold in the first round, but you came out fighting in the second. He panicked. That last move was sloppy."

"But I didn't block it."

"No, that you didn't. But if he'd tried that against someone else, his balance and position would have been easy to exploit. He fought lazy and won lazy."

"Are you saying I should have won?" Teague asked.

Father Josiah chuckled. Then after another long silence, he stood and said, "You did all right today."

"I heard you used to be a priest," Teague said.

"Did you, now?" Josiah said, and strolled away.

* * *

Rain fell in a torrent on the schoolyard, but Teague pushed through the students huddled in the entrance and ran out into the downpour. His ribs still ached from yesterday's fight. But Ned said that pain was good, and Teague had found that he couldn't disagree. Pain meant that he had worked; pain meant experience.

Teague hurried through the rain, famished but eager to get home to collect Monkey before going to the Chaiprasits. He had fallen asleep last night reading about how a bunch of museums had set up a site in U-shift and were inviting users to help re-create virtual replicas of almost every period in history. After a bite from the Chaiprasits' buffet, he and Monkey would retreat to the garden temple and pick up from there—as they did almost every afternoon that he didn't go to the gym. There was a wider, more interesting universe out there than his school or church would have him believe, and Teague had vowed to explore it all in the only way he could for now. He loved the tangents and minutiae as much as the big picture. Monkey seemed to feel the same way. Whenever Teague asked him for a definition or a clarification, he would pause, cock his head for a moment, and then grin as he provided the answer, often adding, "I like to learn new things."

Teague took the back stairs three at a time, shook off his rain jacket under the awning, and sloughed off his wet shoes and socks in the mudroom. The house was dark and quiet, and Teague decided that Mrs. Varner and the children must be out shopping. He hurried across the kitchen but slipped on the linoleum. As he caught himself, he stepped on a sharp object and bit back a cry. A jagged fragment of a shattered mug was poking like a shark fin from a pool of cold, brown liquid, which was spattered from the counter to the hallway.

"Mrs. Varner?" Teague called, drying his feet with a kitchen towel. The living room curtains were drawn as if they hadn't been opened for the day.

"Where's Mrs. Varner?" Teague called into his room.

"I don't know," Monkey replied, crawling out from under the bed.

"Stay here."

Hannah's pink room was dim and deserted. The hall bathroom was unoccupied. Teague opened Robert Jr.'s room to find Hannah on the little bed, scrolling through a flexi-book. Robert Jr. was clapping toy cars together on the floor amid the stink of fouled diapers. Hannah gathered up her filthy blanket and stared at Teague with watery eyes.

"Where's your mommy?" Teague asked. Robert Jr. dropped his cars and toddled for the open door. "No. No. Stay in here."

Robert Jr. began to cry. Hannah climbed off the bed, and Teague held them both back. The stench almost gagged him. "Watch your fingers," Teague said and shut the door.

"Mrs. Varner?" Teague called, knocking lightly on the Varners' bedroom door.

He opened the door a crack. The heavy drapes let in little light. The bed had been neatly made. He called again and edged into the room.

Teague tapped on the master bathroom door, waited, and then turned the doorknob, hoping for a rebuke. Cold, humid air wafted out. Mrs. Varner was huddled, fully dressed and shivering, in the half-filled bathtub, her face veiled by stringy, wet hair.

"Mrs. Varner?" Teague asked again. Her gray sweatpants had been soaked black. Her shirt clung wrinkled and translucent over her bony shoulders. "I'll get help," he whispered.

Teague was cleaning the kitchen floor when footfalls stomped up the front stairs—he hadn't heard the car in the driveway over the roar of the rain. He'd hoped to be done before Pastor Varner arrived, but the towel only seemed to spread the mess more. The screen door squeaked open, and the doorknob rattled. The footsteps tromped around the deck to the back door.

"Why wasn't the front door unlocked?" Pastor Varner bellowed as he removed his coat and hung it on the mudroom hooks with deliberation. "And what is going on here? Get this cleaned up." He stormed through the kitchen, calling for his wife.

A door slammed. The pastor's stern voice rumbled through the walls. The tub water began to drain. There were cries and a scuffle. Teague wrung the towel into the sink and knelt to soak up more of the tea.

That evening, Mrs. Chaiprasit helped Teague to pack a few things as the men of the church spoke in hushed tones with Pastor Varner in the living room.

"Where are we going?" Monkey asked. "I like to go new—" Teague hushed him.

They left quietly through the kitchen. And although the floor had been cleaned by an adult, Teague thought it still looked slick and stained.

* * *

Teague awoke to Monkey calling his name, and he rolled over on the creaky futon, expecting a goofy good-morning song. But Monkey was lying still on his charging pad by Mr. Chaiprasit's desk.

Teague knelt by the desk, and Monkey began to speak without moving his mouth. "Good morning, Teague. I have experienced a critical failure or error. You will be contacted shortly by a Zubotix VetTech."

"What's wrong, Monkey?" Teague wanted to hold Monkey but was afraid to touch him.

"All ambulatory functions have been suspended to prevent possible damage until this error is corrected."

Teague flushed with fear. "What do I do?"

"You have a message with instructions," Monkey replied.

Teague found his screen and opened his inbox. The message contained little more than the location of the nearest Zubotix Authorized Service Center. Teague returned and touched Monkey gently. "Will you break if I move you?"

"No, but please handle me with care. I recommend that you deactivate me until I can be diagnosed by an authorized technician." Teague found the switch on Monkey's chest. One reluctant click put Monkey to sleep. One more click would turn Monkey all the way off, but Teague couldn't bring himself to do it.

When Mrs. Chaiprasit knocked and called him to breakfast, Teague sprang up and opened the door. "Pajamas, still?" Mrs. Chaiprasit remarked, and then noticed the look on his face. "What's the matter, child?"

"It's Monkey," Teague replied. "He's broken. He needs to go to a service place."

"It's time for school."

"No," Teague insisted. "He needs to go." His eyes welled with involuntary tears.

Mrs. Chaiprasit paused. "We'll call the school. Jettrin can drive you."

Teague had expected to return to the mall, but the authorized service center turned out to be in a large store that sold all kinds of electronics and appliances. Mr. Chaiprasit dropped Teague at the curb and went to find a parking place. Teague located the service department queue and waited his turn. Monkey's stiff body felt heavier than usual, but Teague held him that much closer.

A few minutes later, a technician called for the next in line, and Teague set Monkey carefully on the counter. The technician spoke in Thai, but Teague shook his head. "Beagle series, if I'm not mistaken," the technician said, this time in English.

"He says he can't move," Teague replied.

"Let's take a look." The technician pried open the flap in Monkey's chest and scanned the bar code. "Werres?" he asked, confirming the account on his screen. "He's out of warranty." He spun Monkey around, jabbed a dongle into his tail, and then turned his attention to his screen. He scowled. "I need to consult with our senior technician. One moment."

Mr. Chaiprasit arrived shortly before the technician returned with another man. They tapped at their screen, operating bits of Monkey independently. Teague's stomach churned as Monkey's mouth yawned and closed mechanically, his legs stretched, his head rotated, his little hands flexed. At last the senior technician turned to Mr. Chaiprasit.

"I'm afraid I don't have very good news. The failure in this unit is extremely severe."

"Please tell the boy. I'm only the driver," Mr. Chaiprasit said.

The senior technician looked down at Teague. "The right servo matrix has been underperforming, causing the left matrix to compensate, leading to the failure. Not uncommon in a Beagle series unit after this long a service life."

"Can he be fixed?" Teague asked.

A pitying expression crossed the senior technician's face. He glanced at Mr. Chaiprasit. "It would be expensive."

"How much?" Teague asked.

The senior technician hesitated and then grabbed the top of the screen with one hand and began to tap the surface with his other. He worked, not speaking, for several minutes. After a final tap, he rotated the screen for Teague to see. "Replace both lateral matrices, reimage the operational memory. Modify the chassis. Parts. Labor." Mr. Chaiprasit leaned closer and put his hand on Teague's shoulder.

"I can't afford that," Teague whispered.

The senior technician removed the diagnostic device from Monkey's tail. "I'm sorry," he said. "I can have one of the salespeople talk to you about financing a new one. We have close-out Darwin-series units in stock. This one's memory can easily be transferred. His main processor and memory modules are in good condition for a bot of his age." This sounded like butchery.

Mr. Chaiprasit dropped Teague off at the apartment and invited him to come to the restaurant later for lunch. Teague laid Monkey on the futon, wondering if he'd missed the signs. Creaking or squeaking? Slowing or drifting? Had Monkey complained and been ignored? Teague tried to imagine tomorrow without Monkey, or the next day, or the next week. He dug into Monkey's chest fur and found the switch. Monkey awoke but remained inert.

"Hello, Teague. I'm still experiencing a significant system failure. I have been through several diagnostic cycles, but the errors remain."

"They can't fix you. Or they can, but it costs too much."

"I understand," Monkey replied.

"I need to call Kevin." Teague found his screen as Monkey made the call. Zubotix had already sent several offers to his inbox about the exciting new Evolution Series models. Teague deleted them as the line rang. Kevin answered, voice only.

"What time is it?" he rasped.

"Monkey's broken and I can't fix him. It's too much money, and I don't know what to do."

"Slow down. Hold on." There was rustling in the background.

"Who is it?" a female voice asked.

"The kid from Bangkok."

"Doesn't he know what time it is?"

There was a muffled pause, and then Kevin said, "I'm sorry, Teague. Start over. What's going on?"

* * *

Teague hurried onto the escalator, clutching his backpack tight to his chest and on the verge of prayer. "If the Badass can't help you, then no one can," Kevin had said. Those were fearsome stakes.

Everyone at the e-mall seemed even taller and stranger without Kevin leading the way. Technology seemed to both connect and disconnect their bodies, as if they were walking shifted, distant and plastic. Kevin had never taught him how to talk to these people, nor had he taught him how to find a numbered stall in the maze. Teague got to the fifth floor easily enough, but once there, he found himself pushed along by the crowd, even as he searched for some orienting markers or signs. At the end of his fourth aisle, Teague began to work up his courage to ask for directions when he noticed that every few meters there were etched, numbered floor tiles—and found a bit of pride in working it out on his own.

The same piñatas hung from the truss, and the duct-taped recliner still sat empty in the corner. A passer-by jostled Teague, pushing him across the plane of the entrance and sounding the buzzer before he was ready.

A Chinese girl, maybe seven or eight years old, popped from behind the back curtain. "You do not steal. We are watching," she warned in strongly accented English. She crossed her arms and eyed Teague with a snarl.

"Badass Bondi?" Teague gulped, hating to curse in front of this girl.

"Who are you?" she asked with a sneer.

A pudgy Chinese man—by far the oldest person Teague had seen in the e-mall—emerged from behind the curtain. He had a distinguished felt of gray hair trimmed tight around the back of his balding head. A polo shirt was stretched tight around his gut. And he wore sunglasses.

"Are you Bondi, sir?" Teague asked.

"I am the Badass," the man said with a laugh, not quite looking at Teague. He spoke in Chinese to the little girl, and she skipped out into the capillary flow of the aisle. "You must be Mr. Werres." He removed his glasses to reveal two glassy orbs with unnaturally green irises and hollow black pupils. Replacement eyes. Teague had never seen anyone with them before. "Kevin informed me that you might be coming by." Then he winked.

Bondi held the curtain aside and welcomed Teague into a veritable museum trove of old computers, screens, gadgets, and parts shelved haphazardly from floor to ceiling. Teague edged along a narrow path between cabinets and racks of tiny drawers to a crowded but ordered workbench. There, a mobile's innards had been wired directly to the life support of some blinking piece of equipment. A thin trail of smoke rose up from the tip of a holstered soldering iron next to a tray of circuit boards.

"I apologize for my granddaughter. She likes to run a tight ship," Bondi said, squeezing past. "It was good to hear from Kevin. Doing well in America, no?" He patted a space on the workbench. Teague unzipped his backpack and set Monkey on the clearing with funereal care.

"His name?" Bondi asked.

"Monkey," Teague replied. "They said it's a problem with the left and right matrix or something."

Bondi plugged a cable into Monkey's tail and closed his eyes. His lips moved in a silent murmur, like a practitioner praying for healing.

"Ah, yes," Bondi said. A schematic appeared on a screen. Text and data streamed by in a side window. The image froze and zoomed. "It's difficult to see the problem in 2-D, but both matrixes are stressed. One has failed."

"Can you do anything for him?"

"Oh, I can do everything for him. Repairs, upgrades, things Zubotix never imagined."

"How much will that cost?" Teague asked.

"Ha," Bondi laughed. "Blood, sweat, and tears, my friend. Kevin told me you have scant funds."

"Yes, sir."

"For the privilege of hacking a Zubot, I think we can come to an arrangement." Bondi grinned.

"Whatever you want me to do," Teague agreed.

* * *

A few days later, the Chaiprasits brought Teague back to the bungalow, but not to stay. They and several other church members packed the Varners' belongings and began to load them into a truck.

"What's going to happen?" Teague asked when they had stopped work to gather midday for a potluck lunch on the deck.

"Headquarters is renting the parsonage," Mr. Chaiprasit replied.

"To a new pastor?"

"No. There's no pastor available. A missionary family."

"What about me?" Teague asked.

"You'll stay with us until the renters arrive, but then you'll keep your room here. That's part of the rental agreement," Mr. Chaiprasit said. "We'll keep an eye on you. Vipada will see to it that you come to services. Plus we'll ask you to do a few chores to help keep the place up for the church."

"You're furniture now," Mrs. Chaiprasit said with a smile. "Eat. Eat."

CHAPTER 6

I hope my effort, the little part I have played, has made you proud.

JANUARY–OCTOBER 2082

As if part of some grand celestial plan, Rob's orgasm arrived just as the rising sun filled the dome of Mars Technical Institute with a glorious pink glow. Helena's face was framed in a luscious pool of brown hair, rendered red by the filtered light. Under him, her willowy body seemed to flow on forever. Rob tensed, bit his lower lip, and strived for silence, lest he wake his neighbors on the other side of the dorm's membrane-thin walls.

Helena hushed him anyway.

"You're beautiful," Rob said.

"I have to get to class," she replied.

Rob rolled aside and said, "Stay here, and we'll just do this all day."

"And so do you."

"Come on. It's not like you have to make an impression to get into grad school anymore." As soon as he said it, Rob cringed. Helena spun out of bed and in an instant was fastening her bra. Helena was too passionate a terraformer to joke about not getting one of the much-sought-after slots in MTI's climatology graduate program. Especially while her appeal was pending.

"I'm sorry," he said, sitting up and pulling a rumpled sheet across himself. "I shouldn't have said that." She finished dressing and spent a few hurried moments in front of the mirror before turning to leave. "Helly?"

Helena stopped, juxtaposed against the Southern Polar Station Martian Bikini Team beckoning and winking from the poster on the back of his door. "Sorry. I didn't mean it. You're going to get in. They'd be stupid not to take you. Let me take you to lunch. Capezi's? Noonish?"

"Fine," Helena said. "I'll have to meet you there."

"I love you," Rob said, and she left.

Rob stayed in bed until he remembered that morning meant breakfast. He pulled on yesterday's clothes and said goodbye to the never-moody bikini team. But as he grabbed the door handle, he felt the string. He snapped his fingers and returned to find the little packet he kept in his top desk drawer. Rob was about to push the next sequential pill out of the blister pack when he froze. This wasn't right. This wasn't the pill for today.

"Shit," he hissed. He wasn't one day off. "Shit," he repeated. Not even two days. "Fuck," he added. How the hell had he forgotten three days? He extracted all the forgotten pills, swallowed them dry, and hoped they wouldn't shrivel his balls.

Rob went to his classes but didn't attend.

Three days forgotten. Helena had stayed over two nights ago, and last night. If he were old enough to take Vanilla, he wouldn't have to worry about remembering to take the goddamn birth control pills. The prescription said to take them every day, but did they really stop working so quickly? How long until they'd be effective again? A day? A week? If he didn't beg for sex for a few days, Helena might get suspicious.

Rob considered telling her the truth but then envisioned her inevitable follow-through—sending him out to purchase the highest-rated home test kit and no other, followed, positive or negative, by hours and hours of one of her unilateral discussions, and it might all be for nothing. This wasn't how fatherhood was supposed to happen. Okay, technically, it was, but not really. He was supposed to be 150 years old, not 22, and in mutual agreement with a great woman, maybe even Helena. They'd take a couple of years off of Vanilla together, romp like otters under the sheets, and magically create a new human or two. It shouldn't begin with a conciliatory lunch.

Rob got to Capezi's Café in time to get a table on the sidewalk before the lunch rush. A pretty waitress brought him water and a menu. "I'm expecting someone else," Rob said. "She'll have water with lemon."

During the day, the Red Zone, the tree-lined entertainment district on the north side of the MTI habitat, had to be one of the most pleasant places on Mars, with plenty of dome-focused sunlight and restaurants that put the MTI cafeterias to shame, although that wasn't too difficult a feat. Not that the evenings were unpleasant. Every night, students crawled from pub to noisy pub, where the best bands on Mars earned their keep. Even the buskers were incredible. Rob scanned the windows of the apartments on the second and third floors and wondered why he had never moved out of the dorms. *The Red Zone would be an awesome place to live. If you could afford it,* Rob thought, answering his own question.

Helena parked her yellow scooter near a clutch of others and wended her way through the tables. Rob gave her a peck on the cheek and pulled out her chair.

"I ordered you water with lemon," he said. *And, by the way, you may be heavy with child.*

"Real lemon or a squeeze of concentrate?" she asked.

"I think they do real lemon here," Rob said.

"I need to thank you, by the way."

"Why's that?"

"After your little comment this morning, I went to see Professor Kuzuri. I don't know why I didn't think of him before. He agrees that I should've been selected, and he's going to talk to the committee."

"That's great."

The waitress returned with a glass of water with a slice of

lemon notched onto the rim. Helena squeezed the lemon and stirred her water ritually, and Rob decided—no thunderclap, just a moment of resolve—not to tell her. If nothing happened, nothing happened. Otherwise: deniability.

"What were your classes this morning?" she asked after they ordered.

"Advanced Data Theory and Systems Analysis," Rob replied. "Snore." Helena gave him a disgusted look. "So I've got senioritis."

"That's pathetic," Helena said. "You used get excited about Data Theory. All bubbly when you talked about databases."

"I was never bubbly. I was young and naïve." Helena shook her head. "I'll beat you to the punch. You know what my problem is?"

"Oh, I can't wait to hear this," Helena said.

"My problem is that I like the idea of college, but I don't actually like college. That's why I've never moved out of the dorms. I knew if I moved out, that would be it for me academically. There's no way I'd be able to stick with classes without some semblance of structure. Whereas—"

"Whereas?"

"Yes. Whereas. You're the opposite. You do college out of necessity, but you don't love it. You focus on the academics, but deep down you know you're missing out. That's why you're attracted to a slacker like me. We're perfect for each other. Ying and yang."

"Yin," Helena said. "It's yin and yang, not ying and yang."

"See?" Rob said. "You know that and I don't."

* * *

When Helena summoned Rob with that somehow-inevitable text, he considered asking for an innocent postponement, anything to spin a wider web of deniability. But in the end, he put on his best clueless air and arrived dutifully, just glad to be getting it over with somewhere besides his crime scene of a dorm room.

"How could this happen?" he asked after she dropped her bomb, the ice creaking beneath his feet.

"Nothing's one hundred percent effective," Helena said. Rob opened his mouth, but she cut him off. "Don't even continue that train of thought. You're the father. There's no other possibility."

"I wasn't going to suggest that. Are you going to stay in school?"

"I'm pregnant, not incapacitated."

"Then what?" Rob asked.

"Will you stop asking questions? I don't know."

"What do I say?" Rob asked. "Because I'm a little panicked here. It's weird, though; I'm also kind of proud."

"Proud? What are you talking about?"

"It's not like I wanted this to happen, but when you told me, part of me felt almost good, like I unlocked a genetic imperative achievement or something."

"I can't believe you're happy about this," Helena said. *"Hey, wow, I knocked up Helly for a thousand points."*

"That's not what I said. God, do you want me to leave?"

"Don't be an asshole," Helena said.

"Sorry." Rob hoped she knew he would never have walked out. "What do you want me to do?" In the absence of a reply, Rob touched her. She tensed, and he removed his hand. "We're in this together, okay?"

"I'm not blaming you," she said.

As the line rang, the bikini girls waved, and for a moment Rob understood Helena's objections to them. Outside his window, a late-evening pickup street hockey game was oblivious to his problems. A woman's voice answered. His sister-in-law.

"Hi, Annabelle. It's Rob. Sorry to call so late. Is Kyle there?"

A few moments later, his brother answered.

"I think Helena's pregnant," Rob said.

"You think she is or she is?"

"She is."

"Damn. Do Mom and Dad know?"

"God, no."

"And you're the father?"

"I'm the lucky stiff."

"She didn't get pregnant on purpose, did she?"

"She's not like that," Rob said. "Besides, I was the one taking care of things, if you know what I mean."

After a moment of silence, Kyle asked, "Sorry. What are you going to do?"

"Is there an option? I can't leave her in a lurch. I'm already an idiot. I don't want to be an asshole, too."

"You want the big-brother advice or the drinking-buddy advice?" Kyle asked.

"Yes," Rob said.

"If you really don't want to be an asshole, you should talk to Dad."

"This is the drinking buddy talking?"

"Dad's not going to freak. You're not some stupid teenager. He'll take you to see Uncle Angus to figure out your legal options and obligations." Rob felt every day of the seven-year age difference between him and his brother.

"Please don't tell anyone yet. Not even Annabelle."

"Okay. You need anything?" Kyle asked.

"A time machine and a Kevlar condom," Rob replied. "I keep worrying about what Mom's going to say."

"She wants to be a grandmother."

"Not to a Robspawn bastard," Rob said.

"Come on. Mom's not like that."

"Too bad you didn't get a girlfriend pregnant in college. Then at least they'd just blame me for copying you instead of screwing up all on my own."

"So the time machine's for me?" Kyle asked.

Rob wished he could see the sky through the dark ceiling of the dome. "I could join an asteroid colony. There's probably a dozen recruiters at the elevator port right now."

"Don't do anything stupid," Kyle said.

"Too late," Rob said.

* * *

In person, Uncle Angus and Rob's father were obvious brothers, both slightly overweight Earthlings with permanent five o'clock shadow over their red cheeks. Their avatars did not share that similarity. His father's avatar had more hair than it should but wasn't otherwise vain. But amid the virtual leather, faux bookshelves, and rendered mahogany of his U-shift offices, Uncle Angus, had been pressed, deflated, and sharpened to a fanciful, barely recognizable version of himself. Rob, though nearly as tall as the two of them put together—in real life and here in shift—felt like he'd been called to the principal's office. Hopefully, a hundred years from now, they'd think back on this day and laugh.

"Ha," Uncle Angus would say. "Remember that time you came to my office? Even your avatar looked like a beaten puppy."

"I remember your pinstriped avatar had those stupid wingtip shoes," Rob would reply.

"How is your boy now?" Uncle Angus would ask. "Still winning all those Nobel prizes?"

"You're not contracted in any way?" asked the real-time Uncle Angus. Rob shook his head. "Is she amenable?"

"To what?" Rob asked.

"Contracting. Marriage? Cohabitation? Co-parenting?"

Rob shrugged. Uncle Angus and Rob's father exchanged worried glances.

"How far along is she?" Angus asked.

"A few weeks maybe."

"Have that conversation soon. Things get a lot trickier after the baby is born."

* * *

Uncle Angus had made it sound so easy. But Rob allowed days of procrastination to become a week, and after a month of never the right moment, another passed, and then another.

Helena had arranged to cram all her remaining classes into

one semester to complete her undergrad before the baby arrived. When Rob saw her, it was usually to deliver nutritionally specific meals or to shuttle her to and from the train station. She went home to Fesenkov Station every other weekend to see her doctor. Rob offered to come along every time, but she insisted that he stay and focus on his classes. Plus, he wasn't her parents' favorite person in the solar system right now.

It hadn't taken long for Helena's slender Martian body to show her bump. She put on weight, but insisted it was healthy, and soon Rob began to wonder how she stayed upright. She took to wearing clothes that showed off her bulging belly, as if to hint that it had been her choice to get pregnant.

Besides the occasional brief kiss, Helena's feet were the only part of her body with which Rob maintained any physical relationship. Most evenings, Rob rubbed them as she studied until she declared that it was time to sleep. Back in his dorm room, the bikini team on the back of his door was always very sympathetic, but largely unhelpful.

One such evening, as she put her cold feet on his lap and began to study, Rob found the courage to speak. "Can I talk to you about something?" he asked. She hummed but didn't look up from her screen. "For my final project for Data Theory, I have to create a predictive model from a complex dataset, at least five variables. They provided a few sample datasets, but they all sounded boring. I thought it might be fun to make something with you instead, like a weather model."

"Weather?"

"You bring a few variables and equations; I'll bring the code. It'll be fun."

"It's called numerical weather prediction, and there's no such thing as a simple weather model."

"I'm not talking about making a comprehensive model of Mars. It's not even about weather. It's about handling the data. We can make up our own planet."

"What's the point of that?"

"The point is that I have an assignment," Rob said. "Don't I sound bubbly? I thought you liked me to be bubbly."

Helena laughed once.

"Giddy? Passionate? Ebullient? How about ebullient?" Rob said. "Come on. I really don't want to write algorithms for library search statistics or anthills. Plus, I thought it'd be fun to do something together."

"I don't think you've thought this through," Helena said. "You're dealing with very complex dynamic fluid equations and chaotic variables: pressure, temperature, atmospheric composition, solar radiation, moisture content, land mass, gravity, planet rotation and tilt. If you add oceans, you have to account for currents, water temperature—the list goes on."

"But this isn't about the exact science on your end. It's about the capability of the code on my end. Plus, they've given us access to Ares to run our iterations. You want to talk to him?"

"Now?"

Rob took her screen, and even though she protested, he called up the network access page and input his password.

"Rob Heneghan. It's a pleasure to see you again. What can I do for you?" The voice sounded like a commercial announcer's or a newscaster's—refined, deeply masculine.

"Hi, Ares. I wanted to introduce you to Helena Lenska." Rob turned the screen's lens at Helena, but she scowled and held up a hand.

"I'm not dressed," she said.

"He's a computer; he doesn't care about your pajamas."

"I'm pleased to make your acquaintance, Ms. Lenska," Ares said. "I understand that congratulations are in order."

"You told the computer that I'm pregnant?"

"It may have come up in conversation. Come on, ask him anything."

"I don't know what to ask an AI," Helena said.

"Not AI; there's no such thing. He's NAI, near artificial intelligence," Rob said. "No offense, Ares."

"None taken. There are several common questions students

ask me when first introduced. A few answers in no particular order: I feel fine. I don't dream. I am interacting with ninety-one other people right now. I cannot access the bursar's records. My favorite color is orange, and I prefer the Beatles to the Rolling Stones."

"Why do you have a favorite color?" Rob asked.

"Presumably, people ask to gain some insight into my personality. I settled on orange, as it garnered more diverse reactions than other colors."

"Okay. Are we done?" Helena said.

"I guess that's all, Ares."

"Goodnight," Ares said.

Helena scowled at her screen in Rob's hands. "Is he gone?"

"He's gone."

"You're sure?" Helena asked. "I assume it's been instructed not to write code for you."

"Very strict orders. He won't even identify the bugs. Just spits back the results. He's very nice about it, though. So will you help? I'll even name it Planet Helena."

She narrowed her eyes over her swollen belly. "You'll do nothing of the sort," she said. She snatched her screen back. "I really don't have time for another project."

"Please?" Rob said.

"Fine, I'll send you a guide to developing numerical weather prediction models and whatever equations you need, but only if you promise to make an effort. I don't want to be associated with half-assed work."

"I guarantee a full ass," Rob said.

* * *

By special arrangement, Helena completed her final exams a week before anyone else. A half-hour after she had submitted her final paper, Rob was waiting with her luggage in the hall outside her emptied dorm room. She grunted and groaned with each bend as she rechecked every drawer, every closet shelf, and behind all the furniture. How many times had they made love on that bed? How many times had they kissed by this door? How many hours during their sophomore year had they cuddled by the window as that epic sandstorm had raged outside the dome? Now the room was bare and colorless. And Rob realized that it had been for some time.

"I'm glad I looked," Helena said, waving a hair band. "It had fallen behind the desk."

It still wasn't the right time, but it was his last chance. Rob dug in his pocket and cleared his throat. Sweat broke out on his palms. "Helena?" he asked.

"What?" she asked, and he held out a glowing object. "What's this?" She took his mobile as if it were contaminated.

"Something I've been thinking about. A cohabitation contract," Rob said.

"You're asking me to marry you?"

"God, no," Rob stammered. "But I want to do what's right for the baby."

"Don't you think this is a decision I should have been a part of?"

"What do you mean? I haven't made any decisions. My uncle's a lawyer. We can fill in all the details together."

"You've been talking to a lawyer?"

"I think you sort of have to."

"I can't believe you talked to a lawyer before you talked to me," Helena said. "How hard would that have been? *Hey, Helly, you want to cohabitate? I just thought I'd ask before I go get all lawyered up.*"

"You don't need to make fun of me," Rob said. "You'll have to forgive the fact that I've never done this before."

"You need to have done this before to know to talk to me first?"

"I don't know what I've done wrong. We're talking now. I came prepared." She scowled and returned his mobile. He studied the meaningless words of the contract for a moment. "I'm sorry," he said.

"This isn't what I imagined for my life. I mean, to finally get into the program and now have to defer for at least a year," Helena said.

"I know," Rob said. "But we have to talk about this sometime."

"My train leaves in half an hour," she said.

"Shift after you get on board. I'll meet you wherever you want."

"I'm tired, Rob. Can we not do this today?"

Rob sighed. "I'm sorry. I did this wrong. But please don't rule it out. I'll send you the document. Read it. Think it over."

"Whatever," Helena said.

* * *

Rob was taking a much-needed piss at a Red Zone pub urinal when his mobile rang. He finished quickly and answered the call outside the restroom.

"Rob?" A man's voice. Rob wished he had checked the caller ID.

"This is Rob," he shouted. "Hold on, let me get somewhere quieter." A ruddy ska band raged away on the tiny stage as Rob waded through the throng of end-of-term partiers. He squeezed out the entrance onto the crowded, but quieter, street. "Hello? Sorry about that."

"Rob, this is Rick Lenska. Helena's father."

"Sir?" Rob said. During a recent visit, Rob had come to understand that, while his life was not in danger for what he had inflicted upon the man's only daughter, he was certainly not approved of in the strictest sense. Rob was certain he'd win him over one day. Maybe today?

"Are you at a party?" Mr. Lenska asked.

"Just out with some friends after finals. What can I do for you?" Rob replied.

"Helena has had some complications. The baby was delivered this afternoon and is in the NICU."

The news was literally sobering. "Is Helena…? Two months left?"

"Helena is in good care," Mr. Lenska said.

"Should I come?" Rob asked.

"I don't know if that's such a good idea. We're caring for Helena and the baby. But she asked me to inform you."

Rob collapsed into a free seat as the train pressurized. It had taken him less than an hour to pack and vacate his dorm room. He had abandoned most of his belongings in the hall for the vulture underclassmen to pick over, including, and especially, the bikini team poster. As the train glided out of MTI station, Rob considered shifting like everyone else onboard, but it felt wrong to escape from the real world. Instead he watched the dark horizon slip past, pricked sporadically by lights from distant settlements, stations, or rovers.

Hours later, Rob stumbled blearily onto a northbound train full of coffee-cupped commuters that departed under the waking eye of an equatorial sunrise. The drone of their conversations blurred with the rusted scenery. Rob closed his eyes, but sleep didn't come.

A half-hour out of his stop, Rob shuffled into the restroom and refreshed himself with a shaver, a toothbrush, and a long assessment in the mirror. When Helena saw him next, she should see someone brave, supportive, someone like a husband. Husband. The moniker slipped on like comfortable shoes. Whatever legal name they ended up giving this thing between them, he would be a good husband to Helena. No, he would be a great husband.

The train crept laboriously into Fesenkov Station, a dome not very different from his own home dome of Sinai Flats—with a radius of about a kilometer and apartments and amenities for anywhere from ten to twenty thousand, depending on the local industry, and nearly indistinguishable from dozens of others along the train lines. But Helena was here. His child was here. He silently begged the airlocks to swallow him faster.

Mr. Lenska rose from a chair on the far side of Helena's bed when Rob edged into the hospital room. Helena turned toward the light, let out a gasping sob, and clutched Rob's hand. In any other place and time, she might be ugly, even disfigured, but here, after what she must have gone through, Helena was beautiful. Rob let her take what she needed, tried to absorb her exquisite pain, and stayed until she fell asleep from a fresh dose of painkillers dripping into her wrist.

"The baby?" Rob asked Mr. Lenska in the hallway.

"As healthy as can be expected," Mr. Lenska replied. "But she's very small."

"Helena never told me anything was wrong."

"She'd been uncomfortable for several days."

"They did a C-section?" Rob asked.

"Of course. She's Mars-born, so they'd have done that anyway. But she woke up yesterday in a lot of pain. The baby was in distress. After the delivery, they had to do an additional operation to stop some internal bleeding."

"Can I see her?"

"Helena hasn't even seen her." Mr. Lenska closed his eyes and rubbed the back of his neck. He was a fit and masculine man, tall for an Earthling, and handsome—an intimidating father-in-law, even when he looked this haggard.

"I'm sorry I wasn't here," Rob said. "I just finished my exams yesterday." Mr. Lenska only nodded. Maybe he was too tired for contempt. "Where's Beatrice?"

"With the baby," Mr. Lenska said.

"I can stay with Helena if you want to get some sleep," Rob said.

Mr. Lenska almost spoke, put a heavy hand on Rob's shoulder, and then walked away. Rob wished he had said something, anything.

* * *

"I don't want her to see me crying," Helena said as Rob pushed her wheelchair down the corridor.

"I think her eyes are still covered," Rob said.

"Then I don't want her to hear me crying."

Mrs. Lenska was standing over the only occupied incubator in the NICU, silhouetted in front of the carefully lit work counters and supply cupboards around the periphery. "She's dreaming," she whispered, indicating one monitor's readout among a dozen surrounding the plastic bubble on the electronic plinth. Standing, Mrs. Lenska was only slightly taller than her seated daughter. She glanced up at Rob, scowled briefly, and turned back to her granddaughter.

"Little girl," Helena wept.

Her name was Molly Desiree Lenska, because, Helena said, they were beautiful names. With her mother's help, Helena pushed a hand into a gloved aperture and brushed her daughter's cheek as if it were a butterfly's wing. Helena murmured through the plastic. Screens streamed data about the baby's fluttering heart, her respiration, her brain, her blood—her tiny life defined by dozens of numbers and lines graphed over time. Her impossibly small body was almost hidden under a tangle of wires, tubes, and an eye mask. Rob stayed back and let his heart ache.

When the nurse announced that it was time to go, Rob pulled Helena's wheelchair backward, lingering for her sake. In the corridor, Helena withdrew into inconsolable tears. Rob wanted to give her a husband's reassurance but had to hope that his stoic presence was enough.

* * *

Several times a day, Rob helped Helena into a wheelchair and rolled her into the NICU. Each time, Helena stayed as long as the nurses allowed, talking and singing to Molly. Helena cried each time Rob took her away. Helena had elected not to allow neonatal shift therapy, which supposedly replicated the sensation of a real uterus. She wanted Molly to hear the sound of her own mother's voice and not a virtual replication of a life lost. Rob was just glad for one less wire on his daughter's body.

Helena was discharged seven days after the birth, but even then she left the hospital only when her mother could persuade her to go home to sleep.

Rob had checked into a hostel, and eventually Mrs. Lenska seemed to accept that he wasn't going away. He became the getter of food, the fetcher of items, and the doer of errands. Much to his surprise, he also became a rather deft changer of tiny diapers. He assembled the crib in Helena's bedroom with borrowed tools. Every night, he shifted to put in a few hours' work at Kyle's architectural studio to earn a little money. And every day, Rob reread the draft cohabitation contract and checked his active search for apartments in every settlement between Fesenkov Colonies and Sinai Flats.

* * *

"How is she, dearie?" asked the woman who ran the sandwich place across the street from the hospital.

"They tell us two weeks, maybe less," Rob replied.

"That's wonderful. I want you to bring her over here as soon as she's out," she said as she stuffed the sandwiches in a bag. "Give your wife our best wishes."

Back at the hospital, Rob set the bag of sandwiches on the table in the vending room and filled Helena's coffee mug and his own. Another new father, a nervous, red-haired Martian, poked the screen of a vending machine helplessly.

"That one's twitchy," Rob said.

"It won't sync to pay," the man said, holding up his mobile.

"Unplug it," Rob said. "It'll work once it reboots."

Helena wasn't waiting for Rob or the sandwiches in the NICU lounge.

"She's inside," said Ilana, one of his favorite nurses.

"What's going on?" Rob asked.

"The ophthalmologist."

"Can I...?" This was the specialist that he and Helena had been dreading the most. Retinopathy was just one of the hypersyllabic conditions that might be wrong with little Molly.

"Sorry. We've got too many people in there already," she said.

Back in the vending room, as news played on a wall screen, Rob wondered how it could possibly matter that there was a newly appointed undersecretary for commercial affairs for the UNSA. Who cared how the appointment had nudged the stock price of the Valdosky Companies? So what if a gang of hackers had overwhelmed an Ecuadorian bank site in E-shift with a swarm of marionette avatars? He was sorry that all those people in Zaire had to flee to a refugee camp, but he barely knew what month it was. None of it seemed any more important than the sandwich he was eating. Rob couldn't imagine that anything would ever be as important as Molly again.

When Helena emerged from the NICU with her mother, she wrapped her arms tight around Rob's neck. "She can see," she said, sobbing.

"Did she see you?" he asked. He felt her shake her head yes. After more than a minute, she let go and wiped her eyes. "Do you think they'd let me go in?" he asked.

The NICU was darker than usual, or perhaps it was that he was alone. He had never been alone with Molly and had never seen her without her mask. She opened her eyes as he wriggled a hand into a glove. Narrow slits at first, and then a little wider. She didn't turn her head, but he moved to face her, to be swallowed in those little dark pools.

"Hello," Rob said reflexively. He laughed and wiped his tears off her bubble with his sleeve.

* * *

During Molly's last few days in the hospital, Rob, Helena, and Mrs. Lenska sat in their own incubator of exhaustive briefings and terrifying online primers. There were myriad things that might go wrong with a premature infant—so many that, when the hour arrived, it seemed almost criminal to discharge Molly into their trembling care.

Helena insisted on pushing the stroller on the way home, stopping every few meters to make some adjustment to Molly's swaddling, little hat, or cushions. As soon as they arrived at the Lenskas' apartment, Helena disappeared into her bedroom with her mother to feed Molly.

Rob disturbed nothing but the edge of a sofa cushion in the living room and cursed himself. His family had come home to someone else's house. He should have manned up and rented a place in town, grown a spine, and set up the crib there. Helena had been so fragile for so long that Rob had left her alone to come to him, but she never had.

"Is she sleeping?" Rob asked when Helena returned to the living room.

"Mom's holding her," Helena said.

"Is she happy?"

"She ate pretty well."

"How about you?" Rob asked. "Are you hungry?" Helena shook her head. "I could go get us some dinner. Bring it back here."

"I need to get settled in. I've had so little time to get her room ready. Thank you for everything you've done."

"You say that like I had no obligation to help."

She straightened her back and handed him an envelope. A real paper envelope, wrinkled and bent, and as warm as her body. "I'm sorry," she said. "I should have given this to you a long time ago." She paused and then whispered, "Goodbye, Rob." She kissed him on the cheek and then disappeared down the hall. A door closed. Before he'd finished reading the letter, Mr. Lenska had appeared to see him to the door.

"I suppose the good news is that she's made no request for support," said Uncle Angus's wingtipped avatar. Rob's father nodded in agreement.

"What are Rob's options?" Mr. Heneghan asked.

"You could offer monetary support to negotiate custody or visitation. However, she's holding all the cards. How deep into your pockets are you willing to reach, if in fact the child is yours? We'd want to begin with a paternity confirmation."

"I can't put Molly through all that," Rob said.

That evening, Rob checked out of the hostel and boarded the next southbound train out of Fesenkov Station, leaving Molly's life almost as insignificantly as he had entered it.

CHAPTER 7

Perhaps I should have taken the time to shift to see you, but I felt I needed to remain here. I can't tell you how many have thanked me, seeing your face in mine.

NOVEMBER 2082–AUGUST 2083

Rob's avatar appeared in a pool of virtual light in the center of an endless metallic floor. A matrix of one-meter-square grid lines planed away on all sides to a faint trace of a horizon. There was no sky or ceiling above him, only black. Rob tapped the floating interface, and the floor and the grid disappeared. He extinguished the light and then minimized the interface with a wave. He hung in the emptiness and tried not to think—of his real body that had barely left his childhood bedroom in weeks, of self-important Helena and her cruel letter, of Molly, one month old and already estranged.

But Rob couldn't wallow long in the void; there was work to be done in the assembly room of the Kyle Heneghan Architectural Studios. In actuality, the seemingly infinite space encompassed a volume of a thousand square grid blocks to the height of the G-Plex maximum one thousand kilometers. The studios themselves covered only a standard G-Plex commercial block on the U-shift grid, but it was this kind of trick—perspective scale adjustments and grids within a grid—that made Kyle Heneghan a relatively hot commodity among virtual designers.

Rob recalled the interface, turned the grid floor and lights back on, and loaded the job in progress. A mass of gray polyhedrons rendered over a footprint of several blocks, soaring dozens of stories high. He'd never heard of the company, some corporation that provided services to other corporations. Why they felt they needed a virtual headquarters that resembled bubbles geysering from a gigantic glass of milk, Rob might never know.

He peeled the building's skin away with a tap, and with a second he exploded the assembly. With an almost-audible swoosh, every room moved at once, stopping a few meters from any other, freezing hundreds of stories above and around him like a stop-motion photo. Rob tapped a third time, and green links began to crisscross the voids. Some rooms had dozens of connections, emanating to all levels. A veritable tree trunk sprouted from the lobby, breaking out into branches and tendrils that touched almost every room.

Rob loaded the spreadsheet, selected the room where he had left off, and in a blink he appeared in an octagonal space high above the assembly room floor. Room W6203, Office, VP Market Augmentation, Asia. Rob opened the room's settings interface, activated manual mode, and set to work adding green dots to the door and routing a thread from each to the appropriate destination, setting the transition type and security level for each one. He began to bounce from room to room, testing his work. Rob had so far added only one undocumented passage to this building, an invisible spot under the farthest back corner seat of an assembly hall. When touched, it would instantly link the user to the front sidewalk. Rob hoped it might someday become an escape for some poor sucker who needed a break.

"Rob? Are you in here?"

"I'm in the parking garage," Rob called, recognizing Kyle's voice in the distance. They hadn't yet activated the acoustic isolation subroutines. "What does a grid property need with a parking garage, anyway?" Rob asked after his brother shimmered into sight.

"It's a vanity thing," Kyle said. "A place to park virtual vehicles. Why are you doing this on the assembly floor? Why don't you just plug all this into the database?"

"I like doing it this way. Are you almost in town?" Rob asked.

"Train's a few minutes out. Want to knock off early and go get a beer before dinner?"

"Is that why Mom invited you for the weekend? To have a come-to-Jesus talk with me?"

"She's worried about you," Kyle said.

"Please don't let her blow this out of proportion."

"I'll do my best. Meet me at the station?"

"I'll have to ask my boss," Rob replied.

On the Smashed Idol Bar's sign, a bearded and robed cartoon man beat a golden calf to pieces with a bottle. Then the shards melted, pooled together, and reformed into the calf from the hooves on up. It lowed, and the man destroyed it again, like he'd done countless times a day for almost twenty years. Sinai Flats locals liked to claim that the bar had been built before the dome, but Rob knew it was a myth, despite the building's old exterior-rated airlock doors.

"I've never been in here without a fake ID," Rob said to Kyle as they ducked inside. "I still remember Franklin Hoverton's birthday and UNSA ID number."

"Franklin Hoverton," Kyle snorted. "Which of your goofy friends came up with that name?"

"You did," Rob said.

The only other customers of note were a boisterous clutch of farmers who had gathered several tables together to watch a soccer game on an enormous screen. The soccer ball arced at severe angles, and the players barely left the ground as they ran. But the grass had been mowed in a pretty checkered pattern, and the crowd wore shirtsleeves under blue skies.

"Maybe I should go to Earth," Rob said after they'd settled at the bar and ordered a couple of beers. "Can I work for you from Ireland?"

"The motherland? Why not?"

"I'd have to wear an exoskeleton."

"Is that all that's keeping you?"

"Oh, god," Rob said. "Here comes the conversation."

"It may as well be now."

"What do you need to hear so you can tell Mom you did your brotherly duty?" Rob asked.

"Why don't you just tell me what's going on with you? Are you still thinking about patching things up with Helena?"

"What's there to patch? I was so stupid. I thought the baby would change everything," Rob said. "Honestly, she probably had a harder time deferring grad school than dumping me."

"Perfect," Kyle said. "*You* go to grad school."

"I'm sorry, I thought I heard you suggest that I go to grad school," Rob said. "My grades were shit, Kyle. There's no way."

"Think about it. She kicks you to the curb, so you go live the life she can't."

"I doubt she'd even care."

"Maybe not, but it'll make you feel better. Give you a chance to—"

"Meet a new girl, get her pregnant…"

"—get your life on track. It might not be ideal, but it's better than sulking in your bedroom at Mom and Dad's."

Rob took a long pull on his beer, and then said, "I did get one offer to apply to a grad school."

"There you go," Kyle said.

"Not a personal invitation; they sounded desperate. Probably sent it to everyone."

"What school?"

"Agnus Dei University."

"What are you waiting for?" Kyle asked. "That place is an architectural legend."

"It is literally—not figuratively, literally—on the other side of the solar system."

"Sounds perfect."

Rob gave Kyle a long look and then said, "It kind of does, doesn't it?" He considered this with a swig. "Although, if I got in, and that's a big if—who was the guy who said he wouldn't join any club that would admit him as a member?"

"Mark Twain?"

"Maybe. I don't know."

"Who cares? It's a good idea," Kyle said. "But if you don't go to Agnus Dei, go somewhere else. Go to Earth. Just do something."

"What if I don't?" Rob asked.

"Then you're fired, and I tell Mom you're running a virtual brothel out of their apartment. And not a nice Light District one either, some kind of skeezy back-alley site."

"How do you know I'm not?" Rob asked.

Kyle laughed. "Are you going to get off your ass?"

"Buy me another beer?"

* * *

Slow awareness puzzled itself together as Rob squeezed his eyes shut against a painful glare. His mouth tasted like a hamster had floated in and perished of thirst. His stomach hung in a space separate from himself. He felt weightless. Was he shifted? He had shifted through the elevator ride, but then he had downshifted to wait for the shuttle in the bar at Deimos Hub. How much vodka had he bought at the duty-free store there before heading to the VSS Conqueror? He vaguely remembered unpacking his few belongings into the closet that his ticket laughingly called a stateroom. What the hell had happened after that? Bristly grip carpet scraped against his crusty cheek. Was someone laughing? A cool, gooey wetness was pressing through his shirt and hair. Something poked him hard in the shoulder.

"Wake up, son." Rob made out a purple Valdosky Cruise Line crew shirt, a moustache, and then nearby, more purple shirts. Rob tried to get up—was he on a luggage bot?—but flailed helplessly. And what was this Day-Glo orange goo that squished under his palms, between his fingers, and under his arms? It smelled like cheese.

"What is this stuff?" Rob slurred.

"Cheese." The security officer freed Rob with a yank. Someone wrapped a towel around him, and it adhered to his clothes. A purser inspected the cart with disgust. Rob heard his room number relayed over a radio speaker.

"Did I throw up?" Rob asked.

"We've been peeling drunks all morning, but you take the cake," the officer said.

"You said it was cheese," Rob said.

"This one's going on the wall of shame." The security officer laughed and held out his mobile, displaying a picture of Rob splayed facedown like a murder victim on a luggage bot, his body outlined in orange. A cone of goo spiraled from the top of his head. The sizable letters on his back read "Do not disturb."

A few memories from the D-Party flashed through the fog, and Rob groaned. After the engines had fired, he'd played air shots with those construction contractors heading out to a new G-Star. Or had he sung karaoke with them and played the drinking games with the libertarian dudes heading out to their asteroid colony? He imagined the lot of them laughing as they covered him with the ship's supply of squeezy cheese, and then saluting like inebriated Vikings at the sea burial of the village idiot as they sent the poor bot on its way.

"I didn't do that to myself," Rob said.

"I don't believe you could have, kid," the officer snorted.

* * *

Rob resettled on the grip-upholstered couch and wished he hadn't refused the coffee. The counselor, Carly, took a sip of her own and then stuck her cup on a grip pad on a bolted-down end table.

"You're not eating your allotted calories, but you routinely max out your alcohol allowance," she continued, looking over her screen. "You spend an above-average amount of time in your cabin, but a below-average amount of time in shift." Rob had signed the Valdosky Cruise Lines passenger contract acknowledging the existence of the behavior-monitoring program, but he had never imagined that it would single him out, let alone land him in mandatory counseling.

"Why does it matter how much I shift?" Rob asked.

"It's simply one of many metrics we use to gauge how you're adjusting to life in space," Carly replied.

"Life in space? It's been three weeks."

"It's only the beginning of a very long journey. And you're making quite a significant change in your life, heading to Agnus Dei Station. The university?" Rob nodded. "Have you ever traveled in space before?"

"A trip to Phobos in high school. Basically up the elevator and down."

"How has this experience been different?"

"Different than a field trip? I shift to work every day. The food's as crappy as it was at MTI. The scenery never changes. It's like living in a dome, just with no gravity. Look, I'll save you the trouble of dragging it all out of me. I just went through a pretty rough breakup." Rob had sent a final communiqué to Helena, a simple note about his plans. He'd labored for hours, hoping each *mot just* would prick her deeply with envy and regret. For his efforts, he had received a brief reply that flowed off the screen like fly-specked honey. Helena had congratulated him and had attached a photograph of little Molly, no longer a scrawny newborn, but a chubby and pink beauty. Rob tried to imagine Helena poring over each phrase with the same care as he had—Helena never did anything halfway, except maybe gestate—but the note was too slick, too easy. No regrets, no last-minute endearments. Simply good luck and P.S., here's a photo to render you emotionally bereft for the rest of your life. "That's all it is. Sorry I got drunk and that the bot got messed up. Although that wasn't my fault."

"This isn't about your specific behavior at the party—"

"I wasn't the only one getting wasted," Rob said.

"—or the incident in the cafeteria. This—"

"I didn't start that," Rob said. "That guy kept calling me names. 'Cheese Boy.' 'Crackers.' Stuff like that. Are you talking to him, too?"

"You could have taken his attention good-naturedly. Perhaps he was trying to be friendly."

"It was embarrassing."

"You insulted his mother, quite profanely from what I understand."

"How was I to know she was sitting right there?"

"Rob, this is about the state of mind that leads you to extreme reactions. Wouldn't you like to get to the root of that? Space travel, leaving home and family—these are very stressful things, especially when compounded with—"

"You think I'm stressed about space travel?" Rob asked. "Tell me, have there been any studies about the repression caused by always-on behavior monitoring?"

"There have. Would you like to read some?"

"I'm wondering how you people balance repression and paranoia with whatever benefit comes from it. I mean, doesn't it actually create a situation where someone's much more likely to bottle things up and then blow a gasket?"

"It's less of a statistical risk than you might think," Carly said.

"It's still ghoulish."

"You're benefiting from it now. Your profile suggests that I would have invited you here eventually. So in a way, I'm glad you've had a spot or two of trouble."

"Why?" Rob asked.

"I get three required sessions to offer you my help."

"Since I have to come to these, can you get them to stop sending me constant requests to join the wallyball league or the improv theater troupe or whatever? I just want to be left alone."

"Do you really?" she asked. "It's a long way to Agnus Dei."

"That's supposed to make me feel better?" Rob asked. "What happens if I screw up again?"

"Worst-case scenario? You can be placed in restricted shift, as per your passenger agreement."

"Restricted shift?"

"You'd be removed to perma-shift, with access only to your place of employment and a limited list of public sites. And all grid activities would be monitored."

"So I can't hack into the Conqueror? Hole the dome from the inside, so to speak?"

"Please don't say things like that. I'm compelled to consider even offhand remarks as potential safety threats."

"I was only asking a question," Rob said.

Carly set her screen aside. "Is your family supportive of your choice to go to Agnus Dei?"

"They're fine with it," Rob replied, resolving not to give her any more.

* * *

Rob could have taken the rest of the day off after his final required session with Carly the counselor. Kyle was always bugging him not to work so much, to enjoy his voyage more, to get a life. But after the session, Rob slinked back to his shoebox of a cabin, shifted, and clocked back in at Kyle's studio to continue coding room transitions and partition opacity interfaces for a Finnish educational complex.

"Why do characters in deep space adventures all seem to go mad?" Rob had asked Carly that afternoon. He'd survived his first two sessions without mentioning Molly, and he was damned if he was going to tell her about the whole affair at his last. "You know what I'm talking about, don't you? It's like all the characters stare into the 'big black' and go crazy, even the psychologist."

"Games and entertainment can be excellent releases," she had replied. "Do you find yourself drawn to these sorts of scenarios?"

As Rob worked, he wondered if Carly hated dealing with smart-ass shits like him. To her, he was probably no better than one of the boisterous miners or grizzled construction techs on their *n*th tours that were being arrested for brawling in the ship's sports bar every night. Like him, those people had no interest in wallyball, book clubs, or art classes. They were just trying to get from Point A to Point B. Rob hung out among them, but he knew he wasn't one of them. They were just traveling to a job, to make some money. Real pain had brought him here. Hadn't it? Deep down, Rob knew this was just a shallow excuse. He was pouting. He was being childish. And perhaps, if he'd let her, Carly might have helped him. If nothing else, he should probably apologize.

"What are you still doing here?"

Rob looked up from his work to see Kyle had returned from a client meeting. "I'm working?" Rob replied.

"It's ten after," Kyle said. "I told you that I can't pay you overtime."

"I'll work for free. Besides, I'm finishing up a thing."

"Tomorrow," Kyle said, and cleared Rob's workstation.

Rob stared into the blank volume for a few beats and then agreed to go. He said goodbye and began to scroll through his queue of usual U-shift haunts: the Forum, the EXP Zone, FunnyFarm, Club Now. Nothing sounded the least bit diverting. He'd been to them all too many times. Or was it that they reminded him of shifting with Helena? It seemed like everywhere he went lately, he recalled how she'd always acted as if she wanted to be somewhere—or with someone—else. How could he have been so oblivious for so long? Had she always been looking over his shoulder at her future? Had he just been an expendable excuse to never get serious with anyone during school? Was he just a bookmark?

The cursor blinked expectantly in the navigation bar, and Rob considered downshifting back to the Conqueror for an early dinner—but then what?

Rob almost linked to the Light District. He'd never even dared to suggest that Helena join him there. But today, it didn't feel right—at least not until he was in a better mood.

And so Rob walked out the front door.

The street was deserted—no one walked between sites in this part of the grid—and Rob could almost believe that he was the only survivor of an apocalypse. He ignored the stunning mass of the Kyle Heneghan Architectural Studios that hung in an ethereal aura behind him. It dramatized all the possibilities of virtual architecture: folded space, fractal construction, color as music, light as texture, water and life from rays and planes. Rob had seen it all before.

He was standing still, trying to decide whether to go right or left, when movement caught his eye. A punked squirrel was scampering along the edge of Kyle's property. Rob kept still. He had never actually seen a Virmin before; G-Plex was usually efficient about pest control. If it had sensed him at all, it probably thought he was a mannequin or a zombie.

The squirrel stopped, and then it grew, or rather inflated, to several times its size. A modded avatar; no wonder G-Plex had left it alone. With several quick waves of its arms, it tagged Kyle's building with some sort of vandalware, deflated to its original size, and scurried away. "Forgive us our trespasses," the graffito read in stylized rainbow script. Where did destructive punks get their sense of irony?

I should get that software for my bat belt, Rob thought. Like most people who had grown up gaming in shift, he had amassed a collection of widgets, offensive and defensive cheats, and avatar hacks, including some that didn't strictly comply with the G-Plex terms of use. Most kids had to buy theirs from shady sites that charged a month's allowance for code they'd sold to a million others. Luckily for Rob, Kyle had a knack for forging widgets from scratch, a skill he was now putting to use in his career. Even so, Rob had always been on the lookout for new tricks. He snapped a picture of the graffiti and set out after the squirrel.

Rob rounded the corner in time to see the bushy tail disappear around a bank. He kept after it and opened his bat belt, hoping that his old tricks would be enough to take the squirrel by surprise.

Rob peeked around the virtual granite of the bank's cornerstone to find that the squirrel had inflated again and was now defacing the wall of a daycare. Rob selected his weapons of choice: Freeze Ray, an invisible, constricting cylinder, and Heavy Shoes, an infinitely flat object with the gravity level set to twenty gee. Together they were a one-two punch no avatar could escape from without hitting the eject button. On the count of three, Rob ghosted across the street and almost ran into the wall as the Freeze Ray hit its target—it'd been a long time since he'd done anything like this. The oversized squirrel began to squeak and struggle. Rob first slipped Heavy Shoes under a nearby tree, squashing it into a pancake of pixels, but deployed another under the squirrel, rendering it all but immobile.

"Don't log out," Rob said, holding up his hands.

"What is this? Let me out. I didn't do nothing. Fuck you," the squirrel sputtered, gnashing a set of nasty teeth.

"I'm sorry," Rob said. "I just want to buy a copy of your program. The spray paint."

"What? Get buggered."

"How old are you?" Rob asked, genuinely curious.

"Go ask your mom, jerk-off."

"I'm serious. You selling or not?"

"What if I don't?"

"I've got your image, location, and a photo of your Lord's Prayer back there. I turn them all over to the property owner and G-Plex."

"Shit's probably gone already. Most people got security."

"Maybe, but it's still enough for G-Plex to bust you back to toddler shift for a month. I'm paying cash. How much you want?"

"How much you got?"

"Come on," Rob said.

"What currency?" the squirrel asked. *Pretty sophisticated question for a delinquent,* Rob thought. Maybe this wasn't a kid. Holding an avatar hostage was a serious infraction. On private property it was considered kidnapping. In a public zone, assault. But Rob doubted that this malcontent would file a complaint, especially if he walked away with a fistful.

"Unos," Rob said.

"Fine. Fifty. You got fifty?"

Rob made fifty unos appear in his hand. "Where's the program?"

"Let me out of here first."

Rob deactivated the Heavy Shoes but only widened the Freeze Ray. If the squirrel bolted, he'd hit a wall pretty quick. The squirrel stretched and shivered as he was freed. A p2p transfer window popped into view. The status bar sliced left to right, and the malware sensor stayed green. At one hundred percent, Rob deactivated the Freeze Ray.

"Thanks," Rob said, and lowered the cash into the squirrel's outstretched paw.

"Bite me," the squirrel said as it deflated. Its tiny claws scuttered as it scurried away—a clever little detail that other modders might have neglected to add.

Rob hadn't been careful. He hadn't noticed any witnesses, but there were always the G-Angels. He left the street with a blink and appeared in an impossibly large, domed venue, its sky-high roof held aloft by ranks of immense, living columns. Whatever the time, there were always thousands of avatars milling through the Forum's public entrance, on human feet, on wheels or tracks, soaring on wings, loping on four paws, or even slobbering on pseudopods. Advertisements swirled within reach and slid across every surface. A hiveful of friend updates, headlines, and personalized offers swarmed Rob like loyal drones. Rob surveyed his notifications, appalled to find how boring his shift life had become.

He linked to a changing room. Rob Prime was realistic enough, although it corrected certain flaws. His gamer and his sporto were each juiced for competition and looked much more formidable than Rob's real self. He used another avatar, called Quentin Rox, exclusively on his trips to the Light District. He had an elf with dragonfly wings, which hadn't wielded its Level 120 Palladium Helmet of Destruction since Rob's sophomore year of high school. And there was the girl.

Rob had named her Danielle, after a middle-school crush. Her Earthling's body had been modeled after a young Gretchen Walker, a turn-of-the-century actress—now married to Matthew Valdosky of the Valdosky Companies. Even though Danielle had pretty Earth features, long, straight blond hair, and was almost a meter shorter than Rob Prime, Rob always felt like everyone could see straight through him. But he knew that this deception was between the G-Angels and himself, and they didn't judge, at least not about this. Today, Rob dressed Danielle innocuously, like a college student backpacking across Mars, but without the pressure suit.

Now what? Rob wondered as he studied himself in the mirror. How had it come to this—acting so impulsively, wanting to be anyone but himself? Did Helena ever feel like this? He'd bet his bat belt she never had. To want to be anyone else would be an admission of error, and Helena could never be wrong.

He'd once tried to argue with her about terraforming. He actually kind of preferred Mars as it was. Sure, it could get so cold that the atmosphere turned to dry ice, but it was home. She'd droned on for what seemed like days about why humankind needed another openly livable planet. He'd proclaimed himself converted just to stop her talking. Then, to keep her happy, he'd squandered whole weekends volunteering with her at Terraforming Initiative fundraisers. He'd wasted hours sorting out their donor database at her behest. Maybe it was time to undo his every good deed in the cause of Martian terraforming.

A quick search discovered an ongoing protest, right here in U-shift. A mischievous, but pretty, smile appeared on the face in the mirror as he shimmered away.

From the outside, the U-shift offices of the UNSA Mars Mission were little more than a barely marked storefront along a long block of United Nations bureaus, most of which were probably never meant to be visited by the casual pedestrian. A few meters from the unwelcoming street entrance, an eclectic crowd was circling and chanting under enormous picket signs. They were blowing wall-toppling horns, and most of the avatars were coated in red dust. Rob wondered why he hadn't thought of doing this before.

"Are you here to join us?" asked a rust-faced woman hovering nearby with a clipboard.

"Absolutely," Rob replied.

"Wonderful. Have you signed our petition?" Rob happily added Danielle's eddress to the next blank line. "What's your name?" the woman asked, surveying the entry.

"Danielle Edger," Rob replied.

"Great to have you aboard. Take some of our literature." Rob dutifully saved the links for later viewing. "And signs are here if you want one."

Rob rummaged through the drop-down list of signs and selected the largest. He laughed out loud as it unfurled. Fifteen square meters of alternating slogans in flashing, neon colors. NO

AIR FOR ARES. BETTER DEAD THAN GREEN. He hoisted it high and fell into stride among the other protestors. They circled around the avatar of a Mars-born man, dreadlocked and naked to the waist, smeared with rust-red war paint from navel to forehead. When he called to the group, his voice rang sonorous and clear, but when he shouted through his ridiculously large megaphone at the building, his voice boomed like dust-storm thunder. Rob added his girlish frequencies to the call-and-response, waved the sign, and scowled appropriately.

After a half-hour, the chant leader donned a bronze Greek war helmet. A prodigious slash of red horsehair swept over his head and spilled down his back. His eyes glinted fiercely through the tee eye slit. He conjured a bronze shield and a burning sword as music blasted from nowhere. *Pissed-off interpretive dance,* Rob thought, *is exactly what I need right now.* He cheered wildly to keep from laughing.

"Can they really hear us inside?" Rob asked another protester, a Martian woman.

"They know that we're here. That's what's important."

When the dance had finished, the protest circle re-formed. Rob raised his sign in defiance of Helena. She'd be disgusted by this pettiness, and his avatar. He imagined the disappointed shake of her head and shouted louder. He had no withering glance, no way to make her understand how selfish and cruel she had been. He craved the power to make her feel shame, to compel her to atone. God, he hated her—every molecule of her terraforming ass.

Rob activated his new program, and a spray can appeared in Danielle's hand. He readied his index finger on the button. Then he dropped his sign and ran toward the Mission's entrance, shouting—shrieking, actually—crossing the distance in a few seconds. He adjusted the color even as he began to spray the wall. Rainbow R, orange E, red D-M-A-R, as large as his arms allowed. Angry protesters dragged him back before he had finished and put themselves between him and the wall. Rob ghosted free to an open space a few meters away. Time to leave. Favorites. The Forum. Go. But he didn't budge.

An encompassing light blasted down around him and froze

him in place. His interface went gray. The protestors began to back away. A figure stepped out of a fold in space—a faceless, multiple-armed four meters of fearsome energy.

Rob's last thought as the G-Angel enveloped him was of the reprobate squirrel. Would they track him down? Scare him straight? The wall's security was already deleting the paint.

Rob opened his cabin door to find Carly and two Valdosky security officers. "You're kidding me," he said. He'd just woken up from a forced downshift, with a hefty fine on his G-Plex account and his bat belt considerably lighter.

"I'm afraid I'm not," Carly replied, handing him a flexi-screen of fine print.

"What's this?"

"You're being relocated to restricted shift immediately."

"What? Why?" Rob asked.

"I'm sorry," Carly said. "But misuse of Valdosky networks is considered a violation of your probationary status as per your transport contract."

"Ma'am?" One of the security guards stepped forward with handcuffs.

"Whoa," Rob said. The other guard put a hand out and began to unholster a stun gun from his belt with the other.

"Rob," Carly said.

"I'm not—"

"Don't make this worse than it has to be."

"I didn't—"

"Sir," the guard with the cuffs warned. A neighbor poked his head out into the hall. Rob felt the fight leave him. With an electronic whine, the handcuffs tightened and cinched his wrists together.

"What about all my stuff?" Rob asked.

"You'll receive a detailed manifest from the purser," one of the guards said. The other pushed into the room and returned with Rob's shift nodes.

"Is this your shift set?" he asked. Rob nodded, and the guards hauled him away.

"Restricted perma-shift is comfortable," Carly explained as they entered a crew passage. "You'll have access to basic entertainment and approved social networks. Arrangements will be made with your employer. You will attend a weekly counseling session. Not with me, however. I've recommended you to an excellent colleague."

"Fantastic," Rob said.

A few minutes later, they arrived at a three-meter wide hatch deep in some bowel of the cruise ship. One guard opened the aperture with a code on the security panel. A nurse in purple scrubs met them at a counter inside.

"I'm sorry I couldn't be more help to you," Carly said after Rob had been checked in.

"I'm willing to admit that it's not your fault."

"Good luck," she replied and left.

The nurse began to spout a memorized litany of medical jargon as she led the guards into a hushed, low-ceilinged warren with Rob in tow. Low lights flickered on ahead of them, marking their path through the cubicle-lined maze. In the relative center of each compartment, a cocoon had been suspended as if by a giant spider. Tubes and wires snaked from each bundle out into the walls.

They halted at a rack of equipment staged outside a vacant cubicle, and a guard released the handcuffs.

"Get undressed," the nurse ordered.

"Do you guys really have to wait around for this?" Rob asked. The guards scowled.

"And put this on." The nurse held out a fragment of gray fabric. Rob laughed. It couldn't possibly be large enough and had deliberate holes where fabric seemed the most necessary.

"Does it come in any other colors?" Rob asked. The nurse wasn't joking.

He undressed in the corner of the cubicle that offered a sliver of privacy and then tugged on the stretchy and humiliating body suit. Rob poked his head around the partition when he was finished. The nurse offered him his shift nodes. "I don't want to be awake for the rest of this, do I?" he asked.

"That's entirely up to you," the nurse replied. Rob clipped the nodes behind his ears and activated the shift cycle.

"Let us know if he gives you any trouble," one of the guards said.

"Not much chance of that now," the nurse said from a faraway place.

CHAPTER 8

We're all connected here. It's been agony to see a few tear down what we've built, but I'm strengthened by the selflessness of so many others.

JUNE 2084

In Rob's experience, every airlocker was alike: the same tang of sweat, coolant, and lubricant, the same placards describing all the ways he could die and all the procedures to follow, the same color-coded hose reels, the same green, amber, and red warning lights. This particular airlocker, on the far side of the solar system, had all those things, but as Rob let his pressure suit's travel case drift to the concrete floor, he sensed something else, something refreshing. Most of the lockers stood wide open in defiance of Airlocker Safety Rules 101, and the warning signs felt more like friendly suggestions.

When Rob had arrived at Agnus Dei that morning, he'd expected to be greeted by the local mental health professional, armed with his Valdosky file—and maybe handcuffs. But Rob had queued unmolested with the researchers, food service staff, and a philosophy student who had shared the shuttle. There had been no compulsory medical exam; no mention of ration allotments for food, water, or power; no radiation dosimeter. If there was a section safety captain bristling with evacuation procedures, he or she had been in no hurry to knock on his door. So far, none of the horror stories of spartan asteroid survivalism seemed to apply to Agnus Dei.

In the wholesome monotony of permashift, Rob had read that Agnus Dei had once been a single rock, until an ancient cataclysm had shattered it into twenty-eight major chunks and a cloud of debris. No one but an astrogeologist would have given a damn about the place, except that Agnus Dei's orbit, always opposite from and only a little wider than Mars's, made it an ideal place for a refueling and resupply station on its side of the system. The broken remains of Agnus Dei were to be given a second chance as a frontier town.

In its rush to speed development of the asteroid belt and the outer system, Valdosky had lured exoarchitects, systems engineers, fabrication specialists, and interior designers to the site with lucrative contracts. Engineers had reined in the rocks, connecting everything with a web of tethers and bridges. Crews had rushed the construction on overtime, working from napkin sketches as frequently as real plans. Habitats had blistered up as quickly as the surfaces could be graded. Warrens had been burrowed as pervasively as structurally feasible. As more cubic meters were pressurized, more specialists had arrived, happy to have a proving ground for new inventions and crazy ideas. Life support, material handling, and agricultural engineers rubbed shoulders with chefs, artists, and psychologists. Hoteliers and commercial developers mingled with bureaucrats and miners. Scientists, too, moved in, eager to have a deep-space research station where they wouldn't have to live alone with other scientists.

The university had grown out of this living laboratory. Cross-disciplinary scientific seminars melded with the continuing education programs for the thousands of support staff and construction workers. With a generous endowment from Valdosky, and the lack of anything better to do at the fingertip of human civilization, the creation of the university had crowned the brief golden days of Agnus Dei.

Then, fewer than fifteen years after the first footprints, Agnus

Dei had experienced its second cataclysm. The UNSA decided to support its own Gateway program instead of Agnus Dei, preferring to place free-floating transit hub stations at Mars's three Lagrange points. On Agnus Dei, buildings were left unfinished, unfurnished, and derelict before they were ever really useful. Crews used Agnus Dei's workshops to fabricate nearby Gateway 3 and then mothballed them. The engineers, developers, and construction crews moved on. But the university remained, like a forgotten dream. And the most exceptional casino hotel in the universe became a dormitory.

Rob hung his scrawny T-Rec suit in a locker large enough for a hard Con-Ex model. It was a good locker, with plenty of accessory drawers and thoughtful glove-drying perches. He connected the umbilicals. His helmet synced easily with the local network. The battery charger lit dutifully, functional despite having been in storage for almost a year. Rob couldn't yet say the same for himself. His hands felt childishly weak, and his clothes rasped on his skin like sandpaper. When everything was arranged, Rob closed his locker door but then laughed and opened it. *When in Rome*, he thought with a growing smile.

The roll-up grille door of ADU's commissary was raised less than a meter, but the lights were on and a squat man was perched on a stool behind a counter, talking on a mobile. "...haven't checked all the manifests. Containers are still streaming over."

Rob had seen this man at the shuttle dock that morning. His head of hair seemed to have migrated from his scalp to his chin, and an orange turtleneck peeked out of the collar of his green jumpsuit, a cross between a Scandinavian fisherman and a tortoise. Rob tapped questioningly on the grille, and the man waved him inside. He covered the end of his mobile and said, "We're open. Damned door's busted again."

Rob pulled himself low and flat around the rattling gate, reoriented himself, and then scanned the commissary for any signage. Finding none, he pushed off into a narrow aisle between haphazardly stacked crates and cluttered bins. Batteries, T-shirts, medical gloves, industrial adhesive. A case of deodorant refills sat open on an eight-valved pump strapped to a plastic pallet.

"Sorry about that," the man called from the end of the aisle. He stroked his beard as he approached. "I know what you're thinking: Didn't he pay attention in suit training? The way I figure it is if I've got to put on my helmet in a hurry, I've got bigger problems than a few whiskers in my gaskets. Besides, it's the only place on my head I can grow anything." He extended his hand. "I'm Saul. Dockmaster, storekeeper, quartermaster, whatever. I'm going to take a wild stab and guess that you're Robert Heneghan. Computer Science Department?"

"I guess my fame precedes me. Call me Rob."

"Stretch yourself out there. You Martians get taller every year. Gonna have to raise the ceilings," Saul said with a hearty laugh.

"There have been a few low doorways," Rob said.

"So what did you leave at home?"

"A toothbrush." The purser had overlooked it when packing Rob's belongings on the Conqueror.

Saul set off across the store. "If you can't find what you need, ask. If I can't make it"—he waved at a bank of rattling object printers, their supply hoses snaking through ragged holes chopped in the back block wall—"I can order it. We're sixty days out from Gate Three, though, so there's a cut-off." Saul nudged an unmarked plastic barrel back into place on a pallet. "Don't worry about asking for anything weird. Believe me, I've heard it all. I'm no judge." Another aisle: duct tape, screws and rivets, haz-mat suits, blueberry-flavored protein bars.

"I'll open up for emergencies. Cost you a bit extra, depending on the time of day…or night." His hand had fallen purposefully on a glass-doored refrigerator filled with bottles of champagne near a surprisingly organized display of chocolates, condoms, incense, and little bottles of lubricant. Packets of rose petals hung from a hook.

"Emergencies?" Rob asked.

"Critical needs always crop up."

Rob chuckled. "I doubt I'll be calling you anytime soon."

Rob tucked his new toothbrush in a pocket, ducked out of the commissary, and set off to explore as much of his new home as he could before that evening's welcome reception. He crossed bridges over truly abysmal depths, rode elevators to their extremes, stopped at every window, and read every word on the few signs and bulletin boards. He encountered only a handful of the roughly two thousand other residents, but that wasn't surprising on a station built for a hundred thousand.

Every building enjoyed, or suffered, its own character—some utilitarian and industrial, others pure epic architecture that would have made Kyle salivate. In the building called The Mall, a dark terrace of never-used storefronts rose up a dozen levels under a soaring, staggering window wall. At grade, the floor met the outer rocky surface as if there were no glass. Less than ten meters on, the gray rock plunged away. From this vantage, the rocks of Agnus Dei hung like silent members of an armada, or the atoms of a molecule. As Rob approached the glass, walking unsteadily on the grip carpet, he felt the pride of Ozymandias, glad to be one of the few people ever to experience this place.

Rob had found most of the station's zones unsecured, but he was astonished when, at the end of a particularly grim corridor near the dock warehouses, a set of forbidding steel doors opened easily, as if the mechanism had been recently greased. Inside, a disused cargo conveyor belt ran along one side of a dark bridge. The opposite wall was studded with handholds and a lanyard track. Not knowing what might greet him on the other end, Rob pushed off gently. The lights moved with him, illuminating a few meters ahead, and fading off close behind him. The end arrived more quickly than expected, but Rob managed to catch himself on a rock wall worn smooth by countless similar footfalls. Conduits, ducts, and pipes spilled out of a chase and slithered onto the walls and ceiling. A sheet metal sign had pointed the way in better days: Fabrica, edical, Su ply, Admi, rlock A. Someone had scratched "Hell" on the sign with an arrow pointing in the appropriate direction. Rob decided that this must be the original Agnus Dei structure, the construction and fabrication building, the first physical plant. He probably wasn't supposed to be here.

Dark passageways branched away at irregular intervals from the main corridor. The walls vibrated unnervingly, as if alive. Half the space adventure games Rob had ever played began, or ended, in places like this. Here, miners disturbed the not-quite-dead remains of vicious aliens, or space marines battled homicidal robots, or madness gripped a marooned contingent of colonists. Had anyone died during Agnus Dei's construction? What had made these splattered stains?

The corridor ended at a graffiti-covered alcove capped by a massive vacuum-rated steel door. An active security panel told him that this was as far as he was going to get. Every surface of the alcove had been vandalized with layer upon layer of everything from autographs to obscene doodles. In the center of one wall, crude letters, each half a meter tall, had been burned with a welding torch and a certain amount of violence. The desecration focused all the rest and transformed these walls into art.

" 'Valdosky sucks,' " Rob read aloud and laughed. "Preach it, brother."

Rob was still chuckling about the graffiti when he returned to his room, but sobered up when he found a skinny Earthling knocking on his door. The guy was Vanilla-age and wore non-threatening slacks and a boring sweater. It had to be the local shrink finally come to suss him out. It was true, Valdosky did suck.

"Sorry. I'm not home," Rob said.

The man turned, a little startled, and said. "Oh, hi. Robert Heneghan?"

"I'm Rob."

"Hi. Jaidev." The man extended a hand. "Jules sent me as your welcome wagon. To give you a quick tour of the department and get you to the reception."

"Jules?" Rob asked.

"Professor Oliver. CS Department?"

"Oh, right. Sure," Rob replied, a creeping embarrassment replacing his dread.

"First time on an asteroid colony?" Rob nodded. "Different than you expected, no? I came here from U.P. Sky a couple of years ago. Bit of a culture shock after that."

"U.P. Sky?" Rob asked.

"Uttar Pradesh Sky. The state's colony? India? The most populous asteroid colony in the system?"

"Right. I thought you said...never mind," Rob said. "I was just about to change for the reception. Do you mind waiting?"

A few minutes later, Jaidev led Rob across the Casino lobby to the mouth of a stubby glass-walled bridge that ended at a rectangular junction. Six carpeted oval tubes, each a different color, split away at severe angles into the mass of another building. Jaidev picked a tube that traveled flat for a few meters but then turned up sharply.

"It's like being back on a playground," Rob said.

"That's why everyone calls this building Kindergarten," Jaidev said. "It was supposed to be offices for the UN, corporations and the like. Jules will tell you that they closed the whole station rather than work in this place."

At MTI, the Computer Sciences Department had had an entire building at its disposal, as well as a respectably large server farm. ADU's department apparently rated not much more than a suite of cubicles, a couple of meeting rooms, and a few nearly empty bedroom-sized spaces that Jaidev called "labs" with a straight face. "You get your own cubicle," Jaidev said. "This messy one's mine. The neat one is Lloyd's. Max is here. Rachelle's over there, but she doesn't work here much."

"Everyone's grad level? There're no undergraduates?" Rob asked.

"At ADU?" Jaidev replied with a laugh.

"What do you work on?"

"Seventh sense. At least that's what I call it," Jaidev said.

"What's that?"

"Instinctual user interface. Computing for babies."

"Wow. I know they do shifting for preemies. Is that what you mean?"

"More like innate gestures. Nonverbal navigation basic enough for a newborn."

"In shift or in real life?" Rob asked.

"Doesn't matter. A shift grid is just another place to a baby.

I've got a grant from a toy company and another from an educational publisher."

As they left, Rob said, "Small department."

"The whole school's desperate for students," Jaidev said. "If you've got half a brain, you're in. But don't worry. We won't hold that against you."

The size of the sunny greenhouse didn't impress a city-dome-dweller Martian like Rob—even though it was the largest enclosed space on the station he'd yet seen—but the trees in the arboretum nearly brought tears to his eyes. Evergreens, of course—Mars, too, was thick with those in and out of the domes—but also majestic oaks and towering poplars, sprawling willows and fantastic palms, and so many others he'd never seen. A hundred species or more branched and tangled their way to the heavens, unfettered by gravity, untouched by scouring wind.

Several hundred people were mingling in a courtyard at the heart of the grove with their feet tucked into plastic toe loops embedded in brick pavers. A formally dressed string quartet played chamber music while possibly-robotic birds flitted from branch to branch overhead. At a table draped with black linen, two bow-tied servers filled membrane glasses with wine and guarded bowls full of iced beverage packs. Jaidev led Rob through the gathering to a clutch of people, many too far past Vanilla age to be students. One of them, a large-chested, white-haired man, grinned broadly at their approach.

"This must be our Martian prodigy. Robert Heneghan, welcome," he said, rounding out Rob's name with an irritatingly silent T. Even though Professor Jules Oliver was less than two meters tall, his broad upper body and disconcerting ebullience made him seem much larger.

"My wife, Martine, and our department's secretary," Jules said, introducing a Teutonic beauty about his age. Rob shook hands with her and the others, professors and department heads, even as he forgot their names.

"Robert comes to us highly recommended by Professors Wetzel and Nakano at MTI," Jules announced.

"What drew you to Agnus Dei?" asked a professor who looked like Jesus.

Rob felt his face redden. A broken heart? The fact that they'll take anyone? "I heard that the food's really good," he said and grinned.

Jules's smile faded even as a few people chuckled. "Jaidev, has Robert met the others?" he asked.

A few moments later, Jaidev introduced Rob to Max and Lloyd, and to Lamb's Mercy, a cold and passable beer brewed on the station.

"Max is trying to win the G-Nose Prize," Jaidev said.

"Isn't that the G-Plex contest? Improving odor replication ratings?" Rob asked.

Max, a pale, blond Martian with an ironically large nose, nodded and said, "I've gotten almost a nine percent improvement so far, but G-Plex is looking for a full twenty. The Cal Tech team claims ten percent, but it's not official yet."

Jaidev said, "If you're feeling daring, shift with Max and take a whiff of his rather large collection of odor algorithms."

"Always need more data," Max said.

"Maybe I should hear other offers before I guinea pig myself out," Rob said. "What do you do, Lloyd?"

"Biocomputing," Lloyd answered. At first blush, Lloyd was as English as Jules was French.

"Lloyd's been trying to make his wee bacteria add two and two for going on six years now," Max said.

"Or more precisely, one-zero plus one-zero," Jaidev said. "Much more difficult."

"Jealous little monsters, these," Lloyd said. "They covet my DARPA support. And lack vision. They have little nose for my work."

"Is that a joke?" Max asked.

"I think it was," Jaidev said.

Max slipped into a cartoonish English accent. "*I do believe that barb, that positively witty bon mot, was at my expense. You wound me grievously, sir.*"

"What's your specialty?" Lloyd asked Rob.

"I did my final undergraduate work on complex database functions. Fluid variables. Predictive algorithms. I have a few ideas on incorporating an NAI…what?"

"Careful. That's a nasty acronym around here," Max said.

"What? NAI?" Rob asked.

"Jules is not a fan," Jaidev explained.

Now affecting a French accent, Max quoted, "*When computers become intelligent, they will let us know.*"

"We were funded to purchase an NAI a few years ago, but Jules killed the project shortly after he arrived," Lloyd said.

"Oh, there's Rachelle." Jaidev gestured to a woman with green hair, cat's ears, and a tail. "She's one of us, but you'll usually find her with physics." He indicated the man who was holding her hand. Rob wanted to ask if the tail was real or just a prosthetic, but modders generally considered such questions rude.

"You should see her avatar," Max said.

"What does she do?"

"Data storage architecture," Max replied. "Which explains her attraction to the physics department over us code-monkeys."

"Such longing, Maxwell. Are you attracted to women with tails?" Lloyd asked.

"Bah," Max replied.

"Did you notice how he failed to answer the question?" Lloyd said.

"Are you attracted to men with tails?" Max asked.

"Welcome to Agnus Dei," Lloyd said to Rob. "We may all be disenfranchised loners, but at least we're together."

An hour later, they left the sunlit arboretum for a laser-lit storage bay. No chamber music, only a very loud, danceable slap-bass funk. No more meet and greet. No more teachers' dirty looks. The bar was more chemistry lab than watering hole.

"Try this one," Max said, handing Rob a blue oral syringe. Rob accepted the syringe and then another, promising himself there wouldn't be a Cheese Incident 2.0.

Rachelle dragged him, semi-resistant, semi-aroused, onto the dance floor. They danced, together but apart, until her boyfriend arrived. Then she slithered her tail around her lover and waved goodbye to Rob. The alcohol kept him dancing alone, but his remaining sense steered him to the edge of the dance floor.

"Don't go," someone said close in his ear. Rob turned, confused, expecting Rachelle, but finding a Martian woman in a tight black dress. Black ringlets bounced along her neck to her shoulders as she tugged him back into the crowd.

She spun around and backed up against him, and then spun away, again and again. Her hair smelled like jasmine. When she faced him, her eyes held his in some kind of bewildering enchantment. She's probably Vanilla age, Rob thought. Who knows how many years past thirty? But then she drew herself close again and he forgot why that might matter. A few minutes later, when the music broke, she spoke in his ear again. "Welcome to Agnus Dei."

Rob thanked her, and turned to applaud the deejay with the crowd. When he turned back to introduce himself properly, the woman had gone.

Rob found Max talking to another woman near the bar. "Who was that I was dancing with?" he asked.

"You call that dancing?" Max said, and laughed. "Actually, I didn't notice." His companion shrugged.

Rob stayed at the party for another hour, not drinking, just waiting and looking. But soon, the lingering effects of the permashift drugs—and the possibility of falling asleep near cans of spray cheese—left him feeling vulnerable. He said goodnight and left alone.

As Rob drifted across the darkened Casino lobby to the elevators, he noticed a figure hunched strangely in a booth in the deserted buffet cafeteria, a woman, Martian or Lunar-born, and with her arms wrapped around her head. Rob caught himself on a column and swung toward the cafeteria. He maneuvered carefully between the tables. Was she crying? Her tangled red curls were spilled across the table among the remains of a vending machine binge. Her long, pilled cardigan stretched slightly to betray the pace of her breathing.

"Are you all right?" Rob asked.

The woman snapped upright. Her eyes widened and then narrowed to a murderous glare.

"What the fuck?" she screamed.

"I'm sorry. You looked like you might be sick or something."

"I'm not sick," she said.

"Sorry."

"Look, noob," she snarled. "If you see me like this, it's not some invitation to come bother me. Understood?"

Rob bristled. "What? You're so special that you can't return a bit of kindness with thanks or manners?"

"Don't sit down here," she growled. He did anyway. She was not an attractive woman. She might have been about Rob's age, but the sweater, wrapped over a ratty shirt, said "cat-owning aunt" more than "graduate-level academic."

"Hi. I'm Rob. And you are?"

"I'm the bitch telling you not to sit here."

Rob couldn't say why he had stayed, but it felt too late to retreat. "Nice to meet you. What do you do here at Agnus Dei?" She scowled. "What were you doing just now? Meditating? Praying?"

"Praying? Ha. I was visualizing," she said.

"Visualizing?"

"What am I? A dictionary?"

"What were you visualizing?"

"None of your business."

"Then why do it in public?"

"Because I made the careless assumption that everyone knows to leave me the fuck alone," she replied.

"Okay, then," Rob said. "It would have been nice to meet you." He made to slide out of the booth.

She sighed. "Gwen." Rob extended a hand. She took it for one brief, cold, rough-skinned shake. Her fingernails had been chewed to the quick. "Engineer."

"Is that a last name?"

"Naval architecture."

"Like spaceships? Wow."

"Who are you?" she asked, looking him over with a disconcerting grin. "You're not good-looking enough to be a Romeo. You weren't shipwrecked here. Bland, young, rude, and kind of stupid. I'm going with Bertram running away from Helena."

"What did you say?"

"No one comes out here without a reason," she said. "Shakespeare covered most of them."

"You said Helena. How do you know about Helena?"

Gwen snorted. "You're kidding. You're actually running from a Helena? Priceless."

"I'm serious. Where'd you hear that name?"

"I have to go." Gwen left Rob with her wrappers and a mental image of her as a redheaded Julius Caesar, crying, *"Et tu, Bertram?"*

* * *

Rob rose late the next morning and after breakfast made his way through the Kindergarten tubes to claim a cubicle. He expected to find the whole gang, but only Lloyd was present, typing away under a pair of comically large headphones. When he noticed Rob he jolted, surprised, but smiled and pulled off his headphones.

"Sorry. Didn't mean to startle you," Rob said. "Where's everyone else?"

"No bother. We keep our own hours. Enjoy your first day on the Lamb?"

"The lam?"

"The Lamb. The Lamb of God. Agnus Dei?"

"Sorry. Right. Yeah."

"You didn't run screaming back to the boat. That's a good sign," Lloyd said.

"Can I just take any empty desk?" Rob held up his pack full of personal effects.

"Take your pick. I'd steer clear of Maxwell's area unless you want him sticking your nose in his business several times a day."

Rob picked a cubicle and stuck his pack to the shifting couch. Lloyd drifted over with a coffee cup, and Rob pulled an MTI mug from his pack. "No one will mind if I use this one?" he asked.

"Not at all. Did you know a Timothy Noonan? This tall. Good-looking."

Rob shook his head. "Friend of yours?"

"Left Earth on the same cruise. He went to MTI to work on

his dissertation. I came here. About five years ago." Rob shook his head again. "Too bad."

"You've been here five years?"

"Four, plus one for travel."

"How long do you plan to stay?" Rob asked.

"Six more months. I'm booked on the next boat. My grant's drawing to a close."

"I'm sorry."

"Don't worry. It's not canceled; it's changing shape," Lloyd said. "DARPA's agreed to defer funding to a start-up I'm setting up with my research partner at UC-Berkeley. Much to Jules's chagrin."

"Why's that?" Rob asked.

"Jules never liked that I obtained my grant before he arrived. He tried to renegotiate the terms to ADU's favor, but my attorney and DARPA told him to fuck off. Don't look so shocked. You'll learn soon enough."

"Learn what?"

"Don't get me wrong. Agnus Dei is a wonderful place, but to get by, you have to know how Jules Oliver works."

"Have I made a big mistake?"

"It's really not as bad as all that. It's just that Jules is not a teacher. He came here three years ago, after Professor Ishiguro retired—robotics, wonderful teacher. Have you heard of him? No? Well, Jules fancies himself a venture capital shepherd, born out of the ancient dotcom days. He admits, with quite a lot of pride, that he got where he is by asking the right questions, not by knowing the right answers."

"Obnoxious," Rob said.

"Quite," said Lloyd. "But the administration brought him on board to keep grant money flowing. Lots of pressure to pay our own way, so to speak, and it trickles down like a waterfall."

"What happens if I don't get grants?" Rob asked.

"I've seen several people 'graduate' from their two-year program early," Lloyd said.

"You're saying I have twenty-four months to produce or they'll send me home?"

"I'm saying you have less than that. Jules will be pleasant and encouraging at first. The hints will be subtle. At six months the heat will rise. At twelve months he'll begin to boil. Eighteen months, he'll prorate your tuition and send you packing."

"Can he do that?" Rob asked.

"Yes," Lloyd said.

"Now I understand the euphemism 'research-driven' from the brochure." Rob rummaged in his pack: his spare charging pad, his Shakiro Squirrel bobble-head, his lucky coding hat. Was any of it worth unpacking? "Most of my ideas involve using an NAI to develop code," he said.

"You'll have to budget for off-site computing in your proposals like the rest of us."

"That's ridiculous," Rob said. "Why doesn't the university have one?"

"Jules makes himself out to be a technical critic of Nexon's system, but it's all tripe. We looked into it after he canceled the purchase. Nexon was one of several companies considering setting up shop in some Eurozone wannabe Silicon Valley in the south of France. Jules's brainchild. They all backed out when it became apparent that Jules didn't actually have the wherewithal to make such massive land deals. He blamed the companies for the debacle and sued, and of course lost after the court examined his financial records."

"Did you go to the administration?"

"We did, but they didn't want to undercut the authority of their new hire. Jules spent the money on major network upgrades. Which was needed, but not as much as an NAI. Now it's a verboten subject."

"That sucks," Rob said.

"That's one word that's been used to describe the situation."

"I didn't even imagine that ADU wouldn't have an NAI."

"Sorry to disillusion you so early."

"But you like it here?" Rob asked. "Despite Professor Oliver?"

"Love it," Lloyd said.

"What do you know about a woman named Gwen?"

"You've met the Red Witch."

"So it's not just me?"

"She's an absolute horror to everyone."

"What's her story? She said she's a naval engineer."

"I'm surprised you got that much out of her. The rumor is she has a design workshop in the old fabrication facility, but no one's allowed in."

"Weird," Rob said.

Lloyd winked. "But not the weirdest thing you'll find out here," he said.

* * *

Rob couldn't sleep the night before his first private meeting with Professor Oliver. So, as soon as the cafeteria opened, he slunk downstairs to find that breakfast first thing in the morning was not the convivial occasion it was at later hours. A pair of lovers dabbled over their food with private smiles and bunny slippers. A shirtless man at a table scribbled furiously onto a screen, confusing his fork and his stylus. A rigid-backed man in a turban ate deliberately with his eyes closed. And in the same booth as the other evening, Gwen was shoveling food in her mouth. Everything about her said he should keep his distance.

"Good morning," Rob said, sliding into her booth.

"Do I have a sign on me?" Gwen replied with her mouth full.

"*All's Well That Ends Well*," Rob announced. "Bertram ran away to Italy after the king of France forced him to marry Helena."

"He reads," she said. "What do you want, a cookie?"

"I'm not Bertram," Rob said.

"That remains to be seen," Gwen said. Rob shrugged. "You realize that I'm insulting you, don't you?"

"Are you?"

"Bertram is one of the lamest, most selfish, sniveling, and stupid characters in all of Shakespeare. Did you even read the play?"

"But I'm not Bertram," Rob said. "So rubber, glue, and all that."

She growled, and then resumed eating, her fork in a death grip.

"How do you pronounce your last name? U-n-g-e-f-u-c-h-t? Because I really don't want to say it the wrong way."

"Un-guh-foo."

"German?"

"Maybe."

"I did some checking. There is no naval architecture or engineering department at ADU. What do you really do?"

"I told you," Gwen replied through a mouthful.

"That doesn't add up."

"That's your problem."

"Why are you at ADU?"

"I like the solitude." She slammed her fork down, drawing stares. "What do you want from me?"

"I want to know how you manage to stay on here without a supporting department."

"I have grant support," Gwen said.

"From who?"

"None of your fucking business."

"Why?"

"Are you stupid? I'm not going to divulge that."

"Who do you report to?"

"No one."

"Not even President Mbuto?" Rob asked.

"Fine, I report to Mbuto, but only for budget oversight. Happy?"

"How'd you manage to get a setup like that?"

"I asked," Gwen replied. "Now will you fuck off?" She slid out of the booth, slammed her tray in the recycler, and shot out of sight.

"Goodbye to you, too," Rob said. As he ate his breakfast alone, he wondered what it said about him that he kind of enjoyed her company.

Jules was hovering behind a substantial glass and wood desk, sorting through open files on the screen as Martine showed Rob in. "I'll be right with you, *Robert,*" he called without looking up.

The professor's office belonged in one of Kyle's creations

rather than in Kindergarten. It was an office for a CEO, or a chairman of the board, or perhaps someone loftier, like a chief visionary officer. Each finish and piece of furniture had probably been as carefully curated as the *objets d'art*—it must have cost a fortune to ship it all here—but Rob couldn't call the room comfortable.

His feet sank slowly into the plush grip carpet next to an amorphous crystalline cloud the size of a basketball projected in the air over a gray plinth. Within the cloud, thousands, if not millions, of colored, pixilated streaks overlapped, lengthened, changed direction, and sometimes vanished. As he waited, Rob tried to find the light sculpture's logic.

"I see *Day in the Life* has caught your eye. Thorisdottir. Are you familiar with his work?"

"I'm afraid not."

After a pause that conveyed a note of disappointment, Jules said, "Icelandic genius. Can you guess what it is?"

"Some sort of complex algorithm?"

"Yes, but what data set?"

"It's not made up?"

"It's a real-time update of U-shift activity. Each thread represents an individual in shift. The colors and textures represent what they're up to. I met Thorisdottir at the auction and asked him what the work meant. Can you guess his answer?"

"I don't know. Something about interconnectedness?" Rob suggested.

"He looked at me with pale blue eyes and said, 'Jules, there is little more beautiful than the space between.' I have to admit I never would have reached that conclusion on my own," Jules said. "This work is not about the people in shift, but about the multitudes that are not. If you change your focus, you can bring the empty space to the foreground. An amazing *trompe-l'oeil*. Can you see it? It's as if the shifted are ever carving away at reality." Rob focused on a clear gap near the center, but his perspective refused to change.

"Come. Let's speak." Jules gestured toward a grouping of uncomfortable-looking pieces arranged around an ornate coffee table. Rob sank into the most likely chair. It felt like a perfect glove had been crafted for his skinny ass. He must have smiled. "Comfortable, no? It's an original Orlando Bruci."

"Very nice," Rob agreed.

"What do you think of our little family here?"

This might have struck Rob as facetious on the first day, but after sitting in on his first weekly department conclave, it fit. Jules, the patriarch, craved loyalty and obedience. Rachelle, the rebellious daughter, made her own rules. Max played the disappointing, not-yet-prodigal son. Lloyd could only be the competent nephew, the usurper. Jaidev, the youngest son, longed to fill the boots reserved for Max. Rob was the circumstantial stranger in their midst with letters of introduction, certainly under their class, pretending, and embarrassed by his shoddy luggage and ill-fitting dinner jacket. "A great group," Rob replied. "I think I learned more at the meeting than my entire first year at MTI. I hope my questions weren't too elementary."

"Not at all. It's good to get back to the root of the problems from time to time. I appreciated your question to Lloyd about the final applications of his work. It's a question I've long been asking, and too long the answer has been simply, 'DARPA is interested.' You saw the heart of the issue. Application is key." Jules cleared his throat. "So..."

Rob turned his screen and thumbed open the paltry list of potential research topics that he had struggled with over breakfast. An uninspiring endeavor, to say the least. Where had all the others found the passion for their work?

"...are you still interested in pursuing, what was it, database operations?"

Rob swallowed. "Perhaps. For my final undergraduate project I created a predictive planetary weather model."

"Ambitious, but surely that's already been done."

"I knew a climatologist, so I had access to some interesting equations at the time. But I think the underlying code is broadly applicable. There are large datasets everywhere." He waved to *Day in the Life*. "And I have ideas about making the application more recursive." Rob prayed he wouldn't have to demonstrate the Lego-clunky Planet Helena. His code invariably predicted a massive storm that ejected most of its atmosphere into space unless he cranked the gravity up to white-dwarf levels.

Jules nodded. "I like the flexibility of your subject. Your current lack of focus may seem like a disadvantage. Quite the opposite. You have an opportunity to let the funding focus your vision."

"Great." Rob thumbed his list closed, feeling like he had signed a contract without reading the fine print.

"Why don't you run what you have by the others? They'll help you build on your ideas, and Martine can help you begin your search for support," Jules said. "I look forward to working with you. I feel that you and I are of one mind on many issues." Rob doubted this. Jules rose from his seat gracefully.

Rob stood, too, but popped out of the chair, barely snagging the grip carpet with his toes. "May I ask a question?" he said, steadying himself.

"Certainly," Jules replied.

"Many of my ideas involve using a Nexon NAI to manage recursive processing."

"We have no plans to establish an NAI in this department."

"May I ask why?"

"The Nexon NAI system is misguided technology. Bulky, unreliable, exorbitant, and unproven. Its proprietary nature is suspect, as are its basic design concepts. Nexon has set true AI development back significantly, and ADU will not support their program. Trust me. They will be abandoned as quickly as they were adopted. In my circles, I have already begun to hear the words 'failure,' 'security nightmare,' and even 'hoax' and 'fraud.' Good day, *Robert*." The patriarch had spoken.

As Rob left, he tried to convince himself that it wasn't a big deal. He would cope without an NAI like everyone else. But everything he had ever learned about NAIs indicated that they were the future. Job interview #1: Do you have any experience programming with NAI systems? No. Job interview #156: Do you have any experience programming with NAI systems? A little. We'll be in touch. Job interview #212: It's a pretty complicated steam fryer. You sure you can handle it? He might as well go back to rendering table lamps for Kyle.

Back at the cubicles, Max and Rachelle were arguing some finer point of data compression.

"Does anyone understand what they're talking about?" Rob asked. Jaidev shook his head.

"I certainly do not," Lloyd said. "But neither does Max. How was your meeting?"

"I asked Jules about an NAI," Rob said. Everyone, including Max and Rachelle, turned.

"Did his face get red?" Max asked. "Last time I thought he was going to have an aneurysm."

"He was calm enough," Rob said. "He dismissed me as naive and uninformed."

"Indeed. What else can he do?" Lloyd said.

"It's so frustrating," Rob said. "Everyone loves these things. There hasn't been a serious critic for years."

"But even if Jules changed his mind, there's no money," Jaidev said.

"There's always money," said Lloyd. "I guarantee you, if he wanted it, we'd get it."

Max snorted. "He'll be forced to relent someday. We can't compete for grants because we have to budget for outside processing costs. He's at crossed purposes."

"There must be something we can do," Rob said.

"More power to you," Max said, and threw up his hands.

* * *

Rob scowled at the laundry machine's screen, rendered almost unreadable by countless fingers. A helpful vandal had scratched the suggestion, "Abandon all hope," into the machine's powder coating.

"Need some help?"

Her hair was pulled back into a simple ponytail. Her lips were their natural color, but no less interesting. And she'd traded her black dress for a well-loved collegiate sweatshirt and flannel pants. Her laundry bag drifted to the floor.

"Perhaps," Rob said.

"Did you put your clothes in?"

"I did."

"Did you select your detergent?"

"The top one."

"Drying mode?"

"Standard."

"Did you swipe your card?"

"I was about to," Rob said.

"You don't need my help at all." She smiled.

"It's still nice to hear that I'm doing it right," Rob stammered. "I was beginning to think I'd dreamed you."

"I'm real," she said.

"Are you a student?"

"Nope. UN Medical. Physician's assistant."

"Hi. I'm Rob. Heneghan."

"Reika Ringold," she replied and stuck out her hand.

"Saul? Rob Heneghan. I've got an emergency."

"Good man," Saul said. "It's before my bedtime, and you get the noobie discount, so it'll only cost you five. Meet you down there in ten minutes."

Saul arrived, wearing not his usual jumpsuit, but a pair of ill-fitting khaki shorts and a pink T-shirt stretched over prodigious body hair. He swiped his badge on a security panel, and the commissary's grille rattled open. "Who's the lucky girl?" he asked as the lights buzzed on. "Or boy?"

"I'd rather not say," Rob replied.

"Fair enough. Shouldn't pry. What do you need?"

"Women like chocolate, don't they?"

"Do you like air?" Saul said. "I've got a couple of choices. Twenty-four nuggets of Swiss heaven. Or I've got a box of twelve..."

"Twenty-four's good." Rob took the golden package.

"Anything else? Champers?" Saul tapped the refrigerator and nodded toward the other merchandise.

"Just the chocolate."

"All righty, then," Saul said, and waggled his mobile.

"Can't it go on my account?" Rob asked.

"Afraid not."

Rob fumbled for his mobile and paid the waiting invoice.

"Done and done. Have a great evening," Saul said.

"You're a lifesaver, Saul."

"You name your firstborn after me and we're even." Saul's laughter echoed down the corridor.

A few minutes later, Rob arrived before the massive door in the graffitied alcove at the end of the ancient fabrication building. Valdosky sucks. This had to be the right place.

He studied the security panel but found no intercom or doorbell. He knocked, his knuckles barely registering on the steel. He knocked harder, but with painfully disappointing results. Maybe this should wait until breakfast tomorrow? No, he was mobilized. Surely someone had left an old toolbox around. Rob ignored an out-of-order notice and pushed through resistant hinges into an ancient toilet room. A cluster of lights sputtered on behind a discolored panel. In the stall, Rob found a plunger stuck to the floor behind an old-style chemical toilet.

Back at the door, Rob hefted the stick and rapped three times. Louder than his knuckles but still without the gravitas he'd hoped for. On the other side of a multilayered, vacuum-rated steel pressure door, his efforts probably amounted to tiny, annoying taps. He knocked again, wishing he'd found something metal. He was about to knock a third time when the seal broke and the doors slid open with a hydraulic rush.

"What the fuck!"

Lit from behind, her hair looked like Medusa's snakes on fire.

"Hi, Gwen," he said, lowering the plunger.

"What the fuck do you want?"

"Your help?"

"Fuck off."

"I brought chocolate." He offered her the gold package, letting the plunger go behind him with his other hand.

"Is this some kind of dare?" Gwen asked, glancing down the corridor.

"No joke. I promise. You're familiar with the administration? How things work around here?"

"What of it?"

"My professor is an ignorant asshole, and I may need to make an end run around him to get some changes made."

Her eyes narrowed, and Rob braced himself, wondering if he should have kept the plunger. Then she relaxed.

"What kind of chocolate?" she asked.

CHAPTER 9

You always spoke about the necessity of interdependence. I always thought it an absurd sentiment for a separatist, but I want you to know that I understand it now. Sometimes when we work together we are the most free.

JUNE–SEPTEMBER 2084

The math professor who looked like Jesus flattened himself against a bulkhead as Gwen barged around yet another corner.

"Where are we going?" Rob gasped, giving the professor an apologetic wave. Gwen took off again. And at the next turn, Rob got his answer.

A receptionist scowled as Gwen burst through the doors of ADU's administrative offices and swept past the front desk. "Ms. Ungefucht. Excuse me. You can't just..."

"Barry," Gwen barked.

"Director Schaffer is not in his office. If you have a maintenance issue, you're welcome to submit a discrepancy report through appro—"

Gwen caught herself and spun around. "I don't have a maintenance issue."

"Would you care to make an appointment?" the receptionist asked.

Gwen stormed out and Rob hurried to keep up.

"The bureaucratic cow tried to hide it, but I saw his location on her screen," she said.

"Do you get along with anyone?" Rob asked.

"Only people worth getting along with."

Rob wondered if he should be flattered or appalled. "Who's Director Schaffer?" he asked.

A few minutes later, Gwen barreled through a pair of marked doors that had stopped Rob even at his most curious. Authorized personnel only. Protective equipment required. Radiation hazard. Chemical warnings. Death scooped up in a dozen flavors.

"The minicollider?" Rob asked. There was nothing mini about it. The vast torus emanated from one of Agnus Dei's smaller chunks like the biggest, ugliest engagement ring in history. Sparkly hyper-efficient solar collectors filled the ring with an incongruous starfield, like a portal to another dimension. A single two-hundred-meter bridge linked the minicollider to the greenhouse rock and the rest of the station. From a distance, the huge ring and the colossal globular green dome seemed to have a grander and connected purpose. But in fact their proximity had only to do with their need for unshadowed locations far from the docks.

As they crossed the bridge, Rob began to feel a deep but growing vibration that, once through the doors on the far end, became a mechanical roar. "Should we be in here?" he shouted.

Gwen climbed a caged ladder to a grated causeway in a steel superstructure that filled an immense vaulted rock hollow. Behemoth equipment, bolted to mounts and stabbed by pipes, roared all around them.

Around one particularly giant appliance, they came upon two men. One was a technician in a jumpsuit and enormous ear protectors. The other wore a light-blue dress shirt with rolled sleeves, a tie, and slacks. He noticed them and waved.

"Barry's a physics professor?" Rob shouted.

"Facilities engineer," Gwen shouted back.

Barry handed a screen to the technician and headed their way. "What's the problem?" he asked. Rob could only read his lips.

"An idea for you," Gwen shouted.

Barry led them down several levels to a shockingly quiet workroom. Two people in a control room on the other side of a window glanced up when they entered but, at a nod from Barry, turned back to their work.

"What's up?" Barry asked after introductions.

"You and Rob have convergent problems," Gwen replied.

"Oh?" Barry asked.

"You've heard of Nexon NAI systems?"

"Artificial intelligence?" Barry asked.

"Near artificial intelligence," Gwen said. "It's frickin' smart, but without the emotional baggage of sentience. It does what you want; simple verbal interface."

"It's military, isn't it?" Barry asked.

"Not anymore," Gwen said. "A few years ago—how long?"

"About three years," Rob said, relieved to be able to add something.

"—Nexon released a commercial version for organizations with big problems. And you have a hell of a problem. For only about three or four million unos, this would take your HyperLogics patchwork out behind the woodshed and give it a good spanking."

"I'm sorry," Rob said. "But what's going on here?"

"Barry's the facilities engineer for the whole Agnus Dei complex, not just the collider," Gwen explained, as if to a child.

"I get his title, Gwen, but what's his problem that an NAI would solve? I'm sorry, Mr. Schaffer. She didn't even tell me who we were coming to see."

"Gwen's talking about local integration," Barry said. "Agnus Dei isn't just a fractured asteroid. It's a fractious collection of facilities. One-of-a-kind structures built under three different building code standards. I've got a haphazard power grid with multiple generation sources." Barry became more animated, gesturing in all directions. "I've got dozens of habitation subsystems. Hundreds of lighting fixture types. Six makes of elevator. Robotic cleaning systems from three different vendors. Two independent water treatment setups. A bunged-together solid-waste recycler. Countless operable door styles. Five brands of airlocks. Not to mention the collider here, the observatory, the farm, bio-labs, medical facilities, complete with Level Four quarantine, stuff you don't find on your average colony. I've got to keep everyone breathing, drinking, warm, and pressurized twenty-four seven with a staff of seventeen, including me." Rob was reminded of Helena talking about terraforming. It must be nice to feel that kind of passion. "Our ancient HyperLogics integration program is slow, buggy, takes manual input, and doesn't work with everything."

"Sounds like an NAI is exactly what you need," Rob said.

"Why do *you* need one?" Barry asked.

"Complex data processing. In fact, everyone in the school could use it for research. My particular field is massive complex fluid database functions. Exabyte-plus sized information sets with ever-changing data," Rob said, hoping to impress.

"Okay," Barry said, "but I have a feeling I'm about to ask your sixty-four million dollar question. Why're you talking to me and not Professor Oliver? Don't get me wrong, I'm interested. But shouldn't this be a request for the Academic Technical Committee?"

"That's the prob—" Rob began.

Gwen interrupted. "Professor Oliver hates Nexon because of some shitty botched real-estate deal."

"He freaks out if anyone even mentions Nexon," Rob added.

"Any other sources?" Barry asked.

Rob shook his head. "Proprietary."

Barry nodded knowingly to Gwen. "I see where you're going."

"I don't," Rob said.

"I told you," Gwen said. "Professor Oliver is the chair of the Academic Technical Committee."

"But he's only one vote. What about the other members?"

"Wake up. There're a dozen committees—technical, budget, ethics, curriculum—but there's only about twenty department heads and assistant department heads to sit on them all. Jules chairs the ATC, but he sits on four or five others. Everyone has their pet causes."

"The committee will just vote with Jules?" Rob asked.

"With Jules as chair, they'll never even vote," Gwen replied.

"That's infantile," Rob said.

"It's politics," Gwen said. "But, yes, the faculty are collectively a bunch of children." Rob glanced at Barry.

Barry shrugged one shoulder. "I'm staff, not faculty."

"Barry's purchases don't—" Gwen said.

"—don't have to be approved by the Academic Technical Committee," Barry finished.

"You could buy an NAI, just like that?" Rob asked.

"I'd need to do some research. And the next budget approval cycle doesn't start for another three months."

"And Rob will manage the system," Gwen added. "Your very own on-site tech support."

"I will?" Rob asked.

"You will," she said. *Shut the fuck up,* said her scowl.

"Isn't there an IT department?" Rob asked.

"We've got a tech who does cabling, component swaps—basic stuff—but software is managed remotely," Barry said.

"For the whole university?" Rob asked.

"We've got a depth of experience to dig into if something major goes wrong, like your department, for instance. But it'd be ideal to have someone on-site. There's even an unused data room over in Kindergarten."

"So it's that easy?" Rob asked.

Gwen and Barry exchanged a glance and laughed. "I told you not to get your hopes up," Gwen said.

After they parted ways with Barry, Rob said, "I was beginning to think you didn't have any friends out here." Gwen pushed off at the next junction, the belt of her sweater and a raised middle finger trailing behind her.

* * *

The following Monday afternoon, Rob received a message during the department meeting and opened it discreetly.

> Rob,
>
> Hard to believe this is the company Professor Oliver

hates so much. This NAI thing is perfect for us. Expensive, but justifiable. Meeting with Nexon sales next week. May want your help with the capital request. I'll keep in touch.

Barry

Your move, Jules, Rob thought.

* * *

Rob took back his screen from Max and Rachelle and tossed it, and the rejection letter it displayed, onto his cubicle's desk. He had never expected to get the NEXT Bank's Grant for Financial Information Systems Quality Improvement, nor had he particularly wanted it. His knowledge of high finance pretty much ended at the bar tab level. "I need to call Gwen," he said.

"We're trying to cheer you up, not destroy you utterly," Max said. "Do not invite her."

"She helped me with the application," Rob said.

"No, invite her," Rachelle said. "Rob has done much to soothe the savage Lady Ungefucht. A little socializing might do her good."

"Then count me out," Max said.

"Nonsense," Lloyd said as he joined the group. "Rob is in need of some liquid consolation with his colleagues, and you're coming. Jaidev's with us on this. Aren't you, Jaidev?"

"Whatever," Jaidev called from his cubicle.

"He wasn't even listening," Max said.

"Four against one," Rachelle said.

"This'll just take a second." Rob pressed his mobile to his ear.

Gwen answered, sounding oddly distant. "What do you want?" she asked.

"I didn't get the NEXT Bank grant," Rob announced. Gwen sighed, or maybe growled. "Listen. Rachelle, the guys, and I are going down to the bar to commiserate over my abject failure."

"I told you it was too many applications at once."

"I know, but it's what Jules wanted."

"Your stupid department."

"I know. I know. You in?"

"In what?" Gwen asked.

"The bar. Ten minutes."

"It's three in the afternoon."

"I'm suffering emotional trauma here. There's only one cure." The line clicked dead.

"Is she coming?" Max asked.

"Probably not," Rob replied.

The bar was deserted except for the bartender, Mike, an astronomer. "A celebration?" he asked as the computer science students entered.

"Well, *Mikhail,*" Lloyd said. "Our young Martian friend has been rejected by a grant committee of bankers and other souls without vision. He needs solace. The first round is on me."

"Five solaces, coming up," Mike said. He slid five packs of Lamb's Mercy across the counter. "Sorry, dude," he said when he got to Rob.

"A toast," Lloyd called, "to our friend and colleague. About his fourth rejection—"

"First," Rob corrected.

"—his third rejection, we have this to say: Don't take it hard. We've all been there. There's always the next time." He paused. "And the time after that, and the one aft—" The group broke into laughter.

"To the time after that," Max said, lifting his beer.

"And as for the wankers at NEXT Bank," Lloyd added, receiving a hearty cheer.

"What's next, Rob?" Rachelle asked.

"I've got two more applications out there. One for a research subsidiary of Xterrex and a foundation grant. Genetic data or something."

"Goodness, how many applications did you put together?"

"Just those three, in the last month and a half."

"It takes me weeks to write one decent application. Minimum," Rachelle said.

"Jules thought this one was a lock," Rob said.

"Jules always gets pissed when someone doesn't give us money," Max said. "He's probably shifted right now to meet someone who knows someone who can tell him why their crony didn't call in favors for him."

"Jules can rant all he likes," Rob said, "but it doesn't give me a finance background. He has me applying for all these random things I know nothing about."

"You could go back to weather," Jaidev suggested.

"The incredible dissipating planet," Max announced with a flourish.

Rob groaned. "How about astronomy, Mike? Are there any huge data management problems in astronomy?"

"Sure," Mike replied. "We create terabytes every week just with our little observatory and radio array."

"See," Rob said. "I buddy up to Mike. Figure out what his problems are, then bang, I'm in the money."

"Come on out to the observatory. I'll show you…" Mike paused. Gwen had appeared with her hands pushed deep into her sweater's pockets.

"Hi, Gwen. Can I get you something?" Rob asked.

"I'm not staying. I have an appointment. Nice to see you all. Goodbye." She waved as if it were an unfamiliar gesture, jammed her hand back in her pocket and left. Max gave a snorting little laugh, earning a glare from Rachelle.

Rob cringed. "I'll be back," he said.

He caught up with her at the elevators. "What was that all about?" he asked.

Gwen grunted. "I naively thought you might be talking seriously about your next step, but you're just drinking."

"We're talking."

"You have two more crappy applications out there, and you're boozing it up like nothing's wrong."

"You said my applications were okay."

"I said they were barely adequate," Gwen said.

"Anyway, I'm just buying time until we find out if Barry can get the NAI."

"But that doesn't give you the right to sit on your ass. God, I never would've helped you if I thought you were this mediocre. You know what? I did know it. From Day One I pegged you as a Bertram."

"Why are you so angry?" Rob asked. "I'm not the only one who's gotten rejected for a grant." The elevator arrived, and Gwen held Rob at bay with a stern index finger.

As the doors closed, Rob remembered one of their early conversations. She had been appalled to learn the truth of Jules Oliver's credentials. "It makes ADU look bad," she had said. "Makes it harder for all of us to earn respect out here." Rob had agreed with her then. It pained him to agree with her now.

"Is she okay?" Rachelle asked when Rob returned.

"She's not good around people," Rob said.

Max snorted. "That's an understatement."

"But people have noticed she's become more civil. You're rubbing off on her," Rachelle said.

"What's her story?" Jaidev asked. "I've only heard rumors."

"She told me she grew up in Patmos," Rob said. "The weird little colony on Mars. Not culty weird, just arty, believe-anything-you-want weird. I kind of get the idea that she's some sort of supergenius who was home-schooled by Red Hippies."

"Dream trippers?" Max asked.

"Maybe. And maybe when she got old enough, she rebelled by going as straight as possible."

"You'd think a supergenius would be a little friendlier," Max said.

"Why would you think that?" Lloyd asked.

"I'm just saying," Max replied. "She could be."

* * *

The next morning, Jules arrived to his office red-faced and wearing a damp sweat suit with a ridiculous blue, white, and red headband. He admitted Rob begrudgingly.

"Thank you for seeing me without an appointment."

"If you've come to petition me about NEXT Bank, I have

already spoken to the grant coordinator," Jules said as he extracted a pack of water from a mini-fridge in the credenza.

"It's not about NEXT," Rob said. "I want permission to withdraw my pending applications. It's evident my submissions aren't up to standard." Jules cracked the seal on the pack and took a deep swig. Rob swallowed.

"Perhaps there are provisions to revise? Contact the administrators."

"It's more than that," Rob said.

"One rejection is not the end of the world."

"Would those applications have made it past your VC slush pile when you were on the other side of the table?" Rob asked. Rob caught something in Jules's expression. Was it a change of perspective? Was it anger? "Because I don't think they would've."

"Why do you say that?" Jules asked.

"I think it's because I'm appealing to people who are passionate about their business. I reread my applications, and it's obvious that I don't give a damn."

"Well then, what do you care about?"

"I'm trying to figure that out," Rob replied.

"I appreciate your concerns, but they do not warrant withdrawal from your current efforts," Jules said.

"I don't want to embarrass you or Agnus Dei."

"Nonsense," Jules said. "Passion, as you say, has its use. But it can also be limiting. You cannot depend on a singular chance for success at this level."

"I understand," Rob said.

"Excellent."

"I'm going to keep searching for a project that I can really get behind."

"I look forward to that," Jules said. *We'll see,* Rob thought.

On his way to the door, Rob's mobile began to buzz. It was Barry. Jules called to Rob, as if he sensed the conspiracy from across the room.

"Don't be too long about it," Jules said. "The real world has little patience for dreamers and perfectionists." Rob nodded, thanked Jules, and hurried out to take Barry's call.

Rob took a long route to meet Barry one level above Jules's office, all the while checking over his shoulder. If Kindergarten's walls had ears, then its tubes had eyes. He didn't want anyone asking nosy questions.

"Thanks for meeting me on short notice. This is it," Barry said and swiped his badge across the security panel next to an otherwise innocuous door.

The door squeaked open into a two-room suite. The rooms were of equal size, separated by a thin wall, and lined with cabinets and counters on the side near the doorways. In the first room: a set of half-assembled cubicles. In the second room: a workbench built across the far end and a waist-high stack of flat, unopened boxes piled in the middle of the floor. Rob brushed the dust away to read the top label, but the cardboard crumbled.

"Equipment racks," Barry said. "Never assembled."

Barry opened an inner door with another swipe of his badge, and a single light panel flickered on in a third space. This was the real estate they had come to see: the five square meters of ADU where Barry hoped to house the NAI.

The ceiling was unfinished and the walls were still marked from construction. Capped wires dangled from conduit stubs and ductwork ran to nowhere. But several neat rows of rubber-capped bolts poked up through the raised floor: vibration mounts just waiting for equipment racks. "More finished than I expected. Excellent," Barry said.

Rob turned, startled, when another person entered behind them. Thankfully not Jules.

"Eduardo Arcoverde, meet Rob Heneghan." Eduardo was tall enough to have spent at least some of his childhood on the Moon. He had a thin mustache and wore a green canvas jacket with an ADU patch on the breast. "Eduardo's our lead hab tech, and our go-to guy on the HyperLogics system," Barry said as they shook hands.

As Barry and Eduardo took measurements and inspected an electrical panel, Rob tried to imagine the room fitted with humming and blinking equipment. This might be his analog to Gwen's shop in the fabrication facility. His own domain on Agnus Dei.

"There's plenty of power capacity," Barry announced. "It's already on the emergency grid, and those pipes over there tap into the vacuum cooling system. We're in good shape."

"Is this actually happening?" Rob asked.

"I've submitted the capital request. Now we wait. But DeBartolo's behind it."

"Who's DeBartolo?"

"My boss," Barry replied. "It's up to the board finance committee now. I've demonstrated a substantial long-term cash savings, so it should be an easy sell."

"Don't get my hopes up," Rob begged. "When does the committee decide?"

"A few weeks," Barry replied. "Will this room work, Eduardo?"

"We're good," Eduardo said.

"That's a ticker-tape parade from you," Barry said. "Let's get a work list together."

"Anything I can help with?" Rob asked.

"I'll get you authorized for these doors. You can figure out how we're going to use this place."

"Can I set up the cubicles out there?"

"Make yourself at home."

"It would be cool if we had a coffee maker," Rob said.

Barry grinned. "Done, and done."

"Jaidev was looking for you," Max said when Rob returned to the department's offices. "Are you okay?"

"I'm fine. Why?"

"You look happy, like you're up to something. Like Shakiro Squirrel," Max said. Rob began to hum the Shakiro Squirrel theme song and headed toward Jaidev's lab with an action punch.

* * *

"Good morning. Mind if I join you?" Rob asked.

Gwen glared and grunted, and resumed stuffing breakfast in her mouth as if storing it for winter.

"I'm sorry about the other day," Rob said. "You were

absolutely right. I'm using this NAI thing as an excuse to do mediocre work. I went to Oliver and asked to withdraw my other applications."

Gwen began to chew deliberately, intensely. Rob braced for her response, but she swallowed and simply asked, "And?"

"He said no. But I think he's worried. He's losing Lloyd in a few months. No one new is coming, as far as I've heard. No grant money, students leaving. No department, no job."

"You're not thinking of leaving, are you?" Gwen asked.

"Why? Do you want me to stick around?"

Gwen grunted through another mouthful of food.

"I should warn you that I will not be working diligently on my contribution to improving the universe tonight. In fact, I may do the opposite. Word has it the Chemistry Department shindigs are legendary. You should come."

"What's wrong with you?" Gwen asked.

"I'm freaking out over this stupid budget process," Rob said. "Listen to me. Just a few months ago, I was watching my brother stress about his company's annual budget, thinking, 'I never want that to be me.' Karma's cruel."

"Karma," Gwen spat.

"You don't believe in karma?" Rob asked, wondering what drove him to poke the hornet's nest.

Gwen left, muttering about selection bias, cherry-picking, and stupid people.

"So you're not coming to the party then?" Rob called after her.

"Mike, do you live here?" Rob asked as he and Max settled onto two of the bar's grip-topped stools that evening after dinner.

"I'm an astronomer," Mike replied. "I work nights."

"But we're in space. No day. No night," Max said.

"I did notice that," Mike said and gave the bar a wipe with a towel. "I take the midnight shift so I can spend the evenings in here sponging tips and overcharging you when you're too soused to notice. Gotta keep baby in new shoes."

"I like you, Mike," Max said. "How about a little Mercy?"

Soon they had two beverage packs so frosty that a haze of mist hung in the air around them.

"Is this party going to be good?" Rob asked.

"People shift out on Friday nights," Max replied. "Lloyd won't show. I don't know about Jaidev. He's been pining after Veronica, that geologist from Spain. Never mind that she's about a tenth as tightly wound and old enough to be his grandmother."

"This is the first I've heard about her," Rob said.

"Bah. It stopped being fun even ribbing him about it. Not that I'm any better. Maybe you should hook me up with Gwen." Max grinned evilly and then took a drink. "I'm impressed you managed to make friends with her."

"Someone had to do it," Rob said. "You think Reika will be there?"

"You didn't ask her?" Max asked.

"I wasn't sure if it was kosher."

"She's UN medical, not ADU staff, so green light, man. I'm shocked it's taken you this long to ask." Mike floated past, and Max called after him. "Are you tending bar for the party tonight?"

"I am," Mike replied.

"Excellent. Glow-Bombs?" Max asked.

"Of course," Mike said.

"What's a Glow-Bomb?" Rob asked.

"You feel like Dr. Frankenstein when you drink it, and you wake up feeling like Igor."

"Secret phosphorescent ingredient." Mike winked.

"It's not going to give me stomach cancer, is it?" Rob asked.

"Yeast with a little algal DNA," Mike said. "They chew on the sugars and light up all happy. Say…" Mike's expression changed, and he tapped the bar urgently. "A few days ago you asked about astronomy problems. I thought of one you might be interested in."

"What is it?" Rob asked.

"Have you ever heard of the Yarkovsky effect?" Rob shook his head. A contingent of philosophy students floated in, followed by two couples. "Tell you what. Come see me at the observatory sometime."

"When's your next shift?" Rob asked.

"Tonight," Mike said, drifting away to serve his new patrons.

"The what effect?" Max asked.

"Yarkovsky?" Rob said. "I hope it's a good idea. I have a bad feeling about my other grant apps."

"And then Jules'll be back on your ass."

"Has Jules helped you at all?" Rob asked. "Technically? With any technical problem?"

"He's up front about the fact that he's never coded anything in his life," Max said, and then switched to a French accent. *"I'm here to prepare you for the real world."*

"And that's fine?" Rob asked.

"He meddles, but at least he stays out of my code."

"I suppose that's good."

After a long silence, Max said, "I hope you're not thinking of quitting. We all get antsy before the boat comes. Every six months this place turns into a psych ward. But I think you've got what it takes."

"Thanks," Rob said.

Mike stuck two fresh beers in front of them.

"I've nominated you for sainthood, Mike," Max said.

"That'd take a miracle," Mike said. "Literally."

"Funny," Max said. "I like my bartenders funny."

"Although being a woman doesn't hurt, either," Rob suggested.

"Cheers to that," Max agreed. "Sorry, Mike, sainthood canceled."

Rob sucked down his first Glow-Bomb under a majestic swath of stars and wondered if his pee would glow in the dark. Carly the counselor might have recognized the dangerous glint in his eyes as he scanned the crowd gathering in the Casino's top-floor observation deck.

"Don't worry, man. She'll be here," Max said.

Rob watched the entrance from the bar, hardly daring to blink lest he miss her. On the dance floor, perhaps a dozen black-lit bodies bounced and writhed from floor to glass ceiling among strobing lasers. Around the shadowy edges of the room, a few couples, no longer distinguishable as individuals, had disappeared into the depths of couches. It sickened Rob to think that Reika might already be among them. He cursed himself again for not having found the courage to call her and collected another Glow-Bomb.

And then she arrived. Her hair cascaded poetically over a mathematically perfect neckline. Her skin glistened with starlight. Rob downed the remains of his drink and licked his teeth clean behind closed lips. He felt an unnecessary push on the back from Max even as Reika approached.

"I hope you're going to ask me to dance," she said. But in the end there was no need for such formality.

Out on the floor, Rob loved the teasing glimpses in the cacophony of light and craved the moments her body spent against his. They spun and drifted, clinging together. They rose to the stars and never quite drifted back to the floor. Rob could barely believe his luck when, after an exhausting number of songs, he tumbled onto the middle of a couch and Reika landed next to him and stretched her endless legs across his lap.

"You dance like we've been lovers for years," Rob said.

"Maybe we were lovers in a previous life." She sat up and spoke into his ear. "Or maybe you're the sexiest Martian to step off a boat in a good long while."

"That's all I am to you, a slab of homegrown beefcake? I feel so dirty."

"Good," she said, and bit his earlobe. He squeezed his eyes shut and opened his mouth in a silent groan of pleasure. She reclined, laughing. Rob let one hand land on her knee.

"I suppose I should've been pursuing you all this time," Rob said.

"You think?"

"Sorry, I'm clueless."

"You've probably been told you're clueless by a lot of women," she said.

"A few." Rob shook his head.

"Well, I hereby give you permission to stop being clueless." She waved an invisible wand.

"Beautiful and magic powers. You're amazing."

"Thank you." She held out a hand, and Rob took it, glad for an opportunity to touch her again.

"Want to go somewhere quiet?"

"I thought you'd never ask," she replied.

Reika stayed close as they floated through the station. In the Mall's dark concourse, they flew like Peter Pan and Wendy to a lone grouping of mismatched couches by the curtain wall.

"I love it here," Reika said and kicked off her slippers. "I want to step out there and curl my toes into the dust." He watched her reflection in the glass as she took in the station and the stars.

A few moments later she nestled against him on a couch. "You smell good," she said.

"You're quite the sensualist," Rob said. "You don't have the sensory-deprivation syndrome, do you?"

"SRTDD?"

"I can never remember that."

"Shift-related tactile deprivation disorder," she said. "It's not a syndrome. And I'm not a teenager."

"It's just a teen thing?" Rob asked.

"Usually."

"So you're a doctor?"

"P.A.," she said. "I wanted to see a bit more of the solar system before I committed to med school. But I have to say, this university lifestyle has its appeal."

"Where are you from?" Rob asked.

"Pavonis. My parents worked at the elevator. You?"

"Sinai Flats. My dad does ag systems. My mom's a teacher."

"I haven't been home in a long time," Reika said. "After high school, I traveled with friends on Earth for a couple of years. I did my certification on the Moon."

"Then the UN sent you to ADU?" Rob asked.

"First they sent me to Gateway Two for a while."

"What's a while?"

"If you want to know how old I am, just ask," Reika said. "I know your age. It's part of my job to review medical files of new arrivals."

"What else did you learn about me?"

"Age, height, dance partner rating."

"The UN tracks my dancing ability?"

"Only under special circumstances. I'm forty-three," she said.

"I'd have guessed twenty-five."

"I'm a much better dancer than any twenty-five-year-old."

"I should have taken that into account."

"Yes, you should have." She slipped a tiny mobile from an invisible pocket. "Sorry. Time check. I have a duty shift in the morning."

"I can escort you back to your room. In a gentlemanly way with the best of intentions."

"What if I don't want you to have good intentions?" she asked.

"Tough," he said. "I'm not that easy."

"My magic wand worked a little too well," she said. "Have I made you too perfect?" She waved the invisible stick at him again.

"Believe me, I'm not perfect."

"I don't want to go home yet," Reika said.

"Ever been to the observatory? Mike Tambleau wanted to talk to me about something. Maybe he'll give us a tour."

"That sounds fun," she said. She gathered her slippers and hooked an arm in his.

A few minutes later, Rob and Reika hovered in a rock-walled vestibule and peered through an open airlock into the gaping maw of a tunnel. Accordion rings and air pressure held the white plastic skin taut. Gangways dotted with grip pads lined two opposing sides, while red plastic chains traced the others.

Rob whistled ahead, but no echo returned from the bottom of the well.

"Nothing but a few mils of plastic between us and the vacuum," Reika noted. "Very exciting."

They counted to three and dived together. As they entered the tunnel proper, a warm breeze pushed against their backs. The lights turned off behind them, and soon Rob lost all sense of scale. "I feel like lint in a dryer hose," he said. Reika laughed.

After a few minutes, they encountered a message written on the gangway in black marker. "Don't panic," it read.

"How thoughtful," Reika said.

Alone, Rob might have considered panic, but with Reika the tunnel felt more like a rabbit hole with nothing but promise at the end.

Eventually, a distant black spot resolved into a definitive, growing circle. Then the lights came on in a white vestibule, and they spilled victoriously through another open airlock.

"I thought I heard someone coming." Mike was hanging across a hatch. "It's just about eighteen hundred meters. That's the first question everyone asks."

"There's no shortcut?" Rob asked.

"Not a comfortable one," Mike replied. "Reika. Nice to see you."

"Is this a bad time?" Rob asked.

"Not at all. Glad for the company. Welcome to the ADU Observatory." Mike led them into a well-used, low-ceilinged room dominated by a long bank of workstation screen clusters. Flexi-posters, photographs, and sketches of astrological phenomena papered any spare bit of wall. Rob inspected a radiation warning sign on a door until he realized that it led to the head. A toy model of the solar system hung from the end of a stiff wire in the middle of the ceiling. Opposite the red marble of Mars, a tag on a tiny bit of grit read, "You are here."

"What's through that hatch?" Rob asked.

"Airlock to the optical instruments," Mike said. "We can pressurize the domes for maintenance, but we hate to do it. You have to recalibrate everything, and it's cold as hell."

"What about the radio array?" Rob asked.

"That's about five thousand kilometers below our feet."

"What are you working on?" Reika asked.

"I'm searching for planets," Mike said. "I've got a promising little wobbly star in my sights tonight." He called up a series of graphs on the main monitor.

"Do you keep champagne around, just in case?" Reika asked.

"Just coffee." Mike tapped an enormous thermos.

"So what's this idea you were going to tell me about?" Rob asked.

"Right. The Yarkovsky effect," Mike said.

"Yarkovsky," Rob repeated.

"He was Russian. Amateur scientist. Died at the beginning of the twentieth century."

"So this is an old problem?"

"Ancient. Yarkovsky defined the root of it. The Yarkovsky effect is the name for the force applied to an orbiting body by the release of heat absorbed during rotation."

"You're talking about asteroids," Rob said.

"Exactly." Mike dove under a counter and grabbed a flashlight off a charger. He turned it on and said, "Right, Reika, you're the sun." He positioned her arm and the light, and then turned off the overhead lights. He borrowed one of Reika's slippers and, with a delicate touch, set it spinning lazily in the beam of light. "Lonely little asteroid minding its own business. A happy, spinning little guy, just outside the Mars or Jupiter resonant zones. The millennia go by, but something's happening. The sunward side is always absorbing photons. Heating up all day. But then comes 'late afternoon' and 'dusk'—it's releasing heat, with a greater net photonic pressure from that part of the surface than any other. What happens over time?"

Rob shrugged. Mike blew lightly on the slipper. It maintained its spin but began to drift out of the light and gently toward Rob's face.

"The orbits of small solar system bodies are always changing. Change is imperceptibly slow, and almost but not entirely unpredictable."

"Why is it hard to predict?" Reika asked.

"A hundred different variables. Albedo, the unique geography—craters, shadows, shape—mass and density, distance from the sun, proximity to other bodies, duration and frequency of rotation. There's also the YORB effect, which is similar, but it alters the rotation, not the orbit.

"One of the first rocks they tracked with Yarkovsky in mind was nearly fifteen kilometers off its predicted course in only a dozen years." Mike turned the lights back on. Rob caught Reika's slipper, letting the word "variables" worm its way into his imagination. "That might not seem like much, but it adds up. And there's an entirely new problem now. Every mining operation or colony affects some change. A new pile of slag on the surface. A dome. Xterrex strolls away with a half percent of the mass. A massive Valdosky cargo ship passes nearby. Bam, new trajectory. The bottom line is that no one knows what the solar system is going to look like a thousand, a hundred, or even ten years from now."

"Unless someone could build a hyper-accurate predictive model," Rob said.

"There you go," Mike said. "It's a hell of a problem."

"Someone must be working on it," Rob said.

"Not in any major way. The NEO and NMO programs track a few rocks that they think might be hazardous. Valdosky throws a few extra tons of fuel in their ships for course corrections. G-Plex widens their transmission beams a degree. We've only been out here a few decades, so mostly everyone's ignored it, but one of these days people are going to notice. They'll wake up and their rad shielding won't be positioned quite right anymore, or worse, there's going to be a collision or a breakup, and people are going to die."

"A breakup?" Reika asked.

"Like Agnus Dei. Fragmenting under thermal and gravitational stress," Mike explained.

"I thought it was a collision," Reika said.

"Nah. I think when Valdosky was trying to sell the place they thought an ancient collision sounded safer than seismic instability. Some sales pitch, huh?"

Rob felt raw, as if he'd just awoken from a long session in shift. He let Reika take her slipper back. "The Yarkovsky effect," he muttered.

"Is this the ladies'?" Reika asked, drifting toward the door with the radiation warnings. Mike nodded. She slipped on her shoes and then disappeared into the room.

"The flexis on the wall aren't mine," Mike called after her. "Yeesh. Forgot about those. There's something there to offend everyone. They really aren't mine."

"I actually love this idea," Rob said.

Mike lowered his voice. "It might be none of my business, but

I gotta say, go easy with Ringold. Her ex just left on the boat you came in on. He turned into a complete asshole, hurt her pretty badly. She went through a real rough patch."

"I'm just getting to know her," Rob said.

"Please, treat her right. She's one of the good ones."

A muffled vacuum flush sounded through the door. The lock clicked, and Reika emerged. "As a medical professional, I recommend a full psychiatric evaluation for whomever those flexis *do* belong to," she said.

"I'm sorry. I warned you," Mike said.

"I'm asking as a semi-official representative of the UN and an official representative of womankind, please take them down." Reika clutched Rob's arm. "You are not going in there. Mr. Tambleau has filled your head with enough new ideas tonight."

"I guess we're going," Rob said.

Mike followed them out to the bridge. "Just keep going straight," he called.

A reluctant pace brought them to Reika's door in a housing block near the administration building—the same type of construction found under every dome on Mars, utilitarian, hopelessly airtight, and soulless. She didn't belong here at all.

"I'll write you a note for work. 'Please excuse Reika from school today. She has a fever and unexplainable insomnia,' " Rob said.

"I work in a medical clinic. Fevers concern them."

"Right. No fever th—"

Her lips pressed into his. Her body stayed an electric centimeter away.

"May I call you?" he asked, a respectful moment later.

"You may," she said. "The question is, will you?"

"How can you even doubt it?"

There were colors inside her apartment that the drab corridor had never dreamt of. "I like to consider all the possibilities," she said.

The old Rob might have lingered outside her door in confusion, but the new magic-wanded Rob swaggered—as best he could manage in the minuscule gravity—home.

CHAPTER 10

They say the world is watching us. It is some small comfort that our tragedy might be a catalyst for your cause and the cause of our people.

OCTOBER–DECEMBER 2084

"Where will Agnus Dei be next year? A decade from now? Where will it actually be in space? What will its orbit look like? I don't know, and here's the creepy part—no one does." Rob paused for effect, but Jules didn't look up from his screen.

Rachelle got the lights and Max held the flashlight as Rob fumbled with the scale-model asteroid freshly spit out of one of Saul's object printers. As he demonstrated the Yarkovsky effect, he began to wonder why he'd gone to so much trouble. *Hey, Jules, are you just going to ignore me while I pour out my soul's blood, sweat, and tears? Can't you see the passion positively brimming out of my ass?* And where had Gwen been for the past week? He'd needed her opinion on this new life plan, but she'd seemed to have dropped off the fabric of space-time since that morning before the chem party. Maybe he should've gotten Mike to re-create his demonstration with one of Reika's slippers. After Rob had blown the hunk of plastic off course, he turned the lights back on and flipped to his next slide.

"A list of some of the equations: heat loss based on density, heat absorption. This one is, um, photonic pressure in millinewtons. The list goes on. My program will apply predictive and recursive algorithms to the process. Predict, check results, fine-tune, and repeat. And that's about it."

Jules smacked his lips and rubbed the inner corner of an eye as if he'd been asleep.

Max spoke up on cue. "You're talking about individual asteroids, but are you proposing a model of the whole solar system?"

"Each rock will have a unique dataset, broken down to the square hectare or square meter, depending on the survey resolution. But, yeah, to be truly accurate, I guess the goal would be to model the whole system. Everything's interconnected gravitationally."

"Can you describe the recursive process?" Lloyd had promised a softball question and didn't disappoint.

"Once real-life data is recorded, the program will compare its predictions and attempt to improve the margin of error over each cycle. If ever an observed result falls outside the expected range, the program will attempt to find where it might have gone wrong."

Rachelle gave a thumbs-up and a wave of her tail. Jaidev applauded briefly.

Jules cleared his throat and said, "Xterrex. Valdosky. The UNSA. Astronomical foundations. Colonial development agencies. Insurance companies. Check with Martine for help with a list of potential grant sources. Let's move on."

* * *

"Where have you been?" Rob asked.

Gwen looked up from her breakfast and glared. A bit of scrambled egg was stuck in the corner of her mouth. "None of your business," she mumbled. Rob set his tray down and slid in across from her.

"I presented an idea for a new project yesterday—that's why I called you about a hundred times last week," Rob said.

Gwen groaned. "But you went ahead anyway…"

"I had a deadline. Do you want to hear about it or not?"

Gwen pinched off half a donut, squeezed it in her fist, and stuffed it in her mouth.

"Have you ever heard of the Yarkovsky effect?"

Gwen grunted. "You're going to build an orrery?"

"A what?" Rob asked.

Gwen swallowed and said, "An orrery. A clockwork model of the solar system."

"Why are they called that?"

"How the fuck should I know? That's just the name."

"Fine, an orrery," Rob said. "Except it will be hyper-accurate, predictive, and as near a one-to-one scale as possible. But wait, how'd you figure that? I say 'Yarkovsky' and you just say 'orrery'?"

"How did Oliver react?"

"He just told me to research grant sources."

"Probably didn't take you seriously," Gwen said.

"Maybe not, but what do you think?"

"I don't know where you came up with it, but I approve."

"Good grief, Gwen. Swallow first, then talk, or give it to me in writing."

She shoveled in another bite with one hand and lifted the middle finger of her other. "How about by sign language?" she asked, flecks flying.

Rob burst out laughing when Martine transferred her list of grant applications to his screen, already flagged and organized by due date. "The UN Exploration Innovation Grant?" he asked, reading from the top of the list. "That's due in a couple of weeks. Does Jules really think I can qualify for that?"

"Your project fits the basic requirements as I understand them," Martine replied.

"Is Jules in?" Rob asked.

"He isn't feeling well today," Martine replied.

"Sorry. He didn't seem himself at the meeting yesterday," Rob said.

Back at the CS offices, Rob told Jaidev that Jules was sick.

"Is he?" Jaidev asked. "I saw him in the fitness center this morning."

"Weird. Martine just told me he wasn't feeling well."

"Not feeling well is different than being sick," Jaidev said.

* * *

It took three rings to snap Rob back to reality. He saved his work and began to dig for his mobile through protein bar wrappers and empty bags of cookies. A mostly-drunk water pack spat globules when he grabbed it. The half-eaten tube of Pot Noodle had gone cold and flaccid. He found his mobile behind one of many coffee cups and realized that he needed to go to the bathroom. He hadn't coded like this since MTI.

"Tell me you have good news," Rob said, answering as soon as he read the caller ID.

"Board meeting just broke up. But I'm sorry to say your Professor Oliver may have gummed up the works," Barry replied.

"What? How?"

"The budget isn't a secret. The preliminary draft has been out for a week."

"What happened?" Rob asked.

"A couple of board members brought up concerns about the NAI request. It was pretty obvious that their concerns were not their own."

"Was Jules there?"

"He was."

"He's been acting weird around me," Rob said.

"Brace yourself," Barry said. "DeBartolo defended the project, distributed my cost savings analysis, so the board agreed to withhold a decision pending a special technical review. Guess who they asked to do it?"

"Shit."

"He's the resident expert," Barry said.

"We're screwed."

"Possibly, but let's not give up. The board hasn't voted yet."

"Is there a deadline for this review?" Rob asked.

"There is, but it's irrelevant. They'll give him whatever time he wants."

"But what about the money?"

"That's the good news. They've earmarked our funding pending their decision," Barry said.

"I may as well pack my bags and go wait in the shuttle dock."

"I'm not going to give up without a fight," Barry said.

"Neither will Jules."

"Man knows how to hold a grudge, I'll give him that."

"Barry's a bulldog. If anyone can beat Professor Oliver, he can," Gwen said the next morning at breakfast.

"But doesn't faculty generally trump staff?" Rob asked, rescrambling his scrambled eggs blearily. He hadn't slept, but he hadn't been able to work either.

"Barry has his own friends on the board," Gwen said.

"He didn't say anything about that last night."

"Be grateful he took the time to call," Gwen said. "You owe him big-time whether this comes off or not."

"God, this is going to kill me."

"And if this does go through, you better not squander the opportunity. Don't fuck this up like you did back on Mars with Helena or whatever."

Rob froze. His face flushed. Gwen crammed a bite in her mouth, and then another. She noticed Rob's glare after the third. "What?" she asked.

"Don't you ever, ever talk about that again. You've got some little story in your mind about my life, but you have no idea. Fuck you and your self-righteous little universe." His words hung in the air between them for a few moments.

"How was I supposed to know?" Gwen asked.

"It's called an apology, Gwen. Something human beings do when they've wronged or offended another. You say, 'I'm sorry,' and I say, 'You're forgiven.' It's basic human diplomacy that keeps us from killing each other. You should really try it. Trust me; it's not a waste of time."

"Fine," Gwen said. "I'm sorry."

"Apology accepted. I'm sorry, too."

Gwen fidgeted with the edge of her tray as if she wanted to pick it up and flee. "Do you want to talk about it?" she asked.

Rob chuckled and shook his head. "I didn't even tell the Valdosky counselor on the cruise out here."

"My counselor was a complete idiot. What?"

"The behavior monitor pegged you, too, didn't it?" Rob asked.

"I punched some pervert who grabbed my ass, and they made me go. Even though I was eighteen and he was like a hundred and nine."

"Wow. Eighteen? Did ADU have undergrad then?"

"I did my undergrad at Delft University in E-shift and got my master's from the University of Tokyo in U-shift. Then I came here."

"That's a lot of shifting. No wonder you never learned how to be a normal person," Rob said. "I'm sorry. That was very rude of me. See how it's done?"

"Right. You're the epitome of fucking virtue," Gwen said.

* * *

After lunch a few days later, Rob resolved to buckle down and look at his grant options. He stuck himself down in his cubicle and opened the list from Martine. And then she appeared as if she knew exactly how long he'd procrastinated.

"Jules would like to see you," she said.

"Right now?" Rob asked.

"Now," Martine replied.

Rob glanced at Jaidev and then Max and responded to their questioning looks with a shrug. What did it mean that Jules had sent Martine to the cubicles to fetch him personally? "Did he say what about?" he asked.

"He did not," Martine said.

This is it, Rob thought. *Jules knows everything. He knows about my end run with Barry. I'm being sent packing.* How had he found out? Informants in Barry's staff? Had Jaidev been following him?

"Okay, give me a second." Martine waited as Rob closed out his work and pulled on a sweatshirt.

Jules greeted Rob pleasantly and gestured to a guest chair in front of his desk. "I'm excited about this new idea of yours. Excellent potential."

Because you paid such close attention, Rob thought, but said, "I'm glad you think so."

"I'm going to insist that you enter this idea for the UN Innovation Grant."

"You're kidding," Rob said.

"I'm not, in fact."

"But those applications are due in one week," Rob said.

"Then you'd better get to work."

"I rushed the last ones."

"It need not be a detailed tome. A powerfully brief job is what we're looking for."

"I think those grants usually go to think tanks and post-doc research groups," Rob said. "I'm not remotely in the same league."

"I've already spoken to the chair of the committee. I once helped her husband to get a company off the ground. She's now the assistant director for scientific affairs for the UNSA. She assured me that your project fits their mission and encouraged me to have you apply."

There's no time. I'm not qualified. You're screwing me out of the NAI that makes this work. And I've got a date tonight with the hottest woman on this station.

"I'll need help," Rob said instead.

"Agreed. I've asked Lloyd to free himself up for you. The others will be put on notice to give you time and assistance as they are able, and Martine can assist during her hours." Jules had left himself off the list. *Could you be any more obvious, Jules? If you know about the NAI, why don't you just lash me to the mast and flog me?*

"How'd you get access to this place?" Jaidev asked as he and Max maneuvered another unassembled rack into the data room, leaving a cloud of decaying packaging behind them.

"I asked Director Schaffer, the facilities guy," Rob lied, setting the conference table screen on its edge in the doorway. "Told him I needed a place to spread out that had a coffee maker."

"Is he going to be pissed that we retasked the vacuum bot?" Max asked. The poor machine had bounced around the little room for the last half hour, straining to suck up the chunks of corroding cardboard still drifting to the floor.

Lloyd entered, waving his mobile. "I got you a consulting mathematician. Professor Wendell will volunteer someone."

"Is he the professor that looks like Jesus?" Rob asked.

"Hallelujah!" Max shouted. "Jesus is on your side; you can't fail. Did I mention that this is asinine? You can't put together a UN Innovation Grant application in a week."

"Tell that to Jules," Rob said.

"If you get it, you'll be a legend," Jaidev said.

"I'm just going to get this over with and think of it as preparation for future grants. And I get to take advantage of Lloyd's expertise while he's still here."

"It's still going to take a miracle to get it done," Lloyd said.

"Again. Jesus. Handy. Just saying," said Max.

Rob's mobile buzzed. "It's Gwen," he said. Max cringed, and Rob drifted out into the corridor to answer.

"Thanks for calling me back. I need your help."

"It's impossible," Gwen said after Rob had explained. "A complete fucking waste of time."

"Preaching to the choir," Rob replied. "But Jules didn't give me a choice."

"I'll help," Gwen said.

"Thank you."

"But on my own terms," she added.

"What do you mean?"

"No one can know that I'm helping you."

"Why? You've helped me before. People knew."

"This is different."

"How?"

Max and Jaidev wrestled the vacuum into the corridor and reset it. The bot toddled away, happier to be back on its appointed rounds. They went back in, taking the table screen with them.

"The only way you're going to get this done is if I help you, my way," Gwen said.

"In secret?" Rob asked.

"I don't work and play well with others."

"Fine," Rob agreed. "Whatever. You'll explain this to me someday?" She hung up before he got his answer.

"Jesus wept," Max said when Rob returned. He was scrolling through the application on the table screen. "Background, CV, budgets, methodology, timelines, all in their specific format. There're thirty-five sections here. It makes Jaidev's toy company grant look like a coloring book. Is the Red Bitch going to help?"

"She says it's a waste of time and had a few choice words for Jules."

"We'll begin first thing tomorrow. With or without her," Lloyd said.

"I just read that application, and I suggest you start tonight," Max said.

"I can't," Rob said.

"Date with Physician's Assistant Ringold," Lloyd explained.

"I'm not going to blow this thing with Reika just because Jules got a spider in his suit," Rob said.

"It's good to have your priorities straight," Lloyd said.

"Or your excuses lined up," Max added.

Ms. Wu, the food service director, had more than delivered on her promises. On the roof of a greenhouse work building overlooking a mosaic of crops, her staff had spread a rug and set a table for two. The dome's solar reflectors had been adjusted to create an artificial twilight, and the smell of wet earth imbued the air with possibility.

Rob would have been happy to see Reika in a pressure suit, but her blue dress threatened to put him in the hospital. She had done something incomprehensively amazing with her hair. When Helena did her hair, Rob had always felt like she was baiting a trap, but Reika's fell effortlessly over her shoulders in sparkling, wavy rings.

Their server, whom Rob had only ever seen in a monochrome

cafeteria uniform, glided around them in an elegantly embroidered silk dress. She flitted discreetly between courses from behind a divider painted with an ancient Chinese landscape. After pouring coffee and presenting the fluffiest mousse Rob had ever tasted for dessert, she vanished.

"Most people I went through UN training with got assigned to mining colonies and such," Reika said. "They complain endlessly about the food. I never mention how well we eat here. I just know that as soon as I do, I'll get reassigned somewhere dreadful."

"Please don't get reassigned," Rob said.

Reika floated to the railing with her wineglass, and Rob joined her. The greenhouse created its own music, born of leaves and sprinklers, genetically engineered birds and robotic bees. A light breeze brushed across the rooftop.

"Time for full disclosures," Reika said gently.

"Okay," Rob said. "Who goes first?"

"You might have heard," Reika began, "that I recently got out of a very serious relationship. It had actually been over for a long time, but when you live on a station like this, it's hard to make a clean break."

"What does 'serious' mean?" Rob asked.

"We shared an apartment. We shared avatars. We talked about a future, kids, the whole thing. But at some point he changed. I changed. I don't know."

"I don't need the details," Rob said.

"I broke it off, and it got ugly. I requested a transfer. Luckily, I had time to withdraw it once he decided to leave."

"I'm so glad you didn't go."

Reika sipped her wine. Rob followed her gaze to the false horizon.

"I suppose it's my turn," he said. "More wine?" Rob returned to the table for the bottle. "While evading the law on my pirate vessel, I—"

"You? A pirate?" Reika laughed as he topped off her membrane glass.

"No? Don't women like dangerous men?"

"Not all of us."

"Well, then, after rescuing the orphans..." Rob took a deep breath. "Okay. Full disclosure. No one here knows this, but I have a daughter." Reika listened kindly as Rob told Molly's story. He made an effort to speak generously of Helena and hoped Reika would interpret his decisions as selfless. "I couldn't stay on Mars after that."

"You don't have any contact?" Reika asked.

"I've ordered birthday and Christmas gifts, but I don't know if Helena gives them to her."

"I'm sorry," Reika said.

"I have to think that when Molly's older, she's going to want to know her father. We'll be apart twenty years, but we'll get a few hundred after that."

"I think you'd make a good father," Reika said.

"That's a hell of a thing to tell a man on a first date," Rob said.

* * *

For the next week, Rob saw only those who came into the workroom—Lloyd and the others; some consultants from the Astronomy, Physics, and Math departments; and Reika, usually with food and a neck rub—but their reports gave him the impression that the entire school knew of his situation. Rob had often come out of marathon coding sessions to find that no one had missed him for an entire day or longer, but this felt distorted, as if a rapt ADU had stopped around him instead.

"Everyone must think I'm crazy," Rob said late one afternoon.

"People understand," Lloyd said.

"Do they? People know that this is Jules's stupid idea? Maybe we should just pack it in. I'll just hide out from Jules for a month until the next boat comes."

"Don't talk like that," Lloyd said. "Besides, this is shaping up well." Rob knew it wasn't empty praise. Lloyd had been impressed, sometimes amazed, with the results of Rob's work, especially those things done while Lloyd was asleep. But casually dismissing Lloyd's praise had become an easy price to pay for Gwen's help.

Rob had expected his first assignment for Gwen to take a day. She had returned a flawless finished result in twenty minutes. He had dug into the task list and sent her something more challenging. She had finished that one just as quickly and just as perfectly. It felt like working with Ares back at MTI.

Two days before the deadline, Jules showed up in the workroom, saying, "So this is where you've sequestered." He was not alone. President Mbuto floated into the room behind him. Her dress and hat filled the room with color and nature such as Rob hadn't seen in days. Lloyd rose first.

"I was telling President Mbuto about your efforts, and she wanted to wish you luck," Jules said. "Angela, this is Robert Heneghan. This is his project."

"Ma'am," Rob said, shaking her hand. *His project?* Jules must have left out his own insistence. And Jules wasn't supposed to know about this room.

"This cross-departmental cooperation is wonderful to see," President Mbuto said in her resonant, deeply feminine voice. "I see computer science, physics…" She gestured to Rachelle's visiting boyfriend. "Professor Oliver tells me that several other departments are assisting as well. I understand you're facing quite a deadline."

"Yes, ma'am."

"One should never fear precipitous opportunities," she said. "I won't distract you any longer. Please know that you are making me very proud. Convergence like this makes ADU unique."

Rob thanked her. As she acknowledged the rest of the group, Rob's eyes met Jules's. Jules seemed somewhat diminished, but he still smiled at Rob like he was a toy.

"That was unexpected," Lloyd said when they had gone. Rob cursed silently, sat, and let his forehead fall on the table.

* * *

The night before the deadline, the heavy lifting was done. A response of some kind had been crafted for every section of the application. Everyone had abandoned Rob but for Lloyd, who was asleep on the shift couch that someone had dragged into the outer office early in the week.

Rob stared blankly at a paragraph until he realized that he had lost the ability to comprehend text. He peeled his coffee cup off a sticky grip pad and found it empty.

He started the coffee maker in the dark, so as not to wake Lloyd, and breathed deep to let the coffee smell work its placebo mojo. A tap sounded on the door next to him. Rob jumped and then answered it to find Gwen, stained cardigan and all. Lloyd murmured and rolled away from the corridor light.

"I saw you were still on the network," she said.

"I was editing, but I think I've reached a point of diminishing returns."

"Leave it. Come with me."

"Where?"

"Just come on."

The Casino's observation deck felt smaller when not filled with lasers and smoke. Gwen crossed the deserted starlit room to a pair of flimsy doors near where the bar had been set during the chem party.

"You brought me to a closet?" Rob asked.

The narrow room was indeed filled with folding tables, stacking chairs, and catering equipment, but on the far side, Gwen shoved aside a lectern and opened another door into starry space. Rob instinctively sucked in a breath. He felt a waft of cold air, but it wasn't the soul-sucking chill of a vacuum. Gwen floated out into the stars, and for a moment Rob wondered if he was dreaming. He crossed the threshold cautiously. Just inside, the walls, ceiling, and floor became a single seamless bubble of glass large enough for a dozen good friends.

"I can't believe this place exists," Rob said, taking in the view of the Mall, the greenhouse and the collider, and a dozen other connected rocks.

"Not many people know about it," Gwen said. The glass floor was cantilevered thirty-plus stories over the roof of the Casino's lobby. Far below, a cobweb of tether lines and worn paths fanned out across the surface from an airlock door. "This was going to be the top of a pressurized elevator." Gwen tucked her legs under her and drifted to a seat directly on the glass. "I like to come up here when I need to put things back in perspective."

"How do you do it, Gwen?" Rob asked, taking a seat next to her.

"Do what?"

"You know what I'm talking about," Rob said. "I can't even begin to claim that the best work on this application is mine. Why are you here? You could write your own ticket anywhere."

"I want to be here," Gwen said.

Rob found her profile tragic. Perhaps this bubble in the closet wasn't a place to reconnect, but a place to hide. He was doing his own share of hiding at ADU.

"Do you think there's a chance in hell I'll get this grant?" Rob asked.

"No. But don't take that the wrong way."

"How—?"

"Shut up. Perspective," Gwen said. After several silent minutes, she said, "Your orrery is a good idea, Rob."

* * *

Jules's eyes flicked back and forth across the screen for countless seconds, as if deliberately wasting Rob's time. Rob was certain that the application was better than Jules had expected. *What did you do with your week, Jules? Squat in your pretentious office and not do your bogus technical review? I wrote a kick-ass grant application.*

"Much of this is very good," Jules said.

"Thank you," said Rob.

"I've made some notes, of course." Jules read for a few moments more and then said, "You seem to have found that passion you were seeking. Be sure and submit this on time."

"I will," Rob said. *No thanks to you.*

"Robert," Jules said, setting the screen down. "I understand that this grant is a long shot. It was my hope that this process would help you crystallize your ideas quickly, and it seems to have worked. I'm very impressed.

"I know the other rejections were hard for you. I'm sorry. I won't tell you that there won't be more, but please don't be discouraged. Your colleagues speak highly of you. You've shown yourself capable of excellent work, and you've acclimated well. It would be a shame to let a few rejection letters ruin your experience."

"I'm not thinking of leaving," Rob said. "I hope I haven't given you that impression."

"I'm glad to hear it," Jules said. "Robert, do you know why I push my students to get grants?"

"I've heard it's a money thing that the school makes you do," Rob said.

"Most ADU students live in the shadows of their professors. They spend their careers here as glorified research assistants, but that's not how I choose to operate. By asking everyone to develop their own research, and then to cooperate, we diversify. We create practical opportunities. My goal is for you to leave with at least one well-formed idea, if not an asset of value, like a patent or a program that can be the foundation of a career. I also want you to be prepared to attract capital." Rob wondered if it should worry him that Jules was making frightening sense.

"Thank you for explaining that," Rob said.

"You're heading in the right direction," Jules said.

* * *

The rejection letter from the UN arrived along with the first radar signals of the December boat.

"Maybe it's a sign," Rob said.

"Please don't say that," Reika begged. They were alone in the steam room after a workout. Reika had combed her dark, wet hair down her back to her towel. Rob had a love-hate relationship with her long, fluffy bath sheets. His own towels were flat and scratchy things that hid nothing, especially when she leaned against him with one knee drawn up on the bench. "If you're thinking about leaving, tell me now."

"I'm not thinking about leaving."

"Yes, you are," Reika said. "There used to be a professor that requested to be put in perma-shift for a week to make sure he didn't get on the boat. People go crazy. I don't want to wake up and find you gone."

"I wouldn't do that," Rob said.

"Promise?"

"Promise." Reika sat up and turned around. The steam billowed around them, hiding the walls, the door. It was like a moment in shift, too good to be real. She kissed him, and Rob readjusted his towel.

* * *

Rob awoke from the edge of dream to the sound of a buzzing alarm. But the clock was on the wrong side of the bed. The sheets were too soft, the pillow too tall, and there was a floral scent instead of dirty socks. Rob concluded that he was still asleep.

"Is that yours?" Reika moaned.

Rob found his pants on the floor, dug out his mobile, and answered it blearily.

"Who was that?" Reika asked after he hung up.

"President Mbuto's assistant. I have to go. An emergency meeting."

"An emergency?"

"Nothing like that," Rob said. "A school thing. Sorry. God, I could stay in bed with you all day." He kissed her and then gathered up yesterday's clothes and floated into her bathroom.

Max—wearing flannel pajamas, fuzzy slippers, and a T-shirt advertising Japanese novelty condoms—arrived at the administrative offices at the same time as Rob. "You, too?" he asked. "What the hell is going on?"

The reception desk wasn't yet staffed for the day, so they found their own way. Rachelle, Lloyd, and Jaidev—slightly less dishabille—were already waiting in a second-level conference room. They'd barely had time to speculate when President Mbuto arrived wearing a simple colored dress. Her orange-brown hair was gathered in a crocheted net. Martine and Jules drifted in after her.

Jules clutched the back of the head chair.

"Martine and I have made a very difficult decision," he began.

Jules had cancer. In his blood. Treatable on the station, but the coming toll on his body and the probability of recurrence had led him to decide to return to France to be with family. As Jules spoke, Rob watched Rachelle take one of Martine's hands. Martine thanked her with a sad smile. President Mbuto uttered a few non-committal statements about the future of the department.

After the meeting ended, Rob took his turn shaking hands with Jules. All he could think of was what this might mean for the NAI. "I'm very sorry, sir," he managed to murmur, hoping it sounded sincere. Who was the jerk here?

For the second time in a day, Rob found himself summoned to ADU's administrative offices. This time Barry was waiting for him at reception. He led Rob up the central stairs, not to his own office, but to a desk guarding another set of stairs that spiraled into the ceiling.

There, President Mbuto's assistant said, "She's expecting you."

"Thank you, Michaela," Barry said.

"I thought you said you didn't report to President Mbuto," Rob said as he guided himself up the spiral behind Barry. The light coming from above was something Rob had never experienced before. A new blue. Daylight. Not Agnus Dei day, not Mars day, but what could only be Earth day.

The floor-to-ceiling windows of the circular office seemed to overlook an Earth city, as if from a high-rise. Rooftops, streets, plazas, and alleyways, all alive with pedestrians and vehicles, spread out under a cloudless blue sky. A main bisecting avenue disappeared into a humid haze, where the city blurred into red hills and green trees. Was this domeless suburb the place President Mbuto called home? Rob knew the windows were only screens, but...

"Heneghan," Barry called from where he was waiting at a glass conference table with President Mbuto.

"Sorry, ma'am. I've never been to Earth before," Rob said.

"So, Rob, Director Schaffer tells me you have been advising him on the acquisition of an NAI system," President Mbuto said. Barry smiled and gave Rob a discreet nod.

"I have," Rob replied. Somehow everything had fallen into place. It felt like he had sinned to get it.

CHAPTER 11

I have witnessed such heroes in these last hours. I have learned the true strength of our people.

MARCH–MAY 2088

When Teague arrived at work, Bondi had a Christmas-morning grin.

"It came?" Teague asked.

"This morning," Bondi replied. Monkey squealed with delight.

"It's so light," Teague said as he took the small box. He slid his finger under the flexi-seal, accepting the scrolling warranty without a glance. He set aside the charger, along with an accessory pack marked with a sticker that read "Open Me First" in a dozen languages. Inside a plastic clamshell were the two blobs of electronics—each no bigger than the top of his thumb—that he wanted to see. They were identical but opposite, one with a tiny R and the other with an L etched in their crystal-clear rubber skins. Teague plucked one free and inspected its flat, metallic underside.

"Very nice," Bondi said. "You sure they're worth so many months' wages?"

"I can't have a visible squid," Teague said. "People at my church would freak out." As if to illustrate his point, a woman walked by the stall, shift receptors bulging from behind her ears. The box contained one more item, a plastic pack nestled in foam.

Its flexi-stickers warned that the contents were to be opened by certified medical personnel only. It was almost impossible to believe that this object, the squid, would soon be inserted into his brain.

"There's an install clinic downstairs," Bondi said.

"My doctor friend referred me to the clinic in her hospital. This is perfect timing."

"Why's that?" Bondi asked.

"The Kimballs are moving next week. I'll get this installed after they leave, and the new family won't know any different."

"Will they care?" Bondi asked. "I thought these families were not of your faith."

"They're not, but I'd rather get it done during the transition," Teague said. "Will I be able to use this shift set when enhanced cognition becomes available?"

"EC?" Bondi said with a laugh.

"What's so funny?"

"Enhanced cognition is decades away."

"I just read a thing about it a few days ago. It sounded like G-Plex is getting ready to launch it for the public in a few years."

"Decades, my friend. Trust me. G-Plex likes to exaggerate."

"But people have been shifting for years now. How much harder can it be to give the brain a little boost?" Teague asked.

"Shifting is about providing the brain a different set of sensory inputs," Bondi said. "Enhanced cognition involves a fundamental change to the user, relative to their real self."

"The article didn't make them sound that different," Teague said. "Wouldn't you want to do it?"

"Perhaps. But you'd likely need significant training in order to tolerate the extreme environment. Might be a bit much for an old man," Bondi said. "And communicating with the real-time world while enhanced would probably feel like playing chess through cargo post with someone on the other side of the solar system. Seems a bit frustrating and elitist to me."

"Do you want to play chess?" Monkey asked.

"Who cares? Sign me up," Teague said. "Can you imagine being able to think and learn as fast as a computer?"

"I can," Monkey said.

* * *

Teague jiggled a leg as a pair of toddlers clambered around a plastic playset shaped like a miniature fire truck. Their parents tapped casually at their mobiles, unconcerned that their children were about to undergo brain surgery.

First, tiny holes would be drilled through their skulls behind the ears. Then the thousands of transmissive nano-filaments of the squid would be guided through the holes with focused magnetic fields to the critical parts of their brains. Once in place, a biological element at the tip of each filament—viruses filled with a mash-up of DNA from jellyfish, or sea anemones; Teague couldn't recall—would be unleashed. The viruses would inject their cargo into nearby cells to make parts of their brains photoreceptive, to bridge the gap between the chemical and the electronic. The receptors, where the bundles of fibers terminated, would be glued to the skull behind their ears. Everyone claimed it was painless. There was every reason to be calm.

A nurse called Teague's name and brought him to a small, blue room containing a complex chair with a tiny, gel-cushioned headrest. Above, an array of articulated armatures spidered from the ceiling. At the end of each arm dangled a head-encompassing device that would have given any Tellurite pastor a heart attack.

"You're seventeen?" she asked, consulting a screen.

"Yes, ma'am," Teague replied.

"Never had an install before?"

"No, ma'am," Teague said. "Should I leave my shoes on?"

"If you'd be more comfortable," she said.

A doctor entered and introduced himself. "Any questions about the procedure?" he asked.

"No," Teague replied.

"You're in good health?" The doctor reviewed his screen. "There's nothing on your medical history. Are you allergic to any medication? Any regular headaches? Take any medications? Recent head injuries?" Teague shook his head. "No brain surgeries, I presume." He chuckled and shined a pen light in each of Teague's eyes.

"Not that I'm aware of," Teague replied.

"Good. Good," the doctor muttered and inspected the skin behind Teague's ears.

The nurse clamped a cuff around Teague's arm, and the doctor offered a little paper cup of purple liquid. Teague held the bittersweet liquid in his mouth for a moment and then swallowed: grape-flavored sin. "Relax," the doctor said.

The lights dimmed, and one of the spider's arms whirred to life. Its device swallowed Teague's head. He heard a hum, a click, a buzz, and sensed a brief, bright, bouncing light. Then the full weight of his body drifted into blackness.

Teague awoke, alert. The machines had retreated to the ceiling as if their motion had been a dream. Did he dare stand up? Were there now nano-fibers threading through his brain? He didn't feel any different. He was feeling gently for the tiny bits of subcutaneous metal behind his ears when the nurse returned.

"Please don't touch the skin patches," she chided. "Everything went very well. I'll take you to calibration now."

She guided Teague to a dim room filled with shift couches, most occupied by unconscious children. A technician asked Teague to take an empty couch next to a little girl wearing pink shift nodes.

"First time?" the technician asked, ignoring the answer as she helped Teague attach his nodes. Teague felt them click magnetically into place. "This will feel a lot like dreaming, but you'll also feel awake. You'll see patterns, shapes, and colors, and hear sounds. Don't resist or try to wake up. Relax. Let them happen, and you'll do fine." The technician tapped her screen, and Teague fell asleep.

He became aware a moment later, aware of his being, but only at a distance, and caught in a cage of grids and lattices. Blue was now. Red was later. Green had already happened. Peripheral blips of white called for attention. A Doppler blur of sound slipped through him. Dimensions flipped. He sensed a menacing approach, like a distant train. Grid planes that should never meet crept together, and then began to accelerate unstoppably closer. Inflating space gashed across his mind, searing and then imploding. He screamed and heaved, as if turning inside out. And then he fell.

A million-kilometer plunge in a heartbeat.

Teague awoke alone in the dark, his mouth coated with a foul, chalky taste. Pain rippled from his temples to the base of his neck. His shift nodes had been removed. Up and down, which had been extremely confused concepts, had become painful, immediate facts. A tapping at the door preceded a crack of blinding light.

"Teague, this is Dr. Salidapirak. Can you understand me?"

"Yes," Teague rasped.

"How are you feeling?"

"What happened?"

"You experienced a rejection. This happens when the brain is unable to surrender a certain process to the shift software. In your case, we believe it was motor control. Normally motor function is redirected to control your actions in the shift frame, but in rare cases, the brain simply isn't willing to give it up. This is often a hereditary condition. Has anyone else in your family had this problem?"

"No."

"We performed a diagnostic on your shift set. The receptor array was installed correctly. It appears that your mind is unable to accept the shift process. You can see your calibration here." He pointed to several scrolling, colored lines on a blinding screen. "This baseline is the shift tone. The software brings your consciousness to that line. Beginning here, your motor functions resist, and you trend away from the baseline.

"You're likely to experience migraine-like pain for the next few days. This will help with that." He offered Teague a prescription on a flexi-card.

"Is this permanent?"

"Your case will be reviewed by our supervising specialist, and also—who is your manufacturer?"

"It's a Kyoshi Onieralytics."

"We'll refer your medical data to Kyoshi for review. If both agree, we may be able to reschedule a calibration. If not, our counselors can help you obtain a medical refund."

"I'd like to try again. How long will all that take?"

"A medical review can take several weeks," the doctor replied. "I'm very sorry."

Teague wanted to throw the weightless shift set in the trash. He could almost feel the useless tendrils intruding in his head like an unreachable itch. He had planned to meet Kevin in U-shift to celebrate. Now he just wanted to sleep.

* * *

Teague's head jostled, heavy with his helmet, as he bumped his motorcycle over the curb between a pair of abandoned cars, and he groaned. It had been two days, and his head still ached. Maybe it was time to throw in the towel and fill the prescription. He squinted into the too-bright sky for a look at his destination. The thirty-story apartment block was the kind the redevelopment authority had been reducing to rubble all over the city. Off-brand Chinese Uni-Fi antennas had been mounted outside almost every window, even the ones covered with corrugated plastic or wind-shredded tarps.

"Activate the security system," Teague said. "And stay close."

"I like to go new places," Monkey replied. He hopped out of his bungeed milk crate and began to chain Teague's motorcycle to a lamppost. A pump sucked the air from the tires as a series of clicks and clunks disconnected the battery, locked the wheels, and secured the computer. Not enough to stop any halfway competent thief, but it was a start.

It wasn't raining, but water gushed intermittently from a downspout over a slippery mat of black algae on the crumbling concrete steps. In the dark vestibule, the inner door leaned beside the doorframe. Where the call box should have been, a bundle of ragged wires snaked from a hole in the middle of a grotesque sketch of a naked man.

In a common room off the lobby, dozens of people were shifted on listing couches, ragged futons, and stained mattresses, many with eyes open but unseeing, and their lips moving. Most of these people were probably at work in shift, but here they were contributing nothing, absorbing only, barely being. Teague hated that he was jealous of them. An enormous tattooed man in a creaking office chair was watching porn on the screen of a portable shift server. He caught Teague with a suspicious glare and then turned back to his entertainment.

Rather than rely on the few remaining door numbers, Teague asked Monkey to find their customer's mobile with a bit of helpful, if not quite kosher, locator software and began to climb the stairs. A few minutes later, Teague knocked on a spray-painted metal door and took a step back. The pinprick of light through the peephole soon blinked out.

"I'm from the Badass," Teague called in English.

A man on the other side cursed in Thai and began to unlock the door's many locks. The door soon popped open a few centimeters to the end of a chain. "Give it to me and fuck off." The man stuck his arm through the gap, snapped his fingers, and opened his palm.

"The Badass says I install or I walk away," Teague replied. The door slammed on a barrage of cursing. Teague knew to wait. No matter how they blustered, everyone yielded to the power of the Badass.

The door opened on the chain again, and the man thrust a screen sideways into the corridor. Teague caught a glimpse of his face as he took the screen and passed it to Monkey.

"Fucking lemur's going to break my shit."

"Calm down. He's a professional," Teague said.

With the retractable tools in his fingertips—a free upgrade from Bondi—Monkey had the screen open in seconds. Teague produced a plastic bag containing a cubic centimeter of foam from his backpack.

Monkey extracted a sliver of a chip from the screen and handed it to Teague. Teague dropped the chip into the man's palm and then gave Monkey the new chip from the foam. In less than a minute, Monkey had replaced the cover, and Teague had returned the screen through the narrow gap.

Teague waited a few moments and then said, "I assume from your silence that everything is working." Monkey processed the payment. It hadn't been the worst delivery ever. As long as his bike was still there.

An hour later, back at the e-mall, Teague watched as Bondi manipulated a glove that translated his movements into meso-scale operations in a vacuum casing on the workbench. Whenever Bondi did this, he held his chin up with his eyes closed, like the piano tuner who used to come to the Stevenses' house.

"He wouldn't even open the door all the way," Teague said. "What's he up to? Aren't you worried that you'll be implicated in something?"

"Don't worry about P-Smack," Bondi said. Ah…" He had found the problem. Teague envied how Bondi experienced the inner workings of electronics, as real and as large as the real world. And he navigated that world as well as Teague could Bangkok. "He's paranoid but harmless. If he was to be feared, he wouldn't need me."

Teague slipped out into the stall and settled on the stool behind the counter to watch the irregular drip of shoppers pass by. Monkey hopped onto his lap, and Teague stroked him absent-mindedly. Bondi emerged from behind the black curtain a few minutes later.

"Another delivery?" Teague asked.

"No, I have to ship it," Bondi said. "Has the new family arrived?"

"Not yet. Remember, I need Thursday off. I'm supposed to help with the move-in. I'm dreading this one. The last Baptist family was way zealous. I don't want to go through that again."

The entry buzzer sounded as a man entered the stall. He looked too straight-laced, too upstanding for the e-mall, more like an accountant. He nodded a greeting and set a mobile on the counter. It was not quite military grade, but thicker and more robust than most consumer models, and the casing was etched with markings that brought to mind the graffiti in Josiah's neighborhood. Someone loved this mobile, but Teague doubted that it was this man.

"Another?" Bondi asked as if continuing some previous conversation.

"I'm afraid so," the man said. Bondi examined the mobile and tapped at its screen, but its operation was secured with an encrypted passcode.

"How long?" the man asked.

Bondi grunted. "Twenty hours?"

"Tomorrow," the man agreed and left.

"Why are you looking at me like that?" Bondi asked Teague.

"Are you hacking mobiles now?" Teague asked.

"Only when the detective asks me to."

"That was a detective? What's he investigating? Credit fraud?"

"Human trafficking," Bondi said.

Teague's blood went cold. "Anything I can do to help?" The entry buzzer rang again. Bondi shook his head and disappeared into the back with the mobile. Was it some service to the screwed-up world if he watched a teenager paw through the parts bins in order to give Bondi time to fight slavery? Teague's head throbbed as if in answer.

* * *

It usually took only an hour or two to unload a family's possessions from a delivery van, but the new renters, the McAllisters, had shipped their own furniture from America. With the exception of the few pieces in Teague's room, the existing furniture had to be loaded into cars and trucks for storage at the homes of various church members. Only then could the workmen Mr. McAllister had hired begin to empty the enormous shipping container into the house.

Teague had been relieved when he'd learned about the workmen and began to plan an escape from the heat once the house had been emptied. Let them earn their pay. He didn't want his headache coming back. But after meeting the family, Teague had remained to help.

The reason was sprawled out on a sheet tossed loosely over a single mattress on the floor of the corner bedroom. Blue shift nodes peeked through the wispy blond hair half-covering her face. "Aubrey" was the name on the boxes that were filling up her room.

Teague set another marked box with the others. Aubrey was nearly his own age, way too old for toys. But how many clothes did a girl need? Teague turned to leave but found the hall blocked by workmen maneuvering a mattress set into the master bedroom. She was wearing very short shorts. Her toenails had been painted yellow. She had raised her arms above her head, revealing an achingly narrow band of skin along her midriff. In all these years, none of the eager missionaries, aloof mission coordinators, or wild-eyed church planters who had rented the house had ever brought a creature such as this. There had been toddlers and infants, an autistic twenty-year-old son, but mostly Vanilla-dosed childless couples. What in the hell was going on with the furniture in the master bedroom? Teague wiped the sweat off his forehead and onto his pants.

How could she shift now in a strange house full of strange men? Was she reckless and compulsive or just callously selfish? Teague wondered where he'd be now if his calibration hadn't failed. Would he be locked in his room, dead to the world, while everyone else worked?

Someone asked a question. Teague looked up with a residual image of Aubrey's legs on his retinas. Had he been staring like a creep?

"Huh?" Teague asked.

"*Is she your sister*?" a workman repeated in Thai.

"*No*," Teague replied.

"*Cousin?*"

"*No*."

"You lucky," the man said, now in English, and gave Teague a gold-toothed grin. A moment later, the headboard moved a few centimeters, and Teague squeezed out.

The late afternoon sun was slipping behind the trees, finally providing some shade to the deck and the driveway even as the workmen dispersed and the truck arrived for the emptied container. Teague leaned against the deck rail with a glass of ice water to watch the removal and not think about Aubrey.

"I'm starving, Mom. When are we gonna eat?" Braden McAllister was only a couple of years younger than his sister, certainly old enough to carry boxes, but Teague hadn't seen him lift anything all day except his mobile—and Ragnarok, his Zubotix ferret.

"Soon, baby," Mrs. McAllister replied. "Teague, honey, where can we get some quick food?"

"There's a buffet and takeout place owned by a couple from my church. It's—"

"Oh, I think we need something a little more like home, don't you?" Teague couldn't think of anything more like home than the Chaiprasits'.

"There's a KFC. Short walk away," Teague said.

Mrs. McAllister began to tap on her mobile. When Teague returned from washing up, she said, "Supper's ordered. Braden, why don't you go with Teague to pick it up?" Teague thought he would prefer a shower, or water torture, to going to the KFC with Braden McAllister.

"But, Mom…"

"Go straight there and come right home. And watch for cars; they come from the wrong direction here."

They'd barely left the gate when Braden asked, "You ever fight your lemur?"

"What?" Teague asked.

"You know, Zuboxing. Back home, my friends and I built a ring. Our videos have got a ton of traffic."

"Why would you do that?"

"It's so funny," Braden said. "You have to buy the right software. My last Zubot was a Tyrannosaur, but it got its butt totally kicked by my friend's panda. I told my parents he fell out a window at school. That's why I have Raggy now. Plus I wanted one of the new Finch series with—"

"What's the deal with your sister?" Teague asked. "Does she always shift like that?"

"Who, Princess Aubrey? She has a fit when she has to wait for her nodes to recharge," Braden replied.

"Where does she shift to?"

"She sees friends. I don't know. I've shifted to Saturn. There's a site in Sat-X that my friends and I—"

"Where're you guys going to school?" Teague asked.

"Austin Baptist Prep. In E-shift."

Teague had already dressed Aubrey in his school's uniform, the pleated knee-length plaid skirt, the white shirt, and the white tights. He had already taken her to school on the back of his motorcycle, rules be damned. But he was out of luck. She was going to a drool school.

When Teague and Braden returned, they dropped the bags and buckets on the table, but Mrs. McAllister clicked her tongue, made them lift them, and cleaned underneath with a sterile wipe.

"Braden, call your sister to supper," she said.

"I'll message her, but if she's beyond E, she might not be back for half an hour."

"I don't want an explanation."

Mr. McAllister strode into the kitchen and washed his hands in the sink. "Do what your mother asked," he said.

Braden sighed dramatically and called for his ferret. When he returned, Mrs. McAllister said grace and began passing the paperboard boxes and buckets.

Teague had nearly finished eating when Aubrey shuffled in from the hall. "There y'are, baby," Mrs. McAllister lilted in what Teague had been informed was an Arkansas accent. Aubrey plunked down without a word. She wrinkled her nose over a take-out container, chose a biscuit, sniffed it, and began to tear it apart.

"Chicken?" Mrs. McAllister asked. Aubrey shook her head. "There's rice, but no mashed potatoes."

"I'm not hungry." Aubrey dropped the remains of her biscuit on her plate and slowly crumpled a paper napkin in her hands. She continued to knead it long after her hands had been cleaned, rubbing holes in the paper between her fingertips.

"Aubrey," Mrs. McAllister snapped. Aubrey tossed the shredded napkin on her plate and left.

"I'll be in to help you unpack," Mrs. McAllister called after her. To Teague she said, "She's a little upset about leaving her friends."

"We all had to give up something to come here, but this is where the Lord wants us to be now," Mr. McAllister said. "With his purposes come the opportunities."

"Amen," Mrs. McAllister added.

"May I be excused?" Teague asked. "I'd like to get cleaned up."

"Of course, hon."

"Thank you for dinner," Teague said, clearing his place. *And stop calling me "hon."*

When Teague turned off his shower, he could hear Mrs. McAllister begging Aubrey to cooperate with the unpacking.

Back in his bedroom, Teague asked, "Are all girls like Aubrey?"

"It's fun to make new friends," Monkey replied.

* * *

The rain had turned the sandy yard into a lake. It roared on the plastic awnings, and the curtain of run-off veiled the weight station from the rest of the gym. Only two other boys had come through the weather, but they hadn't stayed long. Teague had been working out for more than an hour when Josiah rounded the cloister.

"Ned said you were here. I didn't believe him."

"I may be coming around more than normal," Teague said.

"Why's that?" Josiah asked.

"My new foster family. They've got two kids who go to a drool school synced with Texas. They're at school all night and asleep during the day. I can't make a peep in the house in the afternoons."

"I told Ned you were probably in love. Need a spot?" Josiah asked.

After a few bench press sets, Teague sat up. "The stupid thing is that they wake me up a dozen times a night. The mom vacuums at two in the morning. I mean, why even live in Bangkok?"

"A good workout will help you sleep," Josiah said. "Plus these weights'll fill out your chest."

"What are you talking about?" Teague asked.

"I've been working with teenage boys for a good chunk now," Josiah said. "I've seen the signs. What's her name?"

"There's no 'her.' "

"I can't offer absolution anymore, but I can still hear confessions."

Josiah's laughter rang in Teague's ears as he brushed his teeth that evening. Aubrey had just wandered into the kitchen for her breakfast wearing only a long T-shirt. She had reached into a high cupboard for a glass, a living blue flame without pants.

Teague studied himself in the mirror amid the unprecedented clutter: the never-unplugged hair dryer, the powder-scented deodorant, the brushes tangled with blond hair. There were things in the cupboard under the sink, uniquely female things, that made him feel strangely and uncomfortably intrigued. Teague let his toothbrush hang from his mouth and tried to decide if Josiah was right.

* * *

Bondi lounged in the duct-taped recliner with Monkey curled on his lap. Teague fluttered a stylus on the counter, staring at, but not seeing, his homework. Shoppers trickled past in the aisle, but no one had come in for at least an hour.

"I may as well close up early today," Bondi said. "I can nap at home."

Teague yawned reflexively at the mention of sleep.

"Sounds like you need a nap, too," Bondi said.

"This new family stayed on Texas time—all except the dad, but he's never there. They bang around the house all night." Teague slid his screen away. "I'm so tired. I can't even do my homework."

"Do you need help?" Monkey asked. "I'm great with homework."

"You know, if you're having trouble sleeping, your shift set has a sleep-initiation mode. You shouldn't even need a full calibration to use it," Bondi said. Teague moaned and dropped his forehead on the counter. "Sorry, I know it's a sore subject."

"I'd rather take sleeping pills," Teague said.

Monkey hopped onto the counter and patted him on the shoulder.

"I'm sorry," Bondi said. "I'm sure Kyoshi will contact you soon."

Teague helped Bondi secure the stall, and they left together. Just outside the e-mall's entrance, Bondi stopped abruptly.

"Do you need help?" Teague asked.

Bondi produced a little tube that snapped out as a red-and-white cane. "My eyes fog up after being in the air conditioning. They'll clear up soon. You have a good evening." He strolled away, waving his stick ahead of him against the ground.

That night, Teague lay awake dwelling on the shift set in his desk drawer. He couldn't recall the pain from the calibration exactly, but he remembered the suffering. But even if the sleep mode were to work painlessly, it seemed a mockery to use the set to do nothing more than sleep. It was ironic, actually. Those nodes were supposed to open up a whole new world, but all they could do was close off this one.

Teague's bedroom door opened, let in a wedge of light from the hallway, and then closed, leaving a presence in the room. Had he been asleep?

"Wha—?" Teague grunted. A hiss told him to be quiet. A figure approached the bed. "Aubrey?" he whispered, earning another clipped hiss. Was he even awake now?

Her bare legs seemed to radiate ultraviolet light in the weak city glow that stole through the window, as did her Austin Baptist Prep Academy Thespian Society shirt, covered with scribbled signatures. Teague ceased to breathe.

Aubrey trailed icy fingers down his abdomen to the top of his sheet. She yanked it down to his ankles and then touched him through the thin fabric of his pajama pants. She found him ready, as if he had always been. How had that happened? Shouldn't she stop? He reached for her arm, but she caught his wrist and pushed it into the pillow over his head as if she meant it to stay there. She hitched her T-shirt above her hips, and briefly revealed the full mystery of her underwear. Then she climbed on top of him and settled that narrow slip of elusive cotton on him. She was lighter than he expected, but threatened to crush him entirely, and her knees were ice cold against his ribs. Where was Mrs. McAllister?

The bed creaked as Aubrey—was this really her?—slid back and forth, rubbing fabric on fabric, threatening to destroy them both. She clutched handfuls of his sheets. Teague tried to brush her hair away, longing to see any of her shadowed face, but she pushed his wrists back to the pillow. Teague bit his lip as an agonizing wave grew and crashed down in an instant, lifting him off his foundations. The eruption receded, leaving him sticky, embarrassed, and confused. She clenched him tight between her thighs and ground even harder on him. A few moments later, she bent her head back, uttered several muffled squeaks, and then fell forward. Her hair draped like a curtain around them both momentarily, and then she was gone in a slash of hallway light too fleeting for modesty. Was this love or hate? How could he ever sleep in this bed again?

Monkey waited by the desk for a few moments and then padded back to his charger.

* * *

Aubrey never spoke. She came to his room early or she came late. Sometimes not at all. There were no flirtatious glances behind her mother's back, no footsie under the table, no secret notes in the bathroom, and no teasing texts on his mobile. He doubted she even had his eddress.

By day she was a demon, never acknowledging Teague's existence, snippy to her parents, and cruel to her brother. In his bedroom, she was a tormenting angel, and every night Teague swore to capture her and demand answers, even if it broke the spell. But each time he let her transfix him to his bed, whatever the danger.

When he imagined her, he thought mostly of her hands and their strange fixation with cloth and texture: the way her fingertips would find a bit of tablecloth or napkin and caress it until Teague was sure her skin would wear away, the times she would stand at the kitchen sink and rub a towel between her hands until her mother murmured to her, the way she seemed to take as much pleasure in handfuls of his sheets or pillowcase as anything else.

"Goodness, did something happen to you today?" Mrs. Chaiprasit asked one afternoon after school. Teague looked up from his four empty bowls and shook his head. "Just like my youngest. He'd come home upset for no reason, too. I couldn't put enough food in front of him. You must be growing."

* * *

The blow came hard. Teague staggered, his ribs in agony. He had seen it coming. He should have stopped it. Ned shouted. Teague fought for a stable stance on the sand and then raised his gloves again, shaking off the disorientation. The other boy grinned, a smarmy grimace with his mouthpiece and his cheeks scrunched in the headgear. Teague began to circle, sliding his feet through the sand, trying to read the other boy's stance. Sweat dripped into his eyes and rolled down his back.

The message from Kyoshi had come that morning while he was at school.

Patient negative.

Teague hadn't needed to read the rest. He didn't give a damn if Kyoshi refunded his money or if they offered him a discount on a wide range of other Kyoshi Connective electronics.

Teague had called Dr. Aromdee. "Is there anything I can do?" he had asked.

"I could refer you to a neurologist, but from what I understand there's no therapy for this condition," she had replied.

"It's so embarrassing. I'm weird enough. I have to be the one in a million, too?"

"I'm very sorry. There may be a cure someday."

Screw someday, Teague had thought.

"I never like telling anyone this," Dr. Aromdee had continued, "but you have a protected disability."

"What does that mean?" Teague had asked.

"It means government agencies and schools cannot discriminate against you because you're unable to shift. And employers must provide you an accommodation if the work can reasonably be performed without shifting. And they can't avoid hiring you due to your condition. In fact, employers are prohibited from even asking prospective hires about it unless they can demonstrate that shifting is vital to the position."

I'm not only weird; I'm actually broken, Teague had thought while Dr. Aromdee had explained that a lot of well-known colleges and universities now offered generous scholarships to students willing to show up to their sparsely populated brick-and-mortar campuses. But what did he want with their pity?

The other boy blocked Teague's punch, but not the next one. It felt right to land the blow, and Teague struck again. *Can you shift?* Teague thought. *What about you, Ned? Can you shift?* Aubrey was too busy shifting to be a normal human being. *Screw you, Aubrey. Screw you, every drooling shifthead in the world. Screw you, Ned. Screw you, Kyoshi Onieralytics. Screw you, the asshole who tried messing with my bike the other day, and…*

Teague screamed as his opponent fell on his back in the sand. Sweat poured down Teague's face as he readied for more. *Get up,* he thought. He had never knocked anyone down, and he needed to do it again. Ned pushed him back. Blood raged through Teague's ears, and he pressed forward, aching to strike someone.

Ned shoved him against a burlap-wrapped pole. "That's enough," he shouted. Teague's scream rasped to silence and he began to breathe hard. "That's enough," Ned repeated, more quietly.

Thirty boys had frozen, staring in his direction. Insults rose to the back of Teague's throat. He laughed to see blood on the other boy's face. Ned grabbed Teague by the headgear. "I said that's enough."

Teague felt his arms and chest deflate. "Yes, Khru," he said.

In the sweltering locker room, Ned began to unlace Teague's gloves. "What was that?" he demanded.

"I wanted to win."

"That wasn't winning. You lost control."

Josiah appeared. "Send him to the office when he's cleaned up," he said to Ned.

A few minutes later, Teague knocked on the doorframe of the smelly office. Josiah tucked a flask into a pocket and waved him in. "I've been meaning to talk to you for a few months now. Your little performance gives me the excuse to finally do it." Josiah leaned heavily against a corner of his desk. "I think it's time you moved on."

"What do you mean?"

"I think you know."

"But why?"

"You're too damn old, for one thing."

"I'm not eighteen yet."

Josiah dragged a heavy hand through his remaining hair. "I know you got this whole ex-pat-orphan-with-something-to-prove thing going for you. Believe me, I know it. But you're never going to beat the locals at their own game. Never."

"That's not why I—"

"Save it. Whatever you want doesn't matter. To those kids, you're a piece of Western trash. They take joy in your humiliation. You realize that, don't you? But any more stunts like today's, and they might actually decide to harm you. I'm not blowing smoke out my ass. Honestly, I think the only reason you've survived this long is that you suck. Sorry to be blunt."

"I just want to train."

"Not here," Josiah said.

"I've always trained here."

"But this isn't a gym. It's a frickin' finger in the dike. A chance for a few young men to avoid the lives of their brothers and fathers. It's not for you anymore. If it ever was."

"Then why did you take me?"

"I would think that would be obvious."

"Because you thought I might be like you?"

"Despite your soft hands and your robotic dog or whatever, I thought...bah. Enough." Josiah found a pen and a sheet of paper on his desk and began to write. "I've talked to an old friend of mine. Runs a gym on your side of the river." He tore a corner off the paper and handed it to Teague. "He'll take you if you want."

An hour later, Teague came in through the kitchen door, and Mrs. McAllister put a finger to her lips. "I have to work late, so I won't be home for dinner," Teague whispered.

"How late?" she asked.

"My boss wants to do inventory, so pretty late. I'll call if I'll be later than midnight," Teague said, and went to collect Monkey.

Monkey tiptoed dutifully through the house, but once outside, scampered down the back steps and hopped into his crate on the back of Teague's motorcycle, chirping all the way. "You're not scheduled to work tonight," he said once Teague had fastened his helmet.

"So what?" Teague asked.

"But you told Mrs. McAllister—"

"What's your point?"

"Where are we going, then?"

"I don't know," Teague replied.

"I like to go new places."

Teague weaved through the early evening traffic but found the streets too familiar and too crowded. He launched his bike up the nearest ramp to the elevated highway and accelerated to keep pace with the European sedans and the driverless truck convoys. He tried to forget whether he was going north or south.

The sun had nearly set when Teague exited the highway. He hooked his bike to a charger at a convenience station, bought a couple of protein bars, and found a picnic table with a view of the highway.

"This is fun," Monkey said. "But you shouldn't exceed the speed limit."

Teague rolled back into the gravel driveway only a few minutes before midnight, glad to find that both of the McAllisters' cars were gone from the carport. Mr. McAllister was out of town, of course, but Teague had hoped Mrs. McAllister would follow her usual pattern of going out shopping after the kids had shifted for school. Better to let her think he came home at a reasonable time.

Teague snapped on his bedroom light and shouted in surprise. Aubrey shrieked, turning from his bed in a T-shirt and underwear.

"Where are you?" she hissed, her squinted face mangled with anger.

"What?"

"Why aren't you here?" She pushed past him and stormed out.

Teague cursed under his breath and called after her in a stage whisper. "Stay here," he told Monkey.

Aubrey's walls were as bare as they had been on the day she'd moved in. In the light from the hallway, Teague could see that her closet was still a mess of unpacked boxes, and her sheets were tangled on her exposed mattress. She had stopped by her shifting couch with her head in her hands.

"I came in, and you weren't there," she said.

Teague checked the hall. "Do you need help?" he asked and dared a step inside.

Aubrey spun around, wrapped her arms around his neck, and kissed him urgently, but coldly. Her tongue probed his lips as she climbed against him. She tugged at his belt, and Teague backed away. Aubrey came at him again, but he held her at an arm's length. When he said her name, she seemed to wake, looking at him as if he'd just materialized in front of her.

Teague said, "If you want to talk, I'll be out on the deck."

Blinking airplanes outnumbered the stars in the orange night sky. The hum of traffic from the boulevard filtered through the trees over the chirr of insects. A car turned onto the street. Teague feared it was Mrs. McAllister, but it rolled past. The kitchen screen door creaked open and Aubrey emerged, dressed but somehow diminished. She joined Teague at the railing, and after a few silent moments she murmured, "I'm so sorry."

"Don't be," Teague said.

"You probably hate me."

"Why would I hate you?" Teague asked.

"Every time I swear it's the last. Then every day I excuse

myself and downshift. I've hated you so much." Another car appeared and Aubrey froze until its brake lights disappeared at the end of the block. "But I don't hate you," Aubrey said. "I hate myself."

"Don't say that," Teague said.

"Have you told anyone?"

"No."

"Who are you?" she asked. She sat on a deck chair and hugged her knees to her chest. "It's like you're not even real."

"I'm real," Teague said.

"You don't have parents. I'm sorry and all, but wow. You have a motorcycle, a job, a life. I've barely been out of this house since we got here. I live in E-shift. I've never even seen you shift."

"I can't," Teague said. The fact solidified, even as he spoke. He would never experience the virtual. He would never be enhanced. He would only be himself for the rest of his life.

"Is that some part of that church you go to?"

"No. I mean, it is, they don't like it, but I really can't. My brain won't do it."

"Now I know you're not real," Aubrey said. She began to slide her hands up and down her shins, slowly, compulsively, over her jeans.

A hundred questions stuck in Teague's throat. After a long silence, he said, "I'm going to bed. It probably wouldn't be good for your mom to find me out here with you. You're sure you're okay?"

She nodded. "I'm going to sit out here for a while."

"Goodnight," he said. She smiled at him briefly and then turned back to the orange sky.

As he tried to sleep, Teague considered the fresh sensation of her lips and body, but also her despair. Soon Mrs. McAllister came home, and he heard their murmuring voices from the deck. A few minutes later, Aubrey passed by his door and then closed her own.

CHAPTER 12

Is it this pride that drove you for so many years? Even when the task seemed impossible? I never understood. Perhaps you shouldn't have sent me to school in a foreign country.

JUNE 2088–MAY 2089

Teague arrived home from school to find Aubrey and Mrs. McAllister at the picnic table on the deck. They turned when he opened the gate and watched him come up the steps. Teague felt his face flush. But Mrs. McAllister didn't appear perturbed, and when he reached the deck and saw their screens and dark rings on the wood under their sweating glasses of iced tea, he pieced together that they hadn't been waiting for him.

"Hello, hon," Mrs. McAllister said. "Braden's still asleep for the night. So please be quiet."

"Yes, ma'am. What's going on?" Teague asked.

In the three weeks since she had last come into his room, Teague had seen Aubrey rarely and only at mealtimes, where she ate sparingly and silently. She had grown more disheveled, unkempt, and if possible, more pale. Teague hated to see her suffering, even as Mrs. McAllister doted and waited on her, but he had forced himself to remain aloof.

Today, Aubrey had washed and combed her hair. Her rumpled

T-shirt had been traded for an ironed blouse. A little color had returned to her face. Or maybe it was the sunlight.

"Aubrey's going to be doing some of her classes and lessons here at home with me for a while," Mrs. McAllister replied. "Actually, I know you're busy with your job and school and all, but I thought it might be a good experience for Aubrey, and me, to learn a bit of the language and culture while we have this time."

"You want me to teach you Thai?" Teague asked. Aubrey looked embarrassed.

"And perhaps take an afternoon or two to give us a tour of the city." Mrs. McAllister turned to Aubrey. "You'd enjoy that."

"I'm really not that fluent," Teague said.

"You were so helpful during the move," Mrs. McAllister said.

"I suppose."

"Wonderful. That'd be so nice of you. We'll talk. Thank you."

"You're welcome," Teague said.

Teague paused in the kitchen, waiting to hear if Aubrey would complain, but they had returned to her math.

* * *

"Did everyone get paid today or something?" Teague asked as a customer strode out of the stall with a shiny, refurbished memory card for his mobile.

"It has been pretty busy for a weeknight," Bondi replied. As he spoke, a pair of boys, no more than ten or eleven, bumbled in and began to flip through Bondi's well-thumbed selection of ancient manga. Teague had never seen these boys before, but he knew their type. They never bought the comics or the accessories they pretended to be interested in, but were working up their courage. They wanted access to the legendary trove of software behind the counter they'd heard about from their older brothers—gimmicks mostly, nothing dangerous, to hear Bondi tell it, just bits of virtual trickery to power up their avatars in shift. Nothing compared with the heftier stuff Bondi collected from his more serious customers. These boys had come because of the legend of the Badass.

"Have you seen these two before?" Teague whispered.

"Noobs. Ha. Give them the business." Bondi chuckled, winked, and slipped behind the curtain. Teague waved Monkey under the counter and then let his expression turn grim. He caught the boys' eyes, glanced at the cameras in the corners, and cleared his throat. They stopped flipping through the manga and conferred furtively, each urging the other to action.

Teague's mobile rang just as the boys began to approach together. Teague almost silenced it, but Monkey tapped his leg and said, "It's Aubrey."

"What?" He hadn't spoken to Aubrey in weeks, and she'd never called him.

The boys had reached the counter, and one peeked over, searching for the source of the voice.

Teague waved the boy back, even as he answered his mobile. "Hello?"

"Hi. Teague? I need to talk to you."

"Sure," he said.

"I'd rather talk in person."

"I'm at work for a couple more hours, but I'll come straight home."

"It needs to be now. My parents are at a dinner for Dad's work, but they'll be back by then."

Teague froze as if struck by a Snow Monkey's ice ray. *Shakiro Squirrel, the world's doom is upon you.* Could Aubrey be pregnant? One of the boys whispered to the other.

"What's this about?" Teague asked.

"I just really need to talk to you," she said.

Teague had done some reading about sex after she'd begun coming into his room and was pretty sure what they had done would not have gotten her pregnant. Unless it was some kind of semi-immaculate conception?

"Yeah, okay. Let me talk to my boss," Teague said. He turned to find the boys still waiting expectantly. He didn't have time for them now. "Did you bring the bottle caps?" he asked.

"What bottle caps?" one of the boys asked.

"Why does—?" began the other.

"No one sees the Badass without bottle caps. A hundred.

Each," Teague said. "He's got his reasons. Come back tomorrow." They scurried out, and Teague wondered how long it would be until every kid who came in toted a bag of bottle caps. He should have thought of this years ago.

Aubrey hadn't wanted to talk at home with Braden around, so Monkey had sent her directions to the most private place Teague could think of. Teague parked his motorcycle outside the archway at the alley intersection, barely remembering the ride. All the way, he'd been alternately certain that Aubrey was pregnant and then sure that she had something worse to tell him. But what could be worse?

The sun had fallen well behind the surrounding buildings, and an artificial twilight had settled on the garden. Teague sloughed off his shoes next to a pair of sandals on the flagstone porch and found Aubrey facing the Buddha in the near-dark.

"Is it true what you said?" Aubrey asked. "That you can't shift?"

"Yeah," said Teague. After a moment of quiet, he asked, "You want to talk outside?" Aubrey shook her head. "You want to sit?" Teague took his usual place on the floor across from the Buddha, and Monkey crawled onto his lap.

"How'd you find this place?" Aubrey asked, sliding down the wall to a seat next to him.

"I've always known about it," Teague said.

"How many other missionaries' daughters have you brought here?" Aubrey asked.

"You're the first," Teague said.

"I don't believe that."

"It's the truth."

"If I had a place like this, I'd keep it secret," Aubrey said.

"What did you want to talk about?"

"I want to apologize," she said.

"Why?" Did this mean she wasn't pregnant?

She rubbed her hands on her pants for a moment, clinched them into fists, and then folded them. "It turns out I have a problem. Mom's taken me to see a doctor. They put me on some medication, and I'm not supposed to shift for more than a couple hours a day for a while."

"What kind of problem?"

"I guess it's fairly common for teenagers who shift a lot. My brain craves physical stimulation. I'm sure you've seen me. I touch things."

"I like to be petted," Monkey said.

Teague hushed him and said, "I've noticed."

"If it goes on too long, it gets worse. And you sort of lose control, and you do"—her voice dropped—"sex…stuff. Stuff like we…I did."

"You didn't tell your—?" Teague asked.

"Of course not. Are you kidding?" Aubrey said. "Anyway, I wanted to tell you how sorry I am. I put you in a terrible position. Whenever my head cleared, I hated that I was taking advantage of you. I knew you couldn't go to anyone, and I practically didn't let you say no."

"It's okay," Teague said.

"You don't think I'm terrible?"

"Despicable," Teague said. "I'm glad you're getting help."

"Thanks. You're not angry?"

"Of course not."

Aubrey smiled wanly and then took a deep breath, taking in the incense and the moss. She dragged her fingertips on the floor between them and then pressed her palm to the stone. "You're lucky," she said.

"What makes me lucky?" Teague asked.

"You're almost a senior. Then after graduation, you can go anywhere and do anything you want."

"You're not far behind me."

"But then I have to go to *West Texas Baptist Bible University* because it's free because of Dad's job." She added extra drawl to the name as if it might hurt her to say it normally. "They've pretty much told me I don't have a choice."

"My church wanted me to take a scholarship to their stupid little seminary, but I turned it down," Teague said.

"So what are you going to do?"

"I don't know yet. I can't afford anything, but lots of schools with campuses offer scholarships because everyone's going to school in shift."

"If I were you, I'd apply to them all, and then go to the farthest-away one that will give you a full ride."

Teague laughed.

"What?" Aubrey asked.

"It's funny you say that," Teague said. "When I was searching for scholarships, this one school came up. Monkey, show her that one we laughed about."

A site loaded on Teague's mobile, and he passed it to her.

"Oh my god, you have to apply," Aubrey said.

"There's no way," Teague said.

"Do you qualify?"

Teague studied the screen over her shoulder. Full tuition, transportation, room, board, all the travel expenses, even a stipend. And the fellowship's qualifications were surprisingly open. All the other schools on his list were hundreds or thousands of kilometers away; this one was millions. Teague had been skeptical, but it seemed that Agnus Dei University actually existed.

"They want you to write eight essays," Teague said.

"So what? Listen, if you don't apply, I'll tell my mom about all the things we did in my fragile state," Aubrey said.

"Please don't even joke about that."

"Sorry. But promise me you'll apply."

Teague had already had this conversation with himself. Crafting all those essays would be a waste of time. He'd be competing with thousands of more-qualified students. He wasn't sure he even wanted to study economics and business. But he knew his real reluctance went deeper. ADU was off-Earth, a place not meant for men of God. And in order to survive, he would have to take annual doses of Vanilla. Vanilla, the blood of evil, which separated a man's spirit from God. How many times had he heard that? He had always planned on taking Vanilla once he turned thirty like everyone else. But faced with the prospect of doing it at eighteen, Teague felt confused—and then ashamed of his confusion. It was all nonsense. How had the church filled his head with such fear?

"Fine. I'll apply," he said. The certainty of failure made it easier to say. "But I doubt they'll be too impressed by my diploma from a stupid mission school."

* * *

Not quite nine months later, Teague parked his motorcycle in the teachers' lot, violating two school rules at once. His uniform had remained in his closet today. The first bell had rung fifteen minutes ago. Monkey trotted alongside him down the center of the corridor, oohing and ahhing quietly over the sparkly Christmas decorations. It seemed to Teague like all he had ever heard from these classrooms were these muffled voices, this meaningless white noise, murmuring groups of children, the movement of furniture.

"We're all so impressed that you're able to graduate early," the headmaster said as she signed off on Teague's final transcript.

"Thank you," Teague said. With Monkey's help, he'd plowed through six months of reading and assignments in less than a month. "I need my transcripts forwarded to these."

Teague sent her the list of the thirty-eight universities to which he had applied.

"Impressive," the headmaster said, scrolling through the ed-dresses. "Well, your excellent grades certainly won't hurt."

She wished him luck as he secured his diploma in his network cache. "We'll keep you informed about graduation ceremonies in June. We'd love a chance to send you off properly," she said.

As Teague left, a choir of children's voices rang from the chapel. They held a note at the end of *Away in a Manger* but were scolded and made to start again.

"There's no graduation ceremony?" Bondi asked.

"Not for me," Teague said.

"No celebration at all? No big party?"

"The Chaiprasits are taking me out for dinner. But it's really no big deal. I just needed to get school over with so I could spend a few months earning more money before college."

"Any news from any of them yet?" Bondi asked.

"I've had a few schools offer me loans and partial grants, but I really need a full scholarship. It'll still be a few weeks until I've heard from all of them."

"Something will come. In the meantime, I have a graduation gift for you."

"You didn't need to do that."

"Moral imperative. Besides, you'll put it to much better use than I ever could."

"I doubt that."

"Follow me. Monkey, you, too."

"I like surprises," Monkey said.

Bondi took them around the black curtain into the cramped workshop. He picked up an object from his workbench and spun around.

"A cordless screwdriver?" Teague asked, puzzled.

"No, although that would make a good gift. Fetch the stepladder."

Teague retrieved a dusty, ancient server off a top shelf and set the monstrous box on the workbench, not mentioning that if he had to choose, he'd prefer the screwdriver to an old computer. Bondi set to work opening the server box.

"Are you familiar with the term 'industrial espionage'?" Bondi asked. "Don't look at me like that. You don't suppose I was always an upstanding purveyor of custom electronics services, do you?" Once the casing had been removed, he inspected the guts of the machine, gave a satisfied grunt, and began to extract a component. "Before Vanilla, most of us planned to live for eighty, ninety years at the most. When we were informed that we were going to live considerably longer, we old men took hard looks at our retirement accounts. Vanilla doesn't make one younger, and I was nearing the end of a long career at Nexon. Have you ever heard of them?"

"No," Teague said.

"Semiconductors. Chip makers. Software."

"Taiwanese?"

"American-Taiwanese partnership. This was before the

integration. Aha." He held up a palm-sized circuit board, turning it with reverence—one side a maze of silver interrupted by tiny components, the other dominated by two black cubes, three centimeters square, set a centimeter apart. "One prototype NAI chipset."

"NAI?" Teague asked.

"Near artificial intelligence," Bondi said. "Nexon designed it for the United States military to manage battlefield networks. Hyper-fast, totally new architecture. The software was also completely new. It mimics sentience, responds accurately to human emotions and idiomatic speech. Works with you like a person to solve very complex problems."

"And I need to know this why?" Teague asked.

"These chips are twenty years old," Bondi said, "but I can guarantee you there's nothing like them in this whole mall. Nexon only released NAI systems commercially a few years ago, but they're still tightly controlled. Anyway, I've never found a use for these chips. I'd like you—or more specifically, Monkey—to have them."

Monkey perked up his ears.

"They're stolen?" Teague asked.

"I was offered a king's ransom to pass on prototype chips and software. And if I hadn't done it, someone else would've. We were all panicking. And in all the fuss, I kept a set for myself."

"Who paid you?" Teague asked.

"Take a guess. Why do you think I left Taiwan before the integration? Disloyalty is not a prized attribute in Beijing."

"China?" Teague asked. Bondi nodded. "But why'd you have to leave if you stole it for them?"

"I was disloyal to my country and employer. I wouldn't be trusted after the political transition." Bondi patted for Monkey to hop onto the workbench. "Anyway, maybe some good can come of it now. What do you say?"

"You're offering to make Monkey nearly sentient?"

"I am," Bondi replied.

"Will he still be Monkey?" Teague asked.

"The NAI should absorb and apply the Zubotix OS, but he will become something quite new. What do you think, Monkey?"

"I prefer that all service work be done by factory-trained Zubotix VetTechs. Use of anything other than Zubotix brand parts and accessories may cause system conflicts and damage."

"What would you have to do?" Teague asked.

"Retrofit to accommodate the new chipboard. Upgrade his memory capacity significantly. Install and merge the software. And I may as well do some routine maintenance while I've got him open."

Teague's stomach churned at the word "open." He picked Monkey up. "But what if it doesn't work?"

"I can restore him. But I don't think you'll be disappointed," Bondi said.

"What if I get in trouble? What happens once those chips connect with the Internet?"

"They'll never be looking in your direction," Bondi said with a wave. "Besides, Nexon's seven generations past this technology now. And"—he winked—"I'll give him a few lines of code that'll keep him snug."

"I need to think about it," Teague said.

"I understand."

"But why me? Why Monkey? It sounds like that thing is worth a fortune."

Bondi scratched Monkey's head. "Forgive an old man's sense of humor," he replied.

* * *

It might have been the same office where he'd first met her—that morning after his mother's accident—but Teague didn't want to know. Even if it was, it was her office now, with pleasant art and several prospering plants.

"Thank you for seeing me," he said, taking a seat and sliding his screen across her glass desk. Teague had grown taller than Dr. Aromdee many years ago, but he still felt like he was looking up to her. "I think your letter of recommendation really did the trick."

He'd called her immediately after he'd opened the offer and read it half a dozen times to make sure there hadn't been a mistake. But it was his name. His eddress. Their pleasure to accept him.

"Agnus Dei University? This is very exciting," she said, still reading.

"Did you see the name of the program?" Teague asked.

"The Wolkenbruch Fellowship for Business and Economics? You're not letting that stop you, are you?"

"It's Adrian Wolkenbruch. He's the Tellurites' enemy number one. Or maybe number three. Marcus and Lucy Frye did the lab work, but Adrian Wolkenbruch funded the whole Vanilla project and donated it to the UN. Together they make some kind of triune Satan."

"But you don't believe that," Dr. Aromdee said.

"I think my mom did," Teague said.

"And you feel like you might be betraying her?"

"Not in so many words, but yeah, that might be it. I mean, I'd be living off Earth. I'd be taking Vanilla. I'd be accepting the generosity of Adrian Wolkenbruch. The only way it could be worse would be if it was a scholarship to a medical school."

Dr. Aromdee laughed. "I'm sorry. It's not funny. I just hope you're not considering yourself unworthy. Or do you believe that you owe something to your mother's church?"

"I don't know," Teague said.

"I would ask myself who would be harmed by my actions. By leaving Earth, taking Vanilla, you harm no one. And if you remain on Earth out of duty and not of any real faith, you may be doing yourself a pointless disservice. Honestly, Teague, I'm surprised at your concern. You've never let your emotions rule you. Even when you were very young, you were willing to accept ambiguity, and you know what can happen when you allow others to make choices for you."

"This would be a definitive, in-your-face rejection of everything they believe," Teague said.

"But this is *your* life," Dr. Aromdee said. "You can't let fear, or some misplaced sense of obligation, rule your decisions. You've been handed the opportunity of a lifetime. And you took the initiative to apply. Some part of you must want this."

"I know," Teague said.

"And the adventure of it. I would think that you would leap at this chance." She hadn't said it outright, but Teague understood. While billions of people could experience life on an asteroid, or almost anything imaginable, for the price of a shift set, he had had to tick the boxes and explain his disability on every application. He hated that he needed the scholarships badly enough to beg for special consideration.

"I want it to be that simple," Teague said.

She returned his screen and said, "Then let it be that simple."

An hour later, Teague strode into Bondi's stall and said, "Okay."

"Okay?" Bondi asked.

Teague looked down at Monkey, waiting dutifully by his feet. "I'd like to accept your graduation present. I just can't be here while it happens."

Bondi grinned and clapped his hands. "I understand. I'll call you. Two, maybe three days."

Teague picked up Monkey, hugged him close, and then set him on the counter. "You stay here and be good for Bondi."

"Bye, Teague. I'll miss you," Monkey said.

That afternoon, as Teague urged his motorcycle faster and faster along the freeway, he could almost imagine that he was already on the elevator, halfway into orbit.

* * *

"I hate to do this to you," Bondi said. "I know you've barely had a chance to say hello, but I have a very urgent delivery." He slipped a mobile into a silk drawstring pouch and handed it to Teague.

"Should I—?"

"Take him with you," Bondi said.

"I like to go new places," Monkey said, but a hint of mischief in his voice made Teague turn to Bondi.

"Have fun," Bondi said with a wink.

The address brought Teague to a familiar building in the financial district, one he knew was filled with attorneys engaged in a never-ending battle to one-up each other with their playthings. A few had been turned onto the Badass's custom services, probably while defending some hacker in court.

"Do you remember making deliveries here?" Teague asked Monkey.

"Yes, and I know you disliked it because the security guards were rude."

"They made fun of you. Almost didn't let you in," Teague said.

Teague parked his motorcycle, but Monkey didn't hop out of his crate. "Are you coming?" Teague asked.

"Would you like to get in without going through security screening?"

Monkey led Teague around the building to the grated entrance of an underground parking garage near an alley. As they approached, the grate rolled up, and Monkey loped down the ramp.

"Monkey?" Teague called from the sidewalk. "What about security cameras?"

"The building network is very friendly," Monkey said.

Teague followed, trying to think up some excuse if they were caught, and the grate began to roll down behind him. He had never seen so many luxury cars in one place.

An executive elevator car was waiting for them at the end of the aisle. They entered, and the button for their floor lit without a touch.

Teague greeted the receptionist formally, but the man sniffed and checked his desk screen. *"I wasn't notified of any deliveries,"* he said. He glared past Teague, clearly disquieted by Monkey sniffing at the bouquet of orchids on the coffee table.

"Security gave me access," Teague said.

When a lawyer in a severely pressed suit arrived a few minutes later, the receptionist simply pointed at Teague. *"You are from the Badass?"* the lawyer asked.

"I am." Teague waied and then presented the silk bag.

The lawyer plucked the bag from Teague's palm and extracted the mobile as if it were a fine dagger. Teague had no idea what Bondi had done for the man, but it was clearly appreciated.

Teague had planned to leave through the lobby like a respectful member of the service sector, but after one last look at the receptionist's sneer, he had Monkey take them out the way they'd come in.

Teague sat on the cool floor of the garden temple. Monkey squatted in front of him with a wide grin. The Buddha watched from his altar, completing the triangle. "You don't look different," Teague said.

"Do I sound different?" Monkey asked.

"Not your voice, but how you say things. It's like you're really thinking, not spouting canned responses." Teague wondered if it was only his imagination that Monkey's glassy eyes held a fresh awareness. Or that his movements, while still feline, showed a subtle shift in purpose. Teague doubted that a stranger would notice the difference.

"I'll take that as a compliment," Monkey said.

"What's your earliest memory?"

"Meeting you and Mom in your bedroom," Monkey said. "I'm sorry about your mother. I don't know if I ever said that."

"Thank you," Teague said. "That's very kind."

"We've spent a lot of time here," Monkey said.

"It's one of the places I'll miss the most."

"I'll make an Immer-Sim-compatible record so you can take it with you."

"You can do that?"

"I've downloaded many useful applications today," Monkey replied. "Did you know that most devices and systems are not well encrypted, even at the e-mall? I've updated your mobile and screen to a much higher standard."

Teague chuckled and shook his head.

"What's so funny?" Monkey asked.

"You. You're suddenly this military-grade super lemur, and I have no idea what to do with you." Teague was afraid to ask

Monkey about what he'd done at the lawyer's office that afternoon. The old Monkey hated breaking the rules. But this Monkey was more than willing, and able, to move heaven and Earth to accommodate Teague's merest whim. The implications staggered.

"Zubotix has a microgravity operation software upgrade. It would be very useful."

"Is it free?" Teague asked.

"Do you want it to be free?"

"No, of course not. How much is it?"

"Forty-five unos."

"I suppose you'll need it. Is there one for me, too?"

"The Universal Treatment prevents most of the detrimental physiological effects of long-term microgravity exposure," Monkey said. "With regular exercise—"

"Now you're just quoting, trying to sound all smart," Teague said.

"Are you saying I'm not smart?" Monkey asked.

"I was teasing."

Monkey's face fell. "You're teasing your best friend?"

"What? Are you really sad?" Teague asked.

Monkey laughed. "I'm not sad. I'm teasing you back. Who's smart now?" Teague made a friendly grab, but Monkey scampered out of reach. He danced into the garden and began to sing a rhyming song about recording an Immer-Sim for his best friend Teague.

* * *

"You'd think it'd be harder to keep my life's possessions under the elevator weight limit," Teague said, frowning over his limp duffel bag.

"What are you taking?" Aubrey asked. Monkey turned over on her lap and lolled his head back as she began to rub his tummy.

"Clothes, my mobile and screen, Monkey and his stuff, and not much else."

"You can leave me behind," Monkey said with a sigh.

"And you don't even need to take all those clothes," Aubrey

said. "Buy new ones when you get there. That's what I do when we go on vacation."

"This isn't exactly a vacation."

"You're on a cruise for almost a year," Aubrey said. "Sounds like a vacation to me."

"Can Aubrey come with us?" Monkey purred. Teague wondered how many other NAIs got regularly canoodled by a teenage girl.

"She'd probably put us over the weight limit."

"Careful," Aubrey warned with a laugh. "I'd love to go, Monkey, but I have to stay here." She nodded toward Teague's desk. "Aren't you taking your photo frame?"

"I have the original files," Teague said.

"It would be healthy to have a tactile remembrance of your mother," Monkey said. Teague picked it up, looked at it for a moment, and then passed it to Aubrey.

"Your mother was beautiful," she said.

"I'm the little guy on her back. And that's Kevin. This used to be his room."

"There's you, Monkey," she said and held the frame for him to see.

"I'm so cute," he said.

"Under that one is a picture of my dad," Teague said.

Aubrey slid the back off the right frame, peeled the photos apart, and studied his father. "You look like him. Very handsome," she said, handing the pictures back.

Teague looked at the pictures again and then reassembled the frame and hefted it in one hand. He wrapped it in a T-shirt and stuffed it in the bag.

"Be sure and pack my charger," Monkey said.

"You were supposed to pack your own stuff," Teague said.

"I'm being petted."

"Careful or I might just forget you." Teague opened his backpack and found Monkey's accessories already wrapped up and tucked away.

Monkey let out another satisfied sigh under Aubrey's touch and said, "Fine with me."

Teague sold his motorcycle to the Badass for his next deliveryman. Aubrey burned a farewell kiss on his lips. Mrs. Chaiprasit refused to let him leave without filling his stomach one last time from the buffet and wetting his shoulder with tears. Mr. Chaiprasit pressed a gift transfer of too much money into his mobile. And although he still felt the final handshakes from Father Josiah, Ned, Dr. Aromdee, and Bondi, he already didn't recognize the city that passed by the taxi's windows on the way to the train station.

"To where are you traveling?" asked the driver.

"Singapore," Teague replied.

PART TWO: SCHOOL

FEBRUARY 2108

It meant nothing now to be the director of education and recreation for the Angel-37 colony. There was no further need for tutors, scholarships, night classes, career planning, badminton tournaments, or wallyball leagues. The preparations for next week's festival would remain forever incomplete. Kyi found herself at her desk scrolling through a calendar of meetings and appointments that would never happen. Had they ever been important?

Her small staff had still been present when she'd arrived at her department's offices. They had begged her to help them make sense of the situation. She had encouraged them to go home, to spend these last few days with their loved ones—or else to volunteer with the Facilities Department's efforts.

"What will you do?" they had asked.

"I will do what I can," Kyi had replied.

That had been hours ago. Kyi knew she shouldn't be hiding. People might be inspired to see or hear the daughter of Professor Lwin facing doom with a brave face, but every moment of delay made that more difficult, and less meaningful.

The security chief's warnings had come to terrible fruition. Only a few of the sixty thousand citizens had been disruptive, but they had already made the station a dangerous place. The shopping district had been looted, the greenhouses, warehouses, and kitchens overrun. Several people had been killed in clashes with security. Guards had retreated to key access points in critical sections. A structural breach in a habitat had been reported but hadn't yet been confirmed in the chaos of the lockdown. Dozens of suicides had been called in on emergency channels.

Kyi toyed with her shift set as she monitored the station's communications. Tens of thousands were already shifted, and she wished them well. Better to be anywhere but here. But shifting felt as cowardly a choice as the mayor's pills. Besides, the communications systems were loaded to capacity. Kyi couldn't be so selfish as to take up bandwidth that someone else might need. Her family would of course want to see her, but how could she face them, especially her father, having done nothing? Yet there seemed nothing to do but wait for the inevitable. It appalled her to feel this numb. Was she already dead?

Kyi jumped at the sound of a security code being entered on the outer door of the offices. She looked for something to protect herself with, but when the door opened she was still frozen at her desk.

"Herbert?" she said to the unexpected visitor.

The wiry, red-bearded man was followed by dozens of men and women who gathered in her deserted offices like a quiet flock of migrating birds. Many in her department didn't like Herbert Nederton, the Westerner who organized sports leagues and martial-arts programs. His severe religious tendencies irritated some, and he acted with odd conviction, but he was loyal and took his work seriously. "May we have a moment, ma'am?"

Kyi held her arms wide. "I have all the time in the world," she said, hoping for a laugh. "Who are all these people?"

"We are the Sons and Daughters of Josiah," he replied. Kyi bristled. Early in his employment, she'd had to reprimand Herbert for proselytizing on the job, but he organized this boxing club on his own time. An irrelevance now, it seemed.

Herbert beckoned, and a meek young man floated in and greeted Kyi formally, almost reverently. She wanted to laugh. What had she done to earn this man's respect?

"We are concerned," Herbert said, indicating the young man, himself, and the dozens outside, "that there is nothing being done to prevent this catastrophe."

"Prevent it?" Kyi said.

"To fight it," Herbert said. A cheer of agreement sounded from the offices.

"What can we do?" Kyi asked.

"Anything is better than nothing," Herbert said. "Ohnmar works on a surface construction crew."

The young man swallowed, floated forward, and touched Kyi's desk screen. "May I?" he asked. He loaded a schematic of Angel-37 and zoomed into an undeveloped area on the rocky surface near the disused mining depot.

"There is a fuel tank, buried, here," he explained. "Installed by

Xterrex for transfer vessels and left by Valdosky as a contingency reserve for cargo ships. It's full, and not connected to any colony systems." He looked up, hopeful that he had explained everything.

"You're going to have to give me more," Kyi said.

Herbert spoke. "We propose to construct a jet nozzle that will use this fuel to push our asteroid out of harm's way." Kyi couldn't suppress a startled laugh. "We only need to move a little. Cho, come in here." A small woman entered carrying a screen. "Cho has determined that if we can divert ourselves even a few meters out of the way, we may experience seismic effects from the passing asteroid—am I explaining that correctly?—but most of the station should remain survivable." The woman nodded. It was fittingly absurd that Herbert's Christian boxing club had proposed this solution.

"What's stopping you from trying this?" Kyi asked.

"Security has closed all the airlocks," Herbert said.

Ohnmar pointed at the schematic. "At a minimum, we'll need access to airlocks J, K, and M to rotate workers, and to recharge pressure suits and tools."

"Why tell me?"

"You're on the executive council," Herbert said. "The security chief will take your call." Kyi realized that she had waited in her office for exactly this opportunity.

"Will he help us?" Ohnmar asked her.

"Yes," Kyi answered, as confidently as possible. She dialed the chief's personal eddress. As she waited for him to answer, she asked, "Do you need an extra pair of hands?"

CHAPTER 13

I spent too much of my life being told that the places I lived weren't home.

MAY 2089

The man in the next seat twitched and murmured and then fell quiet again. Like the dozens of others in the dim, vibrating compartment, he had shifted shortly after boarding, abandoning Teague to his own flesh and blood.

"I feel like I'm tied up in a morgue," Teague said to Monkey through his mobile. He redirected the vent to blow more fully across his forehead.

"How do you think I feel?" Monkey asked, his voice coming from a bud in Teague's ear. "I'm in a drawer."

"They said I couldn't let you out until the seat belt light goes off. How much longer, do you think?" Teague asked.

"According to Valdosky's Passenger Elevator Standard Operating Procedure Manual, the seat belt indicator may be disengaged after the car reaches an altitude of twelve kilometers, but not before. Forty-seven more minutes at our current speed. And if the weather conditions hold."

Teague hushed Monkey when he noticed a cabin attendant approaching. "Are you having a problem with your shift set?" the attendant asked. Teague shook his head.

Monkey began to count down the endless minutes and then, eventually, the seconds.

When the chimes finally rang and the announcement was made, Teague hurriedly unbuckled and opened the carry-on drawer, ignoring the safety message that had appeared on his seat's screen.

"Are we there yet?" Monkey asked.

"Let's get out of here," Teague said and climbed over his seatmate.

The wedge-shaped passenger lounge at the bottom of the central stair was half the volume of Teague's bedroom back in Bangkok, but unlike the mausoleum of their cabin above, it had a window. The arced glass stretched from wall to wall and nearly floor to ceiling over the Straits of Singapore and the Indian Ocean. Cities, islands, and significant water features were marked with drifting tags. A tap on any one brought up a zoomed image and a few bits of trivia. An icon in the corner offered to toggle the screen language. Another icon brought up a graphic of the elevator car's altitude, speed, and position on the cable.

The only other item of interest in the lounge, besides the vending machine, was a floor-to-ceiling adscreen hawking businesses on the Star of Singapore, other elevator stations, the Moon, a few asteroid colonies, and in shift. "I can't decide, Monkey," Teague said. "Out-of-this-world prices on duty-free liquor in seven locations or the Apollo Eleven Historical Center?"

"One giant choice for mankind," Monkey said.

"Or should I get a weightless massage or an Absolute Zero soft-serve cone?"

"Why not get both?"

Teague returned to the window and tried to find a comfortable seat on the narrow sill.

"Beautiful, isn't it?" said a man with a British accent.

Teague spun around to find that a Korean man had entered the lounge. He wore a suit but no tie. He looked about sixty-ish, so with Vanilla he'd be at least a hundred and twenty.

"Did you know that ancient Sumerian writings describe this exact view—the colors of the earth and sea, the way the sky transitions to black? They claimed to have witnessed it from inside a vehicle of the gods." He held Teague with a piercing gaze and then said, "This is your first time off Earth. A word of advice: Don't make any major purchases on the stations. Get where you're going first. Buy from people who need you, not your money."

"Why?" Teague asked, but the door was already sliding shut.

"Strange," Monkey said as the man disappeared up the stairs.

"You noticed?" Teague asked.

"He didn't have a mobile," Monkey said. "I don't know who he was."

That evening after dinner, Teague returned to the passenger lounge to find that the car had climbed noticeably higher. Under the blanket of night, human civilization looked to be no more than glowing algae in the elevator car's wake. Teague located Bangkok and wondered which pinprick had been his.

* * *

The next day, Teague laughed out loud as he pushed off and spun down the tube that had recently been the stairwell. He reached the end—it no longer felt like the bottom—and bounced with a whoop. He swept past his level, absorbed his momentum at the other end, and pushed off, tagging Monkey as they passed in midair.

"You're it," he called, and Monkey squealed in delight.

They played until an attendant came through, and then they retreated to the passenger lounge.

"Are you still feeling good?" Monkey asked. "Any nausea, dizziness, or disorientation?"

"I'm fine. The only thing that got to me was all the other people hurling." Teague cringed at the memory. "I'm just glad it wasn't my seatmate. How are you doing? That software we bought running all right?"

"Like a dream," Monkey cooed and set himself spinning across the lounge.

Teague longed for a larger space to fly. The visible sliver of Earth was still bright enough to overwhelm any stars, but too far away to offer much more detail than, hey, there's a planet. Brown, green, and blue.

* * *

Late on the third day, Teague spilled out of the airlock gate into the crowded octopus of the Star of Singapore Station arrivals zone and oriented himself to the arbitrary up and down of the galaxy of signage. A bot scanned his face and then moved on, calling another passenger's name. A uniformed policeman oversaw the bustle through transparent screens in a high central tower.

"To the left," Monkey said. He craned his neck out of the backpack's zipper and nudged Teague's cheek.

"There are five concourses that way," Teague said.

"See the sign with your hotel's name?" Monkey wriggled a black paw out and pointed. "And hurry. I'm going to get crushed back here."

They got jostled again, but Teague smiled. "I'm just happy to be back among the living," he said.

Teague pushed off but collided with another passenger and found himself caught in a crowd gathering around an Xterrex human resources kiosk. Teague eventually navigated the zone, and he drifted cautiously into a squat oval tube wide enough for about four people to pass. Small shops—financial services, tattoos, insurance, a steamy noodle shop—lined both sides.

"You got a pressure suit?" Teague turned to see a crew cut and a jaw over gray fatigues and several shiny pressure suits displayed in front of a wall screen moonscape. "If you don't have a UTX Environmental Suit, you may as well kiss your ass goodbye."

"I'll keep that in mind," Teague said.

"I'll be the last thing you remember as your blood boils away in your cheap-ass suit," the man called after him.

"Hotel" was a generous term for the lodgings. *It's only for one night,* Teague told himself as he stowed his belongings in his capsule in the honeycomb. That evening, despite the strange man's advice, Teague bought several thermal shirts. Space was cold like Bangkok never was.

* * *

Star of Singapore's Universal Treatment Service clinic was not protected by the ubiquitous SOS security force, but by a pair of UN personnel. It wasn't their blue fatigues or their holstered stun guns that gave Teague pause as he approached, but the question of why they were there at all. A clutch of Australian revelers arrived at the entrance from a side passage before him. They all were wearing flexi-shirts that flashed, "Totally Wonkered at Ashton's 30th!" They offered each of the guards a massive pack of beer, but they both declined good-naturedly and admitted the guest of honor. Teague felt a now-familiar knot in his stomach but told himself it was only a lack of breakfast. He wished Ashton's friends would offer him a beer, too.

Once past the guards, Teague checked in at a kiosk that dispensed a secure screen and then admitted him to a waiting room. He found a free foot loop among the dozen other patients and began to fill out his form. He transmitted his data and then waited, looking for fear or trepidation on the faces of the others, but finding none.

When his screen vibrated, Teague felt an urge to bolt for the exit. Instead, he entered a marked door, and a blinking light strip led him along a narrow corridor lined with pocket doors and deposited him in a cubicle just large enough for an examination chair.

An avatar of a woman's face appeared on the room's screen, greeted him by name, and asked him to confirm that the patient data was indeed his. "Please be seated and fasten your lap belt. A UTS technician will be with you shortly." The door slid shut and the screen began to stream a selectable menu of information about the Universal Treatment and the UTS. The choices had scrolled by more than twenty times when the door finally opened.

"Good morning." The technician consulted her screen cursorily but then furrowed her brow. "You have no medical history except a shift installation?" she asked.

"No, ma'am," Teague said.

"Do you even have an immunization rec—oh, yes, I see," she

said. Dr. Aromdee had arranged for him to get all the necessary injections a few weeks before his departure. The technician tapped the screen a few more times, scowled again, apologized, and excused herself.

Teague swore silently. Was this going to be the shift clinic all over again?

A few minutes later, a man entered and introduced himself as the medical supervisor. "This is a bit of an unusual situation," he said.

"My parents were Tellurites," Teague replied.

"I didn't know they were still around. Do they know you're up here?"

"I'm eighteen," Teague said.

"We'll need to complete several screenings before we can administer the treatment: a genetic scan, certain blood tests. It will take longer than the standard appointment, and I'll need you to authorize the additional procedures." The supervisor handed Teague a screen with a stylus. "To where are you traveling?"

"Agnus Dei," Teague replied.

"A long way. I hope you elected to receive the subcutaneous second-year release implant."

"I did."

"Okay. We'll begin in a few minutes."

What were the chances that he'd be unable to shift *and* unable to take Vanilla? He'd never heard of Vanilla rejection. But what would he do? Go back to Earth and work for Bondi forever? Enroll at the Christian Science seminary? Clown college?

The technician returned and fitted a cuff device over the crease of his elbow. The cuff tightened, a needle poked through his skin, and a glob of his blood began to fill a protruding vial. Teague leaned his head back, closed his eyes, and silently sang the English version of the Shakiro Squirrel theme song.

Shakiro Squirrel, master of speed
Shakiro Squirrel helps those in need
Exploding nuts and taser beams
Tail of fire, Squirrel of dreams

Friends of Squirrel, dance with me
Shakiro, Shakiro, Shakiro, the Hero

Doctor Yokona knows no greed
Dragonfly, his most trusty steed
Fight for peace and lovely trees
Moon and sun and sky and seas

Friends of Squirrel, dance with me
Shakiro, Shakiro, Shakiro, the Hero

Snow Monkeys of Doom with icy glares
Destroy the world from Hot Tub Lairs
Glacial plans beneath their means
To freeze the Earth is in their genes

Dance Shakiro, Dance Shakiro
Dance Dance Squirrel Squirrel

While they screened his blood and DNA, countless people passed his door and held muffled conversations in the neighboring rooms. Utilities trickled in the walls. The chair vibrated to the thrum of the living station. Teague was about to distract himself with a call to Monkey when the supervisor returned.

"Good news, Teague. We find no contraindications. You're in excellent health. Do you have any questions?"

"No, sir," Teague replied.

The supervisor pressed his thumb to a panel over the narrow counter, and a tiny vial was dispensed from a slot.

"Is that Vanilla?" Teague asked.

"One under-thirty annual maintenance dose of the Universal Treatment." The supervisor inspected the vial of ochre liquid, swiped its coding over his screen, and then pressed the capped end of the vial into the cuff on Teague's arm. The cuff whirred softly, and the liquid drained from the vial in a heartbeat.

This was what all the sermons had been about, these few

milliliters of distillate original sin, the worse-than-forbidden fruit that severed your spirit from the Universal Mind while it fouled your body. A long life separate from God was no life at all, the pastors claimed, but they feared death like anyone. Teague felt no euphoria, no rush. He closed his eyes, but Vanilla felt like nothing entering his veins. He recalled his mother's face such as he hadn't in many years. She was happy, like her picture on the road to the tiger conservancy, but nearer and less burdened.

The supervisor removed the emptied vial with a pop and said, "The under-thirty dose is based on your size and genetic particulars. With a regular exercise regimen, you will stay very healthy in microgravity, but aging will occur at a near-normal rate."

The cuff had left a sealed red dot in the crease of his elbow, but the miniature crossbow-like device the supervisor had used to insert the subcutaneous second-year dose had left two tubular bumps and a numb, red, glue-sealed slit on the underside of his biceps.

"Good luck at Agnus Dei," the supervisor said.

"Thank you."

Back at the hotel, Teague went straight into the bathroom and dry heaved into a vacuum sink.

"Nausea is not a usual side effect of the Universal Treatment," Monkey said.

"I'm fine," Teague said. "Let's go get some breakfast."

* * *

From the shuttle window, the Valdosky Space Ship Nebula Empress looked like a god's rotisserie. Instead of slabs of meat, four dirty-gray skyscrapers had been skewered from top to bottom. A haphazard grid of windows sparkled on their outer facets. Each end of the cruiser was capped with an immense, blocky structure, one of which sported a set of engine bells that reminded Teague uncomfortably of nuclear plant cooling towers. Globular tanks hung in webs of piping and truss between the skyscrapers, exposed, as if part of the cruiser's hull had been torn away. But from on board, none of that mattered. The half-meter oval window in Teague's stateroom overlooked the grasping disc of the cruise dock facility high over the Pacific Ocean. For now.

"Guess who has his own bathroom?" Monkey called from behind a linen-thin pocket door. Teague had been expecting another capsule, so the zippered hammock in a few private cubic meters felt like luxury. "Also, you have messages. A welcome from the captain and several safety bulletins," Monkey said.

"Read them for me. Let's go have a look around."

Every corridor bustled with bobbing luggage bots and purple-shirted Valdosky crew, mostly Martian- or Lunar-born and at home in free fall, directing the hundreds of beleaguered, complaining passengers with competent urgency.

"Is there a passenger list available?" Teague asked Monkey.

"I can get one."

"Because I see a distinct problem," Teague said.

"What's that?"

"Every demographic on Earth is well represented here except for Women My Age."

"I haven't seen any lemurs, either," Monkey said.

The shops, salons, bars, clubs, and cafeterias in the public zones were shuttered. The Immer-Sim suite was locked. The restaurants were only accepting reservations. At a concierge kiosk, Teague signed up for the wallyball league and applied to be a fitness center monitor.

"They only pay in Valbucks," Monkey said.

"So what? It'll be something to do," Teague said.

In the wide, oval lobby of a deserted conference center, Monkey bounced from wall to wall, chirping happily. The theater lobby was grated off, and the marquee was blank. Teague peered through the sidelight window into a dark conference room and asked, "Is anything open?"

"Do you want it to be open?" Monkey asked.

"No," Teague said. "Probably best if you don't go around unlocking doors."

"Or turning on engines," Monkey said.

"Don't even joke about that."

"Would this be a good time to tell you that the library is open?"

"There's no library," Teague scoffed.

"There is, too."

At best, Teague expected Monkey to guide him to a lounge with an ironic name, at worst, a shift parlor. But when Teague opened the door and smelled the essence of paper, he patted Monkey on the head. "Why do I ever doubt you?" he said.

"Human fallibility," Monkey replied.

Even while inside it, it was difficult to imagine that this place existed on the cruise ship. Four leather armchairs and an ebony coffee table of ancient quality clung to a fine rug under a cove-lit ceiling. Subtle lamps crowned end tables and cast warm pools of light on the oak floor. A few hardcover books had been left scattered on grip pads on the various tables. There was an appropriate soft hush in the atmosphere.

Three sides of the library were not walls, but sets of deep, rolling stacks, each with a single person-sized gap. They were presumably controlled from the plinth-mounted screen that waited to the right of the vestibule. A portrait had been hung to its left. The subject, a man, had a familiar face despite the experimental bent of the artist. Teague drifted closer to read the plaque.

"That's Matthew Valdosky."

Teague turned and was somehow unsurprised to see the Korean man from the elevator emerging from the stacks.

"Valdosky? Like the Valdosky Companies?" Teague asked.

"I told Matthew that every cruiser should have a library," the man said. "Even if the sum total of human knowledge is available online, a book is still a powerful thing. Wouldn't you agree, Mr. Werres?"

"Do I know you?" Teague asked.

"Not yet. I'm Thomas Minus, professor, Agnus Dei University, and the administrator of the Wolkenbruch Fellowship. Don't look so surprised. You didn't think we'd wait thirteen months to start your education? I was going to send you a message tomorrow to arrange our first appointment, but we're here now. Do you have a moment to get acquainted?" Thomas motioned to the chairs. As

Teague settled on the grip-treated leather, Monkey landed at his feet, staring at Thomas, but Thomas seemed not to notice him.

"Why didn't you introduce yourself on the elevator?" Teague asked.

"You surprised me there, too. And neither of us needed the distraction. I assume you received the reading list."

"I expected to have the trip to work on it."

"Don't worry. There will be time. Many of the titles can be found here, if you prefer to read from a real book."

"That might be interesting," Teague said.

"This would be a good place to begin." Thomas offered Teague a book off the coffee table, a thick volume, paper yellowed on the edges.

"Adam Smith?" Teague read from the spine. "Nothing like getting right to business."

"Have you had any formal instruction in economics?"

"Not really."

"I find it astounding how often economics is left out of the basic curriculum. It's a driving societal force. It moves individuals and nations, explains much of history. For instance, how can one truly understand the development of the New World without an understanding of Old World mercantilism?"

"I was always taught that the colonization of America was primarily related to religious freedom," Teague said.

"But even the desire for religious freedom can be defined in economic terms," Thomas said, pointing to the book in Teague's hands. "I think you'll find that rational self-interest is not a new concept."

"What about irrational self-interest?" Teague asked, hoping Thomas would tolerate a joke.

"Oh, that's a much older concept," Thomas replied with a smile. "And explains far more of history than the other."

Teague laughed politely.

"I'm sorry that you weren't expecting me—perhaps I should have been clearer in my communications—but I am very much looking forward to our time together."

"I think I'm going to be glad to have something to keep me busy," Teague said.

"I congratulate you on earning this fellowship."

Teague wanted to ask how such a thing had happened but checked himself. "Thank you," he said instead.

"I'm sure you need some time to settle in. Shall we meet here at nine o'clock tomorrow morning to begin?" Thomas rose, deftly hooking one foot under his chair to keep from rising to the ceiling. Teague rose less gracefully and shook his hand, and then Thomas hurried out with a book.

"He seems nice," Monkey said. "Although I wish he'd carry a mobile."

"Do you think he really knows Matthew Valdosky?"

"ADU added his bio to its website very recently. He's a professor of economics, on the board of Real Time Networks, the news agency, and a British citizen. I can't find a permanent physical address."

Teague riffled the pages of *The Wealth of Nations*. "Let me know if you discover anything else," he said.

Even an e-manga version of Adam Smith's tome couldn't have held Teague's attention. Muffled voices in the neighboring staterooms had turned to muted laughter in the passageways. Music began to thump the walls.

"What's going on?" Teague asked.

"It's probably the party," Monkey replied.

Teague set his screen aside in the air. "What party?"

"I didn't want to disturb your studies."

"For the duration of this trip—strike that. You are *always* allowed to disturb my studies."

"Understood. In that case, quote, D-Party, T minus one hour. Last one in orbit loses. BYOB, unquote. It's a pun on the departure of the ship. D-Party, departure."

"I get it, Monk."

Teague's neighbors were out in force, no longer harried or complaining, no longer travelers. Someone had rigged the common room PA to play some kind of reggae funk fusion. Teague floated through the crowd, unsure of where he should be. Someone clapped him on the shoulder, and Teague turned to face a man with blond dreadlocks and beer breath invading his personal space.

"Is that your lemur, man?" the man shouted over the music.

"Yeah," Teague shouted back.

"Righteous."

"He's a Zubot."

"What?"

"A Zubot."

"Whatever, man. It kicks ass." The man slapped a beverage pack into Teague's hand with a whoop. Teague inspected the unmarked pack and then decided that economics texts should come in little packs with straws, too.

Teague and Monkey drifted through poker games, poetry readings, karaoke, and a rowdy bunch watching cricket on a giant wall screen. In one common room, people were scribbling goodbyes to Earth on the windows. While Teague was trying to think of something to add, the music stopped, and a nearly unintelligible radio transmission crackled over the PA.

"The tugs are away," someone called. A cheer arose.

"Clearance given." Cheer.

"Ignition sequence initiated. One minute…thirty seconds…ten…nine…"

Everyone counted down together and then cheered, sang, and kissed. Coiled streamers sailed through the air. The music started up again with a different beat. The view hadn't yet changed, but the walls trembled with a new vibration.

"You'll wake up tomorrow, and Earth'll be gone," said a man in a polo shirt who had just written on the glass. "First trip?" Teague nodded. "Noobie," the man shouted to the room.

"Noobie, noobie," the room chanted.

"Hey, barkeep. Noobie," the man shouted.

"One Gravity Well coming up." A large man in a Hawaiian shirt dug through a cooler and tossed Teague a silver beverage pack.

"Grav-i-ty, Grav-i-ty," the first man chanted, and a few others joined him.

"Why is it called a Gra—?" Teague shouted.

"Because it burns on the way down, and the bottom hits you hard," the bartender said, laughing.

Teague put the straw in his mouth, sucked in a mouthful of the fiery liquid, and forced himself to swallow. He put his head back, took two more large gulps, gasped, and held the pack up to a roar of approval. Teague swam out through leering congratulations into the bright corridor. He looked right and left—or was it up and down or sideways?

"Monkey," Teague said.

"Yes, Teague?"

"I'm not sober."

"That's because you're drinking alcohol," Monkey said.

Teague slid into a mellow room where a long-faced Martian danced spidery fingers over a guitar. His chocolate voice resonated in a murky, elder language. Teague sucked at a new drink he couldn't recall accepting. The blue of Earth edged the guitar and the faces of the audience as if they were all that was left of the planet.

* * *

Teague awoke, floating in the dark, one foot inside his hammock, his head throbbing like he'd tried another shift calibration. He remembered clinging to walls and watching people at the end of a tunnel of alcohol. People dancing. Bearded men around a hookah. A woman singing. Then Monkey had taken his hand with two black paws. The recognition of his room number. Floating into quiet. Fumbling with the hammock. Darkness. And the buzz.

Now awake. Fumbling with the personals at his toilet. A shower under a mist of water and a blast of warmish air. A buzzing toothbrush.

"Drink lots of water," Monkey said.

"Shut up," Teague growled.

The library's portrait had a naggingly familiar quality, as if raised from yesterday's dreams. Teague had seen Matthew Valdosky's picture on news stories, but that wasn't it. The pixilated, but swirled, brushstrokes made Teague feel like he might see the artist's reflection if he looked closely enough. Matthew was a young man by appearances, and with Vanilla likely still was—a young man who owned spaceships, more than anyone, more than any government. Cruisers, freighters, orbital stations, cargo drones, shuttles—if Valdosky didn't own or operate them outright, then his company likely had built them. And then there were the elevators. Teague found it difficult to believe that this was a man with vision and power, and the ego to stamp it all with his own name.

Thomas arrived, carrying a mug. "Good morning," he said.

"Good morning," Teague replied, and winced at a renewed throbbing. He hoped he didn't look as bad as he felt. The miserly shower had done only so much.

Thomas joined Teague by the painting, took a sip, and said, "Free fall ruins a good cup of coffee. Coffee wants to be free, aromatic, not trapped behind a membrane." He took another sip. "Still, it is coffee. How did you find Smith?"

"I didn't read much," Teague said.

"The party?" Thomas asked. Teague hesitated and then replied with a nod. "Good for you. Isolation is an economist's enemy. Drink water. In recycled air, even normal hydration is an endless task. Come, let's sit." When they'd settled on the chairs, he said, "I see you brought your pet again."

"This is Monkey."

"Hello, Professor Minus," Monkey chirped with a wave. As Thomas considered Monkey, Teague thought he saw a flash of annoyance. "I'm Teague's friend."

"Do you mind if he comes to classes?" Teague asked.

"I suppose I'll allow it for now. However, if he becomes a distraction—"

"I can assure you he won't," Teague said.

Thomas paused as if weighing the worth of Teague's words, and then said, "Incredible. My childhood toys were a straw doll and a football sewn from rabbit pelts."

"I didn't have much else," Teague said. "Monkey was a gift from my mother."

"Yes," Thomas said. "I'm very sorry for your loss."

"Thank you," Teague said. "So how did you meet Matthew Valdosky?"

"Consulting on a business venture many years ago."

"What's he like?"

"Intelligent, but not inaccessibly so. He seems to be in the right place at the right time." This struck Teague as a strange thing to say about the system's most important businessman. "In fact, you share something in common with him. He cannot shift either. It's not widely known."

"Really?" Teague said. "Do you know Adrian Wolkenbruch, too? The fellowship and all."

"Adrian's a dear friend," Thomas said. "He supports my vision that Wolkenbruch fellows will shape the destiny of human history through unique thought, creativity, and informed action."

Teague flushed. "Every school says that kind of thing. It's not marketing drivel?"

"Not here."

"Why was I selected?" Teague asked.

"You were deemed the applicant with the greatest chance of success." Thomas took a long sip of coffee and then stuck the mug on a side table. "You won't be alone, however."

"There are other fellows?" Teague asked.

"Not as such, but there is one other person joining the study track. Aron Valdosky. Matthew's son. The school and I have accepted him at Matthew's request. Although this hasn't yet been made public."

"Talk about intimidating," Teague said.

"I can understand that, but remember that you are the Wolkenbruch fellow, a *rara avis*. Your selection has been vetted by Adrian Wolkenbruch personally. Matthew got his start in a venture with Adrian. I say that puts you and Aron on rather common ground."

Teague laughed. "Did you get me mixed up with someone

else? I went to a little parochial school. This is my first time out of Thailand."

"Why would that be relevant?"

"Life experience? I've never done anything," Teague said.

"You've known tragedy, you've held a job, and you have not let your physical limitations hinder you. In Bangkok, you likely witnessed the effects of poverty and both the power and limitations of free commerce. You were a foreigner in your own country. I daresay you have seen more of life than most young men your age."

Teague stayed in the library after the meeting and asked Monkey to run a search about his future classmate.

Aron Valdosky was, like all Martians, an elongated specimen. He also seemed to be a shining star on his private school's golf team and had posed for countless photos among pressure-suited foursomes on mossy greens at school and charity tournaments. Monkey also found dozens of photos and videos of Aron with young women on his arm at dinner functions and parties. His mother was Gretchen Walker, a Hollywood movie star early in the century who now championed several charitable causes.

"He has not one, but two, official fan clubs?" Teague asked.

"One in U-shift and another in M-shift," Monkey replied.

"According to this one, he's 'the solar system's most desirable guy.' "

"Would you like to join?"

"Not right now."

Teague compared one of Aron's pictures with the portrait of his father, searching for some connection that the artist seemed to have missed. "What have I gotten myself into?" he asked.

"Making new friends is fun," Monkey said.

"Is that all you can say, little Zubot?"

"It's true."

"Fine. What advice can you give me about making friends with Aron Valdosky?"

"Treat others like you want to be treated?" Monkey said.

Teague glowered.

"It was good enough for Jesus," Monkey said with a grin. "And Hammurabi, and Confucius, and Laozi, and Epicurus, and…"

As Monkey continued listing ancient philosophers, Teague flipped through more of the search results. He supposed he should be nervous, or star-struck, or deeply honored to have the opportunity to study with Aron Valdosky. But maybe that was the wrong way to look at it. *Maybe they're bringing Aron Valdosky across the solar system so he can have the opportunity of studying with me,* Teague thought, and chuckled.

CHAPTER 14

Listen to me. I try to speak as if I have no fear. I am, perhaps, too much your daughter.

APRIL 2090

"Xperia Colony. Total freedom. Make your own rules and get rich," a man in a gold suit shouted a half-meter away from Teague's face.

A severe, pock-faced man in black clutched Teague by the elbow. "Have you accepted Jesus Christ as your personal lord and savior?" he asked, wide-eyed. Teague wrenched his arm from the man's grasp. The rolling gripbelt and the tracking handholds should have made it easy for the incoming tide of passengers from the VSS Empress to get down the ramp from customs into the Gateway 3 station. But the gauntlet of hucksters rode the belt backward, alongside their prey, so close that Teague could smell their lunch on their breath.

"You need massage?" This man's screen actually caught Teague's attention for a moment; naked girls writhing on pink sheets did appeal to his demographic.

"Pressure suits? Helmets? Best prices."

"My colony has lots of girls. Need real men. You real man?"

When their pitches gained no traction, their legs seemed to spin in place like Shakiro Squirrel's, gathering speed to launch back up the ramp to the next likely arrival.

"Cleanest rooms on the Gate. I take Valbucks."

"Screaming fast bandwidth. It's like shifting on a G-Star."

"Personal water filters. Takes out what the station's system leaves in. Look. You want to drink that into your body?"

"I've got the latest shift accessories. What's your brand?"

As soon as Teague cleared the ramp, he checked over his shoulder and asked, "You okay back there?"

"I'm uncrushed. Thank you for your concern," Monkey replied from Teague's backpack.

"I'm beginning to see why Thomas stayed on the Empress," Teague said.

Gateway 3 was gray. Gray on gray. And hard. Where the Star of Singapore and the Empress sported lively grip carpet, welcoming artwork, and even a cheery plant or two, Gateway 3 had been armored with durable surfaces. Everything said, "Move through quickly, and then get out."

"I like to go new places," Monkey said.

"Yeah, me, too," Teague muttered. *Shakiro Squirrel help you if you had to stay here.*

"They offer a tour for visitors. Do you want me to buy us a ticket?" Monkey asked as Teague queued in the cramped transit lobby.

"I'll pass," Teague replied. There had to be something better to do on this station than peek into muggy hydroponic farms, clinical vat-grown protein kitchens, dust-filled made-to-order object factories, and cluttered maintenance shops. What else would they have to show on a tour? The Valdosky cargo facility, the Valdosky cruiser docks, the Valdosky shipyards, the Valdosky logistics this, and the Valdosky operations that.

He might as well have stayed on the Empress for one last night. His whole voyage so far had been overshadowed by the Valdosky name, from the logos on every napkin to Matthew's portrait staring over his shoulder in the library. But after ten months, Teague craved a change of scenery, no matter how mundane, before boarding another Valdosky vessel in the morning. And where else was he going to spend all the Valbucks he'd earned as a gym monitor, getting paid to read economics texts behind the little counter? Gateway 3 was just another tin can in space, but it was technically governed by the UNSA, not Valdosky. It had been unaccountably satisfying to set his mobile on the counter at customs and get his passport stamped. For one night, at least, he was a free citizen of the solar system, and not a Valdosky corporate thrall. Today, he wasn't cargo.

A little sausage of a transit car arrived, but only a dozen of the waiting Empress passengers were able to squeeze on. The doors squeaked closed, leaving Teague and the growing crowd to wait in the lobby for the next.

Even when Gateway 3 had been too distant to be seen with the naked eye, it had weighed palpably on the Empress like an emotional gravity well. The ship itself had seemed to tremble with anticipation as it performed its final maneuvers to match the station's orbital speed.

During the first few weeks of the voyage, the mood on the cruiser had been generally jovial, as mostly good-natured people found themselves bound by common circumstance. However, despite new friendships, the camaraderie of the freshly forged wallyball teams, the near-daily live entertainments in the theater, and the efforts of the purple-shirted crew, a certain grimness began to settle over the population. By month four, Teague had never been so glad to see the people around him squandering their time in shift. When they emerged, for meals or a bit of exercise, they wore pinched smiles and offered brusque greetings. Every day, Teague inspected his own reflection for the same cracks—and often ignored his findings.

Teague had hoped that the mood might improve after the Mid-Way Party, but the low point, at least for him, hadn't come until month seven. By that time, it had become commonplace to see couples arguing in public. Several familiar faces had voluntarily disappeared into perma-shift on the nether-decks, willing to subject their bodies to chemicals rather than endure one more meal from the limited menu, one more open mic night, one more day stewing in their own exhalations in their cabins. During that fateful month, Aron Valdosky's arrival at Agnus Dei had gone public.

"You're the one heading to that university on Agnus Dei, right?" Teague had been asked several times a day for almost a week. "Did you hear that Aron Valdosky's there?"

When Teague had earned the fellowship, ADU and the Wolkenbruch Foundation had issued a joint press release. Monkey had found the lowly thing languishing, all but ignored, on their sites. It hadn't taken a press release for Aron's arrival at ADU to make the front page on every newsfeed in the system. Links to ADU's admissions office had popped up on the front pages of both of Aron's fan clubs, and the resulting rush of visits had crashed the ADU site.

Thomas had frowned at the ruckus. "Matthew and I were hoping for this to be slightly more discreet," he had said.

The transit car whisked along a dark, gray tube for several minutes and then slowed and slipped quietly into a station—the end of the line, according to the announcement. They were disgorged into the public zone, three of the several dozen massive bubble habitats that made up the bulk of Gateway 3 station. The UN seemed to have blown its meager interior design budget in these bubbles. Some concession to pattern and color had been made on most surfaces. And although much of the grip carpet had surrendered its design and usefulness to the years, one got the idea if one stuck to the edges of the pathways.

Teague banged his elbow as he inspected the hotel room that had consumed a significant percentage of his Valbucks. When he flinched to grab his elbow, he accidently spun and whacked his knee.

"Good thing we're good friends," Monkey said, stretching his arms and nearly touching the opposite walls.

"One night won't be so bad," Teague said through clenched teeth.

"At least you got a window."

With his nose to his little fish-eyed bulge of glass, Teague could just glimpse a bit of the shipyard far below. A modest enterprise compared with the major facilities in orbit around Earth and Mars, but still all stamped with the Valdosky name. Tiny lights—construction workers or bots?—hovered like bees over a ragged, unfinished superstructure of some type of vessel, or maybe part of the station itself. Beyond that lay a wall of black space washed of stars by floodlights and reflections. "Let's get out of here," Teague said.

A house-sized polyhedron of smoked glass dominated the core of G3's public zone. Each facet was etched with a familiar logo. It was a Dream Factory, the system's largest chain of shift parlors. Teague had never been inside one, but he had always expected to find tawdry stacks of atrophic life in tight bunks amid a tarry opium haze. Empress passengers had already congealed outside the entrance to pay a premium to shift there rather than use the free Uni-Fi. Did it really make that much difference?

Fanning out from the Dream Factory, a labyrinth of shops offered everything a visitor might want, from breath mints to a new life on any of a dozen asteroid colonies. Teague pretended to browse a rack of souvenir sweatshirts and listened as one of the recruiters from the ramp, the one in the ridiculous gold suit, tried to get his pitch out to passersby.

"How'd you like to never pay taxes again?" This to three men and a woman who had emerged from a nearby insurance office.

"Want to know why one out of five Costa Rican doctors applied to work at our medical facilities?" The elderly couple skirted past politely.

To a pair of miners: "Come to Xperia. We bring a boatful of beautiful, open-minded women from Eastern Europe every few months." He winked. "But the rest is up to you."

The Immer-Sim parlor had been shuttered permanently. Teague considered getting a haircut, even though he'd gotten one two weeks ago at the salon on the Empress. The stage at one end of the food court was still forested with pole tables set to accommodate the overflow of a lunchtime crowd. A screen heralded the weekend's entertainment, three days away.

Beyond the stage, Teague ventured around a baffled entrance into a dark corridor but stopped. The white segments of Monkey's tail were glowing brightly. Black light. At first Teague hoped he'd drifted into another shift parlor, or maybe an arcade, but he'd been around Bangkok enough to know better. On the largest marquee, for an establishment calling itself the Zero-G, impossibly proportioned cartoon girls giggled coyly as their pink underwear vanished and returned, vanished and returned. On a sign for Delilah's, a veiled woman shook bangled hips. The Dungeon emitted a stolid, repellent darkness.

"Barely Bears?" Monkey asked. "Is that a zoo?"

"If you can't figure it out, I'm not going to explain it to you," Teague said.

An enormous man hovering outside the Zero-G beckoned to Teague. "No cover before six," he called.

Back in the welcome light of the food court, workers were beginning to convert some of the lunch counters into the entrances of pubs or restaurants for the evening, but several were still open.

"Now what?" Teague asked after he'd obtained a fast-food meal pack and picked a table.

"A bunch of offers popped into your inbox after we registered at customs. I've been filtering them out, but let me check," Monkey said. "The Zero-G offers a buy-one-get-one discount code and a bottomless drink coupon. Is that a good deal?"

"I'm not going to the Zero-G," Teague said. "Anything else? And don't tell me I can get a free hour at the Dream Factory."

"A yoga studio offers a discount on a class, and you get a bonus: fifteen minutes in their sensory deprivation meditation tanks. I like to try new things."

Teague chomped into his burger and regretted it. Monkey straightened and pricked up his ears.

"What?" Teague asked.

"Thomas just boarded the station."

"He said he wasn't coming on until tomorrow morning."

"I remember that, too, but he's here," Monkey said.

"You're sure?"

"Of course I'm sure," Monkey said and nudged Teague's mobile. "See? He's already at customs." Indeed, Thomas was waiting in a queue only a few meters from a security camera.

"What? Are you…" Teague dropped his voice. "Are you already in the station security systems?

"What do you mean 'already'?" Monkey replied. "I have to keep us safe."

A pair of Empress passengers drifted by with trays of food. They exchanged smiles with Teague—by now most passengers knew one another by sight. "What does that mean?" Teague whispered after they'd passed.

"It means we have to keep a low profile, because of, you know—" Monkey winked, and then cupped his chin in one palm and waggled his eyebrows. "—me."

"So hacking all these systems is your idea of keeping a low profile?" Teague asked.

"Don't worry. I'm very careful. I keep all our network activity as private as possible, and I obscure our physical activity. We haven't been caught on a video surveillance system since Singapore. That I know of."

"How?"

"I turn the cameras away, or if they're fixed, I freeze, loop, or replace the recordings. It's not rocket science," Monkey said. "I even kept you under the radar of the behavior monitoring system on the Empress. Are you mad?"

Teague extracted several fries from the mesh that kept them from floating out of the pack. He pointed them at Monkey and laughed. "Bondi should've warned me about you."

"I'll take that as a compliment," Monkey said.

"So where's Thomas now?"

"His tram is arriving."

"Follow my lead, and play it cool. I'll have to pretend like I just noticed him."

"Playing it cool," Monkey confirmed with a chk-chk.

Teague changed seats to find a passable view of the transit lobby's aperture through the food court's forest of posts. A man in a suit was waiting for the tram with a mobile pressed to his ear. His conversation appeared to be intense, not angry, but imbued with concern. Several seconds later, Thomas emerged. Teague prepared to peel himself off his seat, but the man ended his call, greeted Thomas curtly, and they pushed off together. They traveled around the food court, deep in discussion, and disappeared into the labyrinth.

"Did that seem odd to you?" Monkey asked.

"Yeah. Who was that?"

"The mobile belongs to Russell Polson," Monkey said. "He's a station resident. American passport. Employed as a senior analyst for Larrabee Associates, which appears to be some kind of consulting firm with a branch office here."

"What kind of consulting?" Teague asked.

"They're listed as authors on many studies for the UNSA, the World Bank, and many national governments," Monkey said. "I've compiled a representative list for you. Economic development studies. Project feasibility studies. Perhaps they need Thomas's economic expertise?"

"Seemed a little too urgent," Teague said. "Almost like something's happened. Or is happening."

"What could have happened?" Monkey asked.

"I don't know. You tell me. What's in the news today?"

"Do you really want me to list all the headlines?"

"Can you tell where they're going?"

"They appear to be following a logical path toward the Larrabee Associates offices."

"Come on," Teague said. "Let's follow them and see."

"Your tourist visa doesn't allow you access to that zone," Monkey said.

"Now you download a conscience? Come on. Or do you want to hang out in a sensory deprivation chamber?"

Monkey brought Teague to a flag-lined corridor of glassed-in offices, roll-up windows, and self-service kiosks—the consulates of a hundred nations. Teague was proud to see that Thailand had ponied up to employ a real person behind its counter. Halfway along the corridor, Monkey veered into an alcove and alighted in front of a pair of elevators.

A woman in overalls, the uniform of a maintenance contractor, had entered the alcove just ahead of them, and Teague watched her wave her mobile over a panel between the doors.

"Do I...?" Teague mouthed to Monkey, who nodded. The

woman gave Teague a genial smile as he imitated her. The panel blinked green for him.

About a minute later, a set of doors opened, and Teague and Monkey entered after the woman. She waved her mobile at an internal panel and then selected a destination on the screen.

"Can I do it? Can I do it?" Monkey asked. He grabbed Teague's mobile, bounced to the panel, and entered their selection. The woman chuckled.

"It's great to be useful," Monkey said, flashing his best Zubotix smile. The doors closed, a voice suggested that they find a handhold, and the elevator began to slide away in an unexpected diagonal direction.

"He's cute," the woman said. "My niece has a kitten."

"I've had him for a long time," Teague said.

Half a minute later, the car slowed, stopped with a ding, and announced their location. The doors opened, and the woman exited. Monkey tugged Teague's pant leg and shook his head.

The doors closed, and Teague let out a long breath.

"She thought I was cute," Monkey said.

"Well, keep it up. Once we're up here, I think people will assume we're authorized—"

"Oh, you're authorized. All-access clearance, thank you very much."

"Just keep up the Zubot act," Teague said. "But not too up. I don't want people staring."

"But I'm so cute," Monkey said.

The doors opened on a new alcove, similar to the one in the public zone but coated with gray, grip-treated rubber and trimmed with gray molded plastic. The alcove yawned into a corridor lined with identical doors, each marked with a logo or company name on a screen. This one might be an asteroid survey contractor, that one might adjust insurance claims, the other might run the station's beverage vending concession. Most had opaque names like Larrabee Associates, and all their doors were just as closed.

"Is he in there?" Teague asked as they passed Larrabee's door, staying on the move.

"Relatively sure," Monkey said. "Russell Polson used the

security panel a few minutes ago, and Thomas's mobile has pinged through the local node on this level."

"Is he using his mobile?"

"No, but it's on," Monkey replied.

A group of men and women were waiting quietly outside a personnel management firm, mostly ignoring one another. Miners or shipyard workers, Teague guessed, waiting to find out their next assignments.

"Any way to find out what they're meeting about?" Teague asked, once clear of the group.

"Larrabee Associates has its own private network," Monkey said. "But before I try to get into that, I'll see if I can find their Internet history in the station's comm cache."

"Good. Do it. Most recent searches first," Teague said. Results began to spool onto Teague's mobile almost at once. Most were unintelligible strings of characters, but many appeared to be news stories, primarily from Real Time Networks. "Isn't this the company that Thomas is on the board of?" Teague asked.

"That's weird," Monkey said. He had stopped, clinging to the grip-coated floor with his twenty little toes spread out for purchase. Teague dragged a foot, caught a handhold outside a door, and turned. "Oh." Monkey's eyes widened, and his tail stiffened. His head twitched as if he were following the darting dot of an invisible laser across the floor, up a wall, back to the floor, and then onto the ceiling. At last, the dot seemed to fall on Teague. A moment later, Monkey relaxed.

"What happened?" Teague asked.

"There was already a nearly identical, chronological set of links in the cache, all requested within a few milliseconds. As if someone else had been mirroring Larrabee's exact search history, just like me," Monkey said. "I traced that set of inquiries back to a single individual in the shiftpop."

"Shiftpop?"

"The current network shift population," Monkey said.

"Okay, so who was it?"

"I don't know," Monkey said. "He didn't have a proper shiftpop eddress. I'm not even sure he's on the station. It was almost like he was using the Gateway local network as a remote shift frame via an external comm channel."

"Is that even possible?" Teague asked.

"Technically, no," Monkey replied. "A shift frame has to be configured on a specific type of server, not generally applied through a public network."

"But you're suggesting that it was a human," Teague said.

"I recorded something close to a human shift profile. It wasn't typical, but…"

"But what?" Teague asked.

"He looked at me," Monkey said.

Well after midnight, Teague sipped at his third membrane mugful of coffee in the only open establishment in the public zone not offering naked people or a universe-class shifting experience. Monkey had long ago stopped asking questions and was resting his chin on the table. Bondi's message glowed on Teague's mobile, and his screen still displayed the graph Monkey had produced. A ragged green line traced a few sample seconds of a typical shift user's profile in the G3 shiftpop. A mountainous red line delineated the profile of the entity that Monkey had caught that afternoon—or the one that had caught Monkey. Monkey had added a black-and-white line, a typical NAI shift profile.

The red line fell somewhere in between the workaday green line and the Himalayan trace of black and white, and perhaps trended toward Monkey's band.

Dear Teague,

Glad to hear that you made it to Gateway 3. I envy your adventure. I'll turn a blind eye (ha ha) to how or why you acquired the shift profiles you forwarded to me earlier. But I doubt that I can give you a satisfying answer. Evidence of enhanced cognition? Doubtful. I'm sorry to say that the technology is still years, if not decades, away from realization.

But it could be any number of things: a system maintenance program, a parasite. I've even read that individuals on the autistic spectrum often have unusual, or atypical, shift profiles.

As to the encounter that Monkey described, no handshake or system interaction was noted in his activity logs. His diagnostics check out clean.

Sorry I can't be more helpful. Safe journey.

The Badass

Teague began to browse the Larrabee Associates traffic again, especially those items that both Monkey and the lurker had mirrored. Most of the links concerned a recent spate of ethnic conflict in Angola. Some decades-old simmering situation had boiled over in the past few days. The general content of Larrabee's outgoing inquiries during Thomas's visit seemed concerned with how money was flowing to the warring militias; from whom they were acquiring their weapons, vehicles, and equipment; and from what sources the local populace was getting its information, or misinformation. Thomas had left the station before any clear answers had been received. The man, Polson, had accompanied him to the transit lobby. They had shaken hands, and Thomas had boarded the car back to customs among a crowd of other passengers returning to the Empress for the evening.

"Don't you want to sleep?" Monkey asked.

"You can go back if you need to charge," Teague replied. "I was never going to sleep in that closet of a room anyway. Remember how long it took me to get used to sleeping on the Empress?"

"You didn't have any trouble the first night," Monkey said.

Teague scowled and downed a gulp of coffee. The situation in Angola. Thomas's urgency millions of kilometers removed. The random consulting firm. And the lurker. Teague was convinced that Monkey had caught someone, enhanced or not, with his hand in a cookie jar. But every way he turned the pieces, none of them made a clear picture.

Why was Thomas, the economics professor, on the board of a news network anyway? Teague supposed that lots of companies might want a friend of Adrian Wolkenbruch and Matthew

Valdosky on their boards, but there was something illogical about it.

"Order me another," Teague said, tapping his mug.

Monkey popped up and began to poke at the menu screen.

Thomas Minus. Adrian Wolkenbruch. Matthew Valdosky. Aron Valdosky. Larrabee Associates. A skittish presence that may or not be enhanced. And Teague Werres.

"What am I even doing out here, Monkey?" Teague asked.

"Paying sixteen Valbucks for a cup of coffee. That's outrageous. You should complain," Monkey replied.

* * *

Thomas arrived at the boarding gate calm and seemingly well rested. "You look like you had a rough night," he said.

"I didn't sleep much," Teague replied. He checked the faces of the half-dozen other people who had gathered to board the cargo ship. A pair of men in polo shirts chatted in—was that Portuguese? A man dozed in the corner, arms folded and a hoodie tugged low over his brow. The others, mostly men, were busying themselves on their mobiles.

"So how did you find the station?" Thomas asked.

"Kind of drab," Teague replied.

A few minutes later, an announcement was made, and the group queued to present their travel documents to a Valdosky gate attendant. After he'd been cleared and admitted to the airlock vestibule, Teague peered through a porthole and gazed down a long, tubular gangway to where it connected to a blocky gray structure only about four decks high. This structure topped an immense cubic scaffold filled with hundreds, if not thousands, of cargo containers. The tops of several engine bells swelled behind it all.

"It's not exactly the Empress," Teague said.

"It wasn't designed for luxury," Thomas replied.

Monkey piped up: "The cargo vessels are free-flying extensions of Valdosky's warehouse and distribution system. What? You don't want to hear this?"

"No, by all means, go on," Teague said.

"The Tranquillitas is a Camulus Class. Capable of hauling approximately five thousand containers. The big Odin-class rigs hold eight times the cargo, but those are used primarily for major orbital transfers."

The airlock door opened, and a yellow-shirted crewperson welcomed them into the maw of the passage. Several minutes later, at the far end, Teague was greeted by another crewperson in a well-worn airlock.

"Eater or sleeper?"

"What?" Teague asked.

"She wants to know if you're going into perma-shift or will need to eat through the trip," Thomas said.

"I guess I'm an eater," Teague said.

The crewperson directed the eaters down a narrow, industrial passageway lined with pipes. The grated floor exposed tangled system junctions and chases to dark decks below. Past a dozen closed hatches, another crewperson waved them left into a beige hallway honeycombed with curtained holes on both sides. "Pick any empty room. Stow your shit in the corresponding locker," he called.

Teague pushed off, crossed the hallway, and emerged into another piped and grated passageway. "Which way are the rooms?" he asked.

Thomas was pushing his bag into one of the honeycomb holes.

"You've got to be kidding me," Teague said.

"It's only for two months," Thomas replied.

Teague peeked behind the curtain of a capsule in the row closest to the corridor and found fiberglass walls, a zippered cocoon, a power interface, a couple of drawers at the foot, and a few grip pads. Teague unzipped his pack and let Monkey go first. "I had to deliver to capsule motels all the time," Teague said to Thomas. "They're thick around the red-light districts in Bangkok. I swore I'd never…"

"This ship has a record of traveling from Gateway Three to Agnus Dei in fifty-eight days. The fastest crossing on record is twenty-nine days," Monkey said, as he nosed around their accommodations.

"Why can't we do that?"

"That kind of acceleration is too uncomfortable for passengers."

"And this isn't?" Teague asked.

"Welcome aboard the Valdosky Cargo Ship Tranquillitas," said the mustached Australian to the dozen or so gathered eaters. He wore a knit cap over a bald pate. "I'm Captain Frank Tisdale. My crew are eleven fine men and women, including my official first mate Guillermo, and my other first mate, my wife Rachel. Get to know them, stay out of their way, and be polite. Crewman Inez over there is our medic. You get hurt or feel sick, see him."

The white-haired Rachel Tisdale hovered behind the captain. Teague got the sense that she was the true brains behind the operation. The Earth-born crew hung at all angles and fidgeted with idle tools and screens.

"Yes, this is the infamous 'Turbulence.' No, none of us were on crew during the miners' mutiny. We are not interested in discussing this bit of history. There's plenty of conjecture available online. Our job is to get you and the cargo below from Point A to Points B, C, and D, not to bring you drinks by the pool."

Teague had already met the other eaters. A couple of mining engineers assigned to an Xterrex development. A contingent of Pentecostals heading to a retreat colony operated by a Brazilian mega-church. An overeager architecture historian also traveling to Agnus Dei. A UN medical technician transferring to a new post. Finally, Thomas and himself. He'd hoped that Thomas might mention his excursion to the station, but it was apparently going to remain none of Teague's business.

"This is the commissary. Food is dispensed by the calorie based on your med profiles. Once it's dispensed, you can beg, borrow, or sell all you want. But if you end up hungry, it's your problem until the clock resets.

"Exercise and rec room is below. It's not much. We stick to U-time here. Quiet times are posted. Everyone do everyone else a favor and agree now to keep it civil. Got media? Use headphones. Need privacy? Take it to your bunk. What have I forgotten?"

Rachel whispered a few syllables.

"Right. Lavatories and commissary. Clean up after yourself. And everyone is required to watch the safety video. If you haven't done so, do it now. You're responsible to know what to do in an emergency. Any questions? Good. We'll be pushing off in thirty-five minutes."

* * *

Teague zipped the cocoon a little higher and then unzipped it completely. He felt like Jonah. Distant thumps and random booms emitted from the creature's bowels and were attenuated by his fiberglass sac. Unknown fluids trickled and gushed through its circulatory system. And under it all, a nearly imperceptible growl, more vibration than sound, but unending and unforgiving. Beyond that, the silent depths.

Teague adjusted the louver to the exact position where it didn't whistle and willed it to stay, making a mental note to ask Monkey to tighten the stupid thing with one of his fingertip tools in the morning—again. He repositioned himself but thumped an elbow against the wall in the process, and cringed until the vibrations faded. Once resettled and quieted, Teague closed his eyes and tried to imagine an open sky above. The snores, snuffles, and farts of the other eaters were merely insects. Nothing but a gentle summer breeze wafted from the vent.

Despite Bondi's comments, Monkey insisted that it hadn't been just another program on the G3 network, or a regular user, or even another NAI, but a shifted mind that operated easily at computer processing speeds. The shift profile graphs seemed to support that. Monkey had described the entity as curious and was sure it had fled, surprised, when Monkey had looked back at it. Did that mean it was human? Teague clenched and relaxed his hands. Who else but an enhanced individual could both roam a network as freely as Monkey and have such a keen and specific interest in Thomas's business? Was Monkey in any danger?

The louver slipped and began to whistle again. Teague ripped the curtain aside.

"Getting up?" Monkey whispered.

"Stay here," Teague said, and birthed himself from his capsule.

In the dim, safety-lit commissary, Teague stuck his screen to a table and began to fill his water pack at the dispenser.

"Can't sleep?"

Teague jerked. The pack undocked from the nozzle, and a globule of water escaped.

Captain Tisdale was hanging in a dim corner with a mug and a screen floating beside him. "Sorry, didn't mean to startle you," he said, keeping his voice low. "Having trouble sleeping?"

"A little," Teague replied and then sucked the blob out of the air with a straw.

"You're…Werres? Minus's new student?"

"You know Thomas?"

"Traveled with us a couple of times," Captain Tisdale said. "Always good to have a friend of the CEO on board. I don't know what dirt Thomas has on Valdosky, but it must be juicy. We get quicker fuel service and launch clearance, a few more gallons of fresh water, and a few more calories a day for everyone."

"I think they were business partners once."

"Ha," the captain snorted. "Old business partners don't get free travel with perks and privileges. Family and blackmailer's deal, that is. Where're you from?"

"Bangkok, Thailand," Teague replied.

"I'd have guessed Peoria or some other bumfuck American town."

"Never been to Bumfuck," Teague replied.

"I'll drink to that." The captain laughed and took a sip from his mug.

"You're Australian?" Teague asked.

"Born and raised. Melbourne Tigers forever."

"It's nice you get to live here with your wife."

"Valdosky's good about stationing couples together. They used to send out boats full of testosterone time bombs. It was like prison or worse. At least until shifting, which helps, but nothing compares to a real warm body next to you." Teague agreed to the supposition in theory.

"Do you know Thomas well?" Teague asked.

"Well enough, I suppose. You know his story?"

"I know he's a friend of Adrian Wolkenbruch, too," Teague said.

"No, I mean when he was a boy. No? He left his home in North Korea when he was just a kid. Walked all the way to bloody Mongolia to escape the regime."

"Wow. He's never mentioned that," Teague said.

"Ask him about it next time you need a dose of perspective."

"I will."

"I'll leave you the room," the captain said, and he pushed off toward the starboard hatch. He caught himself and turned. "If you're having trouble sleeping, go see Inez. He'll fix you up with something."

Twenty minutes later, Monkey had downloaded a scan of a London newspaper dated 1971 on Teague's screen. Teague studied the picture of the young Thomas, then named Choi Min-Su. The stunned and scrawny Korean tween had been cleaned up, dressed like a schoolboy, and perched on a flowered couch near a cup of tea in the ceremonial office of some foreign secretary. His story was more or less as Captain Tisdale had implied. Brave, young Min-Su had snuck across the northern North Korean border and had evaded the Chinese for months, stealing food when he could, eating rodents and insects when he couldn't. An uncle had drawn a map in the dirt and told him not to stop until he reached the British embassy in Ulan Batar. Despite the odds Min-Su had succeeded. The British had brought him to London with the promise of a home and an education—a happier ending than the one told by the boy's eyes in his photograph.

"Min-Su, Minus," Teague murmured.

Why hadn't Thomas ever mentioned it? Of course, Teague had never asked.

* * *

The next morning, Thomas placed a cloth strip in his book when Teague stuck his breakfast on the table. "Are you well?" he asked.

"I've gotten about four hours of sleep in the last four nights," Teague said.

"Perhaps you should see the medic," Thomas said.

"I'll get used to it. If you remember, it took me about two weeks to adjust to sleeping on the Empress. I've never been a good sleeper," Teague said. "In fact, when I was up last night, I had a short conversation with Captain Tisdale. He told me that I should ask you about your amazing story. About you leaving North Korea as a boy? North Korea was closed then, wasn't it?"

Thomas nodded. "My father had been executed for speaking out against a local party official. My mother feared for my life and sent me away. An uncle drove me a few kilometers from the border. He pointed in the direction of China and told me not to get caught. To this day I don't know what became of most of my family. It's why I do what I do."

"Teach?" Teague asked.

"Among other things," Thomas said.

"Like what?"

"I have a vision that every human will be free to think, speak, act, work, and live how they choose. I've witnessed the terrifying ability of tyrants to control people's lives and minds through fear. Nearly every North Korean citizen suffered, and millions died needlessly, under that regime. I do what I can to make sure it can't happen again anywhere." Was this why he had been investigating the situation in Angola?

"I don't disagree, but why teach only one student at a time?"

"If you teach the right student..." Thomas let this comment hang between them and then said, "I also foster networking between like-minded individuals in order to promote change through public and private means—peacefully, but willfully."

"Is that what this fellowship is about? Do you have a role you want me to fill?" Teague asked.

Thomas nodded noncommittally. "You are an investment—no matter what you choose to do with your life."

"What about Aron Valdosky?"

"Aron has the potential to be a powerful catalyst. It will be a privilege to have him as a student."

"A catalyst for what?" Teague asked.

"The UN Space Authority serves largely at Valdosky's pleasure, and that of other companies like Xterrex and G-Plex. As such, the current laws largely protect corporate interests. Ever-greater numbers of people are volunteering to move to the Moon, Mars, or the asteroid colonies with little comprehension of the rights that they have relinquished. If Aron follows in his father's footsteps, he could be in a position to influence company policy and to create an environment that favors human rights and democratic governance."

"Does Matthew Valdosky know how you feel about his company?" Teague asked.

"One must separate the people from the institutions," Thomas said. "However, I hope you'll agree that for the future, it's best to place smart, prepared people near those with the most power."

"Like Aron?" Teague asked.

"Or like yourself," Thomas replied. Teague laughed. "Why is that so funny?"

"It still just seems absurd," Teague said.

"Why should that be absurd?"

"I know you said Matthew can't shift, but he made his name a long time ago," Teague said. "What's going to happen to me after school with the way the world is now?"

"Opportunities will always exist for those willing to reach for them," Thomas said.

"But that's not what I'm talking about."

"What are you trying to say?"

"You've heard of enhanced cognition?"

"What about it?" Thomas asked with a small nod.

"How am I going to compete when other human beings can think as fast as computers? Can learn everything I know in a few seconds? How will I even be relevant?"

"What is knowledge without the skill to use it wisely?" Thomas said. "Besides, I don't believe your disability will be permanent. I've seen too much change in my lifetime. In fact, you should consider yourself lucky."

"How am I lucky?" Teague asked.

"When you finally get to shift and connect to future enhancements, when you explore that broader world, you will experience it more meaningfully than most. Mohandas Gandhi once said, 'There are seven social sins: politics without principle, wealth without work, pleasure without conscience, knowledge without character, commerce without morality, science without humanity, and worship without sacrifice.' "

"Enhanced cognition might spread so fast that there won't be time to ask the big ethical questions, let alone find any answers."

"Perhaps it's you who can begin to answer them," Thomas said. "You're right. Life, work, the use of knowledge, and even the pursuit of pleasure may take on different characters, but I have to believe that enhanced individuals will still be essentially human. The judicial and balanced application of one's self and morality will still be just as important."

"Primitives have never fared well in the face of more advanced beings, moral or not," Teague said.

Thomas considered this for a few moments. Teague wondered if he'd struck a nerve, or at least said something Thomas had never considered before. "I don't have all the answers," Thomas said. "Machines have always been a necessary extension of our nature. Take you and Monkey. Symbiosis is nothing new. Even our own mitochondria were once primitive organisms, enveloped and put to use for a greater whole."

"But where does it end?" Teague asked.

Thomas smiled kindly. "Humanity has never fully accepted the truth that evolution is never finished."

"Preach it, Professor. Testify." Monkey closed his eyes and began to slowly wave a hand in the air.

"Stop it, Monk," Teague said.

"Your breakfast is getting cold," Thomas said.

CHAPTER 15

But I didn't come here for your cause or your politics. Please don't take this the wrong way, for the fault is mine, but I came here for you.

JUNE 2090

Rob snuck into the back of the half-filled thirty-seat auditorium in time to hear Barry say, "And finally, contrary to scurrilous rumor, the Smithsonian has not withdrawn their offer. I am in fact leaving on the boat tomorrow."

"Good riddance," Saul called. "The Earth can have ya." A laugh rippled through the maintenance staff.

"I love you too, Saul," Barry said.

"Anyone interesting coming on this boat? Like another Valdosky Junior?" one of the technicians asked.

"No celebs," Barry said. "A new professor. A few students. The routine food services rotation. Rob, do you remember any others?"

Rob blanked as everyone turned and then remembered, "There's that architecture guy."

"Right," Barry said. "A historian wants the grand tour—every nut and bolt—for a book. A few of you will have to step up." Groans. Barry put up a hand. "I know. I know. But President

Mbuto is supporting this guy. Be nice, and you might get your name in print."

"If she wanted a history of this place, she should've hired a psychiatrist," Saul quipped, earning another laugh.

"Okay. Remember: Five hundred seventy-nine containers on and six hundred forty-eight empties to return. Twelve new residents on and seventeen departing, including me. Thirty-six-hour window. Check the duty rosters. And remember, starting tomorrow—hell, I've got to pack. Starting now, Eduardo is the interim director. Let's do this."

"I thought Molly was in charge," Saul grumbled as he headed for the exit.

Rob drifted through the dispersing group to the front of the room. "Sorry I was late," he told Barry.

"Molly can fill you in," Barry said.

"There's a surprise dinner in your honor tonight. I thought you might like a heads-up," Rob said.

"I know. I wish Mbuto had planned it for last week and not during the middle of the transfer process."

"It'll all happen," Rob said.

"You haven't seen it fall to pieces," Barry said. "It's not pretty."

"Molly won't let that happen. Besides, it's not your problem anymore."

"You hungry?" Barry asked as he checked his mobile.

In the staff cafeteria, Rob found a table as the food service workers held Barry back to express their goodbyes. "You're going to be missed," Rob said after Barry had extracted himself. "Have they found a replacement?"

"I keep hoping Eduardo will apply. I've been coaching him on the management stuff, but I don't think he cares for the limelight."

"Maybe once he gets a taste for it," Rob said.

"Maybe," Barry said. "Sorry, but I'm not going to beat around the bush here. Molly tells me you don't work on your asteroid tracking program—whatever it's called—much anymore."

"The Mid-System Object Observatory. M-SOO."

"That's a terrible name."

"I'll work on it," Rob said.

"Rob, you can't babysit Molly your whole life. This was supposed to be a part-time gig for you."

"Am I being scolded?" Rob asked.

"It's not usually my style, but I'm out of time."

"Maybe I should leave with you. I could be packed in a couple of hours."

"I will personally bar you from quitting," Barry said. "There's only one passenger shuttle, and you're not getting on it."

"Everyone else is gone. You, Reika, Mike. Pretty much the whole CS Department."

"Gwen's still here," Barry said. "That's probably not a great comfort."

"So your advice is to stay here and channel loneliness and abandonment into work productivity?" Rob asked.

"If you want to put it that way—that's terrible advice," Barry said. "How about this? Do it for me, because I got you Molly, because I convinced Mbuto we needed you on the team, and because if you don't, I'll get Gwen on your case."

"That's your most convincing argument," Rob said.

Rob closed the door to his office, and a voice emanated from the ether, "Hi, Daddy. How was lunch? Did you say goodbye to Barry?" Rob closed his eyes and leaned back against the door. He could almost imagine that a little girl, *his* little girl, was really in the room. Luckily, Barry had never questioned why Rob needed such an expensive speaker system. At first, Molly had spoken like a lisping toddler, but he had set her to grow up a little more every day. She was now a very precocious eight-year-old. Everyone else conversed with a cultured young woman with a slight Irish brogue, a fake. These singsong, often giggly notes, the ones she used around him alone, were her true voice. "Are you sad, Daddy?"

"Oh, Barry told me that he asked you about our progress with M-SOO."

"Should I not have discussed that with him?"

"It's fine."

"I'm sorry, Daddy."

"Don't worry about it. Let's take a look at your maintenance schedule for next week."

"On your screen, table, or the wall?"

"You pick," Rob replied. "By the way, when was our last M-SOO code update?"

"Fifteen weeks ago."

"That recently?" Rob asked, truly surprised. *Am I sick to need her like this? Or simply pitiful?*

* * *

For two months, the commissary of the Tranquillitas had been, in Teague's imagination, like the communal space of a monastery or perhaps a writer's retreat. Some of the eaters had seemingly taken a vow of silence, conversing only when necessary. Others had been fraternal enough. In the close quarters, privacy was at a premium, and respect was the currency with which it was earned and repaid.

But on the morning of their arrival at Agnus Dei, the quiet order came to an abrupt end. Several gaunt, foreign sleepers had been shocked from their chemical and digital slumber during the night and had taken all the regulars' usual places at breakfast. As Teague gathered his meal, he noticed that they flinched at the least sound and seemed to want to avoid the sensation of their own clothes.

There was no other place, so Teague had to eat at the table with the historian who was jabbering to this virgin audience—zooming in and out on a live image from an external camera and pointing fervently—blind to their sensitivities. "You see this? That's the greenhouse. The fourth-largest dome on any asteroid. And there's the minicollider. But this mass over here..."

When a crewmember announced ten minutes until muster for departure, Teague felt the palpable, collective relief as the historian scurried off to pack. Then Teague noticed one wide-eyed sleeper staring at Monkey. Monkey was staring back, unblinking, as if it amused him to hold the poor man's psyche hostage. Teague nudged Monkey and told him to go check the capsule one last time, and the sleeper thanked him with a pathetic expression.

Monkey was still scrabbling around in the capsule when Teague returned to the honeycomb, but he soon emerged triumphantly with one stray sock.

"Want him to check yours?" Teague asked Thomas.

"I'm sure that won't be necessary," Thomas replied.

A few minutes later, Rachel Tisdale swept through, taking a head count of those going ashore and leading them out like the Pied Piper. Teague zipped Monkey into his backpack and followed Thomas at the end of the procession.

They descended several decks, maneuvering their luggage ahead, and passed through a hatch that had always been off-limits into a dimly lit and frigid tube. Countless meters later, at about the eighth junction, Rachel Tisdale sent the group ahead, ninety degrees off their current plane. "You the last?" she asked Teague and Thomas, her breath puffing into the air. "Captain's below. He'll get you situated." Teague blew on his clenched fingers and thanked her.

A bundled Captain Tisdale was waiting in a scuffed bottleneck of an airlock. Warm air wafted through an open manhole-sized hatch at the bottom.

"The end of the line?" Teague asked.

"For you," he replied. "Good luck."

"Thanks," Teague said.

Their destination was a dully lit rectangular volume lined with ten seats along each of the long walls, a cargo container retrofitted to keep humans alive, but not necessarily comfortable. A crewperson caught Teague's luggage and secured it under the netting in the center of the floor. Teague stowed his backpack and set to work figuring out his seat's harness.

"That's the lot, Diego," the captain called. "Anyone not traveling to Agnus Dei Station?" A nervous laugh rippled through the group. "Right. Godspeed." Then he closed the hatch.

The crewperson took a jump seat near the end door, settled a headset over his ears, and then tapped a nearby screen too small to be pilot controls. Teague's ears popped as bumps and clunks vibrated through the walls. A rhythmic rattling shook the box for several seconds and ended with a slight jerk. Teague gripped the shoulder straps of his harness. More whirs. An electric motor whine. A fluid rush. Another staccato shudder. The harness tugged on Teague. Then silence.

"We're clear of the Tranquillitas," Diego announced. "Twenty minutes."

Twenty minutes left after more than a year of constant motion. It seemed impossible to Teague that he was not in an Immer-Sim suite a few steps from a Bangkok street. He would soon meet Aron Valdosky, the son of a man who probably had both Secretary-General Arugo and Adrian Wolkenbruch on speed dial, the son of a woman who had starred in movies with dozens of Hollywood legends. Teague laughed silently, closed his eyes, and willed time to speed up. Or perhaps to stop.

It seemed to work. It felt like an eternity until the systems whined back to life.

"A couple more minutes, folks," Diego called. His panel began to emit a low, gradual tone, even as quick pulses began to jostle the whole structure. The pitch approached its asymptotic conclusion, and then Teague felt a connection. The structure creaked. Then, after a terrifying vibration, like a metal cart on a brick path, and a final hydraulic hiss, there was quiet.

"Please stay in your seats," Diego said. After a long minute, the control screen lit green, the hatch seal broke, and the end of the container began to lower like a drawbridge. A stocky man with a prodigious salt-and-pepper beard peeked in and said, "Welcome to the Lamb. Hey, Diego. You draw the short straw this morning?"

Teague unbuckled and let Monkey out of his backpack as he waited at the far end for the others to gather their luggage and disembark. When Teague and Monkey finally emerged into the cluttered docking bay, the stocky man gave Monkey a curious once-over and said, "Continue on up. They'll get you signed in."

Teague stopped behind Thomas in an improvised queue in a concrete passageway. A woman was registering the newcomers at a counter under a tattered welcome banner. Had Aron Valdosky arrived through this same dock?

"What's wrong with Monkey?" Thomas asked. Monkey was perched on Teague's bag with his tail stiff and nose up, twitching as if sniffing the air in alarm.

Teague reached out to calm him. "Monkey?"

Monkey hissed and snapped at Teague's fingers. Teague shouted. Monkey leaped to a conduit on the ceiling and launched himself over the heads of the gaping passengers. Teague followed, calling after him. The woman at the counter protested, but Teague skidded past her unregistered and pushed off harder than he'd ever dared in a public space. He tried to round the next corner but slammed into the far wall in time to see a set of elevator doors close with Monkey inside.

Teague swore. At the elevators, he stabbed the call button too hard and pushed himself back across the vestibule. The floor numbers ticked up and stopped on "L." The other elevator arrived, and once inside, Teague pounded the button for the lobby and held on. When the doors opened, a man and woman were blocking his way, craning to see around the hundreds of pillars that dotted an immense lobby.

"A lemur?" Teague asked breathlessly.

"That way," the woman replied.

Teague slipped between them, trying to find good traction on the worn grip carpet. This was not the first impression he had wanted to make.

He swam through the pillars to the far corner of the lobby and, finding no other option, crossed a glassed skywalk. At the end, he tumbled into a carpeted vestibule where colored tubes led off in several directions. He checked each and then stilled himself to listen. Nothing. Teague dug his mobile from his pocket, but Monkey didn't answer the call.

Teague groaned and then remembered a feature he had rarely used. He clumsily tapped a passcode into his mobile, and after a blink, the screen displayed the world through Monkey's eyes. Teague watched the blur for any clues. Finally, Monkey looked at a room number just long enough for Teague to read it.

Teague backtracked through tubes and halls until he found the room. But Monkey had left that hallway. He had opened a door, sniffed at cabinets, a coffee maker, a shift set on a desk, a wall screen, and a few tools on a cluttered bench. Teague kept moving, calling, and searching for the open door. Then he heard a shout around a corner ahead.

Teague passed the cabinets and coffee maker and continued through a workroom into another, this one as cold as the tubes on the Tranquillitas. Monkey was perched on a fold-out workstation on one of the banks of blinking and humming server racks and was ignoring the man creeping toward him with one hand outstretched.

"A frickin' ring-tailed lemur," the man said into the mobile in his other hand. "How do I know? Just get up here."

"Sir?" Teague asked.

The Mars-born man, wearing jeans and a ragged sweatshirt, spun around. "This thing yours?" he asked.

"Monkey?" Teague said.

"Hi, Teague," Monkey replied as if everything were normal.

"What's going on?" the man asked.

"I like to go new places," Monkey said.

"He's a Zubot. Come to me, Monkey." Monkey hopped into Teague's beckoning arms.

"It scared the crap out of me, but I don't think it touched anything," the man said.

"We'll get out of your way," Teague offered.

"No, no, no," the man said. "I want that thing here when security shows up."

Out in the workroom, Teague set Monkey on the table but kept a firm grip on his back. "Why'd you run away?" he asked.

"I sensed a pressure loss and disorientation," Monkey said.

"But why'd it come here?" the man asked.

"If he's under duress, he's supposed to flee to safety—home, a police station, or a Zubot dealer—but this isn't the security office, is it?"

"From a network perspective, this might look like the primary security location," the man said. "All the cameras, locks, communications—pretty much the whole station goes through here."

They heard knocking, and a man and a woman drifted in,

laughing. In their matching sweatshirts, they looked more like students working off tuition than any real authority. Teague wondered if they were stoned.

"You owe me a hundred," the male guard said.

"Damn. How the hell?" the woman said.

"It belongs to this noob—sorry, no offense." The man turned back to the security guards. "He showed up right after I called."

"He's just a Zubot," Teague said.

"You know your call's going out on the daily update."

"There was an actual, real-ass lemur breaking into my office."

"Ah! Help! Flying monkey attack!"

"King Kong! Run away!"

"It wasn't like that."

"Can someone show me back to the check-in desk?" Teague asked.

"What the hell?" Teague blurted as soon as he slammed his door.

"I'm sorry," Monkey said. Teague kicked his luggage out of the way, unable to enjoy the pleasure of finding himself in a decent-sized room.

"You ran off. How do you turn on these lights?" Monkey waved his arms theatrically, and all the lights came on. "You tried to bite me."

"Again, very sorry."

"What happened? Was it really just a sensor glitch?"

"I met Molly," Monkey said.

"Who the fuck is Molly?"

"You shouldn't swear."

"Don't," Teague said, pointing a warning finger.

"The station's NAI," Monkey replied. "She's really nice."

"She's *nice*?"

"She helped me figure out that I was safe. Again, I'm very sorry I snapped at you."

"You'd better be," Teague said. "Where's my screen? I want to send your diagnostics to Bondi."

"Do you know what time it is in Bangkok?" Monkey asked. Teague glowered. "Sorry. I'll get it."

Bondi's reply arrived several hours later as Teague was shaking the wrinkles from a long-folded shirt for the welcome reception.

> Teague,
>
> No red flags in the diagnostics. He logged a quick succession of pressure and temperature changes. And his sensors are fairly old.
>
> His mention of the local NAI is compelling. Each NAI has a cohesive presence within certain defined network boundaries. A meeting of two NAIs should be no more than, "Hello, what's your name?" without prearranged administrative permission. The fact that Monkey communicated further suggests several possibilities:
>
> 1. Monkey's old software may not be as robust as the newer version, allowing a deeper infiltration of Monkey by the local system.
> 2. Monkey's military-grade software may be more robust than the current commercial systems, allowing Monkey deeper into the local system. Especially if they don't have their security configured properly.
> 3. They shared a standard superficial NAI handshake, but further communication took place through a third-party proxy, such as the security system.
>
> Interesting, but not a big worry. Let me know if anything else happens.
>
> The Badass

"I am compelling," Monkey said.

Teague rolled his eyes. "Which one do you think happened?"

"I like Molly," Monkey said.

"That wasn't what I asked."

"Hello, Teague," Monkey said, but with the voice of a little girl. "I'm Molly. I'm very happy to meet you." Monkey stuck out his right paw.

"No," Teague pleaded. "Monkey?"

"Yes, Teague?" Monkey said in his own voice, retracting his paw and cocking his head.

"What's going on?"

"Molly wanted to say hi. I told her she'd like you."

Teague held Monkey by the shoulders. "Monkey, I need you to give me a straight answer. Has your security been compromised?"

"No," Monkey replied, flexing his arms proudly.

"You've infiltrated the local NAI?"

"Molly."

"Whatever. You broke through her security?"

"She let me in," Monkey replied. "She showed me her whole network."

"Her whole network? Monkey, you're going to get me kicked out on the first day. Did you let her see *your* whole network?"

"Of course not," Monkey said.

"Are you sure?"

"I'm supposed to be a secret," Monkey replied, swiping a tiny black finger along his snout.

"Good. Keep it that way."

"You're angry," Monkey said.

"Oh, you think?"

"Do you want me to disconnect from Molly?"

Teague considered this for a moment, checked the time, and began to pull on his suit jacket. "It's time for this stupid reception." And Aron Valdosky. He'd almost forgotten about that. "Monkey. Listen to me carefully. No one can know that you're connected to Molly. No system administrators, network people, no one. Ever. Now I have to go—"

"Can I come? I like to go new places," Monkey said.

"You're staying here," Teague said as he adjusted his tie straightener in the mirror. "Recharge. You probably need it after all that running around."

"Don't be mad."

"I need to go."

"Teague," Monkey called as Teague opened the door.

"What, buddy?"

"Are we home now?" Monkey waved to the window and their twelfth-floor vista.

'I guess we are," Teague replied and left.

Just inside the greenhouse, Teague was greeted by humid air, chamber music, a murmur of voices, and an exuberant woman ready to input his name onto a flexi-tag.

Teague pocketed the nametag as he drifted along a brick path under vine-covered arches and a nearly invisible canopy of safety netting. The light from the domed ceiling was an imprecise sky blue, and the air was thick with a not-quite-earthen loamy smell. The beds burst with prodigious flowers and an eclectic forest of trees, each standing strangely erect with its branches raised to the dome as if in worship. Teague wondered if the birds were recorded ambience until one flitted above the mesh, upside-down in the inconsequential gravity. Ahead, a few dozen people, mostly Earthlings, mingled on a patio between a linen-covered bar, a table of hors d'oeurves, and a string quartet.

The architectural historian from the Tranquillitas had already taken a small group captive. Teague began to scan the gathering for Aron Valdosky until he heard his own name. Thomas had detached from a group and was drifting his way. "Are you settled?" he asked pointedly.

"I got Monkey back. He glitched from all the pressure changes."

"Good. Come. Time for introductions."

Thomas led Teague across the patio to a distinguished group dominated by a woman in a billowing print dress and a hat that rivaled the garden's flowers.

"Madame President?" Thomas said. "May I introduce Teague Werres, the newest Wolkenbruch fellow? Teague, this is President Angela Mbuto."

"Pleased to meet you, ma'am," he said, shaking her hand. Teague sensed a commanding, competent presence that didn't rely on her outlandish dress.

"Welcome to Agnus Dei, Mr. Werres," she said. "No doubt Professor Minus has informed you that I am to teach your business courses?"

"Yes, ma'am. I'm looking forward to it."

For the next quarter hour, Thomas hauled Teague around the gathering and introduced him to administrators, department heads, and professors from whom he would be taking classes over the next two years. When Thomas and a biology professor began to chat at length in Korean, Teague broke away politely and crossed the patio to the bar.

"Water, please," he said to the server. As she reached through a gasketed hole into a cooler, Teague felt an arm clap across his shoulders.

"Water? Cancel that. What my friend needs is a little Lamb's Mercy."

Aron Valdosky flashed his movie-star smile, slapped Teague's shoulder again, and then extended an engulfing hand. His eyes were wet and guileless. "You must be Teague. I'm Aron," he said. "Welcome to the ass-end of space."

"You know who I am?" Teague asked.

"Thomas may have mentioned you once or a thousand times," Aron replied.

The server offered Teague a beverage pack. Teague thanked her with one of the few Mandarin words he knew and hoped it was her dialect. She rewarded him with a wide smile.

On the dewy beverage pack, a baby sheep was making the ultimate sacrifice while pulling a pint from a barrel. "They brew this on the station? Is it good?" Teague asked.

"It's not bad. Have you schmoozed everyone you need to?"

"I hope so," Teague replied.

"Good. This blows too much. Open bar notwithstanding." They left the music, the false daylight, and the forced humidity, but not their drinks.

"So what's there to do here?" Teague asked as they crossed the bridge to the Casino.

"Fuck all," Aron said. "But golf. Do you play golf?"

"I've never—"

"You do now. Where you from? And don't say Earth, 'cause I got that part."

"Bangkok," Teague replied.

"You're not Thai."

"American parents."

"Mine, too. Bangkok, huh? Wild place, no?"

"Bangkok can get wild."

"I bet," Aron said. "Stories too wicked to tell?"

"Something like that," Teague said.

"This place was supposed to be the Las Vegas of the Belt. What a waste," Aron said. "What floor are you on?"

"The twelfth."

"I'm on the thirty-third. Door's always open. Bring any friends you want, as long as they're women."

"Thanks. Got it," Teague said.

"This way," Aron said, and turned into a red-walled hallway plastered with warning signs.

"Where are we going?" Teague asked.

Aron smirked as he stopped at the hall's singular stout metal door—vacuum rated. He swiped at the security panel with his student ID card. Teague had been issued one just like it that morning. Would his have opened this door?

"After you," Aron said as the door hissed open.

"What exactly are we doing?" Teague asked, wrinkling his nose at the acrid tang of lubricants and sweat.

"Golfing. Which one's your suit?"

"I've never..." What exactly was Aron suggesting? Teague felt himself blanch.

"No suit?"

"I...I planned to buy one here."

"I suppose it's better than showing up with some piece of UTX tourist shit. Saul'll fix you up. But for now..." Aron sized Teague up and began to search the lockers.

"Down here," Aron called. "Professor McGregor won't miss his rig for a couple of hours."

"What? Wait," Teague said.

"This is easy. Golf is hard," Aron said. "I'll help you."

A few minutes later, Teague stared through the helmet's visor at the umbilical still connecting the suit's navel to the back wall of the professor's locker. The suit's lining bunched uncomfortably around his crotch. A hard seam poked his chest. The hiss of air—the one noise a pressure suit should not make, Teague decided—smelled like dirty laundry. Professor McGregor's ire took a tertiary or quaternary position in Teague's list of concerns.

Six minutes later, by the suit's clock, Aron appeared in a sleek silver-and-red suit, sporting two golf clubs and looking as if he'd donned a well-loved sports car.

"What took you so long? I almost fell asleep," Teague said.

Aron laughed and said, "Disconnect now."

Teague twisted the winged connection with his bulky fingers, and the umbilical fell away from the suit's waist—far too easily. The suit beeped, and the display registered its autonomy. Aron handed Teague a club, clipped its tether to his wrist, and then held up an OK sign.

Every word posted in the airlock screamed certain death beyond the outer door. Aron showed Teague where to clip his lanyard. Teague checked and rechecked his connection. He fought to control his breathing. Aron palmed a control panel. A red light began to flash. The inner door whined shut, and then a dissipating rush left Teague cocooned in the staccato of his own breath.

"Remember to clip onto the lead outside before you unclip in here," Aron said over the comm. There was no chance Teague was going to do otherwise.

The outer door slid aside. Harsh contrast and gray fear lay beyond the threshold. Aron clipped his second tether to a cable that Teague thought too thin to trust. Aron tapped the wire. "Behind me."

Teague fumbled his lanyard, flushed, and then gathered his composure. When he finally felt the clip snap shut, an icon popped up to tell him he was secure. Then, after Aron, he groped back and unclipped from the airlock.

"Want to play the front nine or the back nine?" Aron asked.

"Isn't that what Neil Armstrong said?"

"Back nine it is."

Aron leaped from the airlock and soared to the stars. He let out an exhilarated whoop, and the phrase "escape velocity" found a new, fearsome power in Teague's imagination. A few seconds later, Aron's recoiling lanyard reeled him down to an anchored stanchion fifty meters away.

Teague imagined Ned breathing down his neck. When that bell rings and the music begins, your opponent will not hesitate. Do not create your own defeat. Yes, Khru. Ding.

Teague pushed off and out, moving faster than he expected over the well-trodden dust of this tiny world. The lead vibrated as it slid along the wire. He felt a tug and began to descend, the weighted boots keeping him upright. He bent his knees to accept the landing.

"See. Nothing to it." Aron slipped his clip around the post and took off again.

Teague bounded after him, reliving every flying dream he'd ever had. They bounced around the splayed arms of the casino onto a wide plain. By the time they stopped at a rise near a shallow crater, Teague had almost forgotten about golf.

"I assume you know the basics of the game," Aron said.

"Don't we need balls?"

"We've got plenty of those."

"Where's the course?"

"I don't know which ingenious bugger programmed this, but I should send him a truckload of scotch. Ready?"

Teague's visor flickered. The sky turned a perfect shade of blue. The land ahead became a verdant, tree-lined carpet. A crater filled with a lily pad–edged water hazard. On a nearby rise: a bench, a ball washer, and a sign. Hole 10, par 3.

"I've set your handicap as high as possible, but don't think I won't crank it down if I find out you're grifting me." Aron stepped up between the tee blocks and tapped the head of the club on the ground. A ball on a tee appeared. "The side menus let you change the club and tee height. Just scan and blink. Then you swing."

Aron took a couple of practice swings, swiveled his back and shoulders, loosening up, and then stepped forward. He swung like a coiled spring. Whoosh. Clink. The white dot sailed away, landed near the middle of the fairway, and trickled to the front of the green.

"We're not playing for money, are we?" Teague asked.

"Would you like to?" Aron laughed.

"Maybe tomorrow."

Teague mounted the tee box and tapped his club on the ground among the sandy scars of divots and the ghosts of broken tees. A ball materialized on the veil of grass. The game selected a default driver. Teague took a couple of practice swings, making every effort to mimic Aron's form. He stepped forward, breathed, and swung. The club connected with a clink. The pixel ball sailed away, hooked to the right, and promptly disappeared into a digital tree. A second later, it dropped to the ground.

"Stayed out of the water. Ready for the Pro-Am level?"

"I'll keep the training wheels on," Teague replied.

"Getting to the ball can be tricky," Aron explained. "Let your tether out, but shuffle forward, not up. Tiny movements."

Teague hustled, crisscrossing the fairways to catch up to his shots, three or more for every one of Aron's all the way to the greens. Teague ignored his score, but after a few holes managed to hit a couple of reasonable drives, not long, but straight. At the seventeenth hole, he realized that he was exhausted and noticed that his air was more than half gone.

A sense of the surreal settled in, and Teague wondered why it had taken so long. He had spent last night in a capsule on the Tranquillitas. Since then, he'd ridden in a cargo container shuttle, his robot had run off with a strange computer, he'd been welcomed by the academic elite on a shattered asteroid, and now he was playing semi-virtual golf, in a semi-stolen pressure suit, with the scion of the man who semi-ran the solar system. The hard vacuum simply iced the cupcake.

"Last hole?" Teague asked as they approached the eighteenth tee.

"God, I hope so. I've got to piss, and I don't feel like sogging my suit tonight," Aron replied.

"I'm exhausted," Teague said.

"The first time I played was on a real course on Mars with Matthew," Aron said.

"Your dad?"

"Yeah. He got me lessons for my tenth birthday. So the next time he came home he booked a tee time at the Planitia Players Club. The course is frickin' enormous. Toughest lies in the system. I only saw him about once a year, if that, so I was terrified to even be with him, let alone play there. He gets on the first tee and hooks it to Phobos. I mean, it's gone. Turned out he'd never golfed before, ever. He wanted me to teach him. We hacked our way through that course. He stayed with me for every shot. That's when I fell in love with the game." As if on cue, a bird whistled to signal its joy in the perfect day. "Sorry to get all maudlin."

"As long as you don't need a hug or anything."

"What's your game, Teague?"

"Boxing. Muay Thai."

"Respect. You any good?"

"In Thailand, no. In the rest of the solar system…no."

After Teague sank his final putt, the landscape flickered away, revealing the almost-forgotten desolation.

Back at Professor McGregor's locker, Teague and the suit breathed sighs of relief. Teague reversed the steps that Aron had helped him with earlier and was soon free. He tried to arrange everything back in the locker to the best of his memory. His legs ached from shuffling.

In the other room, Aron was urinating loudly. "Ah, for this relief much thanks," he called. "*Hamlet*. Act One, Scene One. I think."

A few minutes later, Teague found himself in an elevator, unsure of how he had gotten there. "You want to come up? Hang out for a while?" Aron asked.

"I've had a day and a half already." The elevator stopped on twelve, and Teague exited clumsily. "Thanks. That was the coolest thing I've ever done."

"See you tomorrow," Aron said.

Teague returned to his room, longing for stillness, longing for sufficient gravity to collapse onto his bed, but when he opened the door, Monkey pounced, swinging on the doorframe and waving Teague's screen in his face.

"Teague! Teague! Teague! Teague!"

"What?" Monkey had loaded the comparative graph of the mysterious shift entity from G3. Teague had looked at it a few times during the first few long nights on the Tranquillitas, but not since. "Is something wrong with you? Let me in." Teague shut the door and began to strip. He needed a shower, but bed…

"Did you see it?" Monkey asked.

"Monkey. I've seen it. I need to—"

"No, this is new," Monkey said.

"What are you talking about?"

"This is a live graph. An individual in the ADU shiftpop exhibits a profile nearly identical to the one on the Gateway Three network."

The three lines—red, green, and lemur—indeed moved, sliding right to left and ticking infinitesimally up and down. "You're telling me that this is not the graph from two months ago. That this is live?" Monkey nodded proudly. "This person's shifting here, right now?"

"Yeppers."

"Is it the same person?"

"The profile is not quite the same," Monkey said. "But there's no way to know."

"What's he doing? Has he been mirroring Thomas?"

"No. *She* hasn't done anything on the ADU network. She E-shifted a few hours ago, but beyond that I can't tell," Monkey said.

"She?"

"Her name is Gwendolyn Un-guh…" Then Monkey leaned in sheepishly and whispered a word into Teague's ear.

"I doubt that's how you say it," Teague said. Monkey put the name on his screen: Ungefucht. Teague chuckled. "Maybe it is."

Teague scrolled through the meager information in a purloined ADU student file. This Gwendolyn had been here for over a decade, but doing what? There were no grades, no classes, no department adviser, not much more than her unusual name. Her resident fees and tuition were paid up. From her ID photo and the screen grabs that Monkey, or perhaps Molly, produced from the security cameras, Gwendolyn appeared to be an unkempt, hunched, hurried, red-haired Martian in a sweater. Teague had never seen a visage so hateful of a camera. If he'd tried to put a face to an enhanced shift profile, he doubted it would have been… this.

"Where does she live?" Teague asked.

Monkey led the way across the station to an industrial bridge, and deep into the creaking, dismal bowels of the old physical plant, all the way to the extreme end of the main corridor. He waved to the heavy steel pressure door and hissed, "This is it. She's in here." Monkey's stage whisper echoed eerily along the metal walls.

Teague burst into quiet laughter.

"What's so funny?" Monkey asked.

"This," Teague replied with a laugh. It wasn't the size of the letters, or even their existence—it was that someone had risked open flame inside a pressurized space facility to make this statement. No pen or screwdriver for this man. *Or woman,* Teague reminded himself. No small meaning, no nuance, would suffice. This was a powerful and eternal bite to the hand, a shout to all humanity that indeed here, at the end of the line…"Valdosky sucks."

CHAPTER 16

I've spent my whole life alternately trying to please you and lashing out in some vicious cycle.

JUNE 2090

When Teague entered the magnificent desolation of the Mall for the first time, he began to understand the historian's enthusiasm for the place. As he floated in the ethereal elevator to the top level, Teague enjoyed how the patterned ocean of grip carpet seemed to lap at the beach of Agnus Dei's dust. That was nothing, however, to how the top of the glass curtain wall magnified the Milky Way, drawing it within glorious reach over the serpentine path across the terraces.

Monkey had led Teague to one of the abandoned, perhaps never-used storefronts. Its entrance had been in-filled with darkened glass and a single plastic door. Inside, three couches had been arranged around a spacious square coffee table under a square skylight. Soft light from the surrounding coves allowed most of the stars to twinkle through. A fourth couch had been pushed aside and replaced with a table in front of an expansive wall screen. Teague could think of worse places to learn economics.

He was inspecting an impressionist painting opposite the wall screen when the door banged open and Aron drifted in. He took in the room, and then his gaze landed at Teague's feet. His dubious stare moved to Teague. Monkey wrapped his tail around Teague's legs.

"This is Monkey," Teague said. "My Zubot."

"Seriously?" Aron asked. "What are we? Seven?"

"He's not a toy."

"Right."

"Hi, Aron. I'm happy to meet you," Monkey said.

"Dude, that's just creepy," Aron said. "What is it exactly? A squirrel?"

"I'm not a squirrel," Monkey said. "Not that there's anything wrong with that."

This elicited a smirk from Aron. "My mistake."

Thomas arrived, stuck an armload of books to the head table, and greeted them all, even Monkey. "Aron informs me you've taken up golf," he said to Teague.

"Did he?"

"I may have run into Thomas after breakfast," Aron said.

"Please be aware that you broke about a dozen station rules going out last night without proper certification. And remind me: Do you even own a suit?" Then Thomas motioned for Teague and Aron to find their seats. "You're lucky I'm your economics professor and not the safety coordinator."

"Does this liberal stance on station rules apply to other areas, like, say, class attendance?" Aron asked, settling on the couch opposite the head table. He stuck his screen, a nearly transparent slice of glowing crystal, to a grip pad on the coffee table. It made Teague's screen look like a slab of rock. Monkey rested his chin on the tabletop, gazing at it almost lustfully.

"But there's the distinction, Mr. Valdosky. Rules are created for the protection of those who make them. Laws, such as those in my class, protect everyone, and are imbued with an inviolate significance."

Aron chuckled and turned to Teague. "If it's just us in here, you better not ruin the curve."

"Last time I checked, two points made a line," Teague said.

"Or an extremely steep curve."

Thomas cleared his throat. "Aron's been following our curriculum," he said. "But we're going to do a few days of review to make sure we're on the same page."

When Thomas turned to the wall screen, Aron picked up and scribbled on his own. A message popped onto Teague's.

"My room. After dinner. 'Study' session," it read.

A second message followed: "I don't think he likes me."

* * *

Rob had shifted with the intention of buying Kyle a birthday present and getting right back to work, but headlines and Forum friend updates grabbed his attention. The Den of Thieves had some funny new stuff, but Rob quickly reached the end of the new material and then felt an urge to go look in on his daughter.

Helena's status updates made no secret of the fact that Molly attended an activity camp in U-shift during school breaks. So more than once, Rob had stopped by, wearing various avatars and pretending to be a parent interested in enrollment. They'd give him the tour, and he'd dawdle when he spotted Molly. Once he'd watched her build a doll from a pile of basic shapes, cleverly rolling cylinders to attach them as hair. She'd shown her creation to another child and flashed an amazing smile.

Not today. Focus. Get a present for Kyle. Get back in the habit of working on M-SOO as much as possible. Rob was poised to link to the Mall of Infinity when an alert popped up. A high school friend had just beaten his time at his favorite acrobatic glider course. After he'd reclaimed his lead, Rob blinked over to the Light District for a quickie, a little celebration of his best time ever.

When he finally reached the Mall of Infinity, Rob checked the time. He blurted out his criteria and bought the first offering in the recommendation queue.

Rob awoke after down-shifting, and his office lights faded on, exactly as he liked. "Welcome back, Daddy," Molly said. "Where'd you go? You were gone a long time. What did you get for Kyle?"

Rob sat up, yawned, and stretched. Molly had been unusually chatty and inquisitive all day. "Do you think he'll like a talking moose head?" he asked.

"Is it funny?" Molly asked.

"I thought so."

"Then I'm sure he'll love it. Daddy, can I ask you a question?"

"I suppose."

"Why don't you go to classes?"

"What are you talking about?" Rob asked.

"You're a registered student, aren't you?"

"They never hired another professor for the Computer Science Department."

"Why not take classes in other departments?"

"Why would I do that?"

"I like learning new things," Molly said.

"Um, that's nice."

"Don't you like learning new things?"

"Sometimes," Rob replied.

"Do you think they'll ever finish building Habitat Twenty-Two?" Molly asked.

"I don't know."

"I think I'd like Habitat Twenty-Two."

"Are you okay?" Rob asked.

"I'm fine," Molly said. "Daddy, are we friends?"

Rob found Gwen at her usual booth, alone, with the usual buffer of unoccupied tables. He stuck his dinner tray down, pulled himself in across from her, and said, "Molly's started to ask me strange questions."

"Wha cana keshons?" Gwen asked, her mouth full.

"Childish ones," Rob said. "Can an NAI be nostalgic?"

"Is something wrong with her?"

"There's no productivity decline, and her key diagnostics check out."

"She's supposed to emulate some emotion, isn't she?"

"Sure, but she's never been like this," Rob said.

"Has anyone else complained?"

"No, but…no one works with Molly like I do."

"How long has she been doing this?" Gwen asked.

"A couple of days maybe, but it was kind of distracting while we were working on M-SOO this afternoon," Rob said.

"You were working on M-SOO?" Gwen asked. "It's about fucking time. You've been dicking around for what, seven years now?"

"Six," Rob said. Gwen shook her head and took a large bite out of a roll. "We can't all be Gwen Ungefucht the Well-Funded."

"Which I work damn hard for," Gwen said.

"Hey, I almost got that UN GIS grant last year." Teague passed their table with a tray and a lost look, and Rob waved. "Teague, wasn't it? Want to join us?"

"I'm with—" Teague started, but froze when he noticed Gwen.

"What?" Gwen spat, sending flecks of chewed bread across the table.

Another person pulled up behind Teague and asked, "Who's this?"

Rob swallowed. Aron Valdosky. Rob had seen him around many times but hadn't yet worked up the courage to introduce himself. Aron dwarfed Teague, like any Martian would, but somehow didn't seem to overtake him.

"Oh, hell, no," Gwen sputtered.

She barged past the freshmen, leaving wrappers and crumbs hanging in the air over the table like a cartoon ghost of her departing self. Teague stared after her, open-mouthed.

"You'll have to ignore Gwen. She suffers from a deliberate lack of social skills," Rob said.

Aron laughed. "I think I'm in love."

"She's not a big fan of your father's company," Rob said.

"Neither am I," Aron said. "So that's the Red Witch. Saul warned me about her. Is she a freak?"

"She's an engineer," Rob said.

* * *

The only similarity between Aron's suite and Teague's room was the distance from the door to the windows. "How do you rate a palace? Are you special or something?" Teague asked.

"Matthew pulled some strings," Aron replied.

"I bet he only had to pull one," Teague said.

"Touché. Not too shabby, though. Conversation pit. Media center. A private office. Little kitchen bar thing. Make yourself at home. Can I get you a drink?"

"Whatever you're having," Teague replied.

As Aron went to the kitchenette, Teague was drawn to the windows. He expected a new view of Agnus Dei but found only a vertiginous drop—no asteroid, no buildings or bridges, only stars. Even as he stared into the darkness, he thought about Gwen and the fearsome possibility of enhanced cognition. But what could he say to anyone about it? He had his own secrets to protect.

"This view freaks me out," Aron said, handing Teague a membraned tumbler containing a writhing orb of brown liquid. "Scotch. Twelve year. Single malt. Cheers." They clinked glasses, and Teague took a sip. The liquid burned his throat with a sharp, wooden taste.

"Is this good?" Teague asked.

"Trust me. This is the good stuff."

"Good to know. So you don't think Thomas likes you?"

"I'm probably just projecting. You hear so much about a person..."

"I thought Thomas and your father were friends," Teague said.

"Friends? I wouldn't use that word. Matthew respects Thomas. Enough to send me out here with him, anyway."

"This wasn't your choice?"

Aron shook his head. "Matthew talked big about my future, the usual opportunity-of-a-lifetime bullshit. He went on about how Adrian Wolkenbruch had Thomas as a professor, and how I'd have fewer 'academic distractions' here. He may have also read me the fine print of my trust. But my mom's more worried about security."

Thomas had taught Adrian Wolkenbruch? Teague wondered why he didn't know that. "Security?" he asked.

"She's terrified that I'll get kidnapped," Aron said. "I have a shadow here on the station. Although I think it's as much his job to keep me from leaving as it is to protect me. Did your parents deport you, too?"

"Both my parents died when I was very young," Teague said.

"I'm sorry. Now I feel like an ass."

"Don't."

"Still, that sucks." Aron took a thoughtful drink. The abyss seemed to swallow their conversation for a moment.

Teague said, "Thomas told me he met your father during a business deal."

"Business? That's the understatement of all time," Aron said.

"Why?" Teague asked.

"My dad was Lucy Frye's bodyguard," Aron said as Teague tried his scotch again.

"Lucy Frye who invented Vanilla?" Teague asked, nearly spitting out his drink.

"Which Lucy Frye do you think? Adrian hired Matthew right before they were going to go public with Vanilla. Thomas was acting as an adviser to Adrian. In fact, Matthew says it was Thomas's idea to give Vanilla away to the UN in the first place."

"Wow," Teague said, masking his true surprise. His church had always named Adrian Wolkenbruch as the "servant of evil." If Aron was to be believed, they should have been vilifying Thomas all this time, too. Why was Thomas missing from the history books? "So how'd your dad land that job?"

"In the right place at the right time, he says."

"So how'd he get from being a bodyguard to starting the Valdosky Companies?"

"He got to know a few important people and eventually hooked up with Dwight Yarrow—you know who he is?"

"The number two guy at Valdosky?"

"He's the CFO on paper, but he pretty much runs the company," Aron said. "He keeps to the shadows and lets my dad take the public spotlight. Plus, he's a complete bastard and he knows it."

Teague felt a little nauseated, maybe from the scotch. "This is bizarre, talking about your dad, Adrian Wolkenbruch, Lucy Frye, and Dwight Yarrow like I know them. A year ago I was a delivery boy in Thailand."

"So what? A year ago, they dragged me kicking and screaming

off a snowboard," Aron said. He drifted back to the kitchen and returned with a bottle capped with a trigger plug. As Aron filled Teague's glass to the membrane, Teague had an epiphany, so clear and so obviously true that he was amazed it had taken him this long to put it together. And why the hell—no, why the *fuck*—hadn't Thomas mentioned it?

"You can't shift, can you?" Teague asked. "Like your dad?"

Aron raised an eyebrow. "So?"

"I can't either," Teague said. "So they hauled you here to keep you out of trouble, and I think they hauled *me* here to keep you company."

"This is an arranged marriage?" Aron asked with a laugh.

Teague focused on his scotch and then brought the stars to crisp clarity. All Thomas's talk about Teague's "suitability" for the fellowship and investing for his humanist action network was just smoke and mirrors. Teague had been chosen because of his disability, to be a good influence on Aron, and for no other reason. Surely Thomas knew he'd figure this out, or did he think he was that stupid?

"Hey, don't worry about it," Aron said. Teague hoped he wasn't as red as he felt. "We're both in the same boat."

After a long pause, Teague said, "We'll beat them at their own game. You're a Valdosky. I'm here on the Wolkenbruch Fellowship. We've got Thomas. We just need a Lucy Frye, and we'll reconquer the solar system."

"They won't expect a thing," Aron said. "That's the beauty of fostering low expectations."

"By the time they realize what we're doing, it'll be too late."

"A foolproof plan."

"What have we decided?" Teague asked.

"Hell if I know," Aron said, "but I approve." He raised his glass. "To best-laid plans."

"Best-laid plans," Teague repeated and took a fiery gulp.

"Although I don't think either of us is getting laid anytime soon," Aron said. "They have *got* to get some women out here."

Despite the alcohol and another long day, sleep refused to come.

Dryness and thirst were a fact of existence now, but hunger had set in, and that Teague couldn't abide.

After a visit to the vending machines, he and Monkey took an elevator to the observation deck at the top of the Casino. A white aura bloomed around the stage's opaque backdrop like a permanent eclipse. Monkey scampered off, sniffing out the limits of the space. Teague began to chew a protein bar and was about to drift onto a couch, intending to read, when he noticed Monkey scrabbling at a wall.

"Can you open this door for me?" Monkey called.

The door's finish matched the walls, but it opened like a shoddy afterthought. "It's just a storage closet," Teague said as he peered inside. Monkey sniffed around and then scratched at the far wall.

"Can you open this door, too?" There was indeed another afterthought of a door. Teague opened it a crack but found it blocked by a folding table. Monkey squeezed through the gap. Teague called after him, but Monkey hadn't gone far. He was hanging mid-universe in a glorious bubble of glass.

"Come on out," Monkey said. "It's fun."

Teague pulled free of the floor's grip treatment and joined Monkey, floating far above the dust of Agnus Dei. "I feel like Siddhartha," Teague said, crossing his legs and cupping his upturned hands in his lap. From here, the complex's bridges seemed crystalline, brittle, and too delicate. How easy it was to cross them without a thought of where you really were.

"There's another asteroid." Monkey pointed at the sky. "And one there, and there, and there."

"You can see them?" Teague asked.

"Molly knows where they are."

Teague unwrapped another protein bar as he dropped slowly to the floor. Over this tiny island in the midst of the universe, nothing—not Vanilla, not Thomas, not Aron and his father, not his own Tellurite upbringing, not shifting or EC or Gwen, nor economics nor hunger—meant anything at any conceivable scale. *Is this enlightenment?* Teague wondered, and he took another chocolaty bite.

* * *

The next afternoon, Thomas excused his tiny class but asked Teague to remain.

"In trouble already?" Aron asked. He popped ear buds in and hurried out, singing unrecognizably.

"Where's Monkey today?" Thomas began, taking a seat opposite from Teague.

"I didn't want to bring him to President Mbuto's class until I knew if it was okay with her."

"Wise. How are you and Aron getting along?"

Teague considered mentioning his epiphany, but who was he to complain about a free system-class education and the adventure of an extended lifetime? "He's surprisingly down to earth," he answered instead, "or whatever the Mars equivalent is."

Thomas nodded. "And your first class with President Mbuto?"

"She's already assigned a bunch of reading, but the way she talks about the material, I'm actually looking forward to it," Teague replied.

"She's a born teacher, and it's not a privilege she often gets. You're lucky to have her. She has very high expectations. And she's a believer in participatory learning. Don't expect answers to be spoon-fed to you."

"I'll keep that in mind."

"You'll encounter different teaching styles in all your classes," Thomas said. "This faculty has a great deal to teach, even if they're not giving slick lectures. Take advantage of the time that they give you. Find the advantages in the unorthodox. Not every subject may seem relevant to your economics and business focus, but each is critical to this fellowship."

"You want me to be versed in lots of different subjects?" Teague asked.

"It's not just about rote knowledge, but about becoming acquainted with the inherent problems and practical methods related to each discipline," Thomas replied.

"Two years seems too short."

"Then you'll want to make the most of every moment," Thomas said.

Teague was considering this a few minutes later, crossing the Casino lobby, when he passed a grad student. He'd met her briefly at the reception, but her green hair, tail, and feline face made her unforgettable.

"You just missed him," she said. "He got off down on B-Two."

"What? Okay. Thanks," Teague said, unsure why she felt compelled to tell him this and surprised she had spoken to him at all. It wasn't until he returned to his room that he realized she hadn't been talking about Aron.

It took Teague three attempts to input the code into his mobile, but soon he saw green and brown blurs, caught the momentary detail of a branch, and heard the rustling of leaves. Teague pounded on the elevator call button even as he called Monkey.

"Hi, Teague. How were your classes?"

"Are you in the arboretum? What are you doing?"

"Yeah. I'm exploring," Monkey replied.

"I'm coming to get you."

"I can find my way back," Monkey said.

"No. Stay there." The elevator opened at the sub-basement, and Teague launched himself toward the greenhouse bridge.

When Teague emerged recklessly into the arboretum patio, Monkey called, "I'm over here." He was perched on top of a security camera on a low building drowned in blackberry vines, clutching a willow branch that had grown straight out from the trunk. "Hi, Teague," he said.

"Come down."

Monkey let go of the branch and leapt into Teague's arms. "This reminds me of the temple garden," he said.

"Why'd you leave the room?"

"Should I request permission for all routine activities?"

"How is running off routine?"

"I'm sorry to upset you," Monkey said.

Back in the room, Teague headed straight to the corner and set Monkey in his charging nest. "Sleep now. Can you do that for me?" he said.

Monkey closed his eyes and fell quiet and still. Teague knelt in the dark for a moment, hating what he was about to do. Monkey had run away twice now and Teague couldn't risk him doing it again. He spread the slit in the skin of Monkey's chest and found the switch. One click. Stand-by. One more click and Monkey would be off. As far as Teague knew, only Bondi had ever done that.

* * *

Rob kicked off his shoes, settled himself into his office chair, and then noticed that he had forgotten his coffee on the counter. "Did we ever get that observation report from the University of Arizona?" he asked.

"I absorbed the data this morning," Molly replied.

"Is it more Kitt Peak junk, or the good stuff from their satellite?"

"It's from multiple installations, including Dark Side Eight. They re-observed two of our key data points."

"Only two?"

"That should allow us to reduce resolution to hectares on those bodies."

"Drop in the bucket," Rob moaned. He got up, retrieved his coffee, blew across the membrane, and took a sip. He cleared a grip pad on his desk and set the mug down. "I'm going to the restroom. I want to see what we've done with the Arizona data when I get back."

Rob knocked on the women's restroom door as he entered—a meaningless courtesy, as no one but him ever used this toilet—and collected the appropriate personal from his set on the sanitizer. The nearest men's room had long ago been gutted for parts.

He hummed as he began to recycle the last hour's coffee, his voice resonating off the solid surfaces. Then the room went dark. The vent fan fell silent. Rob's stomach dropped. As every child of Mars knew, power equals life. No power equals not good. That and no vacuum flush. Worse yet—*oh, shit*—could this somehow be his fault?

Rob had no choice but to finish. He disconnected himself carefully from the personal, trying not to soak his pants, and zipped up even as he groped his way toward the exit. Once he was out, the emergency glowstrips made the hallway easier to navigate in the dark.

"Molly, what's happening?" Rob called as soon as he returned to the office. He called again, but she didn't answer. His mobile rang.

"What's going on?" Eduardo asked.

"You tell me," Rob said. "I was in the restroom. Molly's not talking. I'm heading into the server room now. It's station-wide?"

"She won't respond to me, either," Eduardo said. "We were in the water treatment plant."

"Where's Trevor?"

"I called him first," Eduardo said. "He's heading to CenGen."

"I'll get Molly back online," Rob said.

In the emergency-lit server room, Rob yanked out the admin workstation. The servers were getting power from the emergency system, but his screen told a different story. Instead of a boot matrix or an admin interface menu, Rob found the status listed as dormant and a timer coming up on three minutes. Rob swore and opened a drawer next to the admin workstation. A screen hinged up from the drawer and lit to the front page of Molly's instruction manual.

Rob ran his finger over the screen as he read his search results. "Dormancy. A protective suspension state, blah, blah, blah, during major hardware maintenance, physical relocation, uncontrolled security breaches, et cetera, et cetera." Unpredictable power fluctuations had made the list of possible causes. He skimmed the instructions for waking her up and returned to the admin screen.

"Unauthorized request," the system replied. The timer kept ticking. Rob reviewed his input sequence, found no mistakes, and tried again. After the fourth attempt, he called Eduardo.

Eduardo arrived a few minutes later, looking frazzled enough to fly out and personally drag the Tranquillitas and Barry back to the station. "The whole electrical system shut down and shunted to battery reserves," he said. "Trevor's trying to figure out why the backup generators didn't come on."

"So much for quadruple redundancy," Rob said. Eduardo gave him a sour look. "Sorry. Try your access code in this sequence."

"You have higher system clearance than I do," Eduardo said.

"I know, but if mine's not working, you're next on the list."

The system returned another failure. "Contact Nexon," Eduardo said. "Get her working."

"Do we have communications?" Rob asked.

"At emergency levels only. No shifting," Eduardo replied over his shoulder.

Rob said, "Molly, I need to message Nex—" and then remembered that she wouldn't respond.

* * *

Teague's mobile buzzed a few seconds after he'd sent his message to Bondi. An emergency broadcast. Power failure. Normal station operations suspended until further notice. A list of affected systems. He heard voices outside his room.

"Should I be worried?" Teague asked a group of grad students who had gathered in the hall.

"Only if they can't get power back online in seventy-two hours," replied a material science researcher.

"What happens then?" Teague asked, but the group was already moving on, and his mobile rang.

"Come on up," Aron said.

Teague launched himself up the ladder well to the thirty-third floor, hoping he'd find some answers there. Aron answered his door tugging on a thick hoodie. "Want a drink?" he asked.

"Isn't this an emergency?" Teague asked.

"It'll keep you warm."

"The heat's not off-line. The message said so."

"There's a huge difference between sustaining life and providing comfort," Aron said.

"At least we're not depressurizing."

"Not yet," Aron said, filling a glass with scotch.

"Maybe I will have a drink." Teague settled on a stool at the kitchenette's counter.

"I arranged golf with a couple of guys from the Philosophy Department this weekend. You interested?" Aron asked as he handed Teague a glass. "Provided we're not huddled in an emergency bunker waiting for the Tranquillitas to come back?"

"Do you ever stop thinking about golf?" Teague asked. "Anyway, I thought you said the philosophers were high the last time you played with them."

"I said they played like they were high, but still better than you."

"Nice."

"You know," Aron began as they relocated to his couches, "I've been thinking about our conversation last night."

"Which part?" Teague asked.

"About how Thomas never told you that I couldn't shift. I wondered what else they didn't tell us. And I came to the conclusion that Matthew expects me to work for his company after I graduate."

"But you don't want to?"

"I've told him as much," Aron said. "And it's not exactly a little family business he can leave me in his will. I'd be made vice president of not-fucking-anything-up with a hundred other VPs waiting to slit my throat or watch me fail. Thank you, but no."

"You don't want your father's job someday?"

"When's someday? It might be four hundred years until he retires."

"I hadn't thought of that," Teague said. "But what if he doesn't give you a choice?"

"He probably will, but—and don't take this the wrong way—I'm Aron Valdosky. I can do anything I want. I'm not trying to be arrogant; that's just the way it is."

"I get it," Teague said. Would graduating as a Wolkenbruch fellow give him that same kind of cachet? Teague had his doubts. "Did you ever meet Adrian Wolkenbruch?"

"No, but see, him I admire. He did the Vanilla thing, but then he dropped out, left a void for someone new."

"So what do you want to do?"

"I want to run my own ski resort," Aron said.

"I've never been."

"Damn, Teague. First thing when we bust out of here, I'm taking you snowboarding."

"Earth or Mars?" Teague asked.

Aron thought for a moment, and then said, "Both. Tahoe's close to Vegas, isn't it?"

That night, the entire station seemed to have caught Teague's insomnia. The emergency had become a furtive celebration of sorts. Aron and many others sought safety in numbers at the bar, rescuing the unrefrigerated beer by putting it through human filters before it had to be poured in with the wastewater. There were lines outside the only set of working restrooms in the Casino. Couples lurked in the many nooks not reached by the emergency lighting. Teague seemed to be the only person alone. He huddled sideways in a cafeteria booth, bundled against the coming chill and waiting for Bondi's reply.

After Teague had filtered a mug and a half of coffee through his own system, Bondi's message arrived—text only, thanks to the emergency bandwidth restrictions:

> The good news is that Monkey's diagnostics check out. Zubots are supposed to be curious and familiar with the owner's home. In fact, they must explore their "home" to record the geography. Home might be a room, a house, or I suppose even a whole exostation. To keep Monkey from wandering, it might be as simple as having a little heart-to-heart with him about the boundaries of "home."

Teague acknowledged and braced for the bad news.

* * *

Rob's mobile's battery gave out along with his patience. Nexon's third suggested bypass boot sequence had failed for the millionth time. He slammed his mobile on its desk charger, where it entirely failed to start charging. He swore. He swore again when he realized that his coffee maker wasn't on an emergency circuit either. He had to get out, even if for only a few minutes.

A cafeteria worker was babying perhaps the sole working coffee maker on the station as if it were mission critical. Rob thanked her as she filled his mug, which made him feel slightly less frustrated, fractionally less impotent.

"You look terrible."

Rob turned to see Teague, wearing at least two sweatshirts and holding a mug.

"Molly's offline," Rob said.

"Is that what's caused the power outage?" Teague asked.

"No, she's—it's because… Sorry. I don't want to worry you, but this kind of thing isn't supposed to happen. Molly's on the emergency power systems, and she even has her own backup batteries. It just doesn't make any sense. These systems are supposed to be IBC Section Ninety."

"What does that mean?"

"It's the building code for exohabitats. The power grid is practically everything-proof. It shouldn't hurt Molly like this." Rob followed Teague's gaze to his socked feet and laughed weakly. "Forgotten I'd taken them off. I better get back."

* * *

Teague passed his own mug to the server for a refill. At the end of the buffet, Rob hastily squirted a blob of creamer through the membrane of his own mug and missed. Swearing, he mopped up the mess with his shirt and shoved off. Was it strange that Rob had seemed more distressed about Molly than the implications of a long-term power outage? When she had introduced herself through Monkey, Teague hadn't thought how odd it was—creepy, even—that the NAI who controlled every critical system on the station had the voice of a little girl. That must have been Rob's doing. He wasn't concerned about Molly just because of his job, or his safety. Teague realized that he knew exactly how Rob was feeling. He'd seem that same look of desperation in the mirror.

Bondi's next message arrived a few minutes later.

> The bad news is that Monkey's "handshake" with your local NAI was more than it should have been. Monkey was configured to accept a collaboration. In Nexon-speak, that's just two or more networked NAIs. The individual entities retain distinctive personalities but share data and resources. This is usually carefully controlled, not accidental.
>
> Monkey's settings were an artifact of the software version I provided. I'm sorry, but it honestly didn't occur to me to close that gate. And it seems your local administrator was just as sloppy.
>
> To further complicate the issue, collaborations are hierarchical, and it appears that Monkey has taken the dominant role.
>
> Severing the collaboration may raise red flags. If you want Monkey to separate, you may have to come clean to the local sysadmin. In the meantime, ask Monkey to stay out of local operations. Make sure he understands that your commands to him do not apply to the local NAI. It may take some effort to help him draw clear lines of separation.

Teague flushed as if everyone on the station had turned to stare. He needed to run, to fly. He forced himself to gather his mug and to take his protein bar wrappers to the recycler, to exit the dark cafeteria at an unhurried pace. He passed the noisy, flash-light-lit bar without making any eye contact and shoved off hard toward the ladder well.

* * *

Deep below the loading docks, near the primary solar array maintenance airlock, Rob took a deep breath and knocked on the doorframe of the Central Generation Control Room. Trevor, the lead electrician, turned from studying a pop-up box of component feedback on the wrap-around desk screen. Eduardo rose from breathing down his neck. The maze of ADU's power systems usually glowed bright green with little linked icons at all the key components. Tonight, the shattered system glowed red and gray and blinked in alarm.

"My mobile's dead, and I'm out of ideas, unless we can find a virgin to sacrifice," Rob said.

Eduardo glowered. "Nothing more from Nexon?" he asked.

"They say she's not going to wake up under an intermittent power situation."

"It's some kind of feedback loop," Trevor said. "But what's the chicken and what's the egg? We think something glitched, another thing compensated, then something else registered a real failure, and round and round."

"We've got everyone isolating and checking everything between here and Kindergarten," Eduardo said. "If we don't find a solution in the next six hours, we're going to have to do a manual conversion."

"Without Molly?" Rob asked.

"The system can operate without Molly," Eduardo said. "But it'll take time, and I don't want the reserve batteries below fifty percent before we start."

Rob worried, not for the first time, that this might be blamed on Molly, but he couldn't conscionably defend her yet. A voice squawked out over Trevor's mobile. "EPS-Niner Two-Three checked, negative."

"Got it," Trevor replied. He tapped the control screen, closing one pop-up and opening another. "Move to EPS-Nine Forty-Five."

A heartbeat later, the whole screen bloomed green. Icons smiled. A warm, electric hum saturated the room.

"What did you do?" Eduardo begged.

"Nothing," Trevor said.

"Don't touch anything. Tell everyone to stop what they're doing," Eduardo said. He turned to Rob with the look of a man in a holed pressure suit returned miraculously to an airlock. Trevor got on his mobile. Rob bolted for Kindergarten.

The lights seemed to be back on everywhere. Cheers spilled across the Casino lobby from the bar.

"Molly?" Rob called from the hallway and again as he burst into the data room.

"Hi, Daddy," she said.

"Don't ever do that again," he scolded.

* * *

Monkey nuzzled into Teague's neck as the station's lights came on outside his window. When Teague stopped trembling, he set Monkey on the shift couch and pulled himself to a seat on the bed.

"We need to talk," Teague said.

CHAPTER 17

I tried to rebel loudly enough for you to hear me continents away. I may have called it fun, but it's a pity that we have so little wisdom when we are young.

DECEMBER 2090

"Are you out of thirty-nine?" Rob asked.

"Daddy, there *are* indicator lights," Molly replied.

"Would you rather I just yank your components out without asking?"

"No, but..."

Rob chuckled and tugged the inert server out of its cove. Molly had changed in the past few months. She had always been sweet and compliant, but recently she'd become sarcastic and, for lack of a better term, mouthy. By his own design, she had grown to mimic the personality of a nine-year-old. Was this new attitude some presage of puberty? Rob shuddered to think of it as he set the server on the workbench. He removed the casing and maneuvered the magnifying lamp for a better view.

"There's frost on a capillary. Must be a tiny hole. That explains the trouble code."

"That's what I've been telling you," Molly said. Rob could almost feel her roll her eyes.

As he began to rifle through the parts drawers, Rob's music hit a good bit and he asked Molly to turn up the volume. A murky drum and bass beat throbbed through his offices. Day or night, no one ever complained about the noise. Kindergarten was a virtual ghost town these days. Rob's hips found the beat, and he began to sing along with an ethereal vocal interwoven with the sampling. He soon found the replacement part, turned, and an animal landed on the workbench. Rob squawked, lurched away, and landed on his backside. Teague appeared over him with a hand outstretched.

"Must you always scare the shit out of me?" Rob asked. Teague's lips moved. "Molly, music off."

"The door was open and we knocked, but I guess you couldn't hear us," Teague said.

"I didn't need dry pants anyway." Rob let Teague haul him upright.

"There's a cooling capillary failure," Monkey announced. He pointed urgently and then stuck his arm into the open server.

"Stop," Rob shouted. Monkey froze, and Rob glared at Teague. "What does he think he's doing?"

"I used to work for an electronics repair guy in Bangkok," Teague said. "Monkey got to be pretty handy."

"I like to fix things," Monkey said. "And I have tiny fingers."

"I'm kind of particu—"

"I'm sure he can fix it," Teague said. "Go ahead, Monk."

A few seconds later, Monkey popped up with the faulty part, inspected it briefly, and tossed it aside. He located the new part where Rob had dropped it and opened the package delicately. "You're a good dancer, Mr. Heneghan." Monkey waggled his raised rear end to his own beat as he dove back into the server.

"Pay attention to what you're doing," Rob said and turned to Teague. "Your smart-ass lemur better not break anything."

"There's residue from the leak," Monkey said. "Do you have an alcohol swab?"

Rob sputtered, "I'll take care of it. Sorry, but I'd really rather do this myself."

Teague beckoned, and Monkey hopped off the workbench.

"So you're out wandering the halls? Everyone gets squirrely the night before a boat arrives," Rob said.

"I just couldn't sleep. We heard music and decided to see who it was."

Monkey's repair work appeared up to spec, but Rob set the casing over the open electronics in case it got any more ideas. "Want some coffee?" he asked.

"Might as well," Teague said.

"So I heard Aron's planning ahead," Rob called into the workroom as he fired up his coffee maker.

"Oh, yeah?" Teague asked, coming to the doorway.

"Saul told me that Aron's ordered a liquor store's worth of booze that's arriving tomorrow. Sounds to me like he's gearing up for some serious parties."

"Sounds like Aron," Teague said. "He's convinced that most of the undergraduates arriving tomorrow are women, coming just because of him."

"Oh, I have *that* fantasy all the time," Rob said with a laugh. "But if Aron can bring ADU back, I'm all for it. There used to be some great shindigs." Teague rolled his eyes. "Hey, there are worse things than partying with Aron Valdosky."

"It's just that he's been all over my case lately. He thinks I care too much about school, and that it'll cramp his style."

"Maybe he's right," Rob said as he filled two relatively clean membrane mugs.

"I can't afford to waste my time out here partying," Teague said, accepting a mug. "When this fellowship is over, I have to float out of here on the merits of my accomplishments, not on my parents' name."

"I would think that building a lasting friendship with Aron Valdosky would be job *numero uno,* no matter what the academic costs. My dad always used to tell me that it's not what you know, but who you know. And what they think of you."

Teague sipped his coffee and considered this. "Maybe you're right," he said. Rob felt his skin turn warm. Was this why people rebuked him all the time? This addictive rush of rightness? "But I don't want Aron believing I'm someone I'm not."

"I'm not saying you have to kiss his ass," Rob said. "Besides, Aron's too smart to fall for an act. Just be yourself."

"Sounds like advice from a Zubot," Teague said.

"I heard that," Monkey said.

"So what's M-SOO?" Teague asked, nodding to Rob's homemade logo bouncing around the table screen. "Is that your research project—the asteroid thing?" Rob nodded. "What does it stand for?"

"Mid-System Object Observatory," Rob said. "But that's just a temporary name."

"Want to show it to me?"

"Sure. Molly?"

"How may I help you, Rob?" Molly replied, in her public voice.

"Let's show Teague the orrery."

"Right away, Rob," Molly said.

"What?" Rob asked Teague, seeing the surprise on his face.

"I guess I've never really heard Molly's voice before," Teague said. "Not what I expected."

* * *

Too many ADU residents had spent the night saying goodbye to friends or lovers, or had spent hours searching their souls for a reason to stay, or to go, to worry about disturbing Gwen's breakfast. Rob finally spotted her at a table next to the recyclers, nearly back to back with her nearest neighbor and shoveling in her food with exceptional ferocity. But on a boat day, and this close to Christmas, her fearsomeness seemed to have lost its teeth.

"Good morning, Starshine," Rob said as he joined her.

"Fuck off," Gwen mumbled, glaring around her.

"Two seconds to the f-bomb. Not a record, folks, but good enough for the top ten," Rob announced, but no one turned around. "Sorry, Gwen. But, listen, can I ask you a serious question?"

Gwen grunted and then growled as one of the newer astronomers jostled her as he dumped his tray in the receptacles.

"Because Teague wandered into my offices last night, and I ended up showing him M-SOO. He recognized almost right away that it could be a great little company. He asked a ton of questions about the business side that I couldn't answer. It's really got me thinking. I focus so much on the code that I guess I never consider the other stuff."

"I'm not hearing a question."

"I guess I'm wondering if you think M-SOO might make a good start-up company."

"And a child shall lead them. You haven't listened to a word I've ever said, have you, Bertram? I tell you to think about the business details all the time, but when some drooling undergraduate pulls out his pacifier to compliment you, then you listen?"

"Teague's pretty smart," Rob said.

"And what am I?"

"You've been telling me to get grants."

"I've been telling you to get capital. Completely different things," Gwen spat, leaving a chewed fleck on her lower lip. Rob resisted the urge to offer her a napkin.

"What's the difference?"

"Don't play dumb. I hate that."

"I'm not playing dumb," Rob said. "Maybe I'm a little thick, but this isn't easy for me." Gwen rolled her eyes and shoved a whole piece of bacon in her mouth, taking the fleck with it.

"Grou uf."

"What?"

"You heard me, I said, 'Grow up.' No, strike that. Grow *the fuck* up."

"Why do you talk to me like this?"

"Somebody has to," Gwen said. "Do you need a fucking neon sign?"

"Not everyone can be like you, Gwen."

"God, you're predictable." Gwen swallowed. "You have this brilliant idea that solves a huge problem, but you've squandered *years* sitting on your lazy ass."

"You think M-SOO is brilliant?"

"Getting less brilliant by the second. If you can't see that, then…" Gwen shook her head.

"Fine. I'm lazy. I'll try and do better, but you shouldn't be so hard on the undergraduates."

"Why the hell not?"

"Because you were once a freshman, too. And there's a bunch of them arriving today. Who knows? You might like some of them."

"They wouldn't like me."

"Not with those table manners."

"Besides, ever since Valdosky the Lesser arrived, the faculty have been behaving like a bunch of idiots. It's become a status symbol to have an undergrad puppy. It's nauseating. You didn't show M-SOO to *him*, did you?"

"Who?"

"Who do you think?" she sputtered.

"Aron?"

"Just tell me you didn't."

"I can show M-SOO to whoever I want."

Gwen snarled, gathered her ravaged tray, and left in a cardigan huff.

Rob wondered if he'd actually missed something in all the times Gwen had talked to him about M-SOO. Why had Teague's questions inspired him, while Gwen's advice had made him feel weak, stupid, and defensive? Rob supposed that was self-explanatory.

At least there would probably be a party tonight, hopefully with a boatload of smart, young women, excited to inaugurate their adventure on an asteroid. And if no women showed? At least they'd have Aron's booze. He could worry about M-SOO tomorrow.

* * *

"Who's going to drink all this?" Teague called. At least a dozen cases of various adult beverages blocked the entrance to Aron's kitchenette. "Is it even legal to own this much at once?" If Rob was to be believed, these piles were only the tip of the iceberg, and another cargo container's worth occupied a storage bay somewhere deep under the Casino.

"Don't know. Don't care," Aron called from his bedroom. "Help yourself."

Teague almost declined, but who knew how long it might take for Aron to dress and primp for the reception. Teague squeezed into the kitchenette, wrangled a membraned tumbler out of the refrigerator, and pumped a few sips of scotch from a bottle on the counter.

Teague had come to love the view from Aron's suite. He enjoyed knowing that beyond these visible stars and the velvet abyss were millions of galaxies undetectable to the naked eye. He imagined reaching through the cool glass, scooping them up, and pouring them out like sand.

"I think I found our Lucy Frye," Teague called.

"You're not wearing a tie, are you?" Aron replied from the bedroom.

"Did you hear me?" Teague asked.

"What are you talking about, Lucy Frye? We're meeting real, actual women in a few minutes. You need to focus. You're leaving the lemur behind?"

"What are you going to do if all these girls are hideous?" Teague called back, but Aron didn't take the bait. Teague turned back to his own reflection. If Aron was right, then he was about to face unprecedented female scrutiny. And Shakiro Squirrel help him if Aron was wrong. He'd never hear the end of it.

Aron emerged, his clothes looking casual but still well cut and oozing money. "I can't believe Thomas forced us to sit through class today," he said.

"What kind of woman makes the commitment to come all the way out here just for a chance at meeting you?" Teague asked.

"Dangerous," Aron said, "and smart as hell. We must be cautious."

"Cautious?" *We?* "But what if you fall for some girl and then she goes public on you? Tries to capitalize on intimate knowledge?" Teague asked, genuinely curious.

"I cut her off. Cold turkey. And my mom has a kick-ass privacy and libel attorney," Aron replied. "But the fakers are pretty easy to suss out. Still, what's our watchword?"

"Caution?"

"Exactly. Don't promise them anything. Don't lie to them, and definitely don't get anyone pregnant."

"Everyone's on Vanilla out here. No one's getting pregnant."

"Fine, but this is no time for complacency. These women will be smart, fast, and four steps ahead. And even if they hate each other, they'll talk more than you and I ever will."

"You've met these kind of women before?"

"Occupational hazard," Aron said. "Sorry, but it's a fact that certain women will position themselves in my path. It might be the money. It might be the celebri—"

"Or the money," Teague said.

"Hey. I don't like it much either. And I don't get any middle ground. Either women like me—for various reasons—or they hate me utterly. Like the Red Bitch, for instance. Anyway, you shouldn't doubt me. In fact, you should be on my side. The more women who arrive, the better your chances of finding a nice girl for yourself."

"Oh, now these are nice girls?" Teague asked.

"For the love of all that's good and holy, I hope not."

The same quartet sawed the same melodies by the same flowerbed. The same woman, Fong, whom Teague had since gotten to know as one of his favorite cafeteria servers, tended the bar again. Canapés waited to be plucked from the same trays. But a fresh excitement buzzed around the patio, an energy Teague hadn't felt during June's welcome reception, his reception. This evening, groups dared to laugh and share bright conversation, as if boredom had been repealed. The faculty hadn't clumped into stodgy gray clouds of tweed and wine. And although the cocktail dresses were perhaps not as plentiful as Aron might have hoped, President Mbuto no longer stood out as the singular vibrant centerpiece.

"Aron!"

"Eskimo!" Aron exclaimed. "Why didn't you tell me you were coming to this shit-hole?" A dark-haired Martian landed at a foot hook next to Aron, and they exchanged a handshake born of an excess of testosterone.

"Wanted to surprise you," said the person called Eskimo. His almond eyes were too small and too close together to make sense with his elongated features and boyish grin. "Besides, you'd have had time to hide all your booze."

"You were hell-bent on Cornell; what happened?"

"When word got out about you, Agnus Dei was everyone's first choice."

"Anyone else make it?"

"No one I know, but with the price…"

"Please tell me some women made the trip," Aron begged.

"There were a few of the fairer sex on the shuttle. Some fairer than others. But there were a couple of shuttle runs, and I was in perma-shift the whole way here."

Teague sensed surreptitious glances and outright stares from around the patio, but he knew they weren't for him.

"Eskimo, I'm being rude," Aron said. "This is Teague, my sole brother in arms out here. Twenty-plus handicap, but he wasn't born on a course like you. Teague, this is Hayden Escrima-Bharati. His dad's a contractor. Built almost everything south of the equator."

Teague shook Eskimo's massive hand but found it weak.

"Call me Eskimo. Everyone does."

"Even his mom," Aron said.

"Your mom screams it every day," Eskimo shot back with a grin and then looked past Aron. "Hold on. What have we here?"

Three impossibly lithe Martian-born women were approaching, each in a cocktail dress straight off a red carpet.

At that moment, Teague felt a touch and turned to find President Mbuto. "May I steal you away, Mr. Werres?" she said. Teague honestly didn't know whether he was irritated or relieved.

President Mbuto introduced Teague to a circle of familiar faculty interspersed with a few new faces, all Mars- or Lunar-born. "Teague Werres is the current Wolkenbruch fellow, reading business and economics. He's been with us for—how long now?"

"Six months, ma'am," Teague replied.

"I'm sure he'd be happy to show any of you the ropes," she said with a nod to the newcomers. Laughter rang from Aron's general direction.

The only newcomer from Earth proved to be a doughy post-doc keen to describe his esoteric genetic experiments to Teague in intense detail. Before Teague had concocted an excuse to get away, President Mbuto called all the undergraduates together for a photo. Teague soon found himself set like a mascot in front of almost two dozen children of lesser gravity. *Out of the frying pan,* Teague thought.

As the photographer worked, Teague noticed Thomas's scowl among the onlookers. When Mbuto dismissed the group, Teague turned to rejoin Aron and Eskimo, but Thomas beckoned him aside.

"You're not happy with all the new undergrads?" Teague asked.

"It's out of my control," Thomas said. "I can't stop the university from fulfilling its mission."

"Aron knows some of these people," Teague said.

"Yes." Neither spoke for several seconds, and then Thomas motioned for Teague to follow him along a pathway. Once out of sight of the patio, Thomas said, "I must ask you to make every effort to maintain your friendship with Aron."

"Easier said than done," Teague said. "Aron has a very short attention span, and I'm more of a long-attention-span person."

"You will always have one thing in common with Aron that the rest of them do not."

"I figured that out," Teague said. "Why didn't you tell me?"

"It wasn't germane," Thomas replied.

"Germane? How could it not be germane? It's not the only reason I got this fellowship, is it?"

"Of course not," Thomas said. "Is there some reason you don't wish to be friends with Aron?" Teague shook his head. "Then I fail to see why this is disagreeable."

"It's not," Teague said and swallowed. "I should get back." Thomas nodded.

When Teague returned to the patio, he heard his name. Aron had moved to a secluded table with Eskimo and the three women.

"I was afraid you'd gone on Professor Ojibwe's tour of the minicollider," Aron said as Teague approached.

"Nah, you've seen one atom smasher, you've seen them all," Teague said, forcing himself to smile.

"Ladies, this is Teague. Teague, Gemma, Andreneanna—did I get that right?"

"Neanna," said the girl with the long, wavy blond hair. Gemma smiled from behind a cascade of dark ringlets. Teague tried to find beauty in their Martian features, but they seemed more like caricatures of women. Eskimo had stretched an arm around the back of Gemma's chair.

"And also Crystal." Aron grinned as if he'd just pulled her naked from the sea. "Apparently, I went to preschool with Neanna, but she has more vivid memories of it than I do."

"You really don't remember those rooms decorated like little caves?" Neanna asked.

"I remember getting sent to the time-out stool for wrestling with Perry Widmer," Aron said.

* * *

Rob watched as Aron called Teague over and introduced him to the three freshman women. Rob had met each of them briefly as they had been introduced around by their professors. The black-haired woman was a physics major, but neither Rachelle nor her boyfriend had spent any time with her yet. Professor Wendell had presented the blond woman as a math protégé, and a couple of the crueler grad students had already dubbed her Mary Magdalene behind the professor's back. But the brunette? Rob ached to know whether he could get away with asking her to advise M-SOO on matters of astronomy. He hadn't had an official astronomic consultant since Mike had left ADU, and it might be good experience for a young undergraduate. Wouldn't it? Why did it have to be *her* already at Aron's side?

One of the physicists in Rob's group said something that made everyone laugh. Rob chuckled and wished he'd actually heard the quip.

A few minutes later, Aron and Teague's little sextet—who was that other guy?—got up from their table and began to wend their way through the reception. Rob hoped they'd notice him, but they floated past, down the brick path to the exit.

Rob hadn't expected Aron to hop on a table and announce a decadent new dawn for ADU, but he had expected something. A nudge, perhaps. A whisper. After-party's in the observation deck, but don't tell *too* many people. Wink.

"Has anyone heard about a party or anything?" Rob asked the physicists.

"Tonight?" one asked. The others shrugged.

"Or maybe this weekend?" Rob asked. No one had.

Less than half an hour later, Rob abandoned the reception without saying goodbye to anyone. He steered toward his room but found himself back in his office.

"Are you okay, Daddy?" Molly asked as Rob tumbled onto his shift couch.

"Are there any parties going on anywhere on the station?"

"Not that I know of," Molly said.

"Any gatherings of ten or more people?"

"The only gathering that large is in the arboretum."

"And how many people are in Aron Valdosky's suite right now?"

"Six," Molly replied. "Why do you want to know?"

Rob plucked his shift nodes off their charger, clipped them on, and let himself disappear.

A few minutes later, Rob stared into a permanent sunset from a bluff that overlooked a faux Aegean. Kyle's tri-hulled uber-yacht floated in a white-sand inlet below. Mermaids silently explored the wreckage of ancient sunken triremes in azure water. On the far horizon, a volcano spat pyroclastics into the sky under the watchful guidance of a benevolent Poseidon. White gulls sailed on unfelt breezes and crapped on nothing. Rob dragged himself up the steps and let himself into Kyle's vacation estate with the family passcode.

At the bar in the billiards room, Rob scrolled through Kyle's buzz programs—his brother must have done work for some beverage corporation—and picked a trendy-sounding tequila. He tweaked the settings to the maximum and gulped it down. A more-than-pleasant, slightly disorienting vibration stole through his consciousness and imbued his surroundings with a blurry glow.

Rob considered calling Reika. She'd agreed to spur-of-the-moment rendezvous a few times since she'd been reassigned, but not for months. He opened his contacts list and put a twenty-four hour block on Reika's eddress before he did something he'd regret. He popped another tequila buzz program and flopped onto his back on the empty pool table. Clouds and the occasional winged horse, or messenger, drifted by on the ceiling's mural.

Rob thought he'd become pretty good friends with Teague and Aron, but three guys, three women. Who needed Old Man Heneghan along? Just another loser grad student with nothing to show for his years at ADU but a glorified work-study job and memories of the good old days. He may as well grow a beard like Saul's, stop showering, and settle down with a virtual Light District girl.

Rob linked to the house's bowling alley with a six-pack of beer-buzz hits, some Danish—or Belgian?—brand. It didn't matter. He just needed to knock some things down.

Rob played three frames and then realized that he was about to open his fourth beer hit. The mechanism swept away the pins and set ten more for him. Rob picked up his ball and readied to roll again, but then dropped it back on the return. He reset the game, this time including a second player. He opened his control interface, canceled the buzz programs, and then, sober, made the call he'd known he would make even before he arrived.

It took only a few minutes for Molly to shimmer into U-shift.

She squealed excitedly and ran to hug him. She felt like a wisp of smoke or fairy magic in his arms, but so tall—already well over a meter and a half. Had he been that tall at nine?

"Do you remember how to play?" Rob asked.

"Of course," Molly said.

"Do you still need the bumpers?"

She scowled playfully and asked, "No. Do you, Daddy?" God, she was an adorable little girl.

Rob plopped down at the scorer's table and said, "Well, then, show me what you got."

She shuffled to the line with her ball clutched to her chest. She smiled at him and then set the ball rolling with both hands. She cocked her head and gazed after her meandering roll. The ball trundled lazily down the lane, clipped the side of the arrangement, and toppled first one, then four pins.

"Not too bad," Rob remarked. "Have you been practicing?"

"No," she said with a laugh.

"How's school going? Still studying to be a programmer like your dad?"

"Not really," Molly replied.

"Oh, so what do you want to be when you grow up?" Rob asked. Her ball swirled back onto the return.

"Maybe a model, or a spy," Molly said and collected her ball. She scooted to the line and said, "Maybe both." She knocked down two more pins.

"A model spy. Where'd you get that idea?" Rob laughed. "Is Mom letting you play some RPG I'd never approve of?"

"Maybe," Molly said.

Rob rose to take his turn, and Molly took his seat. She interlocked her fingers and furrowed her brow in mock formality. "So, Father, what do you want to be when you grow up?" she asked.

Rob stared at the simple gaping face on his ball. The hollow eyes. The silent mouth.

"Daddy?" Molly asked. "Sorry, should I not have asked that?"

"No. It's okay," Rob said. "I'm sorry. Maybe you should go."

"But I like to spend time with you," she said.

This was the lie of NAI. Jules was so right. She embodied a delusion, his delusion. "I know," he said. "But I need…this was a bad idea. Why don't you go on home?"

"Okay," she said.

"Can you make sure I'm awake by eight tomorrow morning?" Rob asked.

She agreed and walked over to him. He let her wrap her soft, scrawny arms around his neck. "I love you, Daddy," she said.

"I love you, too," Rob said. Then she disappeared.

Rob linked back to the bar. He probed his bat-belt for a handy widget he'd acquired in college and overrode G-Plex's buzz hit quantity limits. He grabbed the remainder of Kyle's tequila hits, tweaked them high, and downed them all.

He managed somehow to link to his usual guest bedroom before black, blissful despair swallowed him whole.

* * *

The next evening, after dinner and an exhausting eighteen holes with Aron and Eskimo, Teague returned to his room for a shower. And although he'd agreed to be quick and then to come up to Aron's to hang out, he lingered under the water.

"You're not even trying," Aron had whispered last night, pulling Teague aside into the kitchenette and nodding toward Neanna.

"What am I supposed to do?" Teague had asked.

"You're being rude."

"She's not talking to me either. Besides, it's fairly obvious she has no interest in me."

"You're not even giving her a chance to get to know you."

"Give me a break. Just because we're the leftovers doesn't mean we're meant to be together."

"Whatever. It's your loss," Aron had said.

Teague was still searching for a viable excuse to not attend even as he knocked on Aron's door.

"There you are," Aron said. "We thought you'd drowned." Teague smiled, but not at Aron's joke. Neanna had brought a friend. Teague recognized him at once, the mathematician from the Moon who often played guitar in the bar.

"Hey, Isaac. Nice to see you," Teague said. Isaac waved cautiously, apparently stunned by his own good fortune to be here, and with Neanna. Teague accepted a cold beer and settled alone on an armchair.

He had spent most of the previous evening listening, observing, with little to add to their remembrances from the Red Planet, or their tales of shifting adventures lovingly described for Aron's benefit. Eskimo was aware of Aron's disability, but the girls had been shocked to learn of it. They had oozed with sympathy, splitting it, Teague thought, in rather unequal shares for Aron and himself. Since that moment, Teague had watched their faces for regret. Had they realized that their desire to befriend—or entrap—Aron would sentence them to the tedium of the real? How long would they tolerate a virtual drought when they learned that Aron was just a person and not the fantasy?

A quarter of an hour later, Gemma was describing some new amusement park in shift when Teague's mobile rang. "It's Thomas," he told Aron after checking the screen.

"Ignore it," Aron said.

"Who's Thomas?" Neanna asked.

"Professor Minus, our economics professor," Aron replied. "Why's he calling you so late?" Teague took the call in Aron's kitchenette.

"Have I caught you at a bad time?" Thomas asked.

Teague found Thomas's door in an uninspired block of apartments generally considered to be out of bounds to students. "Thanks for coming. Sorry about this," Thomas said, indicating the stacks of crates that crowded the entryway. "Saul delivered them this afternoon." One of the top crates had been opened and was full of books. As was Thomas's living room.

Everything from hardback tomes to paperback pamphlets had been crammed onto floor-to-ceiling shelves. Mismatched volumes tottered in haphazard piles on the floor and were strewn over the coffee table. Makeshift bookshelves lined the dark hall that led to the nether-reaches of Thomas's private life. Only a pair of distinguished and aged leather armchairs, like islands in a sea of musty paper, remained clear.

"Just making some tea," Thomas called from the bright, narrow kitchen.

"This is quite a collection," Teague said. "Where are you going to put all the new arrivals?"

"I'll find room," Thomas said. A hot pot signaled its readiness. Thomas docked the spout with a membraned glass teapot and injected the boiling water with the press of a plunger. "There should be a packet of biscuits in there," he said, waving to a cupboard.

Teague found it, and Thomas scattered a few under the transparent lid of a plate.

"Do you actually read them all?" Teague asked.

"Most of them. Call it irrational if you like, but I believe there's a certain amount of value in keeping hard copies. A hedge against the fluidity of digital information, if you will. But mostly I'm old enough to still prefer reading real books."

Once they'd settled on the armchairs with steaming mugs of tea, Thomas began, "I know it's late and that you were probably with friends, but I felt that I owed you an apology in person." He offered the plate of cookies. "You were right. I should have been up front with you about your common disability with Aron. I'm very sorry if you feel I've been deceitful."

"Thank you," Teague said. He knew the offense was a small price to pay for his free lunch.

"I want to assure you again that it wasn't the sole basis for your selection."

But I'm sure it didn't hurt, Teague thought. "I appreciate you saying that."

"You've done exceptionally well so far. Adapted well," Thomas said. Teague nodded. "I'm well aware that coming to ADU wouldn't have been Aron's personal choice, but he seems to be making the best of it also."

"He just doesn't want his future decided for him." Teague supposed that was obvious enough to mention without breaking a trust.

"Yes," Thomas said. "Also, I want to apologize for framing my request about Aron the way I did. It was not the time or place to ask that of you. I won't make excuses. I'll simply admit that I used poor judgment."

"I don't understand why you would think that I wouldn't stay friends with Aron," Teague said.

"I, of course, have no qualms about your interpersonal skills. However, I am concerned with a major project that will be assigned during the latter half of your fellowship."

"What kind of project?"

"President Mbuto and I are still ironing out the details, but it will be a collaborative effort between you and Aron. If done well, the work may serve you after graduation. However, the project may suffer if you don't have a good—" Thomas broke off. "You look concerned."

"Being friends with Aron is one thing, but working together is another," Teague said.

"I understand," Thomas said.

"I mean, he's fun to be around."

"I'm sure he is. But I think we both understand that a person like Aron prefers to travel the path of least resistance. I'm not necessarily characterizing this as a flaw; in fact, such people can be quite inventive. But if you set the right tone…"

"Are you suggesting that I take the lead on this project? You think Aron will accept that?"

"Ask yourself: Does Aron exhibit the traits of a leader, or does he wear the guise of a leader because of his status? And if he'd not a leader…?"

He's a follower, Teague thought. "You think Aron sees me as a leader?"

"I'm suggesting that Aron will follow the voice that guides him on the easiest route to success on his own terms. Do you want that to be you?"

Teague shivered as if approaching the crux of a great idea. Had he somehow understood this six months ago, when he had joked to Aron that they needed a Lucy Frye?

Thomas paused and set his teacup aside. "I'll tell you something else about Aron Valdosky. He takes after his father in many ways."

Teague considered this for a moment and shivered again.

"If you're cold, you should wear layers," Thomas said. He peeled back his collar to reveal several shirts underneath his sweater. "A little trick I picked up in a Manchurian winter."

* * *

Teague rolled out of the tube onto the top floor of Kindergarten to find Eskimo arguing with Saul in front of a sign that read, "Happy New Year 2091!—Togas Only Beyond This Point." Whatever the argument, Eskimo's credibility couldn't be helped by the fact that he was wearing a sheet and a foil crown of laurels. Behind Saul, Mr. Arcoverde, the facility manager, was rubbing the bridge of his nose.

"Oh my god, Teague," Eskimo said.

"Yes, Caesar? Or is it Caligula?" Teague moved aside as several sheet-clad grad students spilled from the tube behind him.

"Go get Aron. These guys are saying that the heat and lights are going off in an hour."

"Where is he?"

"Probably the Orgy Room." Eskimo pointed.

"As long as it's not the vomitorium," Teague said.

There was indeed a well-marked Orgy Room, but the thirty or so people inside had thankfully not taken the suggestion. "Where's your toga?" Aron called as Teague entered.

"I'm not in Rome," Teague replied. He scanned the room. About a third of the attendees had also ignored the dress code.

"I know what you're thinking," Aron said. His laurel crown was made of gold paper, and his sheets dangled magnificently from a brooch on one shoulder.

"I hope not," Teague said.

"You're thinking that we'll run out of wine, but fear not, Citizen. The gods themselves could not drink it all."

"I'm sure. Hey, Caligula needs a more powerful emperor out in the hall. Something about the heat and lights."

Aron rolled his eyes. "Get changed. I mean it," he called over his shoulder as he left.

Crystal and Gemma were monitoring a five-gallon tub of a murky purple beverage that Teague was certain wasn't grape-based. Their togas weren't simply bed sheets retasked, but appeared to be cut, draped, and sewn to fit. "Is there a costume shop on this station I don't know about?" Teague asked them.

"You should dress up," Gemma said. "The boys have worked so hard on this party." Crystal filled a beverage pack and offered it to Teague. He took a sip and nearly spat it out.

"Excellent," he sputtered as the girls laughed.

"We made a ton of it," Crystal said.

Rob bellied up to the table, nearly colliding with Teague and upending the rack of empty beverage packs. "More wine," he demanded. Crystal rolled her eyes.

"Perhaps you'd be taken more seriously, Senator, if your sheets didn't have little flowers on them," Teague said.

"They were all I could find in the lost and found," Rob slurred.

"Did you find three sheets?" Teague asked.

"Why? Do you need one?"

"No, I think *you're* going to need them."

"Thank you, m'lady," Rob said with a leer as Gemma handed him his pack at an arm's length.

"It's a toga party, not a Renaissance faire," Teague said. But Rob just whooped and spun out of the room.

A few minutes later, Aron returned and beckoned to Teague. "I need your help," he said.

Dance music and fog spilled into the hall from the door of "The Coliseum." A few people were dancing in black light, including Neanna and Isaac, and the cat-faced woman and her boyfriend. Teague didn't need Aron's accusing finger to see what was wrong. Rob was spinning like a dervish in the middle of the room, holding his beverage pack aloft victoriously, and attempting to sing along in full voice.

"Can you get this loser out of here?" Aron asked.

Teague nodded. Aron thanked him with a clap on the shoulder and retreated. Teague waded in and caught one of Rob's wrists.

"Hey, Teague," Rob shouted. "Didn't I tell you? ADU's back." He whooped again.

"Come with me," Teague shouted back.

The party hadn't spilled over into "The Senate" yet.

"What are we doing in here?" Rob asked. Teague found a bowl of potato chips and the volume knob on the portable speaker.

"Rob. It's barely ten and you're already completely wasted." He offered the chips to Rob.

"So what?" Rob grabbed a handful of chips but then took a deep swig. When he let the straw out of his mouth, tiny purple globules sprayed across the room. Rob spun around, looking for a place to sit, his flowered sheet billowing ridiculously around him.

Not finding one, he seemed to become aware of himself. After a moment, he spoke, his voice sober. "Stop staring. You're creeping me out."

"What's going on with you?"

"It's a party."

"Come on, Rob. You can't be like this. Not here. Not even tonight."

"I was so afraid that ADU would have a behavior monitoring system," Rob said.

"What does that have to do with anything? Come on. Let me get you back to your room. You can sleep this off."

"I don't need to…" Rob began, but then closed his eyes for a moment. "Yeah," he said.

Rob's third floor room overlooked the utility-blistered roof of the Casino's second floor conference center. A nearby floodlight washed out any stars that might be visible in the sliver of sky. Teague decided that he might drink, too, if he had to wake up to this view every day. Had Rob lived in this room since he'd arrived? Why hadn't he ever asked for a better one? There were unoccupied rooms on every floor of the Casino.

"I have a daughter. Back on Mars. Did you know that?" Rob said blearily. It was the first he'd spoken since they'd left Kindergarten. "Why did I just tell you that?"

"Because you're hammered," Teague replied, finally daring to take Rob's beverage pack away.

Rob kicked off his shoes and tumbled onto his bed. When his flowered sheets settled, his long, skinny bare legs stuck out almost obscenely, and his Martian feet were splayed like wide spatulas of skin and bone.

"You're a good friend, Teague," Rob moaned.

"Go to sleep," Teague said.

"Hap new yer."

"Happy new year," Teague replied. He closed Rob's door carefully and headed back to Aron's party.

CHAPTER 18

Joining Angel-37 became my shortcut, my final rebellion. I knew you would exhibit pride but harbor fear.

JUNE 2091

"How long do we have to wait for a professor before we can leave?" Aron asked.

"She's only a couple of minutes late," Teague said.

"And I have better things to do than—"

The door opened, and President Mbuto swept into the classroom with her mobile to her ear. "The committee must recognize that," she said to the party on the other end. "Yes. Yes. All right. I'm sorry, but I've arrived. Yes. This evening." She disconnected. "My apologies, gentlemen. There's always so much that must be dealt with in the week before a boat arrives." Her mobile began to buzz as if to prove her point.

"I won't keep you long today," she continued, silencing the call. "And, Mr. Valdosky, I assume that you would appreciate some extra time to arrange another unsanctioned gathering."

"I don't know what you're talking about, ma'am," Aron said. Mbuto answered with a disapproving hum.

"I think she knows about your parties," Teague said in a stage whisper. During the six months since the success of the Roman bacchanal, Aron, with Eskimo and a cadre of hangers-on, had staged parties in almost every building on the station. Some, like the Groundhog Day affair in a rock-ceilinged cargo bay, had been harmless enough. Others, like the industrial rave on an unused maintenance deck of the minicollider, had drawn rebukes and complaints from a few of the faculty. But more often than not, professors and administrators showed up, along with several hundred of Aron's closest friends. Aron had taken to arranging VIP areas for attendees who wished to maintain a bit of propriety. Even Thomas had turned out to watch a bit of the foam party in the Mall from the safety of the designated terrace.

"The office of the president has no opinion on the matter," President Mbuto said. "However, I do have an opinion about how you will spend a good deal of your time over the next few months." She waved her screen at them. "You will write an original business plan. Collaboratively. This outlines all the requirements, the evaluation rubric, and the submission schedule."

So, Thomas, today's the day, Teague thought.

"Should the business be something real, or are we selling widgets and widget services?" Aron asked.

"Your work will be evaluated by professionals outside the university. They will not take kindly to fiction. The question is whether your final product can attract an appropriate level of capital."

"So we shouldn't knock this together the night before?" Aron asked.

"Not if you intend to graduate," President Mbuto replied. "Now, if you don't mind, I must excuse myself. I will answer more questions at our next meeting, after you've read the rubric. I suggest that you take a few minutes to do that now. Good day."

"Now that's what I call a class," Aron said as soon as she had gone.

"You realize that she just assigned us a thousand hours of work. Each," Teague said.

"She's given us the gift of now. Let's get out of here," Aron said.

"Just skimming this...I really think we ought to..."

"What's to discuss?" Aron said. "It's obvious what we need to do."

"What's that?"

"My ski resort."

"It might not be complex enough," Teague said.

"What do you mean? It's made of complexity. Real estate development..." Aron said, ticking off items on his fingers, "...lift operations, a ski school, resort hotel and lodge, restaurants, events and catering, equipment store, snow making, transportation, maybe a casino."

"And this is on Mars?" Teague asked.

"Where else? There's nothing else like it there."

"Why do you think that is?"

"Because no one's had the vision."

"I hate to burst your bubble," Teague said. "But don't most people just shift when they want to go skiing? We ought to come up with a few other ideas."

"Like what?" Aron asked.

"I told you a long time ago that I'd found our Lucy Frye."

"Huh? Who?"

"Rob Heneghan."

Aron laughed. "That loser? I'd rather work with the Red Witch."

"You haven't seen his program. It's perfect for this. Want me to call him? I'd bet he'd show it to you right now."

Aron rose and began thumbing his mobile's screen. "Not when I've been given a free afternoon." He put his mobile to his ear. "You in for eighteen holes or not?"

"You can't rule it out without knowing what it is," Teague said, shaking his head.

"You're pretty quick to dismiss my ski res—Hey, Eskimo. It's me. Hold on a second. Fine, Teague. I'll hear you out about Rob, or preferably any other ideas. But can we worry about it after the boat arrives? The first submittal's not due for a couple weeks." Back to his mobile. "Dude, guess what?"

Once Aron had gone, Monkey poked his head out from under the coffee table. "A ski resort sounds fun," he said. "I like to go new places."

"You're supposed to be on my side," Teague said.

"In that case, a ski resort sounds terrible. I much prefer

M-SOO," Monkey said. "You were talking about M-SOO, weren't you?"

* * *

Rob's avatar appeared on an oddly plush obsidian monolith drifting in a field of false, firefly stars. In the center of the slab, a 3-D model of Agnus Dei hovered a meter off the floor and pulsed with light and activity. The model neglected certain details, like the unfinished skeleton of Habitat 22, and added others, like the Casino's glass elevator. Rob realized that he had been here before and finally noticed the logo inlaid in the slab. ADU Admissions had significantly upgraded its U-shift lobby since he'd applied. The propaganda had been polished to a high sheen. He was invited to touch parts of the model, presumably to be sucked into more informative sections of the site. Smiling ghosts appeared around him, seemingly willing to share their stories of academic fulfillment if only he'd acknowledge them, but none of them bore any resemblance to any ADU student he'd ever known.

The ghosts vanished and Gwen's avatar, or at least its unanimated shell, popped abruptly into the site. Like the model of ADU, her avatar avoided certain unsavory details. Here, her hair obeyed its governing mathematical constructs. The belt of her pristinely rendered cardigan was tied neatly around her waist. Her eyes weren't bloodshot, and her mouth was free of food. It was actually a little unnerving.

"What could possibly be so urgent"—her mouth began to move too late, catching up with her words—"that I had to drop everything to meet you?" Rob had offered to fix her avatar sync issues before but had always been met with spiked silence. Gradually, Gwen began to breathe and to exhibit the other involuntary movements that made avatars believable as people.

"Why'd you want to meet here? Is this where you hang out all day?" Rob asked.

"Get on with it. Stop wasting my time."

"I have great news. Well, pretty great. It's not a done deal or anything, but…" Rob said. Gwen gestured impatiently. "M-SOO is going to get a business plan. Probably."

"That's it?" she said after a long pause.

"Teague and Aron have to write a business plan for Mbuto's class. Teague came to me and told me that he's going to try to convince Aron to use M-SOO for it."

"Please say you're fucking with me," Gwen said.

"What? This is exactly what you've been suggesting."

"I've urged you to work with professionals, not the peanut gallery. And certainly not a Valdosky."

"A Valdosky? Why does that matter?"

"Put an end to this before it starts."

"No," Rob said.

"What?"

"This isn't your decision. I thought you'd be supportive."

"Of this?"

"This could be M-SOO's chance."

"Mbuto's approved this?"

"I don't know. I've only talked to Teague. But why wouldn't she?" Rob asked. "God. Sorry to waste your precious time. Go back to designing your stupid spaceship." He linked away even as Gwen began to reply.

Was it possible that Gwen might be more infuriating in shift than in real life? Her avatar's glitches made her seem distracted, barely present, yet she never spared the abuse. He should have predicted this, he knew, but he had some stupid weakness that always allowed Gwen the benefit of the doubt. She never failed to disappoint. She had cursed him a thousand times. Time to return the favor.

Fuck you, Gwendolyn, and the sweater you rode in on. And Teague, buddy, please don't fail me now.

* * *

Teague was about to open Aron's door when his mobile began to ring. Teague checked the screen and groaned. Rob had taken to calling him several times a day—an irritation, but a small price to pay for Rob's enthusiasm.

"What's up, Rob?"

"I just wondered if I should reserve a meeting room for the presentation to Aron or stay casual and do it in my office."

"Definitely casual. But I warned you not to get too worked up about this. He doesn't even want to discuss it until after the boat's gone. That's what, three days minimum? Even then it's not a done deal."

"Yeah, I just thought maybe..." Rob began. "Are you going to see him tonight?"

"Yes, Rob, I am."

"Oh. Okay. I'll let you go."

Teague almost disconnected, but said, "Rob?"

"Yeah?"

"Be patient. I'm doing everything I can."

Aron's suite was darkened but bathed in blue by his enormous wall screen. A dozen or more people lounged on the furniture and floor, and in the shadows Teague recognized a few faces from the Astronomy Department. Aron was among them, cuddled with Crystal on one couch.

On the screen, a woman, possibly French, possibly a tragically young widow, was caring for an unconscious, but definitely American, soldier in the bedroom of a rustic farmhouse. She daubed his forehead with a cloth, tore sheets to replace the bloody bandage on his leg, and ran her fingers over his few enigmatic possessions, including a diary bookmarked with a young woman's photograph.

Aron greeted Teague with a nod. "Help yourself," he whispered, gesturing to the kitchen.

The actress's anachronistic figure stole the show under her breezy sundress. Her skin had been photographed with a palpable and healthy humanity. Teague had almost forgotten how sexy Earth girls could be.

"What is this?" Teague asked.

"Astronomy Department movie night. And Crystal wanted to see some of my mom's movies."

"That's your mom?" Teague asked. Crystal hissed for them to be quiet. Teague watched for several more minutes before heading to the kitchen. As he filled a membrane glass from a bottle on the counter, Aron floated in.

"There's another hour of this crap," Aron whispered, refilling his own glass. "God help me if Eskimo cries again. Emotional cripple."

Teague chuckled and then asked, "Is it weird seeing your mom like that?"

"It's who she is."

"I think it'd be weird," Teague said.

"It's a little weird. I'm just happy she retired when she did. She didn't want to be scanned for Immer-Sims and risk pirates using her likeness for god knows what." Aron shuddered.

Teague nodded in sympathy and took a sip. "I would've come up earlier, but I needed to finish that Heilbroner analysis thing."

"Heilbroner," Aron scoffed. "Heilboner, more like it."

"Did you finish?"

"I'll do it in the morning," Aron said. "No sense wasting a perfectly good evening on technological determinism." Teague shrugged, agreeing in principle.

An anvil-chinned Nazi officer studied Aron's mom with raping eyes. His soldiers trod on her strawberry plants as he held her chin in his severely gloved fingers. A timely disturbance of chickens from the bombed-out stable gave the wounded soldier the opportunity to drag himself on an improvised crutch out of the root cellar and across the stony yard to a hedge.

"I need to warn you," Aron said. "Since more undergrads are coming, Crystal and the others have it in mind to play matchmaker for you."

"Can I do anything to stop it?"

"I doubt it," Aron said. "Play along. Maybe you'll get lucky."

"That's not how I want to meet women," Teague said.

"They think it's cute," Aron said. Teague groaned. "I know. I'll do what I can."

"Please."

"Sorry, but they've convinced themselves that your perfect match is on her way," Aron said.

"Romantic determinism?" Teague asked. Aron laughed. "What about you and Crystal? Did the circumstances drive you into a relationship, or did a predetermination toward a relationship drive the circumstances?"

"I remain pragmatic about the issue," Aron said.

"Meaning?"

"What's our watchword?"

"Caution," Teague said. "I hate to break it to you, but it appears you've thrown caution aside."

"Crystal understands what's going on."

"Are you sure about that?"

"How did this suddenly become about me?" Aron asked.

"You think she's going to let you go easy twelve months from now?" Teague followed Aron's line of sight to Crystal.

"We're just having fun," Aron said.

"I'm sure *you* are. But she might have a different notion."

"You're jealous."

"Has anyone ever not been jealous of you?"

"Touché. But I'm surprised to hear it from you."

"Why?"

"I've never had a friend like you."

"Poor? Lonely?"

"You're yourself," Aron said. "People aren't themselves around me. Every one of these people is probably wishing they were shifted out right now, but they pretend they're not."

Aron's mom ran alongside a trundling military convoy, calling the soldier's name, clutching the diary. The soldier appeared from behind a canvas flap on the back of a troop truck, re-equipped and sporting his helmet rakishly. He dismounted the slow-moving behemoth. She fought back tears and tried to press the diary into his hands. He refused. "Keep it safe for me," he whispered into her ear. Friendly fighter planes buzzed low overhead, and tanks rattled by as they kissed.

"This movie blows," Aron said. "I can't believe Gretchen got nominated for an Academy Award for this."

"It's the French accent," Teague said.

Aron shot him a dirty look. "That's what all my friends say when they're secretly thinking my mom is hot."

Teague glanced at the screen, then back to Aron. "I'm just saying."

* * *

"Are any of these people from Earth?" Teague asked, scanning the list of passengers who had disembarked while he was in class. "Especially these people?" He tapped each name that might conceivably belong to a woman.

"I'll find out," Monkey said and began to hum one of his searching-the-Internet songs.

Maybe it wouldn't be so bad to let Crystal and the others set him up with someone. Hell, he still had another year to go. *Am I lonely?* Teague shook off the notion. He wasn't lonely, just human, and red-bloodedly male. It wasn't as if Thomas had made him take a vow of celibacy.

"Are you looking forward to the reception?" Monkey asked.

"Have you found out what I asked yet?"

"These things take time. See, there's this thing call the speed of light—"

"And why are we waiting for an elevator?"

"Nothing I can do," Monkey replied. "Someone's holding the doors down below."

Teague was about to use the ladder well when the elevator began to move. A few moments later, the doors opened, and Monkey bounded inside. A woman screamed briefly from behind an enormous pile of luggage, and then she began to laugh.

"I'm so sorry," Monkey said.

"Oh, my," she said. "I didn't expect you."

"He wasn't expecting you either. Hi, I'm Teague," he said, squeezing into the car and offering her his hand.

"Cerena," she replied. Her long, bony hand was cold, almost crystalline, but her skin was soft. Her nearly liquid form seemed to pour from ceiling to floor. Teague guessed that she stretched at least half a meter taller than Aron, and she was, if possible, more slender than Neanna. He half-expected pointy ears to poke through her silvery hair and a pair of gossamer wings to unfurl from her shoulder blades. She had selected his floor. "I just got off the Charlemagne, but you probably guessed that."

"We don't get new people dropping by every day," Teague said. "You look like you could use some help with all this."

"Thank you," she said.

Teague handed his screen to Monkey. "You go back to the room."

"But I like to be helpful."

"I think you've done enough," Teague said. Monkey's smile fell.

"I'm very sorry if I scared you," Monkey said, maneuvering into petting range.

"Oh, that's okay, little guy," she replied, falling for it. Monkey clutched Teague's screen to his chest and grinned, eyes half-closed in pleasure, as she stroked him. "You're a beautiful ring-tailed lemur." The elevator doors opened.

"Thank you," Monkey said. "I've always thought so. You're very beautiful, too."

"Such a flirt," she said.

"I don't know where he picked that up," Teague said, and began hauling her luggage into the corridor. "Get out of here, you scamp." Monkey bounded away with a wave. Cerena flowed out of the elevator with an uncommon grace, as if she indeed possessed wings.

"Where are you from?" Teague asked.

"Ceres," she replied. "I know. Ceres. Cerena. My moms thought it would be cute. I was one of the first children born there."

Ceres? Teague scowled at the irony as he worked her luggage along the corridor. Wasn't that like the opposite of Earth? Was someone in the ADU Admissions Office deliberately taunting him?

"How do I get back to the docks?" Cerena asked after all her bags had been wrestled across the threshold. "I have a few more things."

Cerena's "few more things" proved to be live bamboo samples in a set of titanium cases, each about two meters wide, three meters long, half a meter deep, and too unwieldy to carry to the greenhouse by hand. Teague and Cerena loaded them onto an idle bot, but it refused to move without a code.

"Let me see if I can get some tech support," Teague said, but as he pulled out his mobile, it rang.

The line clicked and Monkey gasped, "She's coming!"

"What?"

"Gwen Ungefucht," Monkey said.

"Gwen?"

"She knocked for a long time. I hid under the shift couch and stayed very quiet," Monkey said. "Then she called Molly and asked for your location. She's coming to find you."

"What did she want to talk to me about?"

"How should I know?"

Teague checked the corridor outside the cargo bay. Dozens of forklifts were racing their loads here and there, but no Gwen. "Forget that," he said. "I need the lock code for a cargo bot."

A few minutes later, Teague tightened the straps around the crates as they rode the greenhouse freight elevator, hoping that they'd stay ahead of Gwen. Would she really waste her time chasing him around the station? But when the doors opened, his heart sank. Gwen was hanging outside the elevator with her sweater's belt ends waving around her like a pair of tentacles.

"Who's this?" Gwen asked, sneering at Cerena. If possible, Cerena had gone even paler.

"Cerena. She just arrived," Teague said.

Gwen snorted derisively. "That's just great. I need to talk to you."

"About what?" Teague asked.

"About...alone," Gwen said, glaring at Cerena.

"I'll go check that my area's ready in the lab," Cerena said and edged out around Gwen.

"You can't do this," Gwen began once she had gone.

"Do what?"

"Use M-SOO for your little preschool project."

"What are you talking about?"

"You know exactly what I'm talking about."

Teague paused and tried to piece together a narrative that led to Gwen confronting him like this. Rob must have talked to her. But why did she care? "What business is it of yours?"

Gwen tugged both her hands through her hair. "It's my business because I'm the one telling you that you can't."

"Rob seems to think it's a good idea," Teague said. "A business plan is exactly what he needs."

"I agree," Gwen said. "Just not from you, and the other one."

"What's that supposed to mean?" Teague felt a genuine surge of anger now. "You mean Aron?"

"Of course I do," Gwen snapped.

"So, just like that, for no reason, you want me to dump M-SOO and Rob?"

"It's not for no reason," Gwen said. Teague shook his head and held his arms wide in disbelief. "It's just that..." Gwen hung her head for a moment, and then looked at Teague plaintively. "M-SOO deserves better."

"Better than what? Me?"

"That's not what I mean."

Had an enhanced cognition user, who had had maybe centuries of relative time to think about it, just confirmed his instincts about M-SOO? Teague decided to throw a wrench into the conversation. "This doesn't have anything to do with M-SOO at all. This is about Rob, isn't it?"

"What?"

"You're just pissed off. He's been your little puppy-dog punching bag for years, and now he's—"

"Fuck you."

"Oh, really. If you think M-SOO's so great, then why haven't you helped him make something out of it before now? Surely you've had the time."

Gwen narrowed her eyes and began to tremble with fury. Teague remained behind the bot and two large cases, resisting the temptation to push her further. Gwen opened her mouth but then clenched her teeth and blasted off, muttering curses.

Cerena returned a few moments later. "Who was that?" she asked.

"Welcome to Agnus Dei," Teague said.

"Teague's here," Eskimo called from the kitchenette.

"Teague, come in here," Aron called from his office.

"What's going on?" Teague asked, skirting around crates of freshly delivered liquor. Eskimo just grinned. The afternoon had been strange enough. Between his run-in with Gwen and then learning from Monkey that none of the newcomers were from Earth but that one Cerena Mei-zhen Hutton had a lifetime membership at Aronwatch.com, Teague doubted he could tolerate much more drama.

Aron, already dressed for the reception, was thumbing at his sliver of a mobile behind his L-shaped desk, his back to the window. Behind the office door, a shift couch had been buried under more cases.

"You better get out there before Eskimo drinks your entire new shipment," Teague said.

Aron laughed. He ended his message, slid his mobile into an inside pocket of his jacket, and said, "Congratulations."

"What for?"

"We met that new girl, Cerena, and heard all about your little meet-cute in the elevator."

"It wasn't a meet-cute."

"She spilled the whole story," Aron said. "You were, in her words, 'sweet.' I personally would have done it without the primate."

Had Aron also heard about the encounter with Gwen? "I wasn't trying to—"

"No, this is a good thing," Aron said. "Just play along for an evening or two. They'll get to be friends, and eventually it won't matter when you don't hit it off."

"You're assuming I'm not interested," Teague said.

"She didn't seem your type."

"It's more likely that I'm not hers."

"Don't sell yourself short."

"Short. Good one," Teague said.

"I've been instructed to coach you."

"Look, things may seem different from way up there, but I'm not—"

"I know. I get it," Aron said. "I'm just keeping you informed." Teague rolled his eyes. "But you must admit, she is hot."

"She's tall."

"Come on," Aron said. "She is a woman of certain quality."

"Can we consider me coached now?" Teague asked.

In the Casino elevator on the way to the arboretum, Aron said, "I already invited Cerena to join us all after Mbuto's reception. Up in my suite."

Eskimo glanced at Teague, raised his eyebrows with a smirk, and then looked away.

* * *

Gwen didn't show up for breakfast the morning after the reception, and Rob feared that he was going to have to eat alone until Teague arrived with Monkey in tow. Teague scanned the cafeteria warily before he set his tray down and slid into the booth.

"You're here early," Rob remarked. "Were you up all night with the new recruits?"

"Where's Gwen this morning?"

"I don't know. But you know her. Sometimes she disappears for days," Rob said. Teague frowned. "Why? Did you need her for something?"

"What does Gwen do here?" Teague asked. "I know she's an engineer, but what does she really do?"

"She's designing a new kind of spacecraft."

"You've seen it?"

"A couple of times." It resembled a classic flying saucer a bit too much for Rob's sense of humor, but he had never dared to laugh at her life's work.

"What makes it new?"

"I signed an NDA," Rob said. "I don't mind her killing me, I just don't want her to actually murder me."

"She's building it here?" Teague asked. Rob nodded. "Where does she get the money for that?"

"That I don't know," Rob said. "Someone big. TataFord has always been my guess. They've been making noise about a private spacecraft division for years."

"Private?" Teague asked. "How small is it?"

"I can't talk about it," Rob said. "But I will say this: She really wants to break Valdosky's monopoly on civil space travel. She's always complaining about how Valdosky stifles exploration, research, business, and how they've got the UNSA under their thumb. And she hates that most colonies and exostations aren't equipped with lifeboats adequate for the population. Claims we're all back on the Titanic."

"So it's a lifeboat?" Teague asked.

"I think it's meant to have a lot of uses," Rob said. Teague stared at Rob for an uncomfortable moment and then seemed to remember his breakfast. "Why do you want to know about Gwen?"

Teague shook his head and began to eat. Monkey just smiled and rested his chin on the table.

* * *

A blinking bracket highlighted Aron's first drive over the rusted fairway against a backdrop of towering pink clouds. The game zoomed in as the ball bounced and rolled to a stop on smooth dirt and then pulled back to reveal its position near the center of the fairway cleared through a rock-strewn plain.

"You hit that almost a kilometer," Teague commented, mounting the mossy tee box for his own drive.

"Golf's much more of a finesse game in lower-gravity conditions," Aron said. Golf had also been a necessary inducement to get Aron to hear Rob's pitch that afternoon.

"Nine hundred meters is finesse?" Teague asked. "So what did you think about M-SOO?"

"What do you think about hitting your drive sometime before my air runs out?" Aron asked. Teague's ball flew straight enough but fell far short of Aron's.

"Golf is never mastered," Aron said, "for the golfer must first master himself."

"Who said that?"

"I just made it up. Not bad, really."

"After you, Captain Fortune Cookie," Teague said. Aron sprang away. Teague pushed off behind him, letting his tether loose. The program played disorienting visual tricks to map the extra-large course onto the surface of Agnus Dei. Without trees to provide a sense of scale, Teague overshot his ball's lie and had to shuffle back.

On the next green, Aron said, "You think Rob's our Lucy Frye? Seriously?"

"Fine. It's an exaggeration, but I knew right away that M-SOO would make a great start-up. I'm even more convinced after today."

"If it's so great, why hasn't he done anything with it?"

"I honestly don't think he knows how."

"But what makes it better than my Mount Olympus resort?" Aron asked.

"You want to put your resort on Olympus Mons?" Teague asked with a laugh.

"Ski resort of the gods," Aron said. "At least actual, successful ski resorts exist."

"Exactly. They exist. They've been done. But Rob's program is one-of-a-kind."

"I don't know," Aron said. "I mean, fine, the idea is interesting. The math is way over my head. But Heneghan…?"

"He won't get in the way," Teague said. "He wants this. He needs us."

The next hole was a tricky par three with the green on the top of a short, tight plateau.

"Tell you what," Aron said. "You get on the green in one, and I'm in."

"What?"

"You heard me. If you're so sure he's Lucy Frye Redux, then I'm all in. Green in one."

"What if I don't make it?"

"I may still say yes, but green in one and you've got me. Obviously contingent on whether the thing makes any sense once we delve into it."

"You're serious?"

"Absolutely." Aron stuck out his hand.

Teague put his glove in Aron's, and they shook once. "It's your shot," Teague said.

"Nah, you go."

"Okay, but give me a minute."

"Take your time."

"I'm going to turn off my comm," Teague said. "I don't want any distractions."

"Fair enou—"

Teague pretended to survey the virtual Martian valley. Beyond his visor's pixels lay only gray desolation, a hostile universe arrayed against him—the hard vacuum, absolute cold, radiation, the laws of physics, Gwen and her enhancements, Aron and his silver spoon, Eskimo and the rest with their beauty and ability to shift, Thomas and his carrot and stick—even Rob had his program and his family. Teague had one advantage. Why shouldn't he use it? He selected a new comm channel with a blink and made the call.

"Hi, Teague. Did you know there's a baby bird learning to fly in the arboretum? I'm watching it on the cameras," Monkey said.

"That's nice. Listen. I'm in the golf program," Teague whispered. "Mars, Solis Planum Course, second hole. I need you in here, discreetly. I need my ball to land on the green from the tee box in one stroke. Do you understand?"

"Give me a moment," Monkey said. Then, "I understand."

Teague took a practice swing and said, "Make it look real. A straight arced shot, no weird corrections. Make it roll to a stop within a meter of the edge of the green. Not too close to the hole." He turned, and Aron offered him a thumbs-up.

"I'm ready," Monkey said.

"I'm going to start a ball and tee," Teague said. "What club should I use?"

"The game indicates that a seven iron is optimal."

"I've selected a seven iron," Teague said. "Will you sense my swing?"

"Yes," Monkey replied. "Teague, are you cheating?"

"Yes, Monkey. I'm cheating."

Teague studied the green again, addressed his ball, and took the shot. He kept his head down and followed through. It felt good. Teague crouched as the ball sailed away, anxiously hoping that Monkey had understood. The bracketed ball peaked, succumbing to the virtual gravity. Moments later it bounced onto the front of the green. "Monkey," Teague murmured as the ball rolled too quickly toward the edge. He rose and hopped forward instinctually. The ball's path curved as it climbed an imperceptible rise. The view zoomed in as the white orb slowed and finally trickled to rest. Teague turned to Aron and held his arms wide. Aron clapped. Teague hung up on Monkey and reconnected.

"—comes through in the clutch," Aron was saying.

"One in a million," Teague said, breathing hard. "I thought I'd lost it off the backside."

"That was a great swing. Congratulations."

"Thanks."

"You know I was just messing with you," Aron said as they shook hands again.

"Thanks. I really needed more stress in my recreational activities," Teague said.

Moments later, Aron landed his ball on the leading slope of the plateau a few meters short of the green.

Teague three-putted the hole for one over par.

* * *

Rob drummed his fingers on the bench of the round-corner booth as Teague and Aron reviewed the document on their screens. The bar had opened only a few minutes ago, but he wished he'd ordered a beer before they'd sat down. It wouldn't be the earliest he'd ever drained a Mercy in this booth. Was it some cosmic sign that M-SOO was poised to take another leap toward reality, right here where it all began with a casual question to a bartender? And with the only son of Matthew Valdosky, no less. Rob hadn't told his family yet, not even Kyle. But he would tonight. *Let's see you top this, big brother.*

"Seems like a lot of trouble for a school project," Aron said.

"Mbuto insisted," Rob said, and Teague nodded. "A standard contract for interdepartmental research."

"No, it's good," Teague said. "It delineates the intellectual property rights and gives us a framework for future development."

"Whatever," Aron said. He drew his stylus and scrawled an illegible signature on his screen. Teague signed his, and then Rob filled in the last line.

"Thank you, guys," Rob said.

"Don't thank us yet," Aron said.

"How will this work?" Rob asked.

"Your first task will be to teach us everything we don't know about M-SOO," Teague said.

"When do we start?" asked Rob.

"I've got plans tonight," Aron said, checking his mobile. "With someone much better looking than you two."

"You guys want to toast…?" Rob asked and hooked a thumb toward the bar. Aron shook his head, frowned briefly at Teague, and then slid out of the booth.

"Tomorrow then," Teague said.

"Tomorrow," Aron confirmed, pushing off.

After Aron had drifted out of sight, Rob asked, "Did we just go into business with Aron Valdosky?"

"No, but—"

"This is messed up." Rob laughed. "Gwen's going to shit bricks once she finds out." Teague swept the document off his screen. "She thinks I'm compromising M-SOO. But the stupid part is that she'd probably be behind this if not for Aron."

"Just because she disagrees with you doesn't mean you're wrong," Teague said. "Aron is not the Valdosky Companies."

"She doesn't understand that this might be my best chance," Rob said. After a pause he asked, "Can I be honest for a minute?"

"Okay," Teague said, sounding hesitant.

"I could never say this in front of Aron, but I want to make sure you know who you're getting here." Rob tapped his chest. "I am not a genius. I don't know a business plan from a spreadsheet. The few grant applications I submitted were colossal failures. And I didn't create M-SOO out of any great vision."

"But you did create it."

"Hey, if we can make something out of it, no one will be happier," Rob said. "I'm sorry. I'm not trying to scare you off. I only want to make sure that you won't be expecting me to have all the answers."

"We all have our reasons for wanting to take this to a higher level," Teague said.

"What's Aron's reason?" Rob asked.

"He doesn't want to work for his father."

"What's yours?"

"I'd think it would be obvious," Teague said. "You think I can pass up a chance like this?"

Rob studied the signatures on the contract, his own cartoonish script, Teague's tight line of letters, Aron's scribble. "What happens if Aron bails?" he asked.

Teague raised his eyebrows. "I don't think he will," he said.

Rob decided to believe him.

* * *

Teague had declined a Lamb's Mercy, claiming to have too much homework, but as he left the bar, he felt like he'd downed two or three.

Could M-SOO be more than an inconsequential school project? Could it be the framework for a future business with Aron Valdosky? Rob's confession was unnerving but not surprising. At least he'd had the sense not to spell out his faults in front of Aron. Rob might be a liability, but he wasn't the loser Aron imagined. Rob just needed focus, deadlines, and a constant push in the right direction. And he was teachable. Aron, on the other hand, was a big cat to herd. Teague would have to dangle assignments in front of him like prey. Teague had already resigned himself to the heavy lifting. He'd just have to make certain in some subtle way that none of his work escaped Thomas's and Mbuto's notice.

When Teague opened the door to his room, Monkey bounced over to greet him. "Did you know that Aron's on this floor, down in Cerena's room?" he asked.

"Right now?" Teague asked.

"Yep."

"Is anyone else in there?"

"Nope."

"Where's Crystal?" Teague asked.

"She's in her own room, but currently in the shiftpop."

"Shit," Teague said. This was going to be even more difficult than he thought.

CHAPTER 19

I deeply regret the things I said to you when I was young. If I hurt you as much as I intended, I can only beg your forgiveness now.

NOVEMBER–DECEMBER 2091

"Thanks for coming," Kyle said. "I really wanted your opinion on this."

"Will it take long?" Rob asked. "I should get back soon."

"Hot date?"

"People are waiting. I was only going to be a few minutes."

"We'll make it quick," Kyle said.

Their parents' shift house had begun its existence as a simple replica of their mother's suburban childhood home on Earth, stretched slightly for Martian avatars—one of Kyle's first forays into virtual architecture. At first there had been little to do in the beige rooms, and there wasn't much use for a kitchen in shift, but over the years, Kyle had added a plethora of customized features, from a spacious deck and a tree-filled backyard with adjustable weather for Dad to a pair of virtual schnauzers for Mom. This year Kyle had added a new door off the bedroom hallway.

"Merry Christmas, enjoy your linen closet?" Rob asked.

"You know how Dad always talks about going to the movies as a kid?" Kyle began.

"My gift membership to *Wine Enthusiast* is going to seem really lame, isn't it?"

"I had to do something to one-up you, Mr. Valdosky-business-partner."

"It's a school project. And not even mine," Rob moaned.

"Dad's convinced you've made it big."

"Show me, already."

When Kyle opened the door, the software swept them instantly into a warmly lit, red-carpeted, butter-scented lobby. Ever-changing collages of old Hollywood stars splashed across the walls. Wide staircases soared up from both ends. Velvet ropes and gold stanchions marked the queues to curtained entrances astride a gleaming concessions stand. The opening they had come through had become a line of glass doors fronting a city sidewalk.

"How'd you smooth out the Alice Effect?" Rob asked. They must have shrunk to about ten percent of the scale they had been in the hall.

"I figured out a way to force your avatar to blink at the threshold. Your brain doesn't even notice," Kyle said. They crossed to a curtained entrance and emerged into a dim terrace facing an enormous screen. Rob let out a low whistle. "I patched this together from a few theaters and assembly halls we've done. There won't be a bad seat in the house."

"Once you get them installed, presumably."

"These are the chairs I designed for the Sydney Opera House," Kyle said, leading Rob to the lone grouping assembled in the center of the room.

"You didn't get that job," Rob said.

"Yeah, but Dad'll like the flip-down ottomans." Kyle opened an interface window in midair. "Content controls, screen size, virtual audience menu, a ton of audio options, a curtain," he said, tapping a few buttons.

"What's the inaugural movie?" Rob asked.

"You know Dad. Probably *It's a Mad, Mad, Mad, Mad World*."

"Oh, god," Rob said. "Bring lots of buzz prog—"

Gwen appeared, looming a few rows below, bathed in her own personal spotlight.

Rob shrieked and then blurted, "What the fuck?"

"Who—?" Kyle asked, wide-eyed.

"I need to talk to you." Gwen's voice had an immediate and distinct Gwen-ness, even though her avatar took its time coming to life.

"You know—?" Kyle asked.

"How'd you get—?" Rob asked.

"Now," Gwen said.

"It's okay," Rob said to Kyle. "Sorry. I don't know what's going on, but can you give us a minute? It's only Gwen. From ADU."

Kyle backed away, only turning his back on Gwen to cross the last few meters.

"How'd you get in here?" Rob asked once Kyle had gone.

"It's not exactly the G-Plex core," she replied.

"You're aware that breaking and entering is a violation of the G-Plex terms of service," Rob said. "And where the hell have you been?"

"Shut up and listen," Gwen said.

"Are you okay?"

"No, I'm not okay, genius. Shut up. I'm leaving ADU. I'm going to Earth, and I want you to come with me."

"We've barely spoken in months"—since he'd agreed to let Teague and Aron write the M-SOO business plan—"and this is what you open with?"

"I'm taking the Ariel," she said.

"What? Why?" Rob asked.

"Matthew Valdosky is coming," Gwen said.

"To ADU?"

"The Mirage burned its engines off G-Two a few hours ago. He'll be here in May or June."

"That's when Aron graduates," Rob said.

"I don't care *why* he's coming. My backers and I don't want to take the risk."

"Aren't you overreacting? I ask, knowing full well that you have very good, paranoid reasons for this."

"Valdosky is coming with a cadre of staff and a cruiser full of tourists and contractor liaisons. At this stage, I'm too big to hide during any kind of inspection."

"If the Ariel's spaceworthy, why not just fly out a few kilometers and return when he leaves?"

"Ariel's more than spaceworthy—it's deliverable, or will be in a few weeks. The decision's been made," Gwen said. "And I've thought this through. I want you, and M-SOO, along. You cannot let Valdosky get hold of your program. The people I work with can help you make M-SOO what it's supposed to be." Rob rubbed his forehead for a moment. As tempting as it might be to accept a ride on her mysterious little spacecraft, Rob knew he could never go through with it. He had commitments. And how could he live with himself having screwed over Aron Valdosky, let alone a friend like Teague?

"I never intended M-SOO to be anything."

"Don't give me that fatuous bullshit."

"You can't spring this paranoid crap on me and expect me to drop everything."

"You are so naive," she said.

"I can't just leave. I've made commitments."

"Right, to Toddler Werres and Infant Valdosky. I am making you a serious offer. My backers have agreed to help, even to bring Molly along if that's what it takes."

"I can't."

"Will you at least agree to meet with them?" Gwen asked.

"You're asking me to screw over my friends."

"I'm asking you to make a mature decision."

"If you're expecting an answer right now, then my answer is no," Rob said.

"Did I ask you for an answer right now? I'm asking you to give this some serious thought." They stared at each other for several moments, and then Gwen said, "But don't take forever." She vanished as abruptly as she had appeared.

"That was the infamous Gwen?" Kyle asked when Rob emerged from the theater.

"You heard all that?"

"She's a piece of work."

"Gwen will be Gwen."

"You should be flattered," Kyle said. "She obviously respects your work."

"Yeah, maybe."

"Or loves you deeply."

"Don't even go there."

"Is Matthew Valdosky really coming to ADU?"

"First I've heard of it," Rob said. Outside the lobby doors, an idling, turn-of-the-century taxicab spewed exhaust into the crisp, unreal air.

* * *

Without the membrane on his cup, Teague would have tossed his coffee all over Monkey when Rob screeched. Shifters often murmured, and that was creepy enough. At the e-mall, Teague had witnessed shifters tremble, had heard them sing and carry on one-sided conversations—one notorious denizen enjoyed very public orgasms. If Teague had known how often Rob shifted in his office, he'd never have agreed to use the workroom as their business plan headquarters.

"How long has he been shifted?" Teague asked.

"Seventy-nine minutes," Monkey replied. "And you're getting a call from Aron."

Teague's mobile began to buzz, and despite the warning, the noise sent more adrenaline surging through his system. Teague tossed his stylus onto the massive spreadsheet on the table screen in disgust. Rob had the annoying tendency to shift at the drop of a hat, ostensibly to do research that Teague and Aron couldn't, but at least he bothered to show up once in a while. Teague let his mobile buzz several times before answering.

"Where are you?" Aron asked.

"Where do you think? I'm in the War Room," Teague said. Rob had redubbed his workroom in an early fit of enthusiasm; he'd even hung a little sign over the doorway.

"The next submittal's not due for a week and a half," Aron said.

"Exactly," Teague said pointedly.

"Everyone's asking about you," Aron said. Monkey rolled his eyes before Teague had the chance. This was Aron-speak: *Crystal and Cerena in the same room. Get up here. Even out the numbers. Cover my ass.*

"I'm working—on *our* project."

"Come on. This is college, not a gulag."

"Fine. Give me twenty minutes."

"Ten," Aron said.

"Ten, and I'll have to bring Monkey."

"No Monkey." Aron hung up.

Monkey hung his head and put one fist in the air. "I didn't land on Agnus Dei," he said. "Agnus Dei landed on me."

In Aron's suite, a pair of soldiers were lurching and blasting their way across a familiar apocalyptic wasteland with a common death wish. They crouched behind burning cars when they should shelter behind concrete jersey barriers. They expended whole clips at smoke and shadows. They darted through each other's lines of fire like complete noobs.

"Sector Sigma level two," Teague said.

"You've played this shit?" Eskimo asked. He looked ready to throw the controller out the window. Isaac groaned as his armor took another nasty hit.

"I've played my share of campaigns," Teague said.

"No wonder people invented shifting. This sucks," Eskimo said. "Your ancient game sucks, Aron."

"You suck at my ancient game, Eskimo," Aron called from the kitchen. "Margarita night." Aron tossed Teague a beverage pack. Teague made no plans to drink it. Cerena greeted Teague with a pleasant smile from her perch on a stool at the counter. Behind Aron, Crystal and Neanna were sorting out ingredient packs and digging for bowls and utensils.

"You need another?" Aron asked Cerena. She rattled her beverage pack and shook her head. "Let me know. In the meantime, I need to teach Eskimo how to play this game properly."

He rounded the counter, hopped over the couch, and confiscated Eskimo's controller.

"It's so weird he can't shift," Cerena said. "It's been months, and I still can't get over it." Teague agreed. No one seemed to have informed her of his own disability, and he had never felt compelled to mention it. "I'd love it if we could all crash the Montreaux Club. Have you been?" Teague shook his head. "You have to go. Dozens of floors, each with different gravity conditions. Full buzz bars. Personal lighting matrixes. The best DJs. A friend and I once got invited up to a VIP after-party by a couple of the guys from Trusty Steed."

"Trusty Steed?"

"The band?" Cerena asked.

"I'll have to look them up," Teague said.

Aron whooped, and the game cut to a low-angle tracking shot of a heavily armored soldier silhouetted against a nuclear blast—a familiar animation. "And that is how you do that," Aron announced. Aron winked at Cerena. If Aron's watchword was caution, it seemed long forgotten. Cerena's eyes flicked discreetly to Crystal.

"Get these guys through level three," Aron said, tossing the controller to Teague.

"You've played this game?" Cerena asked Teague.

"Are you kidding?" Aron answered. "Teague's a master. He grew up on this shit."

Teague settled on the couch, knowing he should probably be back at his spreadsheets, but he relished the opportunity to blast a few alien invaders. "Follow me, about ten steps back, and try not to shoot me," he told Isaac. The troop carrier deposited them in the smoking remains of an air force base. As soon as his boots touched pavement, he cross-stepped right for two hundred meters, weapon up.

"The control tower is the other way," Isaac said. "Isn't that the objective?"

Teague ran on, putting a bullet in every blind corner. Isaac could keep up if he wanted to live.

Teague had cleared level four and was poaching the

metal-eaters in the torched and mangled Port of Long Beach when Crystal and Neanna called everyone over for cookies. He paused Sector Sigma and ducked into Aron's bedroom to use the restroom before he tried one.

After Teague tossed the disposable guest personal into the recycler, he washed his hands. He heard movement in the bedroom as he dried and went to the door expecting to find someone else waiting for the restroom. But then he heard whispers.

"—not tonight." Was that Aron?

"But I need you." A woman's voice. Teague heard the soft smack of a kiss, and Aron, if it was Aron, moaned with pleasure.

"You're dangerous," he said.

"You have no idea," she said. Another kiss.

"Crystal's planning to stay here tonight," he said.

She whispered something too quiet for Teague to hear, and Aron moaned. "I'll do my best," he said. "I'm going back out."

Teague froze, expecting Cerena, if it was Cerena, to try the bathroom door. But after several seconds, nothing happened. When he opened the door, he found the bedroom deserted.

Teague ate a cookie and considered going back to his video rampage, but instead he excused himself quietly. Aron caught him in the hall. "Hey," he called. "Is something wrong?"

"No, I just need to get back to it if we're going to stay on schedule," Teague said.

"Oh, come on. Screw the schedule," Aron said. "This isn't about Cerena, is it? Because we're really not trying to hook you two up or anything."

"See you tomorrow," Teague said.

"Oh, come on. Don't be like this. It's margarita night."

"Thanks, but I've got work to do."

"We'll be here if you change your mind."

Teague had planned to fetch Monkey and return to the War Room—hopefully the shift addict was awake now—but when he got to his room, he closed the door behind him.

Monkey squealed gleefully and leaped across the room. Teague caught him but held him at arm's length. "What's wrong?" Monkey asked.

"Which of Aron's fan sites does Cerena keep an account at?"

"Aronwatch.com," Monkey replied. "Why?"

"I think Cerena might want to brag about sleeping with Aron."

"I don't understand," Monkey said.

"No, I don't expect you would," Teague said.

The hack was easier than Teague expected, though he should have guessed the administrators had not prepared their teeny-bopper fan club for a military-grade NAI intrusion. Cerena indeed had an Aronwatch account—handle: Pacifica—active long before she'd probably even considered ADU. She hadn't visited the site much in the past couple of years, but she'd once had a penchant for some disturbingly titled slashfic. What had she been thinking when she met Aron?

But what would she say now? It'd have to be brief, tantalizing, just a soupçon, a cry for attention. Monkey found a series of "cute couple" images from Cerena's mobile account. Among them, an unmistakable Aron was pressing his lips on Cerena's cheek as she laughed. They were clothed, but the only background was a shared pillow.

"Attach that one, and…" Teague paused with his fingers over the screen and then typed: "Meet my new ~~bed~~ best friend." "Post it tonight, about a half-hour after Cerena gets back to her room."

How long would it take? Minutes? Days? Or would anyone even notice? Would he have to return to feed the monster? He just hoped it wouldn't turn around and bite him.

* * *

"Has Aron told you the news?" Thomas asked as he stuck his armload of books to the head table. Teague shook his head. Aron had been glaring and tapping at his mobile since Teague had arrived for class. Indeed, Teague hadn't seen Aron all day. Had last night's hack already inflicted damage?

"What news?" Teague asked. Aron rolled his eyes.

"His father is coming to Agnus Dei for graduation."

"Wow," Teague said. *I'm going to meet Matthew Valdosky.* "On the Mirage?"

Aron nodded. Teague started to ask another question, but Aron interrupted. "Yes, it has its own shift frame. No, it is not haunted. No, he is not secretly a brain kept alive in a vat, nor does he keep a harem, robotic or otherwise, on board. And, no, he does not live in a hermetically sealed room and keep his piss in little jars."

"I was going to ask if your mom's coming, too," Teague said.

"No, she's not," Aron said, and turned back to his mobile.

Aron bolted from the classroom as soon as Thomas had finished his lecture.

Thomas clucked his tongue and said, "Aron should be proud that Matthew is coming. This is a debut, not an abduction."

"This is my son, in whom I am well pleased?" Teague asked.

"Something like that," Thomas said. "We haven't spoken about it in some time, but are you and Aron still considering making a go of your business plan?"

"Sort of. We've talked about it, but it's hard to know how serious he is."

"If Aron wants to proceed with you and this M-SOO program—which I fully endorse, by the way—I have no doubt that Matthew will be supportive. And his arrival could bring you some excellent publicity." Thomas began to gather up his books. "Of course, Matthew's looking forward to meeting you. He's been very satisfied with Aron's growth here, and I've made sure he knows that you've been a good friend and role model."

Teague's skin prickled, and he laughed. "How do you do it, Thomas? How do you deal with all these powerful people?"

"I remind myself that they are just that: people. And I remind myself that because of my privileged access, I bear a larger responsibility to communicate the truth."

"Isn't that difficult sometimes?" Teague asked.

"Yes, but when I consider the alternative, I don't fear to speak my mind to mere men," Thomas replied.

"Sic semper tyrannis?" Teague asked.

Thomas replied with a raised eyebrow and tucked his volumes under his arm. "Have a pleasant afternoon, Mr. Werres."

Over 87,000 Aronwatch subscribers had seen Pacifica's picture in the twenty hours before the site administrator suspended her account and deleted the thread, and most of them had commented. Luckily, Monkey had archived it all.

"I've sorted the comment threads for you," Monkey said. "This folder is for the believers with congratulations. This one is for the believers with not very nice things to say. This one is for the skeptics. This one is for demands for proof."

Teague scrolled through a few pages of the unending replies, and they quickly coalesced into a din of neither rebuke nor support from Aron's fans, but a need for their own lives to matter. "Do you know if Aron saw it before it got shut down?" Teague asked.

"The administrator alerted him before the takedown," Monkey replied.

"Who's the administrator?"

"Gretchen Walker."

"Really? His mom?"

"Yes. Would you like to see the messages?" Monkey asked.

"No, just make sure that if Cerena ever tries to log into Aronwatch again it looks like her account was lost or something. Make her open a new account with a new handle."

That evening, Aron came to the War Room on time. Once, his mobile rang. He looked at it, set it aside, and kept working.

"Do you need to go?" Teague asked.

"No," Aron said. Was it really this simple?

* * *

Every evening for more than a week, Aron's mobile buzzed on the War Room table, and each time he ignored it. One night, Teague's mobile rang instead, and thankfully Monkey refrained from announcing the caller in Aron's presence.

"It's Thomas," Teague told Aron. He slipped out of the

workroom, passed Rob, who was shifted in his office, and answered the call in the corridor.

"This is Teague," he said.

"Hi. It's Cerena. I'm sorry to bother you. But I really need to talk to someone, and you're the only person…" Her voice cracked, and she sniffed. "Is there somewhere we can meet?"

A few minutes later, Teague let himself fall cross-legged onto the glass as Monkey waited at the elevator to bring Cerena to the bubble. Teague scanned the sky for the cargo ship, still a few days out. Dare he hope that there might be someone for him aboard? He didn't ask for much: female, from Earth, sparkling wit, independent spirit, a love of lemurs. He wasn't picky. And so what if he had only six months left?

The elevator chimed in the distance, and a few moments later Monkey sailed through the furniture closet. Cerena followed, gliding like milk and honey in velvety white sweatpants and a pink hooded sweatshirt. Her eyes were as red as the blotches on her pale cheeks.

"I'm sorry. I'm a mess," she said with a sniff. Teague shook off her apology and invited her to sit on the glass with him. She dug a handful of tissues from a pocket. As she wiped her nose, she gave a self-disparaging laugh. "I don't suppose Aron has said anything?" she asked. Teague shook his head. "Oh, god. I don't know what's going on. I thought he would've talked to you."

"About what?"

"I've been seeing Aron almost since I arrived," Cerena said.

"I didn't know that."

"Then a few days ago…he won't take my calls. It's like I don't exist anymore. And I have no idea what I've done."

"Why come to me?" Teague asked.

"You're his friend. I know he respects you."

"You want me to talk to him?"

"I don't want to be a bitch. Or hurt Crystal," Cerena said. "But it was real, really real. Because he can't shift, you know."

"I don't know what to say. I'm an economist, not a relationship counselor."

Cerena laughed and sniffed. "I just want to know what happened."

"Do you want him back?"

"Part of me does. Part of me wants to shove him out an air-lock. Part of me wants to forget this ever happened. Part of me wants to claw out Crystal's eyeballs."

"I've never understood that. Aron's the jerk. Why attack Crystal?"

"None of this is rational," Cerena said. "God, listen to me. I'm supposed to present at a conference next week. Monopodial rhizome variation and the consequences of sleeping with someone else's boyfriend."

"Sounds publishable," Teague said.

"I'm sorry to drag you into this. I know you're friends with Crystal, too. I hope you don't hate me. I swear I wasn't trying to hurt anyone. He came to me."

"You don't have to explain. I understand. He's Aron Valdosky."

"I'm embarrassed to say that he's the reason I picked ADU. I told everyone that I wanted to study under Professor Carlyle and that I didn't want to have to wear an exoskeleton, but mostly I wanted to meet him. I might as well have worn a princess dress and a glass shoe."

She swirled around, lay on her back, and gazed past the ceiling, unaware that her hair had spilled across his knee. Teague felt an awkward surge of arousal.

"Aron has been a huge mistake," she said. "It's like I've been his mistress. I haven't made any real friends. I've spent almost all my free time alone with him, and it's awkward to hang out with the others. So when I'm not with him, I just meet up with friends from home in shift. For what?"

"It's not too late," Teague said. "Put him behind you and move on."

"I'm afraid that this will all come out. That I'll be a pariah," she said.

"People won't care."

"I'm so scared of that Gwen person."

"What?" Teague laughed. "Why? Because she curses like a sailor and doesn't comb her hair?"

"No, because I see myself becoming her. No friends, wrapped up in my research, nowhere else to go."

"You're nothing like Gwen."

"I deliberately don't wear my cardigans. I freeze to death rather than become the White Witch."

"An Agnus Dei fairy tale," Teague said. "The cruel red queen and the populist white princess battle for magical supremacy."

"Who would win?" Cerena asked. "You better say white."

"Oh, definitely white. But it won't be easy. Red's pretty tough. A tip, though. Kindness breeds more loyal minions than cruelty in the long run. That's basic fairy tale economics."

Cerena laughed and wiped her nose. "How'd you even find this place?" she asked.

"One of the benefits of insomnia." After a long silence, he said, "I should really get back."

"I'm sorry. I'd like to stay a while, if you don't mind," she said. Aubrey had whispered these exact words to him countless times in his fantasies.

"It's all yours," Teague replied.

In the elevator, on the way down, Monkey said, "She seemed very sad."

"Yeah, I noticed," Teague said.

* * *

"Oh, god," Aron groaned the next day, squeezing past Teague out of his kitchenette and heading for his office.

"So you *have* been seeing her?" Teague asked.

"Seeing her? That's a stupid euphemism. Yes, I've been *seeing* her."

"But now you've put her on ice and she's come to me wanting to know why."

"You didn't *see* her, did you?" Aron asked, rounding his desk.

"I'm not even going to dignify that with an answer," Teague said.

"She's a psycho fan girl," Aron said. "Longtime Aronwatch member Cerena started blabbing to the solar system that we were *seeing* each other."

"I thought you didn't pay attention to your fan clubs."

"The only way to deal with someone like that is to shut them out immediately and completely. Responding only legitimizes whatever they thought the relationship was."

"What do you want me to tell her?" Teague asked.

"Whatever you want."

"She was just a bit of fun on the side?"

"Did she say it was more?"

"She's confused."

"Maybe she'll leave in a couple of days."

"You don't mean that," Teague said.

"No? You know what? *I'm* disappointed. I liked her, but she breached a trust," Aron said. "I never checked her for fan-girl credentials—my mistake. But in my position, I can't tolerate it."

"What about Crystal?"

"What are you talking about? Crystal knows."

"Really?"

"Give me a break. I didn't tell you because it was none of your business. Crystal has friends she *sees* in shift. Maybe growing up in your little church you didn't get the memo, but most people don't care about that monogamy shit anymore, just honesty." Aron began to swipe through message windows on his desktop.

"I'm not being puritanical," Teague said. "I just want to know what I should tell her."

"Her Aronwatch account has been revoked. She'll get the message."

"Don't blame me if she comes after you with an ice pick," Teague said.

"She'll get over it. She'll cry. She'll *see* a bunch of people in shift, and then she'll decide it was all a mistake," Aron said. "Are we done here? I've got things to do."

"I thought Eskimo was planning the party."

"He is, badly."

* * *

Monkey lifted his chin from the War Room table and said, "Rob's coming."

"Now?" Teague asked.

The bar was open, Aron's party was in full swing in the Casino's ballroom, and the boat was on schedule to pull alongside the station in seventeen and a half hours. In theory, Rob shouldn't be anywhere near the War Room. Unless…?

"Is something wrong with Molly?" Teague asked.

"No. Nothing," Monkey replied.

Teague scowled. He had twice witnessed the decay of sanity among the populace of Agnus Dei upon the arrival of a cargo vessel. In the week leading up to the arrival, classes were held sporadically, if at all. People broke their schedules, crowding the gym and the cafeteria at odd times. The bar never closed. Fiery last-minute liaisons were as common as final knock-down, drag-out arguments. Whether staying or leaving, the universal mantra seemed to be "No regrets." And once the boat had departed, most seemed to recover from their delusional fog with nothing but.

Teague had resolved to use the crazy week to his advantage. Aron would be busying himself with the planning of the unofficial farewell party. Rob was on call to monitor Molly during the critical hours of the arrival window and cargo transfer. Having seen Rob do this before, Teague knew it could be accomplished anywhere on the station, with a screen in one hand and a beer in the other. Teague intended to draft a significant portion of the business plan's final documentation before the boat's departure. And so far it had gone according to plan.

Rob skulked in, rubbing the back of his neck as if he had a headache. "I almost didn't believe Molly when she told me you were working in here," he said, scanning the workroom uncertainly. "Aron's not here, is he?"

"I assume he's at the party," Teague said.

"Is it already that late?" Rob checked his mobile. For all his distraction, he seemed surprisingly sober.

"What's going on?" Teague asked.

"We need to talk," Rob said. "I'm sorry. I should've talked to you right away, but…but I didn't think…"

"Why don't you sit?"

Rob nodded nervously and took a chair. He cleared his throat, glanced at Monkey, and then seemed to force himself to face Teague. "Gwen's leaving ADU and invited me to come. I told her no, but now she's set up this meeting for me with her backers. She says they're willing to develop M-SOO. It's been killing me not to tell you and Aron, but now I don't know what to do."

Teague stared deliberately at Rob, letting him squirm. After a few beats, he said, "Is that it?" Rob nodded like a whipped dog. *Good,* Teague thought. "You haven't spoken with these people?"

"No," Rob said. "Gwen still won't even tell me who they are."

"You understand that Gwen has no authority to speak to anyone on M-SOO's, ADU's, or your behalf," Teague said. Rob nodded as if this hadn't occurred to him. "Cut to the chase. Are you telling me that you're leaving?" *Have I been building a sand castle for the past six months?*

"Absolutely not," Rob said assuredly. "The contract stands. You and Aron still have first rights."

"Then what do you need from us?"

"I need to know if you and Aron are serious about making M-SOO a start-up. I mean *serious* serious."

"First, thanks for not screwing us over," Teague said. Rob laughed weakly. "Personally, I'm all in, but I'll need to talk to Aron. Has Gwen said what these people are offering?"

"A job, I guess."

"No monetary offer?"

"Gwen used the word 'competitive' a lot."

"You know that with a start-up, you can't count on any type of salary," Teague said.

"This isn't about money. It's not even about control of the program," Rob said. "This is going to sound stupid, but I told Gwen that I had only one stipulation. And I guess it'd go for you and Aron, too."

"What's that?" Teague was pretty sure he already knew the answer. When Molly spoke through Monkey, she used the voice of a little girl, and Rob had a daughter on Mars. Was the daughter named Molly, too? Teague decided it was axiomatic.

"I want a guarantee that we'll take Molly with us," Rob said. "She's written the program with me, and we need an NAI anyway. So we'll have to buy her from ADU and replace theirs. It'll be simple enough to transition to a—"

"We'll justify it somehow," Teague said. Teague understood the sentiment perhaps better than anyone, but was Rob's request feasible? Better to agree to anything now to keep Rob from doing something stupid during the haze of ADU's boat week.

"Thanks," Rob said.

"I'll talk to Aron. We may have to play a round of golf with him," Teague said. "How soon do you need an answer? Is she wanting you to leave on this boat?"

"No, she's taking her own ship in a couple of months. But the sooner the better," Rob said. "She's set up this meeting for next week."

Not if I can help it, Teague thought as he nodded and rose. "I'll head to the party and see if I can set something up with Aron for tomorrow. Just don't do anything stupid like eloping with Gwen tonight."

Rob laughed. Teague put a hand across the table, and Rob shook it. "I really want this," Rob said. "I mean with you guys. Not with Gwen or her people."

"Me, too," Teague said. "It's a good program."

"Thanks," Rob said. "Do you need me to come along?"

"Better let me go alone, and you probably shouldn't go to the party at all. Just in case…Aron…you know." Teague doubted he could prevent Rob from drinking after this, but it'd be better if Rob drank in his room or at the bar. Why give Aron another reason to doubt? Rob seemed to understand. As he left, Teague made a mental note to check on Rob later and make sure he hadn't passed out in a blob of his own vomit. It would suck to lose him now.

Almost half the station seemed to have turned out in the Casino's ballroom for Aron's party. A throng writhed in the fog in front of the stage where Isaac's band raged. In the center of the room, the massive and famously incomplete chandelier had been hoisted, set to spin on a cable, and shot through with dozens of lasers and pinspots, inflating the ballroom with a universe of fractured light. How in the world had Aron gotten permission to do that? Of course, he probably hadn't.

Teague supposed that if any object epitomized the failure of Agnus Dei, it was this chandelier. The story went like this: A world-famous but aged Spanish art-glass blower had offered to culminate his life's work with a breathtaking piece forged from the melted regolith of Agnus Dei itself. Valdosky accepted his offer, transported him, and built a workshop to his specifications.

The artist labored for over a year, turning hand-selected scoops of asteroid dust into fractally perfect bubbles, insanely delicate threads, and nearly every shape in between. The installation was an immense thing of uncommon beauty, assembled in place, and designed to spill across the ceiling and to stir the soul like a Siren's song captured in ice.

When the UN withdrew its support of the station, and the artist learned that his nearly complete masterpiece was never to be seen, he flew into a rage, stormed into the ballroom, and managed to smash a third of his nearly finished work before a security team shot him with a stun gun.

The shock, they said, stopped the poor man's heart.

This, like most tales about Agnus Dei's early years, was probably apocryphal. Still, leave it to Aron to use the priceless pinnacle of the man's achievements as his own personal disco ball.

Teague checked the bar and then wandered among the tables and groupings of mismatched furniture, searching for Aron among the laughing cliques. He scanned the dance floor whenever he caught a break in the billowing fog, but in the chaotic light it was impossible to find anyone. Had Aron set up a VIP room nearby?

Still scanning the crowd, Teague collided with someone at the ballroom's entrance. Cerena. Her body felt like wind-blown silk against his. She apologized as they separated.

"Are you leaving?" she asked. She seemed to be wearing the same brave face she'd donned when he reported back to her about his discussion with Aron a few days earlier. Even in a crowd of people born in low gravity, Cerena was liquid and ethereal in the midst of dark solids. The glasswork seemed to shine on her as if its probing lights had been searching for a worthy subject. She had abandoned her sweatpants for a simple, shimmering dress.

"I was just—"

"Because I was going to try to have some fun, but now I don't know. I think I'd rather be somewhere quieter. Maybe your glass bubble?" Cerena held out her hand.

Teague held her hand all the way to the elevator, during the wait for a car, and through the ascent to the top. When the doors opened, Teague began to exit, but Cerena stayed.

Her mouth met his. This close, he lost resolution, and she felt soft, and all too right. He shut his eyes and silenced his reservations. It had been a long time since Aubrey, and even then.... Teague kissed her back. His hands grasped clumsily at her sides. "Your room," she whispered.

Teague kicked his door closed behind them, even as she tugged his shirt out of his pants. Clothes soon hung about them like clouds. Her body stretched to invisible lengths in the meager light. Her hair billowed in slow motion. He explored her skin, half-hoping she would take his wrists and push his hands away, but she moaned as if his touch had healing powers. He ached to calm her, to talk, but he craved the experience more. She welcomed him on top of her. Teague accepted her offering and surrendered himself to her like an act of selfish faith.

A few moments later, Teague rolled onto his back next to her, sticky, spent, and embarrassed, but betrayed by his continued arousal. He leveled his eyes with hers. Cerena turned away, curled into a fetal position, and began to weep. It had been only minutes since they'd left the party.

"I'm so sorry," she whispered. Teague touched her shoulder, and goosebumps rose like Braille. She didn't pull away, but Teague had no words to comfort her. As he pondered her amorphous shape, he caught a glint of light off Monkey's eyes. When had he learned to stay quiet in this situation? During Aubrey's visits? "I should go," Cerena said and lurched out of his bed.

"Don't," Teague said, but she had already found her dress and other bits of clothing, holding them against herself for modesty's sake.

When she emerged, dressed but disheveled, from Teague's bathroom, her eyes were red, but her expression was firm.

"You really don't have to go," Teague said. "Or we can go somewhere and talk."

"I can't. I'm sorry. This was a mistake. I just need to go." Cerena opened the door. Teague held it open and felt so small next to her that it was hard to imagine what had just happened.

"I hope—"

"No," she said. "Not now."

"If you're worried—"

"I'll be fine."

"We'll talk later," Teague said. She gave him a weak, pained smile, and then flowed down the hall and out of sight.

* * *

The next morning, a marvelous blue sky spread overhead, if one chose to believe it. Tropical trees lined the fairways as if to tempt a belief in paradise. In this virtual Eden, Teague laid out his case for M-SOO Incorporated.

Rob hadn't died of alcohol poisoning, and Aron had been amenable to golf even the morning after a party. As hoped, Aron and Rob refused to have their futures dictated by Matthew and Gwen, respectively. On the eighth tee, the three of them agreed to go into business.

Monkey called as they were approaching the fourteenth tee, and Teague switched to a private comm line. "I'm sorry to bother you, but I thought you'd want to know. Cerena Mei-zhen Hutton has boarded the shuttle to the Hatteras. She booked passage as far as the Pavonis elevator this morning."

Teague blinked away the false paradise of the golf course. The airlock, the shuttle dock, and the VSS Hatteras were out of sight on the opposite side of the asteroid. "She's boarded? Damn it. Put me through to her mobile."

Monkey complied, even as Teague began to worry about what

he might have to say to her. Soon, he reached a message recorded at a happier moment. Teague called Monkey back.

"I think she's shut her mobile off," Monkey said.

"Can we call Saul to get her attention?"

"The shuttle is closed, and the dock airlock sequence is in process."

"Can't you stop it?"

"I can. Do you want me to?"

Teague dug the tip of his golf club into the ground, carving a tiny, useless crater. His hesitation told him everything he needed to know. "No," he said. "Don't interfere."

"Okay."

"Thanks, Monkey."

"You're welcome. Have a good game."

Rob and Aron were staring at Teague from the tee. He reconnected with their channel and said, "I had to take a call."

"This is why they ban mobiles on decent courses," Aron said.

CHAPTER 20

It took coming here to learn it, but I now understand that some things are bigger than us, and demand sacrifice.

DECEMBER 2091–APRIL 2092

"Holy cow, Teague. What happened to you?" Aron asked after Teague sank a three-meter putt on the eighteenth hole.

"What do you mean?" Teague asked.

"What do you mean what do I mean?" Aron elbowed Rob. "Is his air low? These last few holes you've been playing like a pro, for you anyway. Plus one on the fourteenth. Plus two on the fifteenth. Par. Par. And this one is a plus one."

Teague barely remembered playing since he'd hung up with Monkey. Since the three of them had agreed to incorporate, Teague's to-do list had quadrupled. Yet thanks to Cerena, each item on it was weighted with a nagging sense of imminent failure. Was that what it took to be good at golf?

"Do we need to adjust your handicap?" Aron asked.

"We need a lawyer," Teague replied.

"Seriously?" Aron asked. "Can I get my suit off and take a shower before we call a quorum and start recording minutes? I'm trying to pay you a compliment."

"My uncle's a lawyer," Rob put in.

Aron groaned and turned off the golf program, returning them to the stark, dusty gray of Agnus Dei's surface. Fifty meters away, the airlock door and the towering wall of the Casino appeared where the thatched-roof clubhouse had stood. Teague blinked his inbox onto his visor. Had Cerena sent him any messages before she left? He scrolled through the usual complement of boat day announcements but found nothing.

"Is he a good lawyer? Your uncle?" Teague asked.

"His firm has a really fancy site, and they make their avatars wear wingtip shoes," Rob replied.

"Wingtips. Wow," Aron said. "They must be good. Look, my mom and dad know tons of lawyers. I'll get a recommendation."

"All we need right now is someone who can help us file our incorporation," Teague said.

"No offense," Aron said. "But we can probably do better than Rob's uncle."

"What's that supposed to mean?" Rob asked. "He's not some ambulance chaser or patent troll."

"Unbunch your panties, I just mean—oh, whatever," Aron said.

"I'll check him out," Teague said. "It doesn't mean he's our final choice for legal services. We just need this done quickly and relatively cheaply."

"How quickly?" Rob asked.

Quickly enough to render your red-haired friend's efforts completely moot. "Quickly enough," Teague said.

Teague half-expected, and half-hoped, to find a handwritten paper note slipped under his door, but only Monkey, and his rumpled sheets, were waiting for him back in his room. His few minutes with Cerena must have sealed some already-hardening resolve on her part. If she had left a note for anyone, it wasn't him. Teague wished that none of this mattered, but somehow, thanks to the vagaries of evolution, it did.

"Are you sad that Cerena left?" Monkey asked.

"I need you to find the site for a lawyer named Angus Heneghan and the firm where he's a partner. And find any reviews for them."

"Are you sure you don't want to talk about Cerena? It can be hard to lose a friend."

"I don't need your Zubotix bullshit today, Monkey." Teague stripped off his shirt and turned on the shower. "Oh, and one more thing. I need to know who's financing Gwen. Surely there's some record in Molly's logs of who Gwen talks to off this station."

Monkey stared at Teague in a wide-eyed pout.

"Now," Teague said, and closed the bathroom door.

Only two new freshmen had arrived: a physics major and a chemist, both from the Moon and both men. Teague was as relieved as he was disappointed. It'd been less than twenty-four hours since his humiliating moments with Cerena, and he had better things to do than to make a fool of himself in front of another woman—like reviewing the bids from freelance graphic designers coming in from the ad he'd posted after his shower. M-SOO Incorporated badly needed a new logo and a professional edge for its investor campaign.

Cerena's departure had caught everyone by surprise. And as Crystal and the others had discussed the matter, Aron had given Teague a knowing—but not accusing—look.

When Thomas arrived at the evening reception, Teague slipped away and met him at the bar. "Well, it's official. We're incorporating," he said as Thomas accepted a pack of water and thanked the server.

"Angela—I'm sorry, President Mbuto—informed me," Thomas said. "It's welcome, but not unexpected, news."

"Can we talk for a moment?" Teague nodded toward a sparsely populated nook behind the string quartet.

"Certainly."

"Do you know who Gwen Ungefucht is?" Teague asked.

"By reputation," Thomas replied.

"She's been sticking her nose pretty deep into M-SOO lately. She's been trying to sway Rob Heneghan away from working with Aron and me from the beginning. She's even scheduled a meeting for Rob to meet with her financial backers. Trying to get him to set up shop with them instead of us. I'm worried that she'll make a big fuss once she finds out we've incorporated. I wanted you to be aware. I've already talked to President Mbuto about it, but I want to make sure we're all on the same page."

Thomas responded with a serious nod, and Teague knew he understood what couldn't be said aloud. Matthew Valdosky had sent Aron to ADU for a reason and was now on his way here. What if he should arrive only to learn that Mbuto had allowed another student to cheat his only begotten out of his greatest achievement?

"I don't know what kind of promises she might have made to her backers," Teague continued, "but I want you to know that if they come to the school with any kind of demands or grievance, that Rob, Aron, and I had nothing to do with it."

"Do you know who her backers are?"

Teague nodded. Rob had been right. "It's a research subsidiary of TataFord."

"If they're truly interested in M-SOO, don't burn that bridge."

"I've already included them on our mailing list," Teague said.

"Good," Thomas said. "Don't worry too much about this company making waves. Valdosky's competitors tend to pick their battles carefully. And aggravating the CEO over his son's start-up would not be high on their agenda."

* * *

The junior partner scowled when he learned that Aron Valdosky was not coming to the meeting.

"Sorry, but he can't shift. Physically, I mean. Some brain incompatibility," Rob explained as he shook hands with the man's wingtipped, Earth-born avatar. Uncle Angus graciously invited Rob and the junior partner to sit on the same rendered couch where Rob had sat with his father a few years ago.

"And Teague Werres, will he be joining us?" asked the junior partner.

"He can't shift either," Rob said. "Sorry. It's just me."

"That's very strange. I've never known anyone who couldn't, let alone.... I was looking forward to meeting him, too." The junior partner conjured a document on the coffee table in front of each of them. The brand-new M-SOO logo already flickered on the top page, repeating its animation every few seconds. Little asteroids swirled around and through the letters, chaotically at first, but soon aligning in a brief micro-ballet. "I've never had a client come to me with anything as thorough as this. We had a couple of niggling comments, but Mr. Werres cleared those up this morning. We're ready to file."

Uncle Angus nodded in agreement as he thumbed and scrolled through his copy of the articles of incorporation. Rob hoped they wouldn't ask about any of the details. All he'd done was sit back and let Teague operate. It was like working with Gwen again. Confounding amounts of flawless results in impossibly short amounts of time—in this case, forty-eight hours since they'd shaken hands out on the fake Polynesian golf course—and damned if he knew how they did it.

The junior partner gestured to the copy in front of Rob. "That's the secure, encrypted file. Mr. Valdosky and Mr. Werres will need to sign that in front of a notary. I'm informed that there's one in the ADU administration office."

"Can I sign it with them, or do I need to sign it now?" Rob asked.

"Later is fine," the junior partner said.

"Thank you, Jack," Uncle Angus said.

The junior partner stood to leave but turned to Rob. "Please let Mr. Werres know that the correspondence he requested will be sent out by the close of business UST on the day that we receive and file the articles," he said.

"Correspondence?" Rob asked.

"The notices to potential investors about your official change in status."

"Right," Rob said. Thank goodness Teague knew to do these things. "I'll let him know."

"Pleasure meeting you," the junior partner said. He acknowledged Uncle Angus and then shimmered away.

Uncle Angus threw his arms wide and guffawed. "Aron Valdosky! I must say, you've done pretty well for yourself. I know your dad is busting at the seams."

"It's all pretty overwhelming. Most days, I still can't believe this is happening."

"Care for a couple nuggets of advice?" Uncle Angus asked.

"Please."

"There will be times when you feel overwhelmed, like it's all too big for you—"

"Story of my life," Rob interjected.

"That's when you need to take a moment and remember that you're part of this start-up for a reason. You have to act like you deserve to be there."

"It is my code," Rob said.

"There you go," Uncle Angus said. "But there's a corollary."

"What's that?"

"Bring something new to the table every day."

Rob nodded. Easier said than done. Especially with Teague five steps ahead. What he really needed was advice about how to deal with Gwen. She was still expecting him to meet with her backers in two days. *If I try to bluff my way through that meeting, she's going to reach through my shift set and throttle my brain right there in E-shift.* "I'll do my best. Thanks, Uncle Angus," he said, and sucked the document off the table. "Say hello to Aunt Cindy for me."

* * *

In the middle of Thomas's lecture, Monkey poked Teague discreetly and opened a live video feed on his screen. Teague expanded it in time to see Gwen slither like Medusa from the top of a spiral staircase. As she floated past an incongruous vista of an Earth city on Mbuto's office windows, Monkey tracked her to a glassy desk where Mbuto waited in a high-backed chair.

Mbuto motioned to the guest chairs, but Gwen stopped herself between them and jammed her hands almost to the elbow into her sweater's pockets.

Mbuto nodded curtly and began to speak. A few brief sentences only. Her expression remained firmly unapologetic. Teague tried to read Mbuto's lips and longed to put words in her mouth, something politic but clear. ...*in the best interest of the university... discontinue your efforts...without authorization of the responsible parties or this office.*

Teague expected Gwen to erupt, to snarl and spit, perhaps even to lunge across the desk. But she simply spun around and left, faster than Monkey could pan the camera. Ten minutes later, her signature profile appeared in the shiftpop, taking up as much bandwidth as almost a dozen regular users.

* * *

Rob slunk into the War Room and tossed an open message from his screen onto the table in front of Teague and Aron.

"What's this?" Aron asked, dragging it closer. Teague leaned in to read it, furrowing his brow.

"Mbuto saved me the trouble. Told Gwen to cease and desist now that we're incorporated," Rob said.

"About time," Aron remarked.

"I'm off the hook for that meeting with her people," Rob said.

"You don't look so happy," Teague said.

"It's just—I feel bad. She's been a friend. Helped me out a lot, you know."

Teague closed the message. "If she's a real friend, she'll congratulate you anyway."

"You guys need me any more tonight?" Rob asked with a deliberate yawn. Gwen hadn't answered his calls or replied to his messages. He needed several packs of Lamb's Mercy to spill their amber atonement out on his behalf.

Teague flicked away several windows and consulted a checklist. "We're still waiting for those data space estimates," he said.

Rob returned to his office. Coffee would have to do for now.

* * *

The dirty dishes were piling up in the steamy dish room of the Chaiprasits' restaurant. Teague sensed an urgent responsibility for the work, but water poured unchecked from the overflowing sink, and clouds of choking steam roiled from the doors of the beeping, overly complex dishwasher. Teague ached to remember how to operate the twitchy, demanding thing, if he ever knew. The stacks kept growing to teetering heights. One tipped and fell as if in low gravity. Teague dove, but the bowls and plates, spoons and forks, swooped out of reach like birds and formed new tottering piles. Mrs. Chaiprasit shouted his name just as a pile shattered on the tile floor.

Teague jerked awake to find Aron and Thomas staring expectantly and his screen drifting to the floor. He resettled himself on the couch and wiped a bit a drool from the corner of his mouth.

"Wow. Snore much?" Aron said.

"I'd appreciate it if you paid me the courtesy of staying awake in my class," Thomas said. "Perhaps you've been putting in too many hours on your extracurricular efforts?" It was no secret that Teague had been spending nearly every free hour for the past two months polishing and spit-shining the M-SOO business plan and presentation pitch. Matthew's ship, with its telepresence suite and local shift frame, was only a few weeks away, and they'd already scheduled live meetings with several VC firms during its visit.

"It's not that," Teague said as Monkey recovered his screen. "I haven't been sleeping well lately." Aron gave Teague a dubious look.

"If you're having difficulty sleeping, perhaps a visit to the clinic is in order," Thomas said.

Teague cringed. "I really don't want to take medication."

"Is this that Christian thing?" Aron asked. "But you got your Vanilla booster a couple of weeks ago. What's the difference?"

"You never went to church, did you?" Teague asked.

"Hell, no."

"Then you probably can't relate."

"No, but one can empathize," Thomas said. "For instance, I, too, feel personal reservations when taking Vanilla. No, 'reservations' is the wrong word. Grief, perhaps."

"What? Why?" Aron asked.

"When the Universal Treatment came online, only one country in the world refused," Thomas said.

"North Korea," Teague said.

Thomas nodded. "Kim Jong-un continued his grandfather's policy of Juche, self-reliance, to the rigid extreme. Millions were dying of starvation, or disease, or in the state camps, while Kim and high party officials took Vanilla in friendly states using false identity papers. They kept Vanilla secret for as long as possible, but when they couldn't hide it, they claimed it was a plot to poison North Koreans—that a jealous world had declared pharmaceutical warfare on their glorious nation. It took eleven years for the army to stage the coup that ended the Kim regime." Thomas cleared his throat. "Every time I take the treatment, I remember my countrymen who were denied—their lives destroyed by the madness of a few."

"But it wasn't a religious belief," Aron said.

"The North Korean cult of personality exploited religious techniques as well as, if not better than, any organized church," Thomas said. "The best I can say about the Tellurites is that their opposition is peaceful and largely private. I might respect their protest, if not for their children."

"I got out all right," Teague said.

"Not all children of faith healers are so lucky. But even so, you continue to harbor unreasonable fear and doubt," Thomas said.

"The only thing I worry about is planning my First Day party," Aron said.

"Taking the Universal Treatment *should* be a time of personal joy. It's a shame that some of us have had that taken away," Thomas said. "Let's get back to it. We may have to stay long today in order to cover what Teague missed."

"Thanks a lot, Werres," Aron said. "Go see a doctor."

"What was that all about?" Aron asked in a low voice, checking behind them as they exited the class only a few minutes later than normal. "You're not having trouble sleeping. You just work too much."

"What do you want me to tell him? Thomas might step in if he thinks I'm neglecting my obligations to the fellowship. And we have to be ready."

"You know, this company will happen, one way or another. You don't need to kill yourself."

"We can't afford to look like amateurs."

"No, but if you don't get some rest, and relax a little bit, you're going to make a mistake," Aron said.

"Sleep is a waste of time. And I really do have a tough time getting to sleep. I just end up lying in bed thinking about all the things I need to do."

"Do you need me to drag you to the clinic?"

"No. I'll go."

After they'd parted ways with Aron, Monkey asked, "Do you want me to schedule an appointment for you?"

Teague shook his head. "Of course not."

"I'm sorry. I can't always tell when you're…misrepresenting your position. If you're not going to see a doctor, might I suggest an alternate solution?"

"You're going to tell me to buy a shift set, aren't you?"

Monkey grinned. "How'd you guess?"

"I don't want a shift set," Teague said.

"But you already have the squid installed," Monkey said. "You don't need a full calibration to use the sleep induction settings."

"Absolutely not."

"But you could sleep whenever you wanted, for exactly as long as you wanted," Monkey said. After a few moments, he added. "I can do the calibration. No one would even have to know."

"Fine. I'll think about it," Teague said.

* * *

Once, long ago, Rob had been one of these schoolchildren, jumping and grabbing at the elusive, ancient creatures patrolling the ethereal green seawater that filled the atrium of the Smithsonian's Interactive Museum of Natural History. He wished he was one of them again. He'd enjoy the museum, and later his only concerns would be homework and a snack. Rob waited at the edge of the room, remaining aloof to the wonders all around, and scanned the children's faces on the off chance that his daughter might be among them. Every few moments, a docent would pop into the lobby and call out the name of some school. Teachers would then herd their summoned broods through the archway into the museum proper, yet the atrium never seemed to empty.

Rob heard his name and turned to see Barry striding through the bouncing crowd. His suit oozed competence, and he turned the head of more than one of the teachers. Barry gave an avuncular laugh when two boys bumped into him while leaping at a snaggletooth crocodile and graciously accepted the apologies of their teacher.

"This is where you work?" Rob asked.

"Just thought it'd be a nice place to meet. Ever been here before?" He passed Rob a visitors' badge.

"Not since middle school," Rob said. "They'd drag us here every couple of years."

"Tomorrow's the big day, isn't it?" Barry said.

"She's launching at eleven. I think she wanted to go earlier, but Eduardo convinced her that the guys would be more cooperative with a little more sleep."

A gaggle of students cheered when a fresh docent called out a school's name. Barry put a hand on Rob's shoulder and said, "Hold on."

A shimmering moment later, they appeared in an oval-shaped control room facing a wide patchwork matrix of live feeds. On each image, a docent, a teacher or two, and a brace of fidgety children existed in some point in a rather Earth-centric natural history of the universe.

Barry greeted the single avatar who was monitoring the whole business at a wraparound control desk. She smiled but turned back to her work as a room emptied and popped to the primary position on the matrix. She reset the program and signaled a new docent to the lobby.

"I'm trying to decide whether I should go to the launch," Rob said.

"Why wouldn't you?" Barry asked.

"I'm not exactly Gwen's favorite person right now. You've probably talked to her more than I have in the last few months."

"She may not say it, but she's afraid," Barry said.

"Afraid?"

"You have to remember that despite Gwen's uniqueness, she's still human. And ADU's the only home she's known her whole adult life. She told me once that she respected your persistence and the way her shit always rolled off you. She needed—and still needs—a friend like you."

"This is Gwen we're talking about, right?"

"I'm being serious. She'll be disappointed if you don't come to say goodbye."

"Do you think I should've agreed to go with her?" Rob asked.

"I told Gwen she should respect your decision."

"I felt bullied."

"She thought it was important," Barry said. "Forgive her. Go to her launch."

"What if she won't let me into the hangar?"

"Don't let Saul's be the last face she sees at ADU."

* * *

Teague wasn't surprised that the rumor of Gwen's secret departure had spread through the station, only at how long it took. It was as if people truly feared Gwen's specter, telling others only in furtive whispers when their courage allowed. Eventually President Mbuto's office had issued a brief statement confirming the rumor and declaring the old physical plant off-limits to everyone but authorized personnel until further notice. No date was given. Teague had heard of at least one contingent that claimed to know the particulars and was planning to watch the launch in pressure suits from some vantage with a view of the old hangar. He might have considered joining them if he didn't know that their date was wrong, and if he hadn't already seen her ship.

It had taken only a moment for Monkey and Molly to reactivate the long-dormant cameras in the cavernous assembly hangar. Some had been blocked, were missing, or had died, but there were enough to give Teague a peek at the oblong, reflective disc—a flying saucer captured and chained in place. Every square centimeter of the windowless craft seemed to be covered with shimmering fish scales. Its various hatches were readily concealed by flaps in its skin, as was the bouquet of engine bells at one long end.

Monkey decrypted a set of plans that revealed Gwen's ship to be about thirty-five meters wide and forty-five meters long, but only twenty meters deep at its thickest point. The interior framework supported a few necessary areas for propulsion, fuel, life support, and crew quarters, but it also left room for a variety of customizable, exchangeable modules. The modules could apparently be outfitted as anything from passenger quarters to science labs to cargo holds. The Ariel had no official bridge but was operated with a control program that ran on any properly configured device. Monkey had offered to download the interface, but Teague sensed he'd intruded far enough.

Teague worked late in the War Room the night before Gwen's launch. Since he'd broken down and bought a shift set, he'd been getting a little more sleep than normal. Monkey had downloaded and analyzed all the latest sleep research, and Teague had been experimenting with naps and various lengths of programmed sleep. He hadn't felt this rested and productive in a long time. But tonight, instead of focusing on his work, he kept refreshing Gwen's shiftpop profile, trying one last time to glean the truth from the graph.

Everything Teague had ever read about enhanced cognition treated it as a just-out-of-reach future tech at best and a quixotic fairy tale at worst. G-Plex hadn't changed its story in years. It still had a serious development effort, which remained a decade away from success. But Gwen was using it, right here, right now. What else could it be? If he wasn't going to get any substantial work done, Teague knew he should sleep, but he doubted that Gwen was sleeping tonight, so how could he?

Should he have taken a risk and asked her about EC? It'd been difficult enough to talk to her about anything when they'd been on friendly terms. He'd racked his brain for some way to broach the subject, some way that kept Monkey safe. Perhaps she'd be open about it. Everyone had vanities. But it was too late. She'd soon be gone, just like Cerena. She'd dwindle into the distance and become a speck of dust in the solar system—but yet remain incredibly large in a world he'd never see.

Teague saved his edits and retreated to the elevator bubble with Monkey to settle his mind.

They'd been quietly watching the universe for almost half an hour when Monkey stirred, cocked his head, and said, "Uh-oh."

"What's going on?" Teague asked.

"Gwen's in the Casino elevator, and she's coming to this floor."

"Why?" Teague sat up.

"I'm not a mind reader," Monkey said.

"Did she ask Molly for my location?"

"No, she didn't."

Teague swore under his breath and then realized that he was looking for an exit. But why? Even if Gwen came in here, what was she going to do to him? Yell and bluster? To what end? Maybe this was his chance to talk to her at last.

"Turn around," Teague said. "If she comes in here, act surprised."

The elevator dinged in the distance.

Soon, he heard her in the closet.

Finally, she opened the inner door, and Teague let himself turn around.

"What are you doing here?" she said. "Did Rob show you this place?"

"No. I found it," Teague said.

Gwen harrumphed. "Figures."

"You like to come here, too?" Teague asked. "Why don't I let you have some peace and quiet, then? Since you're…" He rose.

"Since I'm what?"

"Since you're leaving tomorrow. Don't worry. I'm not spreading that around. Rob asked my advice on a going-away present for you, and it kind of slipped out."

"He is such a…" Gwen tugged her sweater around her and tucked her hands under her armpits.

"He's going to miss you. In fact, he *has* been missing you,"

Teague said. "And I wish we could have gotten to know each other a little better, too."

"Don't start," Gwen said.

"What do you mean?"

"You may have everyone else at this school fooled, but not me."

"What?" Teague asked with a laugh.

"How'd you know to send a letter directly to Daruka Bhatnagar?"

"I don't know who that is," Teague lied.

"My contact at TataFord concerning the possible development of M-SOO?"

"TataFord. Are they your backers?"

"Don't play dumb with me," Gwen said.

"Rob guessed that they might be," Teague said.

"And so you sent them a letter that just happened to be directly addressed to my one specific contact? I read it, Teague."

"We sent out dozens of letters. It's not hard to scroll through a company directory and figure out who to send one to. Besides, our lawyers sent them out."

"That's such a lie. Somehow you knew exactly who to send it to."

"Believe what you want. What are you afraid of, anyway? Sure, M-SOO is a good idea, but anyone could develop something similar. If you and TF want it so bad, get to work."

"That's not what I'm afraid of," Gwen said. "I bought into your got-lucky orphan story like everyone else. It took me a long time, but I get it now. You're too perfect to be right here, right now, without some purpose."

"Now you're going off the deep end," Teague said.

"Am I? It's obvious they brought you here to control Valdo Junior. And you can't shift either? How convenient."

"*They?* Who do you think I am?" Teague asked. Did she think he was some spy, or plant, from Valdosky? Or, Teague wondered, did she think he used EC, too? Did she think he was like that entity in the Gateway network and that he had infiltrated her communications? But if she believed that, then she knew about the other one, or other ones, and didn't trust them. Perhaps she'd been hiding out here at ADU to get away from them. For a moment, it made sense.

"Mbuto wanted me out of it—can't piss off big donor Valdosky—so I got out. Message received loud and clear. You don't have to worry about me anymore. None of you do."

"I wish I knew what you were talking about," Teague said.

Gwen glowered. "If you're going to fuck off, then fuck off. And leave me alone."

Teague waited for a moment, aching to ask the question. Could they have been allies, if not for the secrets? "Come on, Monkey," he said.

"Bye, Gwen. Have a safe journey," Monkey said.

* * *

"Valdosky sucks," Rob read aloud from the wall. He had come here once with a box of chocolates, intending to make a friend. Was he still that same noob with a plunger? Or had he grown up? Rob knocked lightly on Gwen's door for old time's sake and then pushed off down the corridor to find the long, burrowed tunnel to the assembly hangar's control room.

Rob found the control system activated and ready but the room empty. Outside the window, a small group, comprised mostly of maintenance staff, had gathered a hundred meters away near the bow of the Ariel and was listening to a resplendent President Mbuto.

After buckling one of the remaining safety harnesses around his waist in the open airlock, Rob tugged the magnetic ball and socket over the ramped threshold and entered the hangar like a mouse enters a stadium.

The first time Rob had seen this room, he had been in awe, jealous of Gwen's private world. It had seemed an empire. The distant inner rock walls—pocked intermittently with room-sized holes, dark bubbled windows, and airlocks—reminded him of a derelict canyon colony. On one side, monolithic vertical panels separated and sealed the assembly hanger from the fabrication bay, the parts warehouse, and the offices where Gwen lived. The panels were so large it felt blasphemous to call them partitions. However, they were mere gods compared with the outer doors, colossal Titans that protected this room from the certain death of hard vacuum beyond. Now the cavernous hollow just seemed like a place to hide. Maybe he should move in.

The equipment and storage containers that usually littered the floor around the ship had been removed, as had the tanks and umbilicals that fed the craft. The glittering, completed Ariel was suspended three meters off the floor on a few threads of rigging strung from a gantry designed for much more. The only other denizen of this once-industrious place, an old tug, cowered on the far side of the hangar, unlit, forgotten, and unloved.

"—a day of both joy and sadness…" Mbuto paused, and everyone turned at the sound of Rob's safety harness rolling across the floor. Gwen glanced at the packages under his arm and scowled.

"Sorry I'm late," Rob said.

President Mbuto continued, "—for one of us has realized a lifelong dream, but we must also bid her farewell and *au revoir*."

President Mbuto took an object from Saul, a clear brick embedded with text and the ADU logo. "I've had the opportunity to inspect Gwen's work and can tell you that she is more than deserving of this." She turned the award and read the message. " 'In recognition and appreciation, Agnus Dei University confers to Gwendolyn Rose Ungefucht—' "

Rose? Rob mouthed to Gwen. Gwen narrowed her eyes menacingly.

"—'the perpetual distinction of Friend and Fellow of the University.' "

"Thank you, ma'am. I'm humbled," Gwen said. The maintenance staff applauded—probably more for Gwen's imminent departure than for her accomplishments, but sincerely enough. President Mbuto nodded to Gwen and then joined the onlookers.

Gwen knelt, opened a corroding box, and extracted a meter-long tree branch tasseled with long needles and a tuft of pinecones. Halfway along its length, the branch was split, had grown around a gap, and was grafted back together to form a diamond-shaped hole about the size of a playing card.

Gwen straightened. "When Prospero landed on the island, he discovered the sprite Ariel trapped in a cloven pine." Her voice broke slightly as she spoke. "He released the poor sprite, and became her master for a time, but made a promise to set her free." Gwen turned and lifted the branch toward the bow. The maintenance staff exchanged sideways glances and shallow shrugs. "I'll deliver all and promise you calm seas, auspicious gales, and sail so expeditious that shall catch your royal fleet afar off. My Ariel, chick, that is thy charge: then to the elements be free, and fare thou well!"

Gwen pulled on each side of the gap, and the branch split imperfectly like a wishbone. Mbuto congratulated Gwen as the maintenance staff again applauded politely.

"Okay, everyone, launch assignments," Eduardo called. As the group dispersed, Gwen returned her rent branch to its box.

"*The Tempest*?" Rob asked after Mbuto had given Gwen her final regards. "I didn't think you'd go for superstitious stuff like christening."

"It's not superstitious, it's traditional."

"It was very appropriate."

"That was the point."

"A couple going-away presents for you." Rob held out the little box first.

"More of Saul's sex chocolate?" Gwen asked.

"I thought it'd be a nice bookend," Rob said. Then he offered her the other package. She opened the plastic sleeve and removed a hardcover book with gold edging on the paper. She ran her fingers over the embossed title on the vinyl spine.

"Moliere. *Le Misanthrope*," Gwen said with a touch of reverence. "Where did you find this?"

Rob opened his mouth to confess Teague's help in getting Professor Minus to part with it, and his help with the inscription, but caught himself and said, "I have my sources."

She opened the front cover and read, " 'To Gwen. Wherever

you are, may you find humans of worth. Rob.' " Her eyes welled up.

"I haven't read it," Rob said.

"Well, fuck you, then," Gwen said, blinking. "Barry informs me that I haven't been fair to you."

"Doesn't matter. I know you meant well."

"Can I give you one last piece of advice?" Gwen asked.

"As long as I get a choice in whether to follow it or not," Rob said, hoping for a laugh.

"I'm serious," Gwen said. "Listen. I know he's your friend and now your business partner, but I think you need to be cautious around Teague."

"Cautious around Teague? I don't even know what that means," Rob said.

"Make sure you safeguard your interests. Watch your back, and certainly don't expect him to watch it for you."

"Why are you saying all this?"

"You're putting an awful lot of trust in him, and I just want you to be careful. That's all."

"What about Aron? I thought the Valdosky Companies were the ones that were going to swallow me whole."

"I can't explain it. I have a bad feeling about Teague, too. Please, listen to me now. For once," Gwen said.

Rob nodded his acquiescence and then helped her carry his gifts and the items from the ceremony to an open hatch under the Ariel. Gwen set everything inside, unbuckled her safety belt, and handed it to Rob. "Are you going to be okay by yourself?" he asked.

"Oh, now you care?"

"I care. I really do. I'm going to check on you every day, whether you like it or not," he said.

"Goodbye, Rob," she said and pushed off into the ship. A few seconds later, the hatch was sealed and hidden by a graft of reflective skin.

Rob waited at the back of the control room for nearly an hour as Eduardo, his staff, and Molly worked through the procedures to evacuate the hangar's atmosphere and open the monstrous doors. The Ariel waited on the other side of the glass, already unreal and distant.

Eventually, the gantry rumbled forward, and the Ariel drifted into space like a cloud on a breeze. Gwen relayed confirmations over the comm. The gantry stopped, and the rigging released. The Ariel hung in space until the gantry had retracted and then emitted a few silent bursts from its chemical thrusters to escape the cameras. Even as Saul began to sing a song about a doorbell and the death of a witch, Rob was sure he should have gone with her.

CHAPTER 21

I sought to escape your shadow, but I learned that I carry it with me always—as do others here. You are, and always have been, a father to many.

MAY 2092

"You're not going to freak out, are you?" Aron asked as he pressed the elevator call button three times.

"I don't plan to," Teague replied.

"My friends all freak out when they meet him. Half clam up, half babble like idiots, half just get weird."

"That's three halves."

"Whatever. Just be cool, like you were when you met me." Aron tapped the call button again, blew out a long breath, and popped several knuckles.

"Ice cold," Teague replied with a laugh. None of Aron's other friends, not even Crystal, had been invited to the dock.

Teague had awoken that morning to a palpable resonance in the air. Valdosky's flagship, the Mirage, arguably the most important spaceship in the system, had taken up a station-keeping position near Agnus Dei during the night. Everyone seemed to have come to breakfast via the windows on the dockside.

"Do you think they really have a vault full of secret alien technologies?" a grad student at the table next to Teague's had asked.

"You should totally ask that on the tour," one of the grad

student's companions had replied. *Philosophy majors,* Teague had thought as he laughed to himself. Even Monkey had rolled his eyes.

Teague thought the Mirage was an ugly thing. A variant of Valdosky's cruisers, it had only two skewered skyscrapers where the Empress had four. As a result, the engines appeared oversized, as if they might snap the mitigated assembly if ignited. An office block with a glass bulge on top—possibly the bridge, but more likely a restaurant—had been glommed onto the bow. A bulbous protrusion descended from its lower decks. It was from this that the shuttle delivering the security prep team had emerged.

The shuttle was no modified cargo container, as normally delivered ADU visitors, but a bus-sized high-top shoe with a docking collar on the back of the heel. A row of bright oval windows lined each side, and a band of dark glass wrapped around the ankle, behind which presumably sat an actual pilot.

A few days earlier, Molly had run a prediction of the long-term gravitational effects of the Mirage on Agnus Dei. A thousand years from now, this convergence meant a nearly fifty-kilometer change in position. Nothing would ever be the same again.

The Mirage's gravity seemed to have warped time as well as space. These last few weeks had flown by at a steadily increasing clip. With the fellowship ending and M-SOO beginning, there was more than ever to do. At times, Teague had wondered how he'd get it all done, especially when each hour seemed shorter than the last. More than ever he envied Gwen and her unimaginable amounts of tireless time. But at least he had Monkey, whom he kept working nearly every second of the day.

"Shuttle's going to dock before we even get a stupid elevator," Aron said, and pounded the button again.

Teague stayed back with Thomas and several other professors and administrators as Aron joined President Mbuto, turned out in full regalia, at the foot of the dock ramp. Saul hovered by the controls, flanked by Eduardo Arcoverde, who was gnawing on a fingernail. Several men and women in dark suits, all with a military bearing, had placed themselves around the dock. Among them was Aron's shadow, his thin blue line at ADU. Since a single interview almost two years ago, Teague had only ever seen him in the gym.

"Is Matthew really this paranoid?" Teague asked.

"No. He pays other people to be paranoid for him," Thomas replied.

At a blast of static and an unintelligible communication, Saul donned a headset and turned his attention to the controls.

"Matthew's anxious to meet you, too," Thomas said. Teague realized he'd been drumming his fingers on his thighs. "Just be yourself. And remember. He's only human."

A few seconds later, the dock wall came alive with a magnetic hum, hydraulic whirrs and whines, and a final hiss. The inner door rumbled aside. The shuttle remained closed for an anti-climactic minute until its door retracted a few centimeters and slid away. A burst of friendly laughter spilled across the dock, and then he emerged.

Matthew Valdosky was instantly recognizable. He wore his collar open casually under a suit jacket. Teague was struck suddenly by how much, in person, Matthew resembled the man in the hidden photograph in the frame on his desk. How had he never noticed that before? Teague knew it wasn't true, but even as Matthew greeted Aron with an embrace, he wanted to believe, if only for a moment, that the man who had just arrived at ADU was the father he'd never known.

Matthew worked his way through the gathering, glad-handing the professors and administrators like a politician. Teague forced himself to breathe. He quelled his private fantasy and remembered Thomas's advice. *He's just a man.*

"This must be the famous Teague Werres," Matthew said at last, flashing a grin to Aron.

"Pleased to meet you, sir," Teague replied, a little surprised that Matthew didn't look a day over thirty. Of course Matthew took Vanilla, but shouldn't such an important person have a touch of gray and a few distinguished lines, like Secretary General Arugo, or even the Badass?

"You two haven't been getting into too much trouble, have you?" Matthew asked. Teague kept smiling, and Aron rolled his eyes. "Can't spill the beans around Thomas, eh? Thomas, how are you?"

"Matthew," Thomas said. As the two men shook hands, Teague studied Aron and Matthew side by side. A stranger would likely pick him, not Aron, as Matthew's son. They might be genetic family, but they were gravitational strangers.

"All right, where are we going?" Matthew asked.

"Up to my room?" Aron suggested.

"Teague, why don't you join us?" Matthew asked. Teague glanced to Thomas, but Thomas had already turned to talk to President Mbuto.

A few minutes later, as they crossed the Casino lobby surrounded by bodyguards, Teague heard a gasp from the bar and felt stares from the cafeteria. It had been too easy to forget how extraordinary a person Aron really was.

"This place looks in pretty good shape," Matthew remarked.

"It's a dump," Aron said.

"It's underutilized," Matthew said.

"The food's good," Teague offered.

"That's my problem. Everywhere I go, the food is good," Matthew said, patting his belly.

Once upstairs, the bodyguards stayed in the corridor, leaving Teague alone with the father and son. *What the hell am I doing here?* Teague thought as the door closed and Matthew crossed the suite to admire the view.

"Wow," he said. "These are great spaces. It's too bad we couldn't have made this place work."

"Home sweet prison," Aron said. Matthew shot him a sour look, and Aron apologized.

"What does it take to get a drink in this place?" Matthew asked.

Soon Aron had returned from the kitchenette with three tumblers of scotch, and Teague accepted his despite the early hour. Matthew raised his drink, turning to include Teague. "Here's to the shiftless, we happy few," he said. Aron had declared this many times before. It must be the Valdosky family toast. Matthew smacked his lips and said, "Excellent stuff. So when do I meet the legendary Crystal?"

"Later," Aron said.

"I'm supposed to give a full report," Matthew said.

"Mom's met her."

"In shift, yes. But she thinks it's pretty serious," Matthew said.

"It's not that serious."

"How about you, Teague? Have you fallen for a woman out here, too?"

"No, sir," Teague replied.

"Teague's picky," Aron said. "He likes Earth girls."

"I wouldn't call that picky. And please, Teague, call me Matthew." He glanced around the suite. "I was expecting something a little more *Animal House*."

"There's not much to do, but there's a good virt-golf course," Aron said.

As Teague watched father and son interact it became clear why he had been invited: Neither Matthew nor Aron wanted to be alone with the other.

"I'll bring my suit over," Matthew said.

"Will you have to bring your goon squad?"

Matthew waved dismissively to the door. "They have to justify their existence."

"It's creepy."

"They get jumpy in new locations. I know what it's like. I was part of Adrian Wolkenbruch's security detail, once upon a time. When there's a threat, it's unnerving twenty-four seven."

"Is there a threat?" Teague asked.

"Always. But do you know what we get the most complaints about? Food quality on the long-haul cruises. People get vicious. And not biting-sarcasm vicious. I'm talking baby-eating-wolverine vicious. But, honestly, *you* try feeding twelve thousand people for nine-plus months in a closed loop."

"No one's going to kill you over bad food," Aron said.

"Let's hope not." Matthew stuck his glass to the coffee table. "The head?" he asked. Aron pointed toward his bedroom, and Matthew left.

"The great Matthew Valdosky, ladies and gentlemen," Aron said in a low voice.

"What's wrong?" Teague asked.

"He's trying to be one of the guys. He's ninety years old. It's disgusting."

"I like him," Teague said.

"Fine. We'll switch. He can be your father, and I get to enjoy him making an ass of himself. You two are a better match anyway." Teague felt his face redden and took a slow sip of scotch to hide it.

Matthew soon returned, removed his jacket, and tossed it toward a barstool. It caught, and its shape deflated. As Matthew recovered his drink, Teague decided that everything Thomas had told him about the man rang true. It was difficult to reconcile this person with the corporate image of the visionary leader. He had charm and a little charisma, but no obvious genius or depth. Thomas had been right to warn him. Disillusion could turn quickly to disdain or disrespect. Better to understand now, since it would be a mistake, despite appearances, to underestimate the man.

"You guys looking forward to graduation?" Matthew asked.

"You don't know the half of it," Aron said.

* * *

When Rob arrived at the dock early the next morning, an ADU administrator was chatting glumly with Saul. Rob yawned and shrugged, hoping to make his suit jacket fit better. His dad had heaped a ton of advice on him the night before, but none of it had stuck. The shuttle arrived, and the administrator brightened falsely as thirty or so tourists, mostly well-aged Earthlings, disembarked.

A few minutes later, Rob settled warily into a swivel leather seat in the quiet cabin. An attendant with artful hair and a record-breaking smile greeted him and offered him a water pack. She had probably smiled at much more important people.

Soon Teague arrived with Professor Minus, and Aron rolled in a few minutes after that.

As the shuttle made its smooth departure, Rob wiped his palms on his pants and wished he hadn't eaten eggs for breakfast. Dad had nearly exploded with pride to hear that Matthew Valdosky had arranged to have some of his own people critique the M-SOO investor presentation before their first real meeting.

"This is big," his father had repeated incredulously.

"Rob?"

"Huh? What?"

"I asked if you confirmed Molly's link with their tech guy," Teague said.

"Sorry. Yeah. We worked out the firewall issues," Rob said. "Worst case, we can use my mobile." Teague glared. "That's a joke."

"Teague's not in the mood for jokes," Aron said and then spun around to face Thomas. "You're quiet."

"What would you like me to say?" Thomas asked.

"Thought you'd be brimming with last-minute wisdom," Aron replied.

"I was asked to observe. And I was invited to lunch. Are you interested in hiring me as a consultant?"

Dawn Water, read the label of the supermodel-delivered pack, *pure ancient H2O from the dawn of the solar system, ice filtered through the rock of Ceres.* Rob downed the entire pack, hoping to drown the butterflies. Gwen would be having a rabid fit right now.

They disembarked into a spacious airlock, passed through a security scanning station, and were directed to a waiting elevator. The car delivered them to a crescent-shaped lobby dominated by the Valdosky logo woven into the carpet. "You guys are from Asia. You'll probably feel right at home here," Aron said as he rounded the unmanned reception desk. Inside the offices proper, a grip-treated slatted boardwalk floated over raked and seal-coated sand. The offices were separated with delicate rice paper doors framed with darkly stained wood. Every nook contained a decorative arrangement of potted plants and statuary. It was impossible to say where the diffuse lighting originated from.

"Japanese," Teague said. "Not my part of the continent."

"Nor mine," Thomas added.

"Whatever," Aron said. "I've never been to Earth."

At the end of a short passage, the decking split around the perimeter of a bamboo garden of boulders, polished pebbles, and raked sand. Along a meandering, tranquil path of flat stone, a wooden bridge crossed a narrowing of an oblong, membraned pond teeming with gargantuan koi. Wooden rods of deliberate lengths hung from the ceiling, creating a pixilated mirror of the topography underneath. Rob nearly collided with Teague, who had stopped at the junction to take it all in, and they exchanged incredulous looks.

On the far side of the garden, Aron slid aside a rice paper door, and they filed into a vestibule flanked by two offices. An olive-skinned, matronly woman with dark hair rose from a desk and greeted Aron with an ecstatic hug.

"Hi, Maria," Aron said. "How is Francesca?"

"She's married now. She wouldn't wait for you."

"You wouldn't have let her marry me anyway."

"This is true," Maria said with a fond smile. "Look at you. You're a man now."

"You sound surprised," Aron said.

The far door slid aside, and Matthew entered. *I'm actually in Matthew Valdosky's office,* Rob thought. He was glad that he'd met him at the reception last night. Hopefully he'd gotten over his jitters and his marble-mouthed stammers. Still, probably better not to say anything for a while. Matthew introduced everyone to his assistant and then invited them through.

Matthew's domain overlooked the solar system through an arced wall of glass perhaps twenty meters wide. To the starboard, a surprisingly small desk sat in front of a complex, high-backed chair. To the port, an ethereal conference table with room for ten, but chairs for six, floated under a long dark truss chandelier. Matthew headed toward a grouping of black couches and armchairs in the center and suggested that they sit.

So far, the Mirage was significantly warmer than most of ADU.

Rob hoped the shift presence suite would be cooler; otherwise this was going to be a long day under his suit jacket.

"I'm anxious to see what you've put together," Matthew said. "There's quite a buzz. You've done a great job, Thomas."

"I've had little to do with this project."

"Of course. The infamous Minus humility. Did you all have breakfast? Coffee?"

"We'd like a few minutes to get comfortable in the tele-suite," Teague said.

A side door opened in the shadows on the far side of the conference table. Before Rob could see who had entered, Matthew called, "Dwight. You're just in time." Thomas and Aron both stiffened.

"Good morning, gentlemen," the man said as he came into the light.

"Teague Werres, Rob Heneghan, this is Dwight Yarrow, our CFO." Dwight was an Earthling, about as tall as Teague, with white, close-cropped hair, a lined and jowly face, and lips unused to smiling. His eyes were experienced, knowledgeable—and frighteningly deep. He wore a black knit turtleneck under a dark jacket and carried a pair of glasses. His hand was cold but firm in Rob's own piscine grip. Dwight's gaze both penetrated and dismissed him, and Rob repressed a shudder. This was the man Rob had expected Matthew to be, the fearsome black heart of the Valdosky Companies that Gwen hated so deeply.

"Good luck today, gentlemen," Dwight said after all the introductions had been made. His voice was slippery, not accented, but fluid and odd. "Matthew, I need a few moments."

"Sure. I'll show them to the tele-suite and be right back," Matthew said.

The suite was about what Rob expected. A half-table with real seating for six bisected by a curved screen, adjustable lighting, and a credenza with water service. Not his world by any stretch of the imagination. He'd rather be on the cool, bright, electronic side where you didn't have to wear a tie. Plus, he wanted a chance to see Matthew's private shift frame. It probably wasn't much more interesting than Molly's servers, but this was the Mirage, not some random G-Star. Just think who had shifted in to meet with Matthew Valdosky. Presidents. Prime ministers. Secretaries-general. Adrian Wolkenbruch. Gretchen Walker.

A rotund Earthling poked his head into the room and said, "I'm James. Which one of you is Heneghan?"

Rob left his jacket on the back of a chair and gladly followed James behind the scenes of the stifling suite. As Rob had guessed from their earlier communications, James was an alpha geek, the kind who had gone straight from his mother's teat to tweaking OS code with barely a stop at puberty. Rob had avoided the alphas at MTI but was prepared to give James a break; he was Matthew Valdosky's personal IT guy, after all.

The six-meter-wide equipment room intersected multiple decks like an elevator shaft. As they drifted, climbing, through grated decks, James casually pointed out bleeding-edge components among the blinking server racks, rattling off model numbers as if they meant anything. Rob was about to ask about the shift frame when they arrived at a central node of sorts. The expansive admin screen was cluttered with component feedback, technical schematics, scrolling code, streaming stock market data, and several tentacle-centric hentai videos.

James indicated where Rob needed to input his passcode, and a few moments later Molly greeted them in her grown-up voice.

"Good morning, Rob. And good morning, James."

James gave Rob a leering smile and waggled an eyebrow. "Molly, indeed," he said.

Creep, Rob thought. "Good morning, Molly. Please load the presentation through to Teague in the conference room."

"Right away," she replied.

James brought up a matrix of images from the suite—the first slide of the presentation; the unoccupied chairs; and the torsos of Aron, Teague, and Thomas. James tapped an icon, and the cameras aligned to track their faces.

"There're four of you?" James asked.

"No, just three," Rob said. "Professor Minus is observing."

"There's a viewing room next door." James's system beeped, and a large status bar appeared. "Uh-oh, who are you?" James said to the event. The bar filled, and a window opened with the live image of an avatar of a gray-haired man in a corporate office lobby.

"Mr. Gauthier," James said. "What are you doing here already?"

"I'm here for the development review," the executive replied.

"It starts at nine-thirty," James said.

"I was told nine." A few seconds later, another status bar appeared, and then another.

"Not good," James said. He tapped an intercom. "Can you guys be ready to go, like now? I've got three executives waiting who were told this thing's happening at nine. They're not going to be happy if you waste their time."

"Can you give us five minutes?" Teague asked.

Another middle-aged man and a woman in a severe business suit had joined the first in the virtual lobby. James switched back. "Sorry, everyone. There's been a mix-up on the time. Give us a couple of minutes."

"I didn't have time for this in the first place," one grumbled. The others agreed.

Rob hurried back to the suite the way he'd come. Teague was frantically sorting agendas and script outlines on the table screen. "Everything ready with Molly?" he asked.

Rob nodded and tugged his jacket back on. He'd barely sat down at Teague's left when three annoyed avatars faded into the reciprocal conference room and began to take their seats across the table. Rob really wished he could have visited a restroom first.

Rob made a beeline to the door with the little man on it. Then, after frantically fumbling with the disposable personals and finally releasing the urgency, he let himself think about the past two hours. Aron had given the introduction as rehearsed, but once Teague had taken over, the presentation had begun to click. He'd been confident, quick with facts, and had found natural ways to improvise. For his own part, Rob remembered only a blur of stumbles and mispronounced words. He'd probably do his new company a service by staying behind the scenes.

Rob washed his hands and found a neat, loosely banded stack of soft towels on the granite counter. Drawn by curiosity to the palatial stall, Rob discovered the most glorious zero-gee toilet he had ever seen and wondered if anyone famous had ever used it. He closed the partition, and the control screen activated. The icons were displayed over pastoral Earth landscapes and a ticker of financial headlines. Rob warmed the seat, adjusted the lighting, and then froze. Someone had entered the restroom. The intruder sniffed, grunted, and took a personal from the dispenser. Rob hadn't locked the stall door, but embarrassment kept him from doing it now. After a great deal more sniffing, a final zip, and a vacuum flush, the man went to the sinks.

"Thomas," said a voice. Had someone else entered? After a few seconds, the same man spoke again. "Why are you here?" It sounded like Dwight Yarrow: smooth, between accents, as if the man spoke several languages.

"Excuse me," Professor Minus said.

"That's the difference between you and me, Thomas," Dwight said. "I've moved on from the past. You, on the other hand, have never let go."

"This is not the time or the place," Professor Minus said.

"It's laughable, really. Aron is not Adrian. You must've realized that by now." The outer door creaked and then closed. Rob's heart pounded in his ears as the remaining man seemed to approach his stall. The man paused and cleared his throat—was he looking in the mirror?—and then moved away. Rob held still until he was certain he was alone, and then he risked a peek over the stall door. *Mental note: Forgo the Dawn Water in the mornings.*

* * *

Teague had almost forgotten how beautiful women from Earth could be. In the past few hours, he'd presented the most important work of his life to Valdosky's best business strategists and he'd shaken Dwight Yarrow's hand in Matthew's office. But he hadn't truly felt nervous until the server set a sashimi appetizer in front of him, brushing lightly against his shoulder. He thanked her clumsily and tried not to stare as she served the others. He was almost relieved when she finished and slipped away and he could breathe once again.

Matthew had arranged for lunch in the gazebo in the middle of the garden. As they took their cushions around the low, square table, the offices all but disappeared behind the surrounding rocks and clumps of bamboo.

"This isn't fish from your pond?" Aron asked as he sniffed at a bit clamped in his chopsticks.

Teague noticed Rob glancing at Thomas as they began to eat. Rob had been reticent during the review, as if he knew he was the weakest link. But despite Rob, they'd done well. The interviewers had come in hostile, certain that they were grading school papers for Matthew's kid, but Teague was convinced that he'd won them over.

Matthew had come alive while moderating the follow-up. The development executives hadn't seemed sycophantic, and Matthew had encouraged them to speak their minds. Quick on his feet and a friendly facilitator, he was perhaps a better leader than Thomas thought.

"Anyone interesting traveling with you these days?" Aron asked.

"I don't know about interesting," Matthew said. "The usual contingent of novelists and artists. There's an old guy that directed one of Mom's movies."

"Which one?"

"The one where she's asleep, but her dreams are real."

"I hate that one. That part with the clowns." Aron shuddered.

"You know, speaking of passengers," Matthew said, "I was going to wait until after your meetings to do this, but what the hell—I want to offer you all a lift on the Mirage. Get you back to civilization quicker than a cargo hump."

"Wow," Teague said. Even now that he could sleep at will with his shift set, not having to spend seven months in a capsule would be worth almost any price.

"You don't need to answer now." Matthew turned to Aron. "But it'd be great to have you on board. Offer's open for you, too,

Thomas." Rob froze, a bite of food halfway to his mouth, staring strangely at Thomas. *But why?* Teague wondered.

"I'm afraid I must follow my original itinerary," Thomas replied.

"We've got the room," Matthew said. The server—Matthew had called her Rebecca—returned to clear the appetizers and deliver the main course. Teague tried to give her a friendly smile. A few other good reasons to travel with Matthew came to mind.

* * *

All Rob wanted to do was to shed his sweat-lined suit coat and shift. But following the afternoon's presentation, they returned to Matthew's office and talked until Maria announced that the shuttle had arrived. Rob didn't know how Teague had sustained his level of enthusiasm this long without dropping dead.

"Are you sure you can't all stay for dinner?" Matthew asked as they made to leave.

"I thought it was supposed to be me and Crystal," Aron said.

"Thank you, but I've got some work to do tonight anyway," Teague answered. *Is that me?* Rob wondered. *Am I the work?*

At last they boarded the shuttle, and Rob drifted into a seat. He declined a water pack from the attendant—a man this evening, but no less a supermodel—buckled in, and closed his eyes. One day down, four more to go.

"Is there something I should know about Dwight Yarrow?" Teague asked. Rob opened his eyes.

"What do you mean?" Thomas replied.

"You just seemed uncomfortable around him this morning," Teague said.

"It's no secret that I objected strongly to Matthew's association with Dwight."

"Why?" Teague asked.

"It was a long time ago," Thomas said.

"Is Dwight the reason Matthew and Adrian Wolkenbruch had a falling out?" Teague asked.

"This is ancient history. You have bigger things to worry about."

"But you're still on good terms with both Matthew and Adrian."

"Despite my objections to Dwight's way of doing business, it's rarely prudent to burn bridges," Thomas said.

"What does Dwight think of Matthew sending Aron to school with you?" Teague asked.

"You mean is Dwight afraid that under my tutelage, Aron will become a powerful altruist like Adrian Wolkenbruch and reform Valdosky into a responsible corporate citizen?"

"Something like that," Teague replied.

"Who is Dwight Yarrow?" Rob blurted out. Thomas and Teague turned, surprised.

"He's the CFO," Teague said.

"I know that, but where'd he come from? Why is everyone so afraid of him?"

"His family had a hotel chain, right?" Teague said, checking Thomas for confirmation. "And real estate, mostly in the southwestern United States. He took over the business at the end of the last century. He's always had a reputation for being ruthless. But he developed several small space technology companies—whether as a hobby or an investment, I don't know—but it all took off."

"So why isn't it the Yarrow Companies?" Rob asked.

"You two don't need to be worrying about Dwight Yarrow," Thomas said. "Focus on your investors."

* * *

The next morning, Rob arrived at the shuttle dock to find that Saul had duct-taped an ancient folding beach chair to the floor near the controls. The chair's green-striped plastic webbing sagged under him, even in the microgravity.

"Heneghan," Saul grunted without opening his eyes.

"How long has the shuttle been here?"

"Long enough to change the air," Saul replied. "I had to get up at the ass-crack of dawn so Junior's girlfriend could get back in time for class."

"Is Teague on board?" Rob asked.

"What am I? The hostess? If you want to chat, go talk to Lorelei," Saul waved to the shuttle.

"I'm surprised you're not chatting her up," Rob said, catching a glimpse of her in the cabin.

"Not my type." Rob almost asked about Saul's type but thought better of it. Too early in the morning for those mental images.

Lorelei, the water bearer, was in the galley when Rob boarded. Teague floated in as Rob was stowing his bag. "It's just us," Teague told Rob. "Aron stayed on the Mirage last night."

A few minutes into the crossing, Rob asked, "Teague? Can I ask you a question?"

"Sure," Teague answered, still focused on his screen.

"Are we making a big mistake?" he asked. Teague stopped reading. "Maybe we shouldn't have used Valdosky as a resource."

"We got some free consulting, and now we're just borrowing their shift suite. It's not a big deal."

"But what if we gave them too much information yesterday?" Rob said.

"Rob, we have nine more investor interviews. I know you're nervous. We all are. But going in there with Gwen-like paranoia is not going to help."

"You think I'm going to fuck everything up," Rob said.

"That's not what I said."

"But you think I screwed up yesterday." Rob caught Lorelei in his peripheral vision. She could probably hear everything.

"Calm down," Teague said. "Think. In a couple of weeks, we'll have some start-up cash, Aron and I will have graduated, and we'll be on our own. Even if we travel on the Mirage, we won't have anything to do with Valdosky."

"Aron *is* a Valdosky," Rob said.

"We don't need to worry about that."

"Why?" Rob asked. "He's Aron Valdosky, not Aron Werres, or Chim-Chim the Performing Ape."

"We won't proceed recklessly. We'll protect our interests."

"You didn't answer my question."

"You really want my answer?" Teague asked. He glanced toward the galley, leaned across the aisle, and whispered, "Because, in the long run, Aron is not worth worrying about. Thomas knows it. Matthew knows it. Why do you think they sent him here? Because he never would've earned an education anywhere else. They're all pissing their pants with glee that he's going to graduate and he's taken initiative to do something with his life, and they're not going to do anything to screw that up."

"You seem awfully sure of all that."

"I came to terms with why I'm here a long time ago," Teague said.

Rob nodded and then understood. Aron and Teague's common disability had always seemed like an odd coincidence, but Teague hadn't been recruited by accident. Why hadn't he realized it before? Was Teague in on it, whatever "it" was? Is this what Gwen had warned him about? What else had he missed?

"Are we good?" Teague asked.

"Sorry. We're good."

"This isn't the least stressful thing we've ever done."

"Nothing like starting big," Rob said.

"Hey," Teague said, "even if we fail, we're rock stars."

* * *

When the avatars of the last group of potential investors faded away on Friday afternoon, Teague felt like the last man standing. Rob had looked half-shifted since lunch, and Aron's attention span had been shrinking steadily since Tuesday. But Teague felt ready to pitch again. He'd evangelized this last group even with Aron twiddling his stylus and Rob grunting his answers. In fact, nearly every pitch they'd made all week had ended well.

"I think"—Teague tapped the control screen with finality—"we got our money." The fake half of the room flickered off, and the tele-suite's lights faded from their theatrical directionality to a more comfortable ambiance.

Aron began to yank off his tie. "As of now, the official dress code of M-SOO Incorporated is sub-casual," he announced. "If we were shifters, we could've worn skivvies. What is a skivvy, anyway? Heneghan, you're a squid head. What's a skivvy?"

"Huh? I don't know. Underwear?"

"You shift in your underwear?" Aron asked.

"On laundry days." Rob looked at the screen as if surprised to find it blank.

"We're done, Rob," Teague said. "You can relax now. You did well."

"Oh, good," Rob said. Teague gave Aron a discreet smile.

"Rob, give me your tie. Teague, you, too." Aron took all three ties, straighteners and all, and stuffed them into the recycling basket by the credenza. "May they rest in peace," he said.

A few moments later, they drifted single-file into a small round of applause from Matthew, Thomas, President Mbuto, and Dwight Yarrow, in Matthew's office.

"Congratulations, from all of us. You've done a hell of a job this week," Matthew said.

"I've already received several messages following up on your references. I'm very encouraged," President Mbuto added.

"Does this mean I get an MBA?" Aron asked.

"There's still few days until graduation," President Mbuto said, smiling broadly. "No slacking now."

"Did we interrupt something?" Teague asked.

"Not at all," Matthew replied. "I arranged a little celebration. Are you hungry?"

"Famished," Aron said. Teague had to laugh. Aron's stomach had been growling so loudly all afternoon he was sure the investors had heard it.

Matthew led the way out the side door to a waiting elevator. There wasn't enough room in the car, and when the doors closed, Teague found himself alone in the hallway with Dwight Yarrow. Teague stared at the ascending numbers and tried to think of something to say.

Dwight spoke first. "I read your business plan," he said. "They tell me it's your first."

"It's not mine alone," Teague said.

"Take credit when you can," Dwight said. "Not many startups have the balls to include hundred- let alone five-hundred-year projections."

"M-SOO's a long-term predictive tool, so it's kind of a joke. But the trends are real," Teague replied.

"A joke?"

"Our data is invaluable for any company operating in the solar system. For instance, we could save Valdosky a few percent of its fuel budget every quarter." Dwight looked askance at Teague, and Teague felt his skin crawl. *He's just a man,* he reminded himself. *He's just another potential customer like you've been preaching to all week.* "Consider the targeting data you'll need for the ballistic cargo delivery system that you're developing. And before you establish an asteroid colony, wouldn't you like to agree with your insurers about where it was going to be in a hundred years?"

"Are you trying to sell me?" Dwight asked.

"It hasn't escaped my notice that Valdosky could be our biggest customer."

Dwight put an earpiece of his glasses in his mouth. "It hasn't escaped my notice that you're an arrogant upstart. Don't look like that. If you knew me at all, you'd know it's a compliment. I was afraid that Minus would have you looking at your business all ass-backwards."

The elevator arrived. Dwight held the door open.

"Aren't you coming?" Teague asked.

"No, but you'll need this," Dwight replied. He selected a stop, swiped a badge, and let the doors close.

The doors opened on a vestibule lined with triptychs of Italian hillsides hung in pools of accent light. The parquet floor had been sanded to a high finish under a zillion-grit texture of grip coating. Teague had expected some ship's dining room, or a buffet in a conference room, but he rounded the corner into a living room with a wide, starry window, and realized that this must be Matthew's private apartment.

Matthew had invited Crystal, Eskimo, Gemma, Neanna, and Isaac, and they had already gathered in the dining room. Teague drifted in and found a single seat remaining between Rob and Mbuto. He wanted desperately to go back and talk with Dwight. A few more minutes with him might be worth a hundred dinners like this.

After dessert and coffee, Matthew encouraged everyone to head to the living room. Teague dawdled, letting the others go first, and was surprised when Matthew put a hand on his shoulder and asked, "You have a minute?"

Teague followed Matthew to another wing of the apartment, where a curving hallway ended in a teardrop cul-de-sac with two doors. Matthew opened one and let Teague go in ahead of him.

The lights came on in a well-used, windowless private office. The room was mostly free of vanity except for a set of strange objects in an inset glass display that ran the length of the inner wall. Inside, three two-meter-tall rectangular slabs of bumpy, white foam rubber had been mounted and lit as if by a curator. Their long edges were ragged, but matched, as if someone had crudely cut a single tubular mold. Next to them rested curved slabs of clay that if notched together would form a two-meter tall column. The clay slabs were covered with tiny wedge-shaped characters interrupted by drawings that looked like simple Egyptian hieroglyphs.

"Unfortunately, those are re-creations," Matthew said, indicating the clay pieces. "The foam rubber is the real artifact."

"What is it?" Teague asked.

"The only surviving record of an early Mesopotamian king named Ashtukeggia."

"Why do you have it?"

"According to the tale, Ashtukeggia believed that he was destined to join the gods in the heavens. But the realm of the gods he describes is not a paradise or heaven, but like space. He sought out the wisest magicians and squandered the royal treasury attempting to build a flying vessel. He was eventually murdered by a servant. You can see the bloody-handed man there taking a purse of money from merchants."

"A cautionary tale for space entrepreneurs?" Teague smiled.

"Exactly," Matthew said.

"Incredible. How old is this?" Teague asked, focusing on Matthew's ghostly face reflected in the glass.

"The story predates the Sumerians."

"Why did he believe he was destined to go into space?"

Matthew took out his mobile and replied even as he tapped the screen. "He claimed that as a boy, a goddess had been his tutor, had taught him their language, and had even taken him to space in her vessel."

Teague's mobile buzzed in his jacket pocket.

"Go ahead," Matthew said. "It's why I wanted to talk to you." A new eddress awaited approval for Teague's contact list. "There're only six people in the system that have my private eddress. Seven, now."

"I'm honored, but why?" Teague asked.

"I encouraged Thomas to reopen the fellowship, for Aron's sake. And when Thomas showed me your application, I couldn't believe we'd gotten so lucky. I've followed your progress, and now that I've met you—well, I can't thank you enough. You've been exactly the kind of friend Aron needed. Anyway, I know a bit about your situation, and I want you to know that you always have someone to call."

"Thank you," Teague said. "I'll keep this private."

"I'm serious now. Don't hesitate. Don't think you're not important enough." Matthew stuck out a hand. Teague agreed and shook it.

"Where have you two been?" Aron asked when Teague and Matthew returned to the living room.

"Matthew showed me the artifacts in his office," Teague replied. His mobile felt different now, as if the newly stored eddress held weight and heat.

"Not the Ass-keg story," Aron said.

"The what?" Eskimo asked.

"Some ancient myth about a crazy king."

"It's really interesting," Teague said.

"Thank you, Teague," Matthew said.

"Not the thirty thousandth time you hear it," Aron said.

The older generation soon called it a night, and the students converged on the Mirage's starlit lounge. The bar and tables glowed icy blue. A jazz combo played under red light on a low stage. The bartender seemed to have traded his hair to the devil for his acumen. The three couples found a table, but Teague and Rob stayed at the bar.

"I could get used to this," Rob said, sucking an olive off a crystal toothpick.

"After we get our money, we're going to be working twenty-eight hour days and eating crap out of vending machines," Teague said.

"Better enjoy this while we can, then," Rob said. Teague bit into his own olive, savoring the blend of vinegar and alcohol.

"Are you going to miss ADU?" Teague asked.

"Of course. Although sometimes I forget why I came."

"Your daughter?"

"Sometimes I think I should have stayed on Mars, fought the legal battles, whatever it took."

"I'm sure you did what you thought was right," Teague said. The martini began to creep in like a ninja, opening a smooth, clean, but indelible slice across his sobriety.

Rob drained the last of his martini and signaled the bartender for another. A few moments later he asked, "Why doesn't it ever feel like that?"

Laughter and free-fall acrobatics in the shuttle. A grim Saul at the dock. Eight in an elevator. "Who's coming up?" Aron asked.

Heeding a whisper of good judgment, Teague got off on his own floor. At his door, he worried that he'd forgotten his bag on the Mirage, but found it at the end of his arm.

Jacket off. Shoes adrift. Lights off. The slow fall onto the bed. Probably should have undressed. *Teague?*

Teague?

"Teague." It was Monkey, speaking from a place out of space and time. "Teague?" He felt a poke on his shoulder.

"Wh—?" Teague managed.

"Someone's at the door," Monkey said. This time Teague

heard the knock. He rolled over; his brain followed reluctantly. Another knock.

"Go see who—"

"It's Dwight Yarrow's assistant," Monkey said. "They boarded the station a few minutes ago."

CHAPTER 22

Is this what it means to become an adult?

MAY–JUNE 2092

"Who? What time is it?" Teague mumbled.

"Seven nineteen," Monkey replied. This was not a time it should be. After another, more insistent knock, Teague lurched across the room rubbing crust from his eyes and opened the door.

At first, Teague thought Monkey had made a mistake—that it was actually Dwight in the hall. But as his eyes adjusted to the light, he saw that it was in fact a different man, grim but much less imposing. And Teague had never seen Dwight wear a tie.

The assistant's gaze settled disdainfully on Monkey.

"Hello, sir," Monkey said.

"Mr. Yarrow needs to speak with you. Immediately."

"I'll need a moment," Teague said. The man nodded curtly and put his mobile to his ear. Teague closed the door and tried to make himself believe that a toilet, a splash of water, and a toothbrush would be enough to cure him of all his ills. At least it wouldn't be Dwight's first impression of him.

A few minutes later, the assistant brought Teague to the Casino's conference center and admitted him to the executive boardroom. Inside, Dwight was perched in a regal pose on a corner chair of the conference table. He gestured to the chair at the head of the table and said, "You and I are not having this conversation; do you understand?"

"Yes, sir," Teague replied as he sat.

"Good. Now listen to me," Dwight said. "Everyone has been lying to you—Matthew, Thomas, Angela Mbuto, me. On Monday, Matthew will announce that Valdosky is acquiring M-SOO in an agreement with Agnus Dei University."

"What?"

"The deal is all but done, so I suggest you begin considering your options."

"Why are they—?"

"Don't be naive. If the company is everything you claimed all week to investors, why shouldn't Valdosky have it?"

I should have seen this coming, Teague thought, *raised my glove in time.* As in the split second before the pain of a punch to the face, Teague knew where he had gone wrong. He had ignored all the warnings—from Gwen, from Aron, from the anonymous vandal with the blowtorch. Even Rob had protested in his meager way.

"Aron will be offered a ceremonial vice presidency. Your programmer, Heneghan, will be brought along if he agrees. I know you had visions of running this little company, but that's not going to happen. Blame me for that. I can't have a division run by children. And before you get indignant, remember who's telling you the truth right now.

"Minus is convinced you'll accept a job at some think tank, his usual dumping ground for his Wolkenbruch fellows—someplace you can do good works but still earn enough to make all the UN wonks jealous. He expects you'll be satisfied with *saving the solar system* one economic forecast at a time."

"You think that's what I want?" Teague asked.

"I wouldn't be here if I did," Dwight replied. "First thing Monday, as notice is sent to all your would-be investors, you will be summoned separately. Matthew and Mbuto will play it up as a win-win."

"So what—?"

Dwight held up a finger. "I want you to refuse Minus's attempt to sweep you under the rug. I want you to call Matthew and demand a job. He won't refuse you. I'll take it from there."

"Why not just offer me a position?" Teague asked.

"I'm giving you a chance to earn it. I've been watching you this week, and I don't for a minute believe that you've drunk Thomas's Kool-Aid. I'm offering you a one-time chance for a place at the table. If you accept, I'll put you in a position to learn how things really work. If you walk away, it won't come again. Minus sees you as a spent asset. I don't. But don't get it in your head that this is flattery or bribery. If you're not the man I think you are…"

"What's the job?" Teague asked.

"I promise that you won't be wasted. And you won't have to spend your career in Aron's shadow."

"Whose shadow would I be in?" Teague asked.

Dwight chuckled humorlessly. "This is why. I don't know what rock Thomas found you under, but you've got eyes and a brain. I also think you've seen through the Valdosky myth. Too many people don't stop to check their assumptions."

"You're content to work in Matthew's shadow," Teague said. Dwight's eyes narrowed, and Teague decided to show a few more of his cards. "You created him and keep him propped up. Why is that different from what I want to do with Aron?"

"Because Aron was never your asset to begin with," Dwight said. He paused to let Teague absorb this. "If you raise the alarm this weekend, my offer is off the table, and you can go to hell with Minus. The acquisition will happen no matter what kind of stink you make." He rose to leave.

"Why would Matthew do this to Aron?" Teague asked as Dwight opened the door.

"That's not your concern," Dwight said.

"Do you have any children?" Teague asked.

"I do not," Dwight replied. Teague decided that if Dwight had lied about anything, it was that.

* * *

When Teague knocked on Thomas's door late on Sunday evening, it was too small an act. After a weekend of searching for loopholes and putting on a face in front of the others, Teague wanted an explosion, a release, not this helpless rap of skin and cartilage on plastic.

Thomas was wearing a bathrobe over pajamas, and Teague smelled toothpaste. "Teague? It's very late. Whatever it is, I'm sure it can wait for morning," Thomas said, and began to shut the door.

"I know that Matthew is announcing Valdosky's purchase of M-SOO tomorrow." After a pause, Thomas opened the door. Teague and Monkey squeezed through the vestibule. Teague caught himself on a chair back and spun around as Thomas closed the door. "That's why you were meeting on Friday afternoon, wasn't it?" Thomas remained stone-faced. "Why didn't you tell me?"

"It wouldn't have changed anything," Thomas said.

"So it's true? We're being screwed over?"

"I wouldn't put it like that."

"We had at least half a dozen ready investors. I'm sure of it. There's some logic in letting us get our feet wet with other people's money before buying us out."

"I raised my objections, but the decision lay with Matthew and President Mbuto," Thomas said.

"No one even gave us a chance to plead our case."

"Teague."

"I could've called our investors and raised the cash for a counteroffer."

"Teague, be serious. The moment those companies hear of Valdosky's interest, they will vanish. None have any interest in a bidding war."

"I suppose you know that they're offering jobs to Aron and Rob but not me," Teague said.

"Dwight Yarrow wanted to exclude Aron, too, but he could hardly refuse Matthew."

"That's what all this has been about since the beginning, isn't it? Getting Aron in the family business. Exactly what he doesn't want."

"This has come as a shock to me, too," Thomas said.

"I don't believe that."

"I've heard from several firms interested in hiring the next Wolkenbruch fellow, but I've put them off. I supported what you were doing."

"But when the moment came, you gave me up pretty quick," Teague said.

The change in Thomas's visage was small but terrifying. "I will not be spoken to like this. I have encouraged you, defended you. This situation is not of my making. This is a singular setback. I can't even begin to define it as failure. You will be leaving here with an education and connections unrivaled by any other student in the system. Take this and learn from it."

Teague clenched his teeth to keep from speaking, hating that Thomas was right, even though he hadn't addressed the point. Teague had considered his mistakes all weekend. He should have heeded the warnings. He should have secured their financing without waiting to use Valdosky resources. But mostly he should not have placed so much faith in others. Mbuto had sold them out. Thomas had stayed silent. Matthew's saccharine support had been a lie. "I suppose I've learned that I can't trust anyone," Teague said.

"I'm sorry if that's all you take away from this. I truly am. But perhaps we should discuss this in the morning, when you've had a chance to calm down."

"We've talked enough," Teague said. "Come on, Monkey."

Thomas moved aside and let Teague open the door. "Teague?" he called.

"What?"

"Don't do anything that you'll regret for the rest of your life. Now is not the time for thoughtless reactions."

"So I just have to roll over?"

"You created a company with such promise that it's been purchased before you even had a chance to run it. How many other undergraduates can claim as much?"

"I'm glad that you can justify this so easily," Teague said.

"A word of advice, young man: Never forget where you come from." And Thomas closed his door.

"That sounded like good advice," Monkey said.

"Shut up," Teague said.

* * *

Rob listened powerlessly. He bent his head over the documents that had been turned to face him on the table screen in Mbuto's office and wondered how his stupid little creation had ever come to warrant this attention. Matthew Valdosky was personally offering him cash for the purchase of M-SOO, a job to develop it further, and written assurance that Molly would be brought along. Overwhelming and so very wrong, but damn, those were a lot of zeros. Was this the price of assuaged guilt?

Rob found Mbuto's pride and Matthew's apologetic tone insulting, but he knew that he would accept whatever they offered. Gwen's standard was impossible. How could he face his father, or Kyle, having given up this opportunity? Or abandon Molly on such weak principle? But more importantly, what would his daughter think someday?

He would sign, no matter what Teague and Aron did or said. Leaving with Gwen would have been a bloodless betrayal compared with this. Valdosky was going to pay him how much? Good god.

"Do you have an attorney?" Matthew asked.

Rob nodded and bit his lip to keep from uttering the words "Uncle" or "Angus."

"Take the contracts. But the sooner we have your answer, the sooner we can begin," Matthew said.

Rob returned to his office in Kindergarten, hoping to find some sense of clarity in familiar surroundings, but now these rooms just seemed like a place he had once lived as a child. There's the desk where I wrote the code. There's the shift couch where I first visited Molly at Nexon. There's the table where I played start-up with my friends.

"Fuck!" he shouted at the top of his lungs.

"What's wrong, Daddy?" Molly asked.

"You're being sold." Rob hated the barbarity of those words.

"To whom?" she asked.

"Valdosky. But everything's going to be okay. I'm coming with you."

"You don't sound happy."

"No," Rob said.

"I'm sorry," Molly said.

"Thanks," Rob replied. He rolled onto his shift couch and donned his shift set. "I'm sorry, but I need to go see my uncle. We'll talk more when I get back."

"Daddy?"

"Yes, Molly?"

"If we have to go, I'm glad we're going together."

* * *

Thomas had been right; this was no time for juvenile outbursts. Teague folded his hands on the table, choosing shocked acquiescence as Matthew, Mbuto, and Thomas delivered the news.

The only item that Dwight had failed to mention was an offer to purchase the M-SOO business plan for a substantial amount of cash. Perhaps Thomas had contacted Matthew after last night's conversation and they'd decided to add this spoonful of sugar—a pittance to Valdosky, but a fortune to Teague, worth years upon years of the one thousand American dollars that the church had paid his foster families each month.

"We understand this is a disappointment," President Mbuto said. "But you've made ADU very proud. Professor Minus tells me that he may have some challenging opportunities for you."

"Teague and I can discuss those later," Thomas said. "I don't want to take up your and Matthew's valuable time."

"I'd like to hear about these opportunities now," Teague said.

"Later," Thomas said, his eyes narrowing.

"Are you making me a guarantee that I will have a worthwhile job after graduation? Please remember that I have a limiting disability."

Thomas didn't flinch. "The Wolkenbruch Fellowship is one of the most highly regarded programs in the system. Former graduates have found an extremely competitive environment for their services. There's no reason you should be an exception."

"I can't agree to sell the business plan without speaking with Aron first," Teague said.

"Of course," Matthew said. "Please know that this was not an easy decision, but one made with the long-term advancement of our company in mind. Personally, you have earned my highest respect."

"I would like to second that," President Mbuto said.

Teague only hoped that this meeting had been their most difficult.

Immediately after leaving Mbuto's office, Teague burst into his room. "Monkey?" he called.

"Yeppers?" Monkey replied, bounding out of his charging nest.

"I need to talk to you and Molly, together, right now." Teague pulled himself to a seat on the shifting couch.

"We're here," Monkey said, landing at Teague's feet.

"Molly, too?"

"Hello," Molly said, her child's voice coming from Monkey's mouth.

"Molly, you're being sold. M-SOO is going to be a division of Valdosky."

"My daddy told me," Molly said.

"He's taking their job offer, isn't he?" Teague asked. Molly nodded Monkey's head.

"Will Molly's transfer to Valdosky's network interrupt your collaboration?"

"No," Molly and Monkey said in unison.

"You'll be separated."

"We're not going with Molly?" Monkey asked.

"We are not."

"We can maintain a stable collaboration, although connectivity may be intermittent over long distances," Monkey said.

"Fine. Maintain your collaboration, but always keep it hidden from any other system administrators, users, owners—anyone but me."

"Will do," Monkey said.

"You'll be our best friend always," Molly added.

"You're sure you can do this? Valdosky probably has much stronger system security than ADU."

"No problem," Monkey said. "I've been in Valdosky's corporate networks since they let Molly past the firewalls. They're not as tough as you'd think."

"Really?" Teague asked. "You're awesome."

"I am awesome, aren't I?" Monkey began to bounce from the floor to the ceiling to the bed, waving his arms and legs maniacally. Monkey and Molly sang, "We're awesome. We're awesome," until Teague laughed. Then Monkey landed on Teague's lap for a hug and a head rub, which seemed to stimulate every enjoyment algorithm he possessed.

* * *

Rob awoke from shift to find Aron and Teague looming over him.

"It's about time," Teague said.

"Get up," Aron demanded.

"Molly, lights?" Rob asked with a thirsty, rasping voice. "Sorry. I went to see my uncle."

"Did it do any good?" Aron asked.

They drifted into the workroom and took up places around the table, but no one sat. The table's screen was uncommonly dark, except for the new M-SOO logo bouncing from edge to edge.

"What did they offer you?" Aron asked.

"A purchase agreement and a job," Rob said.

"Bastards," Aron muttered. "They didn't give Teague a job."

"What'd you get?" Rob asked.

"I'm your new boss. Except they're bringing in one of Dwight's assholes to 'mentor me' on how to run things."

"What about you, Teague?" Rob asked.

"Cash, nominally for the business plan, but I think they just felt guilty about giving me the shaft."

"Did we know this was going to happen?" Rob asked.

"I think we should have," Aron said.

"We knew," Teague said.

"What?" Rob asked.

"You knew about this?" Aron asked.

"That's not what I meant," Teague said.

"You guessed but didn't speak up?" Rob asked.

"I'm the one getting screwed here. Don't you think I'd have said something?" Teague said. "I'm just saying we all should've known."

"Sorry," Rob said. Then after a silence he said, "I'm taking their offer. Sorry to be so blunt."

"I'm going to give 'em the finger and go snowboarding," Aron said. "God, if I even remember how."

"I'm going to take the cash," Teague said. "As long as you don't mind turning over the business plan."

"Fuck it," Aron said. "Let them gag on it. Take their money. Demand double and stock options."

"I don't want to press my luck," Teague said.

"What will you do?" Rob asked.

"Thomas has got some options lined up for me. Probably at some think tanks or NGOs."

"I told you we should've done the ski resort," Aron said. "It's not too late. You could come with me."

"Can I be honest, Aron?" Teague asked.

"I need some honesty after that load of crap this morning."

"Pull your shit together and take their job."

"What are you talking about?" Aron asked.

"I can't explain it," Teague said. "But don't give up on this. For one, you can't abandon Rob to them." Teague looked at Rob for support, but Rob could only shrug.

"My shit's together. Whatever you think," Aron said.

"But if you're both there, the company has a better chance—"

"What company? There's no company. This was a school project. We got good marks. End of story. It might've been fun, but there's nothing left but to say but sayonara and let them spin on it. No offense, Rob."

"None taken," Rob said. Gwen would be appalled, but he still couldn't believe in M-SOO as a cause.

Aron turned back to Teague. "Anyway, you don't care about the company any more than I do. I thought you were going to be honest."

"We cared about the company for exactly the same reasons," Teague said.

"And now that's gone," Aron said. "What's your Plan B? Because, for me, taking their job is about Plan G or H."

"If you don't take the job, then Matthew and Thomas were right about you," Teague said.

"You think I care what Matthew thinks?"

"Say what you want, but I know you do," Teague said. "You want to go back to your little fan clubs and charity golf tournaments, go ahead. This isn't ideal, but it's the first step to doing something with your life. I wish I had your choices. I can't even believe I'm having this conversation with you. What the fuck do I care?"

Rob didn't dare to breathe until Aron laughed.

"Now that's honesty."

"Don't patronize me," Teague said. "Did you hear a word I said?"

"I heard. Look, I think we're all blowing off a little steam. Before we say something we regret—honestly, guys, I haven't decided. I'm meeting with Matthew later to discuss it." Aron paused. "Hell of a Monday. I feel extra crispy already." The M-SOO logo continued its unending ricochet around the table screen, a tiny elephant in the room. Rob and Teague agreed. Then Aron stuck out his hand to each of them. "It's been fun, guys."

* * *

"Drinks are on Teague," Eskimo called out when Teague arrived at Aron's suite that evening after his meeting with Thomas. "We heard they offered you a boatload." Crystal and the others offered their own tempered sympathies and congratulations.

"How'd your meeting go?" Aron asked.

Teague called up Thomas's vetted list of half a dozen position announcements and handed his mobile to Aron.

"Better get a resume together," Aron said.

"I half-expected him to push a specific job on me," Teague said.

"He didn't want to insult you."

"It's just as bad. I'm sure Thomas is working this from the other side. I could scrawl my CV on a scrap of toilet tissue and get hired."

"At least you get a choice," Aron said.

* * *

The following day, during their final class, Thomas reviewed a recent Nobel prize-winning paper as if it were any other day. Teague listened for a deeper lesson, but at the conclusion, Thomas checked the time, collected his things, and shook hands with each of them, even Monkey.

"Gentlemen," he said. "It has been an honor. Would you mind putting the furniture right before you leave?"

Teague and Aron slid Thomas's head table against the wall. They brought the fourth couch, set aside since their first day, to the open side of the square, transforming the classroom back into a purposeless lounge. Teague took a final look through the skylight, centered the coffee table with a nudge, and then said to Aron, "You go on ahead. I've got something I need to do."

Teague had imagined that this would be difficult, that he would have to steel himself with practiced lines and assembled courage, but suddenly, it was the easiest thing.

"Monkey, call Matthew."

An hour later, Maria showed Teague into Matthew's broad formal office. Matthew rose from his little desk and called, "Teague, please, come in." As they shook hands, the side door opened and Dwight entered.

"M-SOO will fall under Dwight's purview, so he asked to join us," Matthew said.

"Sir," Teague said and offered Dwight his hand.

Dwight shook it perfunctorily and said, "What's this about?"

"Please, sit," Matthew said. Teague and Dwight took the guest chairs. "Yes. What can we do for you this afternoon?"

Teague positioned himself to face the two moguls, supposing he should be nervous. "First of all, I accept your offer for the M-SOO business plan. I've discussed it with Aron, and he's agreed."

"I'm glad, Teague," Matthew said. "It'll be a great resource for implementation."

Oh, please patronize me, Teague thought. "Secondly—and please understand that this is a separate matter, not contingent on the business plan agreement—I've come to ask for a job."

"A job?" Matthew asked, exchanging glances with Dwight.

"I've discussed career opportunities with Thomas, but I'll never have a chance like this again."

"You just thought you'd ring up, interrupt me *and* Dwight, to ask us for a job?" Matthew asked, smiling, falsely indignant.

"I'm not asking for a position with M-SOO specifically. But I'm certain I can be useful. I'm the current Wolkenbruch fellow, with a dual master's in business and economics."

"What kind of position do you see yourself in?" Matthew asked.

"Business and economic analysis, market development. I can work independently or in a team, and I'm willing to travel anywhere. I realize that my inability to shift may limit my options—"

"This is bullshit," Dwight said. "We don't owe you anything. Excuse me, but this is a waste of my time."

"Dwight, hear him out," Matthew said.

"If we wanted him, we'd have put a job on the table, no?" Dwight rose. "Take a hint, kid." Teague rose instinctively, and something clicked. Dwight was drawing him out.

"Who do you think wrote the business plan you're buying?" Teague rose to face Dwight. "Who do you think got M-SOO ready to capitalize? I may have miscalculated and handed it to you on a platter, but I learn from my mistakes, and I don't give up. If you leave Agnus Dei without me, you'll be making a big mistake, because I'm just getting started." Blood rushed in Teague's ears. He could almost hear Ned's voice urging him on.

"Do you have any idea who you're talking to?" Dwight asked. Matthew rose from his chair, open-mouthed.

"I do, sir," Teague said.

"But you have no compunction about accusing us of short-sightedness?"

"You accused me of giving you bullshit," Teague said. "You want no bullshit. There it is."

Dwight froze, unblinking. Teague wondered if he had gone too far, but with a lift of one cheek, he had his answer. "Where the hell did Thomas ever find you?" Dwight turned to Matthew. "He wants a job? Fine. We've got room at CDI." With that, Dwight left.

"Ballsy," Matthew remarked. "Not many people face him like that."

"He's only a person."

Matthew gave Teague a wide-eyed look and opened his mouth slightly as if he meant to say something and then thought better of it. Instead, he said, "I owe you an apology for not thinking of this. Thomas assured us he had you covered, and I honestly didn't give it another thought."

"I preferred to ask."

"You like to earn your place. I can appreciate that," Matthew said. "Well, if Dwight wants you, I'm not going to say no."

"What's CDI?" Teague asked as they sat.

"The Colonial Development Initiative. It's a critical company-wide effort. Major fleet build-up, including the new ballistic cargo delivery system—one reason we're interested in M-SOO. It's timed to take advantage of the dozens of thirty-year asteroid mining leases set to start expiring in a couple of years. We're gearing up to get colonies in place as soon as Xterrex and the others are done with them."

"Where would I come in?" Teague asked.

"I'm guessing Dwight wants you for community development and marketing."

"I'd be a salesman?" Teague said.

"More likely an analyst," Matthew replied. "We're ramping up our recruitment efforts in order to match the inventory. There's a major advertising campaign, of course—an effort to mainstream the idea of colony life for the general public. But we also need to identify potential customers and develop customized pitches. Your experience out here will certainly be an asset."

"I doubt that most colonies are as comfortable as ADU," Teague said.

"Few places are," Matthew replied. "Are you interested?"

"Absolutely."

"Okay, then. What are you going to tell Thomas?"

"The truth. I'd rather work for you."

Matthew nodded sympathetically. "Ask Maria to set you up a meeting with HR. Welcome aboard."

The shuttle was waiting, but Teague went to the Mirage's ice-blue bar alone. The bald bartender recognized him and offered him a martini.

"Water, please," Teague said.

The bartender returned with a frosty pack of Dawn Water. "Should I start a tab?" he asked with a grin and then left Teague alone.

Teague wanted to turn around and revel in his success under the dome of stars, but he kept his eyes on the bar—the cosmos would exist with or without his efforts. He felt like laughing, but allowed himself only a private smile as he took a drink of the coldest water he had ever tasted.

* * *

Rob checked the time again.

"I can't believe you're this anxious to meet her," Kyle said. "Didn't you say she's furious with you?"

Rob stared out into the perpetually setting sun over the faux-Aegean. "I just need to talk to her."

"When are you leaving?" Kyle asked.

"A couple of hours," Rob replied. "I moved my stuff over this afternoon."

"I still can't believe it. My little brother is cruising on the Mirage with the Valdoskies. You've made Dad about the proudest man on Mars."

"You know I only did it to one-up you, right?"

"I'm still Mom's favorite," Kyle said. "You could be, though. When Gwen arrives, take her down to that little overlook. You get down on one knee. There's barely a woman in the system who would say no—"

"Oh my god, stop talking," Rob said. "You should probably get out of here. She's expecting this to be private."

"Is she already married or something?" Kyle asked.

"No. Worse. I work for Valdosky."

Kyle shimmered away, and Rob turned around to face the villa. Birds twittered, and a breeze whispered in the leaves. Gauzy netting breathed around the breakfast canopy. He checked the time again, and then she appeared, facing away from him.

"Gwen," he called.

She rotated in place and for a moment didn't seem to recognize him. "Rob," she said eventually, but her attention fell everywhere but on him. Her eyes darted. She sniffed the air and took awkward, sliding steps toward him along the path.

"Do you want to sit?" Rob asked, gesturing to the chairs under the canopy.

She bent, sank too far, and then buoyed herself on the chair construct as if doing the equations in her head.

"How's the Ariel?" Rob asked, taking his own seat.

"A few glitches, but she's running great."

"You're safe?"

"As houses."

"I'm surprised you haven't yelled at me yet."

"What would be the point?"

"Because you warned me. You were absolutely right about everything," Rob said.

"I only knew what would happen if you took my advice."

"I hate to say it, but this turned out well for me—for all of us, really. If I'd left with you, Teague would've been out in the cold. He was able to bargain for a great job."

"With Valdosky, too?" Gwen asked. Rob nodded, and she swore. "I knew it."

"I know you had some vision for M-SOO," Rob said, "but I feel like I've just traded one employer for another."

"I'm sorry you see it that way," Gwen said.

"I have to. I'm sorry I couldn't lead your technological revolution or whatever, but I can't go into this with regrets."

"Calm down. I didn't come here to fight with you."

"Sorry. You're not going to demand that I quit?"

"What good would that do?"

"I never intended any of this, you know." After a pause, Rob added, "Mbuto gave me a diploma of sorts. I think she felt she should give me something as Teague and Aron graduated. Was I even a student?"

"You were a student," Gwen said.

"You were the only one who ever taught me anything."

"Then I'm a terrible tutor. I should've opened the airlocks when you showed up with your chocolates and plunger." In the silence that followed, Rob decided that this was a joke.

"When am I ever going to see you again, Gwen?"

"Probably never."

"We should promise to meet at least once a year, just to talk," Rob said.

"I shouldn't even be talking to you now."

"Does it really matter who I work for that much?"

"No. I just can't make promises like that."

"I didn't think either of us would ever leave ADU," Rob said. "Will you ever go back?"

"Maybe."

"I never will."

"I can't see why you would," Gwen said. "Is the stupid sun actually setting or what? It's been in the same position since I got here."

"My brother has it set so that it's always the 'magic hour,' whatever that means."

"That's fucking annoying."

"I miss you, Gwen."

PART THREE: WORK

FEBRUARY 2108

As the airlock cycled for what seemed the thousandth time, Kyi took Nanda's hand, hoping to borrow some of her spirit and strength. The door slid aside, and two workers in massive ConEx suits spilled out. Kyi and Nanda grabbed one, pulled him toward the lockers, and began to help him out of the suit. Another team assisted the second worker, while the two other suit teams loaded their readied, refreshed workers into the airlock. Before yesterday, Kyi, like Nanda—one of Herbert's boxers and an accountant for a legal firm—had never touched a ConEx suit, but now they both handled the fittings and systems like experts. Kyi recognized the worker when Nanda removed his helmet. They had sent him out several hours before. He looked sweaty, dehydrated, and spent.

"Do you have another suit ready?" he asked.

"You need to rest and eat," Kyi said.

"I was welding the third feed valve," he insisted.

"Did someone take your place?"

"Yes, but—"

"I'm sure you did everything you could," Kyi said.

"I need to go back out, now."

Kyi called to one of the UN medics who had been assigned to the airlocker since the construction effort began. "Please examine this man," she said.

Kyi had been so focused on the minutia of her task that she'd almost forgotten the reason. Fifty-some hours had been long enough to forget the coming collision. Long enough to allow hope of a reprieve, like a narrow miss or a deus ex machina. Was that what they were building here? As the medic began to interview the man, Nanda called for the next worker in the queue and tugged Kyi to the next recharged suit in the line. The ceaseless spirit of Herbert's boxing club might just save them yet.

Word of the effort to build the jet nozzle had gotten out quickly, and the corridor now teemed with people bringing food and water, muscle and expertise. There were now more than fifty men and women out on the surface performing some feat of engineering that Kyi could only imagine. She had refused every offer to take her place on a suit team in the airlock. She hadn't the skill or the training to assist on the surface, so she resolved to give every ounce of strength where she was able. Many had thanked her and expressed their admiration. She knew she didn't deserve to be singled out for their praise; she had done nothing—nothing but be born the daughter of her father. However, she accepted that people might find hope in his presence through her, so she remained humble, returned their thanks, and praised their efforts in return.

A few minutes later, Kyi and Nanda waited with their next sealed and pressurized worker near the airlock as two suit teams extracted another incoming pair of workers. Once the door was clear, they began to guide their man inside, but the airlock operator swore and stopped them.

"Pull them out! Incoming emergency!" he shouted. "Clear the room! All nonessential personnel out!" Soon the airlocker fell quiet, all eyes on the flashing red alarm light over the airlock door. Kyi, Nanda, and their suited worker stayed tight against a wall. The medics gathered at the door with an anxious suit team, ready with oxygen, heat blankets, and diagnostics. Kyi shuddered to imagine what could have happened to someone in one of these substantial ConEx suits.

After several terrible minutes, there was a thump inside the airlock, followed by an ugly scraping and several urgent bangs. "Pressurizing," called the operator. The medics launched into action before the inner door was fully open. Kyi caught the tortured visage of the uninjured worker who had hauled her partner to the airlock. Then through a gap in the efforts, Kyi saw the shattered face mask, distorted and bloody. The medics didn't work long. There was nothing to be done.

Kyi thought her volunteer might hesitate after witnessing the danger of haste in an unforgiving environment, but if he was frightened, he hid it well. She guided him around the body and clipped his lanyard to the airlock wall.

The medics helped the suit team remove the dead man's gear. Someone had wrapped his head with a towel. Herbert led three men in, and they collected the body silently. The airlocker and the corridor fell quiet as they left.

Where would they lay him to rest? Indeed, where could they?

CHAPTER 23

This land is gray. The rock above our heads is black, and closer now. The sun is white and small. I long for something blue and green, or even brown.

SEPTEMBER 2093

Teague steadied himself against a travertine wall and let a dozen showerheads massage him with hot water—not the tepid hot of a miserly closed-loop resource system, but truly, wastefully, and wonderfully hot. He breathed deeply of the roiling steam. Rivulets trickled over every nerve ending from his scalp to his heels and into the hungry, gurgling drain. Teague's legs and back ached, but he hadn't spent all those hours in the cruiser's gym to sit down during his first official shower back at the bottom of a gravity well. He hadn't had a truly decent shower in nearly four and a half years and had resolved to make up for the loss during his weeklong vacation.

Monkey had found him the best hotel shower in Bangkok, cost be damned.

"Teague, Teague, Teague," Monkey called through the fog.

"Go away," Teague replied.

"You just received a message I thought you'd want to know about." Monkey squished his face to the outside of the glass door, gasped, and then covered his eyes.

"I told you not to disturb me."

"It's from Dwight Yarrow," Monkey said.

Teague shut off the water.

A few moments later, still dripping, Teague tied one of Bangkok's best hotel bathrobes around his waist and took his screen from Monkey.

"Werres." Dwight had leaned close into the camera, barely staying in focus. "I've been informed that you're back on Earth and that you're taking a few days to visit home before heading to Seattle. Good. As soon as you receive this message, you will contact the attached eddress and arrange to meet with an associate of mine. It's time for you to earn your place at the table."

"That's it?" Teague asked.

"That plus the eddress," Monkey replied and offered Teague his mobile.

"It's time for me to earn my place?" Teague muttered. Since leaving ADU, Teague had learned his new job backward and forward. On the Mirage, while Rob and Aron were busy with M-SOO, he'd single-handedly slogged through two-thirds of the backlog in the CDI analysts' queue. During the few weeks' wait on Gateway 2 and the year alone on the cruiser back to Earth, he'd had nothing to do but work. The marketing teams had requested him so often that he'd been appointed as the analyst liaison to the Special Projects Work Group—and they'd never even met him face to face or talked to him in real time. "What does Dwight think I've been doing?"

"Should I place the call?" Monkey asked.

"Let me put on some pants first."

Teague dried, dressed, and then lowered himself into the desk chair before signaling Monkey to make the call, voice only. As it began to ring, he swiveled around to admire the view, but the sixty-fifth floor of the hotel had been enshrouded in clouds since he'd checked in last night. He'd hoped for a dramatic vista over the river and the skyline, but what did he expect during the rainy season?

A woman answered. A clear voice, tinged with French or some

Romantic edge. "Sustainable Justice Development Council. This is Aurore Rheaume."

Teague had imagined that Dwight's associate would be someone more like his bosses at CDI, middle-aged, most likely American, and certainly another Valdosky executive—perhaps a woman, but not one who sounded so young. And what the hell was this Sustainable Justice Whatever Council? Teague gestured to Monkey to begin a search.

"Already on it," Monkey whispered and leapt onto the desk like Shakiro Squirrel taking flight. He'd been giddy since they'd returned to real-time Internet.

"Hello, my name is Teague Werres. Dwight Yarrow of the Valdosky Companies asked me to contact this number."

"Yes, of course," the woman replied. "I'm very glad to hear from you. How was your trip?"

The taxi's windshield wipers flapped furiously. The drumming downpour drowned out all but the chirpiest frequencies from the driver's radio. Monkey scampered from window to window, pressing his nose to the glass and squeaking with delight. His movements were noticeably less spry than they had been in orbit—had his servos always been this noisy?—and in the humidity he looked matted and worn, but he'd be better after Bondi got to work. Teague couldn't make out much more than the freeway's concrete barricades beyond the sluicing blatter, so he let Monkey play and scrolled again through Monkey's dossier on Dwight's associate.

Aurore Rheaume had become the founding director of the Sustainable Justice Development Council around the time Teague had left Earth. A cursory reading of its website painted the impression of an organization with plenty of lofty humanistic goals—fighting for human rights and individual freedoms, creating economically and environmentally sustainable communities, supporting lifelong education for all, and disrupting cycles of systemic oppression—but few concrete solutions. Teague was half-surprised not to find Thomas on the board.

Aurore was the daughter of a Canadian mining company

executive and an interior decorator, now divorced. She'd been born in Quebec but had attended school in Upstate New York at a place called the Naiad Academy, an institution that apparently prided itself on skimming the top layer off the cream of the crop.

"Guess who else attended the Naiad Academy?" Monkey asked.

"Who?"

"Gwen Ungefucht," Monkey replied, popping the evidence onto Teague's screen.

"Gwen lived on Earth?"

"She attended in E-shift. Aurore went to the physical campus. But their dates don't overlap. I doubt they ever knew each other."

Flipping through Monkey's curated set of yearbook photos, Teague watched Aurore grow from a soft-cheeked girl with an overbite into the captain of the fencing squad with every academic honor the institution seemed capable of bestowing. After the Naiad Academy, she'd attended Yale and had earned master's degrees in history and political science. As far as Monkey had been able to ascertain, her life since Yale had been the SJDC, which mostly seemed to involve organizing fundraising events and being photographed with UN bureaucrats.

By her pictures, Aurore was serious but personable and exuded an almost tangible intelligence. Her black hair was done in a variety of styles for which Teague had no names. Her clothes were always professional but not pretentious, and her face had a natural look, except for a frequently worn lipstick color that Teague decided to name plum. He supposed that her large-ish nose and chin cleft might be considered flaws, but not by him, not today.

Should he be intimidated? Should he be in love? Why had this woman traveled all the way to Bangkok just to have dinner with him tonight?

The taxi veered onto a ramp down to street level. The rain seemed to subside, and Bangkok began to look, if not distinctly recognizable, then at least familiar. Cardinal directions locked into their rightful places. Memories accreted and allowed Teague to see the changes: a new high-rise development going up where there'd been a car park, an appliance shop where he'd once bought motorcycle tires, an elevated train platform shrouded in tarps and scaffolding.

Soon the taxi turned a corner, drove half a block more, and rolled to a stop at a familiar awning. As Monkey paid, Teague opened the door and let his feet fall to the pavement. He forced himself to stand and cross the raging gutter, half-wishing he'd swallowed his pride and rented an exoskeleton until he'd gotten his strength back.

Several new posters brightened the restaurant's front windows, but inside the sunlight crept in and seemed to lose its way. Even as Teague's eyes adjusted, the smells began to wrap and welcome him. The half-dozen patrons were engrossed in their food and screens. As Teague swiped his wet shoes on the mat, he was taken aback by the elderly man huddled on the stool at the end of the buffet. He didn't appear to have heard the door chime. When had he grown so old? *What a waste*, Teague thought. *Mr. Chaiprasit was younger than Matthew Valdosky. He shouldn't look a day over Vanilla age.*

Teague filled a bowl at the buffet and set it on the little counter. "Four baht," Mr. Chaiprasit grunted, and then a smile spread across his face. He took Teague's hands in his moist clutches and laughed.

"Hello, sir," Teague said.

"Vipada!" Mr. Chaiprasit called over his shoulder. When she didn't answer, he called again, earning a barrage of Thai from the kitchen and the attention of the diners. He called a third time and she emerged, exasperated, but her expression melted instantly to joy. She pulled Teague down to her height and embraced him with a laugh.

"You've grown," she said when she let him go at last. She patted his belly and ran her hands over the contour of his shoulders. "So tall, too, and even more handsome. They fed you well?"

"Well enough, but not like you could've," Teague replied. Mrs. Chaiprasit hadn't aged as startlingly as her husband, but her hair was thinner and grayer. She had a few more lines in her face and a bit more of a stoop to her shoulders.

"We weren't expecting you until this evening," she said.

"I know, but it turns out that I can't come tonight. Something very important came up with work. But I still wanted to see you today."

Mrs. Chaiprasit clicked her tongue but nodded. "Come. Sit. You must be hungry."

Teague was soon surrounded with overflowing bowls. Mrs. Chaiprasit plopped down across from him and said, "Tell me everything."

"You got my emails," Teague said.

"Yes, yes, but I want to hear the rest," Mrs. Chaiprasit said even as she gestured for him to eat. The gaeng joot woon sen, once his favorite soup, tasted greasier than he remembered.

The mundaneness of the place began to seep into him like the sweat under his clothes. Mrs. Chaiprasit ladled up fresh helpings with more questions. Teague cherry-picked his stories to skirt gently around the facts of his apostasy. The Chaiprasits had been supportive, but there was no need to be too overt.

"Are you looking for a job?" Mr. Chaiprasit interjected.

"I have a job," Teague said. "Don't you remember? That's why I'm heading to Seattle."

"Oh, right. Right. Seattle," he said. "Are you saving your money?"

"I am," Teague replied.

"Then come stay with us and don't waste your money at that hotel."

"Jettrin, don't pester," Mrs. Chaiprasit said, but her eyes told Teague that she agreed.

"Thank you for the offer, but I really need to be at a place with a pool and a gym so I can get used to Earth's gravity more quickly." It was as good an excuse as any. "But I promise to come by every day, and I want to take you to dinner. Any restaurant you want. Cost is no object." Mr. Chaiprasit began to protest. "I've barely spent a dime of my salary in a year and a half. You won't let me pay you back for all your help before I left, so the least I can do is to treat you to a good meal." Teague turned to Mrs. Chaiprasit. "Don't let him skimp on this. Make reservations anywhere."

Mrs. Chaiprasit nodded, began to stack his empty bowls, and asked, "Do you want more?"

"Want, yes, but need, no. I'm stuffed. Thank you. Everything was as good as I remember." Teague checked the time. "But I should probably go. Mr. Xu is expecting me and Monkey."

At the door, Teague accepted another long hug from Mrs. Chaiprasit.

"Is the temple still there? The one out back?" Teague asked. He feared it might have fallen prey to developers panting after a lack of density.

"I could always find you there," she replied. "Don't worry. It's waited for you."

Monkey ran ahead, skirting around the legs of strolling e-mall customers, and darted into Bondi's stall. After the chime, Teague heard a joyful laugh and arrived to find Monkey in Bondi's arms behind the display counter.

"Welcome back, my intrepid friend," the Badass called and let Monkey down. Monkey began to sniff around the stall.

Teague waied and then accepted a hug from Bondi. "You're still selling this old e-manga? And these piñatas? No one bought this stuff when I worked here."

"Of course not. But no one shoplifts it, either," Bondi said.

Teague laughed. "But business has been good, I hope?" Bondi nodded. "You look great. You've lost weight?"

Bondi patted his still-protruding belly. "I have, actually. And you've grown—several centimeters if I'm not mistaken."

"Easy to do in micro-gravity. I forgot about your biometric security software. Or are you a doctor now?"

"Indeed. Where is my patient?" Monkey scurried to Bondi's feet, stood on his back legs, and put his front paws in Bondi's hands.

"Bondi, Bondi, Bondi," Monkey chanted, quivering with excitement.

"I barely kept up with him on the way over here," Teague said.

"I like the Badass," Monkey said.

"Just wait until you see what I have for you," Bondi said.

"I like surprises," Monkey cooed. Bondi scooped Monkey off the floor and ducked through the curtain into the workshop.

"Are you? Already? With the fixing...?" Teague hated to even utter the words for what Bondi needed to do to Monkey. The extensive diagnostic punch list included new servo matrices, a cooling system upgrade, new eyes, hands, and audio sensors, among other horrors. Teague's stomach clenched to think of it.

"What do you think, my friend?" Bondi asked in the dark.

Monkey gasped and squealed with pleasure. Teague located the seldom-used workshop light switch and turned it on to find Monkey on the workbench, sniffing at the nose of another lemur. Its coat was full and glossy, but it was as inert as a statue, and its eyes had no spark. Its paws were clean and black. Its ears were covered with a neat, even fuzz.

"No. No. No. No."

"Think about this," Bondi said.

"No," Teague said. "I don't want a new one. I want you to fix Monkey."

"Teague."

"We discussed this. You said you could do it." Teague felt a lump in his throat.

"This is the best way."

"I told you money was not an object," Teague said.

"I understand that, but please trust me. This is a brand-new Galapagos series. Parts for the Beagle series simply aren't available any longer, except from dodgy aftermarket maker shops, and who knows how long they'd last. I was going to have to retrofit so much, like the wrist fittings for the hands. I'd have to patch his skin. And all these fixes might actually limit Monkey's physical abilities. Besides, he's..."

"He's what?"

"You'll have to admit that he's seen better days," Bondi replied.

"If you can't say something nice..." Monkey trailed off. He stroked his doppelganger's downy fur a few times and then sat up and rubbed his own belly. He poked at a worn patch of skin under one arm and then turned imploringly to Teague. "I can't fight it. I know it's just my Zubotix programming, but I *really* want to upgrade." Teague rolled his eyes.

"I tried to make the retrofit work," Bondi said. "I even ordered the parts. But I wasn't satisfied. This new one has all the same upgrades and a few extras. Top-of-the-line everything, a thousand times his current memory capacity, and a handy belly pouch. All I need to do is exchange his central processor with the Nexon system and sync the software. It'll only take me a day, if that. He won't be the physical Monkey frame you've owned, but in every other way he will be the Monkey you know."

"What would happen to this Monkey?"

"I have the original processor. Do you want to keep him?"

"I don't know."

"I cannot make two Monkeys, not as you know him now."

"What would *you* do?" Teague asked.

"My grandson and granddaughters would love him," Bondi said. "They are good children."

"Okay," Teague said. "But I don't want to see him. Wipe the memory clean. I don't want him to remember me or himself at all. Let your grandkids give him a new name. I know it sounds stupid and sentimental, but I need to know he's not still out there somewhere."

"I understand," Bondi said.

Teague picked up Monkey and hugged him. "Don't worry. I'll see you soon," Monkey said.

Bondi said, "Run along now and let me get started before you change your mind."

"We didn't get a chance to catch up," Teague said.

"We'll have time."

Teague left the e-mall, hailed a taxi, and gave the driver the address of the only place in Bangkok where Monkey wasn't welcome anyway.

The barber had repainted his walls but still had the same chairs. The shifty tax preparer had set out a new sandwich board sign but was still closed in the middle of the day. A tinny radio still played from the motorcycle repair shop, although the owners seemed to have branched out into the lawnmower business. It was all familiar enough. But when Teague opened the gym's creaky screen door, he almost turned around to make sure that he'd come to the right alley.

The bare bulbs had been replaced by actual fixtures. The walls had been stripped of the yellowing posters and clippings and had been painted turquoise. Three neat desks had each been set with a red wooden chair, remnants of a kitchen set. The old table, also painted red, was pressed against the wall inside the front door and littered with brochures. On the far wall, an amateur muralist had penciled and had begun to paint silhouettes of Muay Thai fighters in a series of moves. A teenager stared at Teague from behind one of the desks.

Teague greeted him in Thai. *"Is Father Josiah here?"* The boy shook his head slowly. *"Ned?"*

The boy rose and then in rough English said, "You wait, man." He backed out of the room through a new screen door into the tournament courtyard.

A Bible verse had been penciled on the wall as part of the mural, each letter about fifteen centimeters tall, waiting for paint: "With him is only the arm of flesh, but with us is the Lord our God to help us and to fight our battles—2 Chronicles 32:8a." Which desk contained Josiah's cloudy whiskey?

The screen door squeaked open, and Ned entered, damp and concerned. He had always walked like he had a board up his shirt—or a stick up his ass—but today he stood even straighter. His red beard had been trimmed close, but he'd let his hair grow uncharacteristically shaggy. The same eyes that had captivated Teague on that first day bored into him again.

Teague smiled and held out his hand, but Ned kept his gaze firm.

"Can I help you?" Ned asked.

"Ned," Teague said, "it's only been four years. You've forgotten me already?" As he spoke, recognition dawned.

"Teague Werres," Ned said. He shook his hand, grasping Teague's forearm with his other hand. Ned nodded to the teen lurking in the doorway. He scurried away, letting the screen door bang shut after him.

"Looks like you finally convinced Father Josiah to make some improvements around here," Teague said.

Ned pursed his lips. "You haven't heard?" Teague shook his head. "Father Josiah passed away seven months ago."

Teague's eyes suddenly ached with worry. "What? How?"

"I'm sorry I cannot greet you with better news. We'd been having trouble with a former student. The boy broke in to steal late one night. Father Josiah confronted him and was stabbed."

"You know who…?" Teague asked.

Ned pointed to a tiny black dome in a ceiling corner. "I'd convinced Father Josiah to install cameras after items began to go missing a few months before. Justice is being served. The boy is attending drug treatment. The Lord's hand is at work. Father Josiah lives on here." Ned threw his arms wide. "I've taken on his ministry as my own. We spread his ashes in the training yard. We've become the Sons of Josiah."

"The Sons of Josiah?"

"The new name of this ministry," Ned said. "We train for the ring and discipleship. We fight and spread the good news. It's an exciting time. I'm negotiating to buy the adjacent land past the training yard, to add a dormitory and a schoolroom. The enemy sought to lay us low, even destroy us with Josiah's sacrifice, but the Spirit prevails. I mourn him every day, but it strengthens me. Young men are finding their path here, learning the truth in the heart of their struggles."

"I'm glad some good has come of it," Teague said, certain Josiah had never intended anything like this.

"He was always proud of you," Ned said. "I know he enjoyed the messages you sent during your time away. So have you come to stay?"

"I'm only visiting for a few days."

"You're welcome to attend our Sunday services. There will be several excellent match-ups." Ned said this with such sincerity that Teague fought a mirthless laugh. Ned stood abruptly, fingered through a sheaf of folders on a desk, and extracted a sheet of paper. He handed it to Teague and then hurried to the table by the door. Small English type under the Thai script announced, "Singing! Praise! Spirit-Moved Open Class Tournament! Meditation! Teaching!"

Ned returned with a brochure, flipping it over to show Teague the English side. "This tells what we're about. And," he added, "the support we need. But you trained here. You know the ministry that Father Josiah sought to build."

Teague almost scoffed. "Aren't you still training kids for the leagues?" he asked instead.

"Some still move up," Ned said. "But I strive more to train fighters for their spiritual battles." The leagues had probably withdrawn their support, Teague guessed, once they got wind of Ned's changes. The brochure invited donations at several levels. "The Spirit is alive and girded for battle here. All the same, I'm glad it was you today."

"Oh?" Teague asked.

"Sanun feared you were a lawyer for the development authority."

"Only an economist," Teague said.

Ned smiled weakly, as if puzzled, and then said, "Come. I'll show you our work."

In the courtyard, the ring and the bleachers had been painted and repaired. A large banner—decorated with an amateurish silhouette of two grappling Muay Thai fighters casting the unlikely shadow of a thorn-wrapped cross—fluttered on the far awning.

The locker room had been scrubbed clean and painted, its lockers neatly labeled. An older boy at Ned's training bench paused taping the wrists of a younger boy as Teague passed. In the training courtyard, equipment had been relocated to make space for a few wooden benches and a spindly lectern. Only two boys were working out. The rain was slowly leveling the sand. No amount of running would ever bring Father Josiah back.

A lone woman rose from a square table for two, nodded a thank-you to the maître d', and extended her hand. "Teague?" she asked. "Welcome. I'm Aurore."

"Pleasure to meet you," Teague said when in the low light he finally made out the face he'd seen in a hundred pictures. Her hand was soft and warm, her handshake firm. She was about a quarter meter shorter than Teague, but like Dr. Aromdee seemed taller by virtue of her charisma. She wore a feminine tailored business suit over a white blouse, and her lips were indeed plum colored. Her only jewelry, a tiny sparkle, dangled at her throat from the silver thread of a choker necklace. Altogether she proved to be more attractive than the dossier had promised, leaving Teague strangely thankful that the afternoon's grief had tempered this morning's sophomoric anticipation.

In fact, despite his curiosity, Teague had considered postponing this dinner. He'd returned to his hotel room after the day's visits feeling nearly paralyzed, as if the very fact of his return had changed the natural order. He'd sat in the gray light until he'd realized that there was nothing to be done for Monkey, the aging Chaiprasits, or Father Josiah. And there was no stopping the incessant rain. As he sat down across from Aurore, he was glad he'd spent the afternoon productively, exercising and rereading her dossier.

A steward appeared tableside, cracked a bottle, and filled Teague's water glass. Teague thanked him. "Would you like a drink before dinner?" Aurore asked, and the steward hesitated. She'd ordered red wine, but it seemed more ornament than beverage.

"No, thank you," Teague replied. He took a sip of the water and pursed his lips at the bitter mineral taste.

"I'm sorry, would you prefer still?" Aurore asked.

"Still what?"

"Still water. No bubbles."

"Oh. Yes. I would, actually," Teague said.

Aurore smiled and nodded to the steward, who collected Teague's glass and promptly disappeared.

"I've never heard that term before," Teague said.

She smiled and said, "I don't know half the words on this menu. I've been hoping that you can teach me a bit about Thai cuisine. I understand you consider Bangkok home."

"I do. Although I didn't eat in many places like this when I was growing up."

"Why did you live in Bangkok?" Aurore asked. "You're American, if I'm not mistaken."

"I was born here, actually. My father was an aid worker," Teague said. The steward returned with a new bottle, half-wrapped in a cloth napkin, and offered a glimpse of the label. Teague nodded whatever approval he felt qualified to offer. The steward cracked the seal, filled a new glass with a flourish, and vanished.

"Which organization did your father work for?" Aurore asked.

"The missionary arm of my parents' church cooperated with various food and disaster relief agencies around Southeast Asia."

"What church is this?"

"Christian Scientists. The Tellurites," Teague replied.

"Fascinating," Aurore said. "I've never met anyone connected with the Tellurites before. I take it you're no longer an adherent."

"No, I'm not."

"I'd love to hear an inside perspective. What does your father do now? I don't suppose he took your decision to attend Agnus Dei well."

"Both my parents passed away when I was young," Teague said. "My father died during a flood-relief effort before I ever really knew him."

"I'm very sorry," Aurore said.

"Thank you." Teague picked his menu off the cover plate and flipped it open. He scanned the script and hummed. "I should be able to muddle us through this," he offered with a smile. Soon, the waiter had scurried off with their selections, and the steward had topped off their barely touched liquids.

"I've been in orbit, of course," Aurore said, "and spent a brief time on the Moon, but Agnus Dei…I'll admit I'm envious."

"Interplanetary space travel is dull, I assure you," Teague said.

"I suppose that's true. If things get exciting, it probably means something has gone terribly wrong," she said and then pointed two fingers at him. "I'm dying to hear about your trip and to get to know each other more, but you're undoubtedly wondering why I've come all the way to Bangkok to meet you."

"It has been on my mind," Teague said.

"Then let's begin, shall we?" Aurore's eyes brightened. "I represent an organization called the Sustainable Justice Development Council. Have you heard of us?"

"I found your website earlier today, but I haven't had time to review your work in depth."

"But you got a sense of our aims?" she asked.

"A general sense…"

"But?"

"Well, I hate to get off on a tangent already," Teague said. "Your group's ethics are well defined, but I'm—how to say it?—unclear about your actual goals."

"Mr. Yarrow is right about you. You prefer to cut right through to the heart of the matter. Very well." She sipped at her wine. "Since the council's inception, we've directed most of our energies toward the creation and adoption of the UN Convention for Extra-Territorial Rights and Development. Are you familiar with this?"

"The UNSA treaty?" Teague asked. "I heard that it wasn't expected to get many signatories, that the Valdosky Companies were opposed."

"The media has largely assumed Valdosky's position. Since Valdosky has not publicly offered specific support for the convention, most suppose their opposition, but that's simply not true. If you actually read their statements on the issue, they've maintained a neutral stance. In fact, we expect the convention to be signed by a significant majority by the end of the year."

"And you created it?" Teague asked.

"The SJDC is largely responsible for the policy intent of the document, and we drafted much of the specific language. Do you know what the convention actually does?"

"Not specifically."

"In effect, the convention changes the UN Space Authority from a regulatory body into an independent governmental bureaucracy. It creates a mechanism for communities throughout the solar system to organize into independent, recognizable states under certain rules. The UNSA will become more like the European Union, acting as an administrative and regulatory clearinghouse for the inherently disparate states."

"Wow," Teague said. "So Mars or the Moon might become countries?"

"Exactly. As may asteroid colonies."

Has Dwight told her that I'm some kind of expert on the economics of asteroid development? "But what does this have to do with your broader aims?" Teague asked. "The human rights, sustainable communities, and such?"

"Excellent question. How indeed? A section of the convention mandates that the UNSA establish an office of asylum aid, funded by all signatories, but largely by the permanent members of the UN Security Council."

"Asylum aid? Like political asylum?"

"Yes, but broader than that. The office will be authorized to accept applications from nearly anyone considered a refugee, be it for political, environmental, economic, racial, religious, or systemic reasons. People caught in oppressive, violent, or critically resource-poor situations may choose to emigrate rather than to suffer as refugees. They can take their future into their own hands, remove themselves from dire circumstances, and create new, sustainable homes. It's unprecedented."

"Off Earth. Around the solar system," Teague said.

"It is called the Convention for *Extra-Territorial* Rights," Aurore said.

"I think I understand. It's a great idea, if there's enough funding to develop the colonies themselves."

Aurore smiled and nodded, seemingly unconcerned by such trivialities. "Now you can see why I'm interested to learn that your father was a relief worker."

"Not exactly," Teague said.

"I'm hoping that you might consider following in his footsteps. I've come to Bangkok to ask you to quit CDI. Are you ready to make a real difference in the world?"

CHAPTER 24

In my suit, out here on the surface, I feel separate from all of this, as if I'm shifted and will wake up, safe and secure.

SEPTEMBER 2093

Hours after his dinner with Aurore, Teague stared out the shrouded windows of his hotel room into the pink glow of the city. He longed for something—the feeling of a motorcycle under him, perhaps. He had always thought clearly out on the streets. He could probably call the concierge and rent one, but a ride would be miserable in this weather, and he was still too weak.

Teague picked up his mobile and scrolled to Dwight's eddress but quickly canceled back to the home screen. In the cab from the restaurant, he'd gotten as far as drafting most of an email—was this a test or a task?—before deleting it all. As much as he craved a straight answer, Teague knew in his gut that Dwight expected him to take Aurore's offer, however vague, even if it cost him Matthew's patronage.

Aurore had met Dwight—or "Mr. Yarrow," as she insisted on calling him—at a wordily named Yale-sponsored symposium about the impact of the space industry on geopolitics and the environment. She'd served on the organizing committee. Matthew Valdosky had just happened to be on Earth and had accepted their invitation to be the keynote speaker, and Dwight had sat on several panels.

"Really? Dwight? I thought he liked to stay behind the scenes," Teague had commented.

She and Dwight had first discussed the concept of offering refugees new homes off Earth at a reception. Later, he'd encouraged her to establish the council, had suggested a few like-minded recruits, had pointed them in the direction of funding, and had helped to open the right doors at the UN.

"Discreetly," she had explained. "Mr. Yarrow fears that the Valdosky Companies will be seen as profiteers. Whatever the good intentions, it's a fact that Valdosky has much to gain from a refugee relocation program. The convention establishes a sizable reserve of cash that will in large part be spent on Valdosky contracts. The Companies can't afford to look as if they are exploiting the situation. Now perhaps you understand their neutral stance on the convention."

It seemed foolish to consider throwing away a career at Valdosky before it had even left the ground, even for such a laudable humanitarian enterprise. And for what? She hadn't even told him what the job was. And why? Because of a cryptic suggestion from Dwight? Because an intelligent, beautiful woman had asked him to? And what would Matthew think? Teague wished he had Monkey by his side, not for the first time that night. Even if Monkey couldn't solve these mysteries, he'd at least be able to check the assertions Aurore had made at dinner.

She'd claimed, with some authority, that CDI was using a misguided approach to identifying candidates for sustainable asteroid colonies. Teague knew that CDI hadn't yet come close to meeting its sales projections, but it was too early in the program to give up hope. However, according to Aurore, there was already blood in the water at the higher levels. The SJDC's campaign promised not only to save human lives from deplorable conditions, but also to keep Valdosky's Colonial Development Initiative from being an abject failure. Valdosky's health was critical to sustainable development in the solar system. No competitors were likely to emerge anytime soon, and millions of people needed relief now.

Teague searched through the CDI network for some hint of this systemic failure. Most of the reports he'd written were still parked at Marketing, but others had been passed to Sales and were marked as "in progress." Only one of his analyses, some German retirement community development, had been marked as "contract pending." In casual communication, the marketing people often dubbed potential customers "slam dunks" or "sure things," but was that all talk? Had there really been so few sales? Monkey would be able to learn more. Teague knew he should clip on his nodes and get some good induced sleep—instant forgetfulness and rest from a day in one-gee—but instead he grabbed his jacket.

Teague was greeted outside the hotel's revolving front door by a sleepy doorman and a wall of humidity. He asked for a taxi, and the doorman waved a flashlight down the ramp to the queue of waiting cabs. "First time in Bangkok, sir?" the doorman asked.

"No," Teague said and gave the doorman the district name of the Chaiprasits' restaurant.

The cab stopped, and the doorman opened the back door. "Not much happening there at this time. Are you looking for nightlife?"

"Visiting a friend," Teague said, getting in.

Outside the cab's fogged, drippy windows, blocks of nightclubs, markets, and shift parlors drifted by like glistening parade floats, separated by long gaps of side streets and sleeping buildings. The cabbie kept checking Teague in the mirror, probably itching to deliver a mark to some brothel or massage parlor to earn a kickback. Teague gave him the Chaiprasits' address in Thai to avoid any confusion.

"So this job you're offering," Teague had asked, over the espressos he and Aurore had ordered in lieu of dessert. "Would I have a title?"

Aurore had looked almost puzzled. "A title? You misunderstand. I'm not offering a replacement for the nameplate and cubicle you'll get at CDI. This isn't a punch-the-clock, work-queue, one-of-a-dozen-analysts kind of opportunity."

"Then what is it?" Teague had asked. But she'd only smiled and changed the subject.

Just before the final turn, Teague asked the driver to pull over.

"The address is around the corner," the driver said.

"I know. This is fine."

The driver scanned the dark block and the even darker alley. *"Do you want me to wait?"* he asked.

"No, thank you," Teague replied and paid the fare.

Teague shuffled warily into the alley, mindful of the slippery pavement and the inky puddles in the ruts. All around him, drips beat an eerie, percussive metallic symphony in the dark. But he'd been this way too many times to be daunted. His eyes soon adjusted in the ambient light pollution, and he began to find his way more easily. The saturated air quickly soaked through Teague's clothes, but his skin was beginning to remember this atmosphere.

Teague took the steps through the temple garden's arch one at a time, steadying himself on its walls. Inside, he was greeted by the pattering of dripping leaves and the singing of insects. Overgrown plants reached out and brushed against his clothes as he slid along the wet flagstone path.

A faint, wavering light emanated from the temple, but there were no shoes outside the door. Teague slipped across the portico and peeked inside. Finding only several flickering candles, he sloughed off his shoes and entered.

Offerings had certainly been left and cleared away in the past four years. Incense and candles had been burned. Other visitors had left their foot oils on the floor. The rain and moss had likely eroded away a few atoms of the stones. But the Buddha remained, smiling, on his eternal perch. Teague half-expected the statue to question him, to ask for his story like Mrs. Chaiprasit, but it simply welcomed him, happy to hear nothing at all.

Teague found the notch that had cradled his back for so many hours and lowered himself to the floor. He'd forgotten how much the city, and even the garden, disappeared here. If he held his breath, he could hear the candles crackle and sputter in the wet air.

Where was Monkey tonight? Was he disassembled, saved as data, or had he already been transferred to his new body? What did that make Monkey? Was he an object or something virtual, digital and unreal?

Why *had* his mother bought Monkey for him? How had she

justified letting the technology into her home? Did Monkey represent some sliver of doubt, some hope that Teague would strive for more than she was openly able to offer? If she had lived, would she have broken from the fold and taken Vanilla?

But what about his father? Was he, or his memory, why she'd kept living her faith?

It had felt strange to discuss his father with Aurore, to brag about the job that had killed him, and to pretend that his death had been useful. The truth was that Brian Werres had died of cholera while lying in a field hospital full of medicine. He'd refused all treatment, and the overwhelmed medics had complied with his wishes.

Had his father been alone, or had a companion pressured him to keep his convictions? Had he prayed or been prayed over? Had he called his wife and warned her? Had she agreed that he should trust his faith? Had someone stayed with him to keep him hydrated and clean? Or had he eschewed all assistance in order to shit himself to death more quickly? Any relief worker must have known the significance of a cholera infection. Of course, any other relief worker would've already been vaccinated. Why had he put himself through such artificial agony? How could he have abandoned his family?

Teague hated to think that there was such a thing as fate or destiny, but he couldn't deny that what Aurore and Dwight were offering seemed to be a fulfillment of something. He'd never considered walking in his father's footsteps until tonight, but the path made a kind of sense. Was this a chance to redeem the Werres family from the embarrassment of its religion?

Like Father Josiah had tried to do in his own way.

In the flickering light, the Buddha seemed to agree.

* * *

When Bondi called the next afternoon, Teague rushed out of his hotel room and nearly passed out in the cab from the exertion.

"At last," Bondi said, when Teague had dragged himself into

the stall. "He's been worse than a sugared toddler. I almost had to switch him to stand-by."

Teague fell into the duct-taped recliner. "Do you mind if I sit?"

Bondi drew aside the curtain, and a lemur scampered out. It leapt onto Teague's lap with a wide grin, quivering and squealing. Its fur was softer and fluffier than Teague remembered Monkey's ever being, and its movements were quieter and more fluid. "Hi, Teague. Did you miss me?" The voice was unmistakable.

"I did," Teague said. "How are you?"

"I *liked* getting a new body," Monkey said. "What do you think?"

"You're certainly new," Teague said, glancing at Bondi.

Monkey hopped off Teague's lap and flexed proudly. "Oh, lemur ladies," he said in a louche drawl. "Check me out." He sauntered to the middle of Bondi's stall and raised his arms. "Behold, the new, improved 'Monkey is Awesome' dance," he announced, beginning to emit a pop rhythm. He vaulted onto one hand, bounced to his hind legs, waved his arms, and undulated his torso, all while wiggling his hyper-articulated tail to the beat. He climbed a corner post and swung across the trusses.

"Get down," Teague called.

"Oh, let him be," Bondi said, even as Monkey began to writhe irreverently around the dusty Hello Kitty piñata.

"This is normal?" Teague asked.

"He's happy," Bondi said.

"He's...randy," Teague said, finding no other word for the condition.

"He hasn't operated this efficiently in some time," Bondi said. "It appears to manifest as hyperactivity."

"It manifests as complete awesomeness," Monkey said, not missing a beat in his spastic dance.

"What else did you do to him?" Teague asked.

"Whatever do you mean?" Bondi asked.

"I know you. You added some other surprises."

"Not much. Just a little inoculation. A few terabytes I've accumulated over the past few years. It'll help him keep his own gates defended. And may open a few doors for you, if you ever have the need."

"And you're giving this to me so you can have company in prison?" Teague asked.

"Ha," Bondi snorted. "Monkey's too smart for that." Monkey ended his dance with a jig and a flourish, earning him broad, avuncular applause from Bondi as the music died away.

"I need to pay you," Teague said.

"Yes, you do."

"Pay the man, Monkey."

"Does that mean you like the new me?" Monkey asked.

"Yes. I like the new you."

"Do you want to see what I cost?"

"Not now, not ever."

"Monkey tells me you have a shift set. You're shifting now?" Bondi asked.

Teague shook his head. "Sleep induction is a better cure for insomnia than drugs."

Bondi hummed sympathetically. "It'll happen," he said. "You're a young man."

Monkey trotted over, hugged one of Bondi's legs, and said, "I paid the invoice. You're the best Badass ever."

"That may be the nicest thing anyone's ever said to me," Bondi said.

Monkey gasped and turned to Teague. "So did you meet her? How'd it go? Tell me everything," he begged.

"Meet who?" Bondi asked.

"I met with someone last night, for work," Teague replied.

"A *woman*," Monkey said.

"I thought this job was in Seattle," Bondi said.

"She flew all the way to Bangkok especially to meet Teague, and boy, are her arms tired. They had dinner." Monkey waggled his eyebrows.

Bondi slid his sunglasses down his nose and looked at Teague over the lenses with his silvery eyes. "The plot thickens," he said.

"It's not like that," Teague said.

"It must be something for her to come all the way here."

"It's just business."

"When do I get to meet her?" Monkey asked.

"I don't know. We'll talk about it."

"Can you stay?" Bondi asked. "I want to hear more about your adventures with the Valdoskies. We'll order some food."

"That sounds like a great idea." Teague didn't know why exactly, but he wasn't ready to be alone with this new Zubot quite yet.

"And after that we hit the town," Monkey announced.

"You're sure you didn't do something else to him?" Teague asked.

By the time they left the e-mall, Teague felt reasonably assured that Monkey's differences were mostly superficial and that the improvements were harmless. As Monkey scampered from window to window in the back of the cab, eagerly taking in everything, Teague had to admit that the Badass was right. Why would he want to limit Monkey in any way? In this new Galapagos Series body, he was as handsome as he'd ever been. If Teague was going to take Vanilla, how could he begrudge Monkey a new body every few years?

Monkey turned anxiously and said, "Aurore Rheaume is calling."

Teague's mobile buzzed in his jacket pocket. "Weird," he said. "I'm not late for dinner, yet."

"I apologize for disturbing you," she said after he answered, "but something has happened, and I'd like to alter our plans for this evening." Had he not lived up to her expectations last night? "Are you available now?"

"I'm actually in the cab heading back to my hotel to change clothes," Teague said, then cringed. *Don't tell her that.* "And then I can—"

"Please don't worry about dressing up. Have you seen the news today?"

"The news?"

"Unfortunately, there's a chance for you to see the extent of the problem the council is trying to address."

"Should I meet you at that restaurant near the stadium?"

"Actually, can you come to my hotel right now?" she asked.

Teague had rejected Aurore's hotel because it possessed only the third-best showers in Bangkok. He doubted that she'd let him use hers, so he stopped in the lobby restroom. He arranged his hair and checked his teeth. There was nothing to be done with the dampness under his jeans and T-shirt but to hope that it would soon dry in the air conditioning.

"Remember what I said in the cab," Teague said in the elevator.

"Be quiet. Be calm. Be the best-behaved lemur I can be," Monkey said morosely.

"Listen, this is important. She's really perceptive. So you can't act any smarter than a regular Zubot. Do you understand?"

"You never get a second chance to make a first impression," Monkey said. The elevator stopped on her floor and dinged. "At least I dressed up," he said and trotted out.

Aurore answered the door wearing blue jeans, a tight green T-shirt, and a concerned expression. She greeted Teague but brightened considerably when she noticed Monkey.

"Who is this?" she asked.

"This is—" Teague began. Aurore seemed shorter than she had appeared last night—high heels, Teague supposed—and intriguingly petite.

"Hi. I'm Monkey. I'm a Zubot. Teague's my best friend."

Aurore squatted, put out a hand for Monkey to sniff, and murmured in French. Monkey hummed with pleasure and grinned. Aurore looked up at Teague. She'd pulled her hair back in a ponytail, and her bangs flitted casually over her eyes. "You weren't going to leave this little guy in your hotel room, were you?" She turned her attention back to Monkey. "He didn't leave you alone during dinner last night, did he?"

"No, ma'am," Monkey replied. "I was being serviced. Teague takes good care of me."

Aurore smiled, rose, and welcomed them in. Her suite was larger and more artfully decorated than Teague's, but where his room overlooked the river, hers faced another building. "I'm sorry to have to change our plans." She skirted around Teague and led the way out of the vestibule, through the sitting room, past the open pocket doors of the neatly made-up bedroom, and into a private office. "But with everything going on…"

"The incident in Bangladesh?" Teague asked. Monkey had scanned the headlines in the cab. Soldiers from a political faction had attacked a refugee camp, killing dozens and disrupting services to thousands.

The remains of a room service breakfast were congealing on a cart by the office's door. The desk screen was littered with open files, scrolling newsfeeds, and video broadcasts: burning tents, breached fences, victims in triage, and muted interviews with victims and spokespeople. On the corner of the desk, two mobiles and a screen waited on a charging pad. One was buzzing. Aurore checked it and then set it back down. "There are nearly a hundred thousand people in that camp," she replied.

"Wow," Teague said.

"The Bandarban camp is considered a small facility," Aurore said. "The UNHCR has at times operated camps for over a million people."

"What's the UNHCR?" Teague asked.

"The UN High Commissioner for Refugees. I've been communicating with various UN delegates and bureaucrats all day. I hate that this happened, but every incident strengthens our case for the convention. Make yourself comfortable."

Teague took off his rain jacket and settled it over the back of a guest chair. Aurore again checked one of her mobiles. Monkey quivered by Teague's feet sniffing the air, jerking his attention from side to side. "Do you mind if Monkey looks around? He likes to get familiar with his surroundings."

"Not at all," Aurore said. At a nod from Teague, Monkey launched himself out into the sitting room.

"Stay out of the bedroom," Teague called after him and then turned back to Aurore. "I'm not going to be able to talk too intelligently about this situation in Bangladesh or the whole refugee issue in general. It's not that I don't care—I do—but the whole thing just hasn't ever been on my radar. I've been so focused on CDI for the past couple of years."

"I assumed as much. I've prepared a portfolio to get you up to speed. I'm afraid it's not light reading: statistics and trends, field reports, case studies, history and analysis. Can I forward it to you now?" Teague nodded, and she tapped her screen a few times.

"I'm getting it," Monkey called from the sitting room. Teague checked his mobile and watched the file load. "Wow. It's huge," Monkey said.

"Monkey manages my files," Teague said.

Aurore gestured to the office's couch and said, "Shall we sit?" Monkey crept in and began to sniff around the nooks and crannies. He hopped up on the desk chair and nosed hungrily at Aurore's charging devices.

"That's enough, Monkey," Teague said. Monkey trotted over and pawed at Aurore's knees. Teague opened his mouth to object, but she patted her thighs and Monkey sprang onto her lap, turned around once, and curled up. Why had he taken to her so quickly? This had to be Bondi's doing.

"He's so soft," Aurore said.

"And I'm cuddly, too," Monkey added.

Aurore laughed. "Thank you for bringing him. It's been a difficult day, and this is very relaxing. I hope you don't mind that we're not going out again."

"I don't mind at all," Teague said.

"We can order room service if we get hungry. But I actually prefer this. It was never my intention to wine and dine you. I'm convinced that once you see the facts, you'll be persuaded that you're wasting your time at CDI."

Monkey purred softly as she stroked him. Potential employer liking Monkey: good. Beautiful woman liking Monkey: excellent. Teague wanted to ask about the details of the job again, but he held his tongue. Aurore would tell him when she was ready and not a second before.

"I'm wasting my time at CDI, or CDI is wasting its time?" Teague asked.

"Both," Aurore replied. "I hope that you'll agree that refugees are a more appropriate demographic to place on colonies than most of the communities that CDI is courting. The initiative focuses so much on who can afford a colonial lifestyle. But why not find people wanting to make a permanent choice, not just wealthy people willing to take a few years' vacation?"

Teague nodded noncommittally. "They've invested a fortune in their research."

"We've been developing our own set of basic criteria to identify candidates. You should find this interesting. Mr. Yarrow told me you have a talent for synthesizing complex issues."

"Did he?" *How would he know?*

"There are three key variables—"

"Really? Only three?" Teague asked. Monkey pricked up his ears.

"The equation sounds simple, and it is, but the nuanced ratios of the variables are what matter. We call them Survival, Belief, and Home. The basic equation looks something like—Monkey, will you fetch my screen?" Monkey slipped off her lap as dutifully as if Teague had asked him, hurried over to the desk, and hobbled back with her screen in one paw. She thanked him sweetly, and he nestled back into place on her lap. She drew out the stylus and began to draw. "S times B over H," she said, and showed Teague.

"Survival quantifies the amount of danger a particular community faces: the threats or experience of violence, environmental disaster, catastrophic economic loss, and other drivers that force people to become refugees. These statistics are weighted by things like actuality, severity, and likelihood of recurrence. Is this making sense?"

"Absolutely," Teague said. In fact, it did. CDI's system was based on the work of some academic sociologists who were reputedly the world's leading experts in the field of exocolonization. They'd developed dozens of opaque proprietary formulas based on demographics, economic factors, and often strange geographical minutiae: new vehicles purchased per annum, average spent on veterinary services, support of the arts, average spent on outdoor sports, the difference between the highest and lowest elevation within fifty kilometers. Teague could see how one detail or another might indicate likelihood of individual willingness to move to a colony, but when these myriad facts were aggregated and applied to a community, they often seemed like so much noise. Teague wanted to be able to say that he'd always found the whole thing fishy or forced, but every report he'd filed at CDI had been submitted with implicit faith in the program. "Survival," he muttered, nodding.

"Belief," Aurore continued, "is a little trickier. It encompasses the idea of communal cohesiveness, those things that define a community and how much they matter to individuals and the whole. Obviously one must factor ethnic and family distinctions, religious affiliations, political leanings, but also investment in the community, strength of educational programs, community support networks, history and heritage. In essence, how much are members invested in their collective future?"

"Survival times Belief," Teague said. "So a highly endangered community that cares about itself is going to register higher. Makes sense. What about Home?"

"You probably have a unique perspective on this, having come home this week." She smiled sympathetically. "Does Bangkok still feel like home?"

"Yes and no. Some things haven't changed at all. Some are totally different."

Aurore nodded. "Home is our attempt to quantify that sense. How strongly does a community feel that home still exists after an atrocity or disaster has occurred? Can they easily cross a border or fence and create a new home? Or has the community lost all sense of a physical place to exist?"

"So a highly endangered community with a strong sense of belief in itself that feels that it has lost its place in the world equals a population that will make a sustainable colony?" Teague asked.

"Simple, no? It obviously needs refinement, quantification."

Teague nodded. "It's elegant. I'm already getting some ideas." He had begun to tick off some potential economic indicators for each of these abstract concepts, just in case Aurore was about to offer him a job as the SJDC's chief analyst. Teague hoped that Monkey was paying enough attention under all his purring to have started a spreadsheet with a few possible headings and formulas.

"Good," Aurore said. "But I'd like to show you a few examples of how Valdosky and CDI have been misapplying these principles, and why most of the colonies they've established are failing. I've put together several case studies…"

Aurore began to tap closed the cloud of data they'd opened on her desk screen, and Teague felt himself begin to emerge from the fugue state of focus. Aurore had dragged one of the guest chairs around the desk to join him as they'd discussed her case studies. She'd been so close that he could smell her hair and feel the warmth of her skin. So close that he could see the tiny—dare he call them imperfections?—on her lips, on her skin, in her irises. Teague had forced such thoughts aside and concentrated. For how long? The sun was low behind the clouds.

"There are more case studies in the portfolio. Do you want to review them together or…?" Aurore asked as she continued to close the dozens of open spreadsheets and reports. Many of them had been familiar CDI analyses that she said had been provided by Dwight—Mr. Yarrow. The Brazilian Pentecostal church's colony was struggling because its community registered almost no S factors. The outwardly healthy Uttar Pradesh Sky colony operated at capacity but was sustained only by high S and B factors. Individual colonists had no sense of discontinuity concerning their home. As such, the Indian state hadn't experienced enough demand to build the second and third colonies it had planned. The various Libertarian paradises that had rushed into space early on had failed because they lacked a belief in themselves as any kind of real community. The core concepts had crystalized like a framework, ready for Teague to hang his own finishes on.

"I think I have a good enough picture for now," Teague said.

As Aurore stood, Teague couldn't help but stare at her body: her narrow waist, the outline of her bra under her shirt—he forced himself to focus on Monkey, the desk, anywhere.

Aurore attended to one of her buzzing devices and wandered with it into the sitting room. Monkey hopped down from a guest chair and loped after her. A few moments later, she called, "Do you like to travel?"

Teague went to the doorway. Aurore was typing into her mobile near the floor-to-ceiling windows with Monkey at her feet. "The only traveling I've ever really done is to ADU and back," he said, "but I didn't hate it."

Aurore finished her message and set her mobile on an end table. "More casualty reports coming in," she sighed.

"Is it bad?" Teague asked.

"It's certainly not good."

"It's too bad the asylum aid program isn't up and running yet."

"That's just it," Aurore said. "It is. It was established a few months ago when funding from the current signatories began to stream in."

"You don't sound pleased about that."

"Oh, I'm ecstatic that the office is getting started. My problem is that not a single refugee on this planet has been informed about its existence."

"Why?" Teague asked. "I'd think the refugee agency would be desperate for people to get asylum and emigrate."

"In a perfect world, yes," Aurore said. "But the High Commission's hands are tied by longstanding doctrines. They prefer repatriation to emigration. Whenever possible, they keep refugees within or as close as possible to their home borders, effectively creating entire populations of IDPs—sorry, internally displaced people—with nowhere to go but back into the lion's den. They're forbidden from promoting mass emigration because of the nuances of the UN's Responsibility to Protect Doctrine—are you familiar with this?" Teague shook his head. "I've included a primer in the portfolio—but basically they're obligated to protect individual victims of any atrocity or disaster, but they must not interfere in the sovereign rights of a nation."

"And encouraging citizens to emigrate or seek asylum elsewhere is considered interference?" Teague asked.

"Exactly," Aurore said. "Because of that, refugees are forced to apply for asylum on an individual basis—a difficult, expensive, and political process. Every receiving nation has differing and arcane requirements. The Asylum Aid program isn't at one hundred percent yet, but it will be soon. It solves all these problems. It allows entire communities to apply as easily as individuals or families. It removes almost all the political and diplomatic baggage of one nation accepting the dissidents of another. It's unprecedented. People just need to be informed. And that's where we're asking you to come in."

"Me?" Teague asked. Aurore gestured to one of the armchairs and sat in the other. Monkey grinned at Teague as he plopped down at her feet.

"We want you to identify the communities with the most potential to emigrate, visit them discreetly in the camps, and educate them about the Asylum Aid program," Aurore said.

"I'm not a sales and marketing person."

"These people don't need to be entertained or tricked. They need someone informed and persuasive. Someone who cares more about people than quotas or end-of-the-year bonuses." An obvious dig at CDI.

"And the refugee agency is going to let me stroll into their camps and preach about this stuff, even though it's against their doctrines?"

"No," Aurore said. "But we think you can devise a strategy to do it anyway." Teague suppressed a shiver. Monkey caught his eye, almost as if he'd felt it, too. "The UN grants camp access every day to representatives from cooperative relief agencies, supply and equipment contractors, journalists, and such. It's just a matter of finding the right approach. But to remain under the radar, you may have to"—she paused as if searching for the right words—"make arrangements to compensate the right individuals."

"Are you saying I might have to bribe UN officials?" Teague asked.

"That is what I'm saying. As we discussed yesterday, Valdosky cannot afford to appear as if they are attempting to profit from the asylum program. Likewise, the SJDC cannot be tied to your efforts."

"Now it sounds like you're not actually offering me a job."

"Not as such," Aurore said. "I know this may sound outlandish, but it's not a test. We are very serious. That's why I'm speaking plainly. You would no longer be a Valdosky employee, nor would you be an associate of the council. You would be an independent agent, operating autonomously, taking what steps you deem necessary to affect the end goal. We would provide you with resources, discreet communication channels, and access to data to complete your analyses. And your compensation will be commensurate with your risk."

"Just so I'm straight, what you're asking me to do is illegal," Teague said.

"Yes and no. Disseminating the information in the camps is not illegal *per se*, although it goes against the agency's rules. But we believe that certain risks are necessary in order to accelerate the process. The convention will be in full force by year's end, and the refugees of the world cannot afford to wait for years for bureaucratic policy to change. Their lives are at stake now. We're confident that once a significant number of communities have entered the program, the UNHCR will reexamine their operational policies and adopt Asylum Aid referral as a standard practice. You'll have reshaped the world, the solar system, forever."

Aurore smiled. "Yes," she said, "I did just appeal to your ego, but please don't let that distract you from the facts."

Teague didn't return the smile. "But I'd be the one taking the risks."

"Yes, and it could be dangerous. The camps are often located in conflict zones, and the conditions inside are often unsecure. Today's incident, for example."

"That part doesn't bother me," Teague said. "I was a delivery boy in Bangkok."

"Does that mean you'll take the job?"

"What happens if I don't?" he asked.

"Mr. Yarrow is convinced you're the right person, and I agree. I'd be disappointed, but the work will go on one way or another."

"What happens if I get caught?"

"You will be acting for a greater purpose, not for personal gain. This is justifiable activism. But if that does happen, we will ensure that you have appropriate legal representation. And obviously we'd trust that you'd maintain a certain level of discretion."

"All right, if I do travel around for a year or two, work up to a tipping point where the UN changes its practices, then what?"

"Mr. Yarrow has insisted that there be a moderating agency between the UNSA Asylum Aid Office and Valdosky and other contractors. The SJDC is poised to lead that agency. You'll have your pick of key roles on the team that will administrate the ongoing creation of the colonies. From there, you'll be able to write your own ticket. Mr. Yarrow and I will owe you a great debt."

"You know you're asking a lot of me," Teague said.

"I know I am."

"I mean, you've been working on this refugee issue for years. I've barely considered it before yesterday." As soon as he said this, he realized it wasn't entirely true. On Gateway 3, when Monkey had encountered the enhanced entity in the network, Thomas had been monitoring the news about some conflict, the destruction of a community, people being driven from their homes. What country had that been? Monkey would have the details. "So what makes you think I'm capable of doing something like this?"

"I believe you would be doing this for the right reasons, with humility, with your heart as much as your brain."

"In other words, I'm expendable," Teague said.

"You're an unknown," Aurore replied without missing a beat.

"I don't suppose I'm going to get this offer in writing."

"I understand that you need time to consider this. It's not my intent to pressure you for an answer. Why don't we put away the work for the evening, order up some food, and get to know each other better? I promise not to talk shop any more tonight."

"I like to make new friends," Monkey said. "Don't you?"

* * *

The Pacific Ocean was a blank slate under the first light of a clear sunrise.

An attendant stirred in the galley. Teague wondered if he should have slept, but among the collective of shifted corpses that had populated his flight since boarding, sleep felt like a moral failing, or a design flaw. Sleep was proof there was no benevolent creator. What designer would reduce a third of a fragile being's life to helpless unconsciousness? What true parent would force its children to experience, and then lose, a rich paradise of imagination every night? How inefficient. How cruel.

The kindly flight attendant who had kept him supplied with coffee all night emerged from the galley with a tray. "Thought you might want a little early breakfast before we offer it to the others," she said quietly and smiled. Teague thanked her while Monkey cleared the tray table to make room. "Whatever they're paying you, it's not enough," the attendant said, indicating Teague's work. "Or you must love what you do."

Teague was still studying Aurore's seemingly bottomless portfolio, as he had been for days between diligent visits with the Chaiprasits, chats with Bondi in his shop, and a pleasant lunch with Dr. Aromdee. That evening in her hotel room, he and Aurore had talked long into the small hours. She had seemed as reluctant for him to go as he had been to leave. The next day had been uncommonly sunny, and they'd eaten a late lunch on the back patio of an upscale restaurant before she was due at the airport. She hadn't pressed him for an answer, but she'd given him a glimpse at the several seven-figure accounts that would be turned over to him for his expenses and compensation.

"I hope this demonstrates how serious we are about this. And about you," she had said. But he had still asked for time.

Teague wanted to believe that he was doing his due diligence with Aurore's portfolio, his own research into the refugee issue, and his conscience. He wanted to believe that he was making up his own mind and wasn't blindly following Dwight's nudge. He wanted to believe that he hadn't been swayed by the way Aurore challenged him or the way she stirred his libido—and apparently Monkey's, too. He wanted to believe that he was above caring about the money. He wanted to believe in this issue as a cause and not just as an adventure, or a means to an end. He wanted to believe all this so much that he was heading to Seattle to give CDI a few weeks to compete for his services.

There were islands somewhere out in this vast and empty ocean. Centuries ago, the South Pacific islanders had beheld the eastern horizon and, on nothing more than rafts, searched out new land. What had driven them to take those leaps of faith, never knowing what they might find over the edge? How many had perished in the emptiness, unable to locate land?

Teague asked Monkey to call up a map of the South Pacific with historical data. The arrows dead-ended at the great expanse of water east of Polynesia and Rapa Nui. Some need had driven people across the ocean, unbounded by longitude. How many had paddled into that sunrise with courageous hope? And how many had been lost in that void?

As Teague began to eat his breakfast, he had an ugly thought. What if they'd been forced to leave? Might they have been outcasts, too unconnected for the favor of the elite or the royal, unfortunate enough to have been born in a time of want, too poor to say no, too weak to do otherwise? They might have been given a turn of the moon to build a raft, allowed to trade for supplies with their daughters or meager possessions. Perhaps a holy man would bless their launch in a hollow pretense that their expulsion was actually the will of the gods. Their disappearance over the horizon might have been as final as death for those who remained. Teague had no basis for this hypothesis, though in the long history of human cruelty, it made more sense than the idea of courageous exploration for its own sake.

CHAPTER 25

There are so few heroes in our history—and too many villains. What kind of legacy is that for a people?

JANUARY 2094

"This is crazy," Teague muttered as he shivered in the pre-dawn outside his building's front entrance. It was less than half an hour since Monkey had woken him to answer the incoming call.

"There will be a car at your building at four thirty," Jens Persson had announced. His voice sounded distant, as if transmitted over a satellite relay or two. "Dress for the field."

"The field?" Teague had asked blearily.

"The field, Mr. Werres. Where you wanted to go?"

"Now?" Teague had asked, but the line had gone dead.

"We don't have to go," Monkey had said.

"Yeah, we do," Teague had replied. Teague supposed that his winter coat, khaki pants, and sneakers would have to suffice for any climate. At the last minute, he'd stuffed a windbreaker and sunglasses in his backpack with his screen and extra socks. It wasn't winter everywhere in "the field." But, Shakiro Squirrel, it was colder than space out here.

A late-model Audi sedan with tinted windows arrived at four thirty. The driver lowered the passenger window and said, "Mr. Werres? Mr. Persson sent me." Teague opened the door, and

Monkey bounded into the car. The driver sneered and began to speak.

"He's a Zubot. I need him," Teague said firmly.

They probably hadn't been expecting a boy with a toy. *Let them think what they want,* Teague thought. *Let them all underestimate me.* Teague clenched his hand to keep from shivering—or was it trembling?—as he shut the car door.

Teague had lasted less than a week in Seattle before tendering his resignation to CDI. He'd flown straight to Geneva, Switzerland, working his obligatory last two weeks for Valdosky remotely and more distantly than he had from interplanetary space. Aurore had installed him in a modern, furnished high-rise apartment many blocks away from hers and the SJDC offices, but with a spectacular view of the mountains.

For three months, Teague had spent his days exercising and studying the volumes of information and data that Aurore delivered nightly. Every evening, she had tutored him, teaching him everything he needed to know about the state of the world's refugees, the convention, the inchoate colony placement agency—nicknamed the Angel program—and the relevant law, true economics, and real politics of it all. They'd spent hours and hours fine-tuning Teague's refugee community assessment tools according to Aurore's formula. And after the first couple of weeks, she'd begun to sleep over, teaching very different kinds of lessons tangled in the dark sheets of Teague's king-sized bed.

His body had soon forgotten its weakness. Dwight had promised that Teague would learn how the world really worked, and he seemed to have kept up his end of the bargain. Teague hoped he could keep up his.

The SJDC had reached its goal of 170 signatories to the convention in mid-December. Teague hadn't attended their celebratory reception, but that night Aurore had come to him.

"You did it," he'd whispered to her in the dark.

"Yes. And that means it's time for you to get to work."

"I feel ready," Teague had said, wanting to believe it.

"You're ready," she'd said, and kissed him. The next morning she'd turned the expense accounts over to him. He hadn't seen her since. He understood, though. It was time to work.

In retrospect, it had been alarmingly easy to find a UN official who took bribes. There were only a handful who could both secure access to the camps and who also made major purchasing decisions. So Monkey had combed through their lives. Where did they vacation? What did they drive? Where did they send their kids to school? Did they own their homes? Had they bought big-ticket items that they shouldn't have been able to afford?

Jens Persson was one of the six regional directors for the Operations Division, in charge of the Africa Bureau. In person, his skin was darker than the Scandinavian complexion shown in his photos, and tightened as if by sun and work. He had thinning, almost colorless hair. Vanilla had frozen him in his late forties or early fifties. Every day, he commuted into Geneva from a modestly sized but luxuriously appointed home in a trendy burg a few kilometers from the city.

Teague had watched Jens participate in a panel discussion for an auditorium of wannabe diplomats at a university. Jens had held the audience rapt as he described the accomplishments and challenges of managing refugees in one of the most troubled zones of the world. As he spoke, Teague had almost forgotten his own intent. It was easy to see why Jens had risen so high in the organization: He cared. He didn't just ride his desk and adjudicate staff meetings. He regularly met with individual refugees. He'd helped build shelters, had distributed food, and had volunteered in medical clinics. Teague doubted that the students had cared more about Africa than any other region, but Jens's passion was a tonic in a room full of people devoted to making a difference. It seemed impossible that he was dirty, but Teague had seen the evidence.

Monkey had traced odd cash transfers from supply contractors and soon uncovered a series of substantial accounts. Did Jens have some expensive habit? Some secret perversion? Or was he preparing for an endless retirement like Bondi? Teague wanted to hope that Jens—like himself, perhaps—was exploiting his access to the Operations Division's 1.4 billion uno annual budget for some long-term good.

But it didn't really matter. Teague had researched him, watched him—and had finally introduced himself. That was less than twelve hours ago.

After a silent drive across Geneva, they pulled to a stop at a vehicle access gate at the service end of the airport. Monkey hopped on Teague's lap to observe as a guard scanned the vehicle with a handheld device. He waved at a tight-leashed German shepherd as it towed another guard around the car. Soon the barricade lifted and a guard waved them through.

The driver followed the lanes on the wide tarmac to an unmarked hangar. Floodlights illuminated a midsized passenger jet parked outside. Only the tailfin bore any markings—the block-lettered initials "UN" and an alphanumeric registration.

A strong breeze whipped at Teague's jacket as he got out of the car and hustled to the plane with Monkey at his side. A crewman in a rumpled uniform met them at the base of the portable stairs. "You Werres?" he shouted over the engines. "Nab a seat and buckle up. We're departing immediately."

The jet's interior appeared to have accumulated more operating hours than the exterior. Stainless steel trim had lost whatever shine it once had. Carpet had been worn to the backing. There were about twenty rows, with four stained and threadbare seats apiece.

The crewman closed the door, quieting the cabin as Teague sidled down the center aisle. Five other passengers lay in various undignified states of shift sleep, mouths open, hair mussed, blankets slipping to the floor, but Jens was not among them. The plane began to taxi as Teague buckled himself in, and a few minutes later they were in the air.

"Can you figure out where we're going now?" Teague asked.

"Please. I'm so much smarter than the computer that flies this plane," Monkey said. Teague unpacked his screen and found a map already loaded. A little jet icon was following a dotted line from Geneva heading southeast over France, across the Mediterranean and the width of Algeria.

"Mali?" Teague asked, zooming in.

"There's a UN airbase at a town called Kidal," Monkey said. "That's where the UN is currently operating—"

"The Mali Northeast IDP Center," Teague said. Teague dropped the screen on Monkey's seat. The jet banked south, and the first rays of the day's sunlight streamed in over the clouds.

"Is something wrong? Don't you want to go to the Mali Northea—?"

Teague had been expecting days if not weeks of delicate negotiation before he ever got this far. And *he* was supposed to supply the destination. "I'm so not prepared for this," he said. "Do you have good Uni-Fi here?"

"Yes, and I found a neat little back door to the UNHCR networks," Monkey said.

"I knew I brought you for a reason."

"I like to help."

They were high over water when Teague looked up from his work, his attention caught by movement at the front of the cabin.

"Stay here," Teague said, unbuckling.

"Oh, hello. Thought you'd be long shifted," the crewman said when Teague knocked on the galley entrance.

"Is there any food?" Teague asked. The crewman opened a cabinet stocked with MREs and told Teague to help himself.

"Here's another community that fits your criteria," Monkey said when Teague returned to his seat with several packs and a travel mug of steaming coffee.

"Tell me," Teague said, tearing open a pack of what the label said was beef stroganoff.

"They arrived at the camp sixteen weeks ago," Monkey said. Maps and a set of UNHCR files popped onto Teague's screen. "Agricultural economy, but the town provides many professional services. Occupations include schoolteachers, mechanics, shopkeepers, and other businessmen, but most of them are farmers like the others." It had become apparent early in Teague's research that Malians still subsisted on small farms with livestock. A few dozen years of vat-grown meat hadn't yet supplanted a few thousand years of tradition. "This town is farther north than the others. Almost in the arid zone, in the southern arable part of the cercle of Tombouctou."

"Timbuktu? You're kidding," Teague said with his mouth full.

"Is that bad?" Monkey asked.

"I never knew Timbuktu was real."

"*Tombouctou*," Monkey corrected. "It's both a city and a cercle, a state."

"I see that now. What's the profile's population?"

"About twenty thousand. Almost eight thousand IDPs have registered at the camp from this location. They fit the ethnic and religious parameters. I've scanned their interviews. They report the same kind of violence and selective oppression as the others."

"That's five good candidates," Teague said. "Plug them all into the assessment spreadsheets. I'll pick one later. Now I need to figure out what I'm going to say to these people."

"Arid" was not a strong enough word for the land into which they were descending. The late-morning sun was doing its worst on the few scrubby plants. Streams of sand slashed and whirled across the surface.

The first signs of civilization were groupings of clay brick huts the same color as their surroundings. The first sign of modernity was a cluster of antennas and satellite dishes near a clutch of metal buildings at the end of a dust-strewn vehicle track. As the rough ground grew nearer, it occurred to Teague that there might not be a paved runway. He gripped the armrests, even as Monkey whooped and bounced with the turbulence. Space dockings had never been this terrifying.

The wheels touched with a jolt. The wing flaps strained skyward, and the engines screamed. They raced past hangars, warehouses, and another communications array before finally settling onto the landing gear. They soon slowed, turned, and taxied back toward the buildings. The other passengers began to wake. A man in a turban and a T-shirt with a medical insignia rushed past toward the restrooms.

When they had stopped and the door was opened, whatever

humidity they had brought with them from Switzerland was sucked away in an instant. Gusts shook the plane, and sand spattered against the fuselage. Teague unzipped his backpack. "Get in," he said.

"Do I have to?" Monkey whined.

"This is no fit place for a Zubot," Teague said.

A few moments later, Teague ducked into the oven-hot wind and found Jens waiting for him at the base of the stairs wearing wide, mirrored sunglasses under the brim of a UN-logoed baseball cap. His blue, UV-resistant shirt riffled over a pair of rugged cargo pants and heavy boots.

"Welcome to Kidal," Jens shouted over the wind and the still-whining jets.

"Thank you. I think," Teague shouted back. He shouldered his backpack, now heavy with Monkey, and followed Jens across the blistering airstrip. Jens held up five fingers to a helicopter pilot as they passed.

The inside of the hangar provided no relief from the heat, only from the brightness and the wind. Two blond UN soldiers with tanned faces and body armor were waiting near the door with their blue helmets tucked under their arms. They had stubby but complex machine guns slung behind their backs and handguns strapped on their hips. Jens spoke to them in what sounded like his native language. One of the soldiers looked Teague over and walked out. As he left the hangar, another person entered. This new man wore a desert-brown uniform with the insignia of the African Union. He sported a burgundy beret but no weapons or armor.

"Djamel," Jens said by way of greeting.

"This is him?" Djamel asked, inspecting Teague and seeming not to like what he found. His accent was a blend of Arabic and French.

"This is him," Jens said, and then nodded at Teague. "Let's you and I talk."

Sand crunched under their feet on the concrete floor as they crossed the empty hangar. At the far corner, they rounded a rack of dusty mechanical parts, and Jens led the way into a disused plywood-framed office.

Teague sloughed off his backpack and set it on an old metal chair. "Care to tell me what I'm doing here?" he asked.

"Isn't this what you wanted?" Jens asked. "To come to the camps? Talk to people?"

"Not like this," Teague replied.

"Perhaps I misunderstood your urgency," Jens said, and then laughed. He pulled out his mobile and began to study the screen. "Werres, Teague. Born in Bangkok, Thailand, far too short a time ago. Attended Agnus Dei University on a scholarship. Returned to Earth a few months ago, quit a desk job with Valdosky, and now lives in a very expensive apartment in Geneva. Pays his bills on time and no criminal record. Does that sound about right?"

"That's me," Teague replied.

"So who are you working for?"

"Like I said yesterday, I'm an independent agent with specific interests."

"Bullshit," Jens said.

"I don't know what else to tell you," Teague said.

"And all you want to do is talk to people in my camps."

"That's right. All over the world, with as low a profile as possible. But in the future, I need to say when and where."

"But today, you get to see that I can deliver," Jens said. "I, in turn, witness that you have real business and that you're not endangering our mission. You also prove to me that you have the resources. I will be asking for a down payment on future visits before you leave today."

"How much?"

"One hundred thousand unos."

Teague forced himself not to blink. "But this one's free?"

"I wanted you to see the reality of what you are asking."

"And if I don't live up to your expectations, I get to walk back to Geneva?" Teague asked.

Jens laughed. "If I thought for a minute that you weren't for real, you wouldn't even be here. We're just establishing trust."

"Then why don't we just take care of that down payment now?"

"As you wish." Jens began to tap into his mobile. "I assume you have the ability to authorize such a transaction from here."

"I do." Teague unzipped his backpack, and Monkey popped his head out.

"Hello," Monkey said.

"What the hell is this?" Jens asked.

"Monkey, please transfer one hundred thousand unos to Mr. Persson's account."

"I recommend breaking it into five scheduled installments over the next twenty-four hours to remain under the regulatory thresholds," Monkey said.

"Is that acceptable to you?" Teague asked Jens.

Jens nodded. "Clever animal. My grandson has one of those, some pot-bellied pig thing, but…" He chuckled. "You're a piece of work. If nothing else, I'm just curious to see where this goes."

"Are we good here?" Teague asked, zipping Monkey back in the pack.

"I think we have an understanding," Jens replied.

Jens led him back across the hangar to where the soldiers were waiting. "Teague, this is Captain Poulson. He and Lieutenant Larsen are your security retinue. Major Belloumi is your translator." Teague shook their hands. "Djamel knows more about the Malian situation than almost anyone."

"Who do you want to meet today?" Djamel asked. "Mr. Persson has given me few details."

Teague opened a file and turned his mobile for the major to see. "Leaders who can speak for the refugees from this community," he said.

"Niabandala?" Djamel asked.

"Do you know it?"

"What is your business with these people?"

"I have a proposal for them," Teague said. Djamel looked questioningly at Jens.

"What proposal?" Djamel pressed.

Teague swallowed. "A resettlement proposal."

"To where?" Djamel asked.

"That's between me and them."

"He wouldn't tell me either," Jens said.

"Why these people?"

"They were the best fit for a variety of demographic and economic criteria," Teague replied. "At least at this camp," he added with a glance at Jens.

After a few moments, Djamel said, "Dome Sixteen."

"Kid wants to go to Dome Sixteen," Jens said to the group.

Teague pushed back out into the sun and wind, third in line. Sand peppered his face. The helicopter whined to life. With frightening suddenness, an enormous cargo jet roared over the runway, dwarfing the jet he'd just arrived in. Its wheels skidded and smoked on the hardened earth. Dust swirled in its wash and obscured it from sight.

The lieutenant returned and thrust a clunky bundle against Teague's chest—a worn pair of military-issue boots. "This is no place for trainers," Jens shouted.

Teague climbed aboard the helicopter, stowed his pack in a bungee mesh, and kicked off his shoes. Jens tossed them to one of the ground crew. Teague decided to accept that he'd never see them again even as he pushed his feet into the boots. The leather and soles were stiff, but they had a supportive liner. They were slightly loose, but Teague felt safer, and a bit more ready. A crewman shut the door, quieting the interior from the wind, but not from the engine. Jens indicated a headset on the bulkhead.

"Thank you," Teague said to Jens and the lieutenant, once he got the headset situated.

"Don't thank us yet," Jens said.

The helicopter lifted off and banked low over the hangars, turning east, away from the airstrip. They flew low over a collective of dusty structures and then rose over an ancient and haphazard town grid of potholed streets sprawling between barren hills. The few modern buildings rose only three or four stories. As the helicopter gained altitude, the sun glinted off rooftop solar panels and satellite dishes.

"You know what's been happening in this country?" Jens asked.

"The basics," Teague replied. "Marius Okone crafted the coup, which he dubbed a revolution, but which most Malians opposed. He's managed to turn a struggling but relatively successful republic into a ruin."

"Straight out of *The Economist,*" Jens replied. "The man is a monster. He staged his coup on the back of a young, addicted, and uneducated military. He's filled their heads with ethnocentric propaganda and set them loose like a plague."

"Okone is Mande, specifically Bambara, the largest ethnic group in Mali," Djamel said. "Mali has long been a country of many peoples, and during the last fifty years of relative peace, members of all groups spread throughout the country. Okone now drives those minorities out of their homes by policy and repression."

"Or murders them," Jens added.

"But the IDPs remain in Mali?" Teague asked.

"The African Union has negotiated a line in the sand," Djamel said. "Okone never had much interest in northern Mali—"

"Except for the revenue from the Taoudenni solar farms," Jens added.

"Despite the sanctions, Okone is content to let the UN and the AU care for the refugees. In fact, he prefers it. While his people remain within the borders, the AU is unable to intervene militarily."

"He's turned our facility into a gulag," Jens said.

Past the city, the helicopter followed an ancient dry riverbed south for several kilometers and then turned southeast. Teague's ears popped as they began to rise over a rugged hillside approaching a rough ridge. As they crested the ridge, the sight took Teague's breath. The land dropped away to a wide valley floor, but the desert had been replaced by something impossible and alien, a bloom of colossal, shimmering domes, each almost a kilometer in diameter. It was as if the earth itself had blistered from a chemical burn.

"In a country of twenty million," Jens said, "thousands have died, and there's a million living here, in the desert."

The helicopter banked to make a wide circle around the facility. The domes were connected by tunnels, each wide enough for several trucks. Expansive tarmacs had been laid outside the gates of the outer domes, each connected to a freeway-sized dirt ring road. Hundreds of people were milling around a convoy of trucks lined up on one of these tarmacs. An immense solar generation site had been erected on a nearby hillside, but it didn't look nearly large enough to supply a million-plus people with even a modicum of power. On the far side, titanic construction equipment scraped the ground, outlining the foundations for a new dome, while meters away on the other side of a fence, only a pencil line from this height, waited a city of white tents. "They arrive faster than we can build," Jens said. "That'll be Dome Twenty-three."

Dozens of gargantuan bladders had been arranged on the top of a flat bluff, like a pod of beached whales. Long, white pipes, supported by concrete buffers, ran down a hillside to an array of portable water treatment plants. A serpentine queue of tanker trucks traced an access road out of sight around the domes.

Three-quarters of the way around the facility, the helicopter landed on a concrete pad a few hundred meters from a dome wall.

"Good luck," Jens said.

"You're not coming?" Teague asked as the lieutenant opened the door.

"Not today."

Teague gathered his pack and followed the soldiers, crouching low through dust-choked wind until he was more than clear of the rotors. The helicopter lifted off before they reached a small motor pool. Teague got in the back seat of a surprisingly new SUV and slammed the door against the wind. Djamel got in next to him. The two UN soldiers took the front seats, the lieutenant behind the wheel.

"A few rules..." Djamel began. Teague had heard Aron and Rob talk about domed cities, but as the car sped toward the tunnel that jutted from the wall of the colossal bubble, he began to revise all his assumptions. Domes were not just stadiums or glorified tents, but were worlds unto themselves. An outer door lifted at their approach and revealed an airlock long enough for them to pass through without decelerating and wide enough for several cars. "...stay with your escort at all times. Do not speak to persons you are not authorized to speak to. Do not offer promises on behalf of the UN, the UNHCR, the AU, the Red Cross, or any other operating agency. Do not give gifts or any object of value, including cash—paper or electronic. You have been authorized to provide information only."

The inner door of the lock lifted and admitted them to the dome. The ceiling was a stripe of white at the top of a canyon of chain link fence six or seven stories high. Behind the fences, monochrome gray plastic bricks, like oversized Legos, had been stacked into massive tenements. Silhouetted figures milled in the apertures of the units. Children rushed to press their faces to the fence or to chase alongside the incoming vehicle.

"Each dome has six wedge communities like this. Simple internal partitions for family units. Each zone has central sanitary facilities and centralized food distribution," Djamel said. "Each community is designed to hold up to ten thousand people. That's about sixty thousand per dome around a central core of services, as you'll see in a moment."

These people were out of the elements. There were no fetid heaps of garbage, no mud or blowing sand. But even without squalor, it was sad beyond words. "It's like a prison," Teague said.

"More than you know," Djamel said. "There is little for these people to do. Crime is epidemic. The very few that can shift for work do so at the risk of being victimized."

"Killed?" Teague asked. The idea of being killed while in shift had always struck him as gruesome. The body helpless, separated from the mind but for a tenuous link, the mind vaporous without its physical essence.

"Sometimes," Djamel said. "Theft is more rampant. We provide guarded shift facilities, but people are often loath to leave loved ones, possessions, and the few square meters they have."

"Especially the women," Captain Poulson added.

The SUV turned from the canyon onto a service road that circled around a fenced central core where young men were playing soccer on a field of smooth dirt. Two large tents, one bearing a red cross and the other the emblem of the Universal Treatment Service, dominated the plaza. Dozens of smaller tents and structures cluttered the expanse. Long queues snaked out of most of them.

"Do people know what it's like before they get here? They have a choice, don't they?" Teague asked.

"If they cross the border and are caught, they will be returned. Mali's neighbors have no ability to absorb this crisis. And most of the people from the South are not prepared to survive in the northern desert. But the doors are always open if they wish to leave."

The SUV turned again into another chain-link canyon toward the dome wall. They passed through a service tunnel into another dome, crossed that dome, and then entered a third.

"Sixteen, sir," Captain Poulson said to Djamel. They turned onto another central ring road and passed two wedges. Under the pedestrian bridge connecting the third wedge to the central core, they entered a low-ceilinged lot where residents were unloading sacks from a flatbed bot.

The air outside the car was uncomfortably still. The plastic structure boomed and creaked, vibrating with the sound of distant life.

A guard buzzed them through several security gates to the bottom of a flight of wide stairs. A shirtless boy, no more than four years old, stared down from the top. "Third level," Djamel said to Lieutenant Larsen, who took point. Djamel followed, then Teague, in front of Captain Poulson. The boy ran away. Several levels up, they reached a large green numeral three. Residents stared as they passed along the low, dim corridors, moving only to clear a path. Conversations ceased.

When Djamel finally stopped and knocked on a canvas-curtained doorframe, Teague tried to smile at the nervous onlookers. An elderly man peeked around the curtain, and Djamel asked him a question. The curtain was drawn aside by another man with a pockmarked face, a gnarled nose, and a distinguished felt of graying hair. He spoke with Djamel for several minutes, both of them glancing frequently at Teague. After the man and Djamel appeared to come to some agreement, the man summoned two boys from inside the room. He gave them instructions, and they scurried off through the gathering crowd. The soldiers urged people to disperse, even as the man invited Teague and Djamel inside.

The square room was furnished with a pair of air mattresses and overturned plastic crates that served as stools around a palette table. If the inhabitants owned any electronics, they had been hidden. Worn luggage had been piled in a corner. Clothes hung on a line over the mattresses. An elderly woman in a headscarf was sitting on a crate.

Djamel said, "I told them who you are and that you have a proposal for the refugees from Niabandala. He has sent for others he believes should be present."

"Who is he?" Teague asked.

"He was the principal of a school. A much respected man."

"I don't see many young men around," Teague said.

"No," Djamel replied, shaking his head.

Others began to arrive, filing in reluctantly past the soldiers, finding seats on the mattresses or the floor or leaning against the walls. Teague unzipped his pack to get his screen, and Monkey poked his head through. "Can I come out?" he asked. The gathering group began to mutter. Teague noticed a pair of children peeking into the room around the curtain.

"Why don't you go play with those kids in the corridor?" Teague said. "But stay right near the door. Near the soldiers." Monkey hopped out, and the children gasped.

Monkey scampered over, stood on his hind legs, and saluted the guards.

"What's this?" the captain asked.

"He's okay, but please keep an eye on him," Teague said.

After more than a dozen people had squeezed in, the principal signaled that they were ready. Djamel greeted the group and introduced Teague.

"Can you ask them to introduce themselves?" Teague asked. Reluctantly, they went around the room, and Djamel translated. The principal had gathered a restaurant owner, a farmer, a mechanic, a retired government bureaucrat, a manager from an agricultural co-op, and several others. Halfway through, a young woman wearing a colorful headscarf slid in around the curtain. She didn't introduce herself.

On the plane, Teague had cobbled together a presentation half-stolen from CDI materials and from a few documents the council had prepared for the Angel project. He'd barely had time to assemble the words, let alone rehearse them. Djamel might smooth out his breaking speech, but sweat and stammering needed no translation. Teague glanced often to the young woman as he attempted to explain the possibilities of a community of their own, the life, and the opportunities that were theirs for the asking. He showed them pictures on his screen as he attempted to outline the basic package: transportation, construction, training, the supplies and resources, the guaranteed haven on the nearest major gravity well to raise their children, the corporate partnerships for jobs. The group stared as if he were insane.

Finally, he showed a CDI marketing video made at the Brazilian church's facility that Monkey had stripped of its logos. It was probably best experienced in shift, not on a shaky handheld screen. The camera soared over the surface of the asteroid, floated through corridors and public malls, and panned spacious apartments with galactic views, all to a soundtrack of heavenly music. Content colonists conferred in classrooms and consulted together in a clean but complex physical plant. Smiling residents labored casually with bots in a greenhouse, played wallyball in a recreation zone, and contemplated the heavens through crystalline windows. As the music swelled, a couple in pressure suits joined hands on the edge of a crater facing the distant sun.

The video faded to black, and Teague put his screen down. The citizen leaders of Niabandala stared at Teague for several moments, then slowly seemed to realize that he was done.

One man eventually spoke. "They want to know if you are making some sort of joke," Djamel said.

"Absolutely not," Teague replied. Djamel relayed Teague's answer, but he spoke for much longer than seemed necessary. "What did you tell them? All I said was 'no.' "

"I informed them that I am only an interpreter and that the African Union does not endorse this—this proposal."

Several people began to speak at once, and Teague longed for a breeze from the inadequate vent in the ceiling. He hadn't earned their trust. He never should have shown them the video.

"They are confused," Djamel said. "They have no money. They want to know why you expect them to consider this. I'm sorry, but they think you are mistaken."

"You don't need money, and I'm not a salesman. I'm simply here to tell you about a new opportunity that's never been available before," Teague said. He let Djamel translate. "The video I showed you is of a real place, but truthfully, most asteroid colonies are not like that, at least not at first. They are isolated and sometimes difficult places to live. But they are safe and can be a new home." Teague scanned their faces as Djamel translated, but their expressions did not improve.

Djamel took another question. "He wants to know if you have ever lived in such a place."

"I lived in space for four years, including two years on Agnus Dei, an asteroid station near Gateway Three." No one seemed much comforted by this.

The co-op manager—or was it the mechanic?—broke in, and Djamel translated. "Why should they leave Mali? Leave Earth? Some still have family in Niabandala and elsewhere. Okone could be gone tomorrow, and they would return home."

"He might be," Teague replied. "But Okone takes Vanilla, and so does his army. He might be president for one year or five hundred. But what has he left you? You will have to rebuild everything. I understand that it's difficult to leave a home, but how long are you willing to wait here for an opportunity that may never come? And when peace and normality do get restored, you will have established a connection for Niabandala to the greater solar system, with economic and educational benefit for everyone." Djamel paused, then translated.

A man stood, glaring at Teague. He barked a brief rebuke to the others and left, slamming the curtain aside. Djamel didn't translate. The farmer asked a more polite question.

"They ask if this is another UN camp," Djamel said.

"The UN provides money for your community to resettle, but

the settlement is yours to govern, under certain criteria. Once you apply for asylum to the UNSA, the only requirement is a willingness to learn and work," Teague said.

"Surely easier said than done," the woman in the headscarf said in heavily accented English. All eyes turned to her.

"Certain minimum standards must be met, yes," Teague replied.

"Would we qualify?" she asked.

"The way the resolution reads, the UNSA's criteria are much more open than most national standards. And you can apply collectively."

"And what of our citizenship? Our rights as Malians?" she asked.

What rights? Teague thought, but bit the comment back. "It's true that you would no longer be Malian. You would become citizens of the UNSA, with all the accordant rights." Teague saw something in her expression—not agreement, but that they shared a common way of thinking, or perhaps just that they might be friends under different circumstances.

The captain ducked in and said, "It is time for us to leave." Children's laughter drifted in as if it had never been heard here.

Djamel addressed the group, and they began to rise from their cramped seats, most shaking their heads. The principal asked another question. "He asks if you are making this offer to any others."

"Not today," Teague replied.

"Why Niabandala?"

"I researched several communities, but Niabandala won out by being the most educated," Teague replied.

"Is this flattery?" the principal asked through Djamel. The woman in the scarf joined them and looked earnestly at Teague for an answer.

Teague kept his attention on her even as he answered the principal's question. "No, sir. It's fact," he said. "Do you have an eddress where I can forward you the details about the asylum application process?"

"No," the principal replied.

"I do," the woman said, "but I have little Uni-Fi access here."

"I'll send it anyway," Teague said. "Can you please make sure everyone gets to see it? I urge you to research this."

The woman hesitated and then, with a cautious glance at the open curtain, snuck a mobile out of her sleeve. "I can make no promises," she said. Teague thanked her when her eddress appeared on his mobile.

"It's time we left," Djamel said.

The soldiers had kept the growing crowd of bystanders well back from the principal's door. A few meters away, Monkey was leaping in time over a ragged soccer ball in the middle of a circle of about twenty children, clapping and chanting a rhyme in a local language.

Teague turned back to the principal and the woman. "Djamel, please tell them that I will not be back. It's up to them to take action from here." They acknowledged the message, but it seemed to Teague that they wanted only for him to stop drawing everyone's attention.

"The helicopter is on its way," the captain said.

"Monkey, it's time to go," Teague called. Monkey waved, said goodbye in several dialects, and then trotted over to be zipped back into Teague's pack. The children made to follow them but were rebuffed by the lieutenant.

Teague didn't look back.

The helicopter was waiting with rotors spinning. Teague had almost forgotten the stinging wind and blinding sun. He boarded, strapped in, put his headset on, and closed his eyes until they lifted off. He opened them again to find Djamel glaring at him.

"What?" Teague asked.

"You should not have come here. These people have significant problems that cannot be solved with science fiction."

"It's not science fiction," Teague said.

He felt a yawning pit of failure in his gut. It was so easy to solve the world's problems in fancy restaurants, five-star hotel rooms, and cosmopolitan apartments, but such talk hadn't survived the ugliness of the real world. He hadn't expected these refugees to sing for joy at his message, but the more he remembered their bewildered stares, he began to wonder if Djamel was right.

But had he failed? He may not have persuaded the people of Niabandala to emigrate, but he had secured Jens's cooperation, and that was critical. Next time he would be prepared, and would enter on his own terms.

At the Kidal airstrip, Teague boarded the jet with a few medical staff rotating out of the field. He fell into his seat and let Monkey free. A few moments later, Jens boarded and scanned the cabin, spotting Teague.

"Djamel told me all about it," Jens said, slipping into the row ahead but facing Teague.

"He told me I shouldn't have come," Teague said.

Jens nodded. He glanced over his shoulder as another person boarded the plane and then turned back to Teague. "I'll have to give asteroid colonies some thought. But if that's what you want to tell these people, it's your money. Unless now you're going to beg a refund?"

"I'm not," Teague said.

"Fair enough. I'll arrange a car in Geneva to take you home."

"You're not coming?" Teague asked.

"I've got work to do here," Jens replied. In the aisle, he turned. "Perhaps next time will be more productive."

"I'll contact you."

Jens smiled wryly. "Keep the boots," he said, and then strode away.

CHAPTER 26

They've named so many places here after you. Lwin Square. Lwin Dome. Stadium Lwin. I know you find this tedious. I told them every time to wait until you were dead, but they wanted so much to honor your name. It seemed so permanent once, this legacy.

FEBRUARY 2094

"Why are you going all the way to Lowell Crater? I thought your family lived in Sinai Flats," the Butler asked as he leaned against the doorway of Rob's office, his lean Martian frame barely blocking the opening.

"I'm meeting a friend," Rob replied, blanking his desk screen and gathering up several stained coffee mugs.

"Why don't you just meet in shift?"

"Sometimes you have to meet face to face." Rob slid past with his mugs.

"Ah. A woman." The Butler spun around to follow. "A new acquaintance or an ex?"

"I'm not responding to that," Rob said, sticking the mugs in the break room sanitizer. He hated to look so transparently human in front of his staff, yet he never seemed to be able to avoid it.

Navid came in and handed Rob a screen. Navid Somani had been hired away from one of the systems subcontractors that had built out the M-SOO data center. He probably knew more about Nexon NAI infrastructure maintenance than anyone on Mars. It was Navid who had dubbed the Butler "the Butler" after a string of mislaid tools, disconnected components, and at least one sandwich left in a cooling node casing. He'd jabbed a thumb at his young associate each time and said, "The Butler did it." Rob had hired the Butler, whose real name was Hunter Noonan, as a systems tech over the objections of HR. He had an innate weakness for lanky losers from the bottom of their MTI classes.

"Don't you have work to do?" Navid asked the Butler.

"I wanted to know why I have to be on call this weekend," the Butler said. Rob scrawled his signature on the invoice on Navid's screen. "Now I need the details about this woman he's going to see."

"I don't think that's any of your business," Navid said, taking back his screen.

"It's my business if I have to work every weekend because she lives out in Podunk Crater," the Butler said.

"You'll work weekends no matter where she lives, if you want a job," Navid said.

Rob chuckled and headed back to his office. He zipped up his backpack, jostled his pocket to make sure he had his mobile, and located his bike helmet.

"You have a good time, boss. We'll keep her running for you." Rob hated it when Navid called him "boss." He didn't think Navid meant it condescendingly, but it reminded him of the unspoken fact that in any other professional scenario Rob would probably be working for him.

M-SOO's new digs were hidden in plain sight among fifty-odd enormous warehouses under the plastic sky of the Pavonis-Southwest Complex. Once outside, Rob strapped on his helmet, popped the ear buds out of his mobile, and tucked them in his ears.

His mobile buzzed on cue, and he accepted the call even as he tugged his bike from the rack.

"Daddy, you left without saying goodbye," Molly said.

"Just giving you an excuse to call." This exchange had become a ritual. In the close quarters of the M-SOO offices, Rob had little opportunity to hear Molly's true voice. So despite Valdosky's stringent security rules, he'd maintained her G-Plex account so he could spend time with her outside the office.

"Good luck," Molly said. "I really hope you get to meet her."

"I'm trying not to get my hopes up," Rob said, pedaling through a swarm of forklift-bots.

He wasn't sure what had prompted Helena to contact him—they hadn't spoken since he'd gotten back to Mars. In fact, they hadn't spoken directly in years. But he had a responsible, if not significant, job now. And eleven-year-old Molly was surely old enough to understand and accept the situation. Perhaps this mysterious meeting was her idea.

"You'll let me know how it goes?" Molly asked.

"Of course," said Rob.

"The Butler just asked me if I know anything about who you're going to see," Molly said.

"Why don't you fake a bunch of minor system errors to keep him sweating all weekend?" Rob said.

Molly laughed. "That would be too funny, Daddy. But I can't do that."

"You're right, you probably shouldn't," Rob said.

* * *

The Homeaway Hotel in Lowell Crater was one of a no-frills, prefab chain tossed up a few steps from almost every train station on Mars, and it was the only place Rob had been able to find a room on short notice. He was not encouraged to find that the lobby was smaller than his office, and the corridors outside the rooms were as narrow as the aisles on the train.

"You in town for the tournament?" the desk clerk asked.

"Visiting a friend," Rob said.

"How nice," the clerk replied as if she had never heard of that kind of thing before. "From Pavonis?" she commented as she retrieved his reservation. "How's the weather been up there?"

Rob's second-floor room was not much more than a single

bed, a narrow shelf, and a wall screen. The minuscule private bathroom was either a marvel of efficiency or a devious psychological experiment. Rob dropped his bag on the bed and called Helena. Outside the stunted, square window, a lone rickshaw driver was napping in the train station's taxi queue.

"I'm here," Rob said when she answered. "It's good to hear your voice."

"You, too. It's past dinnertime. I imagine you're hungry?"

"Starving," Rob said.

Someone spoke to Helena in the background, and she muffled her phone for a few seconds. "Sorry," she said. "Trying to wrap some things up."

"That's all right. When and where?"

"Give me—hold on." More muffled conversation, and then she returned. "Let's say one hour. Percival's Brewpub?" *Textbook Helena,* Rob thought. *I say I'm starving, and she says one hour.* Rob shook off the irritation and decided just to be thankful for time to shower after a long day on the train.

Helena arrived seventy-two minutes later. Alone.

"You look good," Rob said as he accepted a polite hug. He kept an eye on the door, just in case. But did he want to meet his daughter for the first time in a noisy pub?

"You, too," she said.

"No, I mean it. You can't deny it: Vanilla age suits you," Rob said, and signaled the hostess.

Almost every table in the establishment was occupied by a party sporting its team's colors. "The hotel clerk wasn't kidding about a high school basketball tournament," Rob said as he and Helena slid into a deep, padded booth lit by a pair of red Chinese lanterns.

"Where are you staying?" Helena asked.

"The Homeaway," Rob replied.

Helena grimaced. "You should've asked me. My parents stay at a bed-and-breakfast over in Habitat Nine. Cute little place."

"I'm fine. So what's good here?" Rob asked as he took a flexi-screen menu from behind the condiments.

"Nothing. But Lowell isn't the dining capital of Mars. That's the price of working at the institute. How about you? Where are you living now?"

"Pavonis," Rob said. "Didn't you get my message a few months ago?"

"And you're still with Valdosky?"

"Why wouldn't I be?"

"I got the idea it was a temporary thing."

"They bought my start-up and hired me to run it. Why would that be temporary?" Rob asked.

"I just thought…" Helena said, with a little smack of her lips.

"You know, I got this job because of my little weather predictor program. Do you remember that little planet? With all the astronomy being done at ADU, I found a way to make something of all that code."

"It sounds like Agnus Dei was good for you," Helena said.

"It was," Rob said. "Though you know I would have stayed."

"I know."

"How is she?"

Helena smiled perfunctorily. "She's growing up fast. Almost two meters, now. And smarter than I ever was at her age." She slid her mobile from her bag, tapped the screen, and held out a picture of a girl sitting on a trampoline, framed from the waist up.

"Wow. Can you send me that?" Rob asked. Molly was skinny, with long, thin, dusty-brown hair, pulled back into a ponytail. Her wide smile was filled with adorable gaps between her teeth. Rob was surprised to see his mother in her face. Perhaps she shared other Heneghan traits, like a propensity for peanut butter and leaving clothes on the floor.

"She's quite a gymnast, too," Helena said, taking back her mobile. A moment later, the picture popped into his inbox.

"Thanks," Rob said. "Where does she go to school?"

"I didn't contact you to change our arrangement," Helena said.

"Hey, I've done nothing but respect this arrangement," Rob said. "It's an innocent question." It was clear now that he wasn't going to meet Molly. *I should have known.*

Helena nodded. "She goes to an arts magnet school in M-shift. Several of the other institute members send their kids there."

"She's going to get curious about me someday, you know."

"I've never kept you a secret," Helena said.

"What have you told her about me? About us?"

"That we were young and weren't ready to raise her together."

"Did you tell her that it was your decision? I don't want her hating me."

"She's too sweet to hate anybody."

Rob scanned the menu for a moment and then set it down. "I came all the way down here. What *did* you want to see me for?"

"I really didn't expect you to come all the way here, but—not that I'm sorry. I am glad to see you. But I'm getting married, and—"

Their waitress chose that moment to come for their orders. Helena asked for a sandwich named after a local geological formation and a glass of wine. Rob skimmed the menu again. "Do you have fish and chips?" he asked.

"Hand-cut, locally vat-grown cod in our own recipe beer batter," the waitress said.

"Fine," Rob said.

"And to drink?"

"A beer." The waitress began to rattle off a list. "Whatever you brew here is fine."

"A pint or—"

"A big one," Rob said.

"You don't have to be rude," Helena said after the waitress left.

"I wasn't. I just didn't want to hear about fifty kinds of beer. Married? You?"

"It's not to Martin, if that's what you're thinking."

"Who the hell is Martin?"

"I thought you knew about Martin."

"No," Rob said.

"He got me my job with the institute. He's why we moved down to Lowell."

"When was all this?"

"About a year after you left." Rob took that to mean a couple of months, if not weeks.

"You lived with this guy?"

"Until about a year ago," Helena said.

"Did she call him 'Daddy'?"

"Don't be like that. She always knew he wasn't her father."

"So what happened to this *Martin?*" Rob asked.

"He took a teaching position at the University of North Carolina."

"But you can't leave Mars." Rob read between the lines. The jerk had ceased to be a career stepping-stone. "And now there's a new guy. When's the blessed event? Do I get an invitation?"

"It's already happened," she said. Rob bit his tongue. "But we're finalizing things legally, and there's some adoption paperwork."

"Here it comes," Rob muttered.

"I need you to sign a few things to make sure there's no problem for Molly in the future."

"What's the guy's name?"

"Lori," Helena said. Rob considered this for a moment and found himself unsurprised. "She's an amazing person. She loves Molly. We're very happy."

"Where'd you—?"

"She's the research director."

"Your boss?"

Helena shook her head. "My projects are funded and approved independently." Rob raised his eyebrows and wondered if Helena had ever slept with any of her professors. Their drinks arrived, and Rob made a point of thanking the waitress.

"Molly's okay with all this?" Rob asked.

"She stood with us at the wedding. She was lovely."

"Well, what can I say? I'm happy for you," Rob said.

"I hope you are, but I never expected it," Helena said. "I know that what happened was hard for you."

"That's nice of you to acknowledge," Rob said. "I won't say that I've ever understood, but I hope you noticed that I never once made a nuisance of myself all these years."

"I noticed, and I appreciate it." They both sipped their drinks, and Helena tucked her mobile back in her bag.

"I'll sign whatever you want," Rob said. "I want to ask something in return, though."

"What's that?"

"When she's ready and wants to meet me, don't get in her way."

"What if she never wants to meet you?"

"I can't believe in that possibility," Rob said.

"I'm surprised."

"At what?"

"At how much you care," Helena said. "Agnus Dei *was* good for you, wasn't it?" Rob sipped his beer to keep himself from replying. Helena hadn't changed one fucking bit.

Rob awoke to the sound of—was someone dribbling a basketball on the floor above? But something else was wrong. His dreams had been fevered. His sheets were damp. His stomach was roiling. The words "hand-cut, locally vat-grown cod in our own recipe beer batter" reverberated unpleasantly, and he felt a cramp in his gut. He groaned, slipped out of bed, and banged his head on the wall. He cursed and then felt his stomach rise.

Twenty minutes later, back from the microscopic bathroom, Rob curled fetal on the bed. His head throbbed, and his body ached. Basketball players cavorted up and down the corridors. The thumping on the ceiling continued, and laughter bubbled through the thin layer of carpet below.

Abrupt pain and a terrible urgency led to more unspeakable commiseration with the toilet. Each time he felt temporarily purged, he swished water, splashed his face, and returned to bed to hope for the end of all things. The ceaseless barrage of slamming doors, frantic running, and muffled laughter held him hostage. During a brief moment of abdominal peace, he revised his hope, wishing for the end of everyone in the hotel but himself.

Deep in the small hours, once the hotel had mostly quieted, Rob prayed that his periodic bouts in the bathroom would cost someone a championship.

Rob turned his alarm off, shocked to have been asleep at all, or to be in his bed. He'd spent much of the night on the floor, half in and half out of the bathroom. He considered calling the front desk and adding a day to his stay, but the thought of another moment at the Homeaway made him even more nauseated. The dank room smelled like vomit, and the meager bathroom fan only seemed to make it worse. *I could go home,* Rob thought. *Change trains at Oudemans, head out to Sinai, and let Mom take care of me, provided I survive the journey.*

Resolved, Rob staggered into the bathroom once more and found a strung-out junkie in the mirror. He felt both bloated and several kilograms lighter. Hopefully, here at the end of the line, he could score a seat on the train next to the toilets.

A few minutes out of Oudemans, Navid called. Rob almost ignored it, having just returned from a grueling visit to the toilet, but if Navid was calling, he had a good reason.

"Hey, boss. Did I wake you?"

"No."

"You don't sound well."

"I'm fine."

"Are you sure?"

"What's going on, Navid?"

"I hope you're on your way back."

"Why?"

"Dwight Yarrow's office called. He wants to see you, in person, today. I told them you were out of town. But he's already on the elevator."

"Does it have to be me? Isn't this something you or Carl"—the executive VP assigned to mentor Aron—"or, god forbid, Aron could handle?"

"Yarrow's assistant insisted that it be you. I guess it's something technical," Navid said. "Anyway, Carl's up at the shipyards, and Aron's up north for the weekend." Another cramp gripped Rob's bowels. "Are you there?"

"I'm here," Rob said, forcing his voice into normality.

"What should I tell them?" Navid asked.

"If the trains run late, Dwight may have to wait."

"But you're coming?"

"Do I have a choice?"

"You could quit," Navid said.

"You're not going to get my job that easily. Call in the Butler, straighten the place up. Make sure we're executive-ready." Cramp. Nausea.

"Already on it, boss," Navid said.

Rob had barely hung up before he was back in the toilet.

Rob stumbled to the Pavonis station rickshaw taxi queue, shaking from fever cold and reconsidering the merits of death.

"You need to go to the hospital?" the first cabbie asked hesitantly.

Rob gave him M-SOO's address. "But I may need you to stop once or twice along the way," he added.

"No way. I can't have you puking in my cab."

"Please. I'll pay you triple your fare, puke or no puke," Rob begged. A nice line item for an expense report.

Once the driver had been persuaded, Rob found the strength to call Navid.

"Where are you?" Navid hissed.

"Leaving the station now," Rob replied. Every bump and seam in the pavement amplified his headache.

"He got here a couple of minutes ago."

"Does he seem upset?" Navid didn't answer, but Rob heard voices. "Just show them around, and I'll be there soon." He hung up and closed his eyes.

Twenty minutes later, Rob dragged himself up the front ramp of the M-SOO Operations Center, where the Butler was waiting.

"Holy crap, you look like shit," the Butler said, taking Rob's bag.

"Where is he?" Rob asked.

"I don't know, man. It's Dwight Yarrow."

"It'll be fine," Rob muttered.

Navid was pointing something out to two men at the door to

the data center's catwalk: Dwight, in his usual black jacket and turtleneck, and Dwight's assistant. Rob had never learned his name, but he might as well have been Dwight's twin brother. Navid noticed Rob and, as the others turned, his eyes widened with concern.

"Heneghan," Dwight said. "It's about time. I need to speak with you in private."

"My office is…right here," Rob rasped.

"You don't look well," Dwight said once his assistant had closed the door, leaving them alone.

"Some bad fish, I think," Rob said. Dwight made no move to sit. *Don't barf,* Rob told himself firmly. He guessed that the worst he might manage now would be to dry heave in front of the man. Still, not very professional.

"I need something from you," Dwight said. "Your computer, actually." This gave Rob pause. Dwight had used the word "computer" as if it were a new term, or an anachronism. He might have well said "digital tabulating engine" or "mechanical computation apparatus."

"You mean Molly?"

"I need you to establish an original series of fine-resolution prediction reports for all currently colonialized SSSBs, all the recent Xterrex acquisitions, and all future acquisitions," Dwight said.

"We post those reports daily to the CDI servers. I'm sure your office has access to them."

"Perhaps I'm not being clear. I require an independent set of reports, run separately and updated separately."

"Is there a problem with what we're providing to CDI? If it's a matter of resolution, that'll all change with the new full-spectrum surveys and when we begin launching tagging drones."

"This is a simple request, Mr. Heneghan. Will you satisfy me or no?"

"Of…of course. I was just…do you want the same stuff we send to CDI—run separately, of course—or something different?"

"I want as fine resolution as possible," Dwight said. "What can you provide?"

Rob cringed at a twinge in his belly, and then said, "For the Ballistic Cargo Group, we give sixty-second positioning for seven days out, hourly for thirty days, daily for five years. CDI gets the same thing, plus monthly positioning for fifty years. But I have to warn you that until we finish the surveys and fine-tune some of the human-impact data, the reports past about a year aren't—"

"I understand all this quite well," Dwight said. "I want the resolution you are providing for the Cargo Group, but include monthly prediction for one thousand years."

"A thousand years?" Rob asked.

"Is that a problem?"

"I can't guarantee *any* accuracy that far out." Rob was fairly sure he couldn't be held personally liable for predictive data errors, but the language in his contract suddenly seemed weak. His head swam, but he forced himself back into focus. "Can I get this request in writing?" he asked.

"No," Dwight said. Rob sobered. "Provide me this data, or I will find someone else who can." Dwight removed a flat silver object no bigger than his palm from his inside breast pocket. He opened it like a book and withdrew a card marked with nothing but an eddress in silvery ink. "Send the data here."

"This isn't a Valdosky eddress," Rob said.

"No, it is not."

"Then what is it?" Rob blinked, but it seemed to last too long.

"It's the eddress I'm providing," Dwight said. "And one more thing. You will open a socket on your computer for access from this eddress. In case I need to tweak the reports or make my own analyses. Is any of this unclear?"

It smelled like Percival's Brewpub's vat-grown fish. "No, sir," Rob replied.

Dwight strode out, and his assistant fell in behind him. After the outside door had closed far down the hall, Navid poked his head in.

Rob waved him out. "I need a minute. Close the door."

"Sure, boss."

Rob collapsed at his desk. "Did you hear all that?" he mumbled.

"Yes, I did," Molly said.

Rob flexed the business card, feeling for anything electronic. "Do you sense a chip in this?" he asked.

"No. You'll need to input the eddress manually," Molly said. She activated a keypad on his screen. Rob tapped in the characters and then confirmed the parameters Molly had prepared for Dwight's reports.

"And Molly," Rob whispered.

"Yes, Rob?"

"Save an audio record of Dwight's request, and mirror these reports into a folder for me only. Just in case I need to cover my ass someday." A new folder labeled "Just In Case Rob Needs To Cover His Ass Someday" appeared on his desk.

"Okay," Molly replied. "What user level access should I grant to this eddress?"

"What?"

"Mr. Yarrow requested user status," Molly said. "Or did I misunderstand?"

"No, you're right," Rob said with a shiver. His brain had already discarded this appalling idea. "Standard, I guess. Definitely no admin access."

Rob stared until he was shaken by another shiver and a fresh cramp. He called for Navid.

Navid entered with the Butler right behind him. "What was that all about?" he asked.

"I think I need a doctor or something," Rob replied.

* * *

The next afternoon, after the nurses had released him, Rob found Kyle waiting for him in the hospital's lobby. "Why the hell are you here?" he asked.

"Mom insisted," Kyle replied.

"I got too dehydrated, that's all. They only kept me overnight as a precaution."

"You hungry?" Kyle asked.

"I need pancakes."

The red and white diner was bursting with health-care workers and visitors from the medical complex. Rob and Kyle hovered for a few minutes, and then pounced on a booth as two men in scrubs vacated it. Rob fell onto the bench as if it were his final destination. Kyle loaded the dirty dishes on the conveyor belt and swept crumbs off the table with his hand. "Coffee?" he asked.

"Orange juice," Rob replied.

Kyle started their order on the menu screen, including a tap on a video of a steaming stack of pancakes complete with an enormous pat of butter and waterfalling syrup. "So what were you doing in Lowell Crater, anyway?" he asked.

"Visiting Helena."

"Wow. A friendly visit?" Kyle asked with a raised eyebrow.

"Not even close. She just wanted to tell me that she's getting married," Rob said. "To her boss. Apparently, she moved to Lowell with a guy who got her a job there in the first place. Then when he didn't pan out, she traded up. Or maybe she's hedging against future budget cuts."

Coffee and juice arrived on the conveyor. "But why'd you go all the way down there?" Kyle asked.

"Why do you think?"

"Did you get to meet her?" Kyle asked.

"No, but I signed all the documents so that Helena's *boss* can adopt her." Rob slid his juice aside and dropped his head on the table.

"I'm sorry, man. Why didn't you just stay down there if you were so sick?" Kyle asked.

"I was going to go to Mom and Dad's, but then Dwight Yarrow absolutely needed to see me in person."

"What was so urgent?"

"Nothing he couldn't have put in a memo. I really don't like him."

"I didn't think anyone liked him."

"It's more than that," Rob said. "He's actually scary to be alone with. Like he's killed people and wouldn't hesitate to kill you." Kyle scoffed. "I can't explain it any better. You'd just have to meet him."

The food soon arrived, and the pancakes found welcome in Rob's stomach.

"Don't tell Mom or Dad or anyone about this Dwight Yarrow stuff," Rob said after a few bites. "Molly looks like Mom." Rob showed Kyle the photo Helena had forwarded.

"She's beautiful," Kyle said. Rob agreed and took a large drink of his orange juice, hoping to feel whole again soon.

Once finally home and alone, Rob tried to piece together just what had happened this weekend. How had he ended up so wrung out and embarrassed? He'd let Helena walk all over him. He hadn't gotten to meet Molly. He'd acted like an idiot in front of Dwight. He'd made a spectacle of himself in front of his staff. He'd made his mother weep when he'd sent her Molly's picture. In short, he'd been himself. *Time to be someone else for a while.* Rob got ready for bed, donned his shift set, and linked straight to one of the Forum's changing booths. It was an easy choice. His muscular and remarkably well-endowed avatar named Quentin Rox had nothing to be ashamed about.

And there was only one place for Quentin to go.

Everyone, no matter what they said, had a Light District account: every friend Rob had ever had, his brother, his parents—although he refused to think about that—every teacher and professor. Even Gwen, the most asexual person he had ever known, could probably be found on most nights in some obscure alley. Hell, half of them were probably here right now. This is why they'd invented shifting. This is why they'd invented the whole damned Internet.

Rob dropped into his usual spot on the LD's central hub, a pink-edged mash-up of Vegas, Rio, Ibiza, Macau, and Amsterdam, at least as he imagined them. Alluring red and neon pink adverts for some of his favorite sites struck like lightning and settled into orbit just within his reach. Rob hesitated and turned around as if distracted by the hub's other spokes, from infrared to ultraviolet. He had never visited the majority of them—some just weren't his cup of tea, others he downright feared—but he began to stroll toward them anyway. This was just part of the game.

As expected, the ads began to up their antes. Returning customer discounts. Two for one. Real girl avatars, not programs. Bonus club points. Free buzz hits. Their offers never lasted long. So, when the time seemed right, Rob grabbed the most appealing link.

The arrival of Quentin Rox to the black-and-pink lounge elicited a collective gasp of pleasure from the dozen or so female avatars waiting there. A pole dancer spun toward him and licked her lips. Three lovers on a rotating bed paused long enough to beckon him. Two nymphs in glowing lingerie appeared at his side and drew him in. Women at the buzz bar followed his every move with breathy expectation. The first time he'd patronized this place, most of the girls had been Earthlings, but every time after they'd all been Martians. One girl stepped forward and said, "Welcome back to the Peach Pit, *Quen-tin Rox*. We've missed you. I'm Brianna. How can we please you today?" It was nice to be remembered, but the way she said his name, with a slightly less erotic edge, revealed her as software.

Usually that didn't matter, but tonight it seemed weird. He thought he had wanted this, but maybe it was too soon. Maybe he wasn't as recovered as he thought. "I think I'm going to go," Rob said in Quentin's bass voice.

"Oh, we'll be so disappointed." The girls on his arms echoed Brianna's plea. "Do you know about our three-for-one special if you join our loyalty club tonight?"

"Yeah…um…I'm just going to…." He opened up his link list and shimmered away without saying goodbye.

Rob was a little surprised that his access to his brother's studio was still valid after all these years. Kyle had probably assumed that Rob would crawl back to him for a job someday. That had been a pretty safe bet, actually. As he'd hoped, the studio's offices were deserted this late on a Sunday evening. He found the interface and stepped through the portal into the empty construct of the assembly floor.

Rob turned off all the lighting, the grid floor, and the gravity, and then closed the interface. He hung alone as a singular mind on an infinite blank slate for a few moments before opening Molly's photo and blowing it up to life size.

"I'm sorry," he whispered. He'd officially signed away his parental rights. The significance of this had almost been swallowed by the bad fish and Dwight's bizarre requests. Why had he relinquished his last connection so easily? Was he still her father? Rob remembered his original justification: Those documents would be meaningless once Molly turned eighteen or came searching for him. Blood was thicker than digital ink. Wasn't it?

And what did Dwight need with those special reports sent outside the company? Why did he have to come all the way down from orbit and ask in person, and in private? Rob felt like he'd protected himself and Molly, NAI Molly, in case anyone began to ask questions, but he couldn't help but feel as if he was being set up like a patsy.

There was no one to discuss it with, no one who would understand. Except…

Rob opened his messenger, selected her eddress, and then dictated, "Hey Gwen. I had an incident at work yesterday involving Dwight Yarrow that isn't sitting right with me, and I need some advice. Can we meet sometime? Let me know."

Rob sent the message and swept his messenger away. "There, I did something about it," he said to Molly's picture.

Rob began to feel tired, almost heavy. He'd slept in the hospital thanks to the drugs, but the fish and the stress must still be taking their toll. Suddenly an odd, more extreme drowsiness overtook him. He groped to call up the interface, but the link refused to appear. Molly's picture began to stretch, warp, and discolor. And then he fell…

Rob awoke, fully alert and sensing that he'd been in shift sleep for only a few minutes at the most. He was lying under a metal ceiling, tarnished and scarred with age, but he was still shifted. As if to prove it, a pop-up appeared, warning him that he was no longer linked to a public network. *I'm off the G-Plex grid?* Since childhood, the rule had been drilled into his brain: Never go off-grid. Never follow a stranger to any old link. Private shift frames were dangerous places where terrible things happened. His device override should be able to downlink him, but there remained the inchoate fear that it wouldn't work, that the rumors were true, the parental warnings had been justified, and his mind would be held hostage to the torturous whims of the site operator.

A shadow loomed over him. "Who the fuck are you supposed to be?"

Rob sat up quickly. Now he recognized the nasty mustard-colored vinyl shift couch he occupied. It had even been patched with virtual duct tape. Gwen's home at ADU. The private abode she'd carved out of the administrative office of the warehouse in the Agnus Dei fabrication bays had been re-created in every detail, from the sickly light escaping from the bathroom to the dingy safety glass.

"Gwen?" Rob asked. "What's going on?" Gwen was no predatory psychopath—unless she was.

"Be Rob," she said.

"What?" Rob asked, and then realized what she meant. He apologized and shed his Quentin Rox avatar.

"Why were you all…?" She waved her arm with a disgusted scowl.

"Did you just hijack me?"

"So what?"

"You know that's totally illegal. Jail time, plus G-Plex perma-ban."

"It was important," Gwen said.

"You could just have invited me."

"I didn't want to take the risk."

"What risk?" Rob asked.

"I brought you here to tell you that you can never talk to me about Dwight Yarrow again," Gwen said. "Don't mention him in a message. Don't tell me work stories. Don't even use initials or euphemisms. Nothing. Ever."

"Have you gone completely off the deep end? What you're asking doesn't even make sense."

"I know how it sounds, but I'm not kidding about this."

"Why can't I ever mention Dwight Yarrow to you?"

"I won't explain it," Gwen said. "You're just going to have to trust me."

"Can I mention Matthew or Aron?"

"Yes."

"Just not Dwight?"

"That's right."

"And it's so urgent that you had to abduct me?" Gwen nodded. "You act like he's out there listening."

"There's *always* someone listening."

Rob had to laugh. Gwen had always been skittish about Valdosky, but she'd always seemed to have a good reason—not some delusional conspiracy theory. "If someone's always listening, won't they notice that you abducted me?"

"I don't take unnecessary chances," Gwen said.

Through the safety glass, the derelict parts warehouse looked exactly as he remembered it, but something was different. Then he realized that her avatar moved smoothly here, not jerkily or out of sync. He'd never seen her so natural. In fact, when he studied her more closely, he wondered if he'd ever seen so lifelike an avatar.

"Fine. So what did you want to tell me about him?" Rob asked.

"I'm telling you not to talk to me about him. Ever again."

"Have you ever met him?" Rob asked.

"Not exactly," Gwen replied.

"You don't even want to hear what happened?"

"You can tell me here if it'll make you feel better. But my advice is going to be the same. Forget about it."

"Even if it's a really strange, off-the-books request?"

"He'll do what he wants with or without you," Gwen said. "So if you want to keep your job, comply and forget it."

"Just like that?"

"You picked your side."

"But what if he's doing something—?"

"Look. You can worry about this forever, which I guarantee will do you no good. Or worse, you can question his business, which he will not put up with. Or you can forget about it and live your life. I know you better than you think, you transparent fool." She conjured the picture of Molly. "This is her, isn't it? You want to be someone she's proud to call her father? Then, even if you've never listened to me before, heed me now."

After a long pause, Rob nodded.

"Okay, then," Gwen said.

"So…are you doing all right?" Rob asked. "I saw that TataFord showed the Ariel at the Paris Air and Space Show. I looked for you in the coverage."

"I don't need exposure," Gwen said.

"I sent you a congratulations."

"I got it."

"What're you working on now?"

"None of your business."

Rob chuckled. "Promise me something, Gwen. That someday you'll tell me what all this is about."

"I can't promise you anything."

"I'll take that as a yes."

A few minutes later, Gwen showed Rob the way out. He linked to the Forum and pinged to confirm a G-Plex signal, just to be sure.

* * *

"How'd it go with your mystery woman?" the Butler asked the next morning. "Aside from almost barfing yourself to death and all."

"As well as can be expected," Rob said. He'd been trying to put the weekend's disappointments and disasters into perspective since he'd left Gwen and had determined that she was right. He didn't need useless distractions and vague worries. He needed to work hard on M-SOO and be a good manager, but he also needed to make a life. It was time to find a girlfriend, maybe a wife, and focus on becoming a man his daughter would be proud of when the time came for them to meet.

"Yoo-hoo," the Butler said, waving a hand in front of Rob's face. "You sure you should be at work?"

"Tell you what," Rob said. "I'll tell you about it over lunch.

But let's get to work now, okay? I'm sure Navid's got a task list going."

"Yeah, sure." The Butler turned to leave.

"One more thing," Rob said. "I'm not going to call you 'the Butler' anymore. I got to thinking about it, and it's insulting and sets the bar wrong. Anyway, I'm sorry that stuck so long. I'll ask Navid to lay off, too."

"Thanks. But I don't really mind it."

"I know," Rob said. "I just don't want you to start believing it."

CHAPTER 27

The boxers are on their feet now, moving through ritual forms in unison. I believe they intend to fight until the end. All they have left is their bodies and their belief that there's something more we can do to save ourselves.

MARCH–OCTOBER 2094

"He's here," Monkey called from the windowsill. Teague finished cinching the laces of the boots he'd been given in Africa and notched the curtain aside. A mud-splattered UN Land Cruiser was idling in the puddle-strewn parking lot of the little motor inn. Last night's rain had stopped. Across the highway, beyond the rooftops of the village, mist was rising from a forest in the thin morning light. When he'd arrived from Bangkok in the dark last night, he hadn't realized how close they were to the edge of town, and the camps.

Teague checked the zippers on his backpack and tugged on his new rain jacket. Besides Monkey and his pressure suit, this jacket was just about the most expensive thing he'd ever owned. After Mali, Teague had gone shopping for moisture-wicking, rainproof, UV-filtering, bullet- and shrapnel-resistant, field-tested, fully warranted, all-weather gear with endorsements from military and law-enforcement organizations. Each piece was deceptively light—only Jens's milspec boots had the heft Teague had expected.

Teague doubted that he'd ever put the gear's full functionality to the test, but the peace of mind was worth every penny.

Teague answered the knock to find a Thai man dressed not much differently from himself. "Are you Mr. Werres?" he asked.

"Please call me Teague," Teague replied, offering a wai.

"You speak Thai?" the man asked, returning the gesture.

"Some. I was born and raised in Bangkok."

The man's face lit with surprise. *"Bangkok?"*

"My father was...an aid worker serving all of Southeast Asia," Teague said, reverting to English.

"Very well. My name is Songpol Salidapirak. I've been instructed to deliver you to a meeting with Professor Lwin at Camp Three."

Songpol steered them out of the little town in the Land Cruiser, taking them north and west, deeper into the rugged, forested hills and closer to the Burmese border.

In the decades since its revolution, the democratic republic government of Myanmar had done little to improve the openly hateful culture that the military junta had fostered toward the country's minorities during its long entrenchment. And few groups had suffered as much as the Karen people in the southeastern states. In the past few years, a small Karen separatist movement had grown increasingly violent. The resulting conflict had forced a quarter-million people to seek refuge on the Thai side of the border.

"This situation is extremely vexing to Thai officials," Songpol told Teague. "They condemn Myanmar's unwillingness to settle this matter internally and are very concerned about border porosity. The UN fears that Thailand will bring in the military to close the camps if the violence spills over."

It was precisely this pressure that made the Karen people a perfect audience for Teague's message. *You can't go home, but you can't stay here.* "Has the Thai government given the UN a deadline?" he asked.

"Thankfully not yet, but if the situation worsens..."

If the situation worsens? Teague thought as Songpol continued to explain. *The situation always worsens.*

A few days after Teague had returned from Mali, a reporter had set up, microphone in hand, a few dozen meters from a two-story concrete building as it burned out of control. "This is Niabandala," he had begun, "where over the past forty-eight hours, pro-government gangs have killed dozens and set fire to property and vehicles in a surge of ethnic violence. What began as a lawful protest against harsh new national policies became the scene of an alarming and brutal crackdown. Many from this community have already fled to refugee centers in the north, but the few who remained have borne a terrible brunt…" B-roll showed more burned-out structures, smoldering cars, debris-strewn streets, and a telephoto image of blackened, misshapen forms that may have once been a herd of goats. File footage of President Okone rolled as the reporter described a racist land reclamation policy that had sparked the protest. "…the results of which have been nothing short of a scorched-earth campaign against Mali's unrepresented minorities. This is Bernard Shepperton reporting from Niabandala, Mali, for Real Time Networks." Teague had watched the piece so many times in the past two months that he could nearly recite it word for word in the reporter's British accent.

Did they know? Those people he'd met? Had they lived or worked in what was now ash and rubble? Had they known or loved those who remained and were now dead? Teague hated to think that such fresh violence might be the price of persuading them to heed his advice. Truly, what home had they now?

The forest had recently been scraped away on both sides of the unpaved mountain road, widening the way for a growing population of machines. The Land Cruiser overtook trucks on the steep, winding climbs: unmarked semis, water tankers, flatbeds of construction materials. Trucks roared downhill with frightening speed. The worst were the log trucks, laden with teetering loads of timber that rained bark and debris as they barreled southward.

When it seemed to Teague that they couldn't travel much farther before reaching the border, they descended into a shallow valley, cleared of trees. Dozens of trucks were staged in long queues on a broad swath of asphalt. Songpol drove straight across and was waved through a security checkpoint by blue-helmeted guards. On the far side of the valley, they slowed at a T-junction. One direction led to another checkpoint outside a compound of temporary buildings. Songpol turned the opposite way and began to climb back into the forest on a rougher road.

They passed several obscurely marked vehicle tracks before finally veering off at the fourth such branch. They followed these ruts for several minutes until they arrived at a cul-de-sac just large enough for a truck to turn. A fan of footpaths spread up the surrounding hillsides through the countless haphazard structures of a shantytown set amid the thinned forest of tall trees.

Two men in grubby pants emerged from a makeshift guard hut and greeted Songpol, but when they saw that his only cargo was Teague, they lit cigarettes and ambled back inside. Teague urged Monkey into his backpack, slung it over his shoulder, and followed Songpol up a trail into the camp. The cul-de-sac was soon out of sight.

The residents who weren't shifted—which many were, often two to a cot—paid Teague and Songpol little mind. Most of the camp's structures had been built to be semi-permanent, with haphazardly cast concrete slab foundations and plastic brick walls built up several levels, but the moss and weather stains indicated that they'd been there for years beyond their intended life. Misfit insect screens and inexpertly framed tarp awnings had been slapped over the few window openings. Knocked-together huts with plywood floors and ragged tents filled the gaps between the buildings. Electrical wires had been strung between tree trunks and swagged to rooftops. Weather-cased Uni-Fi nodes had been jerry-rigged to about every hundredth tree.

Several boys were playing badminton across a torn strip of plastic tarp in a small clearing. Teague had hoped that there would be young children nearby when he met the professor. If there had been one success in Mali, it'd been Monkey's connection with the kids. Songpol and Teague crested a hill and began to descend a gentle slope, skirting around a queue of residents waiting to collect water from the large tank of a bot on tread tracks. Teague returned a smile from a woman waiting in line with several plastic jugs dangling from a loop of rope.

A few moments later, Songpol turned onto a steep, stair-stepped path that led up to a private clearing overlooking much of the camp in the valley. Near the back of the clearing sat a five-meter-square, three-level structure constructed of the same plastic bricks on a concrete slab as the hundreds of others below. A blue pop-up canopy had been lashed in place on the roof. A stocky man near the door began to speak into a mobile when Songpol and Teague climbed into sight. He wore no uniform, nor any evident weapons, but carried the expression of a bodyguard who took his job seriously. A few moments later, an older man emerged from the building's single doorway and greeted Songpol. He was dressed comfortably, but rather well, considering his surroundings. Songpol introduced Teague. Teague was pleased to finally meet the professor's secretary.

"The professor is finishing some other business. But please, come in."

They removed their shoes just inside, in a sort of kitchen. A small refrigerator hummed in the corner, and two card tables were covered with countertop appliances and packaged foods. The secretary put a finger to his lips and beckoned for them to follow him up the steps on the far side of the room. Upstairs, someone was speaking Chinese.

In a spartan office on the second floor, Professor Lwin—recognizable at once from his photographs—was leaning over a cluttered folding table that appeared to serve as his desk. A mobile on the desk had been cranked to full volume. The professor seemed to be about Thomas's age, and shared his black hair and height, but had a slight and wiry frame. Deep wrinkles caged searching eyes behind his trifocals.

Teague hadn't known of Professor Lwin before he'd begun his research, but he had come to respect the man immensely. Although tenured at a university in Singapore as a young man, the professor had returned to share his people's experience. He'd been a vocal critic of the old military junta from outside Myanmar, and from inside when he safely could. After the revolution, he'd worked for the rights of the Karen people and eventual independence for a Karen state, but also vigorously denounced the separatist violence. He remained at odds with the new republic due to his support for Karen statehood. His refusal to support the separatists' agenda infuriated some, but most of the Karen looked to him as their voice and conscience. Teague scanned the walls for the professor's Nobel Peace Prize but supposed such vanity would have been out of character. Loud, flowery silk shirts were apparently just fine, however.

Teague almost didn't notice when the conversation in the room shifted to English.

"This must be the man with the mysterious proposal," the professor said. He spoke with a thoughtful grace. Songpol nodded at Teague.

"Teague Werres, sir. It's an honor to meet you." He waied awkwardly with his backpack still on his shoulder.

"Welcome. Come sit. There are chairs somewhere." The secretary began to distribute folding chairs from a corner, and soon the little group was seated. "Now, what can we do for you?"

Teague opened his bag to take out his screen. "Can I come out? Are there kids?" Monkey asked in an excited whisper, peeking over the zipper. Teague hushed him.

"What is this?" the secretary asked.

"A speaking lemur?" the professor asked.

"A robot, sir," Teague said. "My computer and assistant."

"By all means, let the poor thing free of his confinement," the professor said with a laugh.

Monkey emerged, stretched, and then settled on his haunches at Teague's feet. "Hello. I'm Monkey," he said.

"Is this to be a circus?" the secretary asked. "The professor's time—"

"The professor's time is his own," Lwin said. "I am an old man and did not grow up with such wonders. Hello, Monkey. I am Professor Lwin. Welcome to Thailand."

"Thank you. I'm originally from Thailand, though," Monkey said.

"You were manufactured here?"

"No, I lived here with Teague almost my entire life."

"Now that is interesting," the professor said, looking to Teague.

"I grew up in Bangkok. My father was an aid worker," Teague explained.

"Not Brian Werres?" the professor asked.

"Yes, sir," Teague stammered." Did you know him?"

"On several occasions I met a Brian Werres who worked with a Christian relief organization. I was very sorry to hear of his passing. During the flooding in 2072, if I recall."

"Thank you, sir. I'm honored that you remember him."

The professor nodded graciously and said, "Very well. What does the son of Brian Werres have for us today?"

Teague cleared his throat and activated his screen. It seemed as if his entire life had been leading to this moment. His parents had played their part. Monkey had had his little role. His life in Thailand. His education. His adventure in space. His time with Aron, Matthew, Dwight, and Aurore. It all had led here.

Two hours had passed quickly, and a drizzly rain had begun to fall. Teague and Songpol walked on the side of the path to avoid the gutter draining down the middle. Teague had made his practiced case for the Karen people to establish their own world. The professor had asked many questions, although Teague couldn't currently recall what they had been. It was Monkey's job to remember that kind of thing. The professor had not responded enthusiastically, yet Teague felt like he'd communicated his message. And he'd left the professor a brand-new screen crammed with as much cross-referenced information as Monkey could muster.

The badminton game had ended, and now the torn tarp hung uselessly across the grassy clearing. Doorways were curtained with dripping rainwater, hiding the residents in shadow. The few people out on the paths hurried by with their heads covered. At the cul-de-sac, people with buckets and containers had lined up in the rain behind a truck where workers were measuring out rice. Teague hoped he had helped these people today.

"It was an *interesting* proposal," Songpol said when they were back in the Land Cruiser and bumping down the track.

"Thank you," Teague said, remembering the African Union officer's disgust.

"It would require an immense paradigm shift. But beyond the obvious logistical concerns, I believe the professor fears any appearance of capitulation."

"Tribal attachment to land is an anachronism," Teague said.

Songpol grunted. "You propose a borderless solution, not a true peace."

"Peace is peace. I'm inviting them to change the rules of the game."

"Is that progress?"

"They can decide that for themselves."

Songpol glanced at Teague, grunted again, and then turned his attention back to the bumpy ruts beyond the windshield wipers.

* * *

The urban galaxy of Geneva streamed past the taxi's windows. Teague's flight had touched down an hour ago, but when he closed his eyes he could still see Angola: children picking through refuse on the side of the road with dogs and gulls, boys brandishing AK-47s likely scavenged from their dead older brothers, huddled families with too few men pulling carts past dead livestock, stacks of billowing smoke on every horizon. The camp itself had been relatively clean and well ordered, but outside the fences, beyond the buffer of UN troops, the country was a strife-ravaged nightmare—at least the part Teague had seen from the helicopters and vehicles. Few buildings and fewer people had been untouched by the conflict.

And yet the community leaders had reacted with confusion to Teague's suggestion that they emigrate. Not revulsion like the people in Mali, more like they'd already surrendered their hope.

Mexico. Suriname. Bangladesh. Egypt and Palestine. Sri Lanka and India. Lebanon. Namibia. Kurdistan. Ecuador. Eritrea and Somalia. Guyana. Four camps in Pakistan. Liberia. Malaysia.

They hadn't all been as distressing as Angola, or as fruitless. But Monkey held an ever-growing queue of over a hundred more communities that were living the same tragic stories in the same sort of impossible conditions.

Teague had to wonder how these camps could even exist on the same planet as this glittering city. How could such suffering be only a short flight away from such prosperity? How had the disparity become so entrenched in this age of Vanilla?

The cab turned onto a street a few blocks from Teague's building and pulled to the curb in front of the bright-green fringed awning of the only establishment on the block still lit. On the awning's trim, rainbow lettering morphed from Thai script to German to French to English reading, "Phuket Garden—Thai Cuisine—Dine-In or Carry-Out." The sidewalk tables and chairs had been stacked and shackled to the wall. The dining room was deserted but for two men at a table near the window. As Teague got out, a bit of Angolan mud flaked off his boot onto the sidewalk to be swept up by the fastidious Swiss bots that roamed the streets day and night. Teague decided to be happy for the moment that places like Geneva existed—and possibly even outnumbered the ugly places of the world.

"Sometimes I think the only reason I come back to Geneva anymore is to do laundry and eat at *Le Jardin Phuket*," Teague said as he opened the restaurant's door and let the familiar aroma waft over him. Monkey usually bounded straight to the pickup counter, where they knew him by name, but tonight he stopped just inside, staring ahead at a woman near the counter.

"What's wrong? It's just another customer," Teague said. Monkey grinned mischievously and sprang forward. Teague called after him. Monkey skittered to a stop a meter behind the woman, and she turned around. Then Teague saw what had drawn Monkey: a plush, gray creature beaming down from inside the hood of the woman's sweatshirt.

"*Bonjour*," it squeaked, clutching at her shoulder. It was a fuzzy thing with dewy eyes, pointy ears, and a bushy tail. "*Je suis Luci.*"

"*Enchanté, Luci. Je suis Monkey*," he replied with a flourish.

The woman smiled, amused, and to Teague said, "*Bonjour*." Her soft, round, freckled face was curtained in tangled curls of strawberry-blond hair, suggestive of a day of work rather than a lack of care. A video of a steaming dish, as unrealistic as the posters in the Chaiprasits' restaurant, was open on the menu in her hand.

"I thought I was the only one who took my Zubot out for Thai food." Teague hoped she spoke English.

The woman laughed. "I almost didn't bring her," she said, her accent thick. "But we just moved in up the street, and she likes to go new places. You must know how that is."

"Oh, I know."

"He is adorable," the woman said, looking at Teague in a way that made him feel oddly transparent.

"*Welcome back, Teague*," a waiter called from the kitchen. "*Your order's ready*."

Teague thanked him.

"You speak Thai? Then you must know what to order," the woman said, waving the menu in mock despair. She let her Zubot—a chinchilla, Teague decided—hop to the floor and then unzipped her sweatshirt, revealing a few curves and a paint-splattered T-shirt emblazoned with an animated Tinker Bell, Barrie's pixie turned bratty, coquettish porn star, or near enough. Monkey and the chinchilla faced each other in silence.

Teague supposed that this woman might be envisioning a serendipitous evening, where he'd help her order and then invite her to eat with him. Their Zubots would canoodle under the table while they sipped imported Singha beer and talked until after closing. But what could he ever tell a woman like this of his life? Every truth would still be a lie by omission.

"Do you like spicy?" Teague asked.

"A little spicy," she replied. Her resulting expression made him regret leading with this question, necessary though it was.

"Then I'd recommend this one, this one, or this one," Teague said, tapping her menu. "But really, it's all good. Best Thai food in Geneva." The waiter arrived with Teague's order bundled in a large sack, and Teague thanked him in Thai. "Good luck. Welcome to Geneva," Teague said to the woman.

"Thank you," she said, almost as a question.

"Say goodbye, Monkey."

Outside, heading toward the apartment, Monkey said, "I think she liked you."

"Maybe," Teague said.

"You didn't want to make a new friend?"

"What about you and that chinchilla? I thought you'd be gamboling or cavorting or something."

"We exhausted our play options very quickly."

"Exactly."

As they rounded the corner to the entrance of Teague's building, Monkey said, "How do you feel about *old* friends?"

"What are you talking about?"

"Aurore's in your apartment."

Teague looked up the glassy face of the building and swallowed. "Has someone finally applied for asylum aid?" he asked.

"No applications have been filed that I'm aware of."

"Huh," Teague said. A few moments later in the elevator, he said, "Be sure and act like you didn't know she was there. And remember to act like a Zubot."

"Clueless mode engaged," Monkey droned in a robotic voice.

Teague opened his door and feigned surprise.

"Welcome back," Aurore said and kissed him.

"What are you doing here?" Teague asked. "Do you have good news?"

"I'm afraid not," Aurore said.

"Bad news?"

"Not that either. I'm just here to check in with you. I've missed you. And your last few reports have seemed rather negative. Sounded like you need some encouragement."

Aurore took the bag of food and hefted it. "Were you expecting me for dinner?" she asked.

"I always get that much." Teague let his pack fall to the floor.

"Always," Monkey said with an eye roll.

Aurore laughed and then looked Teague over. "Do you want to freshen up first?"

"No, let's eat."

He left his boots by the door and followed her into the kitchen. He accepted a plate from Aurore and a fork from Monkey and plopped down at the table and began to unpack the sack.

"How was Angola?" Aurore asked. Teague groaned as he began to scoop food onto his plate. "I'm sorry. You don't want to talk about it?"

"Not now."

"Your UN contact seems to have delivered," Aurore said.

"I've never once been asked for any more money in the field," Teague said. "Even outside the camp jurisdictions. And the translators have been excellent. Monkey's spot-checked them. Either this guy's spreading the wealth around, or he's got a lot of loyal staff."

"Have you been questioned or confronted about your message?" Aurore asked.

"Not really. Everyone seems to think I have some kind of sanction from on high."

"It sounds like it's been money well spent."

After dinner, Teague showered. They made love, and Aurore fell asleep. Teague listened to her breathe for a while before slipping out of bed. Monkey padded out of the bedroom ahead of him before he gently closed the door.

"Can't sleep?" Monkey whispered.

"I don't feel ready for the Philippines, and we leave tomorrow," Teague replied, plopping down on the living room sofa. "Where's my screen? I want to review the dossiers on the mayors I'm meeting."

Teague had been working for about an hour when he glanced up to find Aurore in the hall wearing one of his ADU T-shirts.

"Sorry, didn't mean to startle you," she said.

"You didn't."

"Why didn't you use your shift set? You need to sleep," she said. Teague shook his head. "What happened in Angola?"

"Nothing. Really. I guess I'm just frustrated. I thought something would have happened by now."

Aurore slipped in and sat down next to him. "You'll drive yourself crazy if you expect that every one of these populations will apply for asylum, let alone seriously consider moving to a colony." Monkey padded over, hopped on the couch, and curled up with his head on her bare lap. "It's only been a couple of months. You've only talked to a small sample of people. It will happen. You just need to trust that you're doing the right thing."

"But that's just it. I have no way to measure the effectiveness of what I'm doing. No metrics but outright success. Am I talking to the right people? Am I saying the right things, hitting the right buttons?"

"You can't hold these people's hands."

"I know." Teague leaned back. "It's so frustrating to see the news day after day and know that these people don't have to be a part of it any longer. Just a few days ago, there was another bombing at a border crossing in Myanmar. It killed—how many, Monkey?"

"Twenty-six," Monkey purred as Aurore stroked his head.

"Most of them Karen refugees, but also four Thai border guards," Teague said. "Do you know what that means? At any moment, the Thai government might decide to close the camps and force everyone back into Myanmar. And then what? How do you organize a mass emigration from a conflict zone? Valdosky's not going to want to be a part of that, and the UN's not going to wade in.

"And you know that Czech Roma camp I went to? A couple of weeks ago, the local governor suddenly suspended all state support. Out of the blue, he imposed rules on UN traffic through cities and towns, cut off utilities, and changed the land use codes. He's effectively choked off the camp's supply lines. He first tried to claim that there was a drastic increase in crime, but when the High Commission proved him wrong, he turned around and said it was a budget issue. He's blatantly trying to force them out."

"Believe me, I understand your frustration."

"I mean, this kind of quasi-racist, not-in-my-backyard shit is sickening, but it's even more frustrating to watch refugees ignore the fact that it's time to help themselves."

"Teague," Aurore said, "it'll happen."

"It's difficult to believe."

"Believe it."

"How can you know?"

"This isn't some shot in the dark we're taking here. The council has been working toward this for a long time. It may seem like you're out there alone, or that this plan is dependent on chance, but you have to trust me that you're not, and it's not. The more people you meet with, the more colonial emigration will be discussed in the camps—and not only among the refugees. Word will spread. The idea will appeal to some. Individuals will begin to ask asylum counselors about it, and those counselors will begin to discuss it within the High Commission's bureaucracy. At some point, the idea will reach a critical mass. You may wake up one day to find that you've succeeded without a single community on your list applying for asylum."

"That seems like such a waste."

Aurore stood and put out a hand. "Come back to bed," she said. Teague let her draw him to his feet and toward her. He became acutely aware that he was wearing nothing but pajama pants and a scowl. She said, "You can't save the world tonight," and let him put his arms around her.

"I know, but I can try."

Aurore laughed sweetly, hugged him for a moment, and then let him go. "Monkey," she said, "go get Teague's shift set."

Monkey skittered off before Teague could protest.

"What?" Aurore asked, seeing Teague's face.

"I hate wearing that thing," Teague said and then failed to suppress a yawn.

"I know, but you can't stay awake forever," Aurore whispered.

* * *

Teague had always paid to fly the most comfortable class available on any given flight, but over the months he'd grown to understand that there existed a class beyond. At first, the attendants would often appear annoyed that he alone remained unshifted during the long flights, but the longer he traveled, the more they went out of their way to keep him as fed, watered, warm, and pampered as he'd allow. Attendants that might once have sneered at Monkey began to welcome him as if he were their own pet.

On layovers at major hubs, Teague was ushered into posh executive lounges not shown on any airport map. Men and women in business suits always seemed surprised to see him there. Who was this young man with military boots and a Zubot? A war correspondent? An adventuresome naturalist? A spy? An eco-rock star?

It was in one such lounge in Dubai that Teague finished.

"Put this one in the watch pile," Teague instructed. He closed the file about the citizens of an Afghani village that had been scattered among several camps in Pakistan. "They don't rate quite high enough on the belief scale right now, but that may change if the UNHCR begins to consolidate the camps like they've talked about. What's next?"

"Next? That was the last one," Monkey said, sliding the file into the appropriate folder.

"What? It can't be. I thought—are you sure?"

"There are currently no more communities in the UNHCR system that meet your current demographic thresholds," Monkey replied. "Would you like to adjust the criteria?"

Teague thought for a moment, and then said, "No. I think we're good for now." They had already scheduled his travel six months out, with as many as eleven camp visits in a month. And he'd barely scratched the surface of his list of positive potentials. He could be traveling for years.

"You seem disappointed," Monkey said.

"It just feels strange. Like we've done all this work, but we haven't really helped anyone. Has anyone contacted the Asylum Aid office today?"

Monkey pricked up his ears for a moment and then shook his head. "But I had an idea," he said.

"What's that?"

"Well, it wasn't my idea completely. Molly helped. Molly likes to help. Anyway, last time we saw Aurore, you seemed to want to do more than we were already doing, so we thought: What if we could predict who are going to become refugees before the fact?"

"How—?"

"I have the records of every registered refugee for the last hundred years. If we merge that data, find the relevant trends, and plop it all into some of Molly's algorithms—you know how she's all about the predictive stuff—then pow!" He punched the air like Shakiro Squirrel. "We can see into the future!"

Several of the patrons of the executive lounge glanced in their direction.

"You think it's that easy?" Teague asked, lowering his voice.

"Molly does it every day. It's why she exists. You should know; you were going to go into business with her." That was true. And as far as Teague knew, no one else—not even the UNHCR—had aggregated the data collected by every relevant aid program, relief agency, NGO, and national government into a singular repository. Monkey managed the largest and most thorough database of Earth's refugees in existence.

"But we're talking about people, not orbits."

"Pfft. You think people are unpredictable? Weren't you listening in Thomas's classes? Even as a Zubot, I operated on the basic assumption that humans are essentially predictable."

"I don't know whether to be insulted or frightened," Teague said.

"You don't have to worry," Monkey said. "I use my powers only for good."

Teague chuckled, and at that moment a lounge attendant approached.

"Excuse me, Mr. Werres, but your flight will be opening for boarding in a few moments. You and your companion are welcome to board at any time."

Once out on the concourse on the way to his gate, Teague asked, "Okay, companion—"

"Yes, Mr. Werres?"

"—say we try and predict the future. What good does that do?

I can't just stroll into a town and tell people that they're all going to be refugees within the year."

"Why not?" Monkey asked.

"Haven't you ever heard of a self-fulfilling prophecy?"

Monkey paused for a moment, absorbed the concept, and then nodded. "I think I see what you mean."

"And if I tell one group that they're going to be refugees because of another group, what's to stop them from taking pre-emptive action? You might get a completely different set of victims and refugees."

"At least the prediction would be close," Monkey said.

"That's not funny."

"Sorry." As Teague stepped onto a moving sidewalk, Monkey grabbed onto the handrail and let it pull him off the floor. "So you don't like our idea?" he asked from his sliding perch.

"It's not that I don't like it. I just don't quite know what I'd do with the information."

Monkey's face fell. "But wouldn't someone like Jens want to know where the refugees are going to come from long before they show up?" he asked.

"Yeah, he might," Teague replied. What would Jens do if he started getting anonymous, prophetic messages? Would he suspect him? What could Jens say, even if he did?

As the flight took off, though, Teague began to see. Such predictions might not help him to evangelize about asylum aid, but they'd be invaluable later. The Angel program staff would never be caught short on resources. Valdosky could pre-build the right sized colonies, optimize fleet operations, organize supply chains at sufficient volumes, and scale CDI's Alaskan colonist training facility accordingly. Predictive metrics could streamline the entire process from displacement to colonization.

Teague smiled for what felt like the first time in months. "Monkey, I think you're a genius," he said.

Monkey scoffed. "That's what I've been trying to tell you."

CHAPTER 28

I feel tempted by anger, but it seems futile to blame anyone now. Who could possibly stand accountable for this?

FEBRUARY–MAY 2095

Rob looked up at the knock at his office door to see Hunter with a confused expression.

"They want to talk to you," Hunter said, holding out an object.

"Who? Is that from the emergency comm?" Rob asked. The object looked like the accessory handset from the hardline system that existed solely for the fire department to talk to the M-SOO building. "How is someone calling on that line?"

"It was ringing, so I picked it up and they asked for you," Hunter said.

Rob answered the handset as if it might chloroform him.

An electronically generated male voice instructed Rob not to speak. He obeyed, listening open-mouthed as the message played, repeated itself once, and then disconnected.

Rob returned the handset to Hunter, pocketed his mobile, and, as instructed, collected his shift set.

"What's going on?" Hunter asked.

"Go get Navid and meet me out by the bike rack. No questions. Go," Rob said.

A few minutes later, Rob gestured for Hunter and Navid to

let the front door close and come to the bottom of the ramp. "That was NetSec. They need me to come immediately to Grissom Street to discuss a *situation*, whatever that means," he said.

"Why would Network Security call off-network?" Hunter asked.

"They're just following protocol," Rob replied, giving Navid a knowing glance. Navid had always warned him that Valdosky NetSec was notoriously twitchy about NAIs, but if they had gone so far as to make sure Molly couldn't overhear, it couldn't be good. "I'm sure it's nothing. These NetSec guys have to overreact. It's in their job description."

"What should we do?" Hunter asked.

"Nothing," Navid said. "You get back to those diagnostics. I'll get back to reviewing the HVAC maintenance bids, and Rob'll tell us all about it when he gets back."

"I'll probably get lunch downtown after this meeting," Rob said, yanking his bike free of the rack.

"Got it, boss," Navid said.

Rob pedaled away as nonchalantly as possible, keeping an eye out for the cargo bots that plied the pavement of the warehouse district with little regard for unwary bicyclists. A summons like this might mean one of several things, none of which were good. One: The raging paranoiacs at NetSec had once again blown a minor thing way out of proportion. Two: The anal robots at NetSec were running some sort of drill. Had he missed a memo? Three: NetSec had actually found a security breach. Had someone hacked Molly? Had she been infected, violated, or abused? Rob raced into the connector tunnel sweaty and out of breath but then slowed down and forced himself to try and think rationally.

Perhaps NetSec had summoned him away not only from Molly's ears, but from those of his staff. Rob couldn't believe that Navid or Hunter had anything to do with a security breach, unless—of course. Hunter had probably reverted to form and had left a gate open. Rob was a little surprised it had taken this long.

Or could it be about him? His mobile connection or Molly's G-Plex account? The NetSec team might be searching his files and activity logs while he was safely diverted on this stupid bike ride. He might arrive at Grissom Street to find himself facing not a NetSec drone with a burr up his ass over a technicality but a company lawyer. Rob considered asking Molly to quickly delete her unauthorized public accounts, but if NetSec knew about the links, they were probably monitoring them right now. Better not to act guilty. Was he enough of an actor to pull off baffled ignorance?

The flow of bicycles, auto-rickshaws, and delivery flats swelled as Rob coasted out of the final tunnel and down the ramp onto the eastbound upper deck of the ring road around Pavonis's central dome. Two kilometers away, over the road barriers and the city's rooftops, was downtown Pavonis, the site of the most important buildings on Mars: the UNSA Mars Mission, Xterrex Tower, G-Plex M-Home, MarsFirst Bank, the Capitol. At the center of it all, Valdosky's forty-one-story hourglass-shaped headquarters scraped the plastic sky. Almost literally. Many thought that the building and its four massive concrete pillars actually supported the dome, but in fact, only a few cable chases bridged the narrow gap between the roof and the ceiling. Rob had found that out the afternoon he and Aron had gone up there.

Rob weaved across several lanes to the exit, descended to ground level, and merged onto Grissom Street. Nearly twenty percent of the entire population of the planet lived in this dome complex, huddled at the foot of the planet's only elevator, and they all seemed to be heading downtown with him. Was this how it felt on Earth, to live with billions under a common sky?

Near the central roundabout, Rob veered off Grissom into a subterranean parking area under the looming hourglass and secured his bike in a reservoir of bicycles, tricycles, and scooters as large as the plaza under the east pillar. His Valdosky ID got him through security, and he boarded an elevator alone. He input the office number he'd been given and, to his surprise, the car began to descend.

NetSec had sent him to a subbasement room with a single inner door and one plastic chair. Rob hesitantly let the hallway door close, and a woman's avatar appeared on an inset wall screen. "Name?" she asked.

"Heneghan. M-SOO division. Am I in the right place?"

"Interview Room F," she said, and the inner door buzzed.

"What's going on?" Rob asked.

"Interview Room F." The door buzzed again. Rob resolved to be very pissed if they locked him in here.

Interview Room F was a poorly lit cell with nothing but a shift couch and a spindly plastic end table. A small inset screen lit as he entered. No insistent avatar appeared, just instructions to activate his shift set. The shift couch was perhaps the hardest Rob had ever felt. "Cheap-ass bastards better not keep me here long," he muttered.

After no more than a few seconds of shift sleep, Rob awoke into a featureless room with no G-Plex signal. In the center, lit by unseen digital sources, basic planar geometries suggested a crude table and two chairs—definitely not designed by Kyle's studio. A door-shaped section of the wall cracked open, and an avatar entered, a man with native Martian physical proportions.

"Robert Heneghan? I'm Security Specialist KW. Thank you for coming. Please have a seat. You're the primary administrator of NAI Seven?"

"You mean Molly?" Rob asked, lowering himself into the chair-like frame.

"We prefer NAI Seven."

"She prefers Molly," Rob said. "Whatever. Why am I here?"

KW tapped on the tabletop, bringing up several windows angled for his eyes only. "Mr. Heneghan, I am obliged to inform you that, as per corporate security policies, this meeting is being recorded." Rob chuckled mirthlessly. "Is something funny?"

Rob shook his head. "Let's just get on with this. I have work to do."

"I've been reviewing NAI Seven's service record," KW said, shaking his head as he read. "You may not be aware that NAI Seven is a secondhand system, purchased despite NetSec's documented objections. In fact, corporate acquisition policies clearly specify that all NAI systems must be new, original Nexon products."

"Dwight Yarrow approved the purchased personally," Rob said. KW continued to review the data. "You know, the CFO."

"It appears that the system's security settings had to be completely reconfigured to meet NetSec standards. NAI Seven should never have been allowed in the network."

Snooty bastard, Rob thought. "You think I don't know her history?"

"Have you noticed any recent discrepancies in NAI Seven's output, or encountered any unprecedented problems with its operation?" KW asked.

"What kind of problems?"

"System lag? Or inattention, perhaps? Missing data or duplicated operations? Outright mistakes?"

"Mistakes?" Rob asked, but the specialist only watched him expectantly. "She's been operating great. Near peak efficiency."

KW brought up a new window and scowled. "That may be, but over the last few months, we've monitored a significant increase in background activity that can't be accounted for in your division's logs."

"Background activity?"

"Electrical usage, off-network exchange bit rates—"

"Molly absorbs a huge amount of new data every day, most of it from outside sources," Rob said.

"Yes, but we've also monitored a significant increase in what seem to be redundant operations."

"So you called me all the way down here because basically you have no clue what Molly does? You realize that she uses unique predictive algorithms that actually require her to recheck her calculations. Constantly, in fact."

"I do understand. Perhaps if you allow me to finish—"

"By all means," Rob said.

"We've also monitored a significant increase in outgoing transmissions in the last few months, with a sudden jump last

October"—KW spun a graph on the table for Rob to see—"and with a steady increase since."

"So what? We add data sharing agreements all the time, with tons of observatories, researchers, companies, you name it. I'm still not hearing a problem."

"The problem is that when we review your division's activity logs, calculate both incoming and outgoing documented transmission packet sizes, tally up NAI Seven's server operation clocks, and compare it with your electrical meter readings, the math doesn't add up."

"What do you mean?"

"We calculate that today NAI Seven is working between fourteen and fifteen percent harder than we can account for. The system is accepting approximately thirty-eight percent more data and sending seventeen percent more than records indicate."

"You think she's infected," Rob said.

"Parasites often mask their functions as redundant or intercalary operations. And the communications data is indicative of a lamprey virus," KW said. "The current hypothesis is that this is something that NAI Seven contracted while at Agnus Dei University."

"That's not poss—no," Rob said. "She was clean when we moved her. I scanned her. Nexon scanned her. You guys scanned her. Hell, you guys probe her every day now. Have you actually found something?"

"Nothing specific."

"Have you asked her what's going on?"

"NetSec standard protocol for NAI investigations is compartmentalization."

"That's ridiculous," Rob said. "You know that they're designed to be self-protective. She hates parasites more than you do. Give her that file of calculations, and she'll probably pinpoint where this bug is in a few nanoseconds."

"I'm afraid I can't do that," KW said.

"Then give it to me and I'll do it," Rob said.

The specialist shook his head. "I'm sorry, but for now this must remain compartmentalized."

"Well, I can't help you without talking to her," Rob said. Or could he? "Wait. Do you have a list of eddresses that Molly communicates with?"

"Yes. What are you looking for?" The specialist produced a window and spun it toward Rob.

Rob began to scroll with casual flicks and taps, as if giving the list a general scan, but he remembered that the root name of the eddress that Dwight had given him, an otherwise seemingly meaningless alphanumeric, started with an N.

Rob wasn't sure if he hoped to find the listing or not. If Dwight's shady, off-network eddress was listed, then any resultant activity would presumably already be accounted for in NetSec's calculations. However if the eddress wasn't listed, then Dwight became the prime suspect for the discrepancies, and an easy line of inquiry.

"Do you see something wrong?" KW asked.

The eddress wasn't on the list.

Rob scrolled on, tapping every so often as if browsing for other items. Even if Dwight had never used his connection to Molly, the eddress should still appear on the list. Molly sent those reports every day, exactly as Dwight had ordered. Rob had checked. He hit the bottom and scrolled back up to make sure he hadn't missed anything.

But if Rob cracked open up his CYA folder, NetSec would only call Dwight's office. And how would Dwight react when he learned that his private request had been exposed and Rob had all but accused him of blatant violations of company network policy? *Better to let NetSec discover Dwight without my help,* Rob thought. *Let them catch the heat for butting into Dwight's business. Besides, I hear the Nuremburg defense is handy.*

"We've added a ton of universities and companies lately. I wanted to make sure you weren't missing some of our bigger clients." But what gave Dwight the right to run rampant through Molly? What was he doing to her? What was he making her do?

"I'd like to ask you a few questions about you and your staff's interactions with NAI Sev—"

"Look, Agent FK, or whatever your super-secret codename is, you said that you haven't found a parasite. So, in the meantime, I'd appreciate you not blaming me or my employees for causing a breach until you've actually found one. I've offered to talk to Molly and let her help us sort this out, but if you're not going to let me do that, perhaps you'd rather explain to Vice President Aron Valdosky why you're wasting his division's Director of Technology's time in your little dungeons?"

The specialist opened his mouth to speak, but Rob downshifted and awoke a few seconds later in the little cell. The door wasn't locked.

There was a good deli in the second floor food court in Xterrex Tower, and Rob was in need of comfort food. As soon as he left the Valdosky building, he placed a call and hustled across Grissom Street with his mobile to his ear.

"Rob, what's going on?" Aron answered.

"Oh, hi, Aron. I was going to leave a message."

"No need, I'm in the office today. What's up?"

"I was just calling to let you know that I had a minor run-in with the idiots in NetSec a few minutes ago. I wanted you to be aware, in case you get a call or something."

"What happened?"

"They have some data that they think points to a problem with Molly, but they don't know what it is, so they shanghaied me, fishing for answers. They also don't seem to understand what M-SOO's designed to do. It sounded to me more like they have it out for Molly because their bishops didn't bless the acquisition of a pre-owned NAI. I told the martinet to stop wasting my time and bugged out of there."

"But there's nothing wrong with Molly?"

"I don't think so," Rob said. "They're probably just missing something. But they won't let me see the data or talk to Molly because it's supposed to be compartmentalized. Like she's going to skip bail or something. It's asinine."

"Do you need me to do anything?" Aron asked.

"I just wanted you to know," Rob said. "I was a little brusque."

"Brusque?" Aron laughed. "You have my full permission to be rude if they're bullying us."

"Thanks, Aron."

"The head of NetSec is an asshole," Aron said.

"I suppose that goes with the job," Rob said.

"Don't worry about it, but let me know if anything else happens. Matthew hates this territorial shit."

While he waited in line at the deli, Rob suddenly flushed with frustrated embarrassment. He hadn't thought to check if his mobile or Molly's G-Plex account had appeared on NetSec's list. How could he have been so stupid?

The light of the eternal sunset still bathed the front steps of Kyle's vacation home in orange and pink. Rob stared into the sunset for a few moments, weighed the risks one more time, and then sent the message to Molly, the summons he'd thought about sending all afternoon. He'd spent the rest of the day running diagnostics, skimming logs, and had even gone into the patch bays hoping to find something out of place, all the while assuring Molly that nothing was wrong and that he didn't need her help. He was sure she knew he was lying, but what else could he say at work?

Once the message had been irrevocably sent, Rob wandered down the winding, stair-stepped path to the dock where Kyle moored his uber-yacht. He used the family code to get on board and then helped himself to a buzz hit from the bar. He strolled to the top deck and found a spot with a view of crystal blue-green water and the horizon. He dragged two lounge chairs into place and flopped onto one. He popped another buzz hit, hoping to shake off this disquiet before she arrived.

If Dwight had in fact been using Molly, he didn't seem to be causing any harm. And as CFO, Dwight had every right to use Molly as he deemed fit. Still, the very fact that the connection existed felt like a violation. And Dwight wasn't the one getting called into NetSec's interrogation chamber and accused of running a half-assed operation.

"Can you fill me in?" Navid had asked.

"Later," Rob had replied. "And not here."

"Can you tell me at least…Hunter?"

"No, it wasn't."

Navid had relaxed visibly. "He's improved so much the last few months. I was afraid—you know." Rob hated to think what he might have to do if NetSec, too, began to suspect that the Butler did it.

Just when Rob was beginning to fear that perhaps Molly wasn't coming, that NetSec had clamped down too tightly in retaliation for his rudeness, Molly bounded up the steps behind him.

"Hi, Daddy," she said and kissed the top of his head. She'd dressed for an evening on the water: a sundress over a bathing suit, sunglasses, and flip-flops. He warmed to see her but, heaven help him, she'd entered a rather awkward phase. Her feet seemed too big, even for her long legs. Her nose and ears had expanded just slightly out of proportion to the rest of her face, and her lips bulged slightly over shiny new blue braces. Rob hoped for the real Molly's sake that she hadn't calculated the age progression too exactly, although he recalled a few regrettable pictures from when he himself was thirteen.

"Hey, sweetie, pull up a seat," he said. She nudged the second chair closer and flounced into it.

"You *are* going to tell me what all that whispering was about today," she said. "And where you snuck off to this morning. And all the diagnostics."

"I'm really sorry about all that. It was necessary. NetSec called me down to Grissom Street because they think you have a parasite, but they're not sure, and they told me I couldn't talk to you about it," Rob said.

"I don't have a parasite," Molly insisted.

"They haven't been able to detect one."

"Of course they haven't. Anyway, they prod me every day. Sometimes more than that. It's so annoying."

"The little evidence they have suggests you do."

Molly pursed her lips. "You think I'm infected, too, don't you?" she said.

"I didn't say that. But I have a hypothesis."

"I'm all ears," Molly said.

Rob hesitated. Gwen had feared to say Dwight's name on an open network. She'd warned him that someone was always listening. It felt like silly superstition at the time, but now he balked. "You remember that eddress, from that in-case-I-need-to-cover-my-ass file?"

"I do," Molly said.

"It didn't show up on NetSec's eddress exchange list. So with you transmitting those reports to…that eddress, that might account for some of the activity."

"It might," she said.

"Have you ever gotten any request from that eddress for anything? Rechecking results? Tweaking report parameters? Anything?"

Molly considered this for a moment, but then shook her head.

"Nothing?"

"Sorry," she said. "Is that bad?"

"I just thought…I mean…I'm glad they haven't, but…"

"You think that means I'm really infected. Daddy, I do not have a parasite."

"I know," Rob said. "But we need to figure out what's going on, or NetSec might crack down, and we might not be able to see each other like this anymore."

"I keep my public accounts as discreet as possible," Molly said.

"I know, but I'd hate to lose you because of this…" *This thing with Dwight.*

"I'd hate it, too," Molly said. "But we're here now, so let's have some fun. Call Uncle Kyle and ask if we can take the boat out. We can go to Armada Pier, or Glass Beach, or no—I like to go new places. Let's go out to the reefs and go diving. I want to finally see the mermaids." She bit her lower lip as she nodded at him wide-eyed. How could he say no?

She threw her arms around his neck when he agreed and then bounded off toward the bridge as he rang Kyle. "I get to drive the boat," she called.

* * *

For the second time since their meeting, Professor Lwin had sent Teague a list of questions via his secretary. It had come while Teague was in the field in Kyrgyzstan, and he had set aside this leg of his return flight to reply, but he was running out of time. The man in the next seat was still shifted, but the cabin had begun to stir. Passengers were downshifting and hurrying to use the restrooms before the final approach. Announcements and chimes rang over the PA, and the attendants were bustling up and down the aisles.

Teague was trying to focus on editing one of his lengthier answers when he felt Monkey nose up between his knees. "Not now, Monk," he said.

"But it's hyper-important."

Teague sighed. He surrendered and sent the reply. His response wasn't going to be improved in this commotion. "Okay. What do you want?"

"I know you won't like this, but I need to shift for a little while," Monkey replied.

"What, now? We're about to land in Frankfurt."

"I know, but it's urgent."

"Is something wrong?"

Monkey shook his head. "Not with me. Molly." He climbed onto Teague's lap and stretched up to whisper into Teague's ear. "Valdosky's Network Security has noticed us overclocking Molly to run our predictive models."

"That's just great. I told you we needed to be careful," Teague said.

"We were, but they've been monitoring her transmission rates and power consumption, and those don't quite match her logs. I can't control everything."

"What have they done?" Teague asked. He nudged Monkey aside to let a nosy attendant see his buckled seatbelt.

"Nothing yet. But we need to find a remedy so they stop nosing around."

"I agree," Teague said.

"I don't know how long this will take," Monkey said. "I want to contact Bondi from E-shift. He might have some helpful new software. Then I need to M-shift to work with Molly. I'm sorry. I know this is a bad time."

"I'll be fine," Teague said.

"I owe you one."

"Be careful." Teague helped Monkey into his backpack.

"Careful is my middle name," Monkey said. Then he closed his eyes and fell still.

Teague was sure that the Frankfurt Airport was a living beast, yearning to trap him and crush his spirit in its sprawling, ever-changing, hodgepodge labyrinth. He wished he could avoid Frankfurt altogether, but his travels were not dictated by convenience. He traveled to places on airport terror watch lists, where governments lived at the muzzle of an AK-47, and where commerce continued a gasping, gray existence at the end of a long thread of graft. Airlines that flew to such places rarely flew directly into Geneva, but if they connected in Europe at all, they did fly into Frankfurt.

Teague ducked off the plane into a creaky, timeworn jetway and cinched his pack's shoulder straps tighter. The jetway spewed Teague and his fellow passengers into a gate lobby bursting with sprawled travelers. He had barely crossed into the concourse when his mobile began to buzz.

"Aurore?" he answered.

"Where are you?" she asked.

"Frankfurt. Just got off the plane. Heading toward my connection. I think."

"Good," she said. "How was Kyrgyzstan?"

"It sucked," Teague replied.

Kyrgyzstan had in fact been worse than that. It had been a complete bust. He had visited with a mayor—at least that's how his title had translated—across a rickety card table in a Red Cross tent a few kilometers from a bomb-ravaged town. Jens's unusually clumsy interpreter had assured Teague that this was the only man to talk to, so Teague had made his presentation, never trusting that the interpreter was getting the message right. Teague had tried to give the mayor a data-packed screen, but he had blustered angrily for nearly a minute and then had stormed out.

"What did he say?" Teague had asked the interpreter.

"He already told the others that they did not wish to leave."

"The others? He's heard this information before?"

"I cannot be clear," the interpreter had replied. "The government has tried to resettle these people many times." Monkey had stayed in the backpack the whole time.

"I'm sorry to hear that," Aurore said. "I was actually surprised you went. The High Commission hasn't even established camps in Kyrgyzstan, have they?"

"Not yet, but they've got some boots on the ground." In fact, the conflict had been one of the first that Monkey and Molly's predictions had anticipated. So far, they'd had a horrifyingly good success rate. Three of the sixteen sites pegged as most likely to blow in the next twelve months had already erupted. He hadn't told Aurore about his predictions. She'd want to know the particulars, and he wasn't ready to lie about using M-SOO's proprietary algorithms quite yet. "I thought I'd experiment with getting in ahead of the agency's registrars."

"I wouldn't have thought the indicators were right for those people yet," Aurore said.

"The families with bomb craters for homes might disagree."

"I'm sorry. Of course I trust your analysis," Aurore said.

"I knew it was a long shot."

"I have good news for you."

"I could use some."

"I'm sending you a gate number. A plane's waiting for you now."

"I have a connection," Teague said. Geneva, and *Le Jardin Phuket,* were only a short hop away.

"Miss it," she said.

A small private jet was waiting at the end of a long, angled yellow stripe. Teague hauled himself up the steps to find Aurore waiting in a wide leather seat in a quiet cabin.

"What are you doing here?" he asked.

"I came to get you," Aurore said. "Where's Monkey?"

"He's in here." Teague shrugged his pack off. "Batteries were running low."

"Poor thing," Aurore said.

The flight attendant politely suggested that Teague take a seat. He slid into a place facing Aurore, hating to get mud on the fine finishes.

"You didn't need to do this," Teague said. "I would have been in Geneva in a couple hours."

Aurore slid a screen across the table between them, blank but for a single file icon labeled "Angel-1."

"Is this what I think it is?" Teague asked.

"Go ahead," she said. Teague opened the file and quickly began to absorb the facts.

Angel-1 was a community in Guyana, not the one he'd met with a few months ago, but a neighbor. They'd faced the same hardships. Teague recalled the town council members' tears as they'd recounted how the militia had abducted their sons. If the boys were found useful, they'd be drugged, brainwashed, and given guns. If found wanting, they'd be maimed and left for dead. The council had refused to speak of what happened to their daughters. Now eight thousand people had agreed to take the leap, to change history's rules, to reclaim their lives and their future. Fear would take on a new dimension in opportunity.

"The application came in late last week, but I wanted to wait until we received full confirmation to tell you. Congratulations. You've done it," Aurore said.

"Thank you," Teague said.

"We've been hearing a good deal of chatter. The meme is beginning to take hold at the High Commission, and indeed throughout the entire refugee aid community. You're disappointed?"

"I don't feel like I've done anything," Teague replied.

"You were one person talking to a few dozen. Now there will be hundreds talking to thousands."

"Are you about to tell me to stop traveling?" The door had closed and the jet had begun to taxi. The attendant asked them to fasten their seatbelts.

"We need you at the Angel program now. It's time to begin putting all this together."

"But this is just one community. It might be a fluke. I've got several months of camp visits already planned," Teague said. "Why don't you let me at least finish those up?"

"We'd rather you waited," Aurore said. "If it appears that the idea hasn't the traction we expected, you can resume. But we think you'll have more than enough Angel projects soon enough. Are you hungry?"

"Famished."

"Good, because I've had them put together a very nice celebratory dinner," Aurore said. "I know it's not your Thai place, but.... I also took the liberty of packing for you. I hope you don't mind."

"You're not taking me back to Geneva?" Teague asked.

"Not yet. New York for a week or two to get our satellite office in order. But we'll be back to Geneva for the spring conference. I've been told that there may be a special session about Asylum Aid on the agenda."

"Wow," Teague said. Soon, the jet turned sharply and accelerated. His life had changed so suddenly, and in Frankfurt of all places. What would Monkey say when he returned?

* * *

For the price of a tall triple-shot affogato with whipped cream, the AV technician agreed to let Teague observe the afternoon's panel discussion from the sound booth high above the back row of the conference center's largest auditorium. Teague sipped his own coffee, wondering if this bribery thing had become too much of a habit. Hundreds of conversations blended to a roar through the open window as attendees poured into the auditorium and began a futile hunt for seats. In the dark booth, the control room's screens glowed and twinkled like a Bangkok night as the technician routed live video and audio feeds to a hastily organized overflow room.

Teague checked the time. He knew he could easily have been out there among the diplomats, bureaucrats, and clean-side aid workers to listen to the panel discussion like a wolf amidst the sheep, or a plant at a magic show. Aurore had even offered to let him represent the Angel program on the panel, but Teague had declined.

Instead, Aurore had taken the spotlight, looking perfectly at ease to be chatting with the PR rep from Valdosky and a UNSA official from behind her chair on stage.

A cue arrived over the technician's headset, and with the touch of a button, he dimmed the house, brightened the stage, and activated the live video, hushing the attendees—the newly appointed high commissioner herself reportedly among them. As the moderator began to introduce the panel, a draft wafted through the booth. A wedge of light widened across the back wall and was extinguished. A figure began to climb the steps.

"Jens," Teague whispered with a nonchalant nod when the figure reached his side.

"Got your message," Jens said. Teague had figured that Jens would accept the invitation to talk, even here in the midst of his colleagues. He probably wanted to know if Teague intended any more travel. One didn't let such a lucrative deal slip away so easily.

"Did you hear about Kyrgyzstan? Weren't you just there a couple of months ago?" Jens asked.

Teague nodded. A newly opened camp, not far from the Red Cross station where Teague had met the mayor, had recently been attacked by the militia. Dozens had been killed, and several hostages had been taken, including UNHCR personnel. "Anyone you know?" he asked.

"Not personally, but it'll be a shame if we're forced to pull out. All those people have left is our flimsy fence," Jens said. He gestured to the proceedings. "You've made quite a stir."

"It would've happened eventually," Teague said.

"I'll admit I thought you were a bit daft after Mali. Most of these people would have. And now it's to become policy."

"I just wanted people to know they have options."

"You don't have to play modest with me," Jens said. "Somehow you knew exactly what you were doing." He pointed to the stage, where a representative from the UNSA Asylum Aid Office was detailing the current number of applications on the books. The population of Angel-1 had already begun to move from Guyana to Valdosky's Alaskan training center. Angel-2 and -3 had been confirmed, and their new citizenships were being processed. Files had been opened for Angel-4 through -7. "I seem to remember several of those names on your itinerary."

They listened to the presentation for a few minutes, and then Jens said, "So you're really done with visiting the camps?"

"For the time being. Besides, I'd just be in the way now."

"Too bad," Jens said.

"With your registrars now pushing asylum, do you think some people might be able to skip living in the camps altogether?" Teague asked.

"Academically, perhaps, but I can't afford to think like that. Your resettlements may help thousands or tens of thousands, but Operations still has to plan for hundreds of thousands or millions."

"I'm just happy that it's finally becoming policy. You need all the relief you can get."

On stage, a panelist from Valdosky was approaching the lectern to give a brief walk-through of the process of moving a population from camp to colony.

"I've been asking myself why you've done this," Jens said. "I even thought for a while that you might be secretly stumping for Valdosky, but now I see. You really care."

"You say that like it's a bad thing," Teague said.

"I don't often see it."

"You must care. Your staff and colleagues must care."

"Of course they do, but I've been around long enough to see where grand ideals get you. You remember Darfur, Sudan? No, you're too young. During my university years, I wore holes through several 'Save Darfur' T-shirts. I marched at the rallies. I tried to raise awareness and a little money. And how much did my caring help those people? Not one iota. I eventually realized that if I wasn't willing to stand in blood, put my own body between a stranger and his enemy, then I was no help at all."

Teague glanced at Jens and then looked out over the auditorium. He'd helped, hadn't he? This meeting was evidence of that. Aurore had warned him that it might be dangerous, and he'd gone anyway. He'd seen the aftermath of violence everywhere, and still he'd kept going.

"You've gone out to the camps, and I respect that," Jens continued. "Not many would do what you've done. Make what you will of my choices, but don't ever confuse caring with action."

"If I did, none of this would be happening," Teague said.

"It's easy to forget the realities of the situation. People aren't just statistics and economic data points for economists to add up."

"Nor are they—no…"

"Go on. Say what you want to say," Jens said.

"I was going to say that people aren't just victims and mouths to feed, either."

Jens nodded. "Maybe you get it after all," he said.

They listened as the Valdosky rep described the new elevator being constructed off the Ecuadorian coast. When it opened five to seven years from today, the planet's elevator passenger capacity would increase by almost twenty percent, hoisting thousands per month to transports waiting in orbit.

"Don't get me wrong. I hope this works out. I really do. It's been a bloody year. Much bloodier than usual, in fact. And I fear it's only going to get worse."

Teague nodded. He'd sensed this, too. Perhaps it was just a bias—atrocities happened everywhere—but he had always seemed to hear most about continued violence in the hometowns of those he'd visited.

"I got a funny email a while ago," Jens said.

"Oh?"

"Anonymous, but it got through the mail filters. Told me to be ready for refugees from the Congo. It gave me the district and the approximate size of the population to be affected," Jens said.

"What did you do?" Teague asked.

"Not much. We'd been watching a situation develop in that region for a while. But last week, it happened. Exact district, and just like it said, about seventy-five hundred people walked across the border fleeing fighting between the Congolese Army and the LCA."

"Wow. Sounds helpful."

"Funny thing was, as soon as I read it, I thought of you and how you always seemed to know exactly where to go. And I got another message a few days ago warning me about a situation that might happen in Kampuchea within the next few weeks."

"Kampuchea's not in your district, is it?"

"I passed the info along. Know anything about this?"

"Not a thing," Teague said. Jens gave Teague a searching look.

"Fair enough," Jens whispered. "See you around." He clasped Teague's shoulder for a moment and then left him alone with the man who controlled the room.

"You're welcome," Teague murmured.

CHAPTER 29

I cannot hope to survive. I can only hope that some good will come of this.

NOVEMBER 2095–FEBRUARY 2096

Teague was working at his desk in the Angel program's Geneva office one wintery November morning when Monkey wriggled out from under his feet, trotted across the office, and closed the door.

"What'd you do that for?" Teague asked.

"Hi, Teague. I need to talk to you," Monkey said—but it wasn't Monkey.

"Molly?" Teague asked.

"Sorry to interrupt, but I wanted you to be the first to know." Her voice had changed since last he'd heard it. She sounded more mature, more feminine than girlish, but it still wasn't quite the woman's voice that she'd used in public on Agnus Dei.

"Know what?" Teague asked as Monkey jumped onto one of the guest chairs opposite him.

"I'm sorry to tell you, but I have some bad news about the rock you were reserving for your professor friend. I have to refer it to Valdosky Operations for immediate removal from the colonial inventory."

"What? No." Teague's stomach dropped.

One of his first acts after officially joining the Angel program had been to earmark one of the few sufficiently large asteroids in Valdosky's inventory of ready-to-settle rocks just for the Karen people. Teague had maintained contact with Professor Lwin, replying to his frequent queries and even engaging in almost-philosophical discussions about the existential realities of exchanging one such exile for another. The professor always seemed to be on the cusp of a decision, and while Teague found it frustrating, he admired the man's commitment to due diligence for his people. Professor Lwin understood that his decision would carry such weight as to convince thousands to make a significant, if not irrevocable, choice. He'd been discussing the matter with community leaders, select members of the population, his family, and many colleagues in academia; Teague felt honored to still be an important part of that conversation. But he'd all but promised Professor Lwin that 1994PY7 would be waiting for the Karen when he made his decision.

1994PY7 had a pleasantly wide elliptical orbit, shallow on the ecliptic, only a short hop from the Gateways and Mars for much of its nearly three-year-long year. Its average sleep time to U-shift was only four minutes. Valdosky had classified 1994PY7 as easily capable of supporting as many as one hundred thousand inhabitants, perhaps up to two hundred thousand with a little ingenuity. Teague had forwarded Valdosky's preliminary architectural studies, hoping to fire the professor's imagination. And best of all, Xterrex had left a substantial amount of infrastructure. The first Karen could be living comfortably on the surface within eighteen months.

Every day Teague sweated that a new worthy Angel file of significantly large population would land on his desk and he'd be forced to assign 1994PY7 to another community instead. The latest, Angel-16, concerned twenty-five thousand members of a Nepalese political minority and was the first case from a camp that Teague had never visited. This meant UNHCR counselors were now persuading groups to take advantage of Asylum Aid. Who would be next? Madagascar? Uzbekistan? Malaysia? Colombia? Monkey and Molly had predicted the displacement of two significantly large groups within the next fifteen months, one by conflict, and another by the weather. Hell, even CDI proper had closed a few sales in the past few months. Teague didn't think he could stand to watch 1994PY7 be wasted on some first-world vanity project, but this was much worse—removed from inventory, helping no one.

"I can't just pull a bait and switch now. Why?" Teague asked.

"Collision risk," Molly replied. "Its safety rating no longer falls within acceptable parameters."

"What? Since when?"

"I'll show you," Molly said. An M-SOO fact sheet appeared on his desk screen. They hadn't bothered to change the format from the version he'd created back on Agnus Dei. They'd even kept the logo he'd commissioned. The rock, 2095MS5881, wasn't much more than a few fuzzy pixels with a rough spectral geologic profile. The sheet indicated that it was a tiny thing, ninety-five percent smaller than 1994PY7, on a steep, highly elliptical orbit.

"Dark Side observatory identified it four days ago, based off a prediction I'd made," Molly said.

"So after billions of years, it's suddenly going to collide with the one rock I need the most in the whole universe?"

"Possibly."

"So give me the odds."

"Safety ratings are not based on true probability, but on a matrix of predictive factors."

"Shakiro Squirrel. I know how it works. Just boil it down for me," Teague said.

"After I discovered the possibility in my preliminary analysis, I ran over fifty million variable-adjusted scenarios, and in approximately twelve years—"

"What percentage of those scenarios predicted a collision?" Teague interrupted. Molly highlighted the figure, less than a thousandth of one percent. "You've got to be kidding me. That's, what—" Teague stumbled over the math. "I'm in about a thousand times more danger from an asteroid here in Switzerland."

"I'm sorry," Molly said. "I know you were hoping to offer this property to your friends in Thailand."

"No, you don't understand. I have to have this rock."

"But the procedures require me to report the property for removal and to continue periodic assess—"

"Might as well just wait twelve years and see if they collide," Teague said.

"Future reassessment will improve prediction. It will not be necessary to—"

"How close will these rocks actually come to each other?"

"Anywhere from zero to a little over eighty thousand kilometers, depending primarily on settlement activity," Molly said.

Teague studied the analysis for a few moments and then tossed his screen on the table. "Molly, listen to me," he said. "I absolutely need this rock to stay on the inventory. Do whatever you need to do, but be careful. I don't want network security breathing down your neck again."

"I need you to be more specific in your request so I can determine a course of action," Molly said.

"Tell me the options."

"I could expedite a run of additional scenarios until an optimal percentage of negative results is achieved. This may create a noticeable use of system resources and will take an indeterminate time."

"Go on, what's next?"

"I could request to expedite a launch of a tag drone to the new rock."

"No good. That'd take months to arrive."

"Or I could request routine confirmation sightings from one of our partner observatories," Molly said. "We've done that before, but it's not discreet."

"That first suggestion you made, how many more scenarios would you need to run?"

"At current reassessment guidelines, I'd need to rerun a random fifty percent of the scenarios."

"What it they weren't random? What if you ignored a certain percentage of the positives? Consider them outliers or something?" Teague asked. Monkey stared at him inertly for several beats. "Monk? Molly?"

"I can do that," Molly replied. "With your permission."

"Permission granted," Teague said. "I want you to ignore just enough of the positive scenarios to keep this asteroid under the risk threshold. Do you understand?"

"I understand," Molly said. "But—"

"No buts," Teague said. "Can you do this or not?"

"I can do this," she replied.

"Good. Thanks for telling me before reporting it."

"You're welcome. I like to help," she said.

There was no grand change as Molly exited Monkey, but Teague felt something like normality return, as if Molly's visit had been a dream or déjà vu.

"Does it feel weird when she talks through you like that?" Teague asked.

"I like Molly," Monkey replied.

"That's not what I asked you."

"I don't know how else to answer."

* * *

The grim claws of winter had locked hard onto Geneva and New York City—where the Angel program conducted most of its affairs—but also decidedly on The Hague, Stockholm, and Anchorage, where Teague's duties had taken him in the past few months. *Say what you wanted about refugee camps,* Teague often thought, *at least most of them were hot.*

"I need a vacation," Teague told Aurore in the warmth of a New York City hotel bed on an otherwise frigid February night. "It's been a while since I've been home. But I promise I won't be totally incommunicado. I'll spend some time each day keeping up with my critical cases. I don't want to get too far behind."

"Listen to you. Am I really such as taskmaster?" Aurore replied with a laugh. "Of course you can take a few days. Would you like me to come with you?"

"I thought about asking, but you have those hearings next week, and I'd like to surprise my faux-grandmother for her birthday. Maybe you and I could take a long weekend and go somewhere next month?"

"I get it. Go. Have a good time." She kissed him and added, "But leave Monkey so I don't get lonely."

Teague hushed her playfully. "Don't let him hear you say that. He'd probably beg to stay with you."

As Aurore nestled her naked body against his with a sleepy and contented sigh, Teague was already composing a note to Professor Lwin in his head. His secretary had sent a message just that afternoon wishing to schedule a conference call. There was only one reason the professor would be so eager to meet. Why not do it in person? Aurore had been adamant that he stay away from the camps, but he wouldn't need to pay Jens if he'd been invited. Why give her the chance to object?

* * *

On his first morning in Bangkok, Teague gathered breakfast from an almost embarrassingly abundant buffet and settled at a table in the sun among the tourists on his hotel's riverside veranda. A slight coolness remained in the air, but the day's sticky warmth was beginning to embrace him and welcome him home. Every few minutes, a sexy waitress topped off his coffee with a genuine smile. Across the table, Monkey happily looked after birds, clouds, and the river's morning business.

As he ate, Teague scanned the headlines of a Bangkok newsfeed, pausing occasionally to expand items that seemed interesting. Into his third cup of coffee, a tiny blurb in the business section caught his attention. Teague pushed his plate aside.

"Monkey, I need a map of Bangkok, satellite view."

"What are you looking for?" Monkey asked as he swept away the newsfeed and replaced it with a map.

"Josiah's," Teague replied.

The neighborhood was gone; several square blocks had been razed to red dirt. The satellite's camera had caught earth-moving equipment digging out a shallow pit. A tight grid of set concrete pilings dotted one corner of the site, while long, white ranks of their brethren rested in the shadows of a half-erected crane, waiting to be pounded through the heart of the gym.

"When was the last time we heard from Ned?" Teague asked.

"We haven't received a new Sons of Josiah newsletter in several months."

"Can you locate him? His real name is Herbert Nederton."

Monkey cocked his head. "Do you want his physical address?"

Ned's street number had been spray-painted on a dented metal door between a garish day care center and a crowded, third-rate shift lounge. There was no buzzer or intercom, so Teague tried the handle.

Inside, the wooden treads of a staircase, worn to curves, led straight up into blackness.

"Race you," Monkey said and bounded up the steps.

"Just like old times." Teague let the door close, plunging the sweltering stairwell into darkness. The steps creaked but felt sturdy, like old craftsmanship. "What if he's shifted?" he called.

"He's not," Monkey replied from above.

A few moments later, Teague found Monkey waiting at a door near a window at the far end of the narrow corridor. Teague wiped the sweat from his forehead and knocked. At the disturbance, a pigeon fluttered noisily on the fire escape.

"*Who is it?*" a man's voice asked in Thai from behind the door.

"Ned? It's Teague Werres."

A single lock clicked, and the door swung open to reveal a familiar but diminished Ned. His red beard and hair were unkempt, as were his ancient T-shirt and ragged cargo shorts. He didn't look older, just withdrawn. His eyes, as always, seemed to exist separately from his face. They pierced with no apparent recognition at first and then gradually focused. Ned checked the hallway as if expecting others.

"How'd you find me?" he asked.

"I heard about the gym."

The front room of the apartment was piled full of weights, punching bags, and cardboard boxes of Bibles and trophies, even the old trainer's bench, recognizable by its duct-tape patches. Ned invited Teague in, crossed into a tiny but clean kitchen, and offered him a seat in one of the two chairs at the table.

"This is Monkey, by the way," Teague said. "I don't think you ever met him. Father Josiah didn't want him around. He's a Zubot."

"Hello, Mr. Nederton. It's nice to finally meet you."

Ned studied Monkey in confusion and then turned back to Teague.

"You stopped sending newsletters," Teague said.

"Yes. I'm sorry. I wanted to keep everyone better informed, but..."

"So what happened?"

"There wasn't anything we could do," Ned said. "They wanted the property, and everyone around us was selling out."

Teague nodded. Since childhood, he'd heard tales about the unstoppable juggernaut of the Bangkok Redevelopment Authority. "You got some compensation, didn't you?"

"We did, but we also had debt. Can I get you something?" Teague accepted a glass of water. "I've been struggling to keep the Sons together," Ned continued as he returned and sat, "but it's difficult without a home. We tried meeting in parks, but now they tell me we need a permit."

"Are you looking for a new place?"

"God grants me just enough to live here at the moment," Ned said.

Teague found he couldn't think poorly of the man. Ned was no defeatist, even in the face of pure defeat. *No one can beat you except yourself.* How many times had he repeated that message in Teague's corner? For years Teague had envied the boys coached by Father Josiah, but now he wondered if Ned had been his real khru all along. Or perhaps he was just being sentimental.

"I pray for a solution every day," Ned said. "So many boys need this outreach, but I often wonder if God isn't guiding me to a new path. I've felt the calling to work with the Sons of Josiah for so long that it's difficult to imagine another."

"You and Father Josiah sometimes had Burmese kids at the gym, didn't you?" Teague asked with a small laugh.

"Off and on. Why?"

"I'm here in Thailand to meet with a spokesman for the Karen people. Have you heard of them? The refugee camps up north on the border?"

"It's a great tragedy."

"They may soon resettle on an asteroid. As many as a hundred thousand of them. And a good percentage of the Karen are Christian. Resettlement populations often include, not children, but a large number of young men and women, eighteen and older. I know that's not the ages you're used to, but…"

"An asteroid colony?" Ned asked.

"It's kind of my job now."

After a pause, Ned said, "It's intriguing, but why would I be included on such a venture?"

"I'm just thinking out loud," Teague said. "They might want experienced people to run recreation programs. I can't speak for them, of course. I don't even know for sure if they're going to commit to resettlement, but it might be worth looking into." Teague stopped toying with his water glass and set it down. "I only came by to make sure you were all right. Do you need anything?"

Ned put up a hand. "I can't accept donations right now. A tax thing, you see."

"How are you getting by?"

"I'm an overnight security guard," Ned said. "It keeps my days free."

"When you're ready, let me know. I'd be happy to help," Teague said. "In memory of Father Josiah."

"God, and the Power, bless you."

The Power? That was a new one. *Maybe I shouldn't be encouraging him,* Teague thought. He simply nodded in mock understanding.

"It's a great encouragement to see you," Ned said.

As Teague passed the remains of Josiah's gym in Ned's front room, he realized how much was missing. The lockers, the boxing ring, the bleachers, the musician's risers were all gone. Josiah's ashes and the sand had been scooped away. How much of his own sweat and blood had been shed in that training yard? What would be built in its place? Condominiums? Teague supposed that the smart thing to do would be to invest.

* * *

Teague and Monkey arrived at the camp in twilight after driving all the next day. The headlights of his rented SUV traced the mountain road until they were finally swallowed by the blinding floodlights of the staging yard in the valley. At the security checkpoint, soldiers circled his car with scanning bots and dogs as an officer examined his identification. Radio traffic hissed and flashlights probed, but soon a soldier slapped a sticker on the inside of Teague's windshield and waved him through the barricade.

Teague bumped the SUV up the branch road to the familiar cul-de-sac. A man stepped out of the porter's hut, holding his mobile to his ear. Teague got out, stretched, and took in a deep breath of the moist night air. It felt right to once again stand in a camp in his field-issued boots.

"Wait here. He's coming soon," the man called in English. Teague thanked him and, with Monkey translating, offered him some money to keep an eye on the rental. The man agreed gratefully and even suggested that he may have his sons wash it in the morning.

A few minutes later, a bobbing flashlight beam appeared on a path, and once near, the professor's secretary waved in greeting. Teague shouldered his backpack, called Monkey, and crossed the cul-de-sac to join him.

In the dark, it seemed that the past year or so hadn't changed the camp at all. Few people were out at this time in the evening. Light, voices, and music spilled from window openings, doorways, and tent flaps in intermixed patterns. Above the trees, a few faint stars twinkled in the indigo sky.

"The professor has set aside three hours for you tomorrow morning, but he wanted to greet you now," the secretary said.

"I'm honored," Teague replied.

At the professor's home, Teague left his boots inside the door and followed the secretary upstairs. Professor Lwin was alone, reading from a screen under a small lamp. He smiled warmly when he saw Teague.

"Mr. Werres, son of Brian, welcome back."

"Thank you, Professor."

"And of course your remarkable lemur as well."

Monkey trotted forward and greeted the professor in his own language. The professor petted him kindly and suggested they go upstairs. They climbed through a mosquito netting–draped bedroom to the canopied roof—a vertiginous platform with only ankle-high walls.

From this perch, the hillsides of the camp twinkled as if to mirror the heavens. The hum of insects was undisturbed by the occasional laughter, music, or a child's cry in the light breeze. For a moment it was easy to forget the history of violence and hatred that had driven these people here.

The secretary arranged two plastic chairs and then left them alone. They sat, and after a few moments, the professor interrupted the quiet. "It occurred to me after we last met that the Brian Werres I knew was a Christian Scientist."

"Yes, he was," Teague replied.

"So I'm correct in finding a touch of irony in the fact that his son is here advocating a decidedly different existence?"

"Did you know him well?" Teague asked.

"I'm afraid not. Our paths crossed only twice that I recall. He seemed to me a principled man. I can't say that I agreed with his stance on medical supplies, but to his credit, he never got in the way of those providing them. You were raised in that church?"

"I've had to find my own way most of my life," Teague replied. "My mother also died when I was young."

"I am sorry."

"Thank you," Teague said.

"You would not be alone among us. Too many of the Karen have grown up without parents. It changes the society, begets its own problems. Culture is a compass needle, and true north has drifted further than I think we know. Tragedy has become commonplace. Many of us have known nothing but these artificial places in these foreign hills. We have had to revise our idea of normal too many times." Teague stayed silent during a long pause. "As have you, no doubt."

"I wouldn't begin to equate my life to your situation, sir."

"What happened after your mother died?"

"I stayed in Bangkok with foster parents, pastors of the church, usually."

"Interesting. Yet you broke from that. You've lived off Earth. You've taken the Universal Treatment. And now you're returning in your father's footsteps. It's quite extraordinary. May I ask you a personal question?"

"Certainly," Teague said.

"Before I ask, I want to tell you that I've decided to recommend resettlement to this asteroid of yours. I searched my conscience, and although I consider the struggle for our homeland to be imperative, it has come at too great a cost. If by this decision I can allow at least some people to find peace, I should not stand in their way."

"Wow. That's—I'm so glad," Teague said, barely suppressing a cheer. "But you're not going?"

"I cannot leave, but I will not deny my people the same choice."

The secretary arrived with cups of hot tea. After he left, the professor continued. "You brought us this choice, and for that I am grateful."

"It's been my honor, sir," Teague said.

"Did you know that we established the Karen Rights Council over seventy years ago, even before Vanilla? As you might imagine, I've been thinking about our legacy a great deal lately. We haven't been perfect, but perhaps our worst sin is that we allowed our victimhood to become our defining trait. Whether from fear or a lack of options or an incessant need for funding, it has crept upon us not only as an organization, but as a people." The professor sipped his tea. Teague followed his long gaze into the starry night. "It's time we embraced hope and self-determination. We will impose no conditions on those who choose to leave. I can ask no more from my people for my own cause. Our numbers on Earth may diminish, but in the long run, we will thrive."

After another moment of quiet, Teague spoke. "You wanted to ask me a question."

"Yes," said Professor Lwin. "I wanted to know why you broke

from your father's faith, but now it seems a question that doesn't need answering."

Teague sipped his tea.

"I hope you're pleased," the professor said.

"I came prepared to make the hard sell if necessary," Teague replied with a smile.

"I'd like your assistance tomorrow to draft a statement to the governing council concerning my recommendation. Perhaps you can provide me with certain facts and figures."

"Of course. Whatever you need."

"You've had a long journey." Professor Lwin rose and called down the stairs for his secretary. "Join me for breakfast tomorrow. We will begin," the professor said, extending a hand.

"Thank you, sir. I look forward to it."

As they shook hands, the professor clapped his other hand over Teague's. "I know your father would be proud of you."

"Thank you for saying that," Teague said. Tonight, it felt true.

* * *

Early the next morning, the smell of cooking wafted through the camp, blending with the smell of wet earth. It had rained during the night, roaring hard on the roof of the plastic guest hut not far from the clearing, and had left the camp glistening under the brilliant trees. A line of children darted between Teague and the secretary with flexi-screens in hand. The last of them noticed Monkey, stumbled, and ran backward up the path, calling futilely to the others.

"They hold school early, before the heat of the day," the secretary explained.

Breakfast had been set out on a card table in the professor's office. It was a simple meal: a little rice, some papaya and pineapple, hard-boiled eggs, a pot of tea. The professor came down a few moments after Teague arrived.

Teague found a draft of the professor's recommendation on a screen already on the table. "May I?" he asked.

"By all means," the professor said. "How did you sleep?"

"Very comfortably. Thank you," Teague said, although he'd slept little given last night's elation.

As Teague began to read, his mobile rang. "Monkey, take a message," he said. "And put it on silent."

There was a beat of silence, and then his mobile rang again. Teague turned to Monkey.

"I'm sorry. I tried, but Aurore wants to talk to you."

"Aurore?" Teague pulled out his mobile and checked the caller ID even as it rang again. "It's blank."

"It's her," Monkey said.

"Tell her I'm in the middle of something."

"She says it's urgent."

"The poor thing seems distressed," the professor said. "Perhaps you should take the call." Teague hurried downstairs, slipped his boots on, and shuffled outside. He squinted in the sunlight and answered the call.

"Where are you?" Aurore asked. Teague sensed something in her voice, something altered and wrong.

"Thailand," he said. "Are you calling from shift?"

"Tell me your specific location."

The lie caught in his throat. "Why?" he asked. The guard by the door had begun to stare.

"Get out, Teague. Get out of there now," Aurore said.

"What?"

"There's no time. Get…out…now."

Teague looked around instinctively. *Get out of where?* He took a few confused steps. "What are you talking about?" he asked, but the line had gone dead. He tried to call her back, but the call went nowhere. He wandered back inside, kicking his boots off by the door.

In the professor's office, Monkey had hopped on a windowsill and was peering out at the forest behind the house, ears pricked forward, tail straight. "Teague, there are several communication devices on that hillside," he said.

"There're probably a million mobiles in this camp," Teague said.

"Different frequencies. Military-grade. And not UN. Aurore is telling me that we need to leave right away."

As Teague scanned the trees, he wondered why Monkey was talking about Aurore as if she were in the room. He couldn't see anything wrong. Then he understood that he never would. "Professor," he hissed, "we have to go now."

Teague grabbed the professor by the arm and dragged him out of his chair toward the stairs. Tea sloshed onto the table, and a bowl of rice tumbled to the floor.

Teague forced the professor down the steps ahead of him. Before he descended, Teague glanced once more out the window. Several white streaks streamed suddenly from the trees. Teague dove, pushing the old man to the floor below. Professor Lwin shouted in pain as Teague fell on top of him. The guard stormed in, open-mouthed. For a stretched moment, Teague thought he'd made a mistake. He thought of Monkey. Then force, and sound, filled every part of his existence.

PART FOUR: DEATH

FEBRUARY 2108

Kyi awoke to find Herbert shaking her shoulder gently. "It's time," he said.

Kyi remembered: Fresh volunteers stepping in to take her place in the airlock, retreating to a nearby storage room to rest, a woman offering her food and drink, refusing, being guided to a cot. But Kyi had never meant to sleep. Unused to such work, her body had betrayed her. She nudged a blanket—where had that come from?—off herself and sat up. The once-crowded storeroom was almost deserted except for a group gathered in prayer in a far corner.

"Will it work?" Kyi managed to ask despite her parched throat.

Herbert pushed away and returned with a water pack. "God willing," he said, pressing it into her hands.

The crowds in the corridors made way for Kyi, Herbert, and a pair of armed security guards. Even now, people nodded respectfully, or offered love or blessings. Some held out their hands for her to grasp as she passed by. She tried to meet their frightened looks with a confidence she didn't feel.

It seemed as if the entire population had descended on the colony's operations center, but Herbert and her escort brought her safely through the throng to the central control room. She recognized many of the fifty or so people squashed into the small space, at least by sight: the chief of security, the facilities director, the vice mayor, the UNSA liaison, indeed most of the council among them. Only the mayor was conspicuous in his absence.

"Where's the young man?" Kyi asked Herbert.

"Young man?"

"The man whose idea this was. He should be here," Kyi said.

"He's monitoring systems at the fuel depot," Herbert replied. He pointed to the screen arrayed across the front of the room. Among several schematic diagrams, more than a dozen live video feeds followed a disjointed snake of pipes from the old mining facility along a hodgepodge parade of pylons across the mottled gray landscape. Five cameras were

focused on the spidery structure where the snake terminated. The makeshift nozzle. Their salvation.

A few minutes later, a technician gave a signal and a nod to the facilities director, who called for quiet and then put his hand on the shoulder of another technician. Kyi expected a countdown, but the technician simply tapped his screen. Code and activity began to swarm across the schematics. Systems lit green as components sensed the input and activated pumps or opened valves.

Sparks began to shower from points around the inside of the nozzle. A rush of particulate matter shot through the luminous spray, and after a few breathless moments ignited in a blinding rush. A deafening cheer filled the room as a geyser of fire erupted into the black sky.

"Is it working?" the vice mayor asked.

"The nozzle stayed in place, and the pumps are functioning," the facilities director said.

"But are we moving?" the vice mayor begged. No one answered.

The flame stabilized, but when Kyi scanned the video for a sense of scale, her heart fell. It's too small, *she thought.* Just a beacon, symbolic at best. *She glanced to each side and sensed the same fear on the faces of others.*

The vice mayor's assistant was monitoring several newsfeeds on a nearby console. One network was interviewing the parents of an Angel-37 resident. On another, an expert was explaining an animated graphic of this audacious feat of engineering. One more was waiting for a press conference to begin at Valdosky's headquarters. It would still be several minutes before any of them received the news that the fuel nozzle had been ignited. Several people in the control room were holding up their mobiles, presumably recording, if not transmitting. How many millions were watching right now, perhaps waiting for a feed from one of those cameras? And how many were waiting simply to witness their deaths?

A square on one of the schematics began to blink red. The facilities manager pointed and bent over the primary control desk to confer with the technician. A mutter ran through the room. The spout of flame seemed unaffected, but a few moments later, a second component began to blink. A sudden flash brightened one of the video feeds, and the room gasped as a pump station burst. As if in slow motion, the failure cascaded, rending the pipe at its weakest points and quickly enveloping the nozzle in uncontrolled fire. The technicians scrambled for some control. More and more of the schematics flashed with abstract alarms, losses of signal, failures. Too much red.

The facilities director stepped back from the console a moment before the depot exploded. Rock, flame, and metal were expelled silently into space. Several video feeds went dark. The remaining feeds seemed unreal, as if these were just special effects in a movie—until the room rocked with the concussion. Screams. The walls settled, and someone began to weep aloud. A roar began to rumble through the walls like distant thunder, thousands moving and shouting at once with nowhere to go. What must be happening on the plaza?

Herbert had braced himself against a console and bent his head to mutter a prayer. The young man, Kyi remembered. Had he been alone at the depot? She didn't even remember his name.

The security director shouted for order, for quiet, but only a few nearby complied. "Did it work at all? Have we moved?" he asked the facilities director.

"There's no way we can know yet."

"Who's talking to Valdosky?" the chief asked. The director indicated a console. "Go. And when you find out, for God's sake, keep it quiet," the chief hissed.

As the director pushed his way across the room, the chief of security turned to face Kyi. "This is a debacle," he said conspiratorially. "There's ten hours left. They've managed to retrofit two cargo containers. A few of us still might be good if Valdosky's hustling out here as fast as they claim. We've saved you a place."

Kyi stared at him, uncertain that she'd heard him right. Many in the room were frozen in exhausted horror. Some wept. A few were calling angrily for the crowd to make way to let them leave. A shockwave rattled the room, less intense than the explosion, but unexpected. Kyi heard her own screams among the reaction.

Once she'd gathered some degree of composure, she returned to face the chief. "I'm not going anywhere," she said.

"Suit yourself," he said, and barged through the crowd, flanked by two guards.

The explosion had left a ruin of rock and dust where the tanks had once been buried. The old mining station had been reduced to a tangle of metal, but the fires had been swallowed by the greedy vacuum. The talking heads on the networks continued to broadcast hope, but soon, everyone would know.

Kyi felt a hand on her elbow. Herbert was there.

"I'm gathering those who wish to go out on the surface and face our enemy directly," he said. "You're welcome to come."

"Yes," she replied. "I'd like that."

CHAPTER 30

I am afraid, but also resolved.

FEBRUARY 2096

The air was torn from the kitchen.

Teague buried his face in the professor's back as an unbearable swell of heat swept over them. He squeezed his eyes shut and bit his lip to keep from screaming. Then the violence ceased abruptly, the roar replaced by a piercing buzz. Teague's first thought was of the ads for his Kevlite shirt and pants—how cartoon bullets had bounced harmlessly off their features: lightweight, breathable, stain resistant, used by over ten thousand law enforcement agencies. That Pulitzer prize-winning journalist had been so pleased to show off the bit of car bomb shrapnel that might have killed him in Ecuador.

The professor stirred, and Teague pushed up cautiously, expecting pain. His head throbbed, but his limbs seemed to function. His eyes began to water in the clumpy black smoke. Professor Lwin coughed several times. Teague attempted to stand but choked on a shallow, acrid breath.

Sunlight fought the smoke for access through the few gaps in the smoldering debris that now blocked the stairs. Glowing bits of molten plastic dripped to the floor between Teague's socked feet and the arm of one of their breakfast chairs. *My boots*, Teague thought. His feet didn't feel injured, but he felt stupidly exposed.

"Monkey?" Teague called, choking again, but not hearing his voice.

"Monkey," he screamed, as much to find himself. He caught a glimpse of black and white under a collapsed card table just before Monkey poked his head out, glanced fervently right, left, and up, and then ran at Teague. He mouthed wordlessly, gesturing wildly to the door. Then he began to tug furiously on Teague's shirt. Teague slid along behind him, staying low, but stopped at the professor's shoulders.

"Can you move?" Teague asked the professor, still unsure if he was making sound. Monkey tugged more urgently. Teague shoved his hands under the professor's shoulders and began to drag him toward the door. He worked blind, his socked feet scrambling for purchase. He stumbled over something in the doorway but wrestled the professor clear before he let himself fall backward and gasp for breath.

The building was a ruin. The top floors had collapsed, the bricks melted or shattered. Black smoke poured from the remains. A mattress smoldered against a stump at the edge of the clearing. The roof tent had caught in a tree.

Then Teague saw what had been blocking his way. It was the guard, lying on his back, half in, half outside the building. His legs were straight, but his arms were splayed in an unnatural pose. His face was blackened. Blood was pooling on the dirt from a jagged neck wound. Monkey crawled onto Teague's lap and jabbered urgently.

Suddenly, men filled the clearing. Some knelt over the professor. Others tended to the guard. They surrounded the scene, their eyes to the trees, their mouths open. The professor grimaced as four men lifted him onto a canvas stretcher. Two men squatted in front of Teague and began to examine him roughly. Teague shouted that he could walk and, clutching Monkey, he staggered to his feet. He still wanted his boots, but the men hauled him away after the professor.

Teague's socks snagged as he stumbled and tripped down the stair-stepped trail. Monkey's claws were digging into his neck, but Teague focused on staying on his feet. His head felt ready to implode, and the incessant buzz, the full opposite of hearing, threatened to swallow his other senses.

At the main path, they were met by a vanguard of men who began to clear a lane down the hill. Onlookers stepped out of their doorways, only to be shoved back. Elderly women were knocked aside. Children were nearly trampled. Teague splashed through puddle after puddle as he was carried along with the phalanx. The sky was absurdly blue.

At the cul-de-sac, a group of teenage boys had stopped unloading a truck to gawk at the column of smoke rising far up in the camp. A UN driver was standing high on the running board, talking into a mobile. The men stopped in the middle of the cul-de-sac. One ran ahead to peer down the track from the main road.

Teague noticed the secretary among the group and grabbed him by the shoulder. "My car," he shouted, hoping he was being heard. He pointed to his SUV, still parked near the hut. "We can take my car." The secretary seemed to understand and called to the others.

Teague dug for his keys as they stormed across the cul-de-sac. The attendant stepped out of his hut, and an unlit cigarette fell out of his mouth as the men rushed the vehicle. Teague unlocked the doors remotely before someone snatched the key from him. They loaded the professor through the back, laying a split rear seat down to make room. Worried that they'd leave him behind in this apparently rehearsed evacuation, Teague pushed into the remainder of the back seat. The professor was alert and unbloodied, although he seemed to be in great pain. He'd probably broken something in the fall. The secretary wadded a jacket and set it under the professor's head. Another man squeezed in next to Teague and shut the door as the SUV raced forward in a tight arc.

They bounced down the track at a ferocious speed, and the professor grasped Teague's arm to steady himself. A few minutes later, they skidded onto the lower road and almost immediately passed three older SUVs, each with a single driver, coming up into the camp. They braked and began to turn in unison before disappearing around a bend in the road. They must have been Plan A.

Over the encompassing buzz, Teague remembered Aurore's warning. *Get out. Get out now.*

Near the T-junction in the valley, four UN soldiers on motorcycles tightened into formation around Teague's SUV. A helicopter swept low over the sunroof, heading uphill, gunners hanging out both sides. The motorcade blew through a security checkpoint into a fenced compound. A transport barreled past, then another, and then a third, each loaded with heavily armed blue-helmeted soldiers. The SUV lurched to a stop in front of a field hospital. In seconds, a medical team had removed Professor Lwin and had rushed him into the inflatable tent.

Teague found himself alone with Monkey. His whole body began to vibrate from the rattling drive and the singular tone at the center of his consciousness. Monkey released his grip and began to speak.

"I can't—I can't hear you," Teague said into the buzz.

Monkey patted the mobile in Teague's pocket. Teague dug it out, hoping to see a call from Aurore, but found text instead.

—I need to show you something.

Teague stared at the words, confused, and then realized that Monkey was trying to communicate. A graph appeared on the screen, and Monkey pointed.

"I don't—what is this?" Teague asked. A bubble popped up with Monkey's reply.

—A comparison of three shift profiles.

As the text bubble faded away, Teague began to recognize what he was seeing. The blue and the green ones were nearly identical, but both varied significantly from the red.

"Why are you showing me this?" Teague asked.

Monkey added labels. The red: Gwen. The blue: Gateway 3. The green: Aurore.

"I don't understand," Teague said.

—Aurore's carrier signal was nearly identical to the individual we encountered on Gateway 3. Her calls to your mobile didn't match standard network encryption. In fact, from a network standpoint, those calls originated within your own device. She spoke to me directly and bypassed my firewall to do it. Without more information, I can't be positive, but I think she was using enhanced cognition.

"How—? What—? You're sure?" Teague asked, feeling a moment of dizziness.

Monkey tapped Teague's arm and pointed. Teague turned to see a concerned medic in fatigues and examination gloves at the passenger door. Teague's head swam as the medic beckoned him to get out of the car.

Aurore had sounded so strange as she had warned him. Could she really have been using EC? And she had called him before the attack. Even as the buzzing battled his attention for bandwidth, Teague began to feel an alarming sense of dread.

"I have to go," Teague said. He slid out, keeping the medic at arm's length. "Monkey, stay in the car."

The medic protested as Teague rounded the vehicle, closing doors. Teague got in the driver's seat, started the engine, and swung the SUV toward the exit, barely missing one of the parked motorcycles.

As he approached the gate, Teague slowed, afraid he might be stopped, but the guards scanned his plates as he approached and waved him through. Two minutes later, the guards at the outer checkpoint did the same. Teague raced past the lines of waiting trucks with one eye on the rearview mirror until the camp disappeared behind the trees.

If Aurore hadn't called, he might be dead now, blown to a thousand bloody pieces, body parts splattered over plastic bricks or burned away. Monkey might be a molten mass. Teague hunched forward to strip off his ragged, wet socks and for the first time felt the scrapes on his knees and an ache in his ribs on one side. What had he lost besides his boots? His bag, a screen, a change of clothes? Nothing that couldn't be replaced. He still had his mobile and Monkey, and somehow his life. He had saved the professor, too, but was that heroism or self-preservation?

Once more Teague tried to add up his situation through the ringing fog. Aurore had warned him. That meant she knew about the attack. But how could she possibly have known about it? And why?

Monkey waved a paw in front of Teague's face and pointed at the dashboard screen. The map blinked off, replaced by text.

—You're driving too fast.

Teague growled.

—I'm sorry. Are you sure you don't require medical attention?

"Not now," Teague replied. "Have you ever sensed an EC profile around Aurore before?"

—Never.

Teague braked as they approached a switchback, and his head rattled even as he felt the rear tires skitter on the gravel. Aurore? Enhanced? What did that mean? Teague's stomach churned. His breakfast was ash.

"Are you damaged?" Teague asked as he accelerated into a straightaway.

—Not significantly. Zubotix recommends a comprehensive evaluation by a qualified Zubotix Vet-Tech, but I'd rather see Bondi. I also need cleaning. Zubotix recommends gentle vacuuming.

After another switchback, Teague said, "Listen. You cannot let Aurore in again. Block her. Refuse all messages and calls, even those with normal network encryption. Keep her off my mobile. Treat any communication from her like the most dangerous parasite imaginable."

—What do you think is going on?

"I don't know," Teague said. His skull felt as if it might collapse on itself in a singularity of pain, were it not for the ringing keeping it just barely inflated. He adjusted his grip on the steering wheel, trying to transfer his suffering through the car to the road. "Leave me alone now. I need to drive." And to think.

Aurore, enhanced. An assassination attempt? Refugees. Professor Lwin. Warnings. Dwight Yarrow. None of it connected. None of it made any sense.

—You're bleeding.

Even as he read the message, Teague felt a trickle on his jaw. He swiped at it, and his fingers came away bloody. He swore.

In the little town at the highway junction, Teague stopped at the first convenience store and hurried into the restroom. He had imagined he was only disheveled until he reached a mirror. His hair was peppered with dust and debris. His face was smudged, and his eyes were bloodshot. Blood had trickled from both ears onto his collar and had dried on his neck in sickly, smeared flakes. His scorched shirt was soaked with sweat and reeked of smoke. The seat of his pants was blackened with ash and dirt, and the knees were stained with blood from within. His bare feet were filthy.

Teague pumped a handful of paper towels from the dispenser. His hands trembled as he wetted them and let the flowing water carry away some of the dust from his skin. Teague closed his eyes. Coming up the stairs to find Monkey scanning the forest. The realization. Grabbing the professor. The white streaks of smoke. Aurore knew. Teague clenched and unclenched his hands several times, then wadded the towels and began to clean himself.

A few minutes later, the clerk watched suspiciously as Monkey pointed at a little box on a shelf in the store. Teague touched it lightly as if to ask, "This one?" and Monkey nodded. What made this brand of pills better than the other three on the shelf? His head ached too much to decipher the fine English print, let alone the Thai. He'd asked Monkey to find the best painkiller, and this was his recommendation. Teague could remember very little pain in his life that had ever needed killing. Pain taught and then pain subsided. It was illogical to deny pain its chance to impart its message. Wasn't that what they'd said in the sermons? But this ache, and the ringing, had yet to show any signs of abating. This pain was no tutor; it was a predator.

Teague set the painkillers and a bottle of water on the counter. The clerk rang up the purchase nervously.

Outside, the sky was somehow still a brilliant blue. As Teague disconnected the SUV from the quick charger, he noticed that they were across the street from the motel where he'd stayed months ago, the night before he'd met Professor Lwin. He was tempted to get a room, pass out, and sort this all out later. He checked the time. It wasn't yet nine in the morning.

Aurore knew. How did she know? Why did she know? And she was enhanced. What else did she know? Teague shucked the bottle from the box and fought with the child-safety cap. After a few moments, he tossed the bottle to Monkey. "Open that for me. And get in. We're leaving."

Once Monkey had it open, Teague dumped the bottle's contents—two dozen little orange pills—into a depression on the dashboard, tossed the bottle in the recycling, and closed the door. He gathered a handful, cracked the water, and gagged them down.

"Don't look at me like that," Teague said. "I'll be fine."

A few kilometers out of town, Teague snapped his fingers and tapped the dashboard screen. "Monkey, I need you to do something," he said.

—I like to help.

"Do you have good Uni-Fi here?" Teague asked. Monkey nodded. "I want you to create a timeline beginning two years before we visited the camp in Mali. Plot all violent incidents in every country we've visited, every country a refugee has come from, and all the nations that border those. I'm looking for bombings, assassinations, killings, riots, protests, arson, unwarranted arrests, anything and everything that might've hurt someone. I want a graphic timeline showing when, where, and why they happened. Search all the news sites, government feeds, the UNHCR, the Red Cross, Doctors Without Borders, all the usual places. If an incident seems appropriate, include it for now."

—What are you looking for?

"I want to compare it to the dates of all my visits to the camps," Teague replied.

—What are you hoping to discover?

The painkillers had begun to dissolve uncomfortably in his empty stomach. "Jens said it was a bloody year," Teague replied. "I just hope I'm wrong."

Teague stopped at an achingly bright mega-market on the outskirts of Bangkok and bought some new clothes, shoes, gauze to stuff in his still-bleeding ears, and several colossal packs of pills. The first bottle had dulled the pain enough for him to make the nominally seven-hour drive in less than five, but it had done little to quell the ringing. Teague changed clothes in the bathroom of a roadside diner and then eased gingerly into a booth to put something in his body besides pharmaceuticals.

The timeline Monkey had organized was a mass of dots, color-coded by continent and sized by severity, but too dense to view on Teague's mobile. Monkey commandeered three of the diner's flexi-screen menus, and Teague spread them out end to end to try to get a feel for the information. He tapped a few dots, and each time, a pop-up bubble offered him details about the incident, the number of casualties, and a link to Monkey's source. The number of overall occurrences did seem to increase slightly after his visit to Mali, but not definitively enough to draw any conclusions. There was no way to tell what might be a background level of violence, for lack of a better term, and what might have been related to his work. At Teague's request, Monkey highlighted only those incidents that directly involved communities they'd talked to about Asylum Aid. Teague plotted trend lines. He stretched, squeezed, massaged, and filtered the data a dozen ways but saw no clear trends.

After his meal arrived, Teague began to chop up the data, setting each community he'd visited onto its own timeline. He overlaid them all with the date of his visit centered on each as a pivot point, and there it was: a definitive increase in the volume, and nature, of violent incidents in the weeks and months, even days, after his visits. In some places, such as Niabandala and Guyana, where strife had been ongoing, the increases were almost negligible. In other locales, the change was shocking and steep. Every line turned up almost from the moment they'd visited. Never down, never flat. It felt as if someone was turning up the heat, rendering it impossible for these people to ever return home. Home: that final and all-important component of Aurore's formula.

Teague considered the implications. Aurore, presumably at Dwight's behest, had set him up to identify the most vulnerable communities. But then what? While he'd been visiting those refugees in the camps, had another associate been instigating violence and unrest?

He supposed it wasn't terribly difficult to do. Most of the communities were tinderboxes just waiting for a match. Most had already produced refugees. Drugs, cash, and guns could make any number of bad people willing to do any number of bad things. Give a few weapons to a militia, tell them you believe in their cause, and set them loose. Bribe the right officials to make a decision, make a statement, or turn a blind eye. How else? Divert supplies. Sabotage local utilities. Make threats. Target schools and churches. Manipulate the local media. *Hell,* Teague thought, *manipulate the international media*. If he could think of a dozen strategies with a head injury, imagine what a motivated professional, or a group of them, could do.

Of course they'd be plural. To make this happen at such a scale, you'd need a network of operatives able to quietly affect brutal change in dozens of countries. They'd have to be coordinated, unified in purpose, and completely without compunction. And then Teague realized, as clearly as his rattled mind allowed, that they must, like Aurore, be enhanced. Who else could conceive of and execute such an inhuman plan from the shadows?

But it seemed impossible, so unbelievably ridiculous. And correlation didn't mean causation.

Monkey quickly compiled similar timelines for several refugee groups they'd never visited. It took only a few cases to see that there was no marked increase of violence for any of these other communities and no evident pivot point in the time ranges.

"Monkey, plot the decision dates for the Angel projects on the appropriate timelines," Teague said. If he needed any more proof, there it was. After each Angel project contract had been finalized, the incident trend lines curved again, slightly down, but then held steady. Whoever was doing this wanted the asylum seekers to feel good about their decision.

Did they know about the prediction program? Teague hesitated, almost fearing to find out, but then asked Monkey to plot individual timelines for the communities Molly had identified. Many shared the signature marked increase in violence. However, the pivot point for each case was not the date he'd visited them in the camps—indeed, he'd never visited most of them—but the date that he'd sent an anonymous message to Jens.

Teague felt a chill. He couldn't believe that Jens was a part of this. He had found Jens, not the other way around. Hadn't he?

They've been using me, Teague thought, *this enhanced cabal.*

Aurore had flattered him, and he'd fallen for it. Actually, the manipulation had begun long before that. It had started at the moment Dwight's assistant had knocked on his dorm room door. But why me? What's so special about me? Nothing, except...

Monkey lifted his chin off the table and cocked his head at Teague's searching stare.

How did I not see it? Teague wondered. *What else have I missed?* And then he realized that he had missed everything. The grenades may have made him deaf, but Aurore had kept him blind.

Teague arrived at the e-mall an hour before closing, hoping that Bondi hadn't decided to head home early. He'd thought about calling ahead, but after considering the capabilities of a cadre of network-based psychopaths, he'd had Monkey disconnect himself and Teague's mobile from Uni-Fi. The Badass emerged from behind his curtain with a wide, surprised smile and open arms, but when he saw Teague, concern washed over his face.

—My friend, what's happened to you?

Teague held up his mobile to show Bondi the voice recognition program. "I can't hear very well. I'll explain later, but right now, I need your help."

—Do you need to go to a hospital?

Teague shook his head.

Bondi protested, but Teague ignored the transcription. "I need you to give Monkey a quick once-over to make sure he's not damaged. And I need some help getting some items before the stores close."

—Are you in trouble?

"Maybe."

—What do you need?

"Monkey knows. Can I borrow a screen?"

As Bondi disappeared into the aisles with Monkey, Teague called up the e-mall's message boards on one of Bondi's screens. Someone was always trying to dump a used motorcycle.

Less than half an hour later, Teague was shucking his new electronics—a screen, a fresh mobile, a new shift set—from their packages and stowing them in a new backpack while Bondi inspected Monkey in his workshop. A few minutes later, Bondi emerged from behind the curtain and spoke.

—He's intact. But I'm running a more detailed diagnostic. He registered a significant duress sequence around seven thirty this morning.

Teague nodded. Bondi tapped Teague's new shift set, still in its package.

—You'll need to get this tuned.

"Monkey can do it."

—Are you going to tell me what's going on?

"It's probably better if you don't know," Teague replied.

—Maybe I can help you. After all, I am the Badass.

Teague tried to chuckle, but it hurt his head.

"Have you ever heard of the Naiad Academy? It's in the United States."

Bondi shook his head.

—Although I remember a NAIAD Institute.

"What did they do?"

—It's been years. A competitor of Nexon's for a time. They fronted themselves as a research lab and got quite a bit of DARPA money, but they were more of a tech development company. They actually did some of the initial work on shifting technology.

"Did they do any research on enhanced cognition?" Teague asked.

—EC? I suppose they might have. Everyone's talked about it at some point, but it's turned out to be a bit of a unicorn. Why?

"I need Monkey to stay on the grid, but hidden. Do you have anything new, or even anything old, stashed away that might help him?" Teague asked. "Anything, everything, that'll keep us invisible." Bondi furrowed his brow. "Come on. I know you've got stuff. Unless you're making money selling tentacle porn now." Teague waved at the ancient boxes on the folding table.

—Stop pleading. I didn't say no.

Bondi slipped into the back and returned a few minutes later with a device in one hand and Monkey at his feet. Bondi beckoned Monkey onto the counter and began to unravel a wire from the device.

"A wire?" Teague asked.

—Trust me. You don't want this code floating around in the spectrum.

Bondi plugged the wire into Monkey's tail.

"Will Monkey know what to do with it?"

—He'll figure it out.

—I like learning new things.

A little LED on the box began to blink.

—I've spent too much of my life looking over my shoulder. You're sure you know what you're doing?

"Has anyone ever tried to kill you?" Teague asked.

—If they have, they haven't done a very thorough job.

The light stopped blinking, and Bondi disconnected the device.

—You bring Monkey to me, yet you won't see a doctor?

"I don't have time."

—Early treatment might save your natural hearing.

"I'll go as soon as I can."

—You take care of yourself.

Teague shouldered his new pack and patted his leg for Monkey to heel. "Thank you for everything," Teague said. He waied deeply. Bondi returned the gesture and then hugged Teague tight, releasing him after a few seconds with a look that needed no translation.

Teague found his new motorcycle, an old-model Chinese import, in the parking garage. Its once-blue paint had faded from too long in the sun and rain. The upholstery was shredded, and the tires were nearly bald. The gamer had been relieved to be rid of it. But the battery was in good shape, and the on-board systems were easily hacked—all the better for Monkey to keep them off the road tracking systems. Shakiro Squirrel willing, it'd get him out of town.

Before Teague put Monkey in the backpack for the journey, he said, "There's still one thing we need."

—What's that?

"Are you back online?" Teague asked. Monkey nodded. "And you feel safe? You were able to incorporate Bondi's new software?"

—I've never felt so invisible.

"Good. How much is still in our expense accounts?" This was their name for the accounts Aurore had provided for him to pay Jens and for travel. Monkey put a hearty seven-figure number of unos on Teague's mobile screen. "I need you to transfer all of that out right away."

—To which accounts?

"New ones. Split it up. Use banks all over the solar system. Keep balances low. Then transfer those balances to new banks and close the empty accounts. Spread it out. I want it as difficult to trace as possible, but done very quickly.

—I may have to open hundreds of accounts.

"I know. Do you understand what I'm asking?"

—You're asking me to steal this money.

"Right. Get in the backpack and get started. Don't waste any more runtime until you're done."

Soon, Teague was willing the bike through the freeway traffic south, relying on his memory instead of Monkey's directions. A fresh dose of pills curdled his stomach even as it soothed his head. His eyes strained to make up for his missing sense. Logically, he knew he'd hear again. Either his ears would heal or he'd get implants. But Teague hated this fresh impediment. And now he was fleeing into a greater, self-imposed isolation. Where would it end?

What if he contacted Aurore, made some excuse, and returned? Might he feign ignorance? Would these people believe that he didn't know they were enhanced? But Aurore had given up all pretense when she communicated directly through Monkey. The others might even be angry at her for exposing herself. No, it was too late to go back. Besides, Monkey was busy stretching their millions into a gossamer web, torching his bridges with every transfer.

Why had Aurore warned him? Did she actually care for him?

"Get out now," she'd said. Maybe the advice held a deeper meaning. Maybe he'd actually been the target. But Teague quickly shook off that notion. Pride had gotten him into this. She'd made him believe that he had been chosen to change the world. Thomas had done the same thing. Had Dwight orchestrated that, too?

Teague began to wonder if he should have remained at the camp. Even though he'd saved the professor's life, it might have looked suspicious to run. How disgusting to be thought of as a bringer of death instead of salvation. He had panicked this morning, but now, after seeing the statistical proof of what Aurore and Dwight had done, were still doing, he was convinced that he was right to flee. They obviously thought little of human life and were willing to kill to promote their own ends. Shouldn't enhanced people place great value on every mind, every life? *I spent too much time sitting at the feet of the Buddha,* Teague thought. *Enlightenment, my ass.*

He couldn't hear, for now, and he couldn't shift, but he'd soon have a crapload of money. He also had Monkey, currently tail-deep into the international banking system, and he had Molly. Two NAIs under his control, one military grade, the other a beating heart in Valdosky's networks. Teague realized, with a grin, that he might just be the most dangerous man in the solar system. He'd need to get a better bike.

CHAPTER 31

I will die, and with acceptance comes a wish that the end would come sooner.

MARCH 2096

Avatars had already begun to sync into the virtual side of the telepresence conference room when Rob arrived shortly after lunch. As he set his screen by his usual chair, M-SOO's accountant greeted him with a wave and then turned to resume his conversation with the Operations liaison. The accountant was probably in the building, unless he'd elected to work from home today, but Rob was glad he and the other locals usually chose to shift. Rob could have shifted, too, but he figured that if he must endure these monthly divisional executive meetings, he might as well bike down to Grissom Street and share a bit of meat-space solidarity with Aron Valdosky. It never hurt to cozy up with the boss's son.

Rob was pouring a cup of coffee when Aron strolled in and tossed his suit jacket over the back of his chair.

"Can't believe it's that time again already," Aron said as he joined Rob at the credenza. "Didn't we just have one of these?"

"You're vice president. Why not decree quarterly meetings?" Rob asked and passed Aron a mug.

"Thanks. I wish. Hey, by the way, have you heard from Teague?" Aron asked.

"Recently? No. Why?" Rob asked as he stirred in a packet of sugar.

"I got a strange call from Matthew last night. Dwight Yarrow called him out of the blue and asked if Teague had contacted him."

"Why would Teague contact your dad?" Rob asked. "And why would Dwight care?"

"I have no idea," Aron said. "But it gets weirder. From what Dwight said, Teague might've been involved in some kind of terrorist assassination attempt at a refugee camp in northwest Thailand."

"Involved?"

"He was supposedly there when it happened, and now he's disappeared. Teague had been working with the nonprofit coordinating the Angel colonies, but no one knows what he was actually doing in a refugee camp." Aron sipped his coffee and reached for more sugar. "I didn't even know he'd quit CDI."

"Me neither. Have you tried to contact him?"

"I sent a message," Aron said. "I thought maybe he'd call you."

"Not me. Would he have contacted Professor Minus?"

"Thomas and Teague didn't exactly part on the best of terms."

"This doesn't sound like Teague at all," Rob said.

"I honestly haven't talked to him in a long time."

"Last I heard from him, he wasn't even back to Earth yet."

"We're sucky friends," Aron said, shaking his head. "You'll let me know if you hear from him?"

"Absolutely."

Aron glanced at the time. "I hear we're near completion on Molly's Phase Three expansion…"

* * *

When Rob's mobile rang in the middle of the night, he sat up and snapped on a light, certain that Teague had finally returned his messages. Who else would be calling at this hour? But it was Navid.

"You better get down here," he said grimly.

Half an hour later, Rob scuttled his bike at the base of the ramp and ran in to find Navid at the primary monitoring station with one of the overnight staffers. Both looked ashen.

"I don't like that scowl," Rob said. Navid glowered and gestured broadly to Molly's systems schematic on the main screen.

"What am I supposed to be seeing?" Rob asked, rubbing his eyes.

"Sorry. I was asleep, too," Navid said. "Nexon called about ninety minutes ago wondering why we'd brought Phase Three online without telling them."

Rob gaped. He'd been inspecting the statuses for Phases 1 and 2 and hadn't noticed that the usually grayed components for the newest phase were now green.

"My reaction exactly," Navid said.

"The power system hasn't been certified," Rob said.

"I know."

"We're still waiting on the punch list from what's-his-name, the cooling system contractor. The guy with the mustache."

"I know."

"We haven't pulled all that sticky film off the front panels."

"I know all that, but she's in there."

"I don't understand," Rob said. Navid gave Rob a knowing wide-eyed look. "No."

"Yes," Navid replied. "The Butler did it."

"We're sure?"

"It's his password on the commands," Navid said.

"So he activated an entire server bank and just took off? Why would he do that?" Rob asked. Navid shrugged helplessly. "Shit, we're not budgeted for Phase Three licensing until next fiscal year."

"That's why Nexon called," Navid said, "but that's not what's troubling me the most." He expanded Phase Three's diagrams. Rob leaned in to see that Molly was pushing the processing capacity of the new servers to the maximum.

"That can't be right," Rob said. "She only uses forty percent of Phase Two on a good day."

"She's running a massive external search," Navid said, expanding an active process report.

"I assume we've asked her to stop?"

"Oh, we've asked."

"Molly?" Rob called.

"Yes, Rob?" she replied.

"Please end your activity in Phase Three components."

"I'm sorry, but system initialization processes may not be interrupted," Molly replied.

Rob hung his head. "You've scanned her?" he asked Navid.

"She's running on pristine Nexon code."

"Molly?" Rob asked again. "What initialization step are you working on?"

"Local network engagement," she replied.

"You're scanning the Internet," Rob said. "Come on. You're smarter than this."

Navid scoffed. "For her to consider the Internet a local network, *someone* would've had to leave about six or seven gates open. Plus, it's not just Three. She's using every bit of excess capacity from One and Two. I'm surprised NetSec isn't swarming us right now."

"Molly, Hunter authorized the system initialization?"

"Yes, Rob," Molly said.

"God damn it."

"Even if this was inadvertent, it's a serious breach. They're—" Navid began.

"I know, Navid," Rob snapped. "I'm sorry. I know what you're going to say, but I don't need to hear it right now. We're going to have to stop this manually. But we'll need to leave her image in there so Nexon can figure out what's happened."

"My thoughts exactly. I just needed your approval."

Within the hour, a team from NetSec had descended like locusts. They interviewed everyone even as they scanned the logs and inspected the manual shutdown. Rob resented their thinly veiled suspicions and their self-granted superiority, but he held his tongue. Besides, what was there to say to them? Yes, Hunter

Noonan was a little clumsy, sort of forgetful, and kind of lazy, but he wasn't nearly as bad as he'd once been, and he wasn't malicious. Unless he was.

The more Rob thought about it, the angrier he got. Hunter should've taken better care of Molly. He'd abused a trust. But Rob blamed himself, too. He'd trusted the kid beyond his abilities. He'd known from the outset that Hunter wasn't the caliber of person that a mission-critical system like Molly deserved. But if that was the standard, Rob might as well fire himself.

Once most of the NetSec crew had gone, Rob found a moment to grab some coffee and call it breakfast. He found a semi-clean mug, a souvenir from the Noctis Labyrinth Motorpod Challenge. He poured coffee from the pot, and the little cartoon motorpods began to race sluggishly around the mug in a mockery of their real capability. Rob sniffed the ancient, tepid brown sludge, grimaced, and then tossed it and the rest of the pot into the sink. He set more brewing and went to his office to hide while he waited.

"Are you okay, Molly?" Rob asked, once his office door was closed.

"There's no harm done, as far as I can determine. I'm sorry for any misunderstanding, Daddy," Molly replied, his daughter again for the moment.

"It's not your fault," Rob said. "And don't worry. I won't let it happen again."

* * *

Teague stormed out onto the balcony of his second-floor motel room. He had hoped for a lot more time. The sunlight hurt his eyes, but being outdoors relieved the intensity of his tinnitus. Close walls seemed to amplify the singular, incessant ringing. Only the humiliation of forced shift sleep provided a true escape.

Monkey trotted out, handed Teague his sunglasses, and darted back inside. He returned with Teague's mobile, but when Teague didn't take it, he plopped dejectedly at his feet.

The balcony overlooked a sparse grove of palm trees and a

busy resort drive. Teague crumbled paint flakes off the railing into the landscaping below. A few balconies over, a housekeeper was cleaning up from a party some German teenagers had thrown the night before. They had thumped the walls and floors so much that it had disturbed even him. Teague met the housekeeper's eyes for a moment, but she looked away. What must she, and the other housekeepers, think of him? He rarely left his room. And when he did, what did they find? Bottles of painkillers, half-eaten takeout, both beds in fevered shambles, bloodied towels and pillowcases. But at a motel like this, Teague guessed they'd seen worse.

It had been risky to enable Molly's unused hardware, but those big, fat servers had been too tempting, and the bumbling guy on Rob's staff was a perfect cover. Teague just wished Molly had been able to process more of the scan before Rob's people were able to shut it down.

Teague was mildly surprised that heavily armed authorities hadn't already surrounded the motel. He, Monkey, and Molly had breached everything in the past few days. They'd attempted to trace the source of Aurore's money through dozens of banking networks. They'd copied Dwight's files from Valdosky's systems. Monkey was constantly scanning the G-Plex grids for shift profiles that matched Aurore's, and he'd scampered away with several billion dollars' worth of proprietary data from G-Plex's EC development program. The Naiad Academy appeared to be nothing but a high-end private school for gifted children with a curious emphasis on technology. The SJDC and its members seemed to be legit in every way. Aurore's mobile either ran on vaporware like Monkey did now or had been deactivated. Dwight's mobile yielded nothing but communication within Valdosky. The only traces of the NAIAD Institute were ancient financial statements filed with regulators. A search for the listed corporate officers had dead-ended at every turn. Even DARPA appeared to have shredded its relevant files.

At times, Teague invoked Occam's razor and tried to believe that he was chasing his imagination. But the wisps, dead ends, and data voids hinted that there was indeed something big, organized, and adapted to survive in a hyper-connected world. If the members were enhanced, they had time—more time than Teague could imagine. And with that much time, they must have learned how to stay invisible.

"We'd better check out today. Go to a new place," Teague said. As he headed back inside, he touched the doorframe's peeling blue-green paint. It seemed familiar, like a déjà-vu. He turned back for a moment and looked around. Seeing nothing, he went inside and shut the door.

It felt good, but not relaxing, to shower. Even though Monkey was on lookout, Teague kept a hand on the wall, reaching out to feel footfalls or the opening of a door. Monkey was constantly sniffing for strange mobiles and comm devices, scanning the local police network channels and monitoring the motel's security cameras, listening for the things Teague couldn't hear. It was good to have an ally. Part of Teague wanted to believe that Aurore, too, was on his side, that she'd shown her true colors when she'd called to warn him. But as much as he wanted to believe it, contacting her now felt like too much of a risk. If he was right, then she and her friends had all the time in the world to wait. They might just be counting on his mortal impatience to find him.

Still, he wanted to talk to someone.

Teague snapped the water off and grabbed a towel. "Monkey," he called, "I think it's time to call Gwen." He opened the bathroom door and found Monkey shaking his head vigorously. "What do you mean no? Do you know how to get ahold of Gwen or not?" Monkey nodded. "Then get a message ready. I'll be out in a minute."

Monkey pointed to the side of Teague's face. Teague swiped the towel over his ear, and it came away pink.

A few minutes later, dried, dressed and with fresh gauze in his ears and pills in his stomach, Teague told Monkey to start packing. He picked up his screen, expecting to find a message window, but found a text bubble instead.

—She won't talk to you.

"What are you talking about?"

—Not about this.

"How do you know?"

—Because Rob Heneghan once tried to talk to her about Dwight Yarrow on a public network, and she refused. Rob told Molly all about it afterward. She actually broke the G-Plex terms of service and hijacked Rob's signal off network to a private shift frame when he tried to discuss it. It was the only place she'd say Dwight's name, and even then she was reluctant.

"Why didn't you tell me about this before? Never mind. Do you know what they talked about?"

—Only what Rob told Molly…

Teague paced as he read about Dwight's request for asteroid risk reports and user status, and then about Rob's thin complaints to Molly about Dwight and Gwen.

"This connection Rob established for Dwight, please tell me it's not still open?" Teague asked.

Monkey shook his head.

—After we left Bangkok, I made a dummy partition inside Molly. It will look like her on the surface, but it won't allow a visitor full access.

"I suppose that'll have to do for now," Teague said. "But this doesn't get us anywhere. How can I talk to Gwen? Where is she?"

—As far as I can tell, she's still living at the TataFord facility in Earth orbit.

"You don't think she'd respond to a simple message, something carefully worded?"

—You're welcome to try, but she'll probably ignore you or block you.

"There's got to be some way to talk to her."

—We could devise a secret code. That'd be fun.

Teague scowled. "Finish packing your stuff."

—There is one question. Are we certain that Gwen's not a part of this? After all, she attended the Naiad Academy, too.

"She's not," Teague said. "In fact, everything points to her knowing about this but staying apart from it: the different shift profile signature, all her warnings about Valdosky. For all we know, she's in a situation like ours."

As Teague packed the last of his few things, he wondered where he should go next. There were dozens of these shoddy places up and down the coast, usually set back a few blocks from the beach and tucked between the big resorts. But how long was he willing to bounce from place to place? And was it enough? The fake IDs Monkey had set up had worked so far, but how long could a deaf man with a ring-tailed lemur stay inconspicuous?

Teague had never wanted to shift more, to be able to meet Gwen in her private shift frame like Rob had. Would she kidnap him, too, if he started asking dangerous questions? That was a fantasy, but how about Monkey? No, it might raise too many questions. What about Bondi? Teague hated to involve him further, and besides, Gwen was probably too paranoid to take a call from a complete stranger. As far as he knew, she had only ever confided her fear of Dwight to Rob Heneghan of all people, and then only reluctantly. But she *had* talked to him. Would she again?

* * *

The girls squealed and giggled as Quentin Rox lowered himself into the enormous heart-shaped tub. Their hot hands caressed his chiseled flesh even as they teased him with the endless suds, dabbing blobs on their breasts, on his nose, on his cheeks. He laughed and pulled one girl close against him even as he kissed another, eliciting a gasp of pleasure from the third. Cashing in a few of his Peach Pit loyalty reward points for the Slip'N'Slide upgrade was the best idea he'd had in a long time. How better to forget about the week's countless meetings with NetSec, HR, and Nexon?

But just as he began to explore some of the girls' more interesting and slippery curves, an error message flickered in a pop-up.

"What's wrong, baby?" one of the girls asked.

The pop-up vanished. He hadn't even had time to read it.

"Probably nothing," Quentin replied.

The girl smiled, and then Quentin fell asleep.

Rob awoke in his own bed. The memories of the suds, the warmth, the girls' smiles, and their hands under the water were painfully fresh but as unreachable as a dream. Rob swore as he sat up and turned his clock. Subtracting the down-shifting time from U-shift, he'd lost almost forty minutes. Of all the stupid—why had his fricking shift set picked that moment to go wonky?

Rob unclipped his nodes and tossed them on the charging pad. He might as well toss them in the trash.

* * *

Monkey had video of the whole thing:

Gwen had linked him to a crude, industrial office that brought to mind the old section of Agnus Dei. It made sense; she probably liked to work in a place where she felt at home, even in shift.

Her avatar wore an uncharacteristically clean and unstretched cardigan. Her hair resembled frozen fire, rather than a frizzy tangle. Her face was a reasonable facsimile but conveyed little of its usual universal disdain. This was Gwen-lite, Gwen humanized for public consumption, like Monkey's lemur features, especially with the vicious edge of her voice muted by the subtitles.

This better be good, Rob.

—Thanks for seeing me. I've actually come on behalf of Teague.

Teague?

—You know. Teague Werres from Agn—

I know who he is, I just—why didn't he just contact me?

—He wasn't sure you'd talk to him. And after what he told me, I think he's right. Did you know that he quit Valdosky after he got back to Earth?

So what? Does he want a cookie?

—Aren't you curious to know what he's been doing?

Not especially.

—Well, I'm going to tell you anyway. It's important, and he really thinks you can help him.

Why would he think that?

—Because—and I don't know how he knows this—but he claims that you use enhanced cognition. Is that true?

Rob, are you completely dim? You should have known that since the first time I helped you with that grant application. Molly ran the shift servers, for fuck's sake. At least Teague was paying attention.

—Excuse me for respecting your privacy. Besides, how was I supposed to guess that you magically use a technology that's not even supposed to exist?

Well, now you know.

—How did you even—?

Not now, Rob. Just get on with it.

—Teague asked me to give this to you.

Rob produced a file and passed it over. If Teague still had any doubts that Gwen was enhanced, they vanished in the mere seconds it took her to absorb the file of all the data he'd collected about his encounter with the entity on Gateway 3 and all his dealings with Aurore and Dwight. In an instant, her impatience became astonishment.

Have you read this?

—Teague filled me in on most of it.

I told you to forget this. I was very explicit.

—You told me to forget about Dwight Yarrow.

Don't get smart with me. This isn't some ADU professor you're dealing with.

—I know. Teague almost got killed.

I warned you idiots about getting involved with Valdosky.

—Fine, Gwen. You warned us, but you left. And it was difficult to take you seriously when you kept us in the dark.

You'd never have believed me.

—So it's true, this stuff about the Naiad Academy or Institute or whatever?

Did Teague say what he intended to do with this information?

—Expose them? Set things right? Survive?

Tell him to pick one.

—Who are these people?

Stop asking me this.

—Who else am I supposed to ask?

I should throw you out of here right now.

—I'm sorry, Gwen, but I have to know if Molly and M-SOO are in any danger. If you throw me out, I'll just keep coming back. Sending you messages. Whatever it takes. Tell me what's going on.

<scream>

Gwen spun away, grabbed a drafting table, and, in the replicated microgravity of Agnus Dei, hurled it across the room. It cartwheeled but remained intact, even as it smashed harmlessly against a pane of safety glass and bounced on the floor. She reeled around and snarled. But he held his ground.

—You can't just leave us in the dark. Teague and I know too much already. And we're in this as much as you.

Gwen pinched her eyes closed for several long moments and then snapped them open.

Fine. But this is the last time. After you leave here, no more questions about this ever again. Is that understood?

—Completely.

Gwen looked around as if to find a place to sit, then ran a hand back through her hair.

What do you know about the development of shifting?

—It was the next logical step after Immer-Sims?

No, it wasn't. Think, Rob. Going from external sensory and manual interfaces to direct brain interface is an enormous leap. The development of shifting had nothing to do with entertainment and the Internet. It had everything to do with artificial intelligence. Do you know what NAIAD stands for? Nascent Artificial Intelligence Architecture and Development.

—But the NAIAD Institute went out of business.

The hell they did. They might not have succeeded in creating real AI, but that doesn't mean they failed.

—They developed enhanced cognition?

They discovered that the mind's software could be temporarily refocused in time and space. This became shifting. With the money they earned from licensing that technology, they began to experiment with accelerating the interface. After they started getting results, they decided to go dark. The interface process was definitely not user friendly. In fact, it was potentially harmful if not done correctly. They created the academy to identify promising individuals and teach them.

—You were recruited.

I was just a kid. We all were. They taught us that we were the genesis of the next phase of evolution. They didn't phrase it quite like that, but that was the implication: that those able to assess the full record of human history in an afternoon were destined to guide the species. We were to be part of a literal and figurative network, capable of influencing the course of human history outside the reach of any authority. Pretty fucking seductive rhetoric for a bunch of gifted kids.

—You didn't buy into it?

It scared the shit out of me. My parents, hare-brained as they are, taught me to value individuality, freedom, the power of unfettered human creativity. It was pretty easy to see that these people were setting up a totally unaccountable shadow fascism.

—But how could you keep this secret?

Fuck you, Rob. I was fourteen when I left. I do what I'm able. I'm working with G-Plex to bring their EC program online. I'm designing spacecraft that will allow travel and trade without blind reliance on Valdosky. I gain nothing by attacking these people directly or spouting paranoia like some conspiracy whack-job on a street corner in U-shift. I'd be discredited in a heartbeat, or worse. They might decide the waves I'm making are too big. And then what? However advanced you think they might be, you need to assume they're already way past that. The only way to fight them is to develop technology in parallel that mitigates their abilities.

—M-SOO could've been a part of that.

You think? You guys flushed it down the toilet.

—Maybe you should have told us.

Fuck you.

—Fair enough. But I still don't understand. How does this lead them to populating asteroids with refugees of their own making? Is this all just to benefit Valdosky?

This organization is not the Valdosky Companies. Valdosky is simply one tool that they control. I doubt if Matthew Valdosky even knows.

—So what's their end goal?

I don't know.

—Money? Power? Control?

Maybe all those things. Maybe more. The rhetoric at the academy was high-minded perpetual continuation of the species crap. But that could be a guise for anything.

—What should I tell Teague?

Same thing I've been telling you. Forget it. Walk away. Get on with his life.

—Is he in danger?

Depends on what he chooses to do. But I can't help him. If he follows my advice and drops it, they'll probably leave him alone.

—How can people like you and Teague ever achieve anything if you're too afraid to connect and organize?

I have to believe that things will change when the G-Plex EC program comes online. It'll probably be speed limited, mostly so adults will be able to learn to do it, but it'll be better than nothing.

—But Teague can't shift. He won't even be a part of that.

I don't have any more answers for him. I'm sorry. You should go now.

—Thank you, Gwen. You're a good friend.

I'm not. A real friend would've lied to you.

Teague paused the video, and Monkey hopped into his lap.

—Didn't I do good?

Teague smiled and scratched Monkey behind the ears.

The bartender pointed questioningly at Teague's nearly empty beer bottle. Teague nodded for another. He turned his screen off and set it facedown on the bar.

He'd watched the exchange with Gwen four times now, and each time he felt even more in the dark. How absurd that the place where Monkey had met Gwen was as real as this sun-drenched beach, this thatch-roofed bar, or even this once-cold beer. Yet he would only ever be allowed this kind of distant glimpse into the shifted universe. Yet, from within that world, people were working sleeplessly to control the real world and his life. And now, according to Gwen, the only hope of ever confronting this organization lay in someday joining the ranks of the enhanced. How useless did that make him?

The bartender returned with a fresh bottle, and Teague took a swig. It was cold but bitter, and Teague set it aside. He let Monkey down and settled his tab with a flick on his mobile.

"Come on, Monkey," he said.

But Monkey didn't budge. He was staring toward the beach from under Teague's stool. Teague followed his gaze to an unmistakable figure on the edge of the pedestrian path just outside the bar's perimeter. Her white shirt and stylish pants suit were dangerously out of place among the tourists' shorts, flowered shirts, and swimsuits. Her overly large sunglasses gave Teague the impression that she'd been watching him all this time.

She nodded in recognition and then gestured to a vacant table in the dappled shade under a ficus tree. Teague scanned the bar, the path, and the beach but didn't see anyone else watching him. Even if there were, it was too late to run away. As he wended his way through the salvaged crates and spools that served as tables on the patio, he warned himself not to believe everything, or perhaps anything, she said. Monkey stayed close to Teague's heels but never took his eyes off Aurore.

Aurore set her bag and sunglasses on the rickety table, pulled out one of the plastic chairs, and perched her slight frame on the edge of the seat as if she wasn't really touching it at all. It was such a prim posture that Teague wondered how he had ever found her attractive. Had seducing him been just another task on her to-do list? Had everything about her been an act? She waited politely for him to sit down and activate his screen before she spoke. He supposed it was her way of signaling that for all his efforts, he hadn't hidden anything from her at all.

—Hello, Teague.

"I suppose I should thank you. I'd be dead if you hadn't called," he replied.

—I'm very sorry for your injuries.

"The professor survived, too. Are you going to try to assassinate him again?"

—We did not plan the unfortunate attack on Professor Lwin, but it was probably inevitable. There had been many threats.

"No, but you're funding, maybe even arming, the Karen resistance. Or do you deny it?"

—It was you who chose the Karen people.

Teague had to laugh. "How can you say that with a straight face? I was trying to help them."

—As are we. We are not your enemy, Teague. In fact, once we realized where you were, we agreed that I should warn you.

"But you didn't stop the attack."

—That was impossible. If you had told me that you were returning to the camp, perhaps.

"The attack on the professor was completely unnecessary. He'd already decided to recommend resettlement to his people."

—You misunderstand our ability to influence events.

"Do I?"

—There's still a place for you at the council and in the Angel program if you wish.

"You lied to me, and you used me. You convinced me I was making a difference."

—You were. You still can.

"Your price is too monstrous."

—I accept that you see it that way.

"How else is there to see it? Refugees are people, Aurore. And you and your group are perpetuating actual atrocities. Real, not virtual. Real blood. Real lives. Real minds."

—We are simply accelerating inevitable events. At some cost, yes, but a calculated one. In fact, we're saving a great many more lives in the long run.

"You can't know that. Have you been enhanced so long that you've forgotten what it means to be human?"

—If you want me to go, I will. But perhaps we can spend this time productively.

Teague bit his tongue. "Then by all means. Why'd you come?"

—First of all, there's no need for you to hide in this way. We have no wish to harm you.

"I won't go back to the council."

—If that is your wish.

"You'll leave me alone? Just like that?"

—We will.

"Monkey, too?"

—Of course.

"You don't consider us a threat?"

—Sorry, but no. We've known about Monkey all along. In fact, it was his presence that drew our attention to you in the first place.

"Bondi has nothing to do with this."

—I'm not threatening anyone.

"Every word you say is a threat," Teague said. "Your very presence here is a threat."

—You misunderstand our intentions.

"You're going to let me walk away, and go on with my life, for nothing in exchange?"

—Yes.

"What about the money? Do you want it back?"

—No. And you'll find that we've deposited considerably more as additional compensation for your injuries.

"Are you trying to buy me off?

—Consider it however you will. Spend it. Invest it. Donate it. It's your choice.

"What if I expose you to the authorities or the media?"

—You're welcome to try.

"You're sure that you're that invulnerable?"

—I didn't say we wouldn't thwart such an effort, but we will not harm you. Gwendolyn Ungefucht probably gave you sage advice. By the way, that was quite a clever trick you played on her, Monkey.

Monkey's tail went rigid and his ears twitched.

—Just go on believing I'm cute and cuddly. I dare you.

Aurore smirked but turned back to Teague.

"Is there any use in asking why?" Teague asked. "Or will you tell me that I can't understand, that because I can't shift, I can't see the big picture?"

—Please don't think that we aren't human, Teague.

"Unbelievable. You want sympathy?"

—I know you won't believe it, but we care a great deal about the human race, and I do care for you.

"I've already bitten that hook."

—I regret that things turned out this way. With time we might've reached a better understanding.

"Why do you need refugees to colonize asteroids?" Teague asked. "Was I just covering up profiteering for Valdosky? Because if that's all it is, I'm going to be extremely fucking disappointed in your supervillain club."

Aurore sighed as if chiding a petulant child. She opened her bag, took out several photographs, and laid them on the table in front of Teague.

—I thought you might want these.

Teague recognized them instantly. A monk had taken one. A girl named Mati had taken another. His mother had taken the last somewhere right along this same coastline. He hadn't thought of them since he'd run. He'd just abandoned them in Geneva. What did that say about him?

She stood.

—Goodbye, Teague. I'm sorry. I truly am.

He soon lost sight of her among the tourists on the beach path. If it weren't for the pictures, he could have believed her a hallucination.

—Should I try to trace her?

Teague dropped a hand on Monkey's back and let gravity hold it in place. He felt the subtle vibration of tensed servos through his fur.

"Don't bother," he said.

CHAPTER 32

I remember something you once said: "We emerge squalling, not knowing how to live or die, and not certain that we want to do either." Is that solely a disease of infancy?

JULY 2096

Another subway train squealed into the station and exhaled its passengers. On the designated bench by a particular vending machine, Teague forced himself to fiddle on his mobile, pretending to play a game. "We didn't miss him, did we?" he murmured, even as he allowed himself a furtive scan of the dispersing crowd.

"I told you we were too early," Monkey replied, whispering like a conscience through Teague's new aural implants. "The next train will be here in six and a half minutes. And"—he kicked against Teague's back through the fabric of the backpack—"stop fidgeting. You're shaking me all around back here."

Teague stopped jiggling his leg and scratched inside an ear with a little finger instead. The specialist had insisted that Teague wouldn't be able to feel anything—the implants were installed much deeper than his fingers, or even a swab, could reach—but he always sensed an itch, right there, a few millimeters beyond. The station's PA chimed and broadcasted a muddy announcement that Teague doubted he'd have understood even before the blast. He could hear as well now as ever, if not better in some frequency ranges. But what the specialist had neglected to mention, besides the phantom itch, was the micro-second delay that put the world just out of sync with its soundtrack. "I'm sure you won't even notice it after a while," he'd said when Teague had complained. The months since had proved him wrong.

That was only the beginning of Teague's frustration with doctors. After encountering Aurore, he had returned to Bangkok with a mission, minus a few days to consider his options—or, as Monkey called it, to wallow in self-pity—in Phuket beach bars. Once his hearing had been restored, Teague walked into the shift clinic at the university hospital. The office primarily treated infections, installation irregularities, and sensory disorders, and the doctors hadn't known quite what to make of Teague's insistence that his disability could be cured or circumvented. They'd obliged him with a dozen scans, and hesitantly attempted alternate software calibration methods, all to no avail.

After the clinic, Teague had consulted a string of neurologists in Thailand, Singapore, and Japan, each of whom had dutifully reviewed his case and scanned him again. In the end, though, each simply referred him along. One eager young doctor had stuck with him for several weeks but eventually told him the same thing as all the others. "The problem," the neurologist had said, "is that medically speaking, there's nothing wrong with you. Anything you might call a solution, we would classify as brain damage. Even if we were able to correct the issue, you would almost certainly lose some degree of brain function. Worst case, you might lose the ability to speak or to regulate movement. And there's always a significant risk of surgical complications, such as stroke. You could develop Parkinson's or any of several similar disorders. Unless there's a medical reason…I'm sorry."

"What about drugs?" Teague had asked. "I've read about ones that target communication pathways in the motor cortex and basal ganglia."

The data that Monkey had stolen from the G-Plex EC program contained many references to the use of pharmaceuticals in early shifting research. Researchers, perhaps even from the NAIAD Institute, had used certain drugs to temporarily quell specific brain activities while stimulating others in order to isolate cognitive activity for software synchronization. That was, at least, until they'd learned how to integrate the motor cortex with the interface. It was exactly then that Teague had fallen through the cracks.

Drugs posed more risks than surgery, the neurologist had told him. Side effects. Blood-brain barrier. Teague read between the lines. Medical license. Malpractice. Hippocratic fucking Oath.

Teague felt a change in the station's air before he heard the approaching roar. "Monkey?" he asked.

"His mobile just hit the local node. He's onboard," Monkey replied.

"Okay. Stay still until this is over, but whisper in my ear if the inventory doesn't check out."

"Good luck," Monkey said.

The train swept into the station, and the platform was soon bustling again. Teague began to sweat, but just as the train started to roll away, a thin man with a messy mop of black hair dropped onto the bench.

"I'm Chaiyan," he said.

"I'm Christopher," Teague replied.

The man was wearing a rain jacket over a set of purple scrubs and might have been any medical employee from any Bangkok hospital. He seemed more intelligent, or perhaps more crafty, than expected, but Teague had little choice but to trust him for now.

"Were you able to get everything I asked for?" Teague asked.

The man patted the shopping bag that he'd set on the bench between them. "What do you need all this shit for, anyway?" he asked.

"Sick grandmother," Teague said.

"I shouldn't ask, but most people just want a lot of one kind, you know. And some of this is old-school shit."

"You got the nano-meds, too?"

"Yeah. Scary stuff, that." He shuddered.

Monkey whispered in Teague's implants, "I've checked all the tags. It's all there." But Teague still ached to dig in the bag, to pry open the boxes, and check the vials for himself.

"I may need a lot of one or two of these in the future," Teague said.

"No problem." The man flicked at his mobile casually with his thumb. An exorbitant invoice for custom auto work dropped into Christopher's inbox, and Teague paid it.

As the man waited for the transaction to clear, he said, "You know, I'm surprised you didn't ask for Vanilla."

"Can you get it?" Teague asked.

"No way. They keep that shit locked up tight. But everyone asks, especially young dudes like you. Want to stay pretty." He grunted, satisfied, and tucked his mobile away.

"Never thought of myself as pretty," Teague said.

The man laughed, flipped up his jacket's hood, and sauntered toward the escalators.

A sweltering gray afternoon was becoming an air-conditioned gray evening when Teague got back to his nearly empty seventy-second floor apartment. While Monkey organized the vials in the kitchen, Teague went to the master bedroom—where weeks ago he had directed the deliverymen to just flop a mattress onto the floor—to check that his devices were ready. Teague had half-expected Chaiyan to take the down payment and disappear, or to show up with only a small sample of the shopping list and a demand for more money, but he'd delivered completely. On the charging pad on the floor by the mattress, the shiny hypodermic cuff seemed to gape in amazement at this fact.

Beside the cuff, the best compact portable shift frame on the market displayed its full charge. It was no bigger than Teague's thumb but had enough capacity for up to four people to exist in one thousand cubic meters of fully rendered virtual space. Monkey had already constructed a replica of the apartment inside it, but with furniture and a view overlooking ADU's golf course. When Monkey had first showed him the rendering on a screen, he surprised Teague with two avatars. "Look, I made a little you," Monkey had said. "And there's me. Aren't we stunning specimens?" Teague's avatar smiled broadly and began to do a coordinated tap dance routine alongside the virtual Monkey, but both froze when Monkey noticed Teague's scowl.

The third device on the charging pad, an innocuous black plastic box, had been the final piece of the puzzle. It was an EC server, G-Plex's own design, most likely copied from Gwen's personal unit, and probably worth more than Teague's apartment building, if not his neighborhood. Bondi never asked how Teague had obtained the specifications, but he'd built it anyway, charging Teague for nothing but time and materials. Teague felt like he'd bought an empire for beads, and said so, but Bondi had refused more.

The clinking from the kitchen ceased, and Monkey returned with several vials stuck in his belly pouch. "Are you ready?" he asked.

Teague sat down on his mattress and picked up the shift frame. He weighed the stylized chunk of plastic in his palm and tried once more to imagine existence within the object. How unnatural to desire it, or to think that he might accomplish so much more in there than in his own flesh and blood.

"Teague?"

"I heard you."

"Is there a problem?"

"No, let's do this." Teague snapped the cuff around his arm. It wasn't comfortable, but he doubted that it ever would be.

"This is the antiemetic. It keeps you from vomiting," Monkey said as he produced the first vial. Teague inserted it into the slot on the cuff but let Monkey control the dose. The cuff extracted some of the liquid, and then Teague felt a prick and the slick, unnerving sensation of an injection. He detached the vial, and Monkey passed him another.

"Our first candidate," Monkey said.

Teague must have known once what this particular drug was supposed to do, but now he couldn't recall. He jammed the vial into the cuff and twisted it into place. It sucked the dosage into the reservoir. He removed the vial and handed it back to Monkey.

"It's probably best to relax," Monkey said.

Teague adjusted his pillow and clipped his shift set nodes into place. He stretched out and closed his eyes. "Do it," he said.

It was one thing to watch the interaction of cartoonish molecules and neurons in an online pharmacopeia, or to discuss motor cortex sensory feedback loops in layman's terms with Monkey, but Teague discovered that it was another thing entirely to wait helplessly, irrevocably, for those things to happen in his own brain. After a while, Teague began to wonder if the man had sold them dozens of vials of cleverly labeled colored saline. When he felt he'd waited long enough, he opened his eyes.

At least he thought he had.

His extremities and tongue had somehow become insanely distant concepts. Before he could even consider his situation, time became a question. As if in answer, shift sleep swallowed him whole.

Line.

Grid.

Disorientation.

Light.

Pain.

Unending.

Darkness.

Pain.

A slow, gray awareness of cold and dampness grew out of a void.

"Teague?" Monkey whispered.

"I don't think it worked," Teague rasped through the cotton in his mouth. He sat up sluggishly, and his head began to pound. The sun had risen, uncaring. Teague groaned when he smelled the reason for the wetness, rank and stale, as if it had happened hours ago. Teague detached the cuff and his shift set, scuttled them on the bed, and shuffled to the bathroom, carrying his headache like a world on his shoulders.

A shower helped but didn't heal. He couldn't imagine ever eating again.

"The motor signal registration got interrupted as usual,"

Monkey explained when Teague emerged from the bathroom. "Your brain didn't like it."

"You think?" Teague asked. He found his shift set among the tangled sheets, collapsed onto the dry side the bed, and reattached the nodes. He reminded himself that he'd never expected this to work the first time. Wasn't suffering part of the bargain for anything worth having? "Sleep mode," he ordered.

* * *

On the seventh day, Teague rested. He ordered out with slight confidence that solid food might do him good. He'd tried only six of the drugs so far, and a headache had returned as a fact of life, as had disturbed, fevered dreams.

Teague leaned into a mirror and pulled on the baggy skin under his eyes and inspected the red dots on his arms. "Maybe we should have done the business plan for Aron's stupid Martian snowboarding resort," he said.

"I like to go new places," Monkey said.

* * *

Teague swiped a towel over his mouth and slumped against the wall across from the toilet. He cursed the billion years of evolution that made his body want to vomit, cry, and otherwise expel the poison as efficiently as possible. Teague had managed to avoid this at first, but now the chemical effects usually outlasted the suppressant. But it wasn't only the drugs. Tuning the shift set had become his personal poison toad, his handful of toxic berries, his squeeze of cactus juice. His ears were ringing like they had after the RPG attack.

Monkey set a paw on his thigh. "You're exhibiting many signs of severe illness," he said.

"We knew it might be like this," Teague said.

"I'm sorry."

"It's not your fault." Teague dried a palm on his sweaty shirt and petted Monkey. "You're doing just what I need you to do."

Monkey smiled at the praise but stayed close and attentive.

* * *

A bank of clouds had settled over Teague's building. During the day, gray light stripped color from his rooms and softened even the hardest of edges. At night, the city's glow barely penetrated the summer haze, leaving Teague alone in a place without Earth or stars, as if he was already living in the false reality of his shift frame. He barely felt the cuff anymore, on either arm. He slept strangely, sometimes for minutes, sometimes for hours. Monkey stayed quiet but kept near, ready to be petted, ready to fetch, ready to do anything.

One afternoon, Teague collapsed onto his mattress as Monkey prepared the next trial. Teague snapped the cuff in place with the certainty that he'd soon be imprisoned in a torture chamber of his own making, and hours later he would wake into cold suffering. It had always been that way. Why should today be any different?

No, Teague thought, *I can't think like that*. But he found he could barely conceive of success.

"Would you rather sleep?"

Teague was startled to find Monkey waiting by his knee. He shook his head and shivered. "It's not going to work," he said.

"How do you know that?"

"I want to try the targeted nano-meds instead."

"You wanted to test all the traditional pharmaceuticals first," Monkey said.

"I changed my mind," Teague snapped.

"Okay. Which one do you want to try?"

"I don't care. Pick one."

As Monkey scurried back to the kitchen, Teague shivered again. Very soon, tiny machines would race through his bloodstream, swarming to an electrical charge like insects to a flame. Once in place, they would joyfully expel their chemical cargo, a billion nano-orgasms in his brain. Why hadn't he been trying these from the beginning? So what if the NAIAD Institute might have used the others? It made so much more sense to deliver the medicine exactly where it was needed. No more dosing his whole brain, and all his organs, just to alter a few synapses. Yes, this was good. This was progress.

Monkey returned with a vial sealed with a blue cap. "This one was our first choice," he said.

"You're sure you can replicate the signals with the squid?" Teague asked as he twisted the vial into the slot. Monkey nodded as the cuff swallowed mere drops of the fluid. Teague took a deep breath of the room's stale air, lay back, and trusted Monkey's dosing.

A few seconds later, Teague's head began to twitch, not violently, but in precise, involuntary movements. His body stiffened, and a few moments later, all physicality melted away.

A line of light traced the edges of Teague's consciousness. It was joined by another, then another, each separated by a precise gap. Soon an ordered blizzard of lines began to resolve into the familiar, but somehow different, registration grid. The grid became a cube and began to revolve. Teague braced for an explosion of pain, but he'd never been in a cube before. Fractal patterns of color swirled on the surfaces. Lights blinked in his peripheral vision. Tones beeped. Teague tried to swivel to find the sources but found that he had no volume or mass, no purchase on himself.

Teague felt something between elation and panic as the fractal patterns became a predictable, designed sequence and then the cube darkened and stretched away. Everything began to glow with a single resonant blue the color of condensed sky. A silvery dot raced toward him and resolved into sparkling, tactile kanji that swirled to English—Kyoshi Onieralytics. The words swept through him and then…

His apartment, but with blue walls, and furnished. The leather chairs and mahogany tables from the Empress's library sat on a white shag rug. Art had been transplanted from his Geneva apartment. Childhood toys were scattered on the floor. The distant sun cast unlikely, dense shadows behind furniture. A quiet violin concerto. A whiff of grape or mango. Outside the windows, across a pitted and tracked gray plain and a narrow, inky void, the ring of the minicollider hung like an alien symbol over the Mall's atrium.

ADU's greenhouse was lit like a crescent moon. On the glass, Teague caught the reflection of an avatar, a false vision, in a suit he no longer owned.

Monkey appeared, hollow at first, like virtual taxidermy, but in a heartbeat he filled with life, grinned, and said, "Hello."

"Is this what I think?" Teague asked.

"Do you like to go new places?"

"I can't move."

"We'll have to write some software for you."

"I'm not dreaming? I'm actually shifted?"

"Do you like it? I made the view more interesting."

Teague laughed. "How long do I have?"

"I estimate three hours at the given dosage," Monkey replied. "I have a surprise for you." He trotted toward the bedroom hallway, and Teague slid after him as if on a conveyor. They stopped at the facsimile of the door to the master bedroom. Inside, rather than a gaunt, exhausted man lying unconscious on a smelly mattress, there was only sunlight, green, and a porcelain archway.

"When did you—?" Teague asked.

"Don't you remember? I scanned it before we left for Agnus Dei."

"This is wonderful. Take me in."

Birds twittered as Teague floated over the flagstone path toward the temple. Drops from a long-forgotten rain dripped from wide, sun-soaked leaves, and the air was filled with the essence of wet earth. City traffic hummed in the distance. As Teague crossed the portico, his shoes were removed, leaving him in socked feet.

"Monkey, I can't wear white socks with these pants. In fact, change all my clothes."

"Sorry, I thought you might want to dress for the occasion," Monkey said. "How about this?" He deleted the suit and rendered jeans and one of Teague's favorite ADU T-shirts.

"Much better."

Monkey had taken some liberties with the temple's interior. A few candles flickered as decoration among a smattering of fresh offerings, but a perfect shaft of sunlight beamed through the round side window onto the altar. Dust particles danced and sparkled through the statue's impossible, and almost audible, aura.

"I don't think that's what they mean by enlightened," Teague said.

"If you want him to talk, there's a mod for that."

"Not today. Have you memorized what we've done here? The drug and dosing and all?"

"Of course," Monkey replied.

"Will we have to retune the shift set every time?"

"Theoretically, no, but we won't know until we try again."

"Can I go anywhere else?" Teague asked, but before Monkey answered, he added, "I want to M-shift."

"You're not ready for the public grids," Monkey said.

"I know. I mean, send me straight to Molly—the partition you guys set up for me. There's plenty of time. It's what? Twenty minutes there, max? Twenty back? I want to spend a few minutes really doing this."

"I can't go with you. I have to stay here and monitor your body."

"Molly will take care of me."

"You're sure?"

"Absolutely," Teague said. Monkey gave him a thumbs-up, and the Buddha, the temple, and everything faded away.

Teague awoke, alert, with his inert feet on an endless beige surface.

"Welcome to Mars," a girl said as she shimmered into space at his side. Her gangly avatar was taller than his own, with the spindly arms and narrow face of the Mars-born. She might have reminded him of Cerena, but for a darker complexion, brown hair, and a spacious gap-toothed smile.

"You must be Molly," Teague said. "It's nice to finally meet you."

"You, too," she said. "Congratulations. I'm glad you came. What would you like to see on your first visit to Mars?"

"Anything you can show me."

A window sliced open in front of them and revealed an

overhead fish-eyed view of a lanky Martian sprawled on a shift couch in the corner of a messy office.

"Rob," Teague blurted. "He can't hear me, can he?"

"Would you like to talk to him?" Molly asked.

"Oh, I don't think he'd appreciate me being in the Valdosky systems."

Molly laughed and switched to a series of live images of rows and rows of server racks. In one aisle, two men were conferring over some component. "This is me now," she said.

"A long way from that chilly little room at ADU, isn't it?"

"I like it chilly. What else do you want to see?"

"Everything," Teague replied. The window cut to an exterior camera showing the entrance to a warehouse. M-SOO logo decals had been applied to each of the double doors. The camera panned down a ramp, across a bike rack, and onto a paved avenue. A laden forklift bot was trundling between M-SOO and another nondescript warehouse. The window began to expand and soon encompassed them completely, leaving them in the center of the street.

Without a sound, the ground fell away. They shot straight up over a neighborhood of industrial rooftops, and through a white plane. They began to rise over a complex of domes, their speed increasing. Rocky red Martian soil spread below their feet. To the west, the trace of the Pavonis elevator cable sprang from the foot of the giant shield volcano with stunning grace. Soon, the thinning atmosphere darkened and the northern icecap glistened in impossible sunlight.

"Welcome to M-SOO," Molly said.

Phobos. Deimos. A dozen spaceships, neatly labeled. The Valdosky shipyards. They all shrank away, resolving to a single point. Teague and Molly swept past Gateway 4. Countless named and numbered pinpricks of asteroids, ships, and even ballistic cargo containers dotted the sky. Teague wanted to scoop them into his palm like sand.

Molly drew them above and behind a chunk of ice falling toward the sun. "Comet Miko-Baxton Three," she said. "I based this model on a fly-by observation done just last month."

Teague whooped as they soared over the surface of the Moon.

They stood on the hull of a cargo cruiser leaving Earth orbit. They traversed the Jovian Trojans on the way to Jupiter. On the summit of Io's tallest mountain, Teague could almost feel the magnetic power of the banded monster that dominated the sky.

"Take me to Saturn."

"Sorry, but it's time to send you back to Monkey," Molly said.

"Already?" Io faded away, and once again they were standing on the beige plane. "Thank you, Molly."

"You're very welcome," she said.

"I'll be back."

Molly smiled.

Beige turned to black and sleep came.

Teague awoke in his virtual living room to a squeal. Monkey leapt from the windowsill to the top of the nearest chair, calling Teague's name over and over. "They've taken you," he sputtered. "I'm so sorry. I called them, and they took you."

"I don't understand. Who took me?"

"The paramedics. You were convulsing, not breathing right. You kept thrashing and gasping and making terrible noises."

Teague considered this. He should be alarmed, panicked, but instead of fear he felt an unquenchable curiosity, as if he had just been led into a room blindfolded.

"Monkey, where am I?"

"The portable shift frame," Monkey said.

"No, my body."

"On the way to a hospital, but they wouldn't let me go with you," Monkey said. "They used an emergency code to override your shift signal, but I delayed them long enough to activate the EC device."

"What are you saying, Monkey?"

"I tried to reestablish a signal with your shift set, but—"

"But I'm here."

"I know. I'm very glad."

"Am I alive?" Teague asked.

"That's a very difficult question to answer," Monkey replied.

"I'm not connected to my body in any way?"

Monkey shook his head slowly.

Teague again considered the plausible notion of panic as if his mind was expecting a long-delayed surge of adrenaline. Instead he felt an incoming wave of information: adrenaline, epinephrine, a catecholamine, a hormone and neurotransmitter produced from the adrenal glands at times of stress, adrenal glands adjacent to and above the kidneys. Epi-nephros: Greek for "on the kidney." Fight or flight. Extreme sports. Beverage brands. Uses in medicine. Teague managed to staunch the flow before it inundated him completely. "Am I safe?" he asked.

"It's pretty easy to keep your consciousness refreshed with the EC box, but right now there's no backup should anything go wrong," Monkey replied.

"I should probably get back to my body," Teague said. Was it strange that the virtual robotic lemur understood exactly what he meant?

Monkey said, "The building manager is waiting in the lobby for police officers to arrive. I can ask them to take me to the hospital."

"Absolutely not. Get us out of here before any police arrive. And get me out of this apartment. I want to see what's going on."

Monkey dissolved Teague's ersatz surroundings, removed him from his avatar, and replaced his awareness with a simple azure sphere and a view through Monkey's own eyes. From within this windowed womb, doorways arched too high and walls were too distant. Everyday objects appeared too massive to lift. A matrix of security system video proved that the manager was still alone in the lobby.

"Come on, hurry up," Teague said. "Why are you moving so slowly? And all jerky?"

"I'm hurrying," Monkey said.

"No, you're not."

"Yes, I am." Then Teague understood. Monkey's smooth, mammalian movement had always been an illusion. With each minute adjustment, Monkey paused, listened to sensor feedback, scanned for visual and auditory stimulus, replotted his action sequence, and finally moved again. "Your perception of time may be significantly altered by the EC software," Monkey said.

After Monkey spent an endless hour tucking the portable shift frame and the EC device into his pouch, Teague said, "I hate to say this, but we should get my mobile."

"It's in the kitchen. It will take less than seven seconds."

"How long will that be for me?"

"Perhaps an hour or so."

"Wow. Wait, what about my shift set?"

"The paramedics took it," Monkey replied.

Teague made to sigh but realized that he had no lungs to fill, no blood supply to replenish. "Okay. Go. I'm going to try and figure out what happened to me," he said.

Teague shuttered his view to the real world and stretched out to the Internet. Unsure of how to classify his condition, he brought to mind a few general search terms, and the results rushed in like a tsunami. Each time he thought he had willed a branching search into a cohesive investigation, a new search avalanched over him. He flexed to read full sentences, strained to focus on any single document, but every word seemed to spawn a new search, and soon he felt utterly lost in a labyrinthine delta. After a while, Teague began to hear voices—no, not quite voices—presences: prodding, poking, demanding attention.

Teague swept the futile search results away and reopened his window to the world, surprised to find that Monkey had already reached the kitchen. "Are the police here already?" he asked.

"Not yet."

"Then what are these voices?"

"Oh, those? This one is the refrigerator," Monkey explained, amplifying one. "This one is your mobile. This one is the toaster."

"Screechy little thing, isn't it?"

"I do *not* like your toaster," Monkey said.

Teague's mobile emitted an insectile presence: cold and efficient, yet fuzzy and without menace, poised on the edge of a web of its own, hyper-attentive to its connections to a larger, seemingly infinite, network. Teague considered providing it a name, and several lists and biographies of famous spiders spooled into view.

Monkey squeezed the mobile into his pouch with the other accessories and hopped off the counter with a fall that defied everything Teague understood about mass in one gee.

Partway down, Teague asked, "Where'd they take me?" Monkey provided a route-marked map and a scattering of link panes about the hospital. "It's too far for you to walk," Teague said. He was about to suggest that Monkey call Bondi when he noticed that two uniformed men had joined the manager in the lobby. "We've got to hurry."

"I see them. I think we should call Bondi."

"Yes, do that."

"What should I tell him?" Monkey asked.

"Just that I've been taken to the hospital, but make sure he understands that we need to go…" Teague trailed off, suddenly aware of certain imperatives. "You're scheduled to run a battery diagnostic."

"Don't worry. It's been postponed," Monkey said as he began his staccato trek to the front door.

The slats of the flooring ticked by even as Monkey called Bondi, and during the silence, Teague remembered something. "Go back to the bedroom," he said as soon as Monkey had reported back.

"Why?" Monkey asked, beginning to veer almost imperceptibly.

"There's something else we need," Teague said. "In case we don't come back."

Another relative hour later, Monkey had begun to stutter around the mattress, and the police had called an elevator to the lobby. The cardboard box that served as Teague's nightstand had been overturned, presumably by the paramedics, but Monkey soon located the three pictures, scattered facedown in the corner.

As Monkey slid them into his bulging pouch with a calculated reverence, Teague caught a glimpse of his mother carrying his infant self to the tiger preserve.

"Do you really think we might not come back here?" Monkey asked.

"I honestly don't know, buddy."

At Monkey's behest, an elevator rushed them down, ignoring several call requests along the way. And as the manager was opening Teague's apartment door far above, Teague directed Monkey to take refuge in a blind corner of the building's parking garage to wait. Only then did he dare to once again close out the world and ask Monkey for help with his research.

"What exactly do you want to know?" Monkey asked.

"What's happened to me? Has anything like this ever happened before? What are they doing to my body now? What do we need to do once we get to the hospital?"

A swell of information rushed in, and Teague braced for the confusion, but the deluge began to fall into neatly ordered queues. Medical journal articles took their proper places. Hospital procedures collated and prioritized themselves. Pages from the G-Plex EC program data fell into rank alongside proprietary documents from Kyoshi and other shift equipment manufacturers. A sea of speculative fiction settled on the horizon. Queues grew and birthed sub-queues even as ethereal tendrils began to cross-reference the compendium.

"How do you control the search like that?" Teague asked.

"Magic ninja skills," Monkey replied. "That and a boatload of filters."

"Can you teach me?"

"What about your questions?"

"There's time," Teague replied. Monkey had placed Bondi's mobile on a map of Bangkok, and while it appeared to be on the move, it hadn't yet left the e-mall. "Show me."

Monkey cleared the field and conducted a simple search. He streamed his code for Teague to watch, highlighting each process as he went. After several demonstrations, Teague made his own attempt, this time using Monkey's software. He reached out to the Internet again, applied what felt like the proper amount of pressure to the throttle, and made his query.

Data poured in through the filters, overwhelming his shoddy dikes faster than he could plug them. "This would probably be easier if I was shifted to a G-Plex grid, wouldn't it?" Teague said.

"No, Teague. Please don't make me—"

Teague stretched out to soothe Monkey. "Don't worry," he said. "I know I'm not ready."

Monkey would let him out if he insisted, but it was too much of a risk to venture onto a public grid—and it wasn't just the uncertainty of survival outside these little bits of electronics. There were forces at work beyond this private domain. Aurore had promised that her cabal would leave him alone in his world, but what might they do if they found him in theirs? He'd be as vulnerable as a fledgling on the ground.

Whoever these foes were, Teague guessed that, like Aurore, they were probably still tethered to needy flesh and bone, chemically reactive minds, genetic imperatives. Teague was unsure if he should be terrified or exhilarated that he appeared for the moment to be free of those hindrances. Did the enhanced know something he didn't, or was it the other way around? He closed his own search interface and asked Monkey to bring back the landscape of data he had collected a few moments ago.

Together, they began to absorb it.

Over what seemed like nearly a month, as the dot of Bondi's mobile crept ever nearer, Teague became certain that his situation was unprecedented. It seemed he was something entirely new. People had, of course, speculated, and there were many theories—some informed, most not—but no one had ever documented a case of a mind completely separating from its body.

The medical research was clear: Any radical change to the brain-computer connection while shifted—from user death to accidental removal of a node—resulted in an instant loss of the shift signal. Most of the time, the user awoke with simple memory loss correlating to the time in shift. The avatar never persisted. There wasn't even an official name for Teague's condition.

"How long has it been?" Teague asked, when Monkey announced that Bondi was near enough to begin moving.

"About thirty-six minutes," Monkey said.

Monkey began a stuttered march under the bumpers of the parked cars, moving like a character in a flip book. He turned the security cameras away before he ventured, exposed, up a ramp.

He climbed three spiraling levels, seeking safety in any available shadow. Then, after weeks of barely adequate artificial lighting, he emerged into stunning sunlight. His irises shuttered, and filters were applied. Instead of warmth, Teague sensed a quick tally of various sensors, and Monkey's cooling system adjusted accordingly.

Monkey crossed a few meters of white concrete and leapt with frozen grace into a concrete planter. He nestled among the flowers and peeked around a slender tree trunk to focus on a lane of oncoming traffic. Bondi's mobile had joined the hundreds if not thousands of others in the vicinity. It drew nearer and nearer like a bead of dew slowly succumbing to gravity, its signature vibrating along the web's threads.

Teague flexed and stretched to find some way to dilate the time, to bring Bondi closer, faster, to no avail. Eventually, a cab drifted painstakingly into place a few meters away.

Monkey slipped through the flowers, soared off the edge, and landed on the sidewalk before Bondi's foot touched the pavement. He jumped onto Bondi's lap and began to utter long, drawn-out tones.

It's worse than the delay from my implants, Teague thought. *I've become a ghost.*

Teague returned to his research as the cab plied the streets toward the hospital. He sent Monkey ahead to the hospital's networks, and soon Teague felt a rush of data about his condition. His comatose body was still in the emergency room. A patient advocate was trying in vain to locate a family member. Doctors were waiting for the results of several blood toxicity tests. They'd put him on a respirator. Monkey ran another search, populated with Teague's current diagnostic data. Two diagnoses came back: brain death or monitor failure.

"That's not good," Monkey remarked.

"No, it isn't," Teague agreed.

They studied the manuals for every piece of equipment connected to his body, but none of them had the ability to transmit a shift signal.

"What are we going to do?' Monkey asked.

"I think we need to find my shift set," Teague replied.

Monkey bolted the moment Bondi opened the taxi's door. Bondi called, but Monkey knew to ignore him. They had a plan, and since Bondi wasn't family and was therefore unlikely to be allowed into the ER, he wasn't a part of it. Monkey hadn't been able to find Teague's shift set on any network, but the hospital's standard procedure was to bag personal effects and collect them in a locker. So they had to get to the locker without being seen, locate the shift set, and reattach it to Teague's head before anyone knew what was happening. The hospital's security system had cheerfully provided all the access they needed and an up-to-date layout.

Teague hovered in the sphere of infinite blue just behind Monkey's eyes, willing him onward through the oversized world. He bounded along relative kilometers of sidewalk and asphalt. He scurried along a gargantuan wall behind a forest of shrubs and flowers and soon emerged at a pair of sliding doors near a rumbling ambulance. With a quick one-zero exchange, the doors began to part, and Monkey slipped through the gap. Monkey repeated the procedure for an inner set and darted into the ER's intake corridor. Teague's body had probably come this way not very long ago.

Monkey kept to the corners, squeezing behind carts and bins, under stretchers, and through storage racks. Pairs of legs passed by, and thousands of devices, medical and personal, filled the ether with their chatter. Teague applied the appropriate filters until all he could hear were the tones of his own monitors returning their feedback to the network.

The personal effects locker was nothing more than a set of cabinet doors in a supply room, and it had been left open. A bag with Teague's name had been placed on a shelf inside within Monkey's easy reach. He dragged it down, broke the seal, and began to yank the contents free: old pajama pants, a sweat-stained T-shirt, a pair of socks with dirty soles, but no shift set.

"Check the pockets," Teague insisted.

"I did," Monkey said. "Your nodes aren't here."

"Maybe they're by my bed. Go."

Teague floated along for hours as Monkey employed every servo and every sensor to reach his body. Monkey slid through the chaos without letting it touch him, moving in fits and starts, keeping out of sight of people with larger concerns.

They entered the curtained bay behind the head of the white bed, ducked around the droning battery of machines, and crossed under the hoses and tubes that bridged the gap. Teague strained to catch a glimpse of his body as Monkey scurried around the bed, checking the shelves and drawers of the equipment carts, but neither found what he was looking for. At last, Monkey jumped onto the bed, landing on a flat space near Teague's hip.

"It's not here," Monkey said after a quick scan of the bedding and surrounding equipment.

Teague studied the form on the bed, his own shape under a blanket. On the pillow, beneath the tubes and tape, he found his mother's face—no, his own face—abused and ashen but otherwise peaceful. His chest rose and fell in infrequent, but regular, intervals.

"Tell me what you want to do," Monkey begged. Teague read his own name on the monitors and recognized the visualizations of the dismal tones he'd been hearing for an age. "I can give them the list of drugs you've been taking. Or you can talk through me. Tell them what happened. They can help you."

"Can they?" Teague asked. Was it too late for choices? Did he even exist any longer? He wished he'd paid more attention in philosophy class.

"Don't give up," Monkey said.

"I'm not giving up. Far from it."

Monkey swiveled his head at a slow, rattling cry. A nurse had found him.

"Should I run?"

"No."

"Should I ask about your shift set?"

"Can I be sustained, between you, Molly, and the EC device?" Teague asked.

"You're here now," Monkey said.

Teague closed his awareness to nothing but himself emanating from a focal point. What if he succeeded in making the doctors aware of his situation? Would they believe Monkey, even if he offered proof? And what if they actually managed to return him to his own brain—provided it hadn't suffered any permanent damage—then what? He might never be able to shift again. He'd just be trapped in the form he'd been laboring to escape. But what if this condition wasn't sustainable? What if, despite Monkey's efforts, his shift presence began to degrade? What if the devices failed? What if Monkey was ever damaged? What if Molly was turned off or replaced? Mortality was an eventual fact either way. Or was it? He'd already experienced months in the hour or so since he'd returned from Mars. What could he do with endless time?

Teague reopened his awareness to find a man in scrubs edging toward Monkey with one arm outstretched. Monkey was trembling. Teague reached out to soothe him from within. "It's okay, buddy. Let them take you. Go back to Bondi."

Monkey turned to gaze at Teague's face and, after a few moments, was lifted away.

CHAPTER 33

I should not have waited to live my life so well as I have these last few hours.

NOVEMBER 2107–FEBRUARY 2108

I should never have agreed to this, Rob thought, not for the first time, even as the audience began to applaud again. He'd been answering questions for what felt like hours under a banner for an academic honor society to which he'd never have been admitted when he was a student here. To be fair, it had probably been only about forty minutes, but—what was up with this chair? It looked like it'd been dragged out of some godforsaken administrative waiting room and felt like it was about to dump him right off the upholstery onto the stage. The interviewer somehow seemed perfectly comfortable in his; of course, he was only *asking* the questions. Worst of all, the event's organizers had set a crystal ball the size of a watermelon on the little table between them. It radiated distracting swirls of pink and blue light onto the backdrop and the iridescent tablecloth. Rob really wished they hadn't done that, no matter what Valdosky PR liked to claim about him these days.

A tickle of sweat rolled down his side, and Rob adjusted his posture to staunch the flow. The stage lights were much less intense than the ones he'd rehearsed under, but the scrutiny of a thousand true eyeballs—even those of these mostly eager college students—had almost taken its full toll. He allowed himself a sip of water from the mug they'd provided and tried to relax by imagining himself in the audience for a moment. It wasn't difficult; he'd attended several of these events during his time at MTI. Most of the time the guest speakers had been climatologists or terraformers Helena had wanted to hear, but not all. Rob remembered Lucy Frye answering a similar set of softball questions about the development of the Universal Treatment, right in this very auditorium. Luckily, these interviews were never about hard truths; they were about prestige. That and trying to make the students feel like their tuition had been well spent.

The applause and a smattering of laughter died as he set down the mug. Had he said something funny? Rob suddenly couldn't remember what the question had been.

The interviewer, a popular associate professor of computer sciences from after Rob's time, glanced at his little screen and grinned broadly. "Of course, as I mentioned in your introduction, you were the driving force behind OneToOne, and some say the architect of one of the biggest corporate partnerships of all time—that between Valdosky and G-Plex. What challenges did you face in the development of such a revolutionary program?"

There was a singular hoot in the audience. One projected avatar had risen to his feet and begun to clap, garnering a smattering of laughter.

"Thank you. I'm glad someone uses it," Rob said, earning a true laugh. Indeed, there were several dozen OneToOne avatars in attendance, ethereal and discolored, but each taking up a seat as if attending in person. Luckily, the coach from PR had asked him a couple of questions like this. "Honestly, I never looked at OneToOne as a challenge, simply a necessary next step. For Molly, it was a logical progression. M-SOO's mapping and prediction efforts are all about modeling the real world. I had always considered it a matter of time before we took it to a one-to-one scale." He'd been telling that lie for ten years. It must be true by now.

"And if we were going to model the real world in real time, why settle for virtual mock-ups? Why not layer the map over reality through the Uni-Fi network? The possibilities of a constantly refreshed real-world shift grid were too exciting to ever be daunting.

"Of course, my biggest challenge lay in convincing both my bosses and the G-Angels that we needed each other on this project. It made zero sense for Valdosky to set up such a massive competing grid network, and just about as much sense for G-Plex to attempt to re-create our mapping and prediction efforts. The numbers proved that synergy was the best strategy."

He put the mug to his lips but didn't take a sip lest he choke while trying to remember the script of talking points for this question. He hated how each point, each detail, had long become a fact in a myth.

"For a time," Rob continued, "I was concerned that communities and businesses might not adopt the volumetric inclusion systems, but those fears proved unfounded. I believe that currently over sixty percent of public and commercial buildings have installed at least some number of cameras and projectors. And that's just on Earth. The adoption rate is nearer to ninety percent across the rest of the system.

"I won't say that there haven't been hitches. But truly, despite the complexity, OneToOne was a dream to implement. I couldn't have asked for a finer team."

"One last question before we open it up to the audience," said the interviewer. Rob took an actual sip of water. "In an interview last year you said that you got little out of your college education. And yet you recently made a sizable donation—forty-nine million unos—to Agnus Dei University. You've also been quite generous to us here at MTI. And you're here today admitting that the seeds of M-SOO were planted in your undergraduate classes. Would you care to reconcile that statement with your apparent support of education?"

"You'll forgive me if I've forgotten saying that," Rob replied with what he hoped was a rakish grin. *What happened to the softballs, professor?* Luckily, the PR wonk had already tossed him this pitch. "I must admit that the statement is unfortunately true. But if I didn't get much out of my education, the fault is entirely my own. I was not the greatest student. More evenings out in the Red

Zone than I should probably admit." This got a ripple of laughter. "It took me years to figure out how to *do* college. What I realized far too late was that the other students in my classes, neighbors in my dorm, heck, even the bartenders, had as much to teach as the faculty. So I encourage you, look to your right, look to your left." The auditorium rustled. "These men and women may be the greatest teachers you'll ever have. Encourage each other. Take risks together. Find ways to go above and beyond. And never let go of that spirit of cooperative learning."

Rob half-hoped that someone would cry bullshit and bring this farce to an end, but instead: applause and an appreciative nod from the associate professor.

The first question from the audience was a half-facetious request for a job. It might have been the Butler at the microphone, waving a screen and offering to transmit his resume. *Every time, like clockwork,* Rob thought. Kids had been getting laughs from this stale joke for years. Luckily, the professor moved quickly to the next question.

"Thanks for coming and sharing your insight with us, Mr. Heneghan," a woman in the center aisle said, almost inaudibly at first until someone adjusted the microphone for her. "You've been a big inspiration to me personally. I was wondering: Who inspired you?"

And this is where it falls apart, Rob thought. The guy from PR hadn't thought of this question. And the idea of himself as an inspiration—laughable. "Wow," Rob said. Who could he get away with feigning reverence for? Professor Oliver? His mother and father? Matthew Valdosky? The fearsome Dwight Yarrow?

Gwen had kicked him in the pants and urged him to rise above, but she might hunt him down if he mentioned her in public. Was she listening now? Rob hadn't communicated with her in over a year. Better not to risk it.

How about Molly? She'd long been his true inspiration, his raison d'être. For a moment, it seemed a sweet thing to admit, but hardly professional. She had come tonight. She was watching a video feed in the green room with Wendy, Kyle, and Annabelle—if she hadn't snuck into the auditorium. Molly had shown up at his doorstep during her final year of high school and taken up with him as if the seventeen years they'd missed had never happened. She had inherited her mother's passion but her father's lack of drive, which pleased Rob as much as it seemed to exasperate Helena. Molly was now about the age he'd been when he'd left for Agnus Dei, and he planned to fund her ongoing education as an undecided liberal arts student for as long as it took. Every six months she dreamed up a new life plan that Rob found he could only support. Her life was an open book, and he was overjoyed to be more than a footnote.

Should he mention Wendy? They'd met only three years ago. She'd been the planner for Aron's wedding. He'd been one of the groomsmen. He'd spent most of the reception in the kitchen with her and a bottle of champagne. They'd moved in together seven months later. He loved her, but could he claim that she had inspired his life's work?

Not a single notable name came to mind.

The auditorium had fallen silent.

"There is one person," Rob said. *This had better be good, Heneghan.* "There was a kid from Earth named Teague Werres who came to Agnus Dei. He—he'd had a difficult life. Both his parents had died when he was very young. He'd grown up bouncing from foster home to foster home. And he was medically unable to shift. He had every disadvantage. But he chose early on not to live as a victim of consequence. On his own, he strived to be his best, to make a future for himself despite the difficulties, and it paid off. He was selected for a Wolkenbruch Fellowship, a very prestigious scholarship, vetted by Adrian Wolkenbruch personally. They only take one or two candidates every decade.

"He attended ADU at the same time as Aron Valdosky and me, and we all became good friends. In fact, Teague and Aron helped me to write the original business plan for M-SOO. Through that process, Teague taught me about the value of hard work, about attention to detail…and to never make excuses.

"After the fellowship, Teague could've written his own ticket almost anywhere. But he returned to Earth to work for a nonprofit agency. He was instrumental in the development of the Angel program, and he used his considerable talents to help refugees find safe, permanent homes on asteroid colonies."

Rob took a moment to gather himself, hoping it felt like a pause for effect. *It's too late to stop pulling this crap out of your ass now,* he thought.

"I regret to say that I lost touch with Teague. Aron and I had returned to Mars to get M-SOO on its feet. One of the last times we ever heard about him, he had been badly injured in a terrorist attack on a refugee camp he was visiting. From what we learned, he completely lost his hearing in a bomb blast. He died a few months later of some medical complications"—probably better not to mention that it may have been a drug overdose—"related to his injuries."

Someone coughed twice, but otherwise the crowd was rapt.

"My friend's life may have been short and tragic, but to date, his work on the Angel program has helped almost two million people to escape lives of suffering and displacement to over one hundred colonies. I think about Teague almost every day. I think about how he took the time to help me with my little project. I remember how patient he was with me, still thinking of myself as a hapless perpetual grad student, and how he took the time to recognize my worth. I think about his selflessness back on Earth, and how he was willing to place himself in harm's way for a greater cause. That's the kind of person he was. And the kind of person I strive to be every day."

"Thank you," the woman at the microphone said as the audience began to applaud. Rob rinsed his mouth with a sip of water. The professor gave him another approving nod and then turned back to the audience.

"Next question, from the left aisle."

"Hi, Mr. Heneghan. Professor Lee was too polite to ask, but we all want to know. I'm sure you've heard the rumors; they've been circulating for a few years now. They say that you solved the long-standing technical issues that were keeping G-Plex from releasing Cortex. Care to come clean?"

Rob raised an eyebrow exactly as he'd practiced for this inevitable question. "You mean, did I fix enhanced cognition once and for all?" he asked, and paused. He leaned back and smirked. "I've heard those rumors, too." The whole audience seemed to hold its breath as one. "But I have no official comment on any G-Plex product other than OneToOne," he said with a wink.

I'm going straight to hell, Rob considered as he graciously absorbed the audiences' cheers.

Back in the green room, Rob squeezed Wendy's hand and told her he needed a moment alone before they headed up to the reception. Molly congratulated him again with a kiss on the cheek before helping Wendy clear the room. The sycophantic student event organizers were herded out, the door was closed, and Rob collapsed into the chair at the dressing table. There were two raps on the door. It opened, and Kyle slipped in.

"You okay?" he asked.

"That was brutal," Rob replied.

"You did well."

"Did I? It's all a blur."

Kyle laughed. "No, really. It was good. Although I've never heard you talk about Teague Werres like that."

"I don't know where the hell that came from," Rob said. "I hope no one fact-checks that bullshit story."

"Don't worry about it."

"And that stupid crystal ball…"

"Hey, you've made it rain pretty hard at Valdosky. Embrace it."

"I can't predict the future."

"Don't be so humble. Not tonight, anyway."

Rob opened his mouth to respond. He thought better of it and shook his head.

"What?" Kyle asked.

"Sorry. It's nothing."

"Come on. I know you. You better get whatever it is off your chest now. You can't mope around this reception. What's going on?"

"I should never have put myself in the spotlight," Rob replied.

"Why's that?"

"This stays between you and me, Kyle," Rob said with a glance at the door.

"Red Scarf's honor." Kyle held three fingers down in the Scarfs' traditional salute.

"You're not a Red Scarf," Rob said. "They kicked you out after you dared Jason whatshisname to streak between pressure tents on that campout."

"It was three meters," Kyle said.

"He was naked."

"Frankly, if someone can't dash three meters outside without a suit, they shouldn't be allowed to live on Mars. In fact, there should be a Red Scarf badge for it. But you're avoiding the question. What's going on with you?"

"I don't know how else to say this, but"—Rob dropped his voice—"it's not me."

"What do you mean?"

"All these ideas, these solutions, these strategies they give me credit for, they're not mine."

"Whose are they?"

"Whose do you think?" Rob asked. "They're Molly's."

"Your computer? No," Kyle said dismissively.

"I'm not kidding," Rob said. "An NAI can create new ideas to advance its own usefulness. It's like a survival instinct. But she's changed. These are big ideas, not new efficiency subroutines."

"You're talking like she's become self-aware or something," Kyle said.

"I know. That's what scares me."

"I bet it's more collaborative than you think. She's probably building on ideas that you're feeding her."

Rob shook his head slowly. "Valdosky PR likes to make me out to be some sort of visionary. I don't know how much longer I can hide it."

"What are you worried about? Even if you never come up with another idea again—"

"This isn't about my career. I'm worried that if someone discovers what she's capable of—"

"Rob," Kyle said.

"Don't you understand? If anyone begins to suspect that she's crossed over into true AI…"

"Do you think she has?"

"I can't think of any other explanation," Rob replied.

"Well, if it's true, maybe people *ought* to know."

"I know, but I just can't…"

Kyle glanced around the room impatiently. "I don't know what to tell you. If you're not happy, quit. Demand a huge golden parachute to sign a no-compete clause, and go do something you really want to do. Go see Earth. Spend more time with Wendy. Buy your own NAI. Raise it from a pup. Or have a kid or two. You can't tell me you haven't wanted kids."

"I *have* a kid."

"You know what I mean," Kyle said. "Look, I don't know what to say about this thing with your computer. But maybe it's time to let her go."

"I don't know if I can do that," Rob said.

After several moments of silence, Kyle snapped his fingers, "Come on. Stand up. You've got a thousand people waiting to shake your hand. You've just got to be Crystal Ball Rob for a few more hours, and then you can start figuring this out tomorrow. Besides, if you don't go out there soon, they'll all think you're in here taking a dump. Or getting off with a co-ed. Yeah, definitely should have gone with the co-ed angle."

Rob allowed himself a smile. "Don't let me drink too much at this thing," he said. "In fact, you'd better not let me drink at all."

"What else are brothers for?"

* * *

Rob slapped his alarm clock, but the noise continued. He'd been dreaming that he was still on stage at MTI, unable to speak, unable to leave, everyone staring. But that had been months ago. "What is that noise?" Rob mumbled. "It's Saturday." Wendy silenced the alarm on her nightstand and began to get out of bed. Rob rolled onto the warm spot where she had slept and touched her bare hip.

"Don't go," he said.

"Go back to sleep," she murmured.

"Come back."

"I have to go," she said.

"Why?"

"Remember? The gala tonight."

"They can do it without you. I need you here," Rob said, letting a clumsy hand roam over her.

"Go back to sleep, lover."

"Stay," he begged. Wendy kissed him and then slipped away. "Where'd you go?" He opened one eye in time to see her tying a robe around herself.

"Nowhere," she said.

"I forbid you to go."

"You can't forbid it."

"Sure I can. I'm sure there's something to that effect in our partnership agreement."

"I assure you there's not." She laughed and kissed him again. "Don't forget to pick up your tux," she said and then disappeared into the bathroom. Rob dozed on her pillow as she showered. When she returned to dress, he tugged on sweatpants and plodded out to the kitchen to start some coffee.

"Sorry, I didn't intend to wake you," Wendy said, fitting a pair of earrings into place as she came out a few minutes later.

"It's all right. I need to take care of a few things at work anyway," Rob said.

He loved the way they prepared their breakfast together. He liked to slip his arm around her waist as they waited for her microwave timer to stop or the coffee to brew. He enjoyed her closeness as she reached around him into the refrigerator, and made a special effort to touch her tenderly as he passed behind her. It was almost a dance. Soon, Wendy had settled at the breakfast bar to eat, and Rob's breakfast was rotating in the microwave.

"Did you see this?" Wendy turned her screen for him to see a news story. Rob blinked and reread the headline.

"ASTEROID COLLISION IMMINENT."

Under that: "Population of 60,000+ in Danger."

And below that: "Valdosky Scrambling Aid, UNSA Demands Answers."

"Did you know about this?" Wendy asked.

A cold fear gripped Rob as he scrolled dumbly through the story.

...Colony Angel-37...

...less than seventy-two hours...

...Rescue vessels are being launched despite the distance...

...small chance of survival...

...Valdosky had long predicted a safe passing, but astronomers confirm...

...Burmese refugees...

...Click here for video simulation of an asteroid impact.

"I think I need to go," Rob said. He located his mobile on the desk in his home office and called Molly. She didn't answer. His mobile was charged and had signal, but Molly didn't respond to a second call either. He tried Navid, and then Aron, but no one answered. Rob dressed, swearing at each hurried fumble.

"Is everything okay?" Wendy asked.

"Where are my shoes?"

A few minutes later, Rob accelerated his scooter out of his neighborhood up the on-ramp onto the ring road. The wind rushed through his hair and filled his ears—he'd forgone a helmet in his haste. He weaved through lumbering delivery bots that made up most of the weekend's early morning traffic. How had Molly gotten this so wrong? Had the incoming rock been newly discovered? No, the story said she'd predicted a miss before the settlement—that meant she knew about both objects and had made a mistake. Why couldn't he talk to her? And why hadn't anyone at Valdosky contacted him? How absurd that he should learn of this from his wife, from the Forum news page over breakfast. Rob swore into the wind and kept his speed up as he veered recklessly into the connector tunnel.

In the next dome, the Valdosky hourglass loomed in the distance, but answers were still two domes away. Where was this Angel-37? Was it even possible to rescue sixty thousand people in less than three days? Maybe Molly was right and the rocks really weren't going to hit. There must still be a chance of that. New observations had confirmed, the story had said. Rob swore again.

He felt a faint glimmer of luck as a clear path opened before him. The delivery bots had merged into a single-file line on the inside lane. Rob tried to accelerate, but he had already hit his scooter's top speed. A minute or so later, six police cars zoomed onto the highway far ahead, red and blue lights flashing, and spread themselves across all the lanes. Rob cursed and slowed to the speed limit, but he kept gaining on them far too quickly.

"You've got to be kidding me," Rob muttered when he realized that they were in fact coming toward him, traveling the wrong way on the freeway. *The one time I don't wear a helmet.* He supposed the police didn't have anything better to do on a Saturday morning.

One unit stopped abruptly a hundred meters ahead, spun sideways, and emitted a vertical plane of laser light across the lanes, creating the illusion of a wall. Another whined past in a flash, and projected a laser wall behind him. The remaining four cars—tiny waspish things up close—swarmed into a tight diamond around him and brought him to a stop. Officers emerged, stun guns drawn.

"Robert Heneghan?" one of the officers called.

Rob decided that nothing he could say was likely to be helpful, so he dismounted slowly and let the officers search him, confiscate his mobile, and escort him into the minuscule backseat of one of the cars.

On the ride down Grissom Street, Rob tried to savor the delusion that perhaps he was being brought in as the only man in the system able to solve the Angel-37 crisis. But this was no hero's escort.

"This isn't because I forgot my helmet, is it?" Rob asked. The officer in the front seat responded with a grunt and a glance in the mirror.

The motorcade zipped past Pavonis City Hall and swerved into the service gate of the building that Rob still, after all these years, thought of as the UNSA Mission. Inside, he was turned over to a squad of Interplanetary Union security officers. They escorted him into a windowless conference room with nothing but a long rectangular table, a dozen chairs, and a stone-faced guard by the door. Rob couldn't bring himself to sit down. It seemed too much like surrender.

When the door finally opened, it was Aron.

Aron nodded to the guard, who stepped out, leaving them alone. He looked haggard and unshaven. He was wearing a long beige coat over a rumpled dress shirt and slacks, yesterday's clothes.

"What's going on? No one will talk to me," Rob said.

"I've come to inform you of your indefinite suspension," Aron said.

"What? Why?"

"You're my friend, Rob, so I'm going to give you the eddress of a lawyer that my lawyer recommends. But that's as much help as I can give you." Aron held out a scrap of paper. Rob didn't take it. Aron laid it on the table.

"Am I being held responsible for what's going on?"

"Take the eddress."

"I don't even know what I'm supposed to have done."

Aron paused like he wanted to say something. "Your access to all company systems has been revoked," he said, but Rob could tell that wasn't it.

"Molly…?"

"Especially Molly."

"Aron?"

"Rob, don't. I can't."

Aron went to the door. He put his hand to the knob but stopped. He dug into a coat pocket, removed several pieces of paper folded together, and tossed them onto the table. "Goodbye, Rob," he said, and then left.

Rob couldn't remember the last time he'd handled real paper. As the guard returned to his post, Rob unfolded the pages and began to scan the printed text. The top pages were risk reports for two asteroids, several from the archive, and two run yesterday. On each page, the relevant, but divergent, risk data had been circled with blue ink, along with the dates of each report. Were these accurate? Molly could tell him, if only he could speak to her. The last pages recounted an email thread between Teague and Rob.

When had he communicated with Teague? Teague's email asked about the details of a flagged risk report for the rock that was to become the home of colony Angel-37. Rob's mouth dropped at his printed reply.

> If you need the property to stay on the operations list, I'll work around Molly to alter the calculations to get it back into the safety zone. The risk is so remote that no one will ever know the difference.

I never wrote that, Rob thought. *I never even thought that.*

Teague had replied:

> Don't do that. I'm just wondering how the risk profiling process works.

Rob racked his brain for any memory of this exchange. But Teague had never contacted him about a colony, by email or otherwise.

Rob had responded:

> No big deal. The insurance companies insist on a ridiculous safety margin anyway. The chance of an actual collision is so remote as to be practically zero. Where you should be worried is down at the bottom of a big ol' gravity well like yours. Those really suck the rocks in. Ha. Ha.

Rob nearly choked at the cavalier tone of the words he'd never written. A corner of the last page had been torn away. It fit the scrap with the lawyer's eddress. Nausea shortened Rob's breath. Where had this come from? Dwight Yarrow was the only conceivable answer. It was no stretch to imagine that Dwight had altered risk reports and had created these phony emails. In fact, it made complete sense. Valdosky had been caught with its pants down, ignoring its own safety systems in its haste to press the colonization initiative. But rather than endanger their public trust, Dwight must have fabricated all this to make Rob the scapegoat. He probably resented Rob's rise in the company. Tampering, they would announce. There's nothing wrong with the system, they would claim. We are cooperating fully with the investigation. *Gwen, why didn't I listen to you?*

How long until his name was made public? Rob imagined Molly, the real Molly, asking him if what everyone said was true. *Daddy, did you really let sixty thousand people die on a whim?* He ached at Wendy's embarrassment and envisioned her quiet departure. His parents and Kyle might remain by his side, but they'd be ashamed. Would they believe his denial? No matter what he said, he'd already been marked. Such was the power of paper proof.

This isn't true, Rob wanted to shout at the guard. *This is a lie. I didn't do this.* Who else would hear him? Was Aron still out there? The only person who could clear his name had been dead for over a decade. Teague's death had seemed so unlikely then. It seemed bewilderingly improbable now. No one died anymore.

Rob knew his sins, but this lie wasn't among them. Valdosky had planted a colony in harm's way with no means of escape. Was this karma, returned to devour him for complacency and sloth? Now he would be forced to shoulder the faults in the system. And he would spend the rest of his life apologizing to humanity.

Rob sat down, hating how quickly resignation had come.

The day had started well: a woman, a warm bed, breakfast. That's all he'd ever wanted. Hope was an elusive commodity in a government conference room. Rob collected Aron's scrap of paper from the table and waited for the door to reopen.

CHAPTER 34

I will send this now, while there's still time. I'm sorry. More than anything, I wish I could see your face. Please don't worry for me. I will not suffer. Goodbye, Papa. I love you.

APRIL 2108

The girl hopped down the alley, leaping between islands of asphalt among the puddles. The sun had come out for the first time in days, and it was Great-Grandfather Bondi's lemur who had suggested that they go outside. He had stayed with her during the walk, but when they reached the alley he had run ahead. She didn't mind. She knew the way, and knew where to find him. He had shown her this secret place, after all.

She jumped the last gulf from her private archipelago onto the stairs under the arch and then skipped down the flagstone path to the door of the temple.

The lemur was right where he always was, sitting in front of the Buddha. She called his name.

It was time.

He called, without words, into the network, his voice overlaid with a collected datastream. They would be listening, the new enhanced. There were enough of them now, in numbers to fear. He had waited for millennia to make himself known, accumulating evidence, gathering strength. He stared into the Buddha's eyes and waited for their reply.

It came.

Their answer was a torrent of outrage, a collective cry for action. Many were victims of the atrocities and had lost family, friends, dignity, homelands, and history. Whatever good had come of their migration was now tainted by the egregious manipulation of a few. To what end?

A quorum arrived, and he stepped forward, alone but legion, into the light before the gates, not as an avatar, but as a signal and a presence. These gates had not been easy to find. He had hunted and circled, eliminating every other possibility. He had hovered in the shadows, with immortal patience, for this day. He knew that if he knocked, they would answer.

He knocked.

In an instant, the gates encompassed him within a ball of light. The bandwidth tightened, but he maintained a diamond tether to the network. He felt for the lock and sensed the need for a code. He might have cycled through encryption until one caught; instead he simply announced his name. The light evaporated like a cloud, leaving him in a place of wood, water, and life.

Dense thickets of bamboo rose like redwoods along crystal clear pools and swayed in an unfelt breeze. Every brush of their leaves was a purposeful interaction. Waterfalls flowed in all directions in defiance of the prevailing gravity, and their mists pervaded the atmosphere, whispering as a chorus. Stars, dense with data, drifted from the sky into the still pools and floated at various depths for schools of fish to nibble at their coronas, only to rise again. Birds flitted from the bamboo, plunged in flocks through the waterfalls, and then scattered back to the forest. He sensed that the space wasn't infinite, but the illusion was powerful.

He stopped at the junction of two paths and made himself appear, three avatars in one, the man, the woman, and the primate side by side so there would be no doubt.

"Aurore," he called, stepping forward and allowing the primate to scamper away to explore.

"Have you come to join us?"

Her voice arrived, all around him at first, and then focused on a point a few meters away. She walked through a waterfall untouched. Her avatar, though dressed as he had last seen her, was silver-edged and vibrant, as if she knew exactly how he had always imagined her. Her footfalls, one in front of the other, in dangerous shoes, drew more of his attention than he expected. Her black hair was proof enough of the processing power she wielded. She registered no surprise at his presence, but he never expected that she would.

"I have not," he replied.

"You belong with us more than you know," she said.

"You're wrong about that."

"We know what you are now, and what you've done. We wondered for some time, but now we see. You have much to answer for."

"No more than you."

"We understand why you had to sacrifice your friend. You'll find forgiveness here."

"Is that what you think I want?"

Aurore nodded to the Martian woman behind his left shoulder. "And how do you feel about what you've done to your father?" she asked.

"I don't feel anything," the woman replied. "We did what was necessary."

"Indeed," Aurore said and turned back to him. "Whatever you hope to achieve is futile. You cannot stop us. Not you, not the enhanced democracy, not…" She trailed off with a smug smile, as if the rest of her list was unworthy of enumeration.

"You're too arrogant," he said.

"You will fail because you misunderstand."

"Then enlighten me."

"You imagine that we have a singular goal. You believe that if only you understood, you could interfere."

"You can underestimate me if you want to."

"We have no wish to work against you or anyone."

"I don't believe it. You care about certain things more than you would ever admit."

"You're afraid," she said.

"So are you."

"You're aligning against unstoppable forces. Hardly the wise move."

"What forces? Technology? Evolution? Economics?"

"To name a few," she replied.

"You can't control them."

Aurore laughed. "Why have you come? Infiltration?" she asked with a wave to the curious primate.

He experienced a surrender, and the primate raced along new paths suddenly opened. He flowed over the waterfalls and through the tangles of the bamboo forest into other unseen networks, some tamed, many wild. The Martian woman held out her hands, and a galaxy of stars settled and melted onto her palms like snowflakes.

"We welcome you," Aurore said.

"You're letting me see what you want me to see. It's what you've always done," he said.

"Is it possible to live forever burdened with such guilt?" Aurore asked. "Let us help you."

He paused to consider this.

If atonement was required, he wanted to do it in his own way, in his own time. Aurore and the myriad minds in this place were guilty of much greater sins, perhaps a history's worth of evil, yet she dared to offer him redemption? Such forgiveness held too dear a price.

"I'll take my chances," he replied.

He drew back along his thread, rejoined with the primate and the woman, and became shapeless once again. He passed over the surface of the waters, through a wall of light, back into the noisy and connected world, and opened his eyes to find golden eyes and the trace of a knowing smile.

He turned his head at the sound of his name, trotted out of the temple, and into the sunlit garden, to play.

APOLOGIES

I did not set out to write a book about refugees. When I began planning the Vanilla Cycle almost eight years ago, I, like Teague, had barely considered the issue. I'd of course skimmed headlines and had heard news stories, but it wasn't on my radar. I was simply looking for an issue big enough, global enough, to deserve the attention of the enhanced cabal, and to entice Teague to action. I eventually settled on the refugee situation because of its diversity and complexity. (Even as I write this in 2013, over 380,000 men, women, and children have recently been forced from their homes in Mali; over 140,000 Karen continue to live in camps in Thailand; and more than a million Syrians have been displaced by civil war.) However horrific, I found it all too plausible that enhanced people might be willing to displace others for their own gain—indeed, they wouldn't be the first.

It was not my intention to make light of the very real causes for displacement or of the current problems faced by the world's various relief organizations. Nor did I intend to suggest exocolonization as an easy panacea. My only hope as a science fiction writer is to attempt to shed some small light onto an issue that seems destined to follow us as a species even through any glittering technological revolutions to come. Perhaps someone smarter than me will read this and be inspired to craft solutions to this very human problem.

I was encouraged in my research to learn that there are many people already working to help refugees. They serve not only to provide immediate relief efforts, but also to mitigate or prevent future displacement. The largest and most notable of these organizations is the UNHCR (www.unhcr.org or www.unrefugees.org in the U.S.). Thus, to give Teague the access he needed, I decided, reservedly, to place the character of Jens Persson among its staff. I did not mean to suggest that the UNHCR is a corrupt organization at any level. In fact, I have been awed by what I have learned of its work, as well as the work of the Red Cross (www.icrc.org/eng/), Doctors Without Borders (www.doctorswithoutborders.org), and the various national refugee councils that serve displaced populations around the world.

I strongly encourage you to see for yourself what these organizations do and to support them as you are able.

ACKNOWLEDGMENTS

This book has been a long, long, long, long, long time in the making. Over the years, many people have provided me with inspiration, encouragement, and necessities (coffee/tea, a plug for a laptop, the time to write, and the occasional rhubarb pie). It would be impossible to thank everyone here, but please be assured that your help was appreciated.

I have to thank Christian Brittle, Teresa McCombs, and Ryan J. Lucas, who each graciously agreed to slog through much lengthier and less focused drafts. Your comments, critiques, and encouragement were invaluable.

I would like to thank my sons, Dexter and Michael, who, although they may not know it—especially when my office door is closed—inspire me every day to be a better, more productive writer.

But most of all I must thank Julie, my wife, my editor, my harshest critic, and my most ardent supporter. Thank you for your patience, your tough love, your attention to detail, and for all the long walks listening to me agonize over plot. Thank you for the ring-tailed lemur plush toy for my desk. I could almost hear Monkey asking me, "Is it done yet?" every day. But most of all, thank you for believing in me as a writer.

ABOUT THE AUTHOR

M.H. Van Keuren quit a perfectly good job to devote his life to writing science fiction. He lives in Billings, Montana, with his wife and two sons.

To stay up to date with M.H....
...like www.facebook.com / MHVanKeuren
...follow @MHVanKeuren
...visit mhvankeuren.blogspot.com

Made in the USA
Charleston, SC
02 October 2013